T0272082

Ivan Bunin

Night of Denial

Stories and Novellas

TRANSLATED FROM THE RUSSIAN AND WITH NOTES AND AN AFTERWORD BY ROBERT BOWIE

NORTHWESTERN UNIVERSITY PRESS
EVANSTON, ILLINOIS

Northwestern University Press
www.nupress.northwestern.edu

English translation copyright © 2006 by Northwestern University Press.
Published 2006 by Northwestern University Press. All rights reserved.

Published with permission of the Ivan and Vera Bunin Estate.

Printed in the United States of America

10 9 8 7 6 5 4 3 2 1

ISBN 0-8101-1403-8

Library of Congress Cataloging-in-Publication data are available from the Library of Congress.

♾ The paper used in this publication meets the minimum requirements of the American National Standard for Information Sciences—Permanence of Paper for Printed Library Materials, ANSI Z39.48-1992.

To the Bowie boy
about to be

»»» CONTENTS «««

Night of Denial

»»» «««

The Grammar of Love

One day in early June a certain Ivlev was traveling to a distant region of his province.

He had borrowed a tarantass with a dusty skewed hood from his brother-in-law, at whose estate he was spending the summer. In the village he had hired a troika of small but sedulous horses, with thick matted manes, from a wealthy muzhik. His driver was that muzhik's son, a lad of about eighteen, vacant, pragmatical; he kept pondering something morosely, seemed somehow offended, had no sense of humor. Convinced that talking with him was impossible, Ivlev began observing his surroundings in that placid and aimless state of mind that goes so well with the beat of hooves and the hollow jangle of harness bells.

The drive was pleasant at first. The day was warm, dingy, the road quite smooth, the meadowlands profuse with flowers and skylarks; from the grain, from the low dove blue rye stretching as far as the eye could see, a pleasant breeze was blowing over the sloping land, bearing pollen dust that occasionally clouded the air, so that from a distance everything looked hazy. The lad sat erect in his new cap and ill-fitting lustrine jacket. Because the horses had been entrusted entirely to him and because he was so smartly dressed, his mien was especially grave. The horses snorted, trotted along leisurely; the whiffletree of the outrunner on the left would scrape against the wheel, then stretch back out, while beneath it the white steel of a worn shoe kept flashing.

"Stopping off at the count's?" asked the lad without turning around as a village came into view up ahead of them, ringing the horizon with its willow trees and garden.

"What for?" said Ivlev.

The lad was silent for a moment; with his whip he flicked off a large gadfly clinging to one of the horses, then answered gloomily, "To have some tea."

"Tea's not what's on your mind," said Ivlev. "You're always trying to spare the horses."

"It ain't traveling ruins a horse—it's fodder," the lad answered in a preceptorial tone.

Ivlev looked around. The weather had turned bleaker, discolored clouds had gathered on all sides, and now it was sprinkling; these unpretentious days always wind up with a violent downpour . . . An old man plowing near the village said that the young countess was the only one at home, but they stopped off all the same. Content that the horses were resting, the lad pulled a cloth coat over his shoulders and sat placidly soaking on the driver's seat of the tarantass, which he had parked in the middle of the muddy yard near a stone trough that was sunk into ground studded with the prints of cattle hooves. He examined his boots, adjusted the breeching of the shaft horse with his whip stock. Meanwhile, in a drawing room that was murky from the rain outside, Ivlev sat chatting with the countess and waiting for tea. From the veranda came a scent of burning shavings, and past the open windows floated thick green smoke from the samovar, where a barefoot wench had poured kerosene over bundles of wood chips that now burned with bright red flames. The countess was wearing a capacious pink dressing gown cut low over her powdered bosom; she smoked, inhaling deeply; she fussed continually with her hair, baring her firm rotund arms to the shoulders. Inhaling the smoke and laughing, she kept leading the conversation around to love, and apropos of this she mentioned her neighbor, the landowner Khvoshinsky, who, as Ivlev had known since childhood, had been mad with love for his chambermaid Lushka throughout his entire life, although she had died in early youth.

"Ah, the legendary Lushka!" Ivlev remarked facetiously, disconcerted by what he was about to confess. "Because of the way that eccentric worshiped her and dedicated all his life to insane dreams of her, I was almost in love with her myself as a boy; God only knows what fancies came into my head when I thought about her, although they say she was certainly no beauty."

"Indeed?" said the countess, not listening. "He died just this winter. And Pisarev—the only one he sometimes allowed to visit him, because they were old friends—affirms that in no other way was he the least bit mad. And I'm convinced of it—he simply wasn't one to be compared with today's lot . . ." Finally, the barefoot wench came in; scrupulously careful of her every movement, she served him a glass of strong grayish tea and a small basket of fly-specked tea biscuits on an old silver tray.

When they started off again, the rain came down in torrents. The hood had to be raised, and Ivlev was forced to sit in a hunched position, covered with the corneous, shriveled apron. Bells on the horses' necks were clinking, emitting a hollow din; little streams ran over their dark and glistening haunches. With grass rustling under the wheels, they passed some sort of boundary amidst the grain through which the lad had driven in hopes of shortening the way. Warm, rye-scented air gathered beneath the hood, blending with the smell of the old tarantass . . . "So that's how things are—Khvoshinsky has died," thought Ivlev. "I absolutely must stop by there, at least for a look at that deserted shrine of the mysterious Lushka." But what sort of man was this Khvoshinsky? Was he insane or was he just overwhelmed, completely absorbed by a single fixation? According to the stories of old-time landowners, the contemporaries of Khvoshinsky, at one time people in the province considered him a man of rare intelligence. But all at once he was stricken with this love, this Lushka; then came her sudden death and everything went to pieces. He secluded himself in the house, in the room where Lushka had lived and died, and spent more than twenty years sitting on her bed; not only did he never go off anywhere, but even on his own estate no one ever saw him. He sat on Lushka's mattress till it wore right through, he ascribed literally all phenomena in the world to Lushka's influence. If there was a thunderstorm, it was Lushka who had visited this affliction upon them; if war was declared, it meant Lushka had so decided; in the event of a crop failure, the peasants had incurred the displeasure of Lushka.

"You're heading for Khvoshinskoe then, aren't you?" called Ivlev, putting his head out in the rain.

"Yes," responded the boy, from whose drooping cap the water was streaming; his answer was indistinct through the din of the rainstorm. "Up along Pisarev Hill."

Ivlev knew of no such road. Provincial hamlets were becoming ever more impoverished and more remote. The boundary came to an end; going at a walk, the horses drew the tilting tarantass down by way of an eroded furrow to the bottom of the hill—into some still unmowed meadows whose green slopes stood out dolefully against the low clouds. Then the road, which kept fading away and reappearing, began to wind back and forth across the bottoms of ravines, through gullies full of alder bushes and osiers . . . Someone's little apiary came into view, several logs standing on a slope in the tall grass, through which wild red strawberries sparkled . . . They detoured around an old dam, immersed in nettles, and a pond that had dried up long ago—a deep hollow grown over with weeds taller than a man. A pair of black snipe darted out of the weeds screeching and flew up into the rainy sky . . . Upon the dam, among the nettles, a massive old bush blossomed with little pale pink flowers—that charming shrub called God's tree—and suddenly Ivlev recalled the locality and remembered that as a youth he had often ridden in this area on horseback.

"They say right here is where she drownded herself," remarked the lad abruptly.

"Is it Khvoshinsky's mistress you're talking about?" asked Ivlev. "That's not true. She did nothing of the kind."

"No, she did, she drownded herself," said the lad. "Only they figure he most likely went crazy from being so poor, not on account of her."

After a brief silence he added brusquely, "We'll have to stop off again . . . at the Khvoshino place . . . Just look how them horses is dragging!"

"Indeed we must," agreed Ivlev.

Tin-colored with rainwater, the road led to a knoll, to a spot where the trees had been cleared; a solitary hut stood there, amidst sodden, rotting wood chips and leaves, amidst stumps and vernal aspen shoots smelling bitter and crisp. There was not a soul around, only the birds sitting in the rain on tall flowers, yellow buntings whose song rang throughout the sparse forest that rose beyond the hut; but when the troika, slushing through the mud, came even with the threshold, a whole pack of gigantic hounds, black, chocolate, smoke gray, tore out from somewhere barking ferociously and began seething around the horses, soaring right up to their muzzles, somersaulting in the air, even gyrating under the very hood of the tarantass. Just as abruptly the sky above them was split by a deafening peal of thunder; in a frenzy the lad began flailing the dogs with his whip, and the horses rushed off at a full gallop amidst aspen trunks, which went flashing past Ivlev's eyes.

Now the Khvoshinskoe estate could be seen beyond the forest. The dogs dropped behind and immediately fell silent, loping back earnestly; the forest parted and once again open fields stretched before them. As evening began setting in, the storm clouds seemed to be now dispersing, now gathering from three sides: on the left they were nearly black, with light blue apertures; on the right they were gray, rumbling with unremitting thunder; and to the west, beyond the manor, beyond the slopes above the river vale, they were turbid blue, with dusty bands of rain through which distant mounds of other clouds showed pink. But the rain on the tarantass was slackening, and Ivlev rose, all spattered with mud, invigorated; he threw back the cumbersome hood and drew in a long deep breath of air, redolent with the dampness of the fields.

He gazed at the approaching estate, seeing at last what he had heard so much about, and, just as before, it seemed that Lushka had lived and died not twenty years ago but almost in time immemorial. All trace of the shallow little river that ran through the vale was lost in cattails, above which a white gull was gliding. Farther along, on a sloping hillock, there were rows of hay soaked dark by the rain; old silver poplars were scattered among them, standing far apart one from another. On an absolutely bare spot stood the house with its glistening wet roof, a rather large house, which had once been white. There were neither gardens nor outbuildings—only two brick columns where the gates had been and burdock growing in the ditches. When the horses had forded the stream and climbed the hill, a woman in a man's summer jacket with drooping pockets appeared, driving some turkey hens through the burdock. The facade of the house was uncommonly bleak: there were not many windows, and all of them were undersized, set back within the thick walls. By contrast, the dismal verandas were enormous. From one of them a young man in a gray gymnasium blouse girded with a wide belt was peering down at the visitors in astonishment; he was dark, with beautiful eyes, very handsome, although his face was pale and freckled, mottled like a bird's egg.

The visit had to be explained somehow. Having ascended the steps of the veranda and introduced himself, Ivlev said that he wanted to examine and perhaps to buy the library, which, according to the countess, belonged to Khvoshinsky; the young man blushed deeply and immediately ushered him into the house. "So this is the son of illustrious Lushka!" thought Ivlev, drinking in everything with his eyes as he walked, often glancing back, saying whatever came to mind just to have another look at the master of the house, who appeared too youthful for his years. The latter answered hurriedly but laconically, nonplussed, it seemed, by both his bashfulness and his greed. He was terribly happy at the prospect of selling the books and assumed they would bring a fine price; this was evident from his very first words, from his quick awkward declaration that you couldn't acquire such books as these for any amount of money. He led Ivlev through a half-dark passage, spread with straw that was rust red from the dampness, into a large anteroom.

"So is this where your father lived?" asked Ivlev, entering and taking off his hat.

"Yes, yes, here," the young man answered hurriedly. "That is, of course, not here . . . Father sat in the bedroom most of the time . . . but of course he came in here too."

"Yes, I know; he was ill," said Ivlev.

The young man flared up.

"How do you mean, 'ill'?" he said, and his voice took on a more resolute tone. "That's all gossip; Father was certainly not mentally ill in any way. He just read all the time and didn't go out anywhere, that's all . . . No, please don't take off your hat; it's cold in here; we no longer use this part of the house."

It was, in fact, much colder inside the house than outside. In the dreary anteroom, papered with old gazettes, a quail cage made of bast stood on the sill of the window, to which the storm clouds gave a somber cast. A little gray bag was hopping along the floor all by itself. Stooping over, the young man caught it and put it on a bench, and Ivlev realized that there was a quail in the bag. Then they went into the parlor. That room, which had windows facing west and north, occupied nearly half of the entire house. Through one window a centenarian weeping birch was visible, all black, standing out against the gold of the ever-clearer evening glow beyond the storm clouds. The whole front corner was occupied by a devotional stand without glass, full of icons that were hung or set within it. Prominent among them, both for size and for antiquity, was an icon in a silver mounting; on top of it, all waxy yellow like dead flesh, lay some wedding candles tied with pale green bows.

"Excuse me, please," began Ivlev, overcoming his sense of impropriety. "Did your father really . . . ?"

"No, that's right," the young man mumbled, understanding immediately. "He didn't buy those candles until after she died . . . He even wore a wedding band all the time."

The furniture in the parlor was rough hewn, but along the wall there were beautiful cabinets packed with tea china and tall, slender, gold-rimmed goblets. The entire floor was encrusted with dead withered bees that crackled underfoot. Bees were also strewn about in the drawing room, which was absolutely empty. When they had crossed that and yet another gloomy room with stove and sleeping ledge, the young man stopped beside a low door and took a huge key from his trouser pocket. Turning it with great effort in the rusty keyhole, he thrust open the door and muttered something. Ivlev saw a tiny cell with two windows. By one wall stood a bare iron cot, by the other two small bookcases of Karelian birch.

"So is this the library?" asked Ivlev, walking up to one of them. Hastening to answer affirmatively, the young man helped him open a bookcase, then began avidly observing every movement of his hands.

That library contained the most bizarre of books! Ivlev opened the thick covers, turned the rough gray pages, and read: *The Accursed Demesne, The Morning Star and Nocturnal Daemons, Meditations upon the Mysteries of the Universe, A Wondrous Peregrination into an Enchanted Realm, The Latest Dream Book* . . . But his hands, nonetheless, were trembling. So this is what he lived on, the lonely creature who had secluded himself forever from the world in this cell and only so recently had left it . . . But perhaps he, this creature, had not been entirely insane? "There is a state"—Ivlev recalled the lines of Baratynsky—"but by what name shall it be called? Nor dream is it, nor wake, it lies somewhere between. Through it the mind's dementia may verge upon the truth."

It had cleared in the west; gold peered from behind the beautiful lilac-tinged clouds and strangely illumined this humble asylum of love, incomprehensible love, which had transmuted a whole human life into some rapturous state of existence, a life perhaps destined to be most commonplace, if not for a certain fascinating, enigmatic Lushka . . .

Moving a bench from beneath the cot, Ivlev sat down in front of the bookcase and took out his cigarettes, imperceptibly examining the room and committing it to memory.

"Do you smoke?" he asked the young man standing over him.

The latter blushed again.

"Yes," he mumbled and attempted to smile. "That is, I don't really smoke; rather, I sometimes indulge myself . . . But then, if I may, much obliged to you."

When he had taken a cigarette clumsily and lit it with trembling hands, he stepped over to the window and sat down on the sill, obstructing the yellow light of the evening glow.

"And what is this?" asked Ivlev, bending down to the middle shelf, which contained only one slender volume, resembling a prayer book, and a jewelry case, its corners finished in silver tarnished with time.

"It's just . . . The necklace of my late mother is in that case," answered the young man, stammering but trying to speak casually.

"May I take a look?"

"Certainly . . . Although it really is quite plain . . . It couldn't be of interest to you."

Opening the jewelry case, Ivlev saw a frayed bit of cord, a chaplet of cheap pale blue beads made of some material resembling stone. And when he looked at those beads, which once had lain on the neck of the woman who was fated to be so loved, whose nebulous image now could be nothing less than beautiful, he was overwhelmed by such agitation that his heart began racing and everything went black before his eyes. After a long, long look, Ivlev carefully put the jewelry box back in its place; then he picked up the book. Tiny, beautifully printed almost one hundred years before, it was entitled *The Grammar of Love, or The Art of Loving and of Being Loved in Return.*

"That book, unfortunately, I cannot sell," uttered the young man with an effort. "It's very dear . . . Father even used to sleep with it under his pillow."

"But perhaps you'll at least allow me to glance through it?" said Ivlev.

"Certainly," he whispered.

Overcoming his constraint, vaguely tormented by the young man's fixed gaze, Ivlev began leafing slowly through *The Grammar of Love.* It was divided into short chapters: "Of Beauty," "Of the Heart," "Of the Mind," "Of Amorous Signs," "Of Fervent Wooing and Resistance," "Of Disunion and Reconciliation," "Of Platonic Love." Each chapter consisted of brief, elegant, at times very subtle maxims; some of them were delicately marked in pen with red ink. "Love is no Mere Episode in our Lives," Ivlev read. "Our Reason gainsays the Heart, but the Latter is not persuaded. Never is Woman so strong as when She arms Herself with Debility. We worship Woman because She holds Dominion over our Ideal Dream. Vainglory chooses, True Love never chooses. The Woman of Beauty is relegated to a secondary Station; first belongs to the Woman of Grace. She becomes the Sovereign of our Hearts; ere we ourselves take Cognizance, our Hearts have become Thralls of Love for All Time . . ." Then came "An Explication of the Language of Flowers," and once again some passages were marked: "Wild Poppy—Sorrow," "Spindle Shrub—Thy Charm is engraved in my Heart," "Periwinkle—Sweet Reminiscences," "Somber Geranium—Spleen," "Wormwood—Bitterness Eternal." In minute script on a blank page at the very end there was a four-line stanza in the same red ink. Craning his neck to look into *The Grammar of Love,* the young man said with a forced sneer, "Father composed that himself."

A half hour later Ivlev said good-bye to him with a sense of relief. Of all the books, he had bought, at a very high price, only that one slender volume. In clouds beyond the fields the turbid golden evening glow grew faint, its gleam mirrored in puddles; the fields were wet and green. The lad was in no hurry, but Ivlev did not urge him on. The lad was saying that the woman driving turkey hens through the burdock was the deacon's wife and that young Khvoshinsky was living with her. Ivlev was not listening. He thought only of Lushka, of her necklace, which had left him with a complex feeling, like what he had once experienced in an Italian village as he gazed at the relics of a female saint. "She has come into my life forever!" he thought. And taking *The Grammar of Love* from his pocket, he slowly reread by the light of the evening glow the poem written on its last page:

Lovers' hearts will say unto Thee:
"Live in sweet dream-realms above!"
And to the grandchild of years yet to be
They will show this selfsame *Grammar of Love.*

Moscow, February 1915

»»» «««

First Love

Summer. An estate in a forested western province.

Torrents of fresh rain all day long, their unremitting din on the plank roof. Murk, dreariness in the hushed manor house; flies asleep on the ceiling. Beneath a flowing aqueous mesh the wet trees in the garden droop submissively, and the red flower beds by the terrace are uncommonly vivid. Conspicuous in the hazy sky above the garden, a stork bustles about apprehensively. Now grown dark and thin, his tail tucked under, rectricial feathers sagging, he stands on the edge of his nest in the crown of a centenarian birch, in a fork between its bare white boughs, indignant, agitated, fluttering up and down, and periodically he makes a loud, wooden, clacking sound with his bill as if to say, "What on earth is going on? It's a deluge, an utter deluge!"

But then, at about four, the rain brightens, becomes sparser. A samovar is set in the passageway leading to the veranda; the balsamic odor of smoke creeps over all the estate.

And before sunset the skies have cleared. Silence, tranquillity. The masters and their guests go out into the pine forest for a stroll.

By now the blue of twilight is glowing.

In corridors cut through the forest, spread with yellow conifer needles, the paths are moist and resilient. The forest is fragrant, damp, and resonant. Someone's distant voice, someone's protracted call or response reverberates marvelously in the far distant thickets. These corridors seem narrow, the vistas where they end are shapely, infinite, captivating in their twilight remoteness. The pine timberland surrounding them is majestically vast, dark, cramped; the mastlike boles of trees are bare and smooth, red at their crowns; down below they are gray, scabrous, mossy, intermingled one with another: mosses, lichens, boughs covered with rot and with something else that hangs down like the greenish frowzy manes of woodland ogres in fairy tales, all of this forms a labyrinth, creates a vague aura of savage Russian antiquity. When emerging into a glade, one delights in the young pine shoots. They have a lovely pallid hue, a verdure delicate and marshy, slender but vigorous, with many branchings; still covered with tiny drops of rain and fine aqueous dust, they seem to be draped in a silvery Indian muslin laced with sequins . . .

Two figures dashed out ahead of the strollers that evening, a small schoolboy-cadet and a big amiable dog; they kept frolicking about, romping after one another. And amidst the strollers sedately, gracefully promenaded a girl who was not quite adolescent, with long arms and legs, wearing a lightweight, cheap plaid coat that for some reason was quite endearing. Everyone was grinning—they knew why he was doing all that dashing about, frolicking so incessantly and feigning joy, the young cadet, who was on the verge of bursting into tears of despair. The girl knew as well, and she felt proud, contented. But the look on her face was cool and fastidious.

1930

»»» «««

In Paris

When he was wearing a hat—walking down the street or standing in a subway car—and the bright silvery sheen of his close-cropped reddish hair was not so noticeable, you might have looked at the freshness of his gaunt shaven face, at the way he stood tall, gaunt and straight in his long macintosh, and figured him for under forty. But the bright gaze of his eyes held a dry melancholy, and he spoke and behaved like a man who had been through a lot. At one time he had rented a farm in Provence, had been steeped in the mordant wit of the region, and in Paris he tended to smile ironically and sprinkle his always laconic speech with those witticisms. Many knew that back in Constantinople his wife had left him and that since then he had been living with a constant wound in his heart. He never revealed to anyone the secret cause of that wound, but sometimes he would inadvertently allude to it—by making joking remarks with an edge when the conversation touched upon women: "*Rien n'est plus difficile que de reconnaître un bon melon et une femme de bien.*"

Once in late autumn, on a damp Paris evening, he stopped off to eat in a small Russian restaurant on one of the dark side streets near Passy. The same location housed something like a delicatessen, and he paused unthinking in front of its spacious window—on the windowsill inside there were conical rose-colored bottles of rowanberry vodka and yellow bottles of *zubrovka* in the shape of cubes, there was a plate containing stale fried *pirogi,* another with meatballs that had taken on a grayish look, a box of halva, a can of sprats; farther back there was a counter with hors d'oeuvres, and behind that counter the proprietor stood, a woman with a surly Russian face. The shop was brightly lit, and he felt drawn toward that light and away from the dark alleyway with its cold and somehow greasy-looking pavement. He went in, bowed to the proprietor, and passed through to a still empty, dimly illumined room that adjoined the store; the tables there were covered with white paper tablecloths. He took his time hanging up his gray hat and long coat on the horns of a standing coatrack, sat down at a table in the most distant corner, and absentmindedly stroking his arms with his fingers, which were covered with reddish hair, he began reading the endless listing of hors d'oeuvres and foods, partly typed out, partly handwritten in violet ink that had run into blurs on the greasy menu sheet. Suddenly a light went on in his corner and he saw a woman of about thirty approaching him; she had an apathetically polite bearing, black hair parted in the middle, black eyes, and she was wearing a black dress and a white apron, which had patches of lace sewn to it.

"*Bonsoir, monsieur,*" she said in a pleasant voice.

She struck him as so attractive that he lost his composure and answered awkwardly, "*Bonsoir* . . . But aren't you a Russian?"

"Yes. Sorry, you just get in the habit of speaking to the clients in French."

"You mean you really have a lot of French people in here?"

"Quite a few, and invariably they order *zubrovka,* blini, even borscht. Have you made your selection yet?"

"No, there's so much of everything here. Why don't you suggest something for me."

She started the recitation in a practiced tone. "Today we've got cabbage soup naval style and Cossack rissoles; you can have marinated veal chops or, if you like, Karski shish kebabs."

"Fine. I'll have the cabbage soup and the rissoles, please."

She picked up the notepad that was hanging from her waist and jotted it all down with the stub of a pencil. Her hands, very white, had a delicate, genteel shape; her dress was worn but obviously came from a fashionable store.

"Will you have some vodka?"

"I wouldn't mind. It's awfully damp outside."

"How about hors d'oeuvres? We've got excellent Danube herring, red caviar that just came in, and Korkun brand lightly salted cucumbers."

He glanced at her again. The white apron with lace patches looked quite nice over her black dress, and beneath the dress were the nicely formed breasts of a healthy young woman. Her full lips were not painted, but were fresh, her hairstyle was simply a black braid rolled up on her head, but the skin on her white hand was sleek, her nails gleamed with a pinkish tint—obviously manicured.

"What should I get for starters?" he asked, smiling. "If it's all right, I'll have just herring with hot potatoes."

"And what kind of wine would you like?"

"Red. The usual thing—the house wine that comes with the meal."

She noted it down on her pad and brought over a carafe of water from the adjoining table. He shook his head.

"No, *merci,* I never drink water, or wine with water. *L'eau gâte le vin comme la charrette le chemin et la femme—l'âme.*"

"Well, I see you think highly of us!" she answered indifferently and went off for the vodka and herring. He watched her walk away—noted her smooth gait, the way her black dress swung back and forth as she moved. Yes, a polite tone mixed with apathy, all the mannerisms and bodily movements of the modest and conscientious waitress. But fine expensive shoes. Where did they come from? There must be an elderly, well-to-do "*ami*" somewhere in the picture. It was ages since he had felt as animated as he felt that evening, thanks to her, and the thought gave rise to a certain irritation. Yes, you go from year to year, from day to day secretly awaiting only one thing—getting lucky in love—you go on living, in fact, only in hopes of that; and it's all in vain.

The next day he came in again and sat down at the same table. At first she was busy taking the order of two Frenchmen and repeating aloud as she noted it down on her pad. "*Caviar rouge, salade russe . . . Deux chachlyks . . .*"

Then she went out, returned, and came up to him with a smile, as if he was no longer a stranger. "Good evening. I'm glad you liked our place."

He sat up straight with a glow of pleasure.

"And good health to you. Yes, I liked it very much. What name do you go by?"

"Olga Aleksandrovna. And you, if I might ask?"

"Nikolai Platonich."

After they shook hands she took up her notepad. "Today we've got some fine *rassolnik*. Our cook is outstanding; he once worked on the cruise ship of the grand duke Aleksandr Mikhailovich."

"Wonderful. Then it must be great *rassolnik*. And have you been working here for a long time?"

"Going on three months."

"Where were you before?"

"I was a saleslady at Printemps."

"I suppose they cut back on the staff there."

"Yes, I wouldn't have left if it were up to me."

It was a good feeling to think, "Well, so there isn't any *ami* in the picture."

"Are you married?"

"Yes."

"And what does your husband do?"

"Works in Yugoslavia. He served in the White Army. Most likely you did too?"

"Yes, I was in the Great War and then the civil war as well."

"I could tell that right away. You're probably a general," she said, smiling.

"Once was. Now I'm writing the history of those wars for a number of foreign publishing houses . . . How is it you're living alone?"

"It's just the way things turned out."

On his third evening at the café he asked, "Do you like the cinema?"

Placing a bowl of borscht on the table, she answered, "Sometimes I find it interesting."

"They say there's some remarkable film showing now at the Etoile. Would you like to go see it? You must have some days off, don't you?"

"*Merci.* I'm off on Mondays."

"Well then, we'll go on Monday. What's today? Saturday? So then, that makes it the day after tomorrow. All right?"

"All right. So I guess tomorrow you won't be coming in?"

"No, I'm going out of town to visit some people. And why do you ask?"

"I don't know. It's strange, but I've somehow got used to seeing you."

He glanced at her with a look of gratefulness and his face colored. "The same goes for me. You know, there are so few times on earth when you're fortunate enough to meet people you like." Then he quickly switched the conversation back. "So it's the day after tomorrow then. Where should we meet? I don't know where you live."

"Next to the Motte-Picquet metro station."

"Well, there you go, how convenient; that's a direct connection to the Etoile station. I'll be waiting for you by the metro exit at eight-thirty sharp."

"*Merci.*"

Jokingly he bowed.

"*C'est moi qui vous remercie.* Just put the children to bed," he added, in order to find out whether she had a child, "and come."

"Thank God, there's a joy that hasn't been granted to me," she answered, as she smoothly swept up his plate and carried it away.

Walking home he felt touched, but he was also frowning. "I've already got used to you." Yes, maybe this really was that long-awaited lucky chance. But it comes awfully late. *Le bon Dieu envoie toujours des culottes à ceux qui n'ont pas de derrière.*

On Monday evening it was raining, the misty sky over Paris glowed a lackluster red. Hoping to have supper with her in Montparnasse, he ate no meal in the afternoon; stopping off at a café on Chaussée de la Muette, he had a ham sandwich and a mug of beer, then smoked a cigarette, went out, and hailed a taxi. At the entrance to the Etoile metro station, he told the driver to stop and stepped out onto the rainy pavement. The trusting cabman, fat, with crimson cheeks, sat there waiting for him. A bathhouse breeze was wafting from the metro entrance, a thick black mass of humanity was coming up the stairway, opening umbrellas as it moved, a newsboy standing by the metro was calling out the names of the evening editions in a shrill duck quack of a voice. Suddenly, amidst the ascending mob, there she was. He felt a surge of joy as he went to meet her. "Olga Aleksandrovna."

Smartly and stylishly dressed, she raised her black eyes, made up with mascara, to his; she looked at him directly, not the way she had in the café. With a ladylike movement she extended her hand, an umbrella hanging from the wrist, while using the other hand to hold up the hem of her long evening dress. This made him feel even happier: she's wearing an evening dress; that means she was thinking as I was, that we'd go out somewhere after the cinema. He turned back the edge of her glove and kissed her white hand.

"Poor thing, have you been waiting long?"

"No, I just got here. Hurry, there's a taxi waiting for us."

More agitated than he had been for ages, he climbed, after her, into the half-dark cab, which smelled of damp leather. As they turned a corner the taxi lurched to one side, a streetlight momentarily illumined its interior. Instinctively he held her by the waist, caught the aroma of powder on her cheeks, noticed her large knees beneath the black of the evening dress, the gleam of one dark eye and her full lips in their red lipstick—this was a totally different woman sitting beside him now.

In the dark theater, gazing at the glittering whiteness of the screen, where low-humming airships were flying, sweeping obliquely with wings widespread, they quietly conversed.

"Do you live alone, or with some friend?" he asked.

"Alone. Speaking frankly, it's horrible. I have a clean little hotel, it's warm, but, you know, it's one of those places where men bring a girl for the night, or for a few hours. I'm on the sixth floor, there's no elevator of course; and the red carpeting on the staircase ends at the fourth floor. At night when it's raining you get this hideous feeling of depression. You open the window and you don't see a soul around anywhere, it's a totally dead city, or there's maybe just one godforsaken light down there below you in the rain . . . I suppose, being single, you live in a hotel too?"

"I've got a small apartment in Passy. I live alone too. I'm a Parisian now of long standing. Once lived in Provence, rented a farm there. I wanted to get away from everything and everybody, live by the labor of my own hands—but the work ended up getting the best of me. I took on a Cossack emigrant as a worker, and he turned out to be a drunkard, a gloomy sort who was quite a terror when he drank. Bought myself some chickens and rabbits—they died off—and my mule bit me so badly I nearly died myself. Now there's a really mean and intelligent animal. But the main thing was the absolute loneliness. My wife had left me back in Constantinople."

"You're joking."

"I'm serious. Quite the usual story. *Qui se marie par amour a bonnes nuits et mauvais jours.* But as for me, I had very little of either one. We were married slightly over a year when she left."

"Where is she now?"

"I don't know."

She was silent for a long time. Some Chaplin imitator in a derby cocked to one side, wearing absurdly oversized shoes that were in shreds, was scuttling, legs widespread, across the screen.

"Yes, it must be quite lonely for you," she said.

"It is. But what can you do, you have to live and bear it. *Patience—médecine des pauvres.*"

"It's an awfully sad *médecine.*"

"Yes, not the happiest of remedies. It even came to the point," he said with a grin, "that I started going through the newspaper *Illustrated Russia*—you know, they've got this one section where they print ads for people looking for marriage or love: 'Russian girl from Latvia, bored, wishes to correspond with sensitive Russian man living in Paris, please send photograph with letter . . . Serious lady, brown hair, kind of old-fashioned but nice personality, widow, nine-year-old son, seeks correspondence with serious intent with nondrinking gentleman over forty who has work as cabdriver or other such to support him materially, must love the comfort of family. Education and intelligence not a requirement.' Now that I can understand completely—not a requirement."

"But don't you have any friends or acquaintances?"

"No friends. And just knowing people is little consolation."

"Who does your housekeeping for you?"

"My housekeeping doesn't amount to much. I make my own coffee, fix breakfast for myself. In the evening a *femme de ménage* stops by."

"Poor thing!" she said, pressing his hand.

For a long time they sat there like that, hand in hand, united by the murkiness, by the closeness of the seats, pretending they were looking at the screen, toward which the light from a booth on the back wall flowed above their heads in a smoky, chalk blue streak. The Chaplin imitator, whose dilapidated derby had run amuck and detached itself from his head, was madly dashing toward a telephone pole, driving the wreckage of an antediluvian car with a samovarlike smokestack belching fumes. The loudspeaker bellowed out its music at full blare, and down below—they were sitting in the balcony—from the basement of the theater, which was swimming in the smoke of cigarettes, desperately joyful guffaws resounded along with the clapping of hands. He leaned over toward her. "You know what? Maybe we could go out somewhere, let's say over to Montparnasse; it's awfully boring here and you can't breathe for the smoke."

She nodded and started putting on her gloves.

Once again they seated themselves in a half-dark cab and gazed at the coruscations that the rain was making on the window glass, which would flare up momentarily with multicolored diamonds from the gleam of streetlights, or with the interplay up in the heights, where blood-red glimmers blended with quicksilver on the neon street signs. Once more he folded back the edge of her glove, kissed her hand at length. As she looked at him her eyes, too, were scintillating beneath their long, coal black lashes; in a movement both loving and sad she extended her face toward his, offered her full lips with the sweet taste of lipstick.

At the Café Coupole they began with the oysters and Anjou, then ordered partridge and red Bordeaux. Drinking coffee with a yellow Chartreuse liqueur, both of them got slightly tipsy. They smoked a lot, and the ashtray was full of her blood-tipped cigarette butts. Throughout the conversation he kept looking at her flushed face and thinking that this was an absolutely beautiful woman.

"But tell me the truth now," she said as she made little pinching movements to pick bits of tobacco off the tip of her tongue. "Didn't you have any affairs over all those years?"

"Yes, I did. But you can imagine what they amounted to. Night hotels . . . And you?"

She was silent for a moment.

"There was one thing, quite a depressing little incident . . . No, I don't want to talk about that. He was just a boy, something like a gigolo in fact . . . But how was it you split with your wife?"

"That was a shameful business. He was a boy too, a handsome young Greek, fabulously rich. After a month or two there was no trace left of that pure, touching little girl who simply worshiped the White Army and all of us in it. She started having dinner with him in the most expensive nightclub in Pera; he would send her gigantic baskets of flowers. 'I don't get it, how could you possibly be jealous over him? You're busy all day long, and he makes me feel happy; for me he's just a nice little boy—nothing more.' A nice boy! And that boy was twenty years old. It was not easy to forget her, the previous her, the way she was back in Yekaterinodar."

When they brought the check, she carefully looked it over and told him not to leave more than ten percent for a tip. After that it seemed even stranger to both of them that they should separate a half hour later.

"Let's go to my apartment," he said wistfully. "We'll sit around and talk some more."

"Yes, okay," she answered, getting up and taking his arm, pressing it up against her.

The night-shift cabman, a Russian, drove them into the lonely back alleyway, up to the entrance of that tall building, beside which rain was trickling down through the metallic glitter of a gas street-light, spattering against a tin garbage can. They entered the vestibule, which lit up upon their entry, then stepped into the cramped confines of the elevator and were slowly lifted upward, embracing and quietly kissing. He managed to get his key into the door before the electric timer turned off the light. He led her into the anteroom, then into a small dining room where one lightbulb burned wearily in the chandelier. Their faces had a tired look about them now. He suggested they drink some more wine.

"Oh no, my dear," she said. "I can't drink any more."

He tried to persuade her. "We'll have just one glass of white wine. I've got some fine Puis on the windowsill outside."

"You drink it, honey, and I'll go get undressed and washed. Then we can have a nice long sleep. We're not children, and you must have known perfectly well that once I agreed to come up here . . . But then, after all, why shouldn't we stay together?"

He was so agitated that he found no way to answer that. He silently led her into the bedroom, turned on the lights there and in the bathroom, which had an open door adjoining the bedroom. The lamp that burned there was bright, warm air wafted from the radiators, while the swift and steady raindrops pounded on the roof. Immediately she began pulling off the long dress over her head.

He went out, drank two glasses in a row of bitter icy wine; then, too impatient to wait longer, he went back into the bedroom. In the large mirror on the opposite wall the brightly lit bathroom was reflected. She stood with her back to him, totally naked, white, sturdily built, bending over the sink and washing her neck and breasts.

"Don't come in here!" she said, and throwing on a bathrobe that left uncovered her ripe breasts, her strong white stomach and taut white hips, she walked up to him like a wife and embraced him. And as if she really were his wife he embraced her too, all of her cool body, kissing a breast that was still moist and smelling of toilet soap, kissing her eyes and her lips, from which she had wiped the lipstick.

Two days later she left her job and moved in with him.

That winter he convinced her to rent a safe deposit box, in her name, at the Lyon Credit Union and to put all the money he had saved in there.

"It never hurts to take precautions," he said. "*L'amour fait danser les ânes,* and I feel like a twenty-year-old. But all sorts of things can happen . . ."

On the third day of Easter week he died in a subway car. He was sitting reading a newspaper when suddenly his head jerked back against the seat and his eyes rolled up.

As she returned in her mourning dress from the cemetery it was a nice spring day, the vernal clouds were floating in patches through the soft Paris sky, and all things bespoke a youthful, eternal life—but for her the end of life.

Back home, she began tidying up the apartment. Out in the corridor, hanging in the *placard,* she saw the light military coat he had worn for ages, gray, with a red lining. She took it off the hanger, pressed it to her face, and keeping it pressed against her she sat down on the floor, shaking all over with sobs and crying out, imploring someone for mercy.

October 26, 1940

»»» «««

On the Night Sea

A steamer bound for the Crimea from Odessa docked in the night at Evpatoria.

On the ship and beside it a scene straight from hell was played out. As winches rumbled the men taking on cargo and the others hoisting it up from an enormous barge below screamed ferociously; wrangling and shrieking, an Oriental rabble laid siege to the passenger ladder, stormed it with an incredible rush of frenzy, swarmed upward with bag and baggage; an electric bulb hanging over the ladder garishly illumined the dense, disorderly procession of filthy fezzes and hoods resembling turbans, goggling eyes, shoulders pushing forward, hands clutching hand railings convulsively. Below, beside the last steps, which the waves periodically lapped over, there was still more clamor, bawling and brawling, stumbling and clutching; oars thudded, boats full of people collided—they would fly high up on a wave, then plunge steeply, disappearing in the darkness under the broadside. And resiliently, as if on elastic, the dolphinlike bulk of the ship pitched now to one side, now to the other.

Finally things began to quiet down.

One of the last to board, a gentleman with straight shoulders, standing very erect, handed his ticket and bag to the porter at the first-class deckhouse; informed that there were no cabins left, he made his way back to the stern, which was dark. In one of the deck chairs, the only chair occupied, he saw the black silhouette of a man, half reclining under a lap robe. The new passenger selected a chair several feet from him. The chair was low, and when he sat down the canvas stretched to form a nice comfortable cavity. The ship rose and fell, slowly drifted, swung with the current. A soft breeze faintly redolent of the ocean wafted through the southern summer night. Summerish in its plainness and tranquillity, with minute modest stars in the clear sky, the night effused a soft, transparent darkness. The distant lights were pale, and since the hour was late, they seemed drowsy. Soon everything on the ship was completely settled; now the placid voices of the crew were audible, the anchor chain clattered . . . Then the stern shuddered, rumbled with churning water and screws. Scattered low and flat on the distant shore, the lights floated away. The ship stopped swaying.

One might have thought that both passengers were sleeping, so motionless did they recline in the deck chairs. But they were not asleep; they were staring intently through the dusk at one another. Finally the first, the one whose legs were covered by the lap robe, asked simply and placidly, "Are you going to the Crimea too?"

And the other, the one with the straight shoulders, answered unhurriedly in the same tone, "Yes, to the Crimea and then some. I'll be in Alupka, and after that in Gagry."

"I recognized you immediately," said the first.

"And I recognized you, and also immediately," answered the other.

"Quite a strange and unexpected encounter."

"Couldn't be stranger."

"In fact, it wasn't that I recognized you, but I seemed to have had, for some reason, a presentiment that you would show up—so that recognition was beside the point."

"I had exactly the same feeling."

"Yes? Very strange. Doesn't it make you admit that life, nonetheless, has its moments—well, singular moments, so to speak? Perhaps life is not at all so simple as it appears."

"Could be, but then maybe there's another explanation: that just this minute you and I conjured up in our imaginations what we now take to be premonitory."

"Perhaps. Yes, that's entirely possible. Even highly probable."

"Well, there you see. We philosophize away, but maybe life is very simple. As simple as that clamor just now beside the ladder. Those fools, crushing each other; where were they all in such a hurry to get to?"

The men fell silent for a moment. Then they began speaking again.

"How long since we saw each other? Twenty-three years?" asked the first passenger, the one under the lap robe.

"Yes, almost," answered the other. "Exactly twenty-three in the autumn. For you and me it's quite easy to calculate. Almost a quarter century."

"A long time. An entire lifetime. That is, considering that life is nearly over for both of us now."

"Yes, yes. And so what? Are we really so terrified that it's over?"

"Hmm! Of course not. Hardly at all. We're lying, after all, when we tell ourselves how terrifying it is; that is, when we try to frighten ourselves by saying, 'Look, you've lived out your life and in some ten years you'll be in the grave.' And just think: the grave. It's no laughing matter."

"Absolutely right. And I'll tell you something even more interesting. You probably know how I am, so to speak, renowned in the world of medicine?"

"But who doesn't know that! Of course I do. And are you aware that your humble servant has also glorified himself?"

"Well, most certainly. One could say I'm your devotee, your faithful reader," said the other.

"Yes, yes, two celebrities. Well, what were you going to say?"

"That thanks to my celebrity, that is, to a certain erudition (God knows how much wisdom; the erudition, nonetheless, is substantial), I can be almost perfectly sure that I have not even ten years to live, but just a few months. Well, at the very most a year. Both I and my colleagues in the profession have come up with the same irrefutable diagnosis: a terminal disease. And I can assure you that, nonetheless, I am living almost as if nothing had changed. I only smile sarcastically. Imagine, if you please, I wanted to show up everyone with my knowledge of all possible causes of death, to become famous and live a magnificent life; and my achievements collapsed on my head—I made the magnificent discovery of my very own death. They might have played the fool with me and deceived me: 'Hold on, old boy, we'll get you through this, what the hell!' But how can they lie and dissimulate with someone like me? It's stupid and awkward. So awkward that they even overdo the frankness, which they combine with touching emotion and flattery: 'After all, dear colleague, there's no point in trying to bamboozle *you. Finita la commedia!*'"

"Are you serious?" asked the first.

"Absolutely serious," answered the other. "But what, then, is the main point? Some Gaius once was mortal, ergo I too will die; but at some indefinite time in the future! Here, unfortunately, we have an entirely different matter: not at some indefinite time, but within a year. And is that very long, a year? Next summer you'll be sailing somewhere again over the ocean blue, while at the Novodevichy Cemetery in Moscow my noble bones will repose. Well, so what? Just that in thinking of this I feel next to nothing. And what's even worse, it's not at all due to some fortitude that the students see in me as I expatiate to them upon my disease and its course as something interesting from the clinical point of view; it's just some idiotic insensibility. And no one around me, people who know my fatal secret, they don't feel anything either. Well, take you, for example—are you afraid for me?"

"Afraid for you? No, I must confess, not really in the least."

"And of course not at all sorry for me."

"No, not sorry either. Another thing is that I can't imagine your believing in those beatific realms where there's neither sorrow nor lamentation but only the little apples of paradise."

"Well, let's just say religious faith is no big thing in your life or mine."

Once again they both fell silent. Then they took out their cigarette cases and lit up.

"And also take this into consideration," said the first, the one under the lap robe. "That you and I are not putting on airs at all; we're not striking a pose for each other or for some imaginary audience. We're speaking really very simply, without any premeditated cynicism, without caustic vainglory, which always provides, after all, a certain compensation: 'Won't you kindly observe the plight we're in? No one else's problems can compare.' We're also conversing simply and falling silent without making the silence bear some meaning, without any stoic sagacity. Generally speaking, there is no more voluptuous animal on earth than man; the shrewd human soul can extort self-gratification from anything. But in our case I don't see even this. That's all the more curious since one must add to our, as you express it, idiotic insensibility, all the singularity of our relationship. You and I, after all, are bonded in a terribly intimate way. That is, speaking more precisely, there should be that kind of bond between us."

"Of course!" answered the other. "What horrendous sufferings, in fact, I put you through. I can imagine what you had to live with."

"Yes, and even much more than you can imagine. You're right, it's horrendous, all that nightmare a man, a lover, or a husband goes through when his wife has been taken away, won over, and for days and nights on end, almost incessantly, minute by minute, he's writhing around in tormented pride. With terrible jealous visions of the happiness his rival is experiencing, and with hopeless, unremitting tenderness—or rather, tender sexual yearning—for the lost mate. At one and the same time he's wanting to strangle her in a fury of hatred and lavish upon her the most abasing professions of devotion, a truly doglike submissiveness. Altogether it's just too hideous to put in words. And besides that, I'm not an entirely ordinary man but a highly sensitive and highly imaginative individual. So just think about what I went through for years."

"Really years?"

"I assure you, not less than three years. Even for a long time after that a single thought of you and her, of your intimacy with her, would scorch me like red-hot iron. It's understandable. Well, say a man, for example, takes your fiancée away from you—that's still tolerable. But your mistress, or, in our case, your wife! The one, excuse my frankness, with whom I've slept, whose every feature of body and soul I know like the back of my hand! Just think what scope there is here for the jealous imagination. How can you bear another's possessing her? It's all simply beyond human endurance. And for what did I nearly drink myself blind, for what did I wreck my health and aspirations? For what did I waste the time when my powers and talent were flourishing most brilliantly? Speaking with no exaggeration whatsoever, you simply broke me in pieces. I recovered, of course, but to what end? My former self, nonetheless, no longer existed and could not exist. You encroached upon the most sacred thing in all my existence! While seeking himself a bride, Prince Gautama beheld Yasodhara, who 'had the shape of a goddess and the eyes of a doe in spring.' In his passion for her, competing with the other young men, he performed the devil only knows what stunts; for example, he shot from his bow with such force that it was heard for seven thousand miles. And then he took off his necklace of pearls, entwined it about the neck of Yasodhara, and said, 'It is her I have chosen because she and I did play in the forest in times long past, when I was the son of a huntsman and she a forest maid. She lingers in the memory of my soul!' On that day she wore a gold-black mantle, and the prince cast his gaze upon her and said, 'She wears a gold-black mantle because myriads of years ago, when I was a huntsman, I saw her in the forests as a leopard. She lingers in the memory of my soul!' Forgive me for all this poetry, but it contains a profound, terrible truth. Just consider the sense of those remarkable words concerning the memory of the soul, and consider how horrendous it is when an outsider transgresses upon that, the most sanctified encounter in the world. Who knows—perhaps I too would have shot with such force that it could have been heard for thousands of miles. But suddenly you appeared."

"Well then, what do you feel towards me now?" asked the man with straight shoulders. "Malice, loathing, a craving for vengeance?"

"Just imagine: absolutely nothing. In spite of the tirade I just delivered, absolutely nothing. Horrible, horrendous. And there you have all the 'memory of my soul!' But then you know that perfectly well yourself. That is, you know I feel nothing; otherwise you wouldn't have asked."

"You're right. I know. And that's terrible too."

"But we, nonetheless, aren't frightened. What sheer horror: that we don't see anything the least bit terrible about it."

"Yes, in fact, nothing in the least. They say: the past, the past! But it's all nonsense. Strictly speaking, people have no past whatsoever. Only a weak echo from some aggregate of all their previous lives."

Once more the men lapsed into silence. The steamship shuddered, pushed on; rising, then subsiding, slowly and regularly came the soft sound of a drowsy wave, sweeping along the broadside; behind the monotonous din of the stern, swiftly, monotonously swiveled the line of the log, which was ticking off something now and again with a delicate cryptic chime: *dzeen* . . . Then the passenger with straight shoulders asked, "So tell me . . . what did you feel when you heard she had died? Also nothing?"

"Yes, almost nothing," answered the passenger under the lap robe. "Most of all a certain astonishment at my own lack of feelings. I opened the morning paper—and gently it hit me in the eye: by the will of God, such and such a woman . . . For want of habit it's very strange to see the name of someone you know, or someone close to you, in that black frame, in that deadly part of the paper, printed ceremoniously in large type . . . Then I tried to grieve, as if to say, 'Yes, it's that very same person, the one who . . .' But 'I heard the fatal tidings from dispassionate lips, / And dispassionate was my response.' Couldn't even wring any grief out of myself. Only a sort of feeble pity . . . And this was the very one who 'lingers in the memory of my soul,' my first, cruel, long-enduring love. I knew her at the peak of her charm and innocence, when she had that almost adolescent trustfulness and timidity that touches a man's heart in untold ways—perhaps because all femininity must have this trusting helplessness, something childlike, a sign that a girl or woman always harbors a future child within her. And it was to me, first of all, in some divine ecstatic horror, that she gave truly everything God had granted her; and I kissed her girlish body, the most beautiful thing on earth, truly millions of times in a frenzy that has no equal in all my life. And because of her I was literally out of my mind, day and night, for years on end. Because of her I cried, tore my hair, attempted suicide, drank, drove cabmen till their horses dropped, destroyed in a fury possibly my best, most valuable works . . . But then twenty years passed—and I looked numbly at her name in that obituary box, numbly imagined her lying in a coffin . . . An unpleasant picture, but nothing more. I assure you, nothing more. But then, you now—you, of course . . . do you feel anything?"

"I? Well no, what's there to hide? Certainly almost nothing."

The ship pushed on. Wave after wave arose hissing ahead, swept past splashing along the broadsides; the pallid snowlike wake that stretched behind the stern seethed and dinned monotonously. A lush breeze was blowing; a tracery of motionless stars lay high above the ship's black funnel, above the rigging and the slender blade of the forward mast.

"But do you know what?" suddenly said the first passenger, as if having just come to his senses. "Do you know what's most important? That by no means could I connect her, the dead her, with that other person I just told you about. No, by no means. Absolutely not. She, the other she, was a completely different person. And to say that I felt absolutely nothing for her, for that other her, is a lie. So then, what I said was inaccurate. That's simply not how it really is."

The other man reflected briefly.

"Well then, so what?" he asked.

"Just that almost everything we've said doesn't amount to a hill of beans."

"Oh, a hill of beans, is it?" said the passenger with the straight shoulders. "That other she, as you express it, is simply you, your imagination, your feelings—in a word, something that is part of you. And so you've been moved and agitated by nothing more than your very own self. Think about it properly."

"You think so? I don't know. It could be . . . Yes, it could be."

"And were you agitated for long even by your very self? Ten minutes. A half hour maybe. Well, a day at the most."

"Yes, yes. Horrible, but it seems you're right. And where is she now? Up there in that lovely sky?"

"Only Allah knows that, my friend. Most likely nowhere."

"You think so? Yes, yes . . . Most likely you're right."

The plain of the unbounded sea lay like a black circle under the buoyant bright cupola of the night sky. And lost in that circular darkening plain, the little steamship numbly and steadfastly held its course. Stretching infinitely behind it was the sleepily seething, milkish-pale wake—to the distant point where the night sky merged with the sea, where in contrast to that milkiness the skyline seemed dark, melancholy. And the log line swiveled and swiveled, sadly and mysteriously ticking off something, severing now and again the delicate chime: *dzee-een* . . .

Having kept silent for a brief time, the men said softly and simply to each other, "Sleep well."

"Sleep well."

Maritime Alps, 1923

»»» «««

Antonov Apples

I

My memory conjures up an early autumn with lovely weather. Warm, light rainfall passed through August, as if falling on purpose for the sowing—rainfall that came just at the right time, in the middle of the month, around the holiday of Saint Lavrenty. "Autumn and winter live well together when Lavrenty waters are calm and rainfall light." Then, with Indian summer, long drifting strands of gossamer settled all over the fields. That too is a good sign: "When cobwebs abound in Indian summer, autumn will be fruitful." I recall an early, brisk, quiet morning. I recall the big garden, golden all over, dried out and sparse in foliage, I recall the arborways lined with maples, the delicate scent of fallen leafage—and the smell of Antonov apples, that fragrant mix of honey and autumn crispness. The air is so pure that it seems not to exist; throughout the orchard voices and creaking carts resound. These are the orchard men, the harvesters who have hired peasants to pour out the heaps of apples so as to send them off that night to the city—invariably in the night, when it's so glorious to lie on a cartload, gazing at the starry sky, smelling the tar in the fresh air, and listening to the long caravan of carts that squeak so cautiously in the darkness as they make their way down the highroad. The peasant heaping up the apples will eat them with a juicy crunch, one after another, but that's the way it's done; never will the harvester stop him, and he might even say, "Go on, then, eat your fill—ain't no problem! Them that pours honey gets to eat honey."

Only the sated clucking of the thrushes (on the coralline red rowans in the garden thicket) breaks the cool silence of the morning, only the voices and the dull clunk of the apples as they're poured out into measuring buckets and tubs. Through the thinning leafage of the orchard you can see the faraway road scattered with straw, leading to the big shanty, and you see that shanty itself, focal point of the whole operation set up by the harvesters over the summer. The pungency of apples is everywhere but here especially strong. Bedding is spread inside the shanty, there's a single-barreled shotgun, a green-tarnished samovar, crockery in the corner. Bast matting is lying around outside, crates, all sorts of frayed odds and ends; there's a dug-out earthen stove in the ground. At noon they cook upon it a marvelous, thin, millet porridge with fatback; in the evening they heat the samovar there, and a long stream of light blue smoke spreads over the orchard, drifts between the trees. But on festival days a sumptuous marketplace fair springs up beside the shanty, and red attire steadily flickers and flows beyond the trees. Spry country girls of the smallholder class throng together, wearing *sarafans* that smell strongly of dye, the manor servants of the "gentryfolk" come up in their comely and crude, uncouth outfits, and the young wife of the village headman appears, pregnant, with a broad-cheeked sleepy face and as full of herself as an unmilked cow from Kholmogorsk. She's got "horns" on her head—braids wound up on both sides of the crown and covered with several kerchiefs—which make her head look enormous. Her legs in half boots with taps stand there obtuse and sturdy; she wears a sleeveless blouse of velveteen, a long folk pinafore, and a homespun skirt—black lilac with stripes the color of brick and edged along its hem with a broad golden selvedge.

"Now, that's one cock-of-the-walk biddy!" says the harvester, shaking his head. "Ain't many left like her these days."

Little boys keep coming up, dressed in white hempen shirts and short pants, no hats on their white towheads. They advance in twos or threes, taking small steps on their bare feet and looking askance at the shaggy shepherd dog tied to an apple tree. Only one of them, of course, does the buying, since all they have to pay with is a kopeck or an egg, but the customers are many and business brisk, and the consumptive tradesman in his long frock coat and rust red boots is in a good mood. Along with his brother, a lisping nimble half idiot who lives with him "out of charity," he jokes and wise-cracks as he sells, and sometimes even "hits a few licks" on his Tula concertina. The orchard is thronged with people till evening; beside the shanty one hears the hubbub of speech, laughter, and sometimes a foot-stomping dance as well.

On clear days, nearing nightfall, the weather turns cold and dewy. After you've breathed your fill in the threshing barn, of the rye grain aromas of fresh straw and chaff, you walk briskly back home to supper past the earthen bank of the orchard. With remarkable clarity voices in the village or the creaking of gates resound through the bitter-cold evening glow. It's getting dark. And there's still another smell: in the orchard a bonfire burns, and the fragrant smoke from the cherry branches wafts densely through the air. Out of the darkness in the depths of the orchard there's a fairyland scene. As if in some corner of hell a crimson flame blazes near the shanty, surrounded by murk, and black silhouettes, as if cut out of ebony wood, flit about near the fire while the gigantic shadows they cast walk amidst apple trees. A black hand, several yards long, takes the whole of a tree in its grasp, or else two legs are distinctly sketched out—two black pillars. And suddenly all of this slidders down from the apple tree—and the shadow extends over all of the pathway, right from the shanty to the wicket gate.

Late at night when the lights are out in the village, when the seven diamonds of the constellation Atlantides sparkle on high, you run out into the orchard again. Rustling through the dry leaves like a blind man, you make it to the shanty. It's a bit brighter there in the clearing, and the Milky Way gleams white above your head.

"Is that you, young master?" someone calls softly out of the darkness.

"Yes, it's me. Aren't you sleeping yet, Nikolai?"

"We ain't allowed to sleep. But it's late, don't you reckon? I believe that's the passenger train I hear coming."

We listen closely for a long while, and we can feel a quaver in the ground. That quaver grows into a rumble, increases and builds until it seems to be just beyond the orchard; ever more rapidly the clamorous wheels beat out their tempo: pounding and thundering, the train rushes toward us . . . nearer, nearer, ever louder and more ferocious . . . Then suddenly it starts getting quieter, subsiding, as if descending underground . . .

"Where's your gun, Nikolai?"

"Yonder, by that crate."

You swing up the one-barreled weapon, heavy as a crowbar, and you rashly fire it off. With a deafening crack the crimson flame flashes out toward the sky, dazzling you for a second and putting out the stars, and a bracing echo crashes and rolls like a hoop out along the horizon, dying out far, far away, in the pure keen air.

"That's the way to do it!" says the harvester. "Throw a scare into 'em, young master, otherwise we got big troubles! They done shook off all the dooly-pears up by the earth wall again."

The black sky is sketched with fiery streaks of falling stars. You gaze for a long time into its dark blue depths abounding in constellations, until the ground starts swaying beneath your feet. Then you rouse yourself and, hiding your hands in your sleeves, you quickly run down the pathway to the house. How cold, how dew-drenched, and how good it is to be alive on earth!

2

"A fruitful Antonov means a fortunate year." Life on the land will be fine if the Antonov ripens up well—that means the grain will ripen well too. My memory conjures up a high-yield crop year.

At daybreak, when the roosters still crow and the peasant huts are black with smoke, you throw open a window onto the cool garden covered with violet-toned fog, through which specks of morning sunlight gleam, and you can't restrain yourself—you order a horse quickly saddled while you run out to wash in the pond. The delicate leafage on the withies along the shore is almost all blown away and their boughs show through against a turquoise sky. The water beneath the withies has turned transparent, icy, and somehow heavy. Momentarily it drives away the languor of the night, and after you've washed and had breakfast in the kitchen outbuilding with the laborers (hot potatoes and black bread with big moist grains of salt), you ride out past Vyselki to go hunting, taking delight in feeling beneath you the slippery leather of the saddle. In autumn come the patron saints' festivals, and at that time of year the common folks are all tidied up, content, the village has a totally different look. And if it's a high-yield year and a whole golden metropolis soars high up in the granaries, if the shrill geese on the river are voicing their resonant morning honks, then things are not at all bad in the village. Furthermore, from time out of mind, from the years of Grandfather, our Vyselki has been famed for its "affluence." Old men and women in Vyselki are long-lived—that's the first sign of a prosperous village—and they are all so strapping and tall, with hair white as the driven snow. Sometimes you hear things like this: "Um-hum, Agatha, now, she's got eighty-three big ones put behind her!" Or conversations of this sort:

"When do you figure on dying, Pankrat? You must be a good hundred if you're a day."

"What's that you say, my good sir?"

"I'm asking you how many years old you might be!"

"Well, I can't rightly say, my good sir."

"Tell me, can you remember Platon Apollonich?"

"Wellsir, yes, I sure do—real clear I recollect him."

"Well, there you are, see. That means you can't be less than a hundred."

The old man, who is standing at attention in front of the master, smiles a meek and chastened smile. As if to say, "What can you do? I'm guilty, I reckon—lived past my time." And he would surely have lived on even longer, had he not stuffed himself on onions for the holiday of Saints Peter and Paul.

I remember his old lady as well. All the time sitting on a bench out on the porch, hunched over, head dithering, gasping for breath, and holding on to the bench with her hands—perpetually pondering over something. "Thinking about all her paraphernalia, I 'speck," said the peasant women, because she really did have a lot of "paraphernalia" in her trunks. But she apparently was not listening; gazing with her purblind eyes at some distant point from beneath brows raised mournfully, head trembling, she seemed to be making an effort to recall something. A large old lady she was, somehow dark all over. Her homespun skirt looked to have barely made it out of the past century, her hempen slippers were the kind they put on a corpse, her neck was yellow and wizened, her blouse with its dimity-cloth patches was always the whitest of white:

"She's all primped up and ready for the coffin." There was a big stone beside her porch; she'd bought it herself for her grave, and a shroud as well—a wonderful shroud, with angels, crosses, and a prayer printed along its edges.

Well matched with the old folks were the peasant homesteads in Vyselki: brick, built in their grandfathers' times. And the rich muzhiks—Savely, Ignat, Dron—had huts of two or three wings, because in Vyselki it still wasn't in style to separate off the generations. In that sort of family they kept bees, took pride in their stallions of the Bityug breed (that steel blue cart horse), and they maintained their property well. On the threshing floors lay dark thick heaps of grossly rank hemp; there were drying barns and granaries roofed with neatly trimmed thatching. The garners and storerooms had steel doors, behind which they stashed their sackcloth, distaffs, new sheepskin coats, harness with decorative plates, grain-measuring vats bound with copper hoops. Gates and sledges were branded with crosses. And I recall that at times it seemed a great temptation to be a peasant. On a sunlit morning you'd be riding around the village, and you kept thinking about how fine it would be to mow, to thresh, to sleep in the threshing barn on a pile of straw, and on holidays to get up with the sun, to the viscous and melodious peal of church bells from the big village, to wash hands and face beside a barrel, and to put on a clean hempen shirt, trousers of the same material, and those indestructible hobnailed boots. If to all that you could add a robust and beautiful wife in holiday finery, a trip to mass, and then dinner at the household of your bearded father-in-law, a dinner with hot mutton on wooden plates, with bread of sifted flour, honey in the comb, and home-brewed beer—well, what more could you possibly want!

In my memory—a quite recent memory—the way of life of the middling gentry had much in common with the life of the rich peasantry, for its prosperity and its down-home old-fashioned well-being. Such, for example, was the estate of Auntie Anna Gerasimovna, who lived some twelve versts from Vyselki. You would ride along on horseback in early morning, and by the time you reached her manor the day was already dawning. Dogs are with you on a leash so you have to go at a trot, but then you're in no hurry anyway—it's so fine in the open field on a cool and sunlit day! The land is level here, you can see far into the distance. The sky is ethereal and so spacious and deep. The sunlight shines obliquely, and the road, rolled smooth after the rains by passing carts, has an oily texture and gleams like railway tracks. All around you the fresh, luxuriantly green winter crops are spread like broad patches of dimity cloth. A baby hawk soars up from somewhere into the crystalline air and freezes in one spot, flicking his sharp little wings. Running off into the clarity of distance, telegraph poles stand out distinctly, and their wires, like the silvery strings of musical instruments, slide along the slope of the clear sky. Merlins are perched upon them, the blackest of black notes on sheet music.

I never knew or saw the time of serfdom, but at Auntie Anna's estate, as I recall, I sensed it. Upon riding into the courtyard you feel immediately that serfdom is still thriving. The estate is small but everything about it is old, solid, surrounded by centenarian birches and withies. The structures near the manor are numerous—built close to the ground but prosperous-looking—and all of them seem to be fused together out of dark oak logs beneath thatched straw roofs. The only one that stands out for its size, or rather, for its length, is the blackened kitchen building, from which the last of the Mohicans of manor house menials are peering out at you—decrepit old men and women, along with the doddering retired cook who looks like Don Quixote. When you ride into the courtyard they all come to attention and then bow toward you with their deep, low bows. The gray-haired coachman, on his way from the carriage house to take your horse, removes his cap right from the start and walks the whole courtyard with head bared. He used to ride postilion for Auntie, and now he drives her to vespers—in winter using a covered sledge with doors and in summer a sturdy wagon bound round with iron bands, like the kind that village priests ride in. Auntie's garden was famed for its state of utter desuetude, for its nightingales, turtledoves, and apples, and the manor house was famed for its roof. It stood at the head of the courtyard right beside the garden—embraced by linden branches. The building was small and squat, but it did not seem possible this house could be a hundred years old, not when it put on that magisterial gaze as it peered out at you from beneath its uncommonly tall and thick straw roof, which had gone black and hardened with time. Its front facade always seemed alive, as if an old face were looking out from beneath a huge cap with its sockets of eyes—windows that had panes with a mother-of-pearl sheen, provided by the rain and the sun. On both sides of those eyes were the verandas—two large old porches with columns. There were always sated pigeons crouched up on their gables, while sparrows by the thousands would be spattering over like rain from roof to roof. And the coziness of that nest would embrace a visitor beneath the turquoise autumn sky!

You walk into the manor house and first of all you catch the scent of apples, then different smells: old mahogany furniture, dried linden blossoms lying on the windowsill since June. All the rooms—the servants' quarters, the parlor, the drawing room—are cool and murky; that's because the house is surrounded by the garden, and the upper panes of the windows are stained glass: dark bluc and lilac. Silence and cleanliness reign, although it seems that the armchairs, the tables with inlaid work, and the mirrors in their slender, spiraling gilt frames have never been moved from their places. Then you hear an intermittent cough, and out comes Auntie. She is small, but like everything around her she is solid. She has a big Persian shawl thrown over her shoulders. She enters with an air of self-importance mixed with cordiality, and immediately, to the accompaniment of endless chat about old times, about who inherited what, the treats begin appearing: first the "*doolies*" and the apples—Antonovs, "belle-madames," "*borovinkas,*" "fertile girls"—and after that a remarkable dinner: boiled ham that's rosy through and through, with sweet peas, stuffed chicken, turkey, pickled vegetables, and red kvass—a strong drink that's the sweetest of sweet. The windows giving on the garden are raised, and a bracing autumn coolness wafts in.

3

In recent years only one thing has braced up the fading spirit of the landowners: hunting.

In former times estates such as that of Anna Gerasimovna were no rarity. Other estates still maintained the grand style while declining into penury; they were enormous in scope, with orchards of fifty acres. True, some of those certainly remain to this day, but they are lifeless now. There are no more troikas, no more Kirghiz saddle horses, no hounds or borzois, no house serfs, and even he whose domain all this once was is gone—the landlord-hunter, such as my late brother-in-law Arseny Semyonich.

From the end of September our gardens and threshing floors were deserted; the weather, as it always does, took a sudden turn for the worse. Whole days on end the wind would shake up the trees and tear at their branches, rains would drench them from morning till night. Sometimes toward evening, amidst the lowering, low storm clouds in the west, the low sun would break through with its quavering gold; the air would take on a crispness and clarity, and a ray of sunlight would produce a dazzling gleam amidst the boughs and leafage, which, like a meshwork come alive, were twitching and churning in the wind. Cold and bright to the north, above heavy leaden clouds, there was the glitter of an etiolated, light blue sky, and from behind those clouds ridges of snowy mountain-billows slowly floated out. You stood by your window and thought, "Could be, God willing, the skies will clear." But the wind did not abate. It churned about the garden, battered the steady stream of smoke flowing from the chimney of the kitchen outbuilding, and once more the ominous shaggy-haired locks of ash-colored clouds blew in. They rushed along fast and low and soon they fogged in the sun like smoke. Its sheen dimmed as the interstice of light blue sky closed over, the garden turned barren and bleak, and once more the rain started spitting . . . first gently, cautiously, then ever more thickly, and finally it turned into a downpour dark and stormy. Then came a long and disquieting night.

After such a belaboring the garden would be almost totally bare, scattered with wet leaves, and somehow hushed and submissive. But for all that, how beautiful it was when once more the clear weather came, the cold and pellucid days of early October, the farewell festival of autumn! Whatever leafage remained would now hang on the trees until the first frosts. Humbly awaiting winter, warming itself in the sheen of the sun, the black garden would stand against a background of cold turquoise sky. And now the plowed fields took on their stark black look, attenuated by the bright green of winter crops that spread their wisps of side shoots . . . It's time to go hunting!

I see myself again at the manor of Arseny Semyonich, in the parlor of the big house full of sunshine and smoke from pipes and cigarettes. There are lots of folks there, and they are all tanned, with weather-beaten faces, wearing tight-waisted light coats and top boots. They have just eaten a copious meal, they're flushed and animated by the clamorous talk of the upcoming hunt, but they don't forget to finish off the vodka after dinner. Out in the yard a horn trumpets and dogs are yelping in all sorts of tones. The black borzoi, Arseny Semyonich's favorite dog, has climbed up on the table and begun gnawing at what remains of the hare under sauce. But suddenly he lets out a terrible squeal and hurls himself off the table, overturning dishes and vodka glasses. Walking out of his study with a hunter's whip and a pistol, Arseny has suddenly deafened the parlor with a shot. The room is enveloped in still more smoke, and he stands there laughing.

"Too bad I missed him!" he says, his eyes agleam.

He's tall in stature, slim, but wide in the shoulders and well built, with the face of a handsome gypsy. His eyes have a wild glitter and he moves about adroitly in his raspberry silk shirt, velvet baggy trousers, and high boots. After frightening both dog and guests with his shot, he declaims in baritone, using a jokingly pretentious voice: "It's time, it's time, put saddle to the swift Don steed, / And hang about your neck the clear-voiced hunter's horn!"

Then he says loudly, "All right, then, time is golden; let's waste no more!"

I can still feel the way I drew the cold air of that clear and moist day into my young lungs, greedily sucking in my breath till they were full. It was just around eventide and I was riding out with Arseny's clamorous band, stirred by the melodious din of the dogs let loose into a deciduous woodland, out in some backwater called Red Knoll or Thundering Glen, spots that by their names alone rouse the hunter's spirit. You ride along on a mean-spirited, squat and powerful Kirghiz horse, holding him firmly in rein, and you feel fused with him, almost as if you are one and the same creature. He whinnies, asking you to let him pick up the pace, he swishes loudly with his hooves through the deep and airy carpet covering of black fallen leaves, and every sound dully resounds in the empty, moist, and crisp woods. Somewhere far off comes the yap of a dog, answered by the passionate, plaintive call of another, then a third—and suddenly the whole forest is clattering with the tumult of baying and barks, as if it all were made of glass. The sharp retort of a shot bursts out amidst all that din—and then things roll into motion, "commence to cooking" somewhere far up ahead.

"Got one, tally-ho!" someone screams in a madcap voice that carries throughout the forest.

"Ah, they've flushed one out!" that intoxicating thought flashes through your mind. You whoop at the horse, and as if breaking your chains you dash off through the woods, oblivious to everything along the way. There are just the trees that flicker before your eyes and the mud from the horse's hooves that flies back and sticks to your face. You come tearing out of the forest and you see a particolored pack of dogs stretched out over the greenness of the earth, and you spur up your Kirghiz still more to head off the prey. Across green meadows you gallop, over freshly plowed fields and the stubble of last year's crops—until you end up, finally, in another oasis thicket and lose sight of the pack, which fades along with its frenzied barking and yowling. Then, wet through and shuddering with tension, you rein in the lathered, wheezing horse and avidly gulp at the icy dampness of the forest vale. Far away the cries of hunters and barks of dogs are dying out, and around you a deathly silence reigns. The timber forest, with an open spot at one end, stands there motionless, and it seems you've made your way into some mysterious palace chambers. Strong smells waft from the ravines: mushrooms, dank leaves rotted through, and wet tree bark. The dampness of the ravines becomes ever more palpable as the woods grow cold and dark.

It's time to find somewhere to spend the night, but rounding up all the dogs after a hunt is no easy task. Prolonged and hopelessly grievous, the sounds of hunting horns ring out in the forest, and for a long time you hear the cries, the curses, and the squeals of dogs. Finally, after dark has set in, the band of hunters comes bursting onto the estate of some bachelor-landowner who is almost a total stranger, filling with its clamor the whole courtyard, illumined by lanterns, candles, and lamps that are borne out from the house to welcome the guests.

Sometimes such a hospitable neighbor lent accommodations to the hunt for several days in a row. At early daybreak, through an icy wind and the first wet snowfall, they rode out into forests and fields, and at twilight back they came, mud-splattered, faces flushed, reeking of horse sweat and of the hides of the hunted prey—and that's when the drinking bouts began. After a whole day in the cold of the fields the bright house full of people was ever so warm. The hunters strolled about from room to room in tight-waisted coats unbuttoned, drinking and eating at random, loudly sharing impressions one with another, in the presence of a robust full-grown wolf, which lay in the middle of the parlor with fluffy tail thrown out to one side, teeth bared, eyes fixed with pain, staining the floor with its pallid, now congealed blood. After the vodka and the food you feel such a sweet fatigue, take such languid pleasure in the drowsiness of youth that you're listening to the murmur of voices as if underwater. Your weather-beaten face is burning, and when you close your eyes the whole earth takes off and floats beneath your feet. After you lie down in bed, on a soft feather mattress in the age-old corner room with an icon stand and lamp, the phantasms of flaming and multicolored dogs flicker by before your eyes, your whole body hums with the sensation of the chase, and you sink unawares, along with all those images and sensations, into a sweet and healthy sleep, having completely forgotten that this was once the prayer room of the old man whose name is linked with gloomy legends of serfdom times, and that he died in this room, probably in this very bed.

When you happened to sleep through the hunt, your rest was especially pleasant. After awaking you lounge for a long time in bed. The whole house is steeped in silence. You hear the gardener warily making his way through each room lighting the stoves, the sound of firewood crackling and popping. In prospect is a whole placid day in the manor house, which has taken on a wintery quietude. You leisurely dress yourself, wander about the orchard, find amidst the wet leafage a cold and wet apple they have missed, and for some reason it seems uncommonly tasty, not at all like other apples. Then you settle down with books—the books of your grandfathers in thick, shagreen bindings with gold stars on the morocco-leather spines. What a glorious redolence they have, those tomes with their thick, rough, yellowed paper, something like the prayer books used in church! It's a pleasant smell, sour mildew, ancient perfume. Fine too are the notations in their margins, large letters with soft, round flourishes made by a quill pen. You open a book and read, "A thought worthy of ancient and contemporary philosophers, the inflorescence of reason and of heartfelt sentiment." Then, involuntarily, you're drawn into the book itself. It's *The Nobleman-Philosopher,* an allegory published some hundred years ago under the aegis of some "*cavalier* bedight with a plethora of honors" and run off at the printing house of the Department of Civil Charity—the story of how "a nobleman-philosopher, having at his disposal the time and capacities for thought, to which avocation the mind of humanity may ascend, once conceived the wish to compose an *orbis terrarum* upon the vast expanses of his own demesne." Then you come upon *The Satirical and Philosophical Works of Monsieur Voltaire,* and you spend a long time reveling in the lovely, fustian style of the translation: "Sires! In the Sixteenth Centennium Erasmus penned his Praise of Folly (affected pause—semicolon); but Ye do vouchsafe me to extol in your presence Reason." Then you pass from the antiquity of Catherine the Great to the age of Romanticism, to the literary miscellanies, the long and sentimentally pompous novels. The cuckoo scoots out of the clock and coos out its derisively mournful coo above you in the empty house, and little by little a sweet and strange anguish begins creeping into your soul.

Here you have *The Secrets of Alexis* and here *Victor, or a Child in the Forest:* "Midnight strikes! The hum of diurnal and the merry songs of the country folk give way to a sacred hush. Sleep extends lugubrious wings over the surface of our Hemisphere, and those fluttering wings disseminate dolefulness and reveries . . . Reveries . . . How frequently do they do no more than prolong an ill-starred suffering!" And before your eyes the beloved old words are glimmering: crags and leafy woodlets, the pallid moon and solitude, specters and phantoms, putti, roses and lilies, "the mischief and sportiveness of young rapscallions," a lily white hand, Lyudmilas and Alinas. And here you find journals with the names of Zhukovsky, Batiushkov, the Pushkin of the lyceum period. And with sadness you recall Grandmother, her polonaises on the clavichord, her languorous declamations of verses from *Eugene Onegin.* And that dreamy old-world life stands before you. Fine and comely were the girls and ladies who once dwelled in the manors of the nobility! Their portraits gaze down at me from the walls, their aristocratically beautiful heads with the old-fashioned coiffures, their long eyelashes lowered over sorrowful, tender eyes in a meek and feminine pose.

4

The smell of Antonov apples is disappearing from the landowners' estates. Those days were so recent, and yet it seems that virtually an entire century has passed. The old folks at Vyselki, down to the very last one, have died off, Anna Gerasimovna is gone, Arseny Semyonich shot himself. The reign of the petty squires has arrived, landed nobility impoverished to the point of beggary. But even the poverty-stricken life of the middling squire has its charm!

Once again I see myself in the country, enveloped in autumn. The days are bluish, morose. In the morning I mount up, taking only one dog along, and I ride out into the field with rifle and horn. The wind rings and buzzes in the barrel of the weapon; blowing hard in my face, it sometimes picks up a dusting of dry snow. All day long I rove about the empty plains. Chilled to the bone and famished, I return at twilight to the manor house, and when the lights of Vyselki glitter up ahead, when up from the manor drifts the smell of smoke and habitation my soul feels a wealth of warmth and comfort. I recall how in our house we loved to "take the gloaming" during that time of day, to carry on conversations in the semi-darkness, leaving the lamps unlit. When I enter the house I find the cold-weather window frames already installed, and this puts me even more in the mood for the placid style of winter. In the footmen's quarters a worker is stoking the stove, and just as I did in childhood, I squat down on my haunches next to a pile of straw, which reeks already with the pungency of winter crispness, and I gaze by turns at the flaming stove and the windows, beyond which, turning blue, the twilight is mournfully waning. Then I go into the kitchen. It's bright there and crowded with people; the peasant girls are chopping cabbage, their knives flashing. I listen to that staccato clunking in concert as the voices sing, in concert, their sadly joyous songs of the countryside. Sometimes a neighbor, another petty squire, will drop by and take me back to his place for a long stay. Yes, the middling landowner's life has its charms as well!

The squire rises early. Stretching himself thoroughly, he climbs out of bed and rolls a thick cigarette of cheap black tobacco, or the even cheaper kind called *makhorka*. The pale light of an early

November morning illumines a plain study with walls bare, with brittle, yellow fox-fur pelts hanging above the bed, and a squat figure in baggy trousers and unbelted peasant shirt, while the mirror reflects a sleepy face with Tatar features. In the warm, semidark manor house a deathly silence reigns. Out in the corridor, on the other side of the door, an old cook is snoring; this is a woman who has lived in the gentry folks' home since she was a small girl. But that doesn't stop the master from letting out a hoarse bellow that carries throughout the house: "Lukeria! The samovar!"

Then, putting on his boots, throwing a light coat over his shoulders, and leaving the collar of his Russian shirt unbuttoned, he goes out onto the veranda. The locked vestibule smells of dogs; lazily stretching, yawning with a squeal, and smiling, the hounds come crowding around him.

"Get down!" he says, in a slow, condescending bass voice, and he walks out through the garden toward the threshing barn. His chest heaving, he takes in deep breaths of the crisp dawn air and the smell of the bare garden with its overnight chill. Half of the trees along the birch-lined arborway have been cut down; the leaves, curled back and blackened by frost, rustle beneath his boots. Silhouetted against the low, gloomy sky, jackdaws with their hackles ruffled up are sleeping on the cockscomb of the barn. It looks like a glorious day for hunting! Stopping in the middle of the arborway, the master gazes for a long time at the autumnal field, at the desolate green of winter croplands across which calves are meandering. Two hound bitches start whimpering at his feet, and Bounder is already on the other side of the garden; leaping across the prickly crop stubble, he seems to be beckoning, pleading to go out into the field. But what can you do now with hounds? The quarry is out in the openlands now, on the plowed earth, the bare, frozen spots. He's wary of the woods because the wind rustles the forest leaves there. Ah, if only we had some borzoi dogs!

They've begun the threshing in the barn. The drum of the threshing machine hums as it slowly gathers momentum. Lazily stretching the traces, digging their hooves into the manure on the path where they circumambulate, the swaying horses harnessed in the driving gear trudge on. Revolving on a bench in the middle of that gear sits the teamster, shouting at them all in a monotone but flicking only one with his lash: the brown gelding, who is laziest of all and who goes right to sleep as he walks, taking advantage of the blindfold over his eyes.

"Move it, girls, move it!" sternly cries the staid old feeder as he dons a loose-fitting fustian shirt. The peasant girls hastily sweep the floor, run about carrying handbarrows and brooms.

"Let her go then!" says the feeder, and the first fascicle of grain, fed through as a test, flies into the drum with a buzz and a squeal, then emerges from beneath it, ascending in the shape of a tattered fan. The drum hums on still more persistently, the work begins in earnest, and soon all sounds blend into the single harmonious drone of the threshing. The master stands at the gates of the barn and watches, sees the flickering of red and yellow kerchiefs, of hands, rakes, straw, sees all of this commotion, this bustling about at a measured pace to the din of the drum and the monotone cries, the whistles of the teamster. Chaff glumings are drifting off in clouds toward the gate. The master stands there and turns gray all over as the glumes engulf him. He keeps glancing off into the field. Soon, quite soon, the fields will go white; soon the first snow will cover them.

Early snow, first frost! We have no borzois, nothing to hunt with in November; but winter is coming on, and we can start getting down to business with the hounds. Then once more, just like in former times, the middling squires will gather together, drink up the last of their money, lose themselves for days on end out in the snowy fields. In the evening on some desolate farmstead the windows of an outbuilding glitter in the darkness of a wintry night. Out there in that small room clouds of smoke are swimming about, suet candles are burning dimly, and they're tuning up a guitar. Someone starts out in a chesty tenor: "At twilight time was when the mad wind blew, / Blew wide my gates, then, raging, rushed on through."

Awkwardly, putting on a pose of jocularity, the others take up the melody, singing with a mournful, hopeless panache: "Blew wide my gates, then, raging, rushed on through, / And white snow choked the path, once fresh with dew."

1900

»»» «««

Drydale

I

What always amazed us about Natalya was her attachment to Drydale.

She who had nursed at the same breast as our father, grown up with him in the same home, lived all of eight years with us at Lunyovo, as one of the family and not as a former slave, not a mere house serf. And for all those eight years she was, in her own words, on vacation from Drydale, from the agonies it had forced her to endure. But there's much to be said for the proverb "Feed a wolf how ye might, he still has eyes for the wood." After she raised us, reared us up, she returned once more to Drydale.

I recall fragments of the conversations we had with her as children.

"You're an orphan, then, right, Natalya?"

"An orphan, yes, that I am. Just like my masters. Your grandmama, Anna Grigorievna, why, she folded her fair hands ever so early and passed. Same as my papa and mama."

"And what was it they died of so early?"

"Death came, and so they passed."

"Yes, but why so early?"

"So it was God willed. The masters sent Papa off to serve as a soldier, for some sinful thing he done, and Mama, well, she went before her time on account of the masters' turkey chicks. Now that, of course, was something I don't recall, how could I, but the menials at the manor used to tell it: said she was serving as poultry girl, with a goodly number of chicks in her charge, and a hailstorm come upon them out in the pasture, whipped them about till they was ever last one dead. Well, she commenced to running, comes tearing up there and seen what it was—and then got shook up to the point where she just give up the ghost!"

"And how come you were never married?"

"Well, my bridegroom ain't grown up yet."

"No, seriously, how come?"

"They say as how the mistress, your auntie, forbade that happening. So that I, sinner that I am, ended up with the glorified standing of a noble young miss."

"Come on now, how could you be a girl of the gentry?"

"Yes sir, that's just what I was: a young gentry miss!" answered Natalya, the trace of a grin wrinkling her lips as she stroked them with her dark old crone's hand. "I am, after all, milk sister to Arkady Petrovich and a second aunt to you."

As we were growing up, we came to listen more and more attentively to what was said in our home about Drydale. More and more clear became things that were unclear before, in ever sharper relief stood out the strange particulars of Drydale life. How could we not feel that Natalya was truly akin to us—we of the ancient, noble lineage of the Khrushchovs—since she had lived almost the same life as our father for half a century? But those landowner-nobles, so it turns out, were the very ones who drove away her father, sent him off to the army, and kept her mother in such trepidation that her heart stopped beating at the sight of some dead turkey chicks!

"Well, it's true," said Natalya. "When things come to such a pass, nothing's for it but to drop dead. The masters would have packed her off somewheres out beyond the Mozhai!"

Later we learned even stranger things about Drydale. We learned that "in all the universe wasn't nobody" more down-to-earth, more kindhearted than the Drydale squires, but we also learned that there was no one more "hot-blooded" than they were. We learned that the old Drydale manor house was dark and gloomy, that our madman of a grandfather, Pyotr Kirillovich, was murdered in that house by his bastard son Gervaska, who was our father's friend and Natalya's cousin. We learned that years ago our aunt Tonia had gone mad too—over an unhappy love—and that she was living in one of the old peasant shacks, next to the impoverished Drydale manor house, playing ecstatic ecossaises on a pianoforte that hummed and jangled with age. We learned that Natalya as well had lost her mind, that when still a young girl she had fallen in love for a lifetime with our late uncle Pyotr Petrovich and that he had exiled her, sent her off to the small farmstead at Soshki. Our passionate daydreams of Drydale were understandable. For us Drydale was simply a poetic monument of times past. But for Natalya? After all, as if in response to some private thought, she had once said, in a voice steeped in bitterness, "Mercy! At Drydale they used to sit down at the dinner table with Tatar *chabouks*! Scares me even to recall it."

"You mean they had horsewhips?" we asked.

"One's same as the other," she said.

"But why?"

"In case there was a quarrel."

"Was everybody always quarreling at Drydale?"

"Forfend us, Lord, they was! No day went by without a war! Hot-blooded, one and all—pure gunpowder."

When we heard those words we listened rapt with fascination, exchanging delighted glances. Long afterward we would conjure up that huge garden, the huge estate, the manor house with its oaken log walls beneath a heavy thatched roof blackened with time—and dinner in the parlor of that house: everyone seated at the table, all of them eating, throwing bones to the hunting dogs on the floor, squinting sideways at one another—and each with a whip draped over his lap. We dreamt of that golden age when we would grow up, and we too would dine with horsewhips on our laps. We understood, of course, that Natalya derived no joy from memories of those whips. But all the same she left Lunyovo for Drydale, went back to the source of her somber recollections. She didn't have a corner of her own in that house, she had no close relatives there, and now she no longer served her former mistress at Drydale, Aunt Tonia, but the widow of the late Pyotr Petrovich, Klavdia Markovna. But then, without the estate and manor, Natalya found it impossible to live.

"Nothing for it—it's what you get used to," she said humbly. "Where the needle is, seem like, that's where the thread must be. Bred in the bone is home sweet home."

She was not the only one to suffer from that attachment to Drydale. Lord, what passionate lovers of reminiscences, what ardent devotees of Drydale were all the others who had lived there!

Aunt Tonia was poverty stricken, living in a shack. Drydale had deprived her of happiness and soundness of mind, even of the resemblance to a human being. But despite all the exhortations of our father to abandon the native nest and settle in Lunyovo, she flatly refused.

"I'd rather go up on a mountain and break stones!"

Father was a carefree man; for him, so it seemed, there were none of those bonds. But strains of deep melancholy sounded as well in his tales of Drydale. Ages ago he had left to live at Lunyovo, the country manor of our grandaunt Olga Kirillovna. But he complained virtually to the end of his days, "One, just one, Khrushchov is left now on this earth, and he's not living at Drydale!"

True, right after making such a statement he would frequently sit in deep thought, staring out the window at the fields, and then suddenly would smile sardonically, taking down his guitar from the wall.

"Yes, indeed, Drydale's a fine place, damn it all to blue blazes!" he would add, equally sincere in that pronouncement as in the ones he had just made.

But even he had a Drydale soul—a soul ruled beyond measure by the power of reminiscence, the power of the steppes and its sluggish way of life, by that ancient sense of family that melded into a single unit the village and the house-serf menials and the manor of Drydale. True, we Khrushchovs were of ancient, noble lineage, our surname inscribed in *Book Six,* and among our legendary forebears many were the aristocrats with age-old Lithuanian blood and many were the Tatar suzerains. But then, from time out of mind Khrushchov blood was blended with the blood of the house serfs and that of the villagers. Who gave life to Grandfather Pyotr Kirillovich? Multivaried are the legends that speak of that. Who sired Gervaska, the one who murdered him? From our earliest years we heard that it was Pyotr Kirillovich. What was the source of such a sharp distinction in the personalities of our father and uncle? The explanations for that are many as well. Yet Father's "milk sister" was Natalya, and he and Gervaska had exchanged crosses. It's time, high time to acknowledge the kinship of the Khrushchovs with their household serfs and the peasants of the village!

Long was the period that my sister and I as well lived in the gravitational pull of Drydale, under the spell of its antiquity. The household staff, the village, and the manor house at Drydale constituted a single family. That family was still under the domain of our forefathers, and even amidst the descendants such a feeling holds on for a long time. The life of a family, a brood, a clan, is deep, gnarled, mysterious, frequently horrendous. But tempered strong it is as well with the force of those dark depths together with its family traditions and its past. In terms of records, written and otherwise, Drydale is no more rich than a nomad settlement in the steppes of Bashkiria. In the realm of Rus folk traditions replace such records. And a folk legend or a song—well, that's the bane of the Slavic soul! Our former house serfs, those passionate idlers and dreamers—where else but in our manor could they have found joyful repose? The only remaining representative of the Drydale squires was our father. And the first language we spoke was that of Drydale. The first narratives, the first songs to touch us—they too were the Drydale ones, Natalya's, Father's. Who else could have sung the way Father did, he who had learned from the servants to sing—with such carefree dolefulness, such caressing reproach, such weak-willed plenitude of soul—of "that true and fine, sophisticated, ladylove of mine"? Could anyone else have told us stories the way Natalya did? And who was more dear to us than the peasants who lived at Drydale?

Spats and quarrels—that's what the Khrushchovs, from time out of mind, were renowned for, just as any family that lives for a long period unified, in close quarters. During our childhood there was such an altercation between Drydale and Lunyovo that for a good ten years Father never set foot across the threshold of his native manor. So it was that we did not visit Drydale in our childhood; we were there but once, and that was on our way to Zadonsk. But then, dreams sometimes can be more vivid than any waking image. Hazy, but ineradicable, was our memory of a long summer's day, the undulating fields and a backwater highway that enchanted us with its scope, with the hollow white willow trees that still survived here and there. We remembered the beehive up on one of those willows, which had found a spot for itself far off the road amidst the grain—a hive abandoned to the will of God, out in the fields by the backwater road; we remembered the sweeping curve below the long, uphill grade, the prodigious bare common upon which gazed the paltry peasant huts with no chimneys; we recalled the jaundiced look of the rocky ravines behind the huts, the whiteness of the flat stones and detritus on the bottom of those ravines. The first event to horrify us had also been a Drydale thing: the murder of Grandfather by Gervaska. Whenever we heard the tale of that murder told, we perpetually conjured up the yellow ravines that trailed away into the distance: it always seemed that having committed his dastardly deed, Gervaska had run off by way of those very gullies, afterward to vanish, "sinking like a key to the bottom of the sea."

The Drydale peasants used to visit Lunyovo for different reasons than the house serfs did; they came to ask for more land. But they too entered our home as if it were their own. They would bow down waist-deep to our father, kiss his hand; then, with a toss of their hair, they would go through the triune kiss on the face with him, with Natalya, and would end up kissing our lips. They brought gifts of honey, eggs, embroidered towels. And we, raised in the fields and sensitive to smells, avid for them no less than for the songs and legends, we remembered forever that special, lovely smell when we kissed the Drydalers, an aroma somehow hempen. We remembered as well how their presents reeked of an old village in the steppes: the honey smelled of buckwheat in bloom and rotted oaken beehives, the towels of rustic pantries and chimneyless huts from Grandfather's time. The Drydale peasants would tell us no stories. But then, what did they have to tell! For them not even legends existed. Their graves are unmarked, and their lives so similar one unto the other, so meager, lives that leave no trace! For the only fruit of their labor and cares was bread, bread in the purest sense of the word, a thing that is eaten up. To make ponds they dug into the rocky riverbed of the Kamenka River, which had been desiccate for ages. But ponds ultimately cannot be relied on—ponds dry up. They built themselves a place to live. But their habitations were not long for this world: one little spark and they burned down to ashes . . . So then, why were we all drawn even to that bare common, to the huts and ravines, to the ravaged estate of Drydale?

2

It was only late in our adolescence that we found ourselves on the grounds of the country estate about which we had heard so much, the estate that engendered Natalya's soul, that ruled over all her life.

I recall it as if it were yesterday. As we were approaching Drydale towards evening a driving rainstorm broke, with its deafening rolls of thunder and dazzlingly swift, fiery serpents of lightning. A lilac-black storm cloud plunged overladen toward the northwest, majestically blotting out half the sky. Clearly defined, flat, and deathly pallid lay the green meadow of grains against that cloud's massive background; bright and uncommonly fresh was the sparse wet grass on the highroad. The wet horses, which seemed to have suddenly become thinner, sloshed along through the blue mud, their horseshoes aglimmer; the tarantass emitted moist susurrations . . . And suddenly, right by the curve that led to Drydale, we saw amidst the tall wet rye a tall and most peculiar figure in a dressing gown and a crumpled mobcap, a figure that was either an old man or an old woman, beating a skewbald, polled cow with a switch. As we came closer the switch began working with greater vigor, and clumsily, twitching its tail, the cow ran out onto the road. Shouting something, the old woman made for our tarantass, and drawing near, she stretched out her pale face toward us. Gazing terrified into those insane black eyes, feeling the touch of that sharp cold nose, and smelling the powerful odor of a peasant hut, we exchanged kisses with the person who had just walked up. Could this be Baba Yaga the witch herself? But on the head of this Baba Yaga there was a tall mobcap sticking up, made of some filthy rag, and over her naked body she wore a ripped dressing gown wet to the waist, which left uncovered her scraggy breasts. She screamed at us as if we were deaf, or as if she intended to initiate a frenzied swearing row. And those screams were what made us realize who this was: Aunt Tonia.

There were screams from Klavdia Markovna as well, but joyful screams, with the rapturous tenor of a girls' boarding school; stout, small, with a little grayish beard and uncommonly lively eyes, she was sitting by an open window in the house with its two large verandas, knitting a cotton sock, then pushing her spectacles up on her forehead and gazing out at the common, which blended into the courtyard. Natalya, who stood on the veranda to the right, made a low bow, smiling quietly—she was ever so tiny, tanned, wearing bark sandals, a red woolen skirt, and a gray blouse cut low beneath her dark, wrinkled neck. As I glanced at that neck, at the slender clavicles, the weary gloominess in her eyes, I recall thinking, "This is she who grew up with our father—long, long ago but right on this spot, where all that's left of Grandfather's oaken manor house, which kept catching on fire, is this place, unprepossessing as it is; and of the garden, only the shrubbery and a few old birches and poplars; of the outbuildings and servants' annexes, just a hut, a granary, a clay storage barn, and an icehouse overgrown with wormwood and pigweeds."

The redolence of the samovar was wafting through the air, and questions came thick and in droves; from out of a centenarian hutch a variety of things emerged: little crystal vases for jam, golden teaspoons worn thin to the texture of a maple leaf, sugar crackers, dry, ring shaped, preserved in anticipation of guests. And while the conversation heated up, taking on a forced cordial air after the long period of animosity, we went off to wander the darkening chambers, searching for the terrace and the way down into the garden.

Everything in those empty, low chambers, which were still arranged the same way as in Grandfather's time, put together with the log remnants of the very rooms where he had dwelled, everything was black with time, simple and crude. In the corner of the footmen's room hung the large black icon of Saint Mercurius of Smolensk, he whose iron sandals and helmet are preserved in the solea of an ancient cathedral at Smolensk. We had heard the tale: Mercurius was a man of the aristocracy, summoned to save the principality of Smolensk from the Tatars—a voice had called to him from the icon of the Mother of God, Hodegetria the Guide. Having decimated the Tatars, the saint fell asleep and his enemies beheaded him. Then, taking up his head into his hands, Mercurius came unto the gates of the city to bring word of all that had occurred . . . It was a gruesome sight, the depiction of that scene by a Suzdal artist, the headless man holding in one hand his deathly bluish head, a helmet on it, and in the other hand the icon of the Hodegetria. This painting, cherished, so they said, by Grandfather, had survived several horrendous fires, had been split by the flames; it was mounted in a thick silver frame and preserved, on its obverse side, the genealogy of the Khrushchovs, inscribed under old-style rubrics. As if in harmony with it there were heavy iron latches at the bottoms and tops of the two heavy halves of the doors. The floorboards in the parlor were inordinately wide, dark and slippery, the windows small, with frames that could be raised. We walked through that parlor, a miniature version of the very one where the Khrushchovs had sat down to dine with their Tatar whips, and we emerged in the drawing room. Here, opposite the doors to the terrace, was where the pianoforte once stood, the one Aunt Tonia played when she was in love with the military officer Voitkevich, comrade of Pyotr Petrovich. And further on gaped the wide-open doors that gave entry to the divan room on the corner—where Grandfather once had his living quarters.

The evening was gloomy. Out beyond the outskirts of the garden with its trees cut down, beyond the silvery poplars and the threshing barn covered by only half a roof, heat lightning was flaring up in storm clouds, revealing for split seconds mountain ranges of rosy golden billows . . . Apparently the driving rain had not touched Troshin Woods, darkly visible far beyond the garden, on slopes beyond the ravines. The dry, warm smell of oaks drifted over from there, merging with the smell of greenery, with the moist, soft wind that stirred the crowns of what birches still remained on the arborway, through the high nettles, tall weeds, and shrubbery beside the terrace. And the profound silence of the night, of the steppe, and of backwoods Rus reigned over it all.

"Tea is now served, if you please," a soft voice called to us.

It was her, the participant in, the witness of all this life and its principal narrator, Natalya. And behind her, gazing attentively with those crazed eyes, bent slightly, ceremoniously glissading across the dark, smooth floor, came her mistress. She still had the mobcap on, but instead of the dressing gown she had donned an old-fashioned barége dress and had thrown over her shoulders a shawl of faded golden silk.

"*Où êtes-vous, mes enfants?*" she shrieked with a smile of gentility, and her voice, clear and shrill, like the voice of a parrot, resounded eerily throughout the empty black chambers . . .

3

Just as charm was there in Natalya, in her peasant simpleheartedness, in all of her lovely and pitiable soul, engendered by Drydale, so there was charm as well in the ravaged Drydale estate.

The old drawing room with its lopsided floors smelled of jasmine. The rotten terrace, gray-blue with time, was drowning in nettles, elder bushes, euonymus; it had no steps left, so you had to leap down from it. On hot days, when the terrace was baking in sunshine, when the sunken glassed-in doors were open and a joyous glassy sheen was reflected in that lackluster oval mirror that hung on the wall opposite the doors, we kept recalling Aunt Tonia's pianoforte, which once stood under the mirror. She used to play upon it, gazing at the yellowed musical notes with headings in intricate flourishes, while *he* stood behind her, his left hand firmly propping up his waistline, his jaw tightly clenched, frowning. Marvelous butterflies would come floating into the drawing room—some dressed in motley calico-print pinafores, others in Japanese array, still others in black-lilac velveteen shawls. Once, just before his departure, he took a wholehearted whack with his palm at one of them, which had paused, palpitating, on the lid of the piano. All that remained was a silvery speck of dust. But several days later, when the servant wenches, in their ignorance, wiped it away, Aunt Tonia went into hysterics. From the drawing room we walked out onto the terrace, sat down on the warm floorboards—and were lost in reveries. Blowing about in the garden, the wind brought to us the gossamer rustle of birches, with their satin white boles specked with black and their widespread green branches; the wind, swishing and rustling, came running in from the fields—and a green-golden oriole chirped out its sharp and joyous call, soaring all by itself above the white flowers in pursuit of the talkative jackdaws, who lived with a plethora of kinfolk in collapsed chimneys and dark attics, where it smells of old bricks and golden light falls in streaks through the dormer windows upon mounds of gray-violet cinders. The wind was abating, drowsy bees were crawling around on the blossoms by the terrace, going about their leisurely business—and amidst the silence one could hear only the steady babble, streaming like incessant light rain, of the silvery poplar leafage . . . We ambled around the garden, made our way out into the tangle of growth on the outskirts of the estate.

There, on the outskirts, which blended into the grain fields, in Great-grandfather's bathhouse with the fallen-in ceiling, that very bathhouse where Natalya once hid the hand mirror she stole from Pyotr Petrovich, some white lapins were living. How gently they came hopping out onto the threshold, how strangely, twitching their whiskers and cleft lips, did they squint their bulging eyes, set wide apart, at the tall eriophorum (called Tatar thistle), at the henbane bushes and thickets of nettles that were choking off the blackthorn and cherry saplings. And in the threshing barn with its roof half gone a horned eagle owl had found himself a home. Selecting one of the murkiest spots, he perched on the straw-flattener poles, his ear tufts sticking up on end, his blind yellow eyes protuberant—and he had a wild look about him, the look of a demon. The sun was going down far beyond the garden in a sea of grain, evening was coming on placid and clear, a cuckoo bird was cooing in Troshin Woods, and the cow-horn fife of old man Styopa, the shepherd, resounded plaintively somewhere over the meadows . . . The eagle owl sat awaiting night. In the dead of night everything was asleep—the fields, and the village, and the manor. That's when the owl did nothing but groan and cry. He would sweep soundlessly around the threshing barn, across the garden, approaching Aunt Tonia's shack; he would softly alight on its roof—and then let out a morbid screech. Auntie would awaken on the bench by the stove.

"Sweetest Jesus, have mercy on me," she whispered, sighing.

Peevishly and sleepily the flies buzzed about, around the ceiling of the hot dark shack. Every night something awakened them. Either a cow scratching its side against the wall of the hut or a rat that raced along over the abrupt jangling of keys on the pianoforte to fall with a crash onto the crockery shards that Auntie had carefully assembled in the corner; or else the old black tomcat with green eyes would return home late from his rounds and lazily appeal for entry to the hut; or, finally, it would be the flight of that eagle owl, prophesying misfortune with his shrieks. And overcoming her drowsiness in the darkness, waving away the flies that kept getting in her eyes, Auntie would arise, grope about the benches, slam open the door—and stepping out onto the threshold, she would launch a rolling pin in an upward direction, taking a wild guess about where to throw it, up into the starry sky. Then the owl would break free from the roof with a swoosh, touching the straw with his wings, and swoon away with a low sweep in the darkness. Almost in contact with the ground, he drifted smoothly until reaching the threshing barn, where, shooting straight up, he alit on its crest. Then, once again, his wailing would waft across to the manor. He sat as if reminiscing about something—and suddenly let out a howl of consternation; he quieted down—and then abruptly went into hysterical moaning, guffawing, and yelping; once more quieted down—then burst out with a series of groans, sobs, and blubbers.

But the nights themselves, dark warm nights with violet storm clouds, were ever so placid. Sleepily running and streaming along went the soughing babble of the drowsy poplars. Heat lightning flashed warily above dark Troshin Woods—and the oaken smell was warm and dry. Alongside the woods, above the plains of oat fields, through an interstice amidst storm clouds, the gravestone marker of Scorpio, a silver triangle, was burning . . . We returned late to the manor house. Having breathed our fill of the dew, the crispness of the steppes, the field flowers and grasses, we climbed warily up onto the veranda and entered the dark anteroom. Often we found Natalya at prayer before the image of Mercurius. Diminutive, barefoot, hands clasped, she stood in front of him whispering something, crossing herself, bowing down low to the icon, which was obscured by the darkness—and she did all this so simply, as if she were having a conversation with some intimate friend who was, like her, simple-hearted, kind, and gracious.

"Natalya?" we called out quietly.

"Me?" she responded quietly and simply, interrupting her prayer.

"How is it you're not sleeping yet?"

"I figure we'll get our fill of sleep in the grave."

We sat down on a large coffer used as a bed and opened the window wide; she kept standing there with hands clasped. The heat lightning glimmered mysteriously, illumined the dark chambers; somewhere far off in the dewy steppes a quail chittered. Awakening on the pond, a duck quacked out in anxious and cautionary tones.

"Been out wandering?"

"Yes, ma'am."

"Well, that's what young folks does. Why, when we was children, we'd sometimes rove the whole night through . . . Out with the dusk and back with the dawn."

"Did people live a good life then?"

"Yessir, they did."

A long silence set in.

"Nanny, how come the owl keeps screeching?" asked my sister.

"No telling why he's screeching, just ain't no getting shed of him. We might could shoot off a rifle and put a scare in him. Way it is now, it just gives you the willies, all the time thinking, 'Is this some kind of sign boding misfortune?' And it frightens the young miss no end. You know what a fraidy cat she can be, scares her to death!"

"How did she get sick the way she is?"

"Well, that's no secret: tears and more tears, and grief . . . Then she commenced to praying. And all the time getting meaner and nastier with us servant wenches, and ever more angry with her brothers."

Recalling the horsewhips, we asked, "So they didn't get along too well?"

"Wasn't no getting along a'tall! Specially after she got poorly, and Grandfather passed, and after the young masters took things over and Pyotr Petrovich, rest his soul, was married. They was all hot-blooded—pure gunpowder!"

"Did they often whip the house serfs?"

"That was never the customary thing with us. Why, I done such a terrible sin! And all that come of it was that Pyotr Petrovich, he ordered my hair clopped off with sheep shears, then to put a sacken shift on me and send me off to the Ukrainian folks' farmstead."

"What had you done that was so terrible?"

But not every time we asked did we get a direct, quick answer to that question. Sometimes Natalya would tell it with amazing directness and thoroughness, but at other times she began stammering, thinking something over; then she would softly sigh, and by her voice (we couldn't see her face in the darkness), we knew that she was smiling sadly.

"What was terrible was . . . Well, I told you that before . . . Young and dumb I was, yes sir. 'He sang out sin, did the nightingale, he sang misfortune in the garden, did he.' And anybody can tell you, it was a young girl's thing, was what mine was."

Then my sister said to her tenderly, "Can you recite the rest of that poem, Nanny?"

Natalya lost her composure.

"It's not a poem, miss, it's a song . . . And I don't recollect now how the rest of it goes."

"That's not true!"

"Come on, please say it . . ."

In a rapid patter of words she finished it off: "'How it was, a song of sin, misfortune's song . . .' That is to say, 'He sang out sin, did the nightingale, drear song he sang, of misfortune, sang he . . . To the gormless lass he gave no peace, she slept no sleep, in the dark night, not she . . .'"

Mastering her constraint, my sister asked, "And were you very much in love with Uncle?"

Natalya answered briefly, in a toneless whisper of a voice. "Very much."

"Do you always remember him in your prayers?"

"Always."

"They say you fell down in a faint when they were taking you off to Soshki."

"That I did, yes ma'am. Us house serfs, we was an awful tender bunch. Weak as a babe in the woods when they got on us. No comparison to some ignorant muzhik smallholder! No sooner did Evsei Bodulya drive off with me than my head went fuzzy with sadness and fear. In the city I near about croaked with the newness of it all. But then, when we drove out into the steppes, what a tender and pitiful feeling come over me! An officer in a carriage was tearing up toward us from the other direction, he looked just like him—and I let out a scream and fainted dead away! And when I come to my senses, I was laid out there in the cart and I'm thinking, 'I feel fine now, just like I'm in the heavenly kingdom!'"

"Was he hard on you?"

"God forbid it being any harder!"

"Well, all the same, Auntie was the most erratic one, wasn't she?"

"That she was, yes ma'am. Let me just tell you this: they even carried her off to the relics of God's Holy Servitor. We had our fill of sufferings with the miss! Might could have been living her life on out right now, same as anybody else, but she turned proud, then got touched in the head. How that Voitkevich did love her, though! But then, what are you going to do?"

"And what about Grandfather?"

"Him? Why, he was feebleminded. Course, there was stuff going on with him too. Back in them times they was all so full of passions . . . But for all that, the old masters never got hoity-toity in the way they treated us folks. Times was when, say, your papa would give Gervaska a reading out at dinnertime—and right he was to do so! But come evening, why they're passing the time out in the yard together, picking out tunes on balalaikas."

"And this Voitkevich, was he good-looking?"

Natalya gave it some thought.

"No, ma'am, I can't lie to you: he was something like a Kalmyk. Real solemn he was, and liked to make demands. All the time reading poems to her, all the time a-scaring her: saying, 'I'll die and then I'll come back for you.'"

"Well, did Grandpa go crazy over love too?"

"That was over Grandmother. There's a different sort of thing, little madam. And our house was so gloomy too—not a happy place to be, the Lord take it. Be so kind as to listen now to these ignorant words of mine."

And then Natalya started telling, in her slow whispering voice, that long, long tale . . .

4

If the legends are to be believed, our great-grandpa, a man of means, did not relocate from near Kursk to Drydale until he was getting on in years; he didn't like our parts, the desolation, the forests. There's a saying about that: "In olden times the woods were everywhere." Some two hundred years ago, when people made their way along our roads, they were making their way through dense forests. The Kamenka River was also enveloped by the woods, as well as the highlands it flowed through, and the village, and the estate, and the surrounding hilly fields. But then, in Grandfather's day it was different. The picture had changed by the time he came along: an expanse of semisteppes, bare slopes; rye, oats, and buckwheat in the fields; a smattering of hollow white willows along the highroad; and on the Drydale rise nothing but bare white rock land. Of the forests only the Troshin Woods were left. The garden, of course, was still marvelous: a broad arborway with seventy wide-branching birches, cherry groves drowning in the nettles, luxuriant thickets of raspberries, acacia bushes, lilac, and virtually a whole grove of silvery poplars on the outskirts, which blended into the grain fields. The manor house had a thatched roof, which was thick, dark, and sturdy. It, the house, gazed out into a courtyard that had, along each side, long rows of outbuildings and servants' annexes, several wings of them, while beyond the courtyard there stretched an endless green common and a wide-sprawling manorial village—large, poor, and carefree.

"Just like the masters, it was!" said Natalya. "The masters was carefree theirselves—no sense of business, no greed for gain. Semyon Kirillovich, your grandpa's brother, divvied up the inheritance with us: he took for himself what was biggest and best, the patrimonial lands got from the tsar, and tossed us a sop of the rest. All we got was Soshki, Drydale, and four hundred head of serfs. And of them four hundred, a good half run off."

Grandfather Pyotr Kirillovich died when he was about forty-five. Father frequently told the tale of how he went off his head. He had fallen asleep in the garden, on a carpet beneath an apple tree, when a tremendous windstorm suddenly blew up and poured down a whole rain squall of apples on him. But among the menials, according to Natalya, they had a different explanation for

Grandpa's imbecility. They said that Pyotr Kirillovich got touched out of pining with love after the death of our beautiful grandmother and that a mighty thunderstorm passed over Drydale just before evening on that day. After that Pyotr Kirillovich—a stooped dark-haired man with black, attentive and caressing eyes, somewhat resembling Aunt Tonia—lived out his days in a quiet state of lunacy. According to Natalya, they never used to know where to put their money, and so he, in his morocco leather boots and parti-colored caftan, gravely and soundlessly would wander about the manor house, and, after taking a surreptitious look around, he would stick gold coins into cracks in the oaken logs.

"That'll be for Tonechka, her dowry cash," he would mutter when they caught him. "It's a safe place, my friends, better there than somewheres else . . . But then, notwithstanding that, it's really up to you—you want me not to do it, then I ain't about to do it."

And after that he'd go right back to doing it again. Or else he'd be rearranging the heavy furniture in the parlor or the drawing room, perpetually anticipating guests, although the neighbors almost never visited Drydale. Or else he'd complain of hunger and take it upon himself to prepare a bread slop porridge—awkwardly grating and macerating scallions in a wooden cup, adding bread crumbs, pouring in a viscous, foaming, flour-based kvass; finally he would sprinkle so much large-grained gray salt on top that his bread slop came out bitter and inedible. Following the midafternoon meal, when life in the manor came to a standstill, when everyone wandered off to a favorite nook for a long siesta, he didn't know what to do with himself, lonely Pyotr Kirillovich, who slept very little even at night. Unable to stand the loneliness, he would begin peeking into bedrooms, antechambers, maidservants' rooms, warily calling out to the sleepers, "Are you sleeping, Arkasha? Are you sleeping, Toniusha?"

And when the angry response rang out—"Leave me in peace, for God's sake, Papa!"—he would hastily reassure them, "All right then, sleep, sleep, heart of my heart. I won't wake you up."

Then he would amble off somewhere else—skipping only the footmen's room, for the lackeys were quite a rude bunch—and ten minutes later he would be back once more on the threshold, calling out in still more wary tones, making up some story: somebody just drove through the village with the coachman's sleigh bells ringing; "Might could be Petenka, home on furlough from the regiment." Or there was a horrendous hailstone cloud blowing up.

"He, the old master, was terrified of thunderstorms, my chickadees," said Natalya. "Even back when I was a teensy little girl, not in a kerchief yet, well, I can recollect it even then. Our manor house was somehow all black inside—not a happy place to be, may the Lord take it. And in summertime a day was like a year passing. We had no place to put all the menials, why, with just the footmen, there was five of them. And everybody knew that after dinner the young masters retired to have their rest, and like them we did the same, being as we was faithful vassals, exemplary servants. And then is when it would not behoove for Pyotr Kirillovich to get to pestering us—specially Gervaska. Calling out, 'You lackeys there, hey. Are you sleeping?' Cause Gervaska raises up his head off the coffer where he's laying and he says, 'You want me to stick a whole clump of nettles down your britches?' And then: 'Who you think you're talking to, you lazy layabout so-and-so?' 'To the imp, the house spirit, sir, half asleep I was.' So then, Pyotr Kirillovich sets off again, wandering through the parlor, through the drawing room, all the time looking out the windows into the garden, thinking, 'Might could be a storm cloud out there?' And it's true, we had no end of storms kicking up back in the old times. I mean to say mighty powerful thunderstorms. Sometimes, it might be, say, shortly after dinnertime, and the oriole commences to fussing, and from out beyond the garden here comes the clouds . . . it goes all dark in the manor house, the weeds and thick nettles are a-swishing about, the turkey hens with their chickies find a hiding place under the terrace . . . a scary business, a real ornery mess it was! And then, my dear sir, why he, Grandfather, he's a-sighing and crossing hisself, he climbs up to light a wax candle next to the holy images, hangs out the funereal towel off Great-grandpa's coffin—that towel used to scare the wits out of me!—either that or he heaved a pair of scissors out the window. That's the first thing you do, the business with the scissors; it works real good against a storm . . ."

There was a brighter spirit about the Drydale manor when the French were living there—first a certain Louis Ivanovich, a man who wore the baggiest of pantaloons that tapered to a tight fit at the bottom. He had long mustaches and dreamy light blue eyes, and he wrapped strands of hair over his bald spot from ear to ear. Later came Mademoiselle Cici, elderly, perpetually shivering from the cold. In those days the voice of Louis Ivanovich would resound throughout the house, hollering at Arkasha: "Leave ze room and do naught come back!" And from the classroom you could hear, "*Maître corbeau sur un arbre perché,*" and Tonechka was practicing on the pianoforte. The Frenchmen were at Drydale for eight years, staying on to keep Pyotr Kirillovich company even after the children were boarded out to study in the city; they finally left just before Arkasha and Tonechka returned from the district capital for the third school vacation break. After that vacation Pyotr Kirillovich never sent either one anywhere else to study; it was sufficient, in his opinion, to send only Petenka off to school. And so the children were left from that point on without further education and with no one to look after them. As Natalya told it, "I was the youngest of them all. Well, Gervaska and your papa was nearabout the exact same age, so they was like the best of friends. Only it's true what they say—wolf and horse ain't no kin. They was friendly together, they swore to be friends for all time, even exchanged crosses, but Gervaska, he wasted no time about getting up to mischief. Once he pretty near drownded your papa in the pond! A mangy reprobate he was, and ever the one to be cooking up some underhand business. Once he says to the young master, 'When you grow up, do you aim to use a whip on me?' 'That I do.' 'No, you won't.' 'How come?' 'Well, just because.' And he had him another bright idea. There was this barrel standing above where the ponds was, right up on the hillside, and he seen it there and egged on Arkady Petrovich to crawl in it and roll downhill. 'First you have you a go, young master,' he tells him, 'and then me.' Well, the young master, he done just what he told him, crawled in there and he pushed him off, and he goes a-clattering down that hill, right into the water he went. Holy Mother, Queen of Heaven! Left nothing behind but a cloud of whirling dust! Well, lucky the shepherds was somewheres not too far off."

While the French were there at the Drydale manor, the house preserved a look of being lived in. Back in Grandmother's time it still had its gentry folk, its masters and mistresses, those in power and those subordinate, and its reception chambers for guests and its family living chambers, and its day-to-day activities, and its holidays. The outward look of all this was maintained while the French were there, but then the French departed and the manor was left with absolutely no one in charge. While the children were small Pyotr Kirillovich, ostensibly, was number one. But what authority did he have? Who was telling whom what to do: he telling the house serfs or they telling him? They shut the lid on the pianoforte, the tablecloth disappeared off the oaken dining table—they would eat without a tablecloth and at no set time; you couldn't get through the vestibule for the borzoi hounds sprawled out there. No one was left to care about keeping things clean, and soon everything—the dark log walls, the dark floors and ceilings, the dark heavy doors and lintels, the old icons that covered one whole corner of the parlor with their Suzdalian saintly faces—everything went totally black. In the dead of night, especially during a thunderstorm, when the garden was blustering about in the rain, the faces on the icons in the parlor would be constantly aglimmer, while over the garden a shuddering, rosy gold sky would open out, gape wide above, and then, in the darkness, the thunderclaps would roll with their fissures and cracks—the dead of night in the manor was ghastly. But in the daytime things were drowsy, empty, and boring. As the years passed Pyotr Kirillovich was getting ever weaker, fading ever more into the background, and decrepit Daria Ustinovna, Grandfather's wet nurse, ended up running household matters. But her authority was roughly equal to his, and the village headman Demian did not interfere with the management of the manor. He knew only how to run the field work, and sometimes he would say with a lazy grin, "No sir, ain't no way I'd be a aggravation to my masters." In his youthful days Father had no interest in Drydale—he was totally absorbed in hunting, in balalaika playing, in his love for Gervaska, who was numbered among the footmen but who would disappear for days on end, off with Father to shoot on the Meshersky Swamps; or he'd be working with him on balalaika riffs, playing the cow-horn fife in the carriage house.

"So it was we got used to that business," said Natalya, "that all he done at home was to sleep. And when he ain't sleeping, that means he's either in the village, in the coach house, or out hunting: in the winter it was hares, in the fall it was foxes, summertime it was quails, ducks, or bustards. He climbs in a light *drozhky,* straps a gun over his shoulder, yells out to Dianka the bitch, and away they go! Today out to the Serednya Mill, tomorrow to the Meshersky Swamps, and day after tomorrow to the steppelands. And always taking Gervaska along with him. He was the ringleader of all that rigamarole, but he made out like it was the young master just dragging him along. He loved him, his enemy, did Arkady Petrovich, truly like a brother, but with him, the longer it went on the more nasty he got with his brazen-faced mockery. Your father might would say something like, 'How about we get out the balalaikas, Gervasy! You can teach me, if you like, how to play "Red sun rolling off beyond the woods.'" Then Gervaska looks at him, kind of sniffs a little smoke out his nostrils and puts on a mean grin: 'First you got to kiss my hand.' Arkady Petrovich went all pale, jumped up, and whapped him, hard as he could, across the face, but him, he just tossed his head and give him a real black look, scowling away like some highway brigand. 'Stand up, you good-for-nothing!' He stands up, stretches his whole self out, like a borzoi hound, velveteen trousers a-drooping down . . . and he don't say a word. 'Ask forgiveness!' He says, 'Sorry, sir.' And the young master is right choking with fury, but he can't think of nothing else to say. 'Well, that's exactly how you better speak to me: "sir"!' he yells. 'Here I am doing my best to treat you like an equal, you good-for-nothing; times are when I even think there's nothing I wouldn't do for you, and you, what do you do? You deliberately antagonize me!'

"A right peculiar business!" said Natalya. "Gervaska mocking and mistreating the young master and Grandpa, and the miss doing the same to me. The young master—and, if truth be told, Grandpa too—why, they thought the very world of Gervaska, and I did of her . . . when I was back from Soshki, that is, and come to my senses a little bit, after the bad thing I done."

5

Only subsequent to Grandfather's death did they start sitting down to dinner with whips, after Gervaska's flight and the marriage of Pyotr Petrovich, after Aunt Tonia became touched and pledged herself as bride to the Sweet Lord Jesus, and after Natalya had returned from that very Soshki. Aunt Tonia got touched in the head and Natalya went into exile for the same reason—over love.

The tedious, dreary regime of Grandfather was replaced by that of the young masters. Taking all by surprise with his retirement from the army, Pyotr Petrovich returned to Drydale, and his arrival had fatal consequences, both for Natalya and for Aunt Tonia.

They both fell in love. They did not notice how they fell in love. At first it seemed to them that "living had just become a happier thing."

At the beginning Pyotr Petrovich set everything at Drydale out on a new path—toward the festive and gentrified. Arriving with his comrade Voitkevich, he brought a cook along with him too, a clean-shaven alcoholic who looked askance, contemptuously, at the ribbed gelatin molds gone green, at the crude knives and forks. Pyotr Petrovich wished to put on the right face for his comrade—to appear high-spirited, generous, and affluent—but he brought it off awkwardly, like a small boy. And he really was little more than a child, with a delicate, pretty-boy look about him, but by nature harsh and cruel, a boy who seemed self-assured but was easily flustered almost to the point of tears, and later on he would long nurse his malice against the one who had upset him.

"I seem to recall, brother Arkady," he said at the dinner table, on the very first day of his return to Drydale, "didn't we have some Madeira that was not half bad?"

Grandfather turned red, started to say something but didn't dare, and just sat there picking at the front of his caftan. Arkady Petrovich was astonished.

"What Madeira?"

Gervaska glanced at Pyotr Petrovich insolently and smirked.

"You may have been so kind as to forget, sir," he said to Arkady Petrovich, making not the least effort to conceal his sarcasm.

"There was, indeed, a goodly bit of Madeira, and nobody knew how to dispose of the stuff. So all of us, we flunkies, ended up filching it. The wine of the manorial estate, and we slurped it down like it was kvass."

"Just what is this now?" screamed Pyotr Petrovich, his face infused with that dark flush of his. "Be silent!"

Grandfather chimed in ecstatically.

"Just so, Petenka! Right you are. *Fora!*" he exclaimed joyously in his weak voice, and nearly burst out crying. "You simply cannot imagine, he's the ruination of me! More than once I've thought, 'I'll just sneak up and crack his head with a copper pestle . . .' God's truth, it's what I thought! 'I'll stick a dagger in his ribs right up to the hilt!'"

But Gervaska came right back at him.

"I have heard tell, sir, that they punish one severely for such as that," he responded, scowling. "Otherwise, I might have entertained similar thoughts my own self: like it's time to send the master off to the heavenly kingdom!"

Pyotr Petrovich later used to say that after such an abrupt and brazen remark he held his temper only because a stranger was present. All he said to Gervaska was, "Out of here, you, this very minute!" And even then he felt ashamed of his rashness—and hastily begged Voitkevich's pardon, training upon him, with a smile, those enchanting eyes of his, which made a lasting impression on anyone who knew him.

For far too long Natalya, as well, could not forget those eyes.

Ever so short was the duration of her happiness. And who would have thought it would end up with that journey to Soshki, the most remarkable event in her life?

The farmstead in the hamlet of Soshki is still there to this day, although years ago it passed into the hands of a merchant from Tambov. It consists of an elongated hut amidst a barren plain, a granary, a well sweep, and a threshing floor, surrounded by melon patches. Of course, that's the same way the farmstead was back in our ancestors' time. Little changed, as well, is the city that lies on the way to it from Drydale. And Natashka's offense amounted to this: she did something she never would have expected of herself; she stole Pyotr Petrovich's folding hand mirror, with its silver mounting.

When she saw that mirror she was so struck by its beauty—as she was by everything that belonged to Pyotr Petrovich—that she could not resist. And for several days, until they noticed that the mirror was missing, she lived flabbergasted by her crime, enchanted by her terrible secret and her treasure, as in the folktale of the scarlet flower. Before lying down to sleep she prayed to God for the night soon to be over, for the morning soon to arrive; a festive air reigned in the manor house, which had come alive, suffused with something new and marvelous with the arrival of the handsome young master, all dressed up and pomaded, with the tall red collar of his full-dress uniform, his face dark in complexion but delicate, like that of the young miss. The festiveness was there even in the anteroom where Natashka slept, on a locker with a lid that raised, and where, jumping up at daybreak, she recalled at once that there was joy in the world, because by the threshold stood, waiting to be cleaned, those ever-so-light little boots, fit for the son of a tsar to wear. But the most awesome and festive thing of all was out beyond the garden, in the abandoned bathhouse, where she kept the collapsible hand mirror in its heavy silver setting—beyond the garden, where Natashka would run in secret while all were still asleep, through the dew-laden thickets, to exult in the possession of her treasure, to carry it out onto the threshold, to open it wide in the hot morning sunshine and gaze at herself until her head spun, and then to hide it again, bury it away and run back once more, all morning to wait upon the one whom she dared not raise her eyes to look at, for whose sake she peered so long into that hand mirror in her insane desire to make him like her.

But the fairy tale of the scarlet flower was brief, all too brief. It ended in disgrace and shame too horrendous for words, so Natashka thought. It ended when Pyotr Petrovich himself ordered that her hair be sheared, that she be made to look a fright, she who had dolled herself up, darkened her eyebrows in the mirror, creating a certain sweet mystery, a nonexistent intimacy between herself and him. It was he who discovered and transformed her crime into an act of simple thievery, the stupid prank of a serving wench, whom, before the eyes of all the house serfs, they seated in a manure cart, dressed in a coarse shift, her face swollen with tears, disgraced, torn abruptly from all that was native and dear to her, and transported her off to some unknown, horrendous farmstead out in the far reaches of the steppes. She knew already that out there, on the farm, she would have to mind the baby chicks, the turkeys, and watch over the watermelon patches; out there she would bake in the sun, forgotten by all on earth; there, where the steppeland days would be as lengthy as years, where horizons drown in the rippling heat haze and it's so quiet, so searingly hot that you'd sleep the sleep of the dead all day long if you weren't forced to listen to the cautious crackling of parched pea fields, to the brood hens fussing about in the hot earth with an air of exemplary housewives, to the placidly somber gobbling of the turkeys one to another, if you didn't have to be alert for the frightening, upward-swooping shadow of the hawk, to jump up and shriek out in a weak voice an extenuated shout: "Shoo!" All this was out there, on the farmstead, where there was no one but a single old Ukrainian crone, who now held in her power Natashka's life and death, who most likely was eagerly awaiting the arrival of her victim! She had a single advantage over those who are being carted along to their execution: the possibility of hanging herself in advance. And that was the only thing that sustained her on the road into exile—into a banishment that she, of course, assumed would last forever.

On the way there in that tumbrel, from one end to the other of the administrative district, many and manifest were the things that she saw! But she had little use for the sights at that time. She thought, or rather felt, just one thing: that her life was finished, that the crime and disgrace were too great to allow any hope for returning to life! One person from her past life remained, for the time being, beside her: Evsei Bodulya. But what would happen after he delivered her into the hands of the Ukrainian crone, after he spent the night there and left, abandoning her for all time in an alien land? After she had cried herself out she felt hungry. To her amazement Evsei looked upon that desire as quite an ordinary thing, and while they were having a bite to eat he conversed with her as if nothing at all had happened. Then, later on, she went to sleep—and upon awakening she found herself in the city. The only thing that struck her about the city was its dreariness, dryness, the stuffiness of the air, and something else that had a hazy-gruesome, grievous feel about it, like a dream you can't relate. Of that day there was little she later recalled. She remembered only that summer in the steppes is hot, that there's nothing on earth more eternal than a summer's day and nothing stretching on longer than the highroads. She recalled that the city streets have places spread over with stones, along which their tumbrel clattered in the strangest way, that the city smells from afar of iron roofs, and in the middle of the town square—where they rested and fed the horse beside the awnings of the snack stands, empty now toward evening—that it smells of dust, tar, rotten hay, clumps of which, tramped into horse manure, are left at the spots where the peasants parked their carts. Evsei unharnessed the horse and led him up to the tumbrel to be fed; he pushed his hot cap back on his head, wiped the sweat with a sleeve, and black all over with the heat, he went off into the hash house and tavern. In the sternest of voices he commanded Natashka to "keep a eye out," and if anything happened to yell like mad all over the town square. So Natashka sat there unmoving, training her eyes on the cathedral, which at that time had just been built, its cupola blazing like a huge silver star somewhere in the distance, far beyond the buildings. She sat until Evsei returned—masticating, in a happy frame of mind—and, a wheatmeal loaf of bread under his arm, began once more leading the horse back into the shafts.

"You and me, little princess, is running just a tiny bit late!" he muttered in animated tones, addressing not exactly the horse and not quite Natashka. "Well, I figure they won't hang us for it! It ain't a fire we're going to. Me, I don't aim to go rushing back neither—the master's horse means a lot more to me than your fat mouth," he said, thinking now of Demian. "He opens up his fat, wide gob, says, 'Now you mind what I'm a-telling you! Anything goes wrong I'll have your britches down and your butt-end on display.' 'Aha,' I'm thinking. 'Now that really hits me where it hurts! Even the masters, why, not even they has ever took down my britches for a whipping . . . you ain't man enough, you black-in-the-rotten-mouth.' Telling me 'Mind!' What's there for me to mind? I reckon I ain't no more jackass than you. If I take it in my head, I won't come back at all. I'll deliver the lass, make the sign of the cross over myself, and then you just watch my dust making tracks . . . The lass, now, she's got me confounded—fool of a wench, what's she fretting and fuming over? Ain't the world full of space? Say a ox-cart driver comes by with a load of fish or grain, or might be some wandering bandura players or some such passing by the farmstead—just say the word and in a flash you end up out beyond great Father Rostov. And then just let them try to find out where you're at!"

And in Natashka's sheared head the thought "I'll hang myself" was replaced by the thought of flight. The tumbrel began squeaking and rocking. Evsei fell silent and directed the horse to the well in the middle of the square. Back where they had come from the sun was going down behind the spacious garden of the monastery, and the windows in the yellow jailhouse standing across the road, opposite that monastery, glittered golden. For a moment the sight of the jail was an even greater stimulus to the idea of flight. Folks just light out, then live on as fugitives! Only they say the blind itinerant musicians take wenches and lads they've kidnapped, burn out their eyes with boiling milk, and then set them up as beggars, and the ox-cart drivers, they carry you off to the sea and sell you to the Nogai tribesmen. Then again, sometimes the masters catch their runaways, clamp them in shackles, and throw them in prison. But as Gervaska says, "Well, it's still people there in them jails, I figure, and not some wild bulls or something!"

But the light on the prison windows faded away, her thoughts were confused—"No, running off is even worse than hanging myself!" Now Evsei had sobered up and stopped his babbling.

"We're running late, lass," he said, his voice turned anxious, as he jumped sideways up onto the edge of the cart.

And having attained the main road, the cart started shaking again, banging about, clattering briskly over the stones. "Ah, best of all would be if I could get him to turn around," said the mixture of thoughts and feelings in her head. "Turn around and gallop back to Drydale—and fall at the feet of the masters!" But Evsei drove on. The star beyond the buildings was not there anymore. Stretching out ahead of them was the bare white road, the white carriageway, white buildings—and holding dominion over all of this was that enormous white cathedral and its new, white, tin-plated cupola, with the sky above it now gone pallid blue and dry. And there, back home, the dew had fallen by now, the garden was fragrant with crispness, the heated stove in the kitchen was sending out its aromas; far beyond the plains of the grain fields, the silvery poplars on the outskirts of the garden, beyond the bathhouse of her cherished dreams the evening glow was burning down, and in the drawing room the doors were open onto the terrace, a scarlet light blended with murk in the corners, and the young miss, with her yellowish, dusky complexion and her black eyes, resembling both Grandfather and Pyotr Petrovich, was incessantly readjusting the sleeves on her airy and loose-fitting dress of orange silk, intently studying the musical notes, sitting with her back to the evening glow, striking at the yellow keyboard and suffusing the drawing room with the exultant-melodious, sweetly despairing sounds of a polonaise by Oginski, appearing to pay not a smidgen of attention to the officer who stood behind her—squat and dark-visaged, propping up his waist with his left hand and following the movements of her swift fingers with an air of concentrated somberness.

"She has hers, and I have mine," said the mixture of thoughts and feelings in Natashka's head on those evenings when she ran with sinking heart out into the cold, dew-laden garden, penetrated into the overgrown stretches of nettles and pungently smelling damp burdock, and stood awaiting the inconceivable: for the young master to descend from the terrace, walk down the arborway, see her, and make an abrupt turn, come hastening up to her with rapid steps—while she would utter not one sound out of sheer horror and happiness.

The tumbrel rattled along. The city was all around them, hot and stinking, the very city that she used to imagine as some fairy-tale thing. In morbid amazement Natashka gazed at the dressed-up people going back and forth along the stones beside the buildings, gates, and shops with their wide-open doors. "And why did Evsei drive this way?" she thought. "How did he get the idea of clattering his cart along through here?"

But now they had driven past the cathedral, had begun descending toward the shallow river by way of dusty hillsides full of ruts, past black smithies, past the rotted hovels of petty tradesmen . . . Once more there was the familiar smell of warm fresh water, of silt, the evening crispness of the fields. The first dot of light flashed in the distance on the hillside directly opposite, in a lonely little dwelling near the swinging beam of the turnpike barrier . . . Now they had broken free of the city, crossed the bridge, ascended to where the barrier stood—and looked into the eyes of the desolate stone road, running off as a white haze into endless distant reaches, into the bluishness of the crisp steppe night. And the horse went at an easy jog-trot, then, having passed the barrier, at a walk. And once again, here on earth and up in the sky, there was the silence of the ever so quiet night—the only sound was the plaintive, faraway whimper of a harness bell. The whimper grew ever more audible, more sonorous—and merged at last with the synchronous tramp-tramp of horses hitched in a troika, with the steady knocking of wheels that were racing along the highway and coming ever closer. A splendid young coachman was driving the troika, and in the *brichka,* his chin tucked into a military greatcoat with a hood, sat an officer. Drawing even with the tumbrel, he raised his head momentarily—and suddenly Natashka saw the red collar, the black mustache, the young eyes sparkling beneath the helmet, which resembled a pail. She cried out, went numb all over, and lost consciousness.

She was struck by the insane idea that this was Pyotr Petrovich, and, with the pain and tenderness that passed like lightning through her high-strung serf girl's heart, she suddenly comprehended what she had been deprived of: nearness to him . . . Evsei rushed to her and sprinkled her sheared, limply dangling head with water from a wooden traveling jug.

After that she came to herself with an attack of nausea—and hastened to lean her head over the edge of the cart. Evsei quickly put his palm under her cold forehead . . .

Later, relieved, chilled, her collar wet, she lay on her back and looked at the stars. Thoroughly frightened, Evsei kept silent, thinking she had fallen asleep—he just shook his head and drove on, ever onward. Running along, the tumbrel was shaking, and the girl felt as if she had no body, that all she had now was a soul. And the state of that soul was such that "all was so fine, just like in the heavenly kingdom."

The little scarlet flower that bloomed in fairy-tale gardens was her love. But she bore away her love into the steppes, into a backwoods that was still more of a primeval wonderland than the back of the beyond of Drydale, so that there, in silence and loneliness, she could struggle with and overcome its first sweet, burning torments, and later on for many a year, forever, to the day she was laid beneath a gravestone, could preserve it, that love, in the depths of her Drydale soul.

6

Love at Drydale was a peculiar thing. Peculiar, as well, was the hatred.

Grandfather, who perished just as absurdly as the one who killed him, just as everyone who perished at Drydale, was murdered that same year. For Intercession Day, the patron saint's festival at Drydale, Pyotr Petrovich invited guests for dinner—and got himself into a state of agitation: would the marshal of the nobility, who had given his word to be there, come? Grandfather was agitated as well, exultant, although no one knew over what. The marshal did attend, and the dinner was a great success. Everything was clamorous and full of gaiety, with Grandfather reveling in the merriment most of all. Early on the morning of October 2 he was found on the floor of the drawing room, dead.

When he retired from the army Pyotr Petrovich made it clear that he was sacrificing himself to save the honor of the Khrushchovs, the family nest, the estate of his birth. He made it clear that, "willy-nilly," he must take business matters into his own hands. He also had to cultivate acquaintances, connect himself with the most enlightened and useful landed nobility of the district, and with others simply maintain relations. At the beginning he managed to do precisely what he had planned, even called on all the middling landowners, even visited the farmstead of Auntie Olga Kirillovna, a monstrously stout old lady who suffered from sleeping sickness and cleaned her teeth with snuff. Already by autumn no one was surprised that Pyotr Petrovich was running the estate like an autocrat. Besides that, he no longer had the look of the fresh, handsome officer home on furlough; he looked like a man in charge, a young squire. When he lost his composure his face was no longer suffused with that dark flush, the way it had been before. He pampered himself, put on weight, went about wearing expensive caftans, decked out his diminutive feet in red Tatar slippers, adorned his small hands with turquoise rings. Arkady Petrovich felt uncomfortable looking into his brown eyes, didn't know what to talk about with him, deferred to him in the beginning on all matters, and was always off somewhere hunting.

On Intercession Day Pyotr Petrovich wished to charm every last guest with his cordiality, as well as to show that he and only he was the number one man of the manor. But Grandfather was a terrible hindrance. Grandfather was in a state of happiness bordering on bliss, but he was tactless, garrulous, and he looked pathetic in his velvet cap with the relic and his new, knee-length blue jacket with its pleated skirts, sewn by the family tailor but fitting him much too loosely. He too thought of himself as the cordial host, and he fussed about from early morning, organizing a certain fatuous ceremony for receiving the guests. One half of the double doors separating the vestibule from the parlor was never opened. But he himself unfastened the iron latches at the bottom and the top of it; first he pulled up a chair, then, trembling all over, he climbed up on it to reach the top bolt. And after he had thrown the doors wide open he stood on the threshold, making the most of the silence of Pyotr Petovich (who was numb with embarrassment and malice but had made up his mind to endure this); he did not leave his post until the final guest had arrived. He kept his eyes trained on the veranda—and the doors to the veranda also must needs be opened; this too, apparently, in accordance with some ancient custom. Catching sight of an arriving guest, he stamped his feet in agitation, rushed to greet him, performed a hasty *pas de bourrée,* a little hop with one leg crossing over the other, went into a low bow, and choking with emotion, he said to each and all, "Well, how glad I am! How glad! So long since you've honored me with your presence! Welcome, I say unto you, welcome!"

It also infuriated Pyotr Petrovich that Grandfather kept informing all and sundry, for some reason, about Tonia's departure for Lunyovo, to Olga Kirillovna's manor. "Tonechka's feeling poorly, got the melancholy; she's gone off to stay with her auntie for the whole fall." What were the guests to think of such a gratuitous declaration? Everyone, of course, already knew about the business with Voitkevich. Perhaps he did indeed have serious intentions, Voitkevich, sighing enigmatically beside Tonechka, playing four-handed with her on the piano, reading "Lyudmila" to her in his hollow voice, or intoning with somber pensiveness, "By the sanctity of the word art thou to a dead man betrothed." But Tonechka flared up with a fury at even his most innocent efforts to express his feelings—for example, when he brought her a flower—

and Voitkevich abruptly departed. After he left Tonechka stopped sleeping at night, sat in the darkness beside the open window, as if waiting for some indefinite period to elapse before deciding it was time to burst into loud sobs—which awoke Pyotr Petrovich. He would lie there for a long time with gritted teeth, listening to those sobs together with the delicate, sleepy soughing of the poplars out in the dark garden beyond the windows, sounds that resembled incessant light rain. Then he would go and try to calm her down. Among those trying to calm her as well were the drowsy serf wenches, and sometimes Grandfather would come anxiously running in. Then Tonechka would start stomping her feet and screaming, "Leave me in peace, out, archenemies!" And everything would end up with abusive vituperations—they would almost come to blows.

"But understand me, why can't you understand?" Pyotr Petrovich hissed furiously after running off all the serf girls and Grandfather, slamming the door, and firmly holding down the latch. "Can't you understand, you viper, what people will think!"

"No!" squealed Tonechka frenetically. "Papa, he's yelling at me, saying I'm in the family way!"

Then, gripping his head in his hands, Pyotr Petrovich would rush out of the room.

Another big worry on Intercession Day was Gervaska: what if he made some careless remark and insulted someone?

Gervaska had grown horribly tall. Enormous, ungainly, but the most prepossessing, the most intelligent of the footmen, he too was attired in a blue knee-length jacket, baggy trousers of the same color, and soft kid boots without heels. He wore a violet kerchief made of worsted yarn wrapped around his thin, dark neck. He had parted his black, dry, thick hair on one side but had eschewed the "Polish woman" style of the times—which left the hair long at the back and on the temples—instead he had a circular bowl cut. There was nothing for him to shave, just two or three scattered and coarse patches of curling black on his chin and at the corners of his large mouth, which they made a joke of: "A mouth that runs from ear to ear; tie it down, 'fore it runs up his rear!" Fibrous like the stem of a weed, very broad and flat across his bony chest, with a miniature head and deep eye sockets, thin ash blue lips, and substantial light bluish teeth, he, this ancient Aryan, this Parsee from Drydale, had been given a nickname: the Borzoi Hound. Gazing at his teeth bared in a grimace, listening to the way he coughed, a lot of people thought, "Won't be long, old hound, before you croak!" But when they spoke aloud their tone was not the one they used with other servants; they addressed this green-about-the-gills young man with dignified formality, using name and patronymic: Gervasy Afanasevich.

The masters feared him too. Their personalities had a feature in common with the menials: you either lord it over someone or you're afraid of him. To the amazement of the other house serfs, Gervaska suffered no consequences for his impertinence to Grandfather on the day of Pyotr Petrovich's arrival. Arkady Petrovich made one curt remark to him: "You, brother, are an absolute swine." To which he received an equally curt reply: "I just can't abide him, sir!" As for Pyotr Petrovich, Gervaska came to him unbidden. Implanting himself on the threshold with that unduly familiar manner of his, long legs in ballooning baggy trousers, out of proportion with his torso, presenting his left knee at an angle to his body, he asked to be whipped.

"I'm a crude lout, sir, and quite hot tempered," he said dispassionately, rolling his large black eyes.

And sensing a hint in that "hot tempered," Pyotr Petrovich lost his nerve.

"We'll get around to that, old boy! There's plenty of time!" he yelled in a sham-stern voice. "Out of here now! I can't stand the sight of you, impudent scoundrel."

Gervaska stood there a moment, silently. Then he said, "It's up to you. Do as you wish."

He stood for a bit longer, twisting a coarse hair on his upper lip, showing the light bluish teeth in his jaw the way a dog might, his face totally expressionless, and then he left. From that point on he was thoroughly convinced of the advantages of that act: putting on a face devoid of expression and keeping replies as curt as possible. Not only did Pyotr Petrovich begin to avoid conversations with him, but he also couldn't even look him in the eye.

On Intercession Day Gervaska maintained that same insouciant, enigmatic manner. In preparing for the holiday they all were run off their feet, giving and taking orders, bickering and abusing one another, washing the floors, applying a bluish cleanser to the dark, heavy silver of the icon frames, kicking at the dogs who got into the vestibule, worrying that the gelatin would not set, that there would not be enough forks, that the cheese and egg blintzes, the pastry twiglets might burn. Gervaska alone was calmly smirking, and he said to the alcoholic cook Casimir, who was raging about, "Easy now, Father Deacon; slow down before you bust your cassock!"

"Make sure you don't get drunk," said Pyotr Petrovich in an offhanded tone, worried on account of the marshal of the nobility.

"Never been a drinker all my life," answered Gervaska, as if speaking to an equal. "It don't interest me."

Later, in front of the guests, Pyotr Petrovich even cried out fawningly, loud enough to be heard all over the house, "Gervasy! Make sure you stay close, please. When you're not around it's like we're missing our hands."

In the most polite voice he could muster, with dignity, Gervaska responded, "You need not fret on my account, sir. I'd not dare to absent myself."

He served the food as never before. He justified completely the words of Pyotr Petrovich, who proclaimed to the guests, "You simply cannot imagine the impudence of that lummox, but he's a positive genius! Got hands that can do anything!"

Could he have foreseen that he was dropping into the chalice precisely that final droplet that would run it over? Grandfather heard his words. He picked at the front of his jacket, then suddenly yelled out across the whole table to the marshal, "Your Excellency! Reach out unto me a helping hand! I hasten to you, as I would to a father, with a grievance against my lackey! Against this one, him—this very Gervasy Afanasevich Kulikov! He's out to annihilate me! Every step I take he's there to—"

They cut him short, commiserated, got him calmed down. Grandfather was on the verge of tears, but they reassured him so amicably and with such deference, tinged, of course, with condescension, that he acquiesced and lapsed back into that childlike happiness of his. Gervaska stood by the table austerely, eyes lowered and head turned slightly to one side. Grandfather noticed that this giant of a man had a head that was far too small, that it would have been even smaller were his hair clipped, that the back of that head was sharp, and right there, at the back, he had a particular abundance of hair—thick, black, crudely barbered, and forming a ledge above his scrawny neck. Because of his tan, the windburn he got out hunting, Gervaska's dark face was peeling off in spots to form pale violet patches. And Grandfather kept darting fearful and anxious glances over at Gervaska, but all the same he cried out joyously to the guests, "All right, then, I forgive him! Only in return I won't let you leave, dear guests, for three whole days! On no account may you leave! I make of you one special request: stay over till after eventide. When evening begins descending I'm just not myself: such melancholy, such a frightened feeling! The storm clouds come drifting in, why, they say they caught two more of Bonaparte's Frenchie soldiers out in Troshin Woods . . . Most assuredly I shall die at eventide—you mark my words! Martin Zadeka made that prognostication."

But he died early in the morning.

He had his way: "for Grandfather's sake" a lot of the guests stayed overnight. All evening they drank tea, and the jam was there in such profusion, all different kinds, so they could keep going back and sampling it, then going back and sampling some more. Later they set out all the card tables, lit so many spermaceti candles that their reflection shone in all the mirrors, and throughout the rooms, smoky all over with the fragrance of Zhukov tobacco, full of clamor and the hubbub of voices, a golden-hued shimmer was gleaming, as in a church. But the main thing was that many guests stayed on to spend the night. Consequently, one could look forward not only to a joyful new day but also to a lot more bustling about and painstaking efforts. But then, if not for him, Pyotr Kirillovich, never would the holiday celebration have come off so wonderfully, never would the dinner have been so sumptuous and animated.

"Yes, yes," Grandfather was thinking that night, still agitated, after he had removed his knee-length jacket and was standing in his bedroom in front of the icon analogion, where slender waxen candles burned, gazing at the black image of Mercurius. "Yes, a grievous death shall befall the sinner . . . May the sun not set upon our wrath!"

But then he remembered that he had wanted to think of something else; hunching over and whispering Psalm 50, he ambled about the room, adjusted the pyramidical pastille that was smouldering on the night table, picked up the Psalter, opened its pages, and with another deep, happy sigh he raised his eyes to the headless saint. Then suddenly the thought he wanted came to him, and he beamed with delight.

"Yes, yes: 'Old man's here, well he's fit to kill; old man's gone, well you'd buy him back!'"

Afraid of oversleeping, of neglecting some matter, he hardly slept at all. Early in the morning, when the rooms, still in disarray and smelling of tobacco, were suffused with that special silence that comes only after a festive occasion, cautiously, on bare feet, he crept out into the drawing room, carefully picked up several pieces of chalking that were lying around beside the unfolded green card tables, and emitted a weak moan of ecstasy when he glanced out at the garden beyond the glassed-in doors: at the bright sheen of the cold azure, at the silver of the morning rime frost that covered terrace and banisters, at the brown leafage and bare thickets beneath the terrace. He opened the door and drew the air into his nostrils; there was still a bitter and spirituous smell of autumnal rot from the bushes, but that smell was losing itself in the winter crispness. And everything was motionless, serene, almost celebratory. Just now peeking out from far back, beyond the trees, the sun illumined the crowns of the picturesque arborway, crowns half bare, speckled with the sparse and minute gold of white-boled birches, and a charming, joyous, ineffably violet tonality ran through those white and gold crowns, silhouetted against the azure. A dog ran by in the cold shade beneath the terrace, crunching through the singed frost and the grass that seemed to be sprinkled with salt. That crunch recalled winter—and with a sense of invigoration, stretching back his shoulders, Grandfather returned to the drawing room. With bated breath he started moving the heavy furniture around, rearranging it; as he dragged it across the floor, looking in the mirror from time to time at the reflection of the sky, the furniture made a snarling sound. Suddenly Gervaska entered the room briskly and soundlessly—without his knee-length jacket, drowsy and "ornery as sin," as he himself later described his mood.

He came in and called out sternly, in a whisper, "Quiet down there! Why are you sticking your nose into what don't concern you?"

Grandfather raised his inspired face, and with the tenderness that had been with him all of yesterday and all through the night, he answered in a whisper, "There you see how you are, Gervasy! I forgave you yestereve, and you, instead of showing some gratefulness to the master—"

"I'm sick of you worse than bad fall weather, you slobbermouth!" interrupted Gervaska. "Out of my way."

Grandfather glanced fearfully at the back of his head, protruding now still more over the scrawny neck, which jutted out from the collar of his white shirt, but he flared up, shielding himself with a card table he had begun dragging off to one corner.

"*You* get out of the way!" he cried in a soft voice, after thinking it over for a split second. "It's you who must defer to the master. You drive me to it, and I'll stick a dagger in your ribs!"

"Ah!" muttered Gervaska in vexation, his teeth flashing, and swinging out with a backhand blow, he struck him in the chest.

Grandfather slipped on the smooth oaken floor, waved his arms about—and struck his temple right against the sharp corner of the table.

Seeing the blood, the senselessly crossed eyes, and the gaping mouth, Gervaska tore from Grandfather's still warm neck the tiny golden icon and the periapt with incense on its frayed cord . . . He looked around, then snatched off Grandmother's wedding ring from his little finger. Then, briskly and soundlessly, he walked out of the drawing room—and vanished without a trace.

The only person in all of Drydale who saw him after that was Natalya.

7

While she was living in Soshki two more big events occurred at Drydale: Pyotr Petrovich was married and the brothers set off as volunteer militiamen to fight in the Crimean campaign.

She returned only two years later—to find she had been forgotten. When she returned she did not recognize Drydale, just as Drydale did not recognize her.

On that summer's evening, when the tumbrel sent from the manorial homestead came squealing up beside the farmstead hut and Natashka came skipping out onto the threshold, Evsei Bodulya exclaimed in amazement, "Mercy, could that be you, Natashka?"

"And who else might it be?" she answered with a barely perceptible smile.

Evsei shook his head.

"Well, you got right homely-looking, you know!"

But the only difference was that she no longer resembled her former self. Instead of a young lass with short hair, round-faced and clear-eyed, she was transformed into a short-of-stature, gaunt and shapely wench, placid, restrained, and gentle. She wore a long, embroidered blouse, a checkered woolen skirt about her waist; although her head was covered in the style of our women, with a dark kerchief, her complexion was somewhat dusky, suntanned, and dotted with freckles the color of millet. And to Evsei, inveterate Drydaler that he was, the dark kerchief, as well as the tan and the freckles, of course, seemed unattractive.

On the way back to Drydale, Evsei said, "Well then, lass, you're bride's age now. Figure on getting married?"

She just shook her head. "No, Uncle Evsei, I won't ever be married."

"Where's the joy in that then?" asked Evsei, even taking the pipe out of his mouth.

Speaking slowly and deliberately she explained: marriage is not the thing for everybody; most likely they'd assign her as maidservant to the young miss, who had dedicated her life to God, and she wouldn't let her be married. And then again, Natashka had had some mighty clear dreams on several occasions.

"What was it you dreamt of?" asked Evsei.

"Oh, nothing much, just weird stuff," she said. "Gervaska back then, well, he near about scared me to death when he told me all what happened, and I got to thinking it over . . . And, well, then come the dreams."

"Is it a fact that he had breakfast there with you? Gervaska?"

Natashka thought for a moment.

"Yes, he did. He come to us and he says, 'I'm here on some big business for the masters, only first off give me something to eat.' Well, we laid out the table for him, like we would for any wayfarer. And he ate his fill, then walked out of the hut, winking to me. I ran out there, around the corner, and that's when he told me every last bit of it; then off he went."

"But how come you didn't yell out to the folks there?"

"Get on with you. He told me he'd kill me. Said I hadn't to say nothing till nightfall. And he told them he was going out to sleep under the granary."

At Drydale all the house serfs looked at her with great curiosity; her girlfriends and coworkers in the maidservants' room kept pestering her with questions. But she gave even her friends the same short, curt answers, as if admiring some role she had taken upon herself to play.

"It was fine," she kept repeating.

And once she said, in the tone of voice of a wandering pilgrim woman, "Many are the ways of the Lord. It was fine."

And quite simply, without delay, she entered into her day-to-day working life, as if she were not the least surprised that Grandfather was gone, that the young masters had set off for the war as volunteers, that the miss had "gone off her head" and was wandering about the rooms the way Grandfather used to, that a new mistress, a stranger to everyone, was ruling over Drydale—small, plump, vivacious, and pregnant . . .

The mistress cried out from the dinner table, "Be so kind, send in that . . . what's her name? Natashka."

Natashka came in soundlessly and briskly, crossed herself, bowed to the corner where the icons were, then to the mistress and the young miss—and stood there, awaiting inquiries and instructions. Only the mistress, of course, made inquiries; the young miss, grown much older and thinner, sharp-nosed, gazing, inertly attentive, with her unbelievably black eyes, uttered not a single word. But the mistress determined that she would be assigned to the young miss. She bowed and said simply, "Yes, ma'am, I understand."

Gazing at her constantly with that same attentively apathetic look, the young miss suddenly leapt upon her in the evening, and, eyes crossed in a frenzy, took delight in cruelly tearing out her hair—because she had awkwardly removed a stocking from her foot. Natashka wept like a child but said nothing; when she went into the maids' room and sat down on the window-seat coffer, stroking her head to remove the torn-out hair, she even smiled through the tears that hung on her lashes.

"Well, she's a nasty one!" she said. "I'm going to have my troubles with her."

Awakening the next morning, the young miss lay for a long time in bed, while Natashka stood by the threshold, head lowered, taking sideways peeps at her pallid face.

"What did you dream about?" asked the miss, in such a lackadaisical tone that someone else might have been speaking through her.

She answered, "As I recall, nothing, ma'am."

And then the young miss, just as abruptly as yesterday, jumped out of bed in a fury, threw a cup full of tea at her, and falling back into bed, shrieked and burst into bitter sobs. Natashka dodged that cup, and very soon she learned to dodge with extraordinary agility. Sometimes, when the ignorant serving wenches answered that question by saying, "I didn't dream of nothing," the young miss would shriek, "Well, make up some lie!" But since Natashka was not much good at lying, she had to develop a different skill: dodging.

Finally they brought a local physician to see the young miss. The doctor gave her a lot of medication. Fearing they were out to poison her, the miss forced Natashka to sample the pills and drops—and she took them all in a row, trying out every last one. Soon after her arrival she learned that the miss had been waiting for her "like the white light of dawn." She reminisced about her, wore out her eyes with looking, when would they get here from Soshki? She fervidly assured everyone that she would recover her health completely as soon as Natashka returned. Then Natashka returned and was greeted with total indifference. But could the young miss's tears have been tears of bitter disappointment? Natashka's heart shuddered when she pondered that. She went out into the corridor, sat down on a locker, and started crying again.

"Well then, do you feel better?" asked the young miss when Natashka came back in later, eyes swollen.

"Yes, better, ma'am," said Natashka in a whisper, although the medicine was causing a sinking feeling in her heart and making her head spin; walking up to the miss, she fervently kissed her hand.

For a long time after that she went about with eyelashes lowered, afraid to raise her eyes and look at the miss, touched by tender pity for her.

"Ah, you're just a polecat in a Ukraine woodpile!" one of her friends from the maidservants' quarters, Soloshka, shouted at her once. More than the others this girl tried to get Natashka to confide her secrets and feelings; but the delights of girlish friendship were spoiled by her brief and simple responses to every question.

Natashka smiled wryly and sadly.

"Well, why not?" she said pensively. "That could be true. Live with crows and soon you're black. Sometimes my heart pines for my Ukrainians even more than for my own dear mother and father."

In the beginning she saw nothing strange about the circumstances of her new life at Soshki. On the morning they arrived only a few things seemed odd to her: that the hut, visible from afar amidst the surrounding plains, was very long and white; that the Ukrainian woman, who was stoking up the oven, greeted her amiably; and that the man didn't listen to Evsei. He, Evsei, blathered on unceasingly—about the masters, about Demian, about how hot it was on the way and what he ate in the city, about Pyotr Petrovich, and, of course, about the hand mirror. But the Ukrainian, Shary, or as they called him at Drydale, Badger, just kept tossing his head about, and suddenly, when Evsei fell silent, he glanced at him distractedly and whined out a song in a nasal voice full of merriment: "Swirling on, whirling on, snowstorm, snowstorm."

Later Natashka began gradually coming to her senses—and began marveling at Soshki, finding more and more charm in it, and finding things that were different from Drydale. Just the hut itself had so much to astonish her—its whiteness, its smooth, level, bog-rush roof. How affluent did the interior furnishings of that hut seem, compared to the slovenly impoverishment of peasant huts at Drydale! What expensive foil icons they had hanging in the corner, what wonderful paper flowers arranged beside them, how beautiful were the multicolored towels that hung above them! And that patterned tablecloth on the table! And the rows of dove blue pots and miniature pipkins on shelves beside the stove! But most amazing of all were the householders themselves.

She could not grasp what, exactly, was amazing about them, but she felt constantly amazed. Never before had she seen the sort of neat, calm and splendid peasant that Shary was. Short of stature, with a head like a wedge, clipped hair coarse and thick with silver, a mustache—he wore no beard—that was also silvery and was thin, Tatar-style. His face and neck, tanned black from the sun, were deeply wrinkled, but those wrinkles too were splendid somehow, defined, necessary for some reason. He walked around awkwardly—his boots were too heavy. Into the boots he tucked his trousers of crude, bleached sackcloth, and into the trousers a shirt of the same material, which hung low beneath the armpits and had a turn-down collar. On the move he was slightly stooped. But neither that mannerism, nor the wrinkles, nor the gray hair aged him; there was none of that weariness of ours, no sluggishness in his face; his small eyes were sharp, with a glint somewhat sardonic. An old Serb who had once ambled into Drydale from somewhere, with a boy who played the violin, this was who Shary reminded her of.

As for the Ukrainian woman Marina, the Drydalers had nicknamed her the Spear. This tall, fifty-year-old woman was shapely in build. A yellowish tan evenly covered the thin skin, not the Drydale kind, on a face with broad cheekbones; a rough-looking face but almost beautiful for the direct gaze and austere liveliness of its eyes—which were sometimes the color of agates and sometimes amber-gray, changing like those of a cat. On her head, like a high turban, she wore a large gold-black kerchief with red polka dots. A short black skirt of checkered wool fit tightly around her elongated hips and her shins, sharply accentuating the whiteness of her blouse. She wore no stockings, putting on shoes with taps right over bare feet. From exposure to the sun her bare shinbones, slender but rounded, had become like polished yellow-brown wood. And sometimes while at work, wrinkling her brows, she sang in a strong chesty voice the Ukrainian song of how the infidels besieged Pochaev—"The glow of eventide descended, / Upon Pochaev even's gloam"—and of how the Mother of God herself "panoplied" in her solicitude the holy monastery. When she sang her voice was so steeped in hopelessness, in wailing intonations, but along with that there was so much majesty, power, menace, that Natashka sat in awed ecstasy, eyes fixed upon her.

The Ukrainians had no children; Natashka was an orphan. Had she lived with Drydale peasants, they would have called her a foundling or sometimes a she-thief, would have pitied her one day and come at her eyes with sharp needles the next. But the Ukrainians were almost cold, yet were evenhanded in the way they treated her, devoid of curiosity and quite sparing of words. In the fall serf women and young wenches from Kaluga were brought in to do the mowing and threshing; they wore brightly colored *sarafans* and for that were nicknamed the gaudy-blouse girls. But Natashka steered clear of the gaudy blousers. They were reputed to be dissolute, carriers of venereal maladies; they were big breasted, brazen and full of mischief; they swore in the nastiest terms and reveled in the nastiness; they speckled their speech with the humor of billingsgate, climbed up on horses like any man would, then galloped like mad. Would that she might have dissipated her grief in an ordinary social setting, speaking frankly, shedding tears, singing songs. But who was there to confide in frankly or to sing with? The gaudy-blouse girls drawled their songs in vulgar voices, taking up the melody with the exaggerated camaraderie of raucous bawlings, with whistles and hiccuping riffs. The only thing Shary sang was a little something in a sardonic, dancey vein. While in her Ukrainian songs, even the love songs, Marina was austere, proud, and pensively somber—"Rustle white willows / By faraway meadows, / Willows I planted myself"—she related in grievously drawn-out tones, then added, lowering her voice, firmly and hopelessly, "Gone is my loved one / Through faraway meadows, / Where white willows rustle, / Willows I planted myself."

And in her loneliness Natashka slowly drank of the first bittersweet poison of unrequited love, suffered through her shame, jealously, the horrid and dear dreams that she often had at night, the unrealized reveries and expectations that long tormented her on quiet days in the steppes. The searing pain in her heart was often overshadowed by tenderness, passion, and despair gave way to submission, to a desire for the most humble and imperceptible existence beside *him,* for a love that was hidden for all time from everyone and expected nothing, demanded nothing. Tidings of Drydale, news that came from there sobered her up. But for a long period no news came, there was no sense of everyday Drydale life—and Drydale began taking on such a loveliness in her mind, became such an object of desire that she could not bear the loneliness and grief . . . Then suddenly Gervaska appeared. In his hasty sharp manner he delivered all the news from Drydale, related to her in a half hour what another could not have managed in a day—up to the point where he "took a backhanded whack" at Grandpa and backhanded him right to death. After that he said firmly, "Well, now I'll be saying good-bye to you, and I mean for all time!"

His huge eyes burning through her while she stood transfixed, he shouted back as he walked out to the road, "And it's high time you got the goosiness out of your noodle! He's about to get married, and you're no use to him even as a lover. So wise up!"

And she wised up. She suffered through that ghastly news, came to herself—and wised up.

After that the days dragged along in measured steps, drearily, like those pilgrim women who walked ever onward along the highroad past the farmstead, who, while resting there, carried on long conversations with her, taught her patience and reliance in the Lord God, whose name they pronounced obtusely, plaintively, and taught her the most important rule of all: never think.

"You think about it, or you don't think—ain't going to go our way nohow," said the pilgrims as they rethreaded the strands of their bark sandals, puckering up their harrowed faces and gazing off limply into the far reaches of the steppes. "Many are the ways of the Lord our God . . . How about if you was to swipe us a onion, be a good girl, now."

And, as usually happens, others would put the fear of God in her—speaking of sins, of the otherworld, predicting untold misfortunes and horrors. Once, following almost directly one upon the other, came two horrendous dreams. She was always thinking about Drydale—at first it was so hard not to think! She thought of the young miss, of Grandfather, about her own future, she tried to tell her fortune, would she be married? And if so, then when and to whom? One time the thoughts so imperceptibly passed over into a dream that she had an absolutely distinct image of a twilight hour on a searing, dusty, anxiously windy day, and of herself running along to the pond with buckets—and suddenly she saw on the clay-dry slope a gruesome, big-headed dwarf of a peasant in rundown boots, hatless, his ginger-haired locks tousled by the wind, in an ungirded, fiery red shirt aflutter. "Grandfather!" she shouted out in her anxiety and horror. "Is it a fire?"

"Now all will be smashed into flinders and fluff!" replied the dwarf, also shouting, but his words were muffled by the fiery wind. "A storm cloud such as none ever seen is a coming! And dare ye not to contemplate marriage!"

The other dream was even more terrifying. It was as if she were standing at noon in a hot, empty peasant hut, which someone had barred from outside, standing with bated breath, awaiting something—and then a huge gray goat leapt out from behind the stove, reared up on its hind legs, and came straight for her, obscenely aroused, with eyes fiery like coals, joyously mad and entreating eyes. "I am your bridegroom!" he shouted in a human voice, briskly and clumsily running up to her, taking small tapping steps with his little back hooves—and his front feet fell on her breast as he swept her up and collapsed upon her.

Jumping up after those dreams from her bedding in the vestibule, she nearly died with the fluttering of her heart, with the fear of the darkness and the thought that there was no one for her to turn to.

"Lord Jesus," she whispered in a rapid patter. "Mother, Queen of Heaven! Heavenly Saints!"

But inasmuch as she conceived of all saints as brown and headless, like Mercurius, she became even more frightened.

When she began pondering over the dreams, certain ideas came into her head: that her years as a maiden were over, her fate already determined—not by accident did it fall to her lot, such an unusual thing as love for a nobleman!—that still more trials awaited her, that she must be like the Ukrainians in their restraint, and like the pilgrim women in their plainness and humility. And since Drydalers love to play a role, to convince themselves of the immutability of something that, supposedly, can't be averted (although they themselves invent this preordained thing), so too did Natashka adopt a role for herself.

8

Her legs went numb with joy when, skipping out onto the threshold on the eve of Peter-Paul Day, she realized that Bodulya had come for her, when she saw that dust-laden, ramshackle Drydale cart, saw the torn hat on the shaggy head of Bodulya, his tangled beard bleached out by the sun, his face, weary and inspired, aged before its time and ugly, even somehow inscrutable with the paucity and disproportion of its features, when she saw that familiar he-dog, shaggy as well, bearing a certain resemblance not only to Bodulya but to the aggregate of Drydale—his back was a turbid gray color, but on his front side, from the chest, from the thick fur trim of the neck, he seemed as if besmirched by the dark smoke of a chimneyless hut. But she quickly got control of herself. On the way home Bodulya babbled whatever came into his head about the Crimean War, appeared at one point to be happy about it, then distressed, and Natashka made her own sober judgment: "Well, reckon somebody's got to put a stop to them Frenchies' shenanigans."

She spent that whole long day on the road to Drydale in a state of anxiety. To look with new eyes upon the old, the familiar, to relive, in approaching the native hearth, things your former self lived through, to notice changes, recognize the folks you encountered. At the spot in the carriageway where it turned off toward Drydale, on the fallow lands overgrown with laburnum, a three-year-old colt was frisking about; an urchin had put a bare foot on the cord of the bridle, grabbed ahold of the colt's neck, and was trying to throw his other leg over his back, but the colt resisted, jerking around and shaking him off. And Natashka felt a joyful exhilaration when she recognized the urchin as Fomka Pantyukhin. They came upon the centenarian Nazarushka, who was sitting in an empty cart in a pose that was old womanly; instead of hunkering down like a male peasant would he had his legs stretched straight out in front of him. Tensed and feeble-looking, his shoulders were raised high; his eyes were colorless, pathetically morose, and he was emaciated to the point where "ain't hardly going to be nothing left to put in the coffin." Hatless, he wore a long, primeval shift that was dove blue with ashes from his lying perpetually on the stove. And once again she felt her heart shudder—recalling how some three years ago that most carefree and kindest of men, Arkady Petrovich, had wanted to whip this very Nazarushka, caught in the vegetable garden with a bunch of radishes and weeping, frightened out of his wits in front of the house serfs, who surrounded him, yelping and laughing loudly: "No, Grandpa, don't be acting contrary on us now. You got to drop your diapers. No getting around it!"

How her heart foundered when she saw the common, the row of peasant huts—and the manor: garden, tall roof of the house, rear walls of the servants' annexes, barns and stables. The yellow rye field, full of cornflowers, ran right up to the edge of the walls, to where the tall weeds and Tatar thistle grew. Someone's white calf with brown spots was swallowed up by the oats, standing amidst them nibbling at tassels. Everything around her was peaceful, simple, ordinary—only in her mind, which was totally fogged over, were things becoming ever more extraordinary, laden with anxiety as the tumbrel rapidly rolled through the spacious courtyard, which was specked with the white dots of sleeping borzois like a graveyard with stones, as for the first time, after two years of living in a peasant hut, she entered the cool manor house, within which wafted familiar aromas of waxen candles, linden blossoms, of the pantry, Arkady Petrovich's Cossack saddle lying on a bench in the anteroom, of the now empty quail cages that hung above the window—and she glanced timidly at Mercurius, whom they had moved out of Grandfather's old quarters into a corner of the anteroom.

Just as before, the gloomy parlor was brightly illumined by joyous sunlight, which streamed in from the garden through the small windows. A baby chick, who was in the house for reasons unknown, peeped out his lonely orphan's peeps as he wandered around the drawing room. Linden blossoms lay withered and fragrant on the hot, luminous windowsills . . . It seemed that all these old things surrounding her had grown younger, the way it always is in houses after a dead man has been carried out for burial. In everything, everything—but especially in the smell of the blossoms—she sensed a part of her own soul, her childhood, adolescence, first love. And she felt sorry for those who had grown up, died, changed—for herself and for the young miss. The girls and boys of her age were adults now. Many of the old folks, who used to sit near the thresholds of the servants' annexes, gazing out, now and again, at God's green earth, eyes dulled, heads shaking with decrepitude, had now disappeared from the world forever. Darya Ustinovna was gone. Gone too was Grandfather, who had so feared death in his childlike way, thinking that death would slowly creep over him, preparing him for that terrible hour, and who had been mowed down by its scythe so abruptly, lightning swift. It was inconceivable that he was no more, that beneath the mound of a grave by the church in the village of Cherkizovo the thing that lay moldering was he, Grandfather. It was also inconceivable that this black, thin, sharp-nosed woman, who was sometimes listless, sometimes frenetic, who could be anxiously garrulous and frank with her, as with an equal, but before she knew it was tearing out her hair—that this was the young miss Tonechka. It was hard to grasp why the mistress of the house was now some Klavdia Markovna, a small, shrill woman with a little black mustache.

Once, glancing timidly into her bedroom, Natashka saw the fateful hand mirror in its silver mounting—and her heart felt the sweet surge of all those former fears, joys, the tenderness, the anticipation of shame and happiness, the smell of dew-laden burdock in the evening gloaming . . . But all her feelings, all her thoughts she concealed, damped down within herself. That old, old Drydale blood was flowing within her! She had eaten the too-vapid unleavened bread, grown on the loamy soil that surrounded Drydale. She had drunk of the too-vapid water, siphoned from the ponds her forefathers had dug out in the bed of a dried-up river. She was not afraid of the enervating daily grind—but she feared the unusual. Even death did not terrify her, but the dreams made her tremble, the nocturnal darkness, storms, thunder—and fire. As if carrying a child beneath her heart, she carried a vague premonition of some inevitable calamity.

That premonition aged her. And then too, she kept hammering into her own mind, unceasingly, the notion that her youth had passed, and everywhere she sought confirmation of that. Less than a year after her return to Drydale there was not a trace left of that youthful exhilaration she had felt as she stepped across the threshold of the Drydale manor house.

Klavdia Markovna gave birth. Fedosia the poultry wench was promoted to nanny—and she, still young, put on the dark, old-womanly dress, became humble and God fearing. The new Khrushchov had barely begun goggling his nescient, milky little eyes, exuding bubbles of saliva, helplessly tumbling forward, overcome by the weight of his own head, and bawling out truculently. But already they were calling him the young master—already the keening babble of age-old ditties was heard in the nursery: "Here he come, here he come, old man with his bag . . . Hey, old man, you, old man! Don't you come in here. You can't have the little master, you can't have him, we won't let you, he won't cry no more . . ."

And Natashka patterned herself after Fedosia, considering herself a nanny too—nanny and companion of the ailing young miss. In the winter Olga Kirillovna died—and she asked to go to the funeral with the old crones, those living out their days in the servants' annexes; she ate the traditional funeral dish of frumenty, which sickened her with its vapid and cloying taste, but upon her return to Drydale she related in a spirit of tender emotion how the mistress lay there, looking "pretty near like she was still alive," although even the crones had averted their eyes from that coffin, with its monstrous corpse.

In the spring they brought a sorcerer from the village of Chermashnoe to see the young miss, the renowned Klim Yerokhin, a well-favored, affluent smallholder peasant with a large, bluish, grizzled beard, with grizzled curls of hair parted in the middle. Businesslike in his affairs, rational and down-to-earth in mundane conversation, he was transformed into a soothsayer-healer in the presence of the sick. His clothing was well sewn and neat to a rare degree—a long, steel-colored waisted coat of coarse undyed cloth, a red sash, boots. His little eyes were crafty and keen, but there was no sham sanctimony in the way he searched out the icons upon making his wary entry into the manor house, his splendid figure slightly stooped. In a businesslike tone he began the conversation. He spoke first of the grain crops, of rains and drought, then for a long time he sat staidly drinking tea, then crossed himself once again. Only after all of this, abruptly changing his tone, he asked after the one who was poorly.

"Evening gloam . . . darkening . . . It's time," he said mysteriously.

As she sat in her bedroom in the twilight waiting for Klim to appear at her door, the young miss was in the throes of a high fever and so overwrought that she could have collapsed momentarily in convulsions on the floor. From head to foot enveloped in terror was Natalya as well, standing beside her. The whole house was hushed—even the mistress, who packed all the wenches into her room and spoke with them in whispers. No one dared light a single lamp, raise a single voice. The high-spirited Soloshka, who was on duty in the corridor—in case Klim called out or issued an order—saw everything go dim before her eyes as her heart pounded in her throat. For there he was walking by her, unwrapping as he passed a handkerchief with some kind of sorcerer's bones. Then, from the bedroom, that sepulchral silence was broken by his loud, peculiar voice.

"Arise, slave of the Lord!"

After that his grizzled head appeared from behind the door.

"The board," he muttered lifelessly.

And on that board, placed on the floor, they stood the young miss, gone cold all over like a corpse, her eyes rolling and bulging with horror. It was already so dark that Natalya could barely make out Klim's face. Then suddenly he began, in a strange voice somehow distanced from the proceedings. "Filat shall come . . . Shall open the windows . . . Throw wide the doors . . . Then call out, saying, 'Misery, misery!'"

"Misery!" he exclaimed with a sudden forcefulness and menacing power. "Go thou out, misery, into dark forests—there beest thy spot! On ocean's expanse, on sea's watery waste," he maundered in a deep-throated, sinister patter. "On ocean's expanse, sea's watery waste, on the Isle of Buyan lies a she-dog bitch immense, on her back a gray and frazzled sheep-fleece dense . . ."

And Natalya felt there were not, nor could be, more horrendous words than these, which transported her soul in a flash out to the brink of a savage, fairyland world of primeval crudity. It was impossible not to trust in the power of those words, just as Klim himself trusted implicitly in them, he who had accomplished genuine miracles with the afflicted—that same Klim who spoke so plainly and humbly, sitting in the anteroom after the sorcery was done, wiping his sweaty brow with a handkerchief and once again preoccupied with his tea.

"Well, two more eventides for us to work with now . . . Then, God willing, we might see it ease off on her a smidgen . . . You got your buckwheat put in yet this year, madam? They say it's a fine year for the buckwheat! Mighty fine!"

In the summer they expected the masters back from the Crimea, but Arkady Petrovich sent a certified letter with new demands for money and news that they could not return before the beginning of autumn—on account of a slight wound sustained by Pyotr Petrovich, requiring a lengthy rest. Someone was sent to the conjure woman Danilovna in Cherkizovo to ask whether the illness would come to a positive resolution. Danilovna started dancing about and snapping her fingers, which, of course, signified that all would be well. That calmed the mistress down. But the young miss and Natalya had other things to worry about. After Klim's treatment the miss felt some relief, but by the end of the Peter-Paul holidays it started up again: once more the melancholy, plus an intense fear of thunderstorms, of fires, and of something else she kept secret, so that the brothers were of little concern to her. Natalya thought little of them either. Whenever she prayed she made mention of Pyotr Petrovich, asking for the preservation of his health, just as later on, all her life, till she herself was in the grave, she asked that peace be upon his eternal soul. But closest of all to her was the young miss, and more and more the young miss infected her with her own fears, with the anticipation of calamities—and with whatever it was she was keeping secret.

The summer was searing, dusty, windy, with thunderstorms every day. Dark and anxious rumors were spreading amidst the peasants—of a new war, of uprisings and fires. Some said that any day now all the serfs would go off to be freed; others said that no, on the contrary, beginning in the fall every last muzhik would have his head shaved as an army recruit. And, as always happens, countless numbers of vagabonds soon appeared, wandering fools and "monks." The young miss nearly came to blows with the mistress over them, for the handouts she insisted on giving them—eggs and bread. Dronya started dropping by, a long-limbed man, ginger haired, ragged beyond measure. He was simply a drunk, but he played the beatific fool. He would be so lost in thought as he walked across the courtyard, straight up to the manor house, that he banged his head against the wall and then hopped back with a joyful look on his face.

"My little tweety birdies!" he cried out in a falsetto, gamboling around and contorting his whole body, including the right hand, of which he made something like a shield to keep off the sun. "Flown away, flown away, my little birdies, way off into the blue yonder!"

In imitation of the peasant crones, Natalya looked at him in the way accepted as proper for looking at "God's People," obtusely and pitying. The young miss rushed up to the window and cried out in a plaintive voice, all in tears, "Dronya, servitor of the Lord! Pray thou for me unto God, I who have sinned!"

And when she heard that cry Natashka could have swooned with the terrible forebodings she felt.

From out of the village of Klichin came "Klichin Tim": small, yellow haired, fat in a womanly way, with large breasts and the face of a cross-eyed infant, dim witted and gasping with corpulence, wearing a white calico shift and little, short calico breeches. Tripping along on his small feet plump with flesh, taking short hasty steps on tiptoes, he made his way up to the veranda, and his narrow little eyes had such an odd expression—as if he had just emerged from underneath water or had saved himself from some inevitable ruin.

"Woe is me!" he muttered, gasping for breath. "Woe! Calamity!"

They calmed him down, fed him, waited for him to say something. But he kept silent, wheezed, and greedily chomped away. When he had chomped up his fill he threw his sack over his shoulder and began searching anxiously for his long walking stick.

"When will you come again, Timosha?" screamed out the young miss to him.

He responded with a shriek of his own, in a voice absurdly high and alto, mangling, for some reason, the miss's patronymic, "Round about Holy Week, Lukyanovna!"

The miss howled at him piteously as he departed, "Servitor of the Lord! Pray unto God on my behalf, for me the sinner, Mary of Egypt!"

Every day, from everywhere there came news of calamities—thunderstorms and conflagrations. And ever stronger at Drydale grew the ancient fear of fire. No sooner did that sand yellow sea of ripening grain begin dimming beneath a storm cloud that emerged from behind the estate, no sooner did the first whirlwind soar out across the common and the distant thunder go ponderously rolling than the peasant women rushed to bear out to their thresholds those dark little boards with the icon paintings, to prepare pots full of milk, which is known to work best for pacifying a fire. From the manor house scissors went flying into the nettles, that terrifying cherished towel was pulled out, the windows all draped, and trembling fingers lit waxen tapers.

As for the mistress, either she was making a pretense or she too was really infected by the fear. Previously she had said that a thunderstorm was a "natural phenomenon." But now she too crossed herself and narrowed her eyes, cried out at the lightning, and in order to magnify her own fear and the fear of those around her, she kept telling the story of some extraordinary storm that thundered across the Tirol in 1771 and killed 111 people in one fell swoop. And the women listening to her took up the thread, hastened to get their own stories in: about a white willow out on the highroad that was hit by lightning, nothing left of it but ashes, about a peasant woman in Cherkizovo struck dead a few days ago by a thunderclap, about a troika somewhere so deafened as it ran along the road that all three horses fell down on their knees . . . Finally, stepping in to join this maelstrom of dervish dancing there came a certain Yushka, a “sin-beridden monk,” as he called himself.

9

Yushka was born a muzhik, but never had he worked a lick, and he lived wherever the Lord might send him, paying for his bread and salt with tales of his utterly idle existence and his “sinful ways.” “Yessir, brother, a peasant I am, but I got brains and look like a hunchback,” he would say. “So why should I work!”

And it was true, he had a hunchback’s way of peering about—caustically, with a knowing air—he had no hair on his face, and, owing to rachitis of the thorax, he held his shoulders slightly raised. He chewed at his nails and kept brushing back his long, bronze red hair with fingers that were slender and strong. Plowing the soil, in his view, was “indecent and boring.” So he had set off for the Kiev Cave Monastery, where he “done some growing up” and from where he was banished for “sinful ways.” At that point he concluded that pretending to be a pilgrim who wandered the holy places, saving his soul, was old-fashioned and would bring little profit, so he had a go at a different sort of sham. Still wearing his cassock, he started openly bragging about his idleness and lustfulness, smoking and drinking to his belly’s content—he never got drunk—mocking the monastery and demonstrating, by way of the most lascivious gestures and bodily movements, what exactly got him exiled from there.

“Well, stands to reason,” he said to the peasants, winking, “that my shenanigans soon had them to grabbing ahold of this slave of God by the scruff of his neck. So then I took off a-rambling my way home, to Rus. Thinking, ‘I’ll get along back there, all right!’ ”

And sure enough—he got along. Holy Rus embraced him, this shameless sinner, with no less cordiality than those who were saving their souls; it fed him, gave him something to drink, a place to sleep the night, and it listened to his stories enthralled.

"So you done swore off work forever?" asked the peasants, their eyes gleaming in anticipation of his caustic, blunt candor.

"The devil hisself ain't about to make me work no more!" responded Yushka. "I'm spoiled rotten, brother! And I got more rut in me than a monastery goat. The lassies now—and I wouldn't take no older woman if they paid me—the lassies is deathly ascairt of me, but they love me anyhow. And why not? I'm prime meat, I am, top rooster. Well, feathers on my tail might not be too pert, but I got bones that's built!"

When he showed up at the Drydale estate he acted like he belonged there, walked right into the manor house. Natashka was sitting in the anteroom on a bench, crooning a song, "Sweeping up the vestibule, found myself a sugar lump . . ." She saw him and jumped up horrified.

"Who are you?" she screamed.

"A man," answered Yushka, quickly looking her up and down from head to foot. "Inform the mistress that I'm here."

"Who's that?" screamed the mistress in turn, from the parlor.

But it took Yushka only a minute to calm her down. He said he was a former monk and not some runaway soldier, as she may well have supposed, that he was on his way back to his homeland—and he asked her to have him searched and then let him spend the night, get a bit of rest. His straightforwardness made such an impression on the mistress that the very next day he moved into the footmen's room and became like one of the household. Thunderstorms kept blowing over, and he tirelessly entertained the mistress and young miss with stories, got the idea of caulking shut the dormer windows to keep the roof safe from lightning, ran out onto the veranda during the most horrendous thunderclaps to show them there was nothing to fear, helped the serving wenches set up the samovars.

The girls looked askance at him, feeling his quick, lecherous eyes on them, but they laughed at his jokes, and Natashka, whom he had already accosted several times in the dark corridor, whispering hastily, "I'm in love with you, lass!" dared not raise her eyes to look at him. She was revolted by the stench of cheap tobacco that his cassock reeked of, and she was afraid of him, terrified.

She already knew with certainty what was going to happen. She slept alone in the corridor, next to the door that led into the young miss's bedroom, and Yushka had once already snapped at her, "I'm coming for you. Ain't nothing on earth can stop me. And if you yell out I'll burn the whole house down to ashes." But worst of all she was enervated by the realization that something *inevitable* was running its course, that the terrible dream she had had was on the verge of realization—the one at Soshki, about the goat—that apparently she was destined at birth to come to ruin along with the young miss. It was now quite clear to them all: in the dead of night the devil himself was getting into the manor house. Everyone now understood what, precisely, besides the thunderstorms and conflagrations, was driving the young miss out of her head, what caused her to moan out sweet and wild moans in her sleep, and then leap up with ghastly shrieks that made the most deafening thunderclaps seem as nothing in comparison. She would howl, "The serpent of Eden, the snake of Jerusalem is strangling me!" Who could that serpent be if not the devil, if not the gray goat that comes to women and girls in the dead of night? And is anything on earth more hideous than his visits in the darkness, on foul-weather nights with unceasing rolls of thunder, with flashes of lightning on the black icons? The passion, the lust in the whisperings of this scapegrace to Natashka, that was something unhuman as well—so how could you resist it? As she thought in the night about that fatal, ineluctable time that would come for her, sitting on her horse-cloth coverlet in the corridor, staring with beating heart into the darkness and straining her ears to catch the slightest crack or rustle in the sleeping house, she was already feeling the first tremors of that serious malady that was, subsequently, to torment her for so long; there was a sudden itch in her foot, a sharp, barbed cramp passed through it, bending and bowing all of the toes inward toward the sole—then it ran with berserk abandon, voluptuously twisting the veins, through her legs, her whole body, right up to her gullet, to the point where she wanted to shriek out even more frenziedly, with even more sweetness and agony than the young miss . . .

The inevitable was fulfilled. Yushka came—on that horrendous night toward summer's end, on the very eve of Saint Elijah the Ministrant, the ancient caster of flame. There was no thunder that night, and there was no sleep for Natashka. She fell into a drowse—and suddenly, as if someone had nudged her, she was jolted awake. It was the very dead of night—her madly pounding heart told her that. She jumped up, looked down one end of the corridor, then the other: on all sides it was flaring up, flaming, the silent sky full of fire and mystery, with its quivering, dazzling, golden and pale azure flashes of lightning. With each flash the anteroom would light up bright as day. She started running—and then stopped as if rooted to the ground: the aspen logs long stacked in the yard beyond the window gave off blinding white flickers with each flare of lightning. She ducked into the parlor. One window was raised, the steady susurrations of the garden could be heard; it was darker there, but that flame gleamed still more brightly beyond the windowpanes; all was drenched in murk for a time, but then in a trice it caught fire once more, shuddering in one spot, then another—and next came a fleeting glimpse of the garden, swelling up, trembling, showing through against a background of that huge, now gold, now white-violet horizon, all the garden with its lace-laden tree crowns, with its specters of pale green birches and poplars.

"On ocean's expanse, sea's watery waste, on the Isle of Buyan," she whispered, rushing back out and feeling she was bringing on her own ruin with those sorcerer's incantations. "There lies a she-dog bitch immense, gray sheep-fleece dense."

And no sooner had she pronounced those words full of primeval menace than she turned and saw Yushka, with his hunched-up shoulders, standing but two paces from her. The lightning illumined his face—pale, with black circles of eyes. Soundlessly he ran up to her, seized her quickly about the waist with his long arms, and squeezing tight, with a single sweeping movement he threw her down, first on her knees and then onto her back, on the cold floor of the anteroom . . .

Yushka came to her again the following night. He came for many more nights after that—and she, blacking out from horror and revulsion, meekly gave herself to him; she dared not even consider resisting or asking the gentry folk or house serfs to protect her, just as the young miss dared not resist the devil who came to take his pleasure with her in the night, just as, so they said, even Grandmother herself, an imperious beauty of a woman, had dared not resist her house serf Tkach, a desperado and good-for-nothing thief, who, in the upshot, was exiled to Siberia, sent to the deportation settlements there . . . But finally Yushka grew bored with Natashka, just as Drydale itself came to bore him—and he vanished as abruptly as he had appeared.

A month later she felt that she was to be a mother. Then, in September, on the day after the young masters returned from the war, the Drydale manor house caught fire, went up in horrific flames, and burned for a long time: the calamity presaged in her second dream had now come to pass. It caught fire at twilight in the middle of a driving rain, from a lightning strike, a golden fireball, which, as Soloshka described it, had leapt from the stove in Grandfather's bedroom and raced off, skipping and jumping, through all the other rooms. And Natalya, upon seeing the smoke and flames, came running at full speed from the bathhouse—where she spent whole days and nights in tears—and she later told how she collided in the garden with someone dressed in a red Ukrainian jerkin and a tall Cossack hat with galloons; he too was running at full tilt through the wet bushes and burdock . . . Whether any of this really happened or whether it was just her imagination, Natalya could not vouch for sure. One fact alone was incontrovertible: the horror that overcame her relieved her of the unborn child.

From that autumn she began to fade. Her life entered the day-to-day routine from which she never parted to the very end. Aunt Tonia was taken to visit the relics of God's Servitor of Voronezh. After that the devil dared not get near her anymore and she calmed down, began living like everyone else—the derangement of mind and psyche was manifested only in that gleam of her wild eyes, in her extreme slovenliness, her frenetic irritability and melancholy moods during bad weather. Natalya had gone along with her to pay homage to the relics—and she too found tranquillity in that journey, a resolution of all the problems that had seemed insoluble. With what trepidation she faced the very thought of meeting Pyotr Petrovich again! Try as she might to prepare, she could not find a way to imagine herself staying calm. Just think of Yushka, her shame, her ruin! But that exceptional way the ruin had come about, the uncommon depths of her sufferings, the fateful something that was part of her wretchedness—after all, was it an accident that the horrible fire almost coincided with her tribulations!—all this, plus the pilgrimage to the saint, gave her the right to look simply and tranquilly into the eyes not only of those around her but into the eyes of Pyotr Petrovich as well. The Lord God himself had lifted his baneful finger and marked her and the young miss for destruction—so why should they be afraid of mere mortals? Returning from Voronezh, she walked into the Drydale manor house like a nun, the meek, simple-hearted servant of all, light in spirit, purged, as if she had just received extreme unction, and she boldly walked up to kiss the hand of Pyotr Petrovich. Only for one brief moment did she feel a youthful, tender girlish quaver in her heart, when her lips touched his small, swarthy hand with its turquoise signet ring.

Drydale went back to its everyday routine. Rumors of the emancipation were in the air, this time better substantiated—and they occasioned great anxiety in both house serfs and village peasants: what would happen in the future, wouldn't it be even worse? Sure, it's easy to say—let's start a new way of life! The new way was in prospect for the masters as well, but they had not yet learned the old way. Grandfather's death, then the war, the comet that steeped the whole country in terror, then the fire, the rumors of emancipation—all of this made rapid changes in the faces and souls of the masters, deprived them of their youth, insouciance, of that tendency to fly into a rage and then quickly return to normal. Out of this came malice, tedium, vexatious faultfinding one with another; the "discord" began, as Father put it, and it ended up with those Tatar *chabouks* at the dinner table . . . Poverty began reminding them of the urgent need to straighten out their business affairs, which had gone to wrack and ruin with the Crimean War, the fire, the debts. But in business matters the brothers just kept getting in each other's way. One of them was absurdly greedy, austere and suspicious—the other was absurdly generous, kind and trusting. Coming, finally, to a compromise of sorts, they decided upon a venture that by all indications would bring them a healthy profit. They mortgaged the estate and bought up some three hundred emaciated horses—herded them in from practically all around the district with the aid of a certain Ilya Samsonov, a gypsy. Their idea was to fatten up the horses over the winter and make a big profit selling them off in the spring. But for some reason toward spring, having laid waste to a tremendous volume of meal and hay, nearly all the horses, one after another, croaked.

The dissension between the brothers grew even more pronounced. It sometimes came to such a pass that they reached for knives and rifles, and who knows how all that might have ended had not a new misfortune befallen Drydale. In the winter of the fourth year after his return from the Crimea, Pyotr Petrovich went off once to Lunyovo, where he kept a mistress. He spent two days at the farmstead manor there, drinking all the time, and set off for home in a state of inebriation. Snow was coming down; the low wide sledge, covered by a carpet, had two horses harnessed to it. Pyotr Petrovich ordered the trace horse, a young, hot-blooded animal who was sinking up to his belly in the powdery snow, to be unhitched and tied to the back of the sledge. He himself lay down to sleep—with his head, so the story went, facing the back. A foggy, dove blue twilight was setting in. Before he went to sleep Pyotr Petrovich shouted to Evsei Bodulya, whom he often took along instead of the coachman Vaska Kazak, fearing that Vaska would kill him, since his house serfs were embittered by the beatings he gave them. Shouting out, "Let's move it!" he kicked Evsei in the back. And the powerful, bay shaft horse, already wet and steaming mist, his spleen gurgling inside as he ran, pulled them laboriously along the snowy road, into the hazy murk of the desolate fields toward the ever-deepening, sullen winter night.

And at midnight, when everyone at Drydale was sleeping the sleep of the dead, there came a hasty and anxious tapping at the window of the anteroom where Natalya slept. She jumped up from the bench, ran barefoot out onto the veranda. The dark silhouettes of the horses were vaguely visible by the veranda, the sledge, and Evsei, standing there with a knout in his hands.

"We got trouble, lass. Calamity," he muttered in a strange, hollow voice, as in a dream. "Horse killed the master . . . the trace horse. Run into the back end of the sledge, fell up over it, and hit out with one hoof . . . Smashed his face all in. He's turning cold already . . . It wasn't me, not me, I swear to Christ!"

Silently descending from the veranda, tramping through the snow on her bare feet, Natalya walked up to the sledge, crossed herself, fell down on her knees, and embraced the frozen, bloodied head, began kissing it and screaming out over all the estate her wild-joyous cry, choking on sobs and laughter . . .

10

When we had occasion to rest from our urban existence in the quiet and destitute backwoods manor of Drydale, Natalya would relate to us, again and again, the tale of her ruined life. There were times when her eyes darkened, froze in a blank stare, and her voice switched over to a splendid, austere half whisper. That's when I always recalled the crude image of the saint hanging in the corner of the footmen's room in our old home. Decapitated, the saint came to his fellow citizens bearing his own dead head in his hands—as testimonial of the tale he would tell . . .

Now even those few material traces of the past that we once encountered at Drydale were disappearing. Our fathers and grandfathers had left us neither portraits nor letters, not even the simplest appurtenances of their everyday lives. Whatever things had been there perished in flames. For a long time there was a sort of chest in the anteroom with dangling shreds of the brittle and bald sealskin that had fringed it a hundred years ago. This was Grandfather's chest with the Karelian birch drawers that slid out, crammed full of scorched French vocabulary lists and prayer books spotted all over with droplets of wax. Then it too disappeared. The cumbersome furniture in the parlor and drawing room got broken up, disappeared as well . . . The manor house was in its dotage, sinking ever deeper. All those long years that had passed over it, from the time of the last events narrated here, were years of slow death . . . Ever more legendary was its past becoming.

The Drydalers grew up living a life that was back-of-the-beyond, gloomy, but complex all the same, having the semblance of a stable existence, of well-being. Judging by the inertness of that existence, judging by the Drydalers' adherence to it, one may have thought it would never come to an end. But compliant, feeble of will they were, "weak as a babe in the woods when they got on us," those scions of the steppeland nomads! And just as the hillocks disappear, one after another, beneath the crude wooden plough that wends its way across the fields, those little mounds above the subterranean passageways and dens of hamsters, so just as quickly, leaving no trace, did the nests of the Drydalers vanish before our eyes. Its denizens were perishing, dissipating, and those who had somehow escaped destruction were somehow whiling away what remained of their days. We visitors came upon no longer a day-to-day grind, no longer a life, but only the recollections of it, a semi-savage prosaicness of existence. As years passed, more and more seldom did we visit our steppeland region. And more and more alien did it become to us, more and more faintly did we feel our link with that way of life and that estate of the nobility from which we had come. Just as we were, many of our fellow clansmen were of distinguished and ancient lineage. Our names are mentioned in the chronicles; our forebears were royal dapifers and medieval field marshals and "citizens of the first rank" in Catherine the Great's formulation, the closest comrades in arms, even the kinfolk of the tsars. Had we been born in parts farther west, had they been known as knights, how steadfastly would we have repeated their story, how much longer still would we ourselves have held out! For an ancestor of knights could not concede that in half a century a whole class of society had almost disappeared from the face of the earth, that so many of us had degenerated, gone mad, laid hands upon ourselves, had drunk ourselves into oblivion, fallen to pieces, or simply had dropped out of sight! He could not have admitted, as I admit, that we have absolutely no precise conception of the life our immediate forebears led, not to speak of our great-grandfathers, that with each passing day we find it ever more difficult to imagine even what happened a half century ago!

The spot upon which the Lunyovo manor stood had long since been plowed over and seeded, just as the lands where many other manors stood had been plowed and seeded. Drydale was still, somehow, holding out. But having chopped down the last of the birches in the garden, having sold off in plots almost all of the arable land, even its master himself, Pyotr Petrovich's son, abandoned it—he went off to find work, taking a job as a conductor with the railways. And hard was the lot of the longtime female denizens of Drydale, living out their final years—Klavdia Markovna, Aunt Tonia, Natalya. Spring gave way to summer, summer to fall, fall to winter . . . They had lost track of those changes. They lived in memories, nightly dreams, in quarrels and worries over their daily sustenance. During summer those spots once broadly enveloped by the grounds of the estate were now drowning in the rye fields of the peasants; from afar the manor house was still visible, surrounded by that rye. The shrubbery, what remained of the garden, was so wildly unkempt that the quail cried out right by the terrace. But summers were nothing! "Summertime is our paradise!" said the old ladies. Long and hard were the rainy autumns, the snowy winters of Drydale. It was cold, there was nothing to eat in the manor house, which was empty and collapsing around them. Blizzards would cover it over with snowdrifts, and a frosty Sarmatian wind would blow right through it from one end to the other. As for heat—well, they heated the house very seldom. In the evenings a meager ray of light from a tin lamp shone from the windows of the old mistress's chamber—the only habitable room. The mistress, in spectacles, wearing a sheepskin coat and felt boots, was knitting a sock, bending over the lamp. Natalya was dozing on a cold stove bench. And the young miss, looking like a Siberian shaman, was sitting in her peasant shack and smoking a pipe. When Auntie was not quarreling with Klavdia Markovna, the latter would place her lamp up on the windowsill instead of on her desk. Aunt Tonia would sit in the eerie, feeble half-light that made it from the manor house out to the interior of her icy hut, which was glutted with the wreckage of old furniture, the flotsam of broken crockery shards, with the pianoforte, collapsed onto its side, stuffed in there on top of it all. So icy was the shack that the hens, toward whose care Aunt Tonia directed all of her efforts, would end up with frostbitten feet when roosting at night on the wreckage and the shards . . .

But now the Drydale estate is totally deserted. All of those mentioned in these annals of bygone years, all the neighbors, all their coevals are dead. And sometimes you think, "Now, really, did these people actually live on earth?"

Only in the graveyards do you have the feeling that they did indeed; you even feel an uncanny closeness to them. But to get to that point you have to make an effort, sit for a time pondering over a relative's grave—if you manage to find it. Shameful to say, but impossible to hide: we don't know where, exactly, they are, the graves of Grandfather, Grandmother, Pyotr Petrovich. We know only that their burial place is beside the eastern, sanctuary side of that old church in the village of Cherkizovo. In winter you can't get there for the waist-high snowdrifts; you just see an occasional cross jutting out from the snow, plus the tops of bare bushes, twigs. On a summer's day you ride down a hot, quiet and empty country lane, tie your horse to the outer fence enclosing the church grounds, beyond which a dark green wall of firs stands baking in the searing heat. Past the backward-tilting wicket gate, beyond the white church with its rusted cupola, there's an entire grove of small, wide-branching elms, ash trees, wych hazels; all is shade and coolness. You wander around for a long time, past bushes, hummocks, and pits that are covered with delicate cemetery grasses, past the stone plaques that are sunken almost all the way into the ground; they are pocked and dimpled from the rain, overgrown with a friable black moss . . . You come upon two or three iron monuments. But whose are they? They have taken on such a greenish golden sheen that the inscriptions on them are illegible. Under which of the mounds lie the bones of Grandmother and Grandfather? God knows! You can be sure of only one thing: they are somewhere around here, close. You sit and think, trying to conjure up all of those forgotten Khrushchovs. And their time seems by turns infinitely far from you and ever so near. Then you say to yourself, "It's not hard, not so hard to imagine." All you have to do is remember that the lopsided gilt cross standing out against the blue summer sky had the same tilt when they were here . . . that the rye had the same yellow look to it as it ripened in the desolate and searing-hot fields, and that here there was shade, a coolness, those bushes . . . and in the bushes, ambling about and grazing, there was an old white nag just like that one, with the mangy greenish withers and pink, broken-down hooves.

Vasilevskoe, 1911

»»» «««

Way Back When

Once upon a time, long, long ago, a thousand years ago, there lived in the Arbat, at the Hotel North Pole, where I lived as well, a certain inaudible, inconspicuous, most humble of the humble Ivan Ivanich, a man already rather old and quite threadbare.

From year to year Moscow lived on, doing her prodigious deeds. He too did something or other and for some reason lived on in the world. He would leave about nine o'clock and return before five. Musing quietly, though not at all sadly, he would take his key from the nail in the lobby, climb to the second floor, and walk down the zigzagging corridor. This corridor had a very complex, very foul odor, dominated by that pungent and stifling substance that they use to polish the floors of sleazy hotels. The corridor was dark and ominous (the rooms had windows facing the courtyard, and very little light came through the transom glass above the doors), and all day long a small lamp with a reflector burned at the end of each of its articulations. But it seemed Ivan Ivanich experienced utterly none of those burdensome sensations that the corridor aroused in people unaccustomed to the North Pole. He would walk down that corridor calmly and simply, and he would encounter his fellow lodgers: a university student with youthful beard and shining eyes, dashing briskly along and putting his arms through the sleeves of his coat on the run; a stenographer with an independent air, tall and alluring despite her resemblance to a white Negro; a small, elderly lady in high heels, always dressed up and rouged, with brown hair, with phlegm gurgling incessantly in her chest—an encounter with this lady was always presaged by the muffled jingle of the bells that were dashing along the corridor on her snub-nosed pug dog, who had a protruding lower jaw and fiercely, senselessly goggling pop eyes . . . Ivan Ivanich, who would bow politely to everyone he encountered, was not at all offended when he received barely a nod in reply. He would pass one articulation, turn into another still longer and blacker, where the red wall lamp was glittering still farther in the distance; he would put the key into his door, then seclude himself behind it until the next morning.

How did Ivan Ivanich occupy himself in his room, how did he while away his leisure time? God knows. His domestic life, in no way manifested outwardly, of no use to anyone, was a complete mystery to us all—even to the chambermaid and floor boy, who disturbed his cloistered existence only when serving the samovar, making the bed, or cleaning the vile washstand, from which the water always spurted unexpectedly, not into the face, not on the hands, but very high and to the side, obliquely. Ivan Ivanich, I repeat, led a life of rare inconspicuousness, of rare monotony. Winter was passing, spring arriving. Horse-drawn trams sped, rumbled, jangled along Arbat Street, people were continuously streaming by one another, rushing somewhere; light four-wheeler cabs went crackling and clattering along, hucksters with trays on their heads screamed out; toward evening a golden, luminous sunset gleamed in the remote aperture at the end of the street, and over all the bustle and din a low bass peal from an ancient pyramid-tent belfry spread melodiously. Ivan Ivanich apparently neither saw nor heard any of this. Neither winter nor spring, not summer nor fall had the slightest apparent influence either upon him or upon his way of life. But then one spring there came from somewhere a certain nobleman with the title of prince, and he took a room in the North Pole and became Ivan's next-door neighbor. And that's when some utterly unanticipated change came over Ivan Ivanich.

What was it about the prince that overwhelmed him? Certainly not his aristocratic standing. After all, that aged fellow lodger of Ivan Ivanich, the little lady with the pug dog, was also a titled personage, but he felt absolutely nothing for her. How could the prince have captivated him? Certainly not by his wealth or appearance. The prince had squandered all his means; he was slovenly, huge and ungainly, with bags under his eyes and loud, labored respiration. Ivan Ivanich, nonetheless, was both overwhelmed and captivated, and above all, his perennial routine went bottom side up. His whole existence was transformed; he was in a state of incessant agitation. He became absorbed in anxious, petty, and ignominious mimicry.

The prince arrived, settled down, began going out and coming back, meeting certain people, fussing over certain matters—exactly in the same way, of course, as did everyone who lodged at the North Pole. Of those a great many had come and gone in the memory of Ivan Ivanich, although the idea of intruding upon their privacy, becoming acquainted with them had never even entered his head. But for some reason he singled out the prince. Upon meeting the prince the second or third time in the corridor, for some reason he scraped and bowed, introduced himself, and, with all sorts of the most complaisant of apologies, asked to be told as precisely as possible what time it was. Having become acquainted in such a clever manner, he simply became infatuated with the prince, made an utter shambles of his usual pattern of life, and began slavishly imitating the prince's every movement.

The prince, for example, went to bed late. He would return home about two in the morning (always by cab). Ivan Ivanich's lamp also began to burn until two. For some reason he would await the prince's return, his ponderous footsteps in the corridor, his whistling snuffle. He waited with joy, almost with trepidation, and at times he even leaned out of his cramped little room so as to see the approaching prince and have a word with him. Walking by leisurely, as if he had not noticed him, the prince would always ask exactly the same question in a profoundly apathetic tone: "Well then, you're not in bed yet?"

And paralyzed with delight, but without the least timidity, without the least subservience, Ivan Ivanich would answer, "No, Prince, not yet. The night is young; it's only ten past two . . . So you've been out enjoying yourself, having a good time?"

"Yes," the prince would say, snuffling and puffing as he struggled to get his key in the door. "I met an old friend; we stopped in at a tavern for a while . . . Good night."

With that the whole matter would end; so coldly, yet politely, would the prince cut short his late-night conversation with Ivan Ivanich, but even this was enough for Ivan. He would return on tiptoe to his room, routinely dispose of all that had to be done before sleeping, cross himself a bit and nod toward the icon corner, climb inaudibly into his bed behind a partition, and fall asleep at once, absolutely happy and with absolutely no intention of deriving selfish benefit from his relations with the prince, not counting a most innocent prevarication to the floor boy in the morning: "Well, I didn't get much sleep again last night . . . The prince and me got to talking again and sat up till the cocks crowed."

In the evening the prince would set a pair of big, downtrodden shoes outside the door and hang out the most capacious of silvery pantaloons. Ivan Ivanich, too, started setting out his wrinkled little boots, which he used to have cleaned only once in a blue moon, and hanging out his tiny britches with their missing buttons, which he had never hung out before, not even for Christmas or Easter.

The prince would awaken early, let out a terrible cough, take an avid draw on a thickly rolled cigarette, then open his door and bellow into the corridor, loud enough for the whole hotel to hear him, "Hey, boy! Bring the tea!" And in his dressing gown, flapping his slippers, he would march off to answer nature's call and stay for long periods of time. Ivan Ivanich started doing the same; he shouted into the corridor for a samovar, and, in galoshes on bare feet, in a wretched summer coat over soiled drawers, he too ran off to nature's call, although previously nature had always called him in the evening.

The prince once mentioned that he was fond of the circus, that he went there frequently. And Ivan Ivanich, who had never liked the circus, who had last been to the circus not less than forty years ago, decided to see one performance all the same, and that night he gave the prince an ecstatic account of how wondrously delightful he had found it.

Ah, spring, spring! The crux of the matter, it seems, is that all this nonsense took place in the spring.

Every spring seems like the end of something overcome and the beginning of something new. This deception was especially sweet and cogent during that Moscow spring of way back then—for me because of my youth and because my student days were ending, but for numerous others simply because it was spring, an unusually marvelous spring. Every spring is a festival, but that spring was especially festive.

Moscow had made it through her intricate, wearisome winter. Then she had made it through Lent and Easter, and once again she felt as if she were finished with something, as if she had cast some burden from her shoulders, had finally attained to something genuine. And multitudes of Muscovites already were changing or preparing to change their lives, to live them somehow all over from the beginning, this time in a different way than before, to start living more sensibly, properly, more youthfully. They hurried to clean their apartments, to order summer suits; they went out shopping—

for shopping, of course (even for mothballs), is a joy! They were preparing, in a word, for departure from Moscow, for vacations at their cottages in the countryside, or in the Caucasus, in the Crimea, abroad, that is to say for the summer, which, so it always seems, will be inevitably happy and long, oh so long.

How many splendid, soul-exhilarating suitcases and new creaking clothes hampers were bought on Leontevsky Lane and at Muir-Merrielees! How many haircuts and shaves were dispensed at Basile's and Theodore's! Sunny, stimulating days followed one after another, days with new aromas, with a new cleanliness about on the streets, with a new gleam of church cupolas against the bright sky, with a new Strastnoy and a new Petrovka, with new, radiant attire on handsome fops and stylish damsels, dashing along Kuznetsky in the lightweight cabs of daredevil hackneys, with the new, light gray derby of a celebrated actor who was also dashing away somewhere on "pneumatics." Everyone was concluding some phase of his previous life, which had not been lived as it should have been, and for nearly all of Moscow it was the eve of a new, inevitably happy life; so it was for me too, even especially so for me, far more than for others, so it seemed to me then. And ever nearer and nearer came the time of my parting with the North Pole, with all by which I had lived my student life there; from morning to night I was bustling, riding about Moscow, absorbed in all sorts of joyous concerns. But what was my neighbor down the hallway doing, that most modest of the hotel's denizens? Well, pretty much the same things we were doing. The same thing, ultimately, had happened to him as to all the rest of us.

The April and May days flowed on, horse-drawn trams sped jangling by, people were rushing continuously, light four-wheeler cabs went crackling and clattering along, hucksters with trays on their heads screamed tenderly, sorrowfully (although what they extolled was only asparagus), a sweet, warm redolence was wafting from Skachkov's pastry shop, vats of bay leaves stood at the entrance of the Prague, where fine gentlemen dined on young potatoes in sour cream; inconspicuously day approached evening, and now the golden, luminous sky before sunset was gleaming in the west, and over the happy, teeming streets a low bass peal from a pyramid-tent belfry spread melodiously . . . Day after day the spring city lived her stupendous multivaried life, and I was one of the happiest participants in that life; I basked in all her smells, sounds, all her bustling vanity, her encounters, business affairs, purchases; I rode along in cabs, went to the Café Tremblay with my friends, ordered iced fish soup with beet tops and onions at the Prague, and tossed off a shot of cold vodka with a bite of fresh cuke . . . But what about Ivan Ivanich? Well, Ivan Ivanich went off somewhere as well, dropped in a few places, attended to personal matters, small matters, inordinately small, and acquired in return the right to continued existence among us, that is, to a room at the North Pole and a thirty-kopeck meal in a hash house across from it. Only that modest right was he earning himself somewhere, somehow, and it seemed that his presence was alien to our hopes for some new life, for a new suit, a new hat, a new haircut, for competing on a level with someone in something, making acquaintances, finding friends. But then the prince arrived.

How could he have enchanted, overwhelmed Ivan Ivanich? But of course the object of enchantment is not important; what is important is the craving to be enchanted. The prince, moreover, was a man with remnants of the grand manner, a man who had squandered nearly everything but who, in so doing, had lived well in his time. So poor Ivan Ivanich, too, conceived the dream of a new life, a spring life, with pretensions to a grand style and even certain diversions. Well, is that really so bad—to turn in later than ten o'clock, to hang out your trousers to be cleaned, to answer nature's call before having a wash? Doesn't that really rejuvenate you—to stop in for a haircut, to have your beard trimmed, shortened, to buy a grayish hat that makes you look years younger, and to return home with a piddling little purchase, even if it is just a quarter pound of some trifle, prettily tied by the hands of a sweet little shopgirl? Gradually, but ever increasingly yielding to temptation, Ivan Ivanich did all of this in his own way; that is, he achieved, within the limitations of his powers and means, almost everything the others were achieving: he made an acquaintance and began mimicking—true, no more than anyone else!—and he amassed spring hopes and brought a measure of vernal profligacy into his life, and took part in the grand ostentation, and clipped his beard, and began returning to the North Pole just before evening with some piddling parcels in his arms. And what's even more: he bought himself a grayish hat and something in the way of luggage—a little suitcase all studded with glistening tin tacks (for a ruble seventy-five)—since he dreamt of going without fail that summer to the Trinity Monastery or the New Jerusalem.

Whether this dream was ever realized and how Ivan Ivanich's sudden surge toward a new life ended up, well, I really don't know. I imagine that it ended, as do most of our surges, rather poorly, but, I repeat, I cannot say this with certainty. And I cannot say because shortly after that all of us, that is the prince, Ivan Ivanich, and I, parted one fine day, and we parted not for the summer, not for a year, not for two, but forever. Yes, no more, no less than forever; that is, never to meet again not ever till the end of the world, which thought, despite all its apparent bizarreness, simply horrifies me now: just think of it—never! In fact, all of us who live on earth together during a particular time and who experience together all earthly joys and sorrows, seeing one and the same sky, loving and hating, ultimately, the same things, and everyone, down to the last man, doomed to one and the same execution, the same disappearance from the face of the earth, all of us should harbor for each other a feeling of utmost tenderness, of poignant intimacy that moves us to tears, and we should simply cry out in fear and pain when fate separates us, since ever present is the possibility that any separation, even for ten minutes, may become eternal. But as everyone knows we are, ordinarily, not the least given to such feelings, and we often part from even those most dear to us in a way that could not possibly be more frivolous. In just that way, of course, did we part as well: the prince, Ivan Ivanich, and I. One day near evening a cab arrived to take the prince to the Smolensk Station—a rather sorry little cab, which cost him maybe sixty kopecks, while mine, to the Kursk Station, ran a ruble and a half and had a frisky gray mare. And so we parted, without even saying good-bye. Ivan Ivanich remained in his gloomy corridor, in his cage with the dingy glass above the door, and the prince and I drove off in opposite directions, each of us having seated himself in his light four-wheeler after shoving tips into everyone's hands; the prince was apparently rather indifferent, but I was brisk and lively, all decked out in new clothes, vaguely anticipating some marvelous encounter during the trip, on the train . . . And I remember as if it were now: I was riding toward the Kremlin, and the Kremlin was illumined by the evening sun; I rode through the Kremlin, past the cathedrals—how beautiful they were, my God—then along Ilinka, redolent of all sorts of ironmongery, candle waxes and oils, where evening shadows already had fallen, then along Pokrovka, now enveloped in pealing, booming bells blessing the happily ended bustle and vanity of the day. As I rode along I not only rejoiced in myself and in the whole world, but I was truly drowning in the joy of being, having somehow instantly forgotten the North Pole, and the prince, and Ivan Ivanich by the time I had reached Arbat Square. And most likely I would have been amazed had I been told that even they would be preserved forever in that sweet and bitter dream of the past by which my soul will live to the grave, and that there would come a day when I would call out in vain even to them, "Dear Prince, dear Ivan Ivanich, where do your moldering bones lie today? And where are they, our common, foolish hopes and joys, our Moscow spring of way back when?"

Amboise, 1922

»»» «««

A Passing

I

The prince died just before evening on August 29. He died as he had lived—taciturn, estranged from everyone.

Glowing with twilight gold, the sun dropped periodically behind the duskiness of delicate storm clouds that were spread like islands above distant fields to the west. It was a calm, plain evening. The spacious yard of the manor was empty; the house, which seemed to have become even more decrepit over the summer, was hushed.

First to learn of the prince's death were the mendicants, who were always roving about the village. They appeared beside the ruins of stone columns at the entrance to his estate and in clashing, discordant voices began singing the ancient folk canticle "On the Passing of Soul from Body." There were three of them: a pock-marked lad in a sky blue shirt with the sleeves cut off, an old man standing very straight and tall, and a suntanned girl, about fifteen years old but already a mother. Holding in her arms a drowsy child, the nipple of her small breast in its mouth, she sang loudly and impassively. Both muzhiks were blind, their eyes covered by whitish cataracts; but her eyes were clear and dark.

Doors were slamming in the manor house. Natasha dashed out onto the front veranda and tore like a whirlwind across the yard to the workers' annex; through the open door of the house a clock on the wall could be heard, languidly striking six. Only a moment later a farmhand ran through the yard, putting his arms into the sleeves of his coat on the run; he would saddle a horse and gallop off to the village for the old ladies. A visitor at the estate, the pilgrim woman Anyuta, whose short-clipped hair made her look like a boy, stuck her head out the window of the annex, clapped her hands, and screamed something after him—her voice doltish, maundering, and ecstatic.

When young Bestuzhev went into the room, the dead man lay supine on the antique walnut bed beneath an old blanket made of red satin, the collar of his nightshirt undone, his immobile, somehow drunken eyes half closed, his dark face thrown back, now paler, long unshaven, with big graying mustaches. The shutters in this room had been closed, as he had wished, all summer—now they were opening them. On the chiffonier by the bed the yellow flame of a candle burned. Tilting his head to one side, his heart pounding, Bestuzhev avidly scrutinized that strange object that was immersed in the bedding and now was growing cold.

One after another the shutters were opened. As it burned out with an orange tint amidst the storm clouds, the faraway setting sun peeped in the windows, through the dark branches of old coniferous trees in the front garden. Bestuzhev stepped back from the dead man and flung open one of those windows. He felt the flow of pure air that was drawn into the room, into that stagnant, complex, medicinal smell. Natasha, who had been crying, entered and began taking out everything that the prince, suddenly gripped by some apprehensive avidity a week before, had ordered dragged into his room and laid out before him on tables and armchairs: a shabby Cossack saddle, bridles, a brass hunting horn, coupling straps for coursers, a cartridge belt. No longer constrained by the knocking and jangling of bits and stirrups, going about her business with a grim, severe expression on her face, she blew out the candle with a forceful puff as she walked past the chiffonier . . . The prince was immobile; his half-open eyes, which appeared to be gazing somewhat askance, were also immobile. A dry evening warmth, blending with crisp air from the river, filled the room. The sun had expired, everything had faded. The coniferous needles of the front garden were dry and dark against that transparent sea of the sky, greenish above and saffron below, off in the distance to the west. Some kind of bird was chirping outside the window, and the noise it made seemed extremely shrill.

"No need to mourn," said Natasha gravely as she came in again; pulling out a drawer of the chiffonier, she removed some clean underlinen, some sheets, and a pillowcase. "The master died easy, God grant us all such a death. And there's nobody to mourn for him; he didn't leave nobody behind," she added, and went out again.

As he sat against the windowsill, Bestuzhev kept gazing into the dark corner, at the bedding where the dead man lay. He kept trying to understand something, to gather his thoughts, to be horrified. But he felt no horror. He felt only astonishment, the impossibility of grasping, comprehending what had happened . . . Was it all really over, and could one speak so freely in this bedroom now, as Natasha had just spoken? "But then," thought Bestuzhev, "she had been just as unconstrained before when she spoke of the prince—for the whole past month—as one speaks of a man who has already left the realm of the living."

From the yard, from the dusk, came a faint, uncommonly pleasant redolence of smoke. It was soothing, it bespoke the earth, the constancy of simple human life. In the darkened meadows by the river the gristmill hummed on steadily . . . A week ago the prince had been sitting on an old millstone by its gates—in a cap, in a waisted coat of fox fur, thin and bent, his face somber, his arms propping him up on the gray, porous rock. An old man who had brought several bins of newly reaped grain to be ground cast a squinting sullen glance at him as he undid the sacking. "Ain't you got skinny now!" he said coldly and scornfully, although he had always spoken to the prince with deference before. "You don't amount to nothing! No, there ain't much of living left in you. What'll you be, about seventy?"

"Almost fifty-one," said the prince.

"Fifty-one!" repeated the old man mockingly as he busied himself with the sacking. "That just can't be," he said firmly. "You're a far sight older than I am."

"You idiot," said the prince, smirking. "Don't you know we grew up together?"

"Well, whether we did or whether not, there ain't much living left in you now," said the old man, and exerting all his strength, he raised the heavy bag full of rye, pressed it to his chest, then hastily, half squatting, he carried it off into the humming, mealy white mill . . .

"You go on out now, young master," said Natasha impassively but pointedly as she entered the room with a bucket of hot water.

And with that bucket, with those words, Bestuzhev suddenly felt frightened. He arose from the windowsill, and without looking at Natasha went out through the vestibule adjacent to the dead prince's room, onto the back veranda. In the dusk beside the veranda Evgenia and Agafya, two old peasant women who had arrived from the village, were washing their hands. One of them was pouring water from a jug, the other was bent over, the hem of her dark dress held between her knees, wringing something out, shaking her fingers. That was even more frightening—those peasant hags. Hurrying past them, Bestuzhev entered the dry garden, its foliage already sparser as autumn approached, mysteriously illumined in its bottomlands by the round, huge translucent moon, which had just appeared amidst the distant boles of trees.

2

Everything in the room where the prince had died was in order before ten; everything was tidy, the bed was gone, there was a warm redolence of scrubbed floors. The body, towering beneath a sheet, looking very large, lay on tables placed diagonally across the front corner, beneath antique icons next to the window, whose upper pane sparkled silver with moonlight. Three thick candles in tall ecclesiastical candlesticks burned transparently at its head, their crystalline fumes quavering. Freshly washed and combed, wearing a new waisted coat, Tishka, the son of the church custodian Semyon, read the Psalter plaintively and hurriedly. "Praise ye the Lord from the heavens," he read, imitating the monastic sisters—"Praise ye him, all his angels: praise ye him, all his hosts . . ." Transparent spears of flame, golden, with bright blue foundations, quavered and darkly fumed on the candles.

The only light in the house was in the footmen's chamber. A table stood beneath the window there, and on this table a samovar was boiling. They were drinking tea: Natasha, pallid and grave in her black kerchief; Evgenia, looking the very image of death; the sorrowfully meek Agafya; the carpenter Grigory, who already had begun making a coffin in the barn; and the church custodian Semyon, an old man with lackluster, leaden eyes ruined by perpetual reading over the dead by the light of a quavering candle. Semyon, who was to replace his son as reader, had brought his own prayer book, covered by some rough, grayish brown material that appeared to be wooden, spotted with wax, the corners of its pages scorched here and there.

"Don't matter how bad you live, it's still hard parting with this good earth," said Agafya sorrowfully as she poured tea from her cup into her saucer.

"Surely is hard," said Grigory. "Had he known, now, he'd of lived different, he'd of forsook all that he owned. But then, we're afraid to have done with earthly lands and chattels; you keep thinking there won't be nowhere to go in your old age . . . Then one fine day it turns out you ain't made it to no old age!"

"Our life runs back like a wave from the shore," said Semyon. "Death, now, they say, must be received with joy and a-trembling."

"Passing, not death, my dear," Evgenia corrected him in a dry, didactic tone.

"Whether it's with trembling or not, don't nobody want to die," said Grigory. "Take just any little gnat, even he's scared of death. That means they've got souls too."

"Not only souls, dear friend, but souls immortal," said Evgenia still more didactically.

When he had finished his last cup of tea, Semyon jerked back his head to shake the sweaty, dark gray hair off his brow, arose, crossed himself, took his Psalter, and walked on tiptoe through the dark parlor and dark drawing room to the body.

"On your way now, dearie," said Evgenia as he left. "And do a right and proper reading for him. When somebody reads good, the sins drop away from a sinner like leaves off a dry tree."

Semyon replaced Tishka, put on his spectacles, and gazing severely through them, he gently picked away the wax from the guttering candles, then slowly crossed himself, spread his book open on the analogion, and began reading softly, with tender and sad conviction, occasionally raising his voice in admonishment.

The door leading into the vestibule from the back veranda was open. As he read Semyon heard someone's feet tramping on the veranda. Two peasant girls, both in their best clothing, in new sturdy shoes, had come to view the dead body. They entered the room shyly and joyfully, whispering back and forth to each other. Crossing herself and trying to step gingerly, one of them approached the table, her breasts quivering beneath her new pink blouse, and drew back the sheet from the prince's face. The gleam of the candles fell on the girl's blouse, her frightened face was pallid and comely in that gleam, and the dead face of the prince shone like ivory. The large, graying mustaches, which had grown thick during his illness, were diaphanous now, the eyes, not completely closed, glistened with some dark fluid.

Tishka smoked avidly in the entrance hall, waiting for the girls to come out. They slipped past, pretending not to notice him. One of them ran down off the veranda, but he managed to catch the other, the one in the pink blouse. Struggling to break free, she said in a whisper, "You got a screw loose? Let go! I'll tell your papa."

Tishka let her go. She ran out toward the garden. The moon, now smaller, white, clear, hung high above the dark garden, and the dry iron on the bathhouse roof glittered golden in its light. In the garden shadows the girl turned around, glanced at the sky, and exclaimed, "What a night—Lord have mercy!"

And her charming, happy voice rang out with joyous tenderness, resounded in the silent night air.

3

Bestuzhev paced from one end of the yard to the other. From that yard, empty, spacious, illumined by the moon, he gazed at the lights in the village beyond the river, at the bright windows of the annex, where he could hear the voices of people having supper. The barn gates were thrown wide open, a broken lantern burned on the tarantass coach box. Standing in a bent position with one leg thrust out obliquely, Grigory slid his plane along a board that was stuck into an old joiner's bench. A red-hazy flame quavered in the lantern, shadows quavered in the dusky barn . . . When Bestuzhev paused for a moment by the barn gates, Grigory raised his exhilarated face and said with tender pride, "Near about got the lid done."

Later Bestuzhev stood for a time, leaning his elbows on the wide-open window of the annex. The cook was clearing remnants of supper from the table and wiping it with a tattered cloth. Two young boys, the herdsmen, were preparing for sleep: barefoot

Mitka was praying on the plank bunk spread with fresh straw; Vanka prayed in the middle of the room. The tousled, ginger-haired stonemason, broad shouldered and very small of stature, in a black shirt covered with flecks of slaked lime, sat on a bench rolling a cigarette; he had come from the village beyond the river to begin work the following day, repairing the walls in the dilapidated ancestral crypt.

From her place on the stove Anyuta spoke, her voice doltish, ecstatic and maundering. "Now you done passed away, Your Honor, you never got nothing through your noggin . . . And you never did give me nothing . . . 'We ain't got it, we ain't got it, just you wait a spell . . .' So now you can wait . . . Go on and wait. Just go on and wait now! You had enough waiting, dearie? You got anything through that head? You know now what you ever got through your thick head, stupid? What would it hurt you, giving out a ruble or two to cover my body! I'm miserable, I'm a freak. I ain't got nobody. Look here at this!"

She tore open her blouse and showed her naked bosom.

"Naked all over. That's right, stupid! And back in the old days I loved you, I pined for you, you was handsome then, you was frisky and tender, just like a little miss! All through your young years you was wasting and grieving over your Lyudmilochka, while she just racked and tormented you, stupid, then she upped and went to the altar with somebody else, and I was the onliest one that truly loved you, but I kept still and told it to my pillow! I might be miserable, I might be a freak, but maybe my soul, now, is like unto the angels and archangels; I was the only one that loved you, and it's only me setting here rejoicing in your mortal end."

Then she burst into wild, joyful laughter and weeping.

"Come on, Anyuta, let's us go read the Psalter," said the stonemason loudly, in the tone you use with children to amuse someone. "Come on, you not scared?"

"Idiot! If my legs was right I'd go for sure; ain't that what you ought to do?" screamed Anyuta through her tears. "It's a sin, being ascairt of the dead. They're holy and immaculate."

"I ain't scared neither," said the mason in a free and easy tone, lighting his cigarette, which flared up with a green flame. "Why if you like, I'll lay with you all night down in the family crypt."

Anyuta sobbed ecstatically, wiping her eyes with her blouse.

Without disturbing the bright and lovely regnancy of the night, making it even more lovely, airy shadows from the white storm clouds passing over the moon fell on the yard, and the moon, gleaming, rode upon those clouds in the depths of the pure sky, above the glittering roof of the dark, old manor house where only one window was lit, the last window—by the head of the quiescent prince.

1918

»»» «««

The Snow Bull

At one o'clock, on a wintry night in the countryside, the plaintive cry of a child carries from the faraway rooms to the study. The manor house, the estate, the village—everything has long been asleep. Only Khrushchov is not sleeping. He sits and reads, occasionally shifting his tired eyes to fix upon the flame of the candles. "How lovely it all is! Even that azure color of the tallow!"

The flames, their golden-gleaming blades with transparent calamine blue at the base are slightly quivering—and the glossy page of the large French book hurts his eyes. Khrushchov places one hand by the candle. The fingers go translucent and the edges of the palm take on a rosy hue. Just as in childhood he stares, lost in contemplation, at the soft, bright scarlet liquid that is his own life, gleaming pellucid beside the flame.

The cry resounds again, louder now—plaintive, pleading.

Khrushchov gets up and goes to the nursery. He passes through the dark drawing room—the mirror, the hanger brackets of the chandelier gently shimmer there—passes through the dark divan room, the dark parlor, sees a moonlit night beyond the windows, the firs of the front garden and that pale white stratification, pressing down heavily on their dark green, long and shaggy paws. The door to the nursery is open, the moonlight is there in a slender strip of haze. Through the wide, curtainless window a brightly lit, snow-laden yard gazes at him placidly, simply. The whiteness of the children's beds has a cerulean hue. Arsik is sleeping in one of them. On the floor the wooden horses slumber; round glassy eyes rolled up, lying on her back, the doll with the white hair is asleep, and the little boxes that Kolya has so carefully collected are sleeping as well. So is he, but in his sleep he has raised up in bed, sat up and burst out crying: bitterly, helplessly. He is small and thin, with a large head.

"What's the matter, my dear?" whispers Khrushchov, sitting on the edge of the bed, wiping the face of the child with a handkerchief and embracing his meager little body, which so moves him when he feels it through the nightshirt, its tiny bones, its chest with the beating heart.

He takes him on his lap, rocks him, gently kisses him. The child presses against him, trembling as he whimpers, then calms down little by little . . . What could be waking him up for the third night in a row?

The moon goes behind a delicate white swell of clouds, the moonlight, paling, melts and wanes—but after a few seconds it grows again, spreads. The windowsills flare up once more, as do the skewed, golden squares on the floor. Khrushchov shifts his gaze from the floor, from the windowsill to the frame, sees the bright yard and remembers. That's it. We keep forgetting to tear down that white monster, the thing the children plastered together out of snow and put up in the middle of the yard, opposite the windows of their room! During the day Kolya takes a timorous joy in it, that humanlike, truncated stump with the bull's horned head and the short arms spread wide. But in the night, sensing through his sleep its terrible presence, suddenly, without even awakening, he dissolves in bitter tears. Yes, the snow ogre is indeed a hideous sight in the dark, especially if you gaze from afar, through the glass of the panes. The horns gleam, and from the head, from the widespread arms, a dark shadow falls on the shining snow. But just you try to tear it down! The children would howl all day long; although, little by little, it's beginning to melt anyway now. Soon spring will be here; already at noonday the thatched roofs of the huts are soaked through and smoking.

Khrushchov carefully lays the child back on his pillow, makes the sign of the cross over him, and walks out on tiptoe. In the antechamber he puts on his reindeer hat and his reindeer jacket, buttons it up, raising his narrow black beard. Then he opens the heavy door in the passageway and tramps down the squeaking path around the corner of the manor house. The moon, hanging low above the sparse garden, which shows through against a background of white snowdrifts, is luminous but pale with a March-like pallidness. Helices from the delicate cloud swell are stretching out here and there along the horizon. An occasional cerulean star quietly shimmers in the deep, transparent blueness between them. A new snowfall has faintly powdered the firm old crust. The beagle hound Zalivka comes running out from the garden, from the bathhouse, with its roof that glistens like glass. "Hello," says Khrushchov to him. "You and I are the only ones awake. It's a shame to sleep—life is so short. You begin to understand too late how fine it all is."

He walks up to the snow ogre and pauses for a moment. Then resolutely, with a sense of pleasure, he kicks at it with his foot. The horns fly off, the bull's head crumples away in white clumps . . . One more kick, and there's nothing left but a pile of snow. Illumined by the moon, Khrushchov stands over it, puts his hands into the pockets of the jacket, and gazes at the glistening roof. He inclines his pallid face and black beard, his reindeer hat toward one shoulder, trying to capture and fix in memory the tint of that gleam. Then he turns around and walks slowly down the path from the house to the cattle yard. In tandem with his legs, through the snow, moves a skewed shadow. Reaching the snowbanks, he works his way between them up to the gates. The gates are frozen not quite shut. He looks into the crack, through which a sharp, northern wind is drawn. With a feeling of tenderness he thinks of Kolya, thinks about how everything in life is touching, everything full of meaning and significance, and he gazes at the cattle yard. It's cold in there, but cozy. A murkiness hangs above the sheds. The fronts of the carts are gray, strewn with snow. Above the yard the blue of the sky holds a few large stars. Half of the yard is in shade, half is illumined. And the shaggy old white horses, drowsing in that light, have a greenish hue about them.

June 29, 1911

»»» «««

The Saviour in Desecration

No, I mean to tell you, sir, not all folks gives glory unto the Lord, but the Lord, he will make known his ways. Now when and on what account, well, that's something only He knows. Here in our parts just look how many there is of the famous icons and cathedrals, holy relics galore! And let me tell you what once we had to happen here. The daughter of one of our local merchants fell sick with a deathly illness, and God above, Heavenly Mother, the things that man done trying to save his child! He sent away for doctors from Moscow, he ordered up the most costly of prayer services, and he took her off to make supplication at the relics in Moscow, then to the Trinity Monastery. He rooted out every last sacred cross or icon for miles around—but nothing helped! Meanwhile, the girl herself, she's on and on repeating the same thing: "I'll get well, I'll be cured, no doubt about it, only not on account of all them things, but by the grace of the Saviour in Desecration."

"Now, that's wonderful," her father says to her, and her mama too. "We believe you and we put our trust in you, only what is this Saviour in Desecration and where is he to be found?"

"Well, it's something," she says, "that I seen in a dream; it was the Good Lord granted unto me that vision."

"That's even all the better," they answered her, "but just what and where is he?"

"Well, you must search for him, go seek him out, here there and everywhere. I don't know where he is my ownself. All I know is he's been desecrated and much abused, he's gone to wrack and ruin and tossed off somewhere just any old way, and all of this happened long, long ago, back under the rule of the Empress Vasilisa."

"Under what Empress Vasilisa?" they asked her. "Ain't never been any such empress."

"Well, I don't know nothing about that," she says. "All I know is he's tiny as can be, pint sized and dinky, and he's like on some sort of just plain black board, with a sacrilegious inscription—that's the long and short of it. Main thing is you must spare no means to seek him out and find whereabouts he is."

So then, wellsir, what do you think happened next? They commenced to clambering over every out-of-the-way garret space in every house and church, went to peeking under bell tower roofs, rooting through pigeon droppings and rubbish, and finally, you know, they found that which they sought? And where do you think they found him? You ever seen that little ramshackle chapel just downhill from the bazaar? Must be a good thousand years it's been standing there rotting, and folks with no morals up to all sorts of shameless shenanigans inside of it, and right there, in the rubbish, is where they found him. And so then, no sooner did they clean him up a little bit, washed him off, wiped him dry, and brought him into that unhappy home, give him to the girl so as she could pray over him, as is meet and proper, press her lips against him and take him upon her breast, no sooner that's done than lightning fast that girl commenced to crying, sobbing, trembling all over with joy untold—and up she stands on her feet. Hopped up, rushed to embrace her papa and mama, and screeched out at the top of her lungs, "Oh dear parents of mine, I'm cured! Call in the priests and order up a service of thanksgiving to be held! For this, yea verily, is he—the Saviour in Desecration. Look here what's written on him!"

And guess what? It all ended up being true. They turned the icon over, and there, on the other side, they seen the inscription: NOT FIT TO BE PRAYED TO; FIT TO BE USED AS A PISS-POT COVER.

We were riding along at a slow trot, and as he told his story the cabman was sitting sideways on the box and rolling himself a cigarette, gazing into his open tobacco pouch. When he finished the story he muttered, "Lord, forgive me my trespasses, for repeating such words as that!"

The lengthy twilight of summer reigned, Rostov the Great was fast asleep. Far up ahead crepuscular sunlight was still glimmering dully, but the city was long since empty, no one was about on the streets; just a single night watchman wandering down the long, dusty avenue, a clapper alarm in his hands. Warmth, quietude, melancholy.

Indescribably beautiful were the churches that stood outlined against the murk of the earth, against the faintly greenish glow of the faraway sunset sky.

Paris, 1926

»»» «««

The Sacrifice

Semyon Novikov, who lived with his brother, shrivel-armed Nikon, was burned out over the Peter-Paul Fast. The brothers agreed to divvy up what was left after the fire; Semyon would resettle on the outskirts of Brod, where he started building himself a log hut by the highroad.

For Saint Elijah's Day the carpenters asked off work to go back home to their farmsteads. Semyon would have to keep watch that night at the building site. After eating supper with the large family of his brother, cramped up in there with flies all over, he lit his pipe, threw his sheepskin coat over his shoulders, and said, "Had enough of the stuffiness. I'm heading out to where they're putting up the shack; be spending the night there."

"You might better take along some dogs," they answered.

"Get on with you!" said Semyon, and off he went alone.

It was a moonlit night. Lost in thoughts of his future farmstead, Semyon did not notice how he climbed, by way of the wide cattle run, up out of the village to the top of the hill, then covered the good two-thirds of a mile along the highroad to his hut—already ceilinged but not yet roofed, standing in an open spot on the edge of the grain fields, its windows black and frameless, the ends of its freshly hewed logs bleakly aglitter in the moonlight at the corners, along with the gleaming tow shreds that protruded from the grooves and the wood chips at the threshold. The low July moon, which had risen over the ravines of Brod, was lackluster. Its warm light was spilling out, dissipating. Ripe grain fields up ahead shone a bleak, gloomy white, and to the north the sky was utterly louring, a big storm cloud was burgeoning up. Blowing on all sides, the soft wind would intensify now and again, start gusting its way through the rye and oats—and they would sound their dry and anxious susurrations. The storm cloud in the north appeared not to be moving, but periodically it twitched with a quick golden shimmer.

Bending down out of habit, Semyon entered the hut. It was dark and stuffy inside. The yellow moonlight that peered through the emptiness of the windows did not blend with the darkness, serving only to magnify it. Semyon tossed his coat on some shavings in the middle of the hut, right on top of a strip of light, and lay down on his back. He sucked a bit on his pipe, which had gone out, thought a few thoughts, and went to sleep.

But then the wind blowing through the windows picked up, and a hollow growling sounded in the distance. Semyon awoke. The wind had intensified—now it was rushing continuously through the fervent clamor of the grains, and the moonlight had grown even bleaker. Semyon left the hut and went around the corner, into the oats, which were white as a shroud, rustling dry and searing hot. He took a look at the storm cloud, dark slate in color, occupying half of the horizon. The wind was blowing right in his face, grabbing at his hair and mussing it, making things hard to see. The lightning flashes made seeing even harder, dazzling him as they flared up ever more perfervid and threatening. Crossing himself, Semyon got down on his knees. Far away amidst the sea of oats, silhouetted against that wall of the storm cloud, a small throng of people headed in his direction. Their heads bared, girded with white sashes over new sheepskin coats, they were struggling along under the weight of a towering icon painted in ancient times, the kind of image that hangs opposite the tsar's gates in the church. The thronged mass was hazy, transparent, but the icon was clearly visible—an austere, awesome face that showed red against the blackness of the board it was painted on; singed by candles, spattered with wax, the icon was enclosed in an old, dove blue, silver frame.

The wind rearranged the hair on Semyon's forehead, pleasantly fluffing it out. Awe-inspired, full of joy, he bowed down to the earth in front of the icon. When he raised his head he saw that the throng now stood stationary, awkwardly holding that majestic icon tipped back. Traced against the storm cloud like a fresco in a cathedral, soaring high was a huge face: that of white-bearded, puissant Elijah in fire-fringed array, seated like the Lord of Sabaoth upon deathly blue billows of clouds, while above him two greenish orange rainbows blazed against that background of slate. Then, his lightning eyes aglitter, his voice merging with the thunder, with the rumblings, Elijah spoke.

"Straighten up and look sharp, Semyon Novikov! Hearken ye now unto me, O ye princes among peasants, for I shall sit in judgment of him, the sharecropper peasant of Yelets District, Predtechev Branch, Semyon Novikov."

And the whole field, which glowed in tones of white all around, every oat ear with every cockle on top came dashing, running up to bow down before Elijah, and amidst that swishing clamor Elijah spoke.

"Thou, Semyon Novikov, incurred my wrath against thee, and I didst desire to wreak my chastisement."

"How come, Father?" asked Semyon.

"Semyon Novikov, it is not meet and proper for a scoundrel such as you to be questioning me, Elijah. Thou must answer what is asked of thee."

"Well, fine, whatever you say," answered Semyon.

"Year before last I sent down a lightning strike to kill thy eldest, Pantelei. Why didst thou bury him in earth up to the waist and resort to sorceries to return him unto life?"

"Forgive me, Father," said Semyon, bowing. "Just hated to lose the fellow. After all, you thyself can imagine how it is; here's somebody to keep me in food and drink in my old age."

"Back a year ago I aimed to slash up thy rye with hail and whirlwinds, knock it all down to the ground. How come thou didst sniff that out somehow in advance, and sold the rye off for animal fodder?"

"Forgive me, Father," said Semyon, bowing. "Somehow kind of had a feeling, and we was hard up."

"And then just a while back, round about the Peter-Paul holiday, didn't I give you a scorching? So how is it you're in such a rush to build back and separate off from your brother?"

"Forgive me, Father," said Semyon, bowing. "My gimpy-armed brother, well, he's bad luck that just won't quit. Way I figured, all this grief come about on account of him."

"Close your eyes. I need to think this out, hold me some confabulations on what is to be thy punishment."

Semyon closed his eyes and bowed his head. The wind was roaring. Through the noise he strained his ears to have a listen at what Elijah was whispering with the peasants, but another rumble rolled overhead and he couldn't make out a word.

"Shoot, we can't think of nothing!" yelled Elijah at the top of his lungs. "You'll have to tell me yourself what you reckon we ought to do."

"Can I open my eyes then?" asked Semyon.

"Ain't no need for that. The blind man's thoughts run deeper."

"You are a funny one, Father," said Semyon with a grave smirk. "What's there so hard to figure out anyway? I'll buy me a three-ruble candle and stick it up by your picture in the icon."

"Where's the money come from? You done spent it all on your building project."

"Then I'll make a pilgrimage to Kiev."

"That's just one more way of blowing air and wearing out bast sandals. And meantime, who's going to run things here?"

Semyon pondered it over.

"All right, then, the little girl, Anfiska, you can kill her off. She ain't but just over a year. I tell you, though, she's a sweet thing. We'll feel for her, but then, what are you going to do? Pretty soon we'll have another one to take her place."

"Hearken unto my words, Orthodox Christians," said Elijah in stentorian tones. "Thou hast my consent!"

Then such a flame ripped through the heavenly firmament that Semyon's eyelids nearly caught fire, and such a thunderclap split the skies that all the earth beneath him shuddered.

"Holy, holy, holy art thou, Lord God of Sabaoth!" whispered Semyon.

When he came to his senses and opened his eyes he saw only a dusty storm cloud, the grains, and himself, on his knees amidst them. Dust was blowing about in a whirlwind on the road, and the moon had bleared totally over.

Semyon jumped to his feet. Forgetting his coat he rushed off for home. On the common pasture a heavy rain caught him. Dark clouds were louring over the darkened ravines. The red moon was setting. The village lay in a deep slumber, but all the cattle in their pens were restive and the roosters were crowing. Running up to his old hut, Semyon heard wails issuing from within. In a sheepskin coat, hatless, gimp-armed Nikon, scraggy and wizened, stood by the threshold with a dull bewildered look on his face.

"You got big trouble," he said, and by his voice it was clear that he was still half asleep.

Semyon ran into the hut. The women were shrieking and milling about in the darkness, looking for a sulphur splint light. Semyon grabbed the matchboxes from behind the icons and lit the lampion. The cradle that hung beside the stove was tossing from side to side—the women kept knocking against it as they bustled past. In the cradle lay a dead little girl, dove blue all over, and the bonnet on her head was smouldering.

From then on Semyon lived a happy life.

Capri, 1913

»»» «««

Transfiguration

The farmstead was prosperous, the family large.

Having spawned children and grandchildren in profusion, the old man passed opportunely to his reward, but the old lady outlived her time; she lived on so long that it seemed there never would be an end to her pitiful and irksome existence.

She and the old man themselves had been the builders and sovereigns of all that extensive, substantial, filthy and cozy nest, which had long since taken root in this spot, had become homey and lived in, with its barn, hollow osiers, its granaries, oldfangled hut in three wings, with its cattle yard, almost barbarously crude, mired in manure and glutted with well-fattened brutes. Once she and the old man themselves had been young, handsome, clever, and exacting, but later somehow they began floundering amidst the young folk, who were ever more numerous and more robust; first in one thing, then in another they began acquiescing to them, and finally they were reduced to utter nullity, grew shriveled, hunched, and wizen, skulked away to rest on the sleeping shelves or on the stove, became estranged, first from the family, then even from one another, until finally they were parted forever by the grave.

After the old man's death the old lady felt an intense unease about her place on this good earth. Her effacement was absolute; she seemed to have forgotten completely that she, she herself was the procreator of all this young, puissant realm in which she had become so superfluous. Somehow she had turned out to be the most insignificant creature on all the farmstead, living there as if out of charity, good for nothing but huddling on the hot stove in winter and minding the chicks in summer, watching over the hut while the others were working . . . No one ever even gave her a thought, so how could anyone imagine her as fearsome!

But then she took thoroughly sick, lay huddled on the stove beyond all dissembling, eyes closed, breathing feverishly and helplessly, with such great weariness that even the hearts of her broad-shouldered daughters-in-law were squeezed with pity. "Mama, how about me fixing you up some chicken or a little milk and noodles? Wouldn't you like something? How about if I put on the samovar?" But she only breathed on in semioblivion, her hand only quivered in a weak gesture of gratefulness.

Finally she released them all—succumbed.

Winter, deepest hour of night. A night that is her last among the living. Raging snow and murk envelop the farm; the whole village sleeps. All of the household sleeps as well; both inhabited wings are full of sleeping people. And over all this wintry night and this squall, over the slumber and remote seclusion of farmstead and village she reigns, the Dead: yesterday's pitiful and cowed little crone has been transfigured into something menacing and mysterious, into the most lofty and portentous thing in all the world, some inscrutable and awesome deity—a corpse. She lies in her coffin in the unheated wing; she is white, like snow, cloistered in the depths of her sepulchral world, head slightly raised by a straw pillow, chin sunk into her chest; a shadow falls from the black eyelashes that are prominent against the white face. The coffin is behind a table, brightly illumined by a whole cluster of wax candles that are stuck to it and blazing torridly, disquietly; it is covered by a brocade funereal pall flimsy with decrepitude, rented from the church. It is placed on a bench beside a small window, beneath the icons; the frigid squall is raging beyond this window, whose dark panes gleam and scintillate with the snow that freezes to their exterior.

The youngest son of the deceased, Gavril, who has recently been married, stands reading the Psalter. He has always been distinguished in the family for good sense and neatness, for his even temper, his love for reading and church rituals. Who, then, could be better suited to read tonight? He had entered the icy room casually, not the least bit fearful of the long night impending, alone with the dead, giving no thought to the night, with no conception of what awaited him; and now he has long had the feeling that something lethal and irremediable has come into his life. He stands and reads, bending toward the hot, shuddering candles; he reads unceasingly, all at the same pitch, maintaining the high ecclesiastical intonations, the elevated tone he had begun with—he reads, understanding nothing but powerless to stop. He feels that there is no salvation for him now, that he is absolutely alone face-to-face with this awesome creature, all the more awesome since it is the very mother who bore him, alone not only in this icy room, but in all the world. He can sense that the night is abysmally deep and deaf, that there is no one he can turn to for protection or help.

What has happened to him? Did he overestimate his presence of mind when he took it upon himself to read over the dead woman late at night, in the hour of universal sleep? Is he stricken with horror, has he lost the capacity to move? No, something much more awesome and marvelous has happened, something miraculous; he is overwhelmed not by horror, but by this very marvel, this sacrament being consummated before his eyes. Where is she now, what has become of her, pitiful, small, squalid with old age, timidity, and helplessness, for so many years almost unnoticed by anyone in their large family, which was coarse with its own strength and youth? She is no more, she has vanished; is that really she, that Something, icy, immobile, breathless, mute, but absolutely distinct from the table, the wall, the pane, the snow, absolutely not a thing, but a being, whose cryptic existence is just as inscrutable as God? Could it really be that what is lying silently in the beautiful new coffin lined with lilac velveteen, with its white crosses and winged heads of cherubim, could this really be the one who was huddled on the stove just the day before yesterday? No, she has undergone a transfiguration—and everything in the world, all the world has been transfigured for her sake, and he is alone, all alone in that transfigured world!

He is spellbound, imprisoned, and he must stand there till dawn and read unceasingly in the extraordinary, eerie and majestic tongue that is also part of that world, its baneful Word so ominous for the living. And he musters all his strength to read, to see, to hear his own voice and stay on his feet, as with all his being, ever more deeply, he apprehends the ineffable, bewitching something that like a liturgy is being celebrated before him and within his very self. Then suddenly the brocaded funereal pall on the chest of the corpse slowly rises a bit and still more slowly sinks back—she's faintly breathing! And still higher and brighter gleam the flames of the candles, shuddering, dazzling, and everything around him is transmuted into unremitting rapture, which numbs his head, shoulders, and legs. He knows, he still can understand that this is the frigid wind blowing through the window from the storm outside, that this is what whiffs up the pall and flutters the candles. But it's all the same—that wind too is she, the demised one, from her wafts that unearthly icy breath, pure as death, and it is she who at any moment will arise to judge the whole world, all the world of the living, so contemptible in its beastly sensuality and its transience!

Today Gavril is a youthful-looking muzhik with gray, neatly combed hair. He does not manage the farmstead; he has left the managing to his brothers and his wife. The occupation he has chosen is unnecessary for a man of his means but is the only one he loves—coachman.

He is always on the road, and the road, the distant expanses, the view of sky, fields, woods, changing with the seasons, the coach box of cart or sleigh, the swift pace of a pair of faithful, sensitive horses, the sound of the harness bell, and a long conversation with a congenial passenger—all of this affords a happiness that never betrays him.

He is casual, affable. His face is clear and gaunt, his gray eyes truthful, unclouded. He is not talkative, but to a worthy man he is willing to tell the tale, difficult to convey, resembling a yuletide story, but, in fact, truly miraculous, the tale of what he went through by his mother's coffin on her last night among the living.

Paris, 1921

»»» «««

The Gentleman from San Francisco

The gentleman from San Francisco—neither in Naples nor on the Isle of Capri did anyone remember his name—set off for the Old World along with his wife and daughter, on a trip that would take all of two years, solely for the sake of recreation.

He was firmly convinced that he had every right to a rest, to pleasure, to a journey excellent in all respects. Two arguments supported this conviction: first, he was rich, and second, he was just getting around to living, notwithstanding his fifty-eight years of age. Up to then he had not lived, but simply existed; by no means a bad existence, true, but he had, nonetheless, always staked his hopes on the future. He had worked incessantly—the Chinese laborers he took on by the thousands knew all too well what that meant! And finally he saw that much had been accomplished, that he was almost on even terms with those he had once taken as models, and he decided he wanted a breather. People of his circle were wont to initiate their enjoyment of life's pleasures with a trip to Europe, to India or Egypt. He proposed to do the same. Primarily, of course, it was he himself he wished to reward, for all those years of hard work; but then he was also glad that his wife and daughter would have this opportunity. The wife was not one distinguished by acute sensibilities, but then of course all elderly American women are passionate travelers. As for his daughter, a girl who had come of age and was somewhat sickly, well, for her the trip was simply a must—apart from the beneficial effects on her health, do not trips often afford the possibilities of fortuitous encounters? Now and again you end up sitting at the same table with or examining frescoes beside a multimillionaire.

The itinerary worked out by the gentleman from San Francisco was extensive. In December and January he hoped to enjoy the sunshine of southern Italy, the monuments of antiquity, the tarantella, the serenades of promenading troubadours, and what men of his age feel with a special acuity, the love of young Neapolitan girls (even if they, perhaps, expect something in the way of remuneration); for Carnival he intended to be in Nice and Monte Carlo, where the very cream of society gathers at that time, where one person may indulge his passion for automobile or sailboat racing, another roulette, a third what is commonly referred to as flirting, and a fourth the shooting of pigeons, which soar up from their columbaries so beautifully above the emerald lawn, against a backdrop of seascape the color of forget-me-nots, and then come crashing right back down to earth in small white clumps; he wished to devote the beginning of March to Florence, then arrive in Rome for the Passion of Our Lord and hear the Miserere sung there; his plans also included Venice and Paris, bullfights in Seville and bathing on the English islands, and Athens, and Constantinople, and Palestine and Egypt, and even Japan—but that, of course, would be on the way back home . . . Well, in the beginning everything went marvelously.

It was the end of November, all the way to Gibraltar they had to sail in icy murk, through storms of wet snow, but they sailed along engulfed in well-being. The passengers were many, the ship the renowned *Atlantis*—resembling a massive hotel with all modern conveniences, with a late-night bar, oriental baths, with its own newspaper—and life on *Atlantis* flowed along with a measured smoothness: they arose early, to the blare of bugles that resounded stridently through the corridors, in that early crepuscular gloom when day was slowly, inauspiciously breaking over the gray-green watery wasteland, over its ponderous waves rippling in the fog; donning their flannel pajamas, they drank coffee, chocolate, cocoa, then soaked in the bath or did exercises, stimulating their appetites and a healthy frame of mind, put on their vestments of the day and went off to have breakfast; until eleven o'clock it was customary to stroll the decks briskly, breathing in the cold crispness of the ocean, or, for renewed stimulation of appetite, to play shuffleboard or other games, and at eleven to fortify themselves with bouillon and open sandwiches; so fortified, they enjoyed a read of the newspaper while placidly awaiting luncheon, which was even more munificent and varied than breakfast; the next two hours were given over to relaxation; long wickerwork lounges were set out on all of the decks, and the travelers lay covered with lap rugs, gazing at the cloudy sky and the foamy sea knolls that flickered alongside the ship, or lapsing into a sweet drowse; sometime after four, refreshed and raised in spirits, they were treated to strong, fragrant tea and biscuits; at seven the bugle blares heralded what constituted the foremost aim of all their present existence, its crowning moment . . . And that's when the gentleman from San Francisco hastened off to his plush cabin—to get dressed.

In the evening hours the tiers of *Atlantis* gaped out in the darkness with their multitude of fiery porthole eyes, and a huge throng of menials worked away in the underchambers of the ship, in the kitchens, sculleries, and wine vaults. Swelling beyond the walls, the ocean was frightful, but they gave that no thought, firmly trusting in the power their captain held over it, that red-haired, corpulent man of monstrous proportions, who was always somehow somnolent, resembling a huge idol in his uniform with wide golden chevrons, who very seldom left his mysterious quarters to make an appearance among the people; periodically the siren in the forecastle would howl in infernally somber tones and screech with a frenzied malice, but few of the diners could hear that siren—it was drowned out by the sounds of a marvelous string orchestra, elegantly, incessantly playing on in the double-toned dining hall with its festive inundation of lights, with its surfeit of ladies décolleté and men in tails and dinner jackets, slender lackeys and deferential maîtres d'hôtel, amidst whom one, he who took orders only for wine, even wore a chain around his neck like a lord mayor. The gentleman from San Francisco appeared much younger in his smoking jacket and starched linen. Desiccate, short of stature, with a cut to him not quite right but solidly sewn, he sat in the golden nacreous glitter of that palatial hall, a bottle of wine on his table, goblets and finely faceted wineglasses, a curly bouquet of hyacinths. There was something of the Mongol about his yellowish face with the trimmed silvery mustache, his large teeth gleamed with golden fillings, the sturdy, bald head had the look of aged ivory. His wife, a large woman wide in the hips and placid, was dressed affluently but in keeping with her age; decked out in elaborate but light and transparent attire, in a dress low cut but guileless was the daughter—tall, thin, with magnificent hair charmingly coifed, her breath wafting aromatic essences from violet lozenges, with the most delicate of pink pimples adjacent to her lips and between her shoulder blades, which were faintly powdered . . . Dinner went on for over an hour, and after dinner the dancing began in the ballroom, during which time the men—including, of course, the gentleman from San Francisco—propped up their legs in the bar, puffed away on Havana cigars till their faces went raspberry red, and drank their fill of liqueurs served up by Negroes in red camisoles, men whose whites of the eyes resembled hard-boiled eggs shelled. The rumbling ocean swelled up in mountains of black beyond the walls, the squall whistled steadfastly in riggings heavy with snow, the ship shuddered all over as it tried to cope with it, the blizzard, and with those mountains—like a plow it split into two halves their quavering mass, which now and again would boil up and send out high-flying queues of foam; in death-laden anguish the siren whined; suffocating in fog up in the turrets, chilled stiff with cold and crazed with the unbearable intensity of looking stood the sailors on watch; like the somber and searing bowels of Hades, like the last, ninth circle of hell, was the subaqueous womb of the ship—down where gigantic furnaces cackled out their hollow call as they gnawed away with red-hot jaws at heaps of coal flung crashing into them by men who were naked to the waist, drenched in acrid, filthy sweat, crimson skinned from the flames; while here, in the bar, legs hanging jauntily over arms of their chairs, they sipped cognac and liqueurs, swam in waves of heady smoke, and in the dance hall everything glittered and flowed with light, warmth, and joy, and couples would now be whirling away in waltzes, then bent into the curves of the tango—and the importunate music kept beseeching, in its sweetly shameless mournfulness, over and over, for one and the same thing . . . Amidst this scintillating throng there was a certain man of great wealth, clean shaven, elongated in build, wearing an old-fashioned tailcoat, there was a famous Spanish writer, there was a cosmopolitan beauty, there was an elegant couple in love, who attracted everyone's curious glances as they openly displayed their happiness: he would dance only with her, and they pulled all of this off in such a delicate, charming way that only the captain knew Lloyds had hired this couple to play at love for good money, that they had long been sailing, on one cruise ship after another.

At Gibraltar the sun gladdened them all, it was like early spring; a new passenger appeared on board the *Atlantis,* attracting the interest of everyone—the crown prince of a certain Asian nation-state, traveling incognito, a small man, all wooden and broad across the face, narrow-eyed, in golden spectacles, slightly off-putting—for the way his large mustache showed transparently through to the skin, like a dead man's—but on the whole, nice, down-to-earth, and modest. In the Mediterranean Sea a large and multicolored wave, like the tail of a peacock, swelled up, and amidst the bright splendor and absolutely clear sky it was cleaved by the tramontana that blew gaily and rabidly into their faces . . . Then, on the second day, the sky began to blanch, the horizon fogged over; they were nearing land, Ischia appeared, Capri; through binoculars they could discern what seemed lumps of sugar poured out at the foot of some dove blue something of a mountain—and that was Naples . . . Many of the ladies and gentlemen had already donned light winter coats lined with fur at the top; little by little the meek Chinamen, bowlegged adolescents with tar black pigtails down to their heels and girlishly thick eyelashes, always speaking in whispers, dragged out to the stairwells lap rugs, walking sticks, suitcases, *nécessaires* . . . The daughter of the gentleman from San Francisco stood on deck next to the prince, who, by a happy circumstance, had been introduced to her the evening before; she pretended to look intently into the distance where he was pointing and explaining something to her, hastily relating some narrative in a soft voice; because of his short stature he looked like a boy amidst the other passengers, he was not the least handsome and had an odd appearance—spectacles, bowler hat, English mackintosh, the hair of his meager mustache resembling horsehair, the delicate, swarthy skin on his flat face seemingly stretched tight and somehow faintly lacquered—but the agitated girl listened to him with no comprehension of what he was saying; her heart beat in his presence with an ecstasy beyond understanding; everything, everything about him was different from all the others—his dry hands, his clean skin beneath which ancient royal blood was flowing; even his European, quite ordinary, but somehow uniquely tidy apparel harbored some ineffable charm. Meanwhile, the gentleman from San Francisco, wearing gray gaiters over his shoes, kept glancing at the famous beauty who was standing beside him, a tall, remarkably built blonde with eyes painted up in the latest Parisian style, holding by a silver chain a minuscule, hunched lapdog with only manged-out patches of fur left on its back, talking to it incessantly. And his daughter, in a flustered state of awkwardness, tried not to take notice of him.

He had been quite generous en route and, therefore, he trusted implicitly in the solicitude of all who served him food and drink, waited upon him from morn till evening, anticipating his slightest desire, watched over his cleanliness and peace of mind, dragged about his things, summoned porters, delivered his trunks to the hotel. That's how it was everywhere, how it was during the voyage, how it now must be in Naples as well. Naples was growing larger and drawing near; brass on their instruments gleaming, the musicians had thronged together on deck, and suddenly they deafened everyone with the triumphant strains of a march; the giant of a captain, in parade uniform, made an appearance on his bridge, and like a gracious pagan god he waved his hand in benediction toward the passengers. When the *Atlantis* had finally entered the harbor, had swung its multitiered mass, studded with dots of humanity, sideways up against the embankment, when the gangplanks had clattered into place, what multitudes of *portiers* and their assistants in peaked caps with golden lacings, what a variety of *commissionaires,* whistler urchins, and strapping tatterdemalions bearing packets of colored postcards rushed up to greet the gentleman, offering their services! Smirking at those ragamuffins, he walked over to the limousine of that very hotel where the prince might well be staying, calmly muttering through his teeth the words in English or Italian.

"Go away! *Via!*"

From the very beginning life in Naples took on a regulated order and flow: early morning it was breakfast in the dimly lit dining room, it was a cloudy sky that held little promise and a mob of guides at the doors of the vestibule; then came the first smiles of a warm, pinkish sun, the view, from a balcony hanging high, of Vesuvius, enveloped to its pedestal in glittering matinal vapors, the silver nacreous ripple of the bay and the delicate outline of Capri on the horizon, the miniature donkeys that trotted along way down below, hitched to two-wheeler carts, and detachments of toy soldiers marching off somewhere to buoyant, provocative music; then—it was out to the limousine and a slow drive through the narrow and damp streets teeming with people, amidst tall, many-windowed buildings, it was having a look at the deathly clean and uniformly, pleasantly lit (but boring, like looking at snow) museums or at cold churches smelling of wax, all of them, everywhere, featuring exactly the same things: a majestic entryway covered by a heavy leather portiere, and inside a vast emptiness, silence, the quiet flames of a septet candelabrum burning with reddish glow in the depths of the church on an altar draped with laces, a solitary old crone amidst the dark wooden pews, slippery gravestone slabs underfoot and someone's "Deposition from the Cross," always renowned; at 1:00 P.M. it was brunch up on Mount San Martino, where at midday a good many people of the best sort congregate and where once the daughter of the gentleman from San Francisco nearly was sick to her stomach—she thought she saw the prince sitting in the dining hall, although newspapers had placed him now in Rome; at five it was tea back at the hotel, in an elegant salon ever so warm with its carpets and blazing fireplaces; then, once again, preparations for dinner, once again there was that mighty puissant gonging that resonated on every floor, and again the files of ladies décolleté, silkily rustling down staircases reflected in mirrors, again there was amplitude and hospitality flung open in that palatial dining room, and the red jackets of musicians on the estrade, and the black mob of lackeys beside the maître d'hôtel, who with extraordinary mastery ladled out a thick pink soup into bowl after bowl . . . Once more the dinners were so sumptuous, with food and wines and mineral waters and sweet dishes and fruits, that around eleven in the evening chambermaids would make their rounds of the rooms, bringing rubber hot water bottles for the warming of stomachs.

December, however, came off none too successfully; when you spoke to the porters about the weather, they could only shrug remorsefully and mumble that they couldn't recall a year as bad as this, although it was not the first time they had occasion to mumble the same and to cite the awful things transpiring everywhere: on the Riviera there were unprecedented downpours and snowstorms, in Athens there was snow, Mount Aetna was all snowed over too, you could see it shine in the night, tourists were fleeing Palermo, saving themselves from the frosts . . . Every day the early morning sun played the same trick: by midday, invariably, the grayness set in and the sky began dripping rain, which grew ever more thick and cold; that's when the palm trees by the hotel entryway took on a tin-plated gleam, the city seemed especially dirty and crowded, the museums just too monotonous, the cigar butts of chunky cabmen (in their rubber wraps aflutter like wings in the wind) seemed unbearably rank, their energetic cracking of whips over thin-necked nags clearly a sham, footwear on the *signori* sweeping the tramcar rails seemed an awful abomination, and the women shuffling along in the rain through the mud, their black heads uncovered, seemed grotesquely short legged; not to speak of the dampness and the stench of rotten fish that wafted from the frothing sea by the embankment. The gentleman and the missus from San Francisco began bickering in the mornings; their daughter might start out looking pallid, head aching, but then she might liven up, delighted with everything, and when she did she was endearing and beautiful; beautiful too were the tender, complex feelings aroused in her by meeting a man who was not at all handsome, within whom there flowed wondrous strange blood, for after all, in the end it's not at all important just what awakens the soul of a girl—be it money, or glory, or genteelness of birth . . . Everyone assured them that things were not at all like this in Sorrento or on Capri—things were warmer and sunnier, and the lemons were blooming and morals more upstanding and the wine more natural. And so the family from San Francisco decided to embark with their many trunks for the Isle of Capri, intending to take it all in, to roam about the rocks up where Tiberius had built his palaces, have a look at the fairy-tale caves of the Blue Grotto, and listen to the Abruzzian bagpipers, who spend the whole month before Christmas wandering the island and singing their praises to the Virgin Mary; after that they would move on to Sorrento.

On the day of their departure—such a memorable day for the family from San Francisco!—there was not even any sun in the morning. Blanketed to its very foundation in heavy fog, Vesuvius stood low and gray above the leaden swells of the sea. The Isle of Capri was not visible at all—as if it had never existed on earth. And the small steamer making for the island so pitched from side to side that the family from San Francisco lay flat on their backs, on the settees in the sorry little passengers' lounge of that ship, legs wrapped in lap rugs and eyes clamped shut with seasickness. The missus suffered, so she thought, most of all; several times the spasms overcame her, she felt she was dying, and the cabin maid who ran up with a basin—she who had rocked upon those waves for years now, day after day in searing heat and chilling cold, remaining, through it all, indefatigable—only laughed. The young miss, terribly pale, held a slice of lemon in her teeth. Lying on his back in an ample coat and a large peaked cap, the mister never unclenched his jaws the whole trip; his face had gone dark, his mustaches white, his head ached oppressively; thanks to the bad weather these past few days he had had too much to drink in the evenings and had spent too much time admiring "tableaux vivants" in a number of dives. The rain lashed at the shuddering windowpanes, dripped down off them onto the settees, the howling wind rushed through the masts, and periodically, in concert with a wave that swooped down, it flipped the little steamer right over on its side, and when that happened something rolled and crashed around down below. At the stops along the way, Castellammare, Sorrento, things quieted down a bit; but even here there was a horrible pitching and heaving; beyond the windows the seashore, with all of its cliffs, gardens, Italian pines, its pink and white hotels and its smoky, curly green mountains flew up and down as if on a swing; boats were knocking against the sides of the ship, a damp wind blew through the doors, and without shutting up for a single minute, trying to entice the travelers, standing on a rocking wooden barge under the banner of the Hotel Royale, a lisping urchin shrieked out his shrill pitch. And the gentleman from San Francisco, feeling as befitting his age very old, was thinking, with anguish and malice now, about all those greedy little people who reeked of garlic and called themselves Italians; during one of the stops he opened his eyes and raised himself up on the settee, and he saw beneath a rocky overhang a heap of such miserable stone hovels, steeped through and through with mildew and plastered one to another right along the waterfront beside the boats, beside some kind of rags, tin cans, and brown nets, and he recalled that this was the genuine Italy to which he had come to enjoy himself, and then he was stricken with despair . . . Finally, already in twilight, the blackness of the island began drawing near, seemingly perforated at its base with red dots of flame, the wind grew softer, warmer, more fragrant; through the now-resigned waves, lambent like black oil, swam gold boa constrictors of light from the pierside lanterns . . . Then suddenly there was the clamor of the anchor and its splash in the water, the frenzied cries of boatmen, vying with one another, drifted in from all sides—and immediately one's soul felt unburdened, the passengers' lounge took on a greater resplendence, you felt like eating, drinking, smoking, moving about . . . Ten minutes later the family from San Francisco climbed down onto a big barge, fifteen minutes later they had stepped out on the stones of the embankment, and then they seated themselves in the bright little rail coach and were drawn straight up the slope to a droning sound, amidst the picket stakes of the vineyards, half-collapsed stone fences, and wet, gnarled orange trees covered here and there with straw awnings, amidst the splendor of their bright orange fruit and the thick, glossy leafage that was gliding backward, downhill, past the open windows of the coach . . . Sweet is the smell of the earth in Italy after a rain, and each of the islands has its own special aroma!

The Isola di Capri was damp and dark that evening, but now it livened up for a moment, sparked with a gleam here and there. At the crest of the mountain by the funicular platform, a mob of locals stood waiting, those duty bound to give a proper welcome to the gentleman from San Francisco. There were other travelers arriving as well, but not the sort deserving of attention: several Russians who had settled on Capri, bemused and bearded slovenly types in spectacles, collars raised on their bedraggled overcoats, and a gaggle of long-legged, roundheaded German youth in Tyrolese outfits, rucksacks slung over their shoulders, the type that required nobody's services and clutched their money close to the vest. Calmly situating himself apart from both those groups, the gentleman from San Francisco was immediately noticed. He and his ladies were quickly helped out of the funicular, people ran up ahead of them pointing out the way; once again urchins surrounded him, along with those hefty Capriote peasant women who balance on their heads the cases and trunks of respectable tourists. Clattering through a small square went their wooden clogs, across what seemed some operatic stage set with electric orbs rocking in the moist wind above it, while a horde of gamins gave birdlike whistles and began turning somersaults—and as if crossing that stage, amidst them strode the gentleman from San Francisco, toward some medieval arch beneath buildings fused into a single mass, beyond which the roadway, a sonorous little street with a vortex of palm fronds above flat roofs to the left, with blue stars in a black sky on high just ahead, led sloping upward toward the hotel entryway, which glittered in the distance. And it seemed as if that damp stone town on a rocky island in the Mediterranean Sea had come alive in honor of the guests from San Francisco, that it was they who made the hotel manager so iridescent with joy, that the Chinese gong had been awaiting only their presence before clanging out on every floor (just as they stepped into the lobby) its clarion call to dinner.

The polite, fastidiously bowing hotel manager who greeted them, a young man exemplary in his elegance, startled the gentleman from San Francisco momentarily; he suddenly recalled that on the previous night, amidst the tangle of images beleaguering him in his dreams, he had seen this very persona, a man resembling exactly this one, in the same morning coat and with the same mirror-smooth, slicked-down hair. Astonished, he nearly stopped dead in his tracks. But since for untold ages his soul had lacked even a mustard seed of so-called mystical feelings, his amazement immediately dimmed; walking down the hotel corridor, he jokingly mentioned to his wife and daughter this strange conjunction of dream and reality. But the daughter reacted by glancing at him with alarm; her heart was squeezed with a sudden anguish, a feeling of terrible loneliness on this alien, dark island . . .

An important dignitary visiting Capri, Reuss XVII, had just departed, and the guests from San Francisco were allotted the very same suite he had occupied. Providing for their needs would be the most comely and able of the chambermaids, a Belgian girl with a waist slim and firm in its corset and a starched cap in the form of a little serrated crown, together with the most prominent valet de chambre, a coal black Sicilian, fiery eyed, and the most nimble bootboy, small and plump Luigi, who had held no small number of such positions in his time. Scarcely a minute passed before the French maître d'hôtel was gently rapping at the door of the gentleman from San Francisco, having come to inquire if the esteemed guests would be taking dinner, and in the event of a positive response, of which, of course, there could be no doubt, to announce that today's menu included rock lobster, roast beef, asparagus, pheasant, and so on. The floor was still heaving beneath the feet of the gentleman from San Francisco—so thoroughly had he been jerked about by that crappy little Italian boat—but leisurely, with his own hands (although unaccustomed and not very skillfully), he closed the window that had banged open upon the entry of the maître, letting in aromas of the distant kitchen and of wet flowers in the garden, and with unhurried precision he answered that they would indeed have dinner, that their table must be situated far from the doors, well back into the dining room, that they would be drinking the local wine, and to each and every word the maître d'hôtel responded, "*Oui,*" in the greatest variety of intonations, all of which, however, meant only that there was no doubt, nor could there be any, about the probity of desires expressed by the gentleman from San Francisco and that everything would be done exactly as ordered. Before leaving he tilted his head to one side and asked demurely, "Will that be all, sir?"

Having received a sluggish "Yes" in reply, he added that today there would be a tarantella danced in the vestibule—performed by Carmella and Giuseppe, renowned all over Italy and throughout "the entire world of tourists."

"I saw her picture on some postcards," said the gentleman from San Francisco in a voice devoid of expression. "And this Giuseppe, is that her husband?"

"Her cousin, sir," answered the maître d'hôtel.

Pausing for a second, thinking of something but saying nothing, the gentleman from San Francisco dismissed him with a nod.

Then, once again, he went through a ritual that was something like preparing for a wedding: he switched on the electricity all over the room, filled every mirror with reflections of light and brilliance, of furniture and wide-open trunks; he began shaving, washing himself, constantly ringing the bell, while other impatient bell calls, encroaching upon his, raced simultaneously through the corridors—calls that issued from the rooms of his wife and daughter. And Luigi in his red apron, making grimaces of horror that reduced the chambermaids to laughing tears (as they ran past him with Dutch tile buckets in their hands), with an agility characteristic of many portly men, Luigi rushed head over heels in response to the rings, and tapping on the door with his knuckles, with sham bashfulness, with a deference pushed to the point of idiocy, he would ask, "*Ha sonato, signore?*"

Then from beyond the door came the slow and rasping, offensively polite voice, "Yes, come in . . ."

What was he feeling and thinking, the gentleman from San Francisco, on that evening so portentous for him? Like anyone who has suffered through the rocking and pitching, he simply was very hungry, he savored in his mind the first tablespoon of soup, the first gulp of wine, and as he went about the mundane matter of getting dressed he experienced even a certain elevation of spirits, which left no time for feelings and contemplations.

After he finished shaving and washing, after inserting with care a bridgework of several teeth, he stood in front of the mirrors with his silver-rimmed brushes, moistening, then ordering the remnants of nacreous hair on his swarthy yellow skull; he pulled a pair of cream-colored silk underdrawers onto his sturdy old man's body with its waistline thickening from a high-calorie diet, and on his dry, flat feet he put black silk socks and ballroom slippers; bending into a curtsey, he straightened his black trousers (stretched high up his body by silk suspenders) and his snow-white shirt with protruding dickey, inserted cuff links into his sparkling-clean cuffs, then began the agonizing process of fastening the neck stud beneath the stiff collar. The floor was still swaying beneath him, the tips of his fingers were hurting, the stud kept biting hard into the flaccid skin at the hollow beneath his Adam's apple, but he was persistent, and finally, eyes glittering with the effort, face dove blue from the squeezing pressure of the collar tight against his throat, he got the job done—and sat down enervated in front of the pier glass, the whole of his image reflected there and reduplicated in the other mirrors.

"Oh, this is awful!" he muttered, hanging his sturdy, bald head and not trying to understand, not thinking about just what was awful; then, in a habitual way, he examined intently his short fingers with their gouty hardened spots at the joints, with the large and bulging almond-colored nails, and he repeated, with conviction, "It's awful . . ."

But just then, as if in a pagan temple, came the stentorian clang of the second gong, reverberating throughout the hotel. Hastily arising, the gentleman from San Francisco pulled still tighter the tie against his collar and the open waistcoat about his stomach, put on his smoking jacket, tucking in the cuffs, and looked himself over one more time in the mirror . . . "This Carmella," he thought, "with her dark skin and the fakey look in her eyes, resembling a mulatto, in her florid outfit with the color orange prevailing, I bet she can put on quite a dance." With that he briskly left his room, and stepping across the carpet to the next suite, his wife's, he asked loudly how long they would be.

"Five minutes!" responded the resonant, and now buoyant, girlish voice from the other side of the door.

"Wonderful," said the gentleman from San Francisco.

He set off at a leisurely pace along corridors, down staircases covered with red carpeting, looking for the reading room below. The menials he encountered squeezed tight up against walls to let him pass, and he strode on as if oblivious to their presence. Up ahead of him was an old lady who was late for dinner, in a bright gray silk dress, round shouldered, with milk white hair but décolleté; she scurried along at full tilt, laughable in the way she waddled, chicken-style, and he easily overtook her. Beside the glassed-in doors of the dining room, where all had gathered now and begun eating, he stopped next to a table crammed with cigar boxes and Egyptian cigarettes, selected a large Manilla, and tossed three lire on the table; out on the winter veranda he took a glance in passing through the open window—a delicate breeze wafted over him out of the darkness, the crown of an old palm tree was dimly visible spreading its fronds, which seemed gigantic, out over the stars; he heard the distant, steady hum of the sea . . . In the reading room, cozy, quiet, and illumined only above the tables, some gray-haired German stood rustling the newspapers, a man resembling Ibsen, in round silver-rimmed spectacles and with the dumbfounded eyes of a lunatic. Looking him over coldly, the gentleman from San Francisco took a seat in a deep leather armchair in the corner, beside a lamp with a green shade, put on his pince-nez, and twisting his neck up out of the collar that was choking him, he shielded himself completely with the newspaper page. Quickly he ran through the headlines on several articles, skimmed a few sentences about the never-ending Balkan war, flipped the page over with a habitual gesture—when suddenly the lines flamed up before him in glassy splendor, his neck went taut, his eyes protruded, and the pince-nez flew off his nose . . . He fell forward with a jerk, tried to gulp in some air, and emitted a bizarre wheezing noise; his lower jaw fell open, lighting up the whole of the mouth with the gold of its fillings, the head collapsed onto one shoulder and began quivering, the shirt dickey spronged out and curled back—and the whole of his body, writhing and pushing back the carpet with its heels, slid down onto the floor, desperately struggling with someone.

If not for the German in the reading room the hotel staff might have quickly and smoothly put the quietus on this awful business, might have seized the gentleman from San Francisco by head and legs and whirled him off, through back passages, to some far distant point—and not a single one of the guests would have learned what he had been up to. But the German burst shrieking out of the reading room, roused the whole place, all of the diners. Many of them leapt up from their meals, many ran blanching to the reading room, questions rang out in all different languages—"What was it? What happened?"—and no one answered in words that made sense, no one understood, since to this very day the thing that people marvel at most of all on earth, the thing they always and ever refuse to believe, is death. The manager flitted about from one guest to the next, trying to restrain those who were running, to calm them with hasty assurances that this was nothing, a trifle, a little fainting episode on the part of some gentleman from San Francisco . . . But no one was listening, many had seen the valets and bootboys tearing tie, waistcoat, and crumpled smoking jacket off that gentleman, even, for some reason, removing the ballroom shoes he wore over black silk socks on his flat feet. Meanwhile, he was still fighting. He was stubbornly struggling with death, doing all in his power to overcome it, this thing that had so suddenly and rudely pounced upon him. He was twisting his head, wheezing like something whose throat has been cut, rolling his eyes like a drunk . . . After they had rushed him into room 43 and placed him on a bed—it was the smallest, the worst, the most damp and cold room, at the end of the lower corridor—his daughter came running up, her hair undone, the cleavage of her bosom raised by a corset, and then his wife, a large woman all dressed to the nines for dinner, her mouth rounded in horror . . . But by then he had stopped twisting his head.

Fifteen minutes later, somehow, everything in the hotel had returned to normal, although the evening was irreparably spoiled. Some guests returned to the dining room and finished their meals, but in silence, with offended faces, while the manager approached first one table, then another, shrugging in a feeble and decorous gesture of aggravation, feeling guilty though not at fault, assuring one and all that he could certainly understand "how unpleasant this was," giving his word that he would "do all incumbent upon him" to eliminate the unpleasantry; they had to cancel the tarantella, all but the most essential lights were dimmed, the majority of guests went into the city, to a beer hall there, and it was so quiet that the ticking of a clock was clearly audible in the vestibule, where a lone parrot was muttering in wooden tones, fussing about in its cage before bedtime, then contriving to fall asleep with one foot absurdly propped on the top rung of its roost . . . The gentleman from San Francisco lay on a cheap iron bed beneath crude woolen blankets, faintly illumined by the light of a single gas jet on the ceiling. An ice pack drooped down over his wet and cold forehead. The dove blue, already-dead face was gradually cooling, the hoarse gurgle that rippled from the open mouth, illumined by a golden sheen, was weakening. It was no longer the gentleman from San Francisco who was wheezing—he was no more—someone else was wheezing. The wife, daughter, doctor, the menials stood there watching him. Suddenly that which they expected and dreaded came to pass—the wheezing sound stopped. And slowly, slowly, before the eyes of them all a pallor flowed over the dead man's face, then his features took on a brightness, a delicacy of line . . .

The hotel manager came in. "*Già é morto,*" said the doctor to him in a whisper. Face dispassionate, the manager shrugged.

Tears running silently down her cheeks, the missus went up to him and said timidly that they should move the dead man back to his room now.

"Oh no, madam," hastily, in a tone of propriety but without a trace of politesse and not in English, but in French, objected the manager, who had no interest now in the trifling sum that the visitors from San Francisco might leave in his hotel cash boxes. "That's totally out of the question, madam," he said, adding, by way of explanation, that he valued quite highly the suite she spoke of, that if he were to do as she wished then all of Capri would learn of this and tourists would begin avoiding that suite.

Staring at him through all this with a strange look, the miss sat down on a chair, covered her mouth with a handkerchief, and began sobbing. The missus immediately dried her tears, her face flared up. She raised her voice, began making demands, speaking in her own language and not yet aware that from now on they would get no respect whatsoever. With courteous dignity the manager put her in her place: If madam did not care for the hotel policies, he would not be so bold as to detain her; then he announced firmly that the body must be removed at dawn, that the police had already been informed, their representative would arrive momentarily to complete the necessary formalities . . . Was there at least a plain, ready-made coffin to be found on Capri? asked madam. Unfortunately not, by no means, and no one would have time to make one now. The matter would have to be handled somehow differently . . . For example, he received English soda water in large and long cartons . . . the partitions from one such crate could be removed . . .

In the night the whole hotel slept. They opened the window in room 43 —it gave onto a corner of the garden, where, beneath a high stone wall serrated on its crest with broken glass, a stunted banana tree was growing—they switched off the lights, locked the door, and left. The dead man remained there in the darkness, blue stars gazing in at him from the sky; a cricket, with somber lightheartedness, began chirring on the wall . . . Out in the dimly lit corridor two chambermaids were sitting on a windowsill, darning. Up walked Luigi, in slippers, with a heap of linens over his arm.

"*Pronto?* (Ready?)" he inquired anxiously in a resonant whisper, indicating with his eyes the terrible door at the end of the corridor. Then, with a buoyant wave of his free hand in that direction, he said in a shouting whisper, "*Partenza!*"—the "All aboard" word they cry in Italian railway stations by way of dispatching trains—and choking with soundless laughter, the chambermaids let their heads fall on each other's shoulders.

Briskly skipping along, he ran up to the door itself, rapped faintly upon it, and tilting his head sideways he asked in an undertone, with the utmost of deference, "*Ha sonato, signore?*"

Then, squeezing his throat tight, pushing forward his lower jaw, raspingly, sluggishly and somberly he answered himself, as if from the other side of the door, "Yes, come in . . ."

At dawn, when it was growing white outside the window of room 43 and a moist breeze began rustling the torn fronds of the banana tree, when a light blue morning sky had lifted and spread over the Isle of Capri, and gilded against the sun that was rising beyond the distant blue mountains of Italy, the pure and distinct summit of Monte Solaro appeared, when the stonemasons had set off for work, those who were mending the island's pathways for the tourists, a long soda water crate was brought to room 43. Soon thereafter that box had become much heavier—it pressed hard against the knees of the junior porter, who rode with it in a sprightly one-horse cab along the white highroad, meandering back and forth down the slopes of Capri amidst stone fences and vineyards, ever down, down, to the very sea. The cabdriver, a puny man with red eyes, wearing an old suit jacket with sleeves too short and down-at-the-heels shoes, was hung over—he had been playing the bones all night at the trattoria—and he kept lashing the robust little horse in its Sicilian-style getup: bells galore jangling on a bridle with colored wool pompons and clattering along the edges of a tall, copper harness pad; a bird's feather, two feet long, protruding from the trimmed fringe of the forelock and fluttering in the wind as it hastened along. Oppressed by his profligacy, his vices, the driver said nothing—last night he had been cleaned out, down to the last lira. But the morning was fresh, and in this sort of air, with matinal sky and sea, the hangover soon fades away and the light-hearted spirit soon returns; not to speak of that consolation of unexpected earnings provided by a certain gentleman from San Francisco, he who was twisting his dead head about in that crate behind the cabman's back . . . The little steamer, floating like a water beetle far below, on the delicate, bright blueness that so viscously, totally encompasses the Bay of Naples, was sounding its final horns for departure—and they echoed zestfully over all the island, every bend of which, every hill crest, every rock was so distinctly visible from everywhere, as if there were no air at all. At pier-side the junior porter was overtaken by the senior, who raced up in a limousine with the miss and missus, pale, their eyes sunken from the tears and the sleepless night. Ten minutes later the little boat once again roiled up the water and hurried off, for Sorrento again, Castellammare, bearing away from Capri forevermore the family from San Francisco . . . And peace and calm settled in once again on the isle.

Two thousand years ago on this island there lived a man who was unspeakably vile in the satisfaction of his lust and who, for some reason, held sway over millions of people, subjecting them to cruelties beyond all measure, and he is stamped for all time in the memory of mankind, and multitudes of travelers from around the world still assemble to look at the ruins of the stone house where he lived, on one of the very steepest upgrades of the island. On this marvelous morning all those who had come to Capri with precisely that aim were still asleep in their hotels, although little mouse gray donkeys with red saddles were being led up now to the entryways of those hotels, and again today, having awoken and eaten their fill, the young and old American men and women, German men and women must needs clamber up on the backs of the donkeys, behind which, again, must needs be running, by the rocky pathways ever uphill to the very summit of Monte Tiberio, those indigent Capriote crones who drive on the donkeys with sticks in the hands of their sinewy arms. Secure in their knowledge that the dead old man from San Francisco, who intended to go along with them (but had, instead, only spooked them with that reminder of death), was now safely packed off to Naples, the travelers snoozed away in a deep slumber, and things were still quiet on the island, the stores in the city still closed. The only focus of commerce was the marketplace bazaar in the *piazzetta*—huckstering fish and green vegetables—and its only patrons were the common people, among whom, as usual absolutely idle, stood Lorenzo, that tall old ferryman, that lighthearted rake and handsome figure who was renowned all over Italy, who had served countless times as the model for painters; he had brought, and already sold very cheaply, two lobsters that he caught in the night, now rustling in the apron of a chef from that same hotel where the family from San Francisco had spent the night, and now he could calmly stand, till evening if he wished, gazing around with regal mien, posed in his tatters, with his clay pipe and that red woolen beret pulled down over one ear. And down the precipices of Monte Solaro, by way of the ancient Phoenician path hewed out of the crags, down its stone steps from Anacapri came two Abruzzian mountaineers. One was carrying bagpipes beneath his leather wrap—a large goatskin bellows with two sounding pipes—the other had something like a wooden fife. As they walked along, the whole country, joyous, beautiful, sunlit, lay spread out beneath their feet: the stony humps of the island, almost all of which was visible below them, and that fairy-tale azure in which it swam, and the shimmering haze of morning above the sea to the east, beneath a dazzling sun, which was already burning hot as it rose ever higher, and the foggy cerulean mountain masses of Italy, still quavering as they do in the morning, those near and far ridges whose beauty cannot be expressed in human words. Halfway down they slowed their pace; above the road, in a grotto cut into the cliff wall of Monte Solaro, all radiant in the warmth and brilliance of the sun was the Mother of God in white-as-snow plaster vestments and a regal halo that was rusty gold from inclement weather; meek and merciful she stood, with eyes uplifted toward the heavens, toward the eternal and beneficent cloisters of her thrice-blessed Son. They bared their heads—and poured out their naive and humbly joyous praise to the sun, the morning, to her, the Immaculate Intercessor for all who suffer in this nasty and beautiful world, and to Him, born of her womb in the faraway land of Judea, in a Bethlehem cavern that served poor shepherds as refuge . . .

Meanwhile, the body of the dead old man from San Francisco was on its way home, to the shores of the New World, to the grave. Having experienced many indignities, much negligence on the part of humanity, having spent a week peregrinating from one port-side warehouse to another, it ended up, once again, on that same famous ship, the one that so recently had borne it, with such solicitude and deference, to the Old World. But now it was concealed from the living—placed in a coffin coated with tar and lowered deep into the blackness of the hold. And again, once again the ship set off on its long ocean voyage. In the night it sailed past the Isle of Capri, and sad were its lights, slowly fading into the dark sea, for one who watched from the island. But out there that night on the ship, under the bright glitter of the ballroom chandeliers, the dance floor, as usual, was crowded.

The dancing went on the next night, and yet again the next—once more amidst a rabid snow squall that roiled over the ocean, which soughed out its funereal mass, swelled with its mountainous billows arrayed in the silvery froth of mourning crepe. Because of the snow the countless fiery eyes of the ship were barely visible to the Devil, who, from the crags of Gibraltar, from the rocky gates between two worlds, gazed after the ship as it sailed off into night and blizzard. The Devil was massive like a cliff, but massive was the ship as well, with its multiple tiers, its multiple smokestacks, created by the arrogance of the New Man with an old heart. The blizzard raged about in its rigging and blasted through the wide throats of its stacks, which had turned white with snow, but it was steadfast, firm, majestic and awesome. On the very highest level, towering alone amidst the whirlwinds of snow were the cozy, dimly illumined quarters where, immured in a vigilant and fitful drowse, over all the ship sat ensconced in glory its corpulent cynosure, the captain, who looked like a pagan idol. He could hear the oppressive howls and furious shrieking of the sirens, smothered by the squall, but he was calmed by the proximity of what he, ultimately, understood least of all, the thing on the other side of his wall: that seemingly armored cabin that now and again was filled with mysterious hums, quivers, and the dry crackle of blue lights, flaring up and exploding around the pallid face of the telegraph operator, with that metallic semihoop on his head. At the very bottom, in the underwater womb of the *Atlantis,* dimly gleaming with steel sheen, rasping steam and oozing boiling water and oil was the fifteen-ton looming mass of the boilers and various other machines, that kitchen, stoked on its underside by hellish furnaces, within which the progress of the ship was cooked—forces awesome in their concentrated power were gurgling there, transmitted to the keel itself through an underground passage without end, a round tunnel weakly illumined by electric light, where slowly, with a rigor insufferable to the soul of man, a gigantic shaft revolved in its oil-drenched conduit, as if some live monstrosity were stretched out in that tunnel, which resembled the orifice of a gun barrel. But in the middle ground of the *Atlantis* the dining salons and ballrooms were spilling out light and joy, murmuring with the voices of the finely dressed throng, spewing the fragrance of fresh flowers, singing with the notes of a string orchestra. And once again they twirled in sinuous torment in amongst that throng, colliding at times with a spasmodic jerk, amidst the sheen of the lights, the silks, diamonds, and naked shoulders of women, that slim and agile pair of hired lovers: the sinfully modest girl with eyelashes lowered, with her innocent coiffure, and the strapping young man with black (as if pasted on) hair, face pallid with powder, in the most elegant of lacquered footwear, in a tight-fitting tailcoat with long skirts—a handsome figure of a man he was, resembling a huge leech. Nobody knew that this pair was fed up to the gills with shamming the bliss of torment to the shamelessly mournful music, nor did anyone know what was down there deep, way deep beneath them, on the bottom of the dark hold, alongside the gloomy and searing bowels of the ship, which kept on ponderously surmounting murk, ocean, and squall . . .

October 1915

»»» «««

The Saints

The manor house was full of guests—visitors were often received, and when they came they would stay on for lengthy periods. A bright, frosty night sparkled its stars beyond the thin panes of the antiquated windows. The Dutch tile stoves were stoked up so hot that you couldn't even get near them. Festive lamps burned in all the rooms, and in the most distant, the divan room, there was even a chandelier, softly lambent with the crystal that time had turned a swarthy gold. They were dealing cards on three green tables in the drawing room, beneath tall candelabras and the gleam of their candles. The table in the dining room was covered with dishes, hors d'oeuvres, and multicolored decanters. Now and again the guests would come out of the drawing room, fill shot glasses, clink them, then poke about the food with forks and return to the card games. In the buffet room, where a pail-sized samovar was bubbling, the old buffet cook, all atwitter, had quarreled with Agafya Petrovna. Hissing and brandishing a silver spoon at Ustya, who was filling the cut-glass jam dishes, he poured out glasses of black tea and sent the trays off to the drawing room. Piles of wonderfully smelling winter coats, fur hats, and long-waisted *poddyovkas* made of fox fur were strewn about the footmen's room, and way back there, in Uncle's quarters, was where Arsenich sat.

The children looked into the footmen's room and the buffet, then stood watching the cardplayers in the drawing room. For lack of anything to do they swiped wooden plates of sausages off the table in the dining room, peered through the lower panes of the windows. They could see the depths of the sky with an occasional speck of a star, the snow, which sparkled saltlike under moonlight, a long wavy shadow of smoke from the kitchen. Farther on, beyond the white meadows, there were high slopes overgrown with a thick, dark coniferous forest, to which the moon lent a fairyland silver tonality at the treetops. Mimicking the guests, the children were speaking to one another using the formal language of adults.

"Mitya, hey, Mitya," said the bashful Vadya. "Do you intend on going in to see Arsenich?"

"And what about you?" asked Mitya, in that austere tone of voice he always used. "I certainly will be going."

Sneaking a look into the drawing room and the buffet—they were not allowed back in the frigid part of the house where Arsenich was—the children meandered, as if leisurely strolling, past the parlor, then suddenly scooted through the small door beside the corner stove—into the vacant quarters where their uncle the hunter had lived and died and where Arsenich stayed when, two or three times a year, he came to visit his masters.

The manor house lived its life, gay and festive, while these rooms lived theirs—a meager life, alien to all. But Arsenich took pleasure in his proximity to that other life, the first one. Two or three times a year they announced to the mistress that he was standing out by the veranda. She sent word that he was to occupy Uncle's rooms, and Agafya Petrovna would provide him a samovar, sausages, white bread, and a small carafe of vodka. Sitting the whole day all on his lonesome, Arsenich drank tea, smoked, shed sweet tears, and late at night—at the same time as the masters—he turned in, tired and deeply moved, sleeping on the straw beside the stove. After this went on for a week he would seek an opportunity to meet with the mistress, and bowing deeply before her, he would take her hand a number of times and kiss it, then depart for the village where he lodged with a local peasant. And this was called having a visit with the old masters.

Uncle's quarters consisted of two rooms. It was dark in the first room now, but a pair of white and thick interlacings of mysterious moonlight cut through the darkness and spread across the floor. There was the smell of Uncle's saddles and of rats. In the other room a thick tallow candle in a black tin holder blazed, shuddering gloomily, on the kitchen table beside the now cooled samovar; thick waves of smoke were wafting about. They had sent Arsenich some tobacco, but it was weak, Turkish, and to get the full narcotic effect he had to smoke continuously without a break. These rooms were badly heated, the window was filigreed with gray rime, and the frosty air blew in. One corner contained a large black painting hung in lieu of an icon: in the arms of a barely visible Mother of God lay the figure of the naked Christ just taken down from the cross; his body, gleaming wooden and yellow, had a wound with coagulated blood beneath the heart, and his dead face was reclining backward. As frowzy as gray froth on boiled milk, red-faced and unshaven, in Uncle's threadbare dress jacket, Arsenich sat on a stool beside the table, one foot, in a winter felt boot, tucked up underneath him. He was smoking a thick hand-rolled cigarette, and in a joyful state of pensiveness he was shedding bitter tears, ignoring the large teardrops that were dripping down his nose. As usual the children, training their curious eyes on him, walked up to the table and began staring at the dove blue, senescent hands, the collar of that dirty nightshirt (also one of Uncle's), and the red crumpled face with its pinpricks of bristly silver. Turning away in embarrassment, Arsenich began searching his pockets for that gruesome handkerchief of his.

"Are you smoking your big stogies again?" asked Vadya, resting his large, bright eyes on the old rag, so long and carefully preserved.

"That I am again, sir," answered Arsenich in a submissive whisper, flashing a quiet and joyful smile.

"And drinking vodka?" asked Mitya.

"Been drinking that too, accursed thing that it is."

"All of it?"

"All of it, yessir," whispered Arsenich. "Only for the love of God, don't say nothing to your mama about my tears. They're not on account of that, nosir. You yourself will vouchsafe to know—this is not the first time for the tears."

"I wouldn't tell for anything," said Mitya resolutely. "And you?" he asked Vadya. "You won't tell either, will you?"

Vadya, who was thinking about something else, blushed, hastily crossed himself, and shook his head. Laughter and the murmur of voices drifted in from the parlor. Someone, taking a break from the cards, was playing the polka called "Anna" on the pianoforte. Those time-honored sounds were suffused with joy and sadness. Listening and thinking his own thoughts, Vadya asked, "Are you poor?"

Arsenich sighed.

"Poverty, sir, is no sin, and then again, even folks who dwell in affluence may come to no good end," he answered. "Your mama, bless her heart, gives me my monthly allotment of grub, plus a silver ruble for money, and Lord knows, what I pay for my living quarters ain't much, twenty-five kopecks a month. So what it comes down to is I've got no quarrel with God."

"You'll die pretty soon now," said Mitya.

"There you've said the gospel truth. I figure it might even be this very winter."

"And were you once a hunter?"

"Nosir, that was something the Lord never granted. I worked for your grandpa as buffet cook."

"Are you crying over Grandpa?"

"Well, come now, sir, how is it I should cry for him!" said Arsenich. "Why he, by the by, passed on way back in eighteen and forty-eight. And he lived, by our reckoning, a goodly long life—eighty-seven years and then some. No, just now I was weeping over the harlot and martyress Elena, bemoaning her unfortunate fate."

From beneath the stove a mouse scooted out, made as if to dash for the table, but then ran off into the dark room. The children followed its movements with shining eyes, then put their elbows up on the table and began concentrating, once more, on Arsenich's glossy sleeves, the veins of his wrinkled, pink neck.

"Was she executed?" asked Vadya, recalling the other martyrs who were the constant subject of Arsenich's tales.

"As you would expect," answered Arsenich. "Only not with a sword and not by torture, but something even worse."

"Do you feel sorry for her?"

"That I do, yessir. Only the reason I'm crying, by the by, is not so much out of pity, but on account of my sensitive heart. Now, that business, according to legends of yore, came about like this," said Arsenich, trying not to look at the children, averting his eyes, which had gone red again. "Once upon a time there lived, by the by, the most arrant of harlots you can imagine, name of Elena, a girl of well-to-do lineage, an exemplary beauty and heartless coquette . . ."

"And where did she live?" asked the children, coughing from the smoke. "In the forest primeval?"

"Nosir, it was later on that the Lord sent her unto the forest, thereto to live and suffer for her faithful love, but first off she dwelt in the capital city, in spacious and wonderful quarters with feasts and merrymaking, traipsing about, anon, unto balls and masquerades—to put it simply, she indulged herself in salacious lechery for big money. For she was, by the by, not really a gentlewoman all the same, and amongst the masters they called her Adele, and she took money, consequent upon thereof, from any and all both drunk and sober, even, perchance, she would not disdain a mere copy clerk, had he the means to pay. Be that as it might, the first and foremost of princes and counts paid court unto her, spending all they had on buying her presents, and a goodly many even laid hands on themselves on her account. Wellsir, and she, in such wise, didn't even lift an eyebrow, for she was, by the by, without feelings toward men, just like Niobe, nourishing no affection for no mortal. She harbored eternal and endless grief in her soul, though. Yessir, such agues of grief as there's no way even to tell it!"

"And did you ever go to see her?"

"Not to be thought of, such a thing!" said Arsenich. "I, sir, am just a lackey, nothing more than a manor-house serf. Why, the masters, they'd run me out of there with sticks; and they'd be right and proper in so doing!"

"And Grandfather?"

"Well now, your grandpa, that's a different thing, except that he, back then, why, he might not even have been born onto the earth just yet. For this, my dear sir, was way back in olden times, and such as them things could never happen nowadays, in this soulless age we live in . . . But then, let me go on laying it out for you. So this Elena, then, was simply the greediest of harlots, and scores of the masters came to naught, by the by, on account of her comeliness, like worms in coles and cabbages. Only then, one day, such as it was quite late in the evening, her number one *kammerdiener* valet came up anon to her boudoir and proclaimed forthwith that a young and splendid count, from the retinue of the Sovereign Empress herself, did desire an audience with her directly. She was sitting, by the by, at her dressing table in nothing but a peignoir nightgown, combing with a matchless tortoiseshell comb the luxurious waves of her curls, and she answered unto him: Well, I would be much obliged, but it's too late now; even as is, she says, on account of my avarice, I've been as if boiling in pitch the whole livelong day, and so receiving him and giving pleasure unto him, well, it's out of the question now. I'm taking me a bath with perfume in the water and then I'll retire to bed, being as I'm all eaten up with the misery and I hate each and all long sith and can't even bear to look at folks. The servant departed, but directly he come back in again and he says, well, it's like this and that and the other and such . . . The count has gambled away at *shtoss* the whole of his worldly goods and wishes to expend the very last of his means—at these words Arsenich had difficulty controlling his voice—says he desires to expend the last of his means on one night of quintessential love . . . And, well then, being, by the by, seen in to her, he didst captivate her unspeakably with his youth and languorous sorrow, and then and there they decided they'd die together, one death at the same hour and even same second. But the Lord Jesu hisself, apparently, judged the matter not as they! Could be it was she, the Holy One, whose will was done," said Arsenich, raising his inflamed eyes and directing them toward the Mother of God in the painting. "Why, all kinds of them goddesses, they never could suffer the way we do and have tenderness of feeling, they did naught but nourish their own passions, but her now, why, She herself in her love, She went up to the very cross to lament. Only then it was the Saviour saith unto her, 'Weep thou not, my Mother, Virgin Mary, for my torment means Eternal Life from this day forth and forever and ever amen.'"

Arsenich burst out crying and fell silent for a moment, pressing a sleeve to his face, which was awash in tears.

"That's all?" asked the children quietly, after waiting for him to continue.

"Nosir, that's still not all," said Arsenich with a sigh of relief. "Like I was laying it out for you, well, they decided posthaste for to die, and, of course, the young count passed on in nothing flat, but the poison couldn't quite get to her and directly she come to herself, and she remained alive on God's green earth, in order, by the by, to suffer and be rewarded from then forthon for her first and last love . . . A man, now, you see, it don't work that way with him. A man can be loving the object of his love while tempted by others, but a fair damoisel, she won't never allow herself such as that, and she might, on account of suchlike, do sinful things, being as she's not found one worthy of her. Well, and that's how it was with this here business. Of course, she changed even in countenance, thinned out, became still more beautiful than before, and shucked off completely, by the by, all the soulless ways of high society, started acting remissful of her courtesan's duties, and not for all the riches on earth would she agree again to betray her own body, having pledged her love for one man to the very grave. So after that, a short time it was, or a long, but the mistress of the establishment got to feeling, as it was, aggravated with her, and commenced anon to maltreat her in one way and another. But she, not responding whatsoever unto these villainies and despites, gathered together in the wee night hours everything, by the by, the semiprecious gems and brooches that she had received as gifts, tied up her Dutch underthings into a knotted bundle, and upped and made for the primeval forest, thereto where only the eagles alone are creeching and the lynxes are rollicking amidst the oaks. So then, she took along with her just that knotted bundle and, by the by, a benediction from her mother, which being an icon of Saint Nicholas Servitor of God, with its silver and gilt metal framing, and she trudged along beside the boundaries of the fields, just following her nose and weeping bitter tears, no lesser than what I'm doing right now. Of course, it was from joy she was crying, 'cause she's broke away, you see, into freedom, walking under skies of blue, and she finally comes upon a huge herd of sheep.

"The shepherd asked her who she was, anyway, and she went right up to him without no fear whatsoever, gave over unto him her priceless bundle with all her rare treasures, and she strips off her luxuriant raiment and crinolines, then asked him to trade her his beggarly tatters. He, to be sure, was tickled pink and jumping for joy, right quick he peels off his crummy homespun mantle and covers therewith, by the by, her near-about naked body. So then she made him a low bow and moseyed off on her way in the guise of a poor pilgrim woman, and thereto she come to a quiet nunnery, a splendiferous cloister for women it was in that primeval forest, and she asted the elderesses to take her on as a simple novice and she commenced to saving her soul along with them damoisels there, making her orisons, by the by, for forgiveness of sins and beseeching unto God with all her might for life eternal, everlasting."

"There where the flesh consumeth away," added Vadya, recalling previous stories Arsenich had told.

"Nosir, not consumes away," said Arsenich, "but quite on the contrary, attains unto a joy that surpasseth all understanding. And so, by the will of Almighty God, such a unforeseen thing was what was to happen next. An ancient elder turned up in that nunnery, he being a onetime serf-painter who had come wishing to sequester himself amidst the nuns, seeking serenity perdurable. He would do, by the by, all sorts of icons, reams of holy paintings for the church they had built them there, and when he seen her beauty and torment, the way she took to the most menial of tasks, he starts in aploring her to paint her in the guise of the Queen of Heaven, Joy of All Who Sorrow. And she fell down at his feet, adjuring him in the name of the Lord Jesu not to do it. 'I am a humongous sinner,' she says, 'I have been cursed with eternal woe, with a mortal sin, and I bear within my soul a terrible secret.' Well, what she near-about admits is that she, to that very moment, cannot bid adieu to her love for a certain man, but she goes on to say, 'And, after all, the clothing I'm vested in would never allow it, forsooth, being as here I am wearing a poor black cassock, nor can I remove it not for even one moment, inasmuch as I have made an avowal unto God . . .' Only thing is that the elder, well, he remained indurate, by the by. He says, 'The clothes will pass muster, for you are pale and fair like a marble ensemblage of sculpture, and the color black, why nothing could befit you more.'

"So then, in the upshot, he complained unto the very mother superior. And she, why she ups and orders that portrait to be made straightaway. The elder, of course, rejoiced forthon immeasurably, went about doing his task on a daily basis, until all that was left to be painted in was a golden nimbus about the head and off he would tote it thereto, into the church. And that's just what they reckoned on doing, figuring to just paint in, you see, that halo and consecrate that exquisite icon, so as to hang it up, by the by, in the temple, when suddenly a terrible, unspeakable thing come to light. It turns out that the maiden Elena . . . well, to put it in simple words, she was heavy burdened with child, enceinte, and just ain't no way to hide this no more for Nature herself will be not denied . . . Lord God Almighty," exclaimed Arsenich, shaking his head. "What were the nuns to do! The world all around is verily a soulless place, but here she is bringing to their cloister the fruit of love! She had never known that condition before, since she could not, without loving, conceive a child within her womb, and now, as bad luck would have it, she had indeed loved, and, after all, once she was no more a simple maiden, but a pregnant mother, how could she, in that case, have engaged forthon in lechery?"

"Did they order her put to death?" asked Mitya.

"Nosir, worse. In the night-dark of night-black they run her off into the woods," said Arsenich. "And now be so kind as to consider what she, in that case, must have felt? Maybe only Thecla the Anchoress ever underwent such travails as this, in the dream she kept having, in the torments her soul traversed. But then, for all that, just her one small white handkerchief, which she give to a beggarly old man and which an angel tossed upon the scales, putting the devils to shame, why that's what saved her, ended up outweighing all of her sins!"

"But why did they run her off into the woods?" asked the children.

"Well, where else might they run her?" answered Arsenich. "Naturally, into the primeval forest impenetrable . . ."

"Where the eagles screech," added Vadya.

"Yessir, truly said, where the eagles screech and where a truculent beast might well consume her," repeated Arsenich in a tone of bitter exultation. "Where the forest murk was unremitting and just one rock-cliff cave was to serveth as her refuge! And there in that cave was she obliged to give birth unto the child, to diaper him, by the by, with whatever she could manage, and she tore, thereto, her last shirt into strips for swaddling bands, and here it was that all sorts of lynxes might be yowling about, gazing from the oaks with their green eyes, and here flew roaring the very Bird of Play—Arsenich put a strong emphasis on the *l* of the word—the Bird of Play was soaring around, white all over with black wings, whirling and cackling out, wishing, by the by, to scutch at the child and flutter him dead with her wings . . . And of course they, a helpless young 'un and its mother, could not bear such abject torment, all the hunger and cold and the profanation, and they upped and passed on right then and there, being as she had not only not a drop of milk in her breasts, but not even a crumb of bread left for refection-subsistence.

"And then what happened right after that, why what a sudden miracle it was! The beasts, the birds, well they all commenced to sobbing, to wailing their grief over her, and such a whirlwind rose up throughout the woods that in the dead of the night-dark of night-black the entire cloister was awakened by the noise, and the ancient one, the elder-painter, why he leapt up, by the by, in his bedchamber there in the studio, and he hears amidst the terrible hubbub some voice, enjoining him to go out right quick into the forest, and dressed just as he was he run out and woke everybody up, called for the mother superior, called for the very oldest elderess-sister, and so they, the all three of them, set off, they did, with lights and with torches, heading thereto, for that very impenetrable forest. But out there, by the by, lay nothing butcept a body unbreathing! A primeval thicket, and laying beneath it, beneath the kind of pine tree they call a cedar, they seen that mother of ineffable grace, all white like snow in her cassock of black, her shroud, with a dead child at her barren breast—and burning roundabout her head is a fiery nimbus, lighting up all of her pale visage and her cassock. In a word, that very halo that the elder-painter had durst not to paint in on his icon, after he come to learn of the sin of Elena, of the life she had led in the secular world! Now is that, sir, not a great miracle, is that not a sign?" exclaimed Arsenich ecstatically and bitterly, looking at the children with entreating, reddened eyes, which made his disheveled gray hair seem even whiter.

"Did they carry her back to the monastery?" asked the children.

"Wellsir, to be sure they did, where else could they carry her to? And, of course, they sung her funeral obsequies and interred her remains right there in the church with homage unbounded, as if they were holy relics; even buried the child alongside her, and all in tears they pressed up to kiss her hand . . . Perchance it was then they recalled the precepts given unto us by the Holy Apostles, who said, 'Remember ye that a multitude, a great foison of sins are canceled out by love!'"

The dark candle blazed like a burning splint light. Arsenich fell silent and long sat thinking, saying nothing and gazing at his hand, at the rag crumpled up in it. Staring intently and gravely at the candleholder, Mitya poked about at the spots run over with cooled tallow. Vadya kept his motionless, now-drowsy eyes trained on the flame. In the parlor they were playing the polka "Anna" again, and someone yelled out, laughing, "Don't let him, don't!" Vadya suddenly came out of his stupor and asked in a hoarse voice, "And will you be a saint?"

Arsenich started shaking his head.

"Oh, my dear sir, what a grievous sinful thing you're saying! Why, I'm like some kind of hound dog. Lived out my livelong life at the heels of the masters, not a single day of suffering have I known! For what would I deserve such a reward?"

"And did you make up all that stuff yourself?"

"Lord forbid! I hear all the stories amidst the common people, or I collate them down out of books. Folks get together and I sit and read—I have the most splendid of books from olden times . . . It's true, my soul is of a bygone age. Not by my just deserts, but the Lord hath granted unto me a great gift. That gift is something the elders of Valaam Monastery are vouchest safe to receive, but only at the last of their far ancient years, and even then not all of them. This marvelous gift is known as the gift of tears. And then again, by the by, I do so love the poetry of words, just can't tell you how much!"

Then, gazing at the children with his sorrowfully joyful eyes, Arsenich declaimed in a style of the old times, singsong: "I prithee, do this, it's my deathbed behest: / Plant thee a fir tree on the grave where I rest!"

In the snowdrifts outside the window sleigh runners were squealing, the horses made squeaking noises in the snow, and sleigh bells jangled as they neared the veranda. Someone was driving off into the bright, frosty night, into those hazily silver woods, which stood out there in fairyland darkness along the slopes beyond the meadows.

They were playing the polka "Anna," dancing in the parlor, and Arsenich, eyes closed, smiling, nodded his head in time to the music.

"O-ho, but the secular life is a fine thing as well, yessir!" he said with a sigh. "And were it left to my will, I would live my earthly life for a goodly thousand years!"

"How come?"

"Because, dear sir, I would fain to go on living, looking, and marveling at God's green earth . . . For quite a spell today I got myself upset, cogitating upon dear Elena, she of eternal sorrow, but then I recalled, by the by, the great martyr Boniface, and I wept three rivers of tears with the joy of it all! He was a man of lowly origins too, a serf and slave plain and simple. But of a totally different stamp—an arrant scalawag he was, a dissolute sapsucker, nocount and proud of it . . . On the icons they paint him, by the by, as brown haired, but in the *Lives of the Saints* it's stated clear and straightforth: yellow headed he was, and then again he was specked in freckles as it be, stumpy in stature, with joyful eyes and something of a fakery in their gaze, not like Elena the Sufferer. He was in the city of Rome, serving the grand lady Aglaida as major-domo of the dining room, attending, by the by, upon her table—and, well, he captivated her soul. In the *Lives,* of course, this is told in quite a heartless way—they write that she, being not married, dissipated herself in sin, bowed down and succumbed to her lusts, and lived in unlawful cohabitation with her slave Boniface. But if one is to judge this case in human terms, then, could be this is what happened: she spied him, she looks him up and down, and she smiles a crooked smile, thinking, 'Now there's a fine fellow.' And that's when she fell in love with him and brought him near unto herself.

"Well, they lived such a life for a year, for two, her fussing over him, as it was, like a child. There are, you know, them kind of damoisels, tender and charming, devout of soul, although they abide evermore in sin, can't refuse folks nothing, thereto, on account of their kind nature . . . So he's with his boonfellows day and night, off a-twanging on one guitar or another, quaffing wine. In the *Lives* they have it like this: he being awash in the tempests of passion, mired in sin long sith—while she, well, she's setting at home sewing him something, as it be, thinking soft thoughts of him; she forgives him all his infidelities, like a mother. Wellsir, time don't wait for no mortal man, and her years, by the by, was running on, and she begun to pondering on her fate; now and again, I reckon, she would have herself a quiet cry. And, as they say, she finally got up the nerve. 'My dear,' she says, 'my beloved, I havest one cherished dream on my mind. I have sacrificed all for you, fearing, thereunto, neither humanfolk nor the Good Lord, but we are living still, nonetheless, out of wedlock, our bond unacknowledged. We must bring holy relics forthon into our household, for to shed the light of grace upon our home. I beg of you, fit out a ship, carry therewith ye silver and gold, fragrant and precious shroud cloths with the image of Christ in his grave, for to twine about these venerable relics, by the by, and set out sailing for the land of Cilicia, the city of Tarsus. A multitude of zealots most pious dwellest there, folks who have laid down their heads for the love of Jesu.' Well then, of course he agreed to do it, he fitted out a sailing ship, covering its decks, by the by, with divers carpets and silks from far Shamakha, and along with his friends and boonfellows, with wines, music, with all the servants of the court, he set sail . . ."

"And on the way did they run into a storm?" asked the children.

"No sir, on the contrary, they all of them made it quite safely to them faraway lands. They tossed out their anchors there, lowered their sails, and him, he moseyed off for the city of Tarsus, to the guest house there, so he could, you see, rest up, have a walk round, then get on with his business early the next morning. So he walks, by the by, past the city gates, heads up the street thereto, and of course he's footloose, without a care in the world, humming an aria to hisself, when suddenly he hears a humongous clamor. Well, naturally, he right quick runs up there and what he comes upon is a inhumane, murderous spectacle. Folks is swarming around all over the marketplace square, a-raged and hand waving, screeching out demands for executions, and in the midst of the square sits a cruel inquisitor, subjecting Holy Christians to the most fearsome of torments. He orders one of them cut in half, another to put out his eyes, another to have his head lopped off. And down on his knees in front of him there's an elder, bent beneath the sharp blades of a double-edged sword, and in his final hour he crieth out, 'Hallowed be the name of the Lord Jesus Christ, our pure, sweet Saviour!' And when he heard that, Boniface, who, by the by, was the most dyed-in-the-wool scalawag, why then he was like just lit up all over—in the *Lives* it says it plain and clear: his spirit was raised up in the name of the Lord. So he rushed right into the midst of the crowd, leapt out in front of them all, and he upped and took up, not even thinking, the cry of the martyrs: 'May the name of the Lord God be praised! What are you doing, heartless pagans, let me through—for I too most verily desire to suffer for my Saviour!'

"Well then, naturally, they all run up and start to going on at him—horrified on his account, trying to talk him out of it, saying, 'Have fear, by the by, for thy life, come to your senses, why thou art a guest from foreign lands, what business thereto is this of yours?' But he don't back off one iota, saying, 'I'll hear naught of this, you are unworthy to flatter and dissuade me. I curse and fie upon all your marble and graven images, go ahead and smite off my head!' And he rent with a single stroke all of his multicolored raiment, fell on his knees in the midst of the square, bent down his head before them . . ."

"And accepted execution by the sword," added Vadya quietly.

"Yes sir, he accepted execution by sword, my dear precious little one!" exclaimed Arsenich, and taking him by the hand, he firmly pressed upon it his cold lips with their drops of hot tears. "Well, I never!" he whispered then, turning away and groping about on the table for his handkerchief. "If I ain't just gone to the dogs, gone plumb to pot!"

Wiping his face, he took a two-ounce pack of tobacco out of his pocket, and sighing with relief, began rolling a thick smoke. For a long time the children went on looking, first at his gray head, then at its large, trembling shadow on the wall, while listening to that discordant sound of voices, the table talk and laughter in the parlor.

"Do you like Boniface most of all?" asked Mitya in that austere tone of his.

"A sinful man," whispered Arsenich, hastily bending down to tongue-lick the paper on his rolled cigarette. "I do so love his panache!"

Capri, January 23, 1914

»»» «««

Zakhar Vorobyov

A few days back Zakhar Vorobyov, of the village of Aspen Grange, dropped dead.

His hair was a blend of ginger and light brown, he was bearded, and he was so tall, so much larger than the ordinary person, that you could have put him on display at a country fair. He himself was aware that he belonged to a different breed, something like a grown-up amidst children who must, nonetheless, pretend to be one of them. Another feeling haunted him for all of his forty years, a nebulous sense of loneliness. In olden times, so the story went, there were many such as him, but the breed was going extinct. "There's one other fellow like me," he would sometimes say, "but he's living way out yonder, roundabout Zadonsk."

His even temperament, incidentally, was a marvel of consistency. His health was fine to a rare degree, his physique a wonder to behold. He would have been handsome if not for that bearlike brown tan of his complexion, the slightly upturned slant of his lower lids, and the perpetual, glassy tears that hung on those lids beneath big light blue eyes. His beard was soft and thick, with a bit of a waviness, so that you felt like touching it. From time to time, in the gentle way peculiar to giant-sized men, he would smile in amazement, toss back his head, and his fervent, red, animal-like mouth would open slightly to reveal the marvelous young teeth. A pleasant smell wafted from him: the ryelike whiff of a steppeland dweller, blended with the smell of tar from his solidly cobbled boots, the sour stench of his tanned sheepskin coat, and the peppermint aroma of snuff; he did not smoke but he dipped.

He had a predilection for anything linked to olden times. The collar of his austere, rough-hempen shirt, always clean, did not button up but was fastened by a slender red ribbon. From his thin belt a copper comb and a copper ear pick hung. He was still wearing bast sandals up to age thirty-five. Then his sons grew into adolescence, the farmstead prospered, and Zakhar bought himself some boots. In winter and summer alike he went around in his sheepskin coat and fur cap. And that sheepskin he left behind when he died was in fine shape, quite new; the greenish blue pleats, the narrow chevrons of multicolored morocco leather on its beautifully backstitched breast front were still unfaded; the bear brown sealskin—on the trimming of the coat front and collar—was still coarse and lush. Zakhar loved cleanliness and order; he loved everything new and well made.

His death came like a bolt out of blue skies.

It was the beginning of August. He had just knocked off quite a journey by way of a circular route. From Aspen Grange he walked to Red Burnout to attend a court hearing on an action brought by a neighbor. From Burnout he covered the some fifteen versts to the city—to meet with the mistress of the estate where he was sharecropping. He took a train from the city to the village of Shipovo and then set off walking for Aspen Grange by way of Livelong; so there you tack on still another ten versts. But none of that was what did him in.

"Huh?" he would have said in amazed and regally austere tones, with that velvet bass voice of his. "Forty versts?"

Then good-naturedly he would add, "Tell me another one, son! Why, I could do a thousand versts at one go."

In was First Saviour Day. Sauntering through the Shipovo railway station, which was always under repair in summer and was splashed up with whitewash, he remarked jokingly to a man he knew, the coachman of the squire Petrishev, "Now, in honor of the holiday I might could use just a little bit of a snort."

"Not a bad idea. Count me in if you're buying," answered the coachman.

"No can do, I'm all spent out; only made it here by way of a freight train," said Zakhar, although he was far from short of money. The coachman winked to his crony, the village constable Golitsyn. A muzhik from Shipovo, the boozehound Alyoshka, attached himself to the group and the four of them left the station together. Zakhar and Alyoshka went on foot, while the coachman climbed into a tumbrel with a pair of horses harnessed to it—he had come to pick up Petrishev, but the latter had not been on the train—and the constable got in his light sulky. Wasting no time Alyoshka started pushing for a bet: could Zakhar drink three liters of vodka in an hour?

"Do I get vittles to go with it?" asked Zakhar, striding out down the dry road with the wheel ruts slashed across it, beside the tall mare of the constable. Periodically he would force the shaft back down and adjust the crooked harness gear.

"You can have anything you want, long as it don't cost over a half ruble," said the coachman, a morose and dim-witted type.

"And if you lose," added Alyoshka, who was a ragamuffin peasant with a fractured nose, "then you pay it all back three times over."

"You want it that way, then so let it be," responded Zakhar condescendingly, already thinking about what he would get for food.

Not only was he not wearied by his journey to Burnout—where the legal business had been settled splendidly, with agreement on both sides—not only had two days in the city heat not left him enervated and spent, but he was even in a state of animation and pulsing with strength. With all his being he yearned to do something absolutely extraordinary. But what? Drinking three liters is, God knows, a paltry little matter, nothing novel there. He could flabbergast the coachman and make a fool of him, but that was no big thing either. Yet all the same he readily agreed to the wager. As he sat down to eat and drink his first aim was to savor the food—he was ravished with hunger and every morsel was sweet. Second, he wanted to enjoy himself by telling the story of the hearing.

It was a hot day, but the broad expanses of yellow fields around the village, all dotted with hay bales, already had an aura of the approaching fall, something soft and clear. The main square of Shipovo was covered with thick dust. Separating the square from the village were woodpiles, a bakery, a wine shop and post office branch, the light blue house of the merchant Yakovlev with its front garden, and his two shops, which had that peculiar cut to the timber framing at their corners. Some pine planks serving as steps lay in a heap beside one of those dark shops. Zakhar sat there on the planks, drank, ate, talked, and gazed out at the square, at the rail tracks gleaming in sunlight, the swing-beam barrier of the humpbacked rail crossing, and the yellow fields beyond the rails. Sitting beside him, Alyoshka was having a bite to eat as well: cheap bread made from mill sweepings. The village constable—he was a dull, dust-laden man with mustaches clipped close, in a shabby uniform coat with orange epaulettes—he, along with the coachman, smoked, one seated on his sulky, the other in the tumbrel. The horses dozed, waiting patiently for the order to set off pulling. And Zakhar told his story.

"How did it all come out?" he said. "Well, it come out in a tie. They compromised. These court wranglings, confounded goosiness, I never had no use for it, never sued nobody. My old man, bless his soul, he wouldn't have no truck with the squabbling. And this squabble we just had us was the same stuff and nonsense. Biddies get to clucking at one another, then the rest of us, like nincompoops, has to jump right into it."

He had already made short work of three bottles—drinking out of a wooden ladle Alyoshka had found in Yakovlev's courtyard. He went about his business with such ease, so sure of himself that he took no notice of what he was doing. The coachman, the constable, and Alyoshka did all in their power to act calm, although each was praying deep in his soul for Zakhar to collapse and die. But he just unbuttoned his sheepskin coat, pushed his fur cap back off his forehead, and went red in the face. He ate two dried fish, a huge clump of scallions, and five long loaves of French bread, and he put such concentration into his eating, ate with such relish that even his adversaries were in awe of him. In animated tones, with a touch of sarcasm, he went on with his tale.

"What a crazy bunch of shenanigans, them hearings! I wasn't even about to go, no way. I hear tell somebody's got a subpoena out. Well, they went on subpoenaing and subpoenaing, no getting shed of them, and I keep on saying I ain't going. Only then suddenly the big cheeses comes to Burnout, and the magistrator his own self sends word for me to be there. 'Well,' I'm thinking, 'why don't you croak and get out of my life!' But what are you going to do, I didn't have no choice. I grabbed a hunk of bread and took off walking. The heat was something out of this world, dust on the road like charred grass on a burned field; why even your feet is sweating up a storm. Well then, anyway, I made it to Burnout. Right fast I moseyed along and finally moseyed on in there."

Holding the nearly empty bottle under his arm, he let the bright liquid run out into the darkness of the ladle, filling it right up to the rim. Then, smoothing down his mustache, he pressed his moist lips to the vodka, which smelled of plenitude and pungency. He drew it in slowly, enjoying himself, as if he were drinking spring water on a hot day, and when he had drunk it to the dregs he wheezed, turned the ladle over, and shook out the last few drops.

Then he carefully placed the bottle on the ground beside him. The coachman kept his morose gaze trained on him; the constable, who had contrived to set the watch a full fifteen minutes ahead, exchanged worried glances with Alyoshka. After he put the bottle down Zakhar snatched up two or three long strands of scallions, broke them off, and stuffed them into a large wooden saltcellar, mixing them with the big grains of gray salt, then chomping away with a scrumptious, succulent crunch. His eyes, bloodshot and teary, looked terrifying, but he was smiling, his chesty bass voice was sonorous and caressing, pleasantly sardonic.

"So anyway, all right then, I showed up," he said, masticating and puffing out his nostrils. "And what I seen was there was folks all over the place out there on the street, and under a willow tree in the cool of the shade sets the magistrate man in his spiffy spring suit coat, with his little light brown dickey beard; he's got him a table there with I mean any manner of books and papers, and alongside of him (Zakhar gestured with his hand to the left) sets the police constable scribbling away with his little pencil, one of them kind got eight different sides to it. They called forward the peasant Semyon Galkin, from Obukhovsky village. 'Galkin!' they says, and he says 'Yeah!' 'Come here forth,' they says. He rambles up there and they commence to questioning him. But he don't even look at the police, he takes him a pear out of his pocket and stands there eating on it. The police yells at him, 'Get rid of that pear!' He don't pay him no mind, just goes on gnawing away, finishing it off . . ."

"I'd take that pear and whap it upside his head," remarked the coachman.

"You and me both!" agreed Zakhar, breaking into pieces his seventh and last loaf of bread. "Stands up there demolishing his pear! Magistrator man turns to the police, says, 'So then, Mr. Constable, this here is that very same peasant Semyon Galkin that when I come the last time to do the inventory, why he refused to pay the court-ordered sum of forty-eight rubles and eighty kopecks, and when I set about to inventorize how much there was of his timber holdings and his grain, well, then him, this here very Galkin with his coassociates, the two brothers Ivan and Bogdan, they all upped and seated theirselves on the wood, them log beams longside the shack, and did not allow me to proceed with my inventory. Then, when I proceeded to enter into his shack, well, he like as if for no particular reason asted his wife whereabouts was the hand scale, which was said about me and I took it as applying to me, and Bogdan meantime walks up to the window with a scythe on his shoulder, when there wasn't no hay to be cut, haymaking all long since done. And being as I was alone, well I was obliged then to depart the premises. Be so kind now as to call forth his wife Katerina and his mama Fyekla and to enter her testimony into the official record. And what's furthermore, into the protocol of interrogerated persons enter the testimonial of the church warden, peasant Fedot Levonov. And record, what's additionally, that on the aforesaid day, well, the village headman Gerasim Savelev made hisself totally scarce and at my demanding that he show up, well he did not show up, and when I was leaving out of Galkin's place and heading off to the shack of Mitry Ovchininkov, where my gelding was at that time presently located, and was passing past his shack, why he sicced his he-dog on me while he hisself was hid behind his gates which I seen him quite clear, and whistling, but thank the Lord it so turned out that the he-dog did me no bodily harm though he come tearing up at me right against my chest, pounced up on me ramble-scramble like he was out of his mind, all thanks to Mitry, who jumped out with a whip and used it to get him offen me.'"

Carried away by the refinement of his story, Zakhar seemed to have been reading the final words from a written text. After mimicking the pronouncements of the magistrate in a firm, sonorous voice, he started to go on without pausing for breath, but Alyoshka lost his patience.

"Tell the rest of it later! Drink up! Mr. Police, kindly check out your watch."

"No problem, he'll make it," answered the constable with a wink at Alyoshka.

But Zakhar did not notice that.

"Don't get your drawers all in a twist, you snub-nosed scoundrel!" he barked out good-naturedly. "Give me a chance to finish the story! I know how much time I got—I'll drink it all, you need not worry yourself about that!"

His feet were firmly implanted on the edges of his hobnailed boot heels—he was making a proud display of the boots, pulling up, occasionally, just for show, on the boot tops—his face was red, but not yet drunken. Executing an exaggerated low bow to a muzhik driving by in an empty cart, who had looked back at Zakhar and given him the once-over, he blew out his breath with a loud puff through the nostrils, took the coat breast of his hot sheepskin in both hands, moved the collar back off his neck, and went on talking, enjoying the vividness of the scenes that occupied his imagination, the play of his thoughts.

"'Katerina Galkina!'" he intoned loudly from deep in the chest, acting out all the different parts. "'Come forth to be questioned. Move it up closer, right up to the table!' She moves it. 'Did you hear what His Honor the magistrate just said?'

"'Yessir.'

"Well, she's stuttering and crying, can't make no sense of nothing she says.

"'Is it correct that your husband made mention of a hand scale in regardance to His Honor the magistrate?'

"'Well,' she says, 'on that account ain't no way I can know. My husband was fixing to weigh out some rye chaffings.'

"'So then, you do hereby deny that fact of the matter?'

"'I don't know nothing about none of that. On near-about anything that comes up Fedka pulls a lone oar. You ast him if you like; then we can wind this business up, and less fuss for all of us.'

"They called for the old lady. Fyekla. She's a feisty biddy with one leg shriveled up; answers questions like she's spoiling for a fight. 'The property,' she says, 'is mine. I don't make no payments on what my son owes, by rights of my belated husband it all belongs to me, and my son ain't got nothing but the pants that he wears.'

"'Well then, whose son is he?'

"'Mine.'

"'Being as he's your son, then ain't nothing to be discussed further; that there property's got to answer for nonpayment of debts. So move on and don't mouth off no more, or I'll place you under arrest for two days on bread and water.'

"In a word, he put the genuine quietus on the old lady. Then he ast where's the church sexton Fedot Levonov? His girl Vinadorka steps up.

"'Whereabouts is your papa?'

"'He's in the storeroom shed, having his after-dinner rest.'

"'Run over there and fetch him back here. Tell him the authorities is requiring his presence.'

"And anyway, well, he don't live but just across the yard—"

"Right close, you mean he was?" interrupted the constable, exchanging quick glances with Alyoshka and the coachman. "I see . . . Well, go on and finish off your story. I must say, brother, you are one mighty fine storyteller!"

He was babbling whatever came to mind, just to distract Zakhar's attention. Taking out his pocket watch and concealing it between his knees, he moved the hands forward still another ten minutes. Meanwhile, his face beaming with the compliment, Zakhar puffed out his breath even more forcefully, tossed his head to get the hot thick fur of the sheepskin away from his shoulder blades, and blurted out in still more animated tones, "You got it! But listen up now and stop interrupting me, or else I might get ornery . . . So I seen this stubby old man come creeping out from that low-built storeroom. He walks cross the road to his cottage—not wearing no hat, in a new pink peasant blouse unbelted, got the collar undone on account of the heat. Then he comes back out of the shack in a new warm longcoat, green sash about the waist, fur cap in his hands. Walks over. Thick hair, gray headed, in a hairdo like a ram's horns, laying on both sides. Shakes hands with the police, then the magistrator (got money, seem like, this old bird). Goes to whispering something or other in their ear, pointing over to Senka. Then whips out a big old leather pocketbook, starts to counting off three-ruble notes with these stumps of his hands all frostbit. After that he yelled for Vinadorka. Told her get a samovar heated up, invited over the police and magistrator to drink some tea. 'Come have a look at what I got out hunting; show you my bees too, and some new crockery I just bought. And take a gander at my filly. She's a fine light color, spotted all over with dapples!' He's a-laughing and squinching up his face, rotten tooth roots showing in the red of his mouth. 'Ain't no way you can't take a look at her, it's the law of the horses says you got to. And then, we might could make us a deal on her, like what we was talking before.' Then he laughed again, made a hissing sound when he laughed, like a snake. He sashayed on off toward his cottage, smoothing down the dust on the road with his boot, strutting his stuff—"

"Strutting along, putting on the dog," interrupted the constable again, taking up his pocket watch. "But you ain't got but five minutes left now. You're going to have to swig it all down in one gulp."

Zakhar's face suddenly took on a different look.

"What?" he shouted sternly. "You're lying, you are! No way a whole hour went by!"

"It sure has, brother, it sure has went by!" chimed in the coachman and Alyoshka. "Drink up, now. Drink up!"

Zakhar drew in his breath like a blacksmith's bellows and closed his eyes.

"Hold it!" he said. "This ain't right. You been flimflamming me. Give me another half an hour. Main thing is I'm all sweated up. This heat! It's August. The hell with you, I'll just buy you some vodka my own self, but you can stick on more time. At least let me finish telling this story about the hearing!" he said morosely.

"Aha! He's a backslider!" shouted the coachman sarcastically. "None too eager when push comes to shoving back!"

Zakhar trained his fierce bloodshot gaze upon him. Then, without saying a word, he grabbed the bottle by its neck, drained it into the ladle right up to the rim, and slurped it all down. After that, panting a bit, he said rudely, "Well? That make you feel better? And now I'm finishing off my story!" he added with the stubborn insistence of a man who's been drinking. "Lookee here just how drunk you got me, or could be you ain't got the guts to look?"

Then suddenly those terrible eyes of his sparked once again with merriment, his face resumed its self-important, good-natured expression.

"So now you're obliged to listen to what I'm a-saying!" he bellowed out from deep in his chest, and he went back to narrating, but with less smoothness and coherence than before.

"Well then, directly they called out for the conjure man Vasily Ivanov. This here fellow is skinny to the bone, in a gray longcoat, hemp-looking hair hanging about the temples, and a little wedge of a beard. Got his face squinched up even worst than what the old man did, on account of the sun, or maybe just out of being the underhanded schemer he is . . . damn if I know which. It turns out he poisoned this old heifer with a magic potion. Give her some kind of healing stuff, is what he done, tells her take it in a little teensy glass, but she ups and right quaffs it down in great big gulps . . . They called him up to the table.

"'State your name.'

"'Vasily I reckon is what it is.'

"'And who give you the right to practice medicine, you scoundrel?'

"Course, early on sometime they had already done made them a deal. Vaska, likely as not, had slipped them a little something. In front of folks, though, you always got to fuss and carry on, just for the fun of it. So they proceeded to asting questions, on and on, and then finally stopped and yelled at him: 'Out of my sight now, you! Get off into them woods over yonder!' He puts this look on like he's ascairt: hat back on his noggin and right quick skeedaddled off into the aspens . . . Wellsir, that's where the whole business just petered out. The police, he took a look into his little hand mirror, hoisted up his saber on his hip, and folded his papers together.

"'Well then, what about if we was to step on over to old man so-and-so's place?' he says. 'Sure would like to give my gelding a little more rest.'

"'And what time is it getting to be?'

"The police draws out his brand-new pocket watch, silver plated, takes a peek.

"'Thirty-eight past the hour of twelve.'

"'All right, then, we can drop by. Duty bound to take a look at what he got out hunting; old man's right proud of that.'

"So up they got and went off to drink tea. Well, the country boys hung around there, they was all sprawled out, perched like crows on a pile of logs longside of the shack, kicking up a commotion. Some of them saying it ought not to have come down to selling off property for debts. Others said it was none too swift getting the big cheeses in a huff. Some skinny drink of water was raising the most sand of all, going at it whole-hog with one old man. This drink of water yells out that we folks just ain't living right, other countries has got it better, take just the Kirghiz peoples now, why even they've got a leg up on us—leastways they got a great big prairie-land territory where they can live. But the old man yells no, we got things better here . . ."

It seemed to him that he could have gone on talking indefinitely, making it ever more entertaining and telling it better and better. But the coachman and village constable were done listening, convinced now that their wager was lost; not only had Zakhar drunk and eaten them out of house and home, but now he had to go blabbing on endlessly with this stupid story of his. They whipped up their horses and drove off, cutting him short right in the middle of a word. As for Alyoshka, he sat there awhile longer playing yes-man, then asked for four kopecks to buy tobacco and traipsed on off to the station. Zakhar, disgruntled with his collocutors and feeling that the vodka he had drunk was far from enough, was left alone. He sighed, tossed his head to move the sheepskin collar back off his neck, and experienced, still more intensely than before, that surge of power and those vague desires. He got up, went into the wine shop, and bought a bottle of vodka. Then he sauntered off down through an alleyway and out of the village, headed along the dusty road into the open fields, amidst the boundless space of sky and yellow farmland. Sundown was approaching but it was still baking hot. Zakhar's sheepskin glistened. To the right of him a huge shadow with a radiance surrounding its head fell upon the golden, parched stubble of the crops. Pushing the hot fur cap to the back of his head, folding his hands behind him underneath the sheepskin, Zakhar strode resolutely along on the firm earth beneath the layer of dust; like an eagle, unblinking, he glared at the sun, then at the broad expanse of recently mowed steppeland that spread before him, resembling a capacious desert of sand, then at the countless hay bales that were scattered all over those fields, looking from afar like caterpillars—and all along the skyline, all around the hay bales innumerable circlets, raspberry colored, violet, malachite green, were dancing about before his teared-up and bloodshot eyes.

"Well, I am sure enough drunk!" he thought, feeling a sinking sensation in his heart and its throbbing beat in his head. But that in no way damped down his hope that today there would be something extraordinary in store for him. From time to time he stopped walking, took a drink, and closed his eyes. Ah, that's good! It's good to be alive, only I just got to find a way to do something out of this world! Once again he surveyed the broad horizon. He looked up at the sky—and all of his soul, simultaneously sardonic and naive, overflowed with the craving for some monumental feat. He was a man not like any other, and he was firmly convinced of that, but what of any import had he done in his time, how had he manifested his powers? Nothing, he had done nothing! Once he carried an old woman along in his arms for five versts, but that was hardly worth mentioning, a joke; why just say where, and he'd tote to that spot a dozen old nanny goats like her!

His imagination, inebriated and avid for visual impressions, demanded work. He picked up his pace, firmly resolving not to let the sun overtake him—to make it to Livelong before it set—and all the time his mind was racing, thinking. The bottle was about to run dry. Plus which, he felt the need to have just a bit more—so he dropped in and bought another from the lame shopkeeper at the wine kiosk out on the Livelong highroad. The sun was going down; rising up from the east to replace it was a full moon, pale as a cloudlet on the dry, level blueness of the skyline. Barely perceptible, a fragrant evening haze wafted over from somewhere through the ever-cooler air; red rays with an orange tint were sprinkling their way from the left across the prickliness of widely spaced field stubble. Red dust rose beneath Zakhar's boots, and every hay bale, every Tatar thistle, every blade of grass exuded its shadow. "Oh no, you don't! You ain't catching up with me!" thought Zakhar, gazing at the sun, wiping the sweat from his brow, and recalling the Bityug breed stallion he had once lifted up by the front legs at a country fair—to prove his strength on a bet with the locals—then the landowner Khomutov's cast-iron driving gear last summer, the way he dragged it out off the threshing floor in the barn, and then again the old beggar lady he had lugged along in his arms, ignoring her terror and her pleas to "leave me go and let me be."

He stopped with legs spread wide, and their shadow fell in huge pillars upon the crop stubble. Removing the bottle from the deep pocket of his sheepskin, he held it up against the sunlight and grinned with pleasure when he noticed that the bottle and the vodka inside it had turned a rosy pink. Throwing back his head he poured out the vodka into his gaping mouth, not touching the bottle with his lips, and then he reared back to launch that bottle higher than the highest and most delicate hazy cloudlet in the depths of the heavens above. But then he thought better of it and restrained himself—"I'm already flat broke as it is!"—sticking the bottle back in his pocket he strode on, taking pleasure in his recollection of the beggar lady.

"Gracious, that was some wonderful old biddy!" he thought, glancing first at the sun, then at the peasant huts going gray beyond the distant bales. Not long since he was walking along through a fallow field. Looked up and saw a beggar woman lying on a heap of dried manure, moaning. He was already well lit up, and as usual when under the influence, his soul was avidly seeking some mighty feat; made no difference if it was a good deed or a bad . . . could be that something good, rather than bad, would do best.

"Grandma!" he yelled out, rapidly approaching the old lady. "Are you about to pass on, or what? Has somebody did you in, huh? What was it you done and who was it you done it to?"

Dressed in tatters, eyes closed, her pallid face caked in dried blood, the old lady stirred herself and let out a groan. "How come you're not talking to me?" barked out Zakhar sternly. "Being as I'm asting you something, how is it you don't answer? You mean you figure on just laying there like that? Pretty soon now they'll be driving livestock through here, and you'll have a ram butting you about, giving you all sorts of grief . . . Get up now, and I don't mean maybe!"

Glancing at him as he towered there huge and menacing, the old woman suddenly gave a squeal. "Nosir, please, don't you touch me. Even as is, I been tossed by a bull. Have a little sympathy for a poor unfortunate!"

"Ain't no way I can feel for you!" bellowed Zakhar with still more menace, suddenly feeling a surge of pity and tenderness for the old lady. "Get up, I told you!"

She raised herself a bit but fell right back down and squealed still louder. Then, overcome altogether by the pity, Zakhar snatched her up in his arms and tore off, almost at a run, for the village. Wrapping both arms around his oxen neck, suffocating in the vodka fumes he reeked of, the old woman was bounced and shaken about, while he was holding back his tears and rapidly muttering something, trying his best to soften his bass voice: "What is it with you then? Got a screw loose or something? What's there to be ascairt of? Hush, now, I'm telling you, hush up and don't think nothing about nobody! Forget about it all!"

"No sir, I can't take no more!" answered the old lady. "Ain't no happiness I can see for myself, alone on this earth I am. All my born years nary a thing to drink, not a sweet morsel to feed on."

"And I'm a-telling you, now, stop your whining!" said Zakhar. "We all got a tough row to hoe! Sorrow don't play no favorites! Hang on and never say die!" he barked out over all the fields, feeling a sudden burst of impetuous joy. "Eat straw but keep your tail feathers pert! And now I'm about to do you the honor of delivering you to where I make my humble home! As for that there bull, why you ought to be thrashed for that. What you doing roaming around, rambling here and there? How'd you get in amidst the herd? You belong to be associating with the other biddies. With them you can always have you a palaver. But take a bull now, a bull ain't about to lick your hand and call you dearie."

"Oh, stop," moaned the old woman, laughing now through her tears. "You done shook my soul a-loose from my body."

And Zakhar yelped out with still more menace, "Grandma, shut up! Or else I'll take you and chuck you right off in that ditch—you'll land so hard you'll never gather back up all the bones again!" Then, mouth wide open, he roared with laughter, rocking the old lady back and pretending he was about to heave her off the edge of the slope.

As he walked briskly into Livelong, glancing proudly at the lackluster-raspberry sphere that had not yet touched the horizon, his spine was wet, his face sweaty and dove blue from the rush of blood that suffused it, hammer beats from his heart were pounding in his head. It was deathly quiet. Not a soul about anywhere. A level, pale blue of evening sky over it all. There was a faraway thicket darkening at one end of a hollow. Above it hung the full moon, which was aglow now with radiance. A long bare green pasture and a row of shacks beside it. Three enormous, mirror-smooth ponds and, linking them, two broad, manure-based dams with bare, dry willows growing on them—white willows with thick boles and thin, withy-switch branches. On the other side another row of shacks. And how distinct all of this was in that brief interval between day and night: the contours of gray roofs, and the green of the pasture, and the steel slate of the ponds. One of them, to the left, gave off a rosy pink gleam; the others were two mirror-smooth chasms seemingly stamped with the image of the moon's reflection, with every tree bole, every twig.

"Mercy me, why don't you all just croak!" said Zakhar with a loud sigh, pausing there. "It's like the whole place is pushing up daisies!"

He felt like bawling out so frenetically that this entire petty little scrag of humanity, sequestered in its huts, would pour out in horror onto the common. "Oh no, no," he thought, shaking his head. "I'm crazier than a coot, I'm soused . . . It ain't decent what I'm thinking, it's wrong . . . I got to get on home right now . . . I'm going home."

Then suddenly he felt such a burst of hideous, deathly grief, blended with spite, that he could only close his eyes and stand there. Taking on the shade of a copper kettle, his face came unhinged from his light brown beard; his ears swelled up with the rush of blood. As soon as he closed his eyes thousands of malachite green and crimson circles started leaping up out of the darkness in front of him, he felt his heart sink, then the heartbeat broke off—and the whole of his body went swooning off softly into an abyss. Ah, got to get home now, into the threshing barn, lay down in the straw! But he stood there awhile longer, opened his eyes, and instead of turning off to the left, toward Aspen Grange, he strode out stubbornly onto the highroad, crossing the dam and making for the wine shop.

Oh, the grief that lay spread out there on that endless, desolate road, in those bleary plains beyond it, in that silent evening on the steppelands! But with all of his power Zakhar resisted the grief, kept talking incessantly, drank still more greedily to break the back of the grief and to get even with that lame-legged proprietor with the ginger red curls and the steady glare of his white eyes, he who had bustled about with such a vile sense of joy when Zakhar proposed a bet: could he, Zakhar, or could he not drink two more bottles of vodka? Smeared with whitewash, the wine shop had a strange, alabaster look in contrast to the wan azure of the eastern horizon, where that circle of a moon was ever more transparent and refulgent. Outside next to the shop there was a little table and a bench. In calico print blouse and calfskin boots worn down to a reddish color, the shopkeeper idled about next to the table, propping himself up on one leg and poking at the ground with the boot tip of the other. He had set out for display a hind shank of meat, and with extraordinary adroitness and speed, like a monkey, he was gnawing sunflower seeds, his eyes ever fixed on Zakhar. Meanwhile, chest raised, gritting his teeth, his huge fingers squeezing the edge of the table as if with ironclad pincers, licking his dried lips, his every word broken up by impetuous gasps, hardly aware of what he was saying and relentlessly receding into some black abyss, Zakhar hurried, rushed on to finish his story about how he had carried the old lady.

Then suddenly, with a sweeping movement of his whole torso, he arose, kicked at the table, sent it flying, along with the tinkling clatter of the bottle and the faceted glass, and said hoarsely, "Listen here! You!"

The shopkeeper had already opened his mouth to shout at Zakhar for this scandalous behavior, but when he looked up into the white and dove blue face, he was struck dumb. And mustering the last of his strength, holding off the bursting of his heart until he said these final words, Zakhar got them out.

"Listen. I'm dying. Job's done, it's knocking-off time. Don't want to get you in no hot water. I'll just leave . . . I'm going."

With that he walked away with firm strides to the middle of the highroad. When he got to the middle he bent his knees—then heavily, like a bull, he crashed down on his back, arms widespread.

That moonlit August night was a gruesome thing. From all directions peasant women and little urchins came silently running to the tavern; exchanging words in restrained and anxious tones, the muzhiks came up as well. In the most transparent of haze moonlight hung over the desiccate crop stubble. In the middle of the highroad an object enormous and awesome was gleaming white, all aglitter: someone had covered the dead body with a calico cloth. And barefoot women, briskly and silently walking up, crossed themselves and meekly placed copper coins at the head of that heap.

Capri, February 1912

»»» «««

Glory

Oh no, my dear sir, Russian glory is a slippery thing to grasp! Why, it's so steeped in guile that it's worthy of a whole research project. Right here we have, the way I look at it, one of the keys to all of Russian history. And then again, please excuse me, but you're still young and green about the gills. Better you listen to what I've already figured out. In my free time I've always got the spectacles on my nose, forty years now been lucubrating over the books, and then again, I've had my share of experience in life, why, on a number of matters I could compete with Klyuchevsky himself. So don't go to looking at me askance, figuring you've got a second-rate antiquarian bookseller sitting here. Especially when it comes to these God's People you mentioned. Why, there you've hit upon the acme of my expertise. So now just allow me to present you a few examples from that rogues' gallery, and these are not legendary types from time out of mind. They're completely authentic folks, my contemporaries.

Take, for one, the Peasant Beard. He came from Voronezh. Spent years living in relative obscurity, then suddenly got a lucky break. One fine day a walnut ornamental box goes missing in the house of a certain colonel of the reserves. The police are sniffing all about, but soon they lose the scent and end up with beans for results. What's to be done? Well, they went rushing out to the jerkwater districts, look ing for soothsayers. And the low-class jerkwaters round about Voronezh, Orel, Kursk, or Tambov, why, they're swarming like maggots with soothsayers. So, anyway, they sashayed into one little cottage out there, and they came upon quite an assemblage. There's a couple dozen peasant wenches standing around, eyes streaming tears of tender emotion as they gaze upon this here sainted servitor of the Lord. And meantime, the sacrosanct one is having his tea. Over in the icon corner they've laid a table, on that table there's a samovar bubbling away, and there at the table sits a complacent muzhik, got a child's pink sash wrapped about his waist and a beard that takes up his whole chest. He peers bright-eyed from under his brows and sips away without surcease, and he's slurping that tea not from a cup, not from a glass, but right out of a slop basin. He drinks it all down, uses a sleeve to wipe the sweat off the bald spot on his head, licks his lips, and puts in another order in a whispering voice.

"Pour it on, and sweeten it up a little bit sweeter!"

He's got himself in such a sweat, you see, that even his voice is hoarse. And the wench up front, the most imposing and comely one, she falls all over herself hustling up to the table, fills the slop basin to overflowing, heaps in the sugar, then steps back again—stands there weeping, gazing at him cow eyed. Then he goes at it, puffing and blowing like a bull calf.

"Who is this man?" the gendarmes asked.

"One of God's People, Your Honor. He drinks tea and don't do nothing else."

"Who are you, anyway?"

He answered without a trace of constraint.

"Me? I'm the peasant named Beard. I love tea."

"Can you conjure up how a certain thing got stolen?"

He gulped down some tea and said in a rapid patter of words, "I do readings, old buddy, but only on a empty stomach. Come back tomorrow, long about morning time."

Next day they fetched him early in the morning, took him off to the colonel's place, and told him to commence with the soothsaying.

"Nosir," he says, "that won't work. It ain't the way my folks taught me. First thing you got to do is to pray. Pray now. Everybody pray."

So they all prayed: the district gendarme, the sergeant and all the other police, the colonel and his whole family, all six daughters. Even old grandma, they brought her in. But after the praying was done, it turned out that the Peasant Beard couldn't soothsay—didn't know how. They ushered him out the door, naturally, with a few pokes in the neck, but guess what? From that day on the glory of the Beard began growing by leaps and bounds. Hordes of people started following after him, showering him with money, with goodies of all sorts. The richest of the merchants made bows to the ground in front of him, bickering one with another for the right to invite him over. And he graciously accepted the invitations, sat there as guest of honor, and drank himself bonkers on tea. He drank away and issued orders: "Pour it on, and sweeten it up sweeter this time!"

You don't believe me? You think it's impossible that for twenty years they worshiped him like a holy icon, simply for the way the man could emasculate a ten-quart samovar? You say, "Well, okay, he might could have drunk tea, but, nevertheless, there must be more to it than that. He quite likely distinguished himself in some other way, at least once in a while. Well, maybe, for example, he'd come up with a divinely inspired lie, or at least have the decency to play the fool." But no, nothing of the sort! He just kept drinking tea and scarfed up the glory!

But let's proceed a bit further now. Next we have a certain Fedya; he also hailed from Voronezh. Went by a somewhat unfragrant nickname: Fedya the Swill Man. But, once again, he earned himself a glory that was monumental. Had a nice cottage in the jerkwaters, two grown children, a son and a daughter; they ran a little shop with the utmost of business efficiency. Meanwhile, for all of fifteen years, their papa's out wandering the streets. Dark face with no beard, unblinking dark eyes—and never says a word. That is, to be precise, he just sings. You stop him, ask him something, and he comes hulking right up, stares you out of your noggin, and all the while he's bawling out something from the Holy Scriptures. Got a voice that's just hideous. And he's hideous himself: greasy hair, barefoot, dressed, of course, in tatters. He wears an iron pot holder on his head with its legs in the air—his royal crown. His primary occupation is scavenging in offal. No sooner do the bells peal for vesper services then he's off for the edge of town, and he pokes about with his stick until dark, in the ravines where the swill workers have poured out the city's refuse overnight. He roots and roots around till he's dead on his ass—then heads on home to sleep. And what else? Well, once again, nothing else! You ask, then how come they shower him with money, pastry buns, hand him all sorts of treats? How come they grab his hands and kiss them, and not only his hands, but also that foul-smelling stick of his? Wellsir, I don't know, I don't know! Try philosophizing over it yourself—we've got a matter here that could bear some philosophizing.

Next off we might wish to recall Kiryusha of Borisoglebsk, Kiryusha of Tula, or Xenofont the Accursed . . . The first Kiryusha was a muzhik who came from the big trading village near the city of Borisoglebsk. Had a fresh-faced look on his ruddy mug. One fine day he sprinkled some shredded rags on his head, took off his shoes, donned a woman's skirt, picked up some scrap-iron fragments, and from thenceforth he made a name for himself in the city. He chose a big holiday, Trinity Sunday, and he headed straight for the cathedral, to evening mass. And there, of course, up in the most prestigious spots at the very front, stood the cream of the city, all the different ranks in their parade uniforms. It was hot, stifling, there's this unimaginable crush of people, the sun is blazing right down from out of the cupola, and the birch-tree foliage on the floor and along the walls lies there wilting, wafting a suffocating stench like a dead body. Then suddenly the terrible bellow of a cow resounds throughout the church. Carrying on with his mooing sounds, Kiryusha pushes through the crowd and makes straight for the pulpit. Naturally, the gendarmes soon have him snatched up by the scruff of the neck and are seeing him back out the door, but the deed is already done. The whole cathedral, and then the whole of the city is astonished, in a state of alarm. And that cow act he put on for Trinity, well, Kiryusha kept it up for three whole years. He went around for three years speechless, just mooing. He mooed, he blew on a ram's horn of Jericho, and he prophesied through making various gestures. If he stuck a finger into his fist—that meant a wedding. If he put together his teensy hands to form a cross—that meant a death. Then one day, in the fourth year of all these shenanigans, he counted his takings, saw that his capital added up to a nice round figure, and off he scooted for home. There he built himself a little cottage, laid out a front garden with hollyhock bushes, and, well, so on and more of the same, etcetera. Just your run-of-the-mill swindler? Goes without saying. But what about the glory? Did he garner any glory? You bet he did, just as the other two I've lumped in together with him, that is, the Kiryusha from Tula and the fellow named Xenofont. This Tula Kiryusha was small of stature and quite a handsome fellow. He was well versed in the Holy Writ and a sweet-voiced singer to boot. On his chest, over his gray waisted coat, hung a little pouch, and what it contained, well, "mortal man best not peek in there, my dear sisters and widow women and goodwives!" Xenofont now, well for some reason, he called himself the Accursed. A young lad he was, pockmarked, long-limbed, decked out as a novice in a monastery. And the aggregate of his holy foolery consisted only of shambling about the city and drinking tea with burghers' and merchants' wives, invariably flavoring that tea with the oil used to light lamps. Once again you'll ask, wasn't he just a plain-and-simple flimflam man? And once again I'll concur: you're absolutely right. One has a mysterious pouch hanging down on his chest, the other drinks lamp oil—and nothing more than that. Wherein, then, lies their secret? Could it consist only of the pouch and the oil?

Proceeding further, from the portrait gallery of suchlike types I'll show you a couple more, who, at first glance, also appear to be exceedingly ordinary figures: Feodosy of Khamovniki and Petrusha of Ustyug. Feodosy was another one who got fed up with being an everyday yard porter, so he too took off his shoes one fine day, invested himself with penitential chains (that is, he simply wrapped a dog's chain around his body), hired on as his apprentice a certain bum named Petrusha, and set off a-prophesying. Once more you're thinking, "Well then, all the same, he must have had at least some talent for that?" But once again I must disenchant you: not even a trace of talent! His prophesying was egregiously uninspired, and what's more, he had a look about him that was far from prophetic: an ordinary, bald-headed muzhik round about forty years old, with the most merry and impudent of eyes. Petrusha was even more mundane. A base and sorry visage, the mind of a chicken, a disposition vile and lusty. He addressed all women and wenches as "pussy-willow bud," "tweety chiff-chaff," or "little canary bird," and his gluttony was something preternatural. He had a special weakness for milk noodles and watermelons. When he saw a melon he would shake all over and scream, "Temptation, temptation, enormous temptation!" Then he would wrap it in a bear hug, take it upon his knees, and dig in a paw, scraping it out to the very bottom. One more time you'll try to tell me that lowlife scoundrels don't count, and that, therefore, these two servitors of the Lord don't belong in the gallery. But, in the first place, the very point I'm making is how many scoundrels and degenerates there have been and continue to be among our celebrated folks. And, in the second place, I must remind you that my aim has never been to expose. I'm getting at something completely different, at how we Rooskies are inveterate fans of degenerates and scoundrels, and that's what makes us truly remarkable, the way we "go hankering, like some old village biddy, after false prophets." Now, there's a subject worthy of the utmost of attention.

Furthermore, by no means do I acknowledge that, for example, Feodosy and Petrusha are nothing but scoundrels. Nosiree, in certain respects these are remarkable people. You just imagine for yourself all the most carefree slipshodiness, the most shameless ease with which that same Feodosy roamed his away across the land, amidst his fellow Rooskies, whom he considered down to the last man, ever and eternally, the most consummate of dunderheads, considered, of course, not with his mind, but, so to speak, with all of his natural essence. Now really, isn't that, in its own way, a kind of genius? And Petrusha has something of the genius in him as well. Just try to conceive, once again, of something extraordinary in amplitude: a walking insatiable belly, its zoological strivings directed exclusively toward one goal—toward a noodle, a watermelon, toward "little canary birds" and "sweetie pies." I would suggest that nowhere except amidst the Rooskies will you meet with such a quintessence of the primordial, the zoological. And believe you me, the rabble (unbeknownst, of course, to themselves) are in awe of precisely this terrible power of zoological integrity.

To that same species belongs the celebrated Ivan Stepanovich Likhachov. He was called Likhachov (Daredevil) because for years he worked as one of those reckless-driving cabmen. Once he was sitting parked with his cab in the Soboli district—you know of course what that was, a whole block of whorehouses—and he climbed down off his coach box and transformed himself into a wandering preceptor of the saintly life. Put on a cassock, a velvet skullcap—and set off to walking. He was no less prophetically bald than Feodosy and just as complacent. He spoke with the most vulgar of eloquence, delivered the most hackneyed of admonishments, meanwhile, of course, keeping an eagle eye out for how many five-kopeck pieces some tender-hearted sap is digging out of the handkerchief she just unwrapped. It's a subject that's also, in my opinion, of rare interest! Here, as you can see, we have a man who acquired, while sitting for donkers years on a coach box beside whorehouses, a remarkable view of the world, of life and humanity!

Next. Vanyusha Somersault. Why was he Somersault? Because he turned somersaults, ambulating, in large measure, in the shape of a wheel. Astounding! He could cover maybe five, ten versts that way. Then, add to this his countenance: he had the look of a wrinkled boy of forty, with sly little eyes and the loose-hanging hair of a woman; that hair, mind you, was clipped short, considering, of course, that you can't wheel-walk very comfortably with long hair. He was celebrated, by the way, for making a pilgrimage to Kiev with Matryona Makarevna herself, head Madonna of all the female holy freaks in Moscow. In fact, this was not a simple pilgrimage but one in many respects phenomenal. Just imagine, if you will, that this very Matryona Makarevna rounded up in Kiev, and took back with her to Moscow, a good hundred head of the most exemplary idiot women and blockhead men, selected for the chaotic ugliness of their outward appearance and their inner nature! The hair on your head, my good sir, will stand up and twitch when you conjure in your mind the image of that horde of humanity: they're shambling along with all sorts of makeshift pikestaffs in their hands, bedizened in raiment befitting their dignity.

Well, with that pictorial representation allow me, for now, to conclude. I'd think that's enough for the first session. I'll give you just one last example: Danilushka of Kolomna. This character came from a family that was fanatically pious, rich, and austere. He was the only son of a dyed-in-the-wool schismatic, a literalist Bible reader and zealot, and he took up holy freakery in the early years of his adolescence. He let his hair grow long—take note of this amazing feature, the passion for feminine hair!—he took off his trousers, put on a woman's shift—once again, a woman's!—and after that he would get himself all slathered up over three and only three things: money, playing at knucklebones, and dancing at the sight of a dead man. He was extraordinarily handsome in a dark Eastern way, and so nearsighted that the only thing folks ever called him was the blind bitch. But his skill at knucklebones soon gained him glory all over the district, for he had no equal as a knucklebone player. He could be standing a good half verst away from the target, but he'd fling out that long arm of his, and on the first throw he'd slice away the whole setup beneath the rack. He played, he won, and he got rich. He had entire sacks full of knucklebones and dingers of such quality that for any one of them a good player, a connoisseur of the game, would willingly serve three years as a workhorse for the village priest.

He played, he accumulated property, sold it, traded, and then buried his profits somewhere underground. He also cached away what he earned for dancing at funerals over corpses. Now, there's a weird business for you. A wild great hulk of a man, a handsome morose fellow with blue-black hair down to his shoulders, wearing nothing but a shift and going barefooted summer and winter (even in the most bone-chilling frosts)—and he spends day after day either playing knucklebones or running off to funerals. He played as if he were any normal person, only his taciturnity and appearance distinguishing him from others, and whenever he heard there was a dead man in the suburban jerkwaters or in the city, well, off he goes at a trot to the church service. He would burst right in and begin his frenetic dance around the coffin; on and on he danced to the point of collapse. And that's not all! He even ran off to Moscow when he heard that Semyon Mitrich had died—I assume you're acquainted with the preeminence of that persona amidst the freaks of holy foolery? Well, anyway, he came to "dance him off into the Kingdom of the Lord," and, in exchange for his dance, to stuff his money purse tight with the contributions of the flabbergasted rabble. That purse was always hanging down over his chest, and you can just imagine how it clattered and rang with five-kopeck pieces while he performed his frenzied stompings and whirlings!

So, in conclusion—guess how he died? He was ripped asunder in a beastly fashion by his compatriots for setting fire to a church. A strange thing had been going on in the jerkwaters for some time: fires had been breaking out and no one could understand why. It turned out that this was the work of Danilushka, that he had come up with a passion for something new: arson. They found out because not a night went by without a fire, and always the first to arrive at the conflagration was Danilushka, doing his little dance. As he lay dying, he confessed, "I wanted to send off all of Kolomna like a flame in the wind and to dance it away into the heavenly kingdom."

June 27, 1924

»»» «««

Ioann the Weeper

There's a new railway station named Sinful; there's an old village on the steppes bearing the same name.

On summer days the Southeast Express makes a stop at that station. Everything about it, the station, is bare and dreary. The government-standard brick building is still too red. Instead of a platform there is sand. Crossing the sand to the station itself is no easy task, and what's the point anyway? The building is empty and desolate; it has, as yet, no buffet, no book stand. But the train is spectacular. Rich people on their way to the Caucasus sit gazing through the open windows of its massive, dust-laden cars: a celebrated, monstrously stout artiste in his little gray silk hat, a comely dark woman with a lorgnette, a Persian man from Baku gazing steadfastly at her with his sleepy eyes, a slim Englishman with a pipe in his teeth, silently, attentively surveying those vast expanses of plains, surpassed only by the prairies of North America . . . Taking a leisurely stroll along the boards beside the train, a wide-bodied old general with tiny feet puts on an absentminded look while secretly basking in the way the gendarme by the station doors stood to attention when he saw him, enjoying the thought that he, the general, is riding to take the waters on an expensive train, that he can stroll about without his hat, modestly, secure in the knowledge of his dignified, and in all respects proper, existence. Beside the restaurant car that wafts the smells of kitchen vapors, with its plate-glass windows displaying multicolored flowers on snow-white tablecloths, stand clean-shaven lackeys in frock coats with golden buttons, along with the sweaty cook and his kitchen boy—this scene appears identical to what the Englishman has observed in Egypt and on the French Riviera. And that huge American steam engine, all hot and glistening with oil, steel, and copper, shudders with the power that bubbles up inside it, impatiently restraining itself. The sleeve extending from the pump house is rumbling as it fills the deep tender. And now the water has run over the edges, they hastily ring the bell at the station doors, and the general, silver spurs jangling, hurries back to his coach.

The train disappears into the steppes. A peasant who came to the station for reasons known only to him had long been standing in the sand, thinking, "Now, when the machine gets on its way, well I'll just take on off my own self." The Englishman had fixed his eyes on that muzhik, marveling at his fur hat, his sheepskin coat, and the primordial thickness of his beard, which looked faded in the sun. The muzhik gazed at the Englishman as well, but in an absentminded way, for this train had nothing whatsoever to do with his village. He was not thirsty, but after the train disappeared he drank, nonetheless, two mugs of warm water from the barrel at the station; grunting in feigned satisfaction, he wiped his mouth with one hand and wandered off home. He ambled along at a leisurely pace. The time of day was indefinite, not exactly afternoon, not quite evening; at such a time there's nothing to do and no inclination to think. The weather too was indefinite—the sun had gone behind a cloud, and even in the sheepskin he didn't feel hot, although, of course, he could have done without it. The road from station to village ran through a common pasture, skirting the large manor house of a prince and the stone church opposite it, with its graveyard. When he drew even with the church the peasant took off his fur cap and crossed himself, making a low bow. For beyond the church enclosure, beside the sanctuary and next to the grave of that prince who had quarreled with the tsar himself, reposes the blessed Ioann the Weeper, holy fool in Christ.

All, of course, have long forgotten the antiquated estate of the prince. Its manor house is uninhabited; dark and wild is its garden. The graveyard is bare, hummocky. The stone church is painted a dark brown color. Its grounds encompass quite a few scattered, broad, cast-iron grave markers, and right beside the windows of the sanctuary two enormous brick sarcophagi jut out; they too are covered with cast-iron markers. Anyone unfamiliar with the legends of Sinful reads in great amazement the inscriptions on these plaques, telling of those who rest beneath them. One bears the name of the prince and grandee and the other that of his slave, the peasant from Zemlyansk: Ivan Emelyanov Riabinin. The words go like this: such and such a peasant, born and died in such and such years, and below that, IOANN THE WEEPER, HOLY FOOL FOR THE SAKE OF CHRIST OUR LORD. Only on the brink of his demise did the prince, the grandee, make his peace with God and his fellow man. In keeping with his wishes, that plaque over the princely grave has no ornamentation, nothing except a name and the initial words of a penitential psalm of David. The marker of the holy fool, on the other hand, a man who expressed no wishes whatsoever prior to his death, is adorned with poetry and with one of his most beloved lamentations. A HOLY FREAK, A SLUMMOCK HE WAS IN THE EYES OF THE WORLD, reads the line dedicated to his memory by some anonymous poet. And beneath that come the bitter and terrible words of the prophet Micah, the words on the fool's lips when he died: WEEP I WILL AND CRY, WALK I WILL LIKE ONE PLUNDERED, HOWL LIKE THE JACKALS AND WAIL LIKE THE OSTRICHES!

Those on their way to take the waters, riding the express train, know of the prince—from books. But in the village of Sinful his image is hazy. The village knows only that some hundred years ago he came to live out his days in backwater Sinful, that he was short of stature and eccentric, that the occasion of his arrival was marked by strange behavior. He was informed early in the morning on New Year's Day that a priest had arrived with the clergymen of the parish. "Show him into the parlor," said the prince—then forced him to wait for ages. Suddenly emerging from a side door, walking into that cold room with the high ceiling, unshaven, wearing Morocco boots and a dressing gown lined with rabbit fur, he asked the priest abruptly, "To what, my dear sir, do I owe the pleasure?" The priest lost his composure and answered timidly that he would like to hold a service. And the grandee is reported to have said to him with a sarcastic laugh, "So go right ahead, sir, and this time make it a funeral requiem."

"But may I make so bold as to ask your eminence: for whom?"

"For the old year, my dear sir, for the old year!" said the prince, and he set about dragging in the other clergymen, who dared not disobey him. On that same day he issued his first command—half a hundred blows with a birch rod were to be administered to Ivan, who had leapt out at him wailing and barking from a fir grove onto the swept arborway where the prince was taking his constitutional.

Those who travel through the station of Sinful on pilgrimages, to bow down before God's Holy Servitor of Voronezh, have never even heard of the servitor of God from Sinful. But in the village of Sinful itself, here is the story they tell of him. Vanya grew up, they say, in a decent, God-fearing family; his parents had been resettled by the prince to the outskirts of Zemlyansk City. From his earliest years he loved the Holy Writ. His mama pleaded, his father bowed and scraped: take a wife, my son! But he cried, sobbed, asked the Good Lord for a vision, made plans to go to the Athos monastery. With the vision come unto him a trial: heed thy father's words. He arose with the break of dawn, told his pa he would mind him. The wedding was held, the newlyweds were left alone together in the nuptial bedroom, but they didn't never even touch one another and came out, both of them, in tears. Ivan set down to work, as was his wont, at the reading of divers holy writings. The day was fine and frosty, snow had fell in the night, and now it was specked with tracks and footprints. Everybody went to church, the bride went along with her new kinfolks; only Vanya stayed home by hisself, not desirous of going even unto the church. He looked out the window and seen that the fellow who worked for the village priest was driving up to the window in a new sledge, pulled by a crow black steed—a dandy of a horse that was, belonged to the priest, grain fed. So this old boy walks up and knocks with the handle of his whip. "Vanya, your pa says come to the church and bring the new bark sandals and twenty kopecks in change." Vanya said, "But I don't know where Pa's money is." "Behind the icons," said the priest's boy. (In our parts it's always that way—every little note, every novena list, they stick all the odds and ends behind the holy paintings in the icon corner, and back in them times they had no qualms about stashing money there too.) Anyway, naught's to be done, Vanya got the cash, put on his cloth coat, went out and mounted a sleigh, drove off in a kneeling position. Off he goes through the village, whereupon he seen way up high on a mountain the Holy Temple of God, and he said, "Lord Jesus Christ."

And no sooner said than lookee there: he's setting out in the steppelands in a open field on the snow and frost, he's unbooted, coat off, but he's got them new birch-bark sandals on his feet, with his old, crappy pair hanging by a cord over his shoulder, and he's a-sobbing and carrying on. They heard tell of this in the village, got them up a cart to go fetch Vanya, fixing to take him off and face a town meeting, 'cause they figure he's some kind of tramp. But he's just a-wailing and sobbing, going at everybody like a he-dog on a chain and yelling out clear across that field, "I will, walk I will like one plundered, howl I will like the ore-striches!" Well, of course they were all over him, the whole kit and caboodle, they grabbed him, tied him up, and carted him off, but on the way back to the village they come upon his father. "I get home from church," he says, "my son ain't nowhere to be seen, and then what do I spy but a line of footprints running off behind the threshing floor and drying sheds. I head on out there," he says, "following the tracks in the snow, and lo and behold, them footprints are off of brand-new birch-bark sandals, and why, one print to the next, it measures over twenty foot!"

Thus ends the hagiography of the saint as told by the village of Sinful. But the only ones who faintly recall him are the old country wives, living out their long earthly sojourn at the dead estate of the prince. His whole life through, they say, Ivan rambled around behaving indecently. For quite a long time he was chained up in his father's hut, he gnawed at his hands, at the steel chain, he bit at anyone who got near him, screaming out repeatedly his favorite phrase: "Give me pleasure!" And he was beaten mercilessly, both for his frenzied ways and for that incomprehensible demand. Once he broke loose, disappeared, and later turned up doing weird things. He made the rounds of the hamlets, barking incessantly and baring his teeth, rushing up on landowners and others of high status, howling through his tears, "Give me pleasure!" He was scrawny and gangle-shanked, he went about in nothing but a long shift made of sackcloth and belted with a piece of rag; he carried mice in his shirt front, scrap iron in his hand, and be it summer or winter he never wore a fur cap or anything on his feet. Eyes bloodshot, foam on his lips and hair in a tangle, he chased after people and people ran from him, making the sign of the cross. He was afflicted with some disease, which covered all of his face in a white, quicklime crust that made his scarlet eyes still more hideous. He was in a particular frenzy when he came to Sinful, having heard of the prince's arrival.

The prince ordered them to take away his scrap iron, had him whipped in his presence—the stable grooms cried as they tied down the Weeper, who howled and bit at them. The prince said, "There you have it, Ivan, your pleasure. I could put you in shackles and let you rot away in prison, but I, my dear sir, bear no grudge. Rove about at will, prophesy, bellow, but see to it you hector me no more. And inasmuch as you fail to temper your furor, then I will steadfastly provide you with that very pleasure for which you scream when likening yourself unto an ore-strich." But since Ivan did not temper that furor, since almost on a weekly basis he frightened the prince in the cruelest fashion, leaping out at him from behind corners and flinging his mice at him, then nearly every week they dragged the fiercely bellowing Weeper off to the stables.

In the old village of Sinful the past is soon forgotten, what was is soon transformed into legend. They have honored the memory of Ivan the Weeper for so long only because he stood up to the prince himself, and because the prince astonished everyone with his deathbed injunction. When, sick and wasting away, he was informed of the demise of Ivan, who had died out in the fields on a rainy autumnal day, he said resolutely, "Inter that bedlamite beside the church, and me, the grandee-prince, lay me next to him, side by side with my vassal." So Ivan Riabinin became Ioann the Weeper, and the image of him in the village of Sinful is the same as that painted on the walls of the church—half naked and savage, like a saint or prophet.

Every autumn a spare, homely woman in mourning attire arrives at the railway station of Sinful; with a handsome spindle-legged cornet on her arm she debarks from the express train and sets off for the church, accompanied by the stationmaster. By the enclosure of the church they are greeted, with bows, by a portly priest in a black chasuble and a lay reader with a censer. Low storm clouds stretch over the fields, a damp wind is blowing, but the priest and the reader stand with heads bared. Entering the church grounds, the cornet removes his hat too, as does the stationmaster, who brings up the rear of the procession and whose calm demeanor suggests that he has come along only for the sake of politeness. He stands with the same polite and placid mien behind them all as the redolent incense smoke begins diffusing through the air, spreading over the terrible brick sarcophagi, and the priest circles around them, censing and bowing, proclaiming "eternal memory" for the prince and his slave. The cornet prays distractedly. Young as he is, impeccably dressed, he places one leg so that the sharp knee juts out, crosses himself with tiny cruciform gestures, and inclines his small head with a deference not quite brought off, in a bowing style used by those who seldom think of saints but who press perfunctory lips to their images because, all the same, they worry about spoiling their own happy lives through some saint's disfavor. But the lady is crying. She has raised her veil in advance, as she gets down on her knees at the grave of Ivan Riabinin—because she knows that the tears will well up in her eyes momentarily. "A holy freak, a slummock he was in the eyes of the world," she reads from the gravestone plaque. These words touch her. And the terrible words of the prophet Micah, the mention of the jackal and the ostrich, suffuse her with trepidation and anguish. And down on her knees she sheds sweet tears, one hand, gloved, leaning on a thin umbrella handle, and the other—sky blue, diaphanous, with rings—pressing to her eyes a cambric handkerchief.

Capri, February 18, 1913

»»» «««

I'm Saying Nothing

In those days young Alexander Romanov, whom everyone called Shasha, lived with his father in the village, in a house with an iron roof, and his father, Roman, used to beat him.

Roman fancied himself top dog in the neighborhood; he would even proffer his hand to the gentlemen landowners when they met. He ran a shop in the village and a mill on its outskirts, and he was making big money buying up the squires' wooded lots and selling the trees for timber. Makar, his brother, had nothing to eat. Shambling in rags around the common pasture of the village, he would warble meekly, removing his hat, "Greetings, brother!" And well-fed Roman, who had the look of a church deacon, would answer from his porch, "Don't you come sniffing up, lunkhead, saying, 'Brother this, brother that!' Bow down first and then head on off to where you was headed, and don't be talking no small talk at me." So how was Shasha, the lone scion of such a man, to feel? He went promenading about the village in a long, tight-waisted coat made of broadcloth, in boots with tops that glistened, improvising polka tunes on an expensive mouth harp. Girls and young men who met him would cast looks of admiration upon his meanderings; it was enough to make chills run down the spine of a celebrity. But Shasha would respond to those looks with a morose, even truculent glare. He seemed to have spent all of his youth preparing for the role he would play later on to such perfection.

At the peak of his prosperity Roman began declining, muddling up his business affairs. Bearded and grizzled, long in the paunch, wearing a coat of smooth cassinette that looked like a priest's cassock, he would liven up only in his cups; when sober he was sullen and deliberately rude. But he maintained, nonetheless, his fame and his power. Out on the common, beside the church opposite his windows he had a school built, became its patron, and periodically he made the teacher get down and grovel at his feet. He could still treat a guest to sprats, or to sour-tasting lobster in a rusted tin along with that sparkling wine from the Don region called Tsimliansk, and while he was treating he would scream in his ruffian's way, "Drink up, nincompoop!" But it was time, the time was ripe to replace him. Who would do it? There was no replacement. Shasha was delving ever more deeply into his act, playing the role of one grievously offended, and the only contact between him and Roman consisted of his father's dragging him around by the "pompadour." Shasha, so he said, could make an angel cuss a blue streak; you just couldn't resist dragging him around. So he grabbed him by the hair and dragged, and the more he dragged, the more intolerable Shasha became.

Who was he to take no pride in the household, in the might and the swaggering mien of his father? In front of guests Roman would shout at him, "Why can't you loosen up a little bit, you lunkhead!" That was just the way the merchants behaved, those whom his father emulated, and what should make you prouder than that—to feel like a son of the merchant class? Sometimes Roman would even brag on him, smugly declaring to a guest, "Hold on, I want to show you my boy!" Then his bellowing roar would envelop the house. "Shasha, get in here! Mikolai Mikhailich wants to take a gander at you!" But mercy, what an entrance Shasha would make into that room where his father sat with a guest! Face blushing scarlet, peering up from under scowling and grimacing brows, holding his arms twisted in stiff knots like pretzels, he came tripping in with stiff-legged little steps, pigeon-toed, so prissified that he might have been dancing the fifth figure of the quadrille. Scraping a foot in front of the guest, he quickly skipped away to the window or the lintel, puffing out his nostrils, gnawing at the hangnails on his fingers, responding to questions with an absurd brevity and curtness. How could you not beat him? The guest would leave. After seeing him off, Roman would walk up to Shasha without a word; then, swinging back his arm in a broad, sweeping gesture, he would clutch him firmly by the hair. In silence Shasha pulled his head from the grip of that clenched paw, and hopping out into the anteroom, he pounded his chest with one fist.

"All right then, Pa! I'm saying nothing! Always nothing!" he hissed menacingly.

"You little she-ninny, you little bitch!" howled Roman. "It's just for that not saying nothing and that pussyfooting around is what I'm whipping you for! You're asking for it your own self! Why? How come?"

"When I'm dead in the grave my remains will know all!" answered Shasha enigmatically, in his most ferocious voice.

As if he weren't born with a silver spoon in his mouth! He always had money to burn, he dressed like a dandy. At the evening parties he chased after the priest's flirtatious daughters and those of the district gendarme, dancing with them to the music of a hurdy-gurdy. But he payed court to them in a snide sort of way, with abrupt flashes of rudeness. And that's not all. Even when he was face-to-face with himself, gazing in the mirror and teasing up the red-black fleece on his head with a steel comb, he would put on a vitriolic squint. His nose was mashed flat, his voice hoarse, he had the look of a convict at hard labor, and the peasants nicknamed him Hangman. Not much of an honorific, you'd think! But no, he took pleasure in that name too.

"Polecat in a woodpile!" said the peasants. "He don't like nothing, don't nothing go the way he wants!" And he did all in his power to justify the things they called him. "Who is that there? Is that polecat Shasha?" asked Roman in disgust. "Well, them kind of polecats is worthless as a cobble on a bridge! He's a fool, a play-actor, born nocount shiftless and nothing more. How come he's squinching his face up? What the hell else does he need?"

Shasha glared at him with a venomous sneer and kept his silence. "Look at him, lookee there!" said Roman. "Look at what he's making out of hisself!" But Shasha screwed up his brows still more; he had convinced himself now that something horrendous was frothing up inside him. "Oho, Pa!" he hissed, as if unable to restrain himself. "Oh, I could just tell you a certain thing or two!" Lowering Roman, with those flaccid bags beneath his eyes, put on a harrowed grin. "So what is that thing or two? Huh? Come on now, say it!"

"You talking to *me* then?"

"I'm talking to *you* then!"

"When I'm dead in the grave my remains will know all!"

"Well, what will your grave know then? Are you drunk, you good-for-nothing?"

"Yeah, drunk!" answered Shasha. "Drunk! I'm saying nothing! Nothing!" Then, on the verge of tears, Roman reared up again bearlike, seized him once more by the head of his hair, and dragged him around in an ecstasy of suffering.

He made a splendid marriage as well—to the daughter of the steward who ran the estate of a local nobleman, a good-looking, freckled girl with an easy laugh. It was an amazing ceremony. Since the landlords lived abroad, Shasha rode to the church in the squire's carriage, and in awe of that carriage, the priest went to such extremes of congratulation on the occasion of his holy matrimony that Shasha thought he was being mocked. The wedding banquet was held in the manor house too. Wine flowed in rivers, and accompanied by enraptured shouts, Roman pranced out onto the dance floor and stomped the parquet, shaking mirrors and chandeliers. One of the squire's footmen did an outstanding imitation of a locomotive. He blew the hollow sound of the whistle into his fingers, then began tapping out the slow and cumbersome rumble of the accelerating train, ending his performance with his legs in a frenzied gallop. The church sexton drank himself silly on cognac, then dropped dead on the way home. Collapsing into a manure pile in his own yard, the deacon was nearly trampled by sheep. A miserable autumn dawn cast its pale blue light from out of the fog into the smoky reception halls of the manor house, where the lights still burned, where the hoarse voice of the hurdy-gurdy was still gasping out the strains of the dance *lezginka* or the *vyushki,* where those in charge of the ball, the bridegroom's attendants, soaked wet in the heat and the fuss, were still shouting and the young ladies were danced out, their eyes glazed over with fatigue. But Shasha could not spare even his own festivities. Pretending to be drunk, convinced he was in a fit of jealousy over his young wife and a certain youngish landlord, he suddenly stepped on the train of her dress as she waltzed, and it ripped away with a loud tearing sound. Then he rushed to grab a knife, tried to cut his own throat, and when they disarmed him he burst into ranting sobs and tore off his white cravat, summoning up the memory of his dead mother.

As these things always go, having ascended to the heights, Roman would, inevitably, tumble all the way back down again, back to the poor peasant hovel where he had begun. Soon after the wedding it turned out that he was entangled, hand and foot, in snares of debt. Now he was a fright to look at. His bluish gray beard had gone totally white. His face resembled the dirty gray, milked-dry udder of a cow. His eyes took on a deadened glaze, his slack belly hung down flaccidly. And Shasha rejoiced ("I told you so, I told you!") and set about maliciously finishing him off. He raged around, scandalized, demanding a division of property. Green with malice, ursine Roman advanced upon him, aching to maim him. But it was too late; he didn't have the strength anymore! Brought down by the realization of his impending dishonor and poverty, he drank himself into oblivion. Abandoning all shame, he moved his lover, a cook who was the wife of a soldier, into the house. To spite his father Shasha slept with her too. Meanwhile, he wore down his wife with his jealousy and fears. He would disappear from home and send her notes with the peasants: "Farewell for all time, my blessing on the children." At the bottom there would be a drawing of a grave with a cross. In the upshot of it all, Roman was felled by a stroke, and nothing was left of his wealth but the windmill on the outskirts of the village. Shasha's wife took the children with her and ran off to one of her lovers.

Impoverished, on his last legs, Roman moved from the village out to the mill. Grinding his teeth with rage, wifeless and impoverished as well, Shasha followed after him. The mill could have provided a good living, but what did Shasha care about that? Misunderstood as always, unappreciated and fated to live among enemies, those who wished him ill, he had only one recourse: to say nothing, nothing! But now? He could have made thousands just on the mill; put two, three hundred rubles into a new stanchion and new millstones and you'd have carts of grain clogging up the road coming and going. But where would he get the money? Only to idiots does good fortune crawl up out of the blue, while fate takes a sharp and clever fellow and rends him limb from limb!

Nowadays Roman's table was set, in lieu of sprats and Tsimliansk wine, with a hunk of bread and a grain ladle for water, but that was not his problem—he would have eaten anything with the same relish. His problem lay in the agony of injured pride, the most fierce of human agonies. Now he slept on a cold stove, in a large lopsided hut with an earthen floor and holes in the corners. In the mornings he trundled over the threshold with a long walking stick in his hand. Goosefoot and tall weeds had overgrown the outside of the hut, nettles were encroaching upon the enormous frame of the roofless windmill. All of this was built upon a bare hump in the fields, next to a passing road. And Roman ambled out to that road and stood with his trembling cold paws gripping his stick. He wore no hat, the wind blew about his gray, matted hair and his gray beard—the beard of a peasant Job. He went barefoot, in his workaday britches, in a long shift that was dirty with garbage and ashes from the stove. His legs were thin, his torso long and slack. People drove by, those who had known him in his glory and wealth, those who used to tremble in his presence, the very ones he had treated to meals and lorded it over. And Roman—not for nothing was he Shasha's progenitor!—took pleasure in presenting to them his squalor and shame, and he even bowed low to the earth before them. Meanwhile, Shasha frequented pot houses and dives, reveling in his abasement, drinking away what little was left from the past and collecting bruises from peasant fists for his sharp tongue. Especially horrendous were the torments he earned every year on July 15.

By the time that business began Roman already had croaked—ah, what malicious pride Shasha took in his death! The soldier-husband of the cook returned from his army service. He needed her like he needed last year's snow. Nonetheless, when he learned she had been the lover of Roman and Shasha he felt duty bound to avenge his sullied honor. Wisely he timed his vengeance for a day when the village was crowded with people.

Every year on July 15, during the patron saints' festival known as Kiriki, they hold a fair in the village. The cold rain streams down, and there is little to suggest it is summer: just the jackdaws in the openlands, the denseness of the grain and grasses, and the skylarks trilling their songs in the rain as the wind blows them slantwise across the fields. Meanwhile, on the village common, a nomadic tent hamlet is being assembled. Tradesmen have come from the town, and the villagers find it unusual and strange to see these city folks in their long-skirted frock coats. Setting things up, crowding the common, they have transformed the simple rustic scenery with their firmly built, canvas-covered carts full of goods neatly packed. Along with the merchandise they have brought in the smell of a bazaar—samovars are steaming and smoke is wafting from grills where mutton fries. Already they stand, early on the morning of the fifteenth, behind the counters piled with peppermint-flavored pastries, shoehorns, haberdashery, and the peasants with their women and urchins keep driving up in the light rain, drawn in from all directions to this tent city. Their wagons clutter the common in such dense throngs that there's no room left for a pin to drop, and over all this glut of bodies, this din of voices, over the hubbub and screech of carts the holiday clangings of church bells announce the mass.

Enveloped in those peals, in plain view of folks who drive down the muddy byway past the windmill, Shasha stands beside his threshold, devil-may-care in demeanor, stooped, holding in one hand a grain ladle with water and with his other, wet hand rubbing his bearded, pockmarked face, still puffy from sleep. How changed is this stumpy peasant in down-at-the-heels boots from the former Shasha! He has a calmer look about him, but he's even more morose than before. His hair, just as terribly thick, has taken on a peasant-style shagginess. After washing his hands and face he tears at that mane with a wooden sheep's hatchel, combs his tangled, round-shaped beard, clears his throat with a hoarse, hacking sound, and squints sideways into the mirror—at his broad spongy face with its flat nose. He has not forgotten that he looks like a hangman. And it's true, he really does, even more so now. Done with his grooming, he puts on the faded red calico shirt that he keeps for festive occasions. On ordinary days he is numb with boredom, with sleeping too long, with the realization that no one pays attention or listens to him; they're fed up to the gills with his boasting about how rich he once was, his hints of the secrets he harbors in his soul, his vile, cock-and-bull stories about the wife who ran off. But today is a holiday, today he will perform in front of a huge mob; today he will be horribly beaten, knocked senseless while that mob looks on. So now he has begun getting into his role; he is wrought up, his jaws tightly clenched, his brow contorted. After dressing himself he puts on a carrot orange cap with a visor and sets off firmly, resolutely, walking his stiff-legged walk, for the village.

The strangest thing of all is the pious manner he adopts to begin that day. He makes straight for the church, and looking at no one but feeling deep in his soul the eyes of everyone upon him, he bows and crosses himself with broad, sweeping gestures. Inside the church he pushes his way straight through to the pulpit, where he once had the right to stand, and at that moment his contempt for the peasants seeps down to the very marrow of his bones. In stern, abrupt terms he reminds them, as one who has the power, that it wouldn't be a bad idea to make way. And the peasants hastily move aside. Lowering up like a bull from beneath his brows at the officiants, at the icons, to the very end of mass he prays austerely and fervently, arrogantly showing them all that he alone knows exactly when to bow and make the sign of the cross.

Just as austerely he strolls around the fairgrounds after mass, proud that he has already had a bit to drink, that like an equal he can approach a tradesman beneath his canopy, can greet him with a handshake, lean on the counter, take a bunch of sunflower seeds to gnaw on. He can get in that tradesman's way, blather on about the city, about how business is going, can, a time or two, raise his voice at the wenches who rush up to the counter in herds like sheep, crushing one another, at the peasant with a sack under his arm—in that sack a suckling pig fidgets about. This proprietor of the pig has tried out every last penny tin whistle, every last harmonica, and just can't make up his mind which one to buy.

Flowing out of the church, the congregation has now flooded the whole common, the bell towers are pealing, the beggars are bawling out in nasal voices, the livestock and fowl brought in for sale at the Kiriki festivities are mewling and cackling. Amidst the dense mob, spitting out sunflower husks and slipping in the mud between the tents, a multitude of drunks materializes. Shasha has managed a few more drinks himself, and now he feels that his time has come! Having exhausted his palaver with the tradesmen, he sets off with resolute strides toward the carousel. A boundless mass of humanity is teeming there, gaping till its noggin spins at the round and round of flashing wooden steeds and their riders. Nearly the whole village is there, and a head taller than anyone stands the soldier-husband. Shasha's hands turn cold, his lips are quivering, but he acts like he doesn't notice his enemy. He walks up to acquaintances, talks loudly and snorts with laughter, while waiting, on his guard. And then the soldier, in a new visored cap with the white price tag still stuck on, newly shaven and well fed, with sleepy blue eyes, comes staggering up pretending to be soused. He walks straight toward Shasha with a full head of steam, as if he can't see anything there, and he strikes him with a shoulder in the chest. Gritting his teeth, Shasha moves aside and resumes his conversation. But the soldier comes back, walks past again, and slams his shoulder one more time into Shasha's chest! Then, as if losing patience at such insolence, enraptured Shasha squinches up his face, which is already hideously contorted, and mutters through his teeth, "Oho, fellow! As if I hadn't found a way to poke you too!"

Immediately reining in his bent body, the mad rush of its forward progress, the soldier comes staggering back and bellows out like one possessed, "Wh-what?"

Then, amidst the festive hubbub, the clatter and the tinkling bells of the madly whirling carousel, amidst pretend compassion in the ecstatic cries, the oohs and aahs of the mob making way for the combatants, the soldier stuns and bloodies Shasha with the very first blow. Trying to use an old peasant technique, to get his fingers into the mouth and tear away at the lips, Shasha charges him like a wild animal, then falls slam-bang into the mud, out cold beneath the steel-tapped boot heels, which render horrible kicks to the chest and shaggy head, to the nose, the eyes, already glazed over like those of a slaughtered ram. The people making the aahing sounds are struck with wonder: what kind of dim-witted, stubborn so-and-so is this? After all, he knew in advance how it would turn out! Why would he walk right into it? A good question. Why did he? And then again, what was the point of going steadfastly and doggedly about, day after day laying waste to his ravaged homestead, striving to eradicate every trace of what Roman's wild genius had created so adventitiously, craving incessantly the insults and the shame, the beatings?

During mass, in the path to the parvis of the church, by the enclosure the gruesome people stand in two rows. Holy Rus, thirsting for self-abnegation, despising all restraint and labor, all things mundane, with a passion for any and all masks—the masks of tragedy and those of grotesque foolery—from time out of mind and without number has Rus engendered such folk. What faces, what heads stand here! Like those on the Kiev church frescoes and on the Kievan cheap folk woodcuts, depicting devils but Christian zealots too—the legendary desert fathers! There are ancient patriarchs with such desiccated heads, such sparse strands of long gray hair, such narrow lines for noses and deeply sunken chinks to hold their unseeing eyes, as if for centuries these patriarchs had lain in the cave tombs where they were immured back in the days of the Kievan princes, caves from which they have now emerged in half-rotten tatters, placed their beggars' sacks (crossed one over the other) upon what is left of their bodies, hung them over their shoulders on bits and pieces of straps, and set off to tramp the aggregate of Holy Rus, through all her forests, prairies, and the winds of her steppes. There are blind men with huge snouts, strapping peasants built close to the ground, resembling shackled prisoners who have callously murdered dozens of souls. They have heads that are solid-block square, their faces look to have been hacked out with an ax, and their bare legs, covered in dove blue blood, are preternaturally short, just as their arms. There are retards, fat about the shoulders and fat in the legs. There are hunchbacks whose heads are wedge-shaped, as if they were wearing sharply pointed fur hats made of black horsehair. There are dwarfs, perched on their bowed legs like dachshunds. There are foreheads pinched in from the sides to form a skull in the shape of an acorn cap. There are bony old ladies completely noseless, the spitting image of Death herself . . . And all of this, flaunting its show of ragamuffery, its wounds and its boils, sits wailing Old Church Slavonic descants, in crude bass voices and castrati altos, in lubricious tenor tones, singing about purulent Lazarus, about Alexis, Man of God, who, in his thirst for beggary and martyrdom, left the paternal abode and went out "knowing not whither he was bound."

Screwing up brows over dark orbs of eyes, intuitively, with a refined, acute instinct like that of some primordial creatures, these people can sense in an instant, can anticipate the approach of a hand that gives alms. They have already scarfed up a good many bread crusts, ring-shaped rolls and peasants' copper coins stained green with cheap tobacco. After the mass, their singing now more vibrant and importunate, they flow out amidst the sea of country folk to the fair. Following them come the cripples—legless, creeping along on their bottoms or on hands and knees, or lying on their procrustean beds, the pushcarts. Here's one of those carts. It contains a tiny homunculus with calm, milk blue eyes, some forty years of age and wrapped about the ears in a peasant wench's kerchief, thrusting out from beneath his rags a slender violet little hand with six fingers. A lively-eyed boy with sharply pointed ears and fox-fur fluff on his head is wheeling him along. And here comes a peasant with a broad white face, his body all smashed and mutilated, missing a backside altogether, wearing one mildewed bast sandal. He too has been obviously beaten somewhere—as severely as Shasha—for all of his kerchief, his ear, neck, and shoulder are caked in dried blood. In his long sack he has pieces of raw meat, roasted ribs of mutton, bread crusts, millet. A piece of leather is sewn to the underside of his pushcart seat. Now he has bent and twisted himself, fidgeted around, and then set off crawling, scraping his bottom through the mud, kicking out ahead of him the unshod leg, which is bare to the knee and specked with lime-colored scabs, oozing pus and pasted over with bits of burdock.

"Take a gander, Orthodox Christians, lookee over here at this: according to legends of yore, this is the illness called leprosy!" screams out in a merry brisk recitative the pockmarked tatterdemalion who walks beside him, his impresario.

Now these are the people whom Shasha has joined. He lived another three or four years at the mill; he celebrated three or four more fairs; he did battle another three-four times with the soldier. Kind people would bring a jug with a wooden lid and pour water over him, the unbreathing, speechless Shasha. He would slowly recover his senses; not opening his eyes all the way he would drag his wet head along the ground, grievously moaning through clenched teeth, "All right, then, good people! Always nothing! I'm saying nothing!"

After that they carried him back to the mill; he lay two weeks on the stove, gradually getting better, and soon there he was again, making the rounds of the pot houses, bragging, lying, defaming everything and everyone, beating his chest with a fist and threatening all of his foes, in particular the soldier. But then one year an unfortunate Kiriki festival rolled around. The soldier fractured his arm with a boot heel, splintered the bridge of his nose, kicked out his eyes. Now Shasha is blind and crippled. The soldier's wife has left him, kind people have taken the mill and the land for debts. And Shasha has found quiescence; now, bone for bone, flesh for flesh, he's a full-fledged member of the beggarly horde that stands on Kiriki Day by the church enclosure. Wearing tatters, barefoot, thickly bearded, his hair cut butch-style, with straps of sacks hanging over his shoulders in the form of a cross, he screws his brow into a wild grimace above the kicked-out eyes with sockets skinned over, and he huskily bawls, along with the others, the ancient, heartrending religious songs of the mendicants. Each singer making what contribution he can, the choir somberly bleats away. The resonant voices of the leaders, screaming every syllable, stand out:

> "Three sisters once lived, three Marys of Egypt they were,
> They divvied their riches three ways:
> One share they gave to the unseeing body,
> Another they gave unto prisons and dungeons,
> The third share they gave to the churches and temples.
> Adorn not thy body with fine raiment,
> Adorn thee thy soul with sedulous alms giving.
> These thy alms will stand high in the eyes of Heaven,
> Like a candle before the Holy Icons of God!"

Then the harsh voice of Shasha breaks through and sounds forth:

"That time will come,
When the earth, the heavens will shake,
When all of the stones tumble down,
When thrones of kings crumble,
When sun and moon dim,
And the Lord will unleash a river of fire!"

Merging, blending, attaining an ominous power and solemnity, the whole choir bellows in stentorian strains:

"The Archangel Michael
All earthly creatures will hector,
Will blow out the tidings on his horn,
Announce it unto all mankind:
Ye have lived your lives
By your own willful wills,
Went not to the church,
Slept through the matins,
Ate in the time of late vespers;
Here is the paradise that awaits you:
Hell Fires ever burning, unquenchable,
Torments ever aching, unendurable!"

September 14, 1913

»»» «««

Noosiform Ears

Many recalled crossing his path on that dark and cold day, an unusually tall man who was hanging about near the Nikolaev Station and at various points along Nevsky Prospect, a man who called himself the former seaman Adam Sokolovich. With an air of elusive gravity he stood on the sidewalk by Ligovka gazing at the statue of Alexander III, at a chain of streetcars that formed a circle around the square, at the shadowy figures of passersby, at cabdrivers and draymen moving toward the station, at a huge mail car emerging from under the station arch, at a hearse, which bore away amidst all this bustle a squalid, bright yellow coffin unaccompanied by mourners. He stood on the Anichkov Bridge, staring gloomily at the dark water, at barges gray with dirty snow; he rambled along Nevsky, carefully scrutinizing goods in the store windows. Not to notice and not to remember Sokolovich was impossible, and those who encountered him experienced a feeling of vague unpleasantness, a kind of malaise, and turned away thinking, "What a horrible man!"

His clothing—boots, tight trousers, heavy woolen overcoat spattered in back with mud, British leather cap—appeared to have been worn indefinitely, continuously, in all kinds of weather. Unusually tall, thin and ungainly, with long legs and big feet, his face freshly shaven except for a yellowish, rather sparse, American-style trimming of hair beneath his powerfully developed jaw, his somber visage intense and malevolent, he stood for hours in front of show windows, steadily gnawing at the mouthpiece of his cigarette, his long arms thrust in his pockets. Was he really so interested in all those neckties, watches, valises, and stationer's wares? It was immediately obvious that he was not, that he was one of those strange people who roam the city from morning till night solely because they can think only while in motion, out on the street, or who, having no home to go back to, prowl around in expectation of something.

He spent the evening in a cheap restaurant not far from Razyezhaya, accompanied by two nondescript sailors.

The three sat wearing their coats in that cold and dingy room, at a little table placed awkwardly by the wall, and Sokolovich's seat was particularly uncomfortable. Directly facing his back, a small roundheaded Tatar stood at a snack counter in the interior of the room; on the wall in front of him hung a placard advertising a certain beer, depicting three happy men-about-town with top hats pushed back on their heads and frothing beakers in their hands; to the right an icy dampness kept blowing in from the street with the incoming patrons, and to the left the waiters, running back and forth to the counter, kept stirring up the air. Near that counter a stairway of three steps ascended—to a narrow corridor filled with cooking odors and the pungent smell of gas—and through an open door a billiards room was visible, dark in its upper half, bright below, where balls were meeting with a brisk clatter and headless men ambled about in waistcoats with cue sticks on their shoulders—their heads were lost in the murk. Seating himself in that awkward position at the table, Sokolovich took a pipe from his coat pocket; knitting his brow, he stared intently at the beer ad. The sailors conversed with the waiter who had just come up to them, while Sokolovich, packing his pipe with tobacco, said languidly in his hollow voice, addressing no one in particular: "Why is it people collect all kinds of nonsense, but they don't collect advertising matter, that is, the historical documents that portray human ideals most precisely. For example, don't those dandies there really express the aspirations of nine-tenths of all mankind?"

"You're nothing but a son of a Polack," hostilely responded one of the sailors, Levchenko.

"I'm a son of humanity," said Sokolovich with a kind of strange solemnity, which might be taken for irony. "My being Polish hasn't kept me from seeing the world and all its divinities. It hasn't kept me from working as a driver either . . . There's really no pleasure comparable to that, you know, watching the street rushing toward you, and some lady beautiful in a dither up ahead, not knowing which way to fling herself."

When he had spoken, he lit the tobacco and propped an elbow on the table, cradling his pipe in his massive left hand; there was no shirt beneath the cuff of his coat, and he had a bluish tattoo on that flat, elongated hand: a sinuous Japanese dragon.

All evening they drank Caucasian cognac from cups, pretending it was tea, munched on pink peppermint sweets, and smoked to excess. Like all working-class people, perpetually affronted by life, the sailors talked on and on, each trying to speak only of himself, searched their memories for the basest deeds of their enemies and oppressors, boasted—one of them supposedly had poked a feisty first mate "right in the proboscis," the other had tossed a boatswain overboard—and they kept up a steady argument, screaming incessantly, "All right, do you want to make a bet?"

Sokolovich sucked on his pipe, worked his jaw, and maintained a morose silence. Although he had frequented every sort of dive from Kronstadt to Montevideo, he never drank heavily, preferring only ginger beer or absinthe. On that evening he kept pace with his drinking companions, but the cognac had no apparent effect on him. This also provoked the sailors, the more so because, as they later acknowledged, they were always irritated by Sokolovich's powerful and repulsive face, by his tendency to act enigmatic and pensive, and by their ignorance of and lack of insight into his character, his past, or his present homeless and idle life. At one point Levchenko, who had wasted no time getting drunk, screamed at him, "You're a funny bird, you are! It's us who's treating you, so why don't you be sociable instead of just sitting there dragging on your stinking pipe?"

Rudely and dispassionately Sokolovich cut him off.

"Do me a favor, stop the bellowing. It makes me angry. Time and again I've told you that alcohol has little effect on me and doesn't afford me any particular pleasure. My sense of taste is blunted. I'm what they call a degenerate. Understood?"

Levchenko lost his composure and answered with unnatural flippancy.

"Well now, don't you go putting on airs neither! What is it I'm supposed to understand? If you was degenerate you'd be sick, you'd have a weakness for drink, but you're telling me just the opposite. You could kill a man with one hand, but you say—"

"What I say is true," interrupted Sokolovich, raising his voice. "All degenerates have some perceptions and faculties that are sharpened, heightened, and others that, on the contrary, are dulled. Understood? Strength has nothing whatsoever to do with it."

"And how do I recognize this here degenerate if he's full of beans and vinegar?" Levchenko asked mockingly.

"By the ears, for example," answered Sokolovich, half serious, half mocking. "Degenerates, geniuses, tramps, and murderers all have noosiform ears, that is, ears shaped like a noose—the very thing used to choke the life out of them."

"Well, you know, anybody can kill if they fly off the handle," the other sailor, Pilnyak, put in casually. "Once in Nikolaev I was . . ."

Sokolovich waited until he had finished, then said, "Of course, I suspect, Pilnyak, that ears of this sort are characteristic not only of so-called degenerates. As you know, a craving to kill, and, for that matter, to indulge in all sorts of cruelty, is latent within everyone's soul. There are even some who, for any number of reasons, feel an overpowering urge to commit murder—due, for example, to atavism or to some hatred for humanity that has mysteriously developed within them. They kill with complete impassivity, and after they've killed someone they aren't wracked with pangs of conscience, as people like to think; on the contrary, they return to normal and feel a sense of relief—even if their wrath, hatred, and secret craving for blood have had loathsome and pitiful consequences. And it's altogether high time to throw out this fairy tale about the torments of conscience, the horrendous agony that murderers supposedly go through. People have done enough lying about how blood makes them shudder. We've had enough novels contrived about crimes with punishment; it's time to write about crime with no punishment whatsoever. A killer's attitude depends on his point of view toward murder and on what he expects to happen later: will it be the gallows or decorations and praise? For example, do those who condone family vendettas, duels, war, revolution, and public executions really feel so tormented and horrified?"

"I read Dostoevsky's *Crime and Punishment,*" remarked Levchenko with a certain pomposity.

"Did you now?" said Sokolovich, casting a ponderous glance at him. "And did you read about the executioner Deblair? He recently died at his villa in the environs of Paris, aged eighty, having lopped off exactly five hundred heads in his day; he was acting on the orders of his highly civilized government. Penal records are also crammed full of accounts of extremely cruel tranquillity characteristic of our most bloody criminals, of their cynicism and their morally edifying expatiations. But it's not a matter of degenerates, headsmen, or convicts. All the books of humanity—all those myths, sagas, folk epics, stories, dramas, novels—they're all full of the very same accounts, and do they ever make anyone shudder? Every little boy is enthralled by Cooper, where all they do is take scalps, every gymnasium student learns that the Assyrian rulers papered the walls of their cities with the skin of prisoners, every pastor knows that in the Bible the word "killed" is used more than a thousand times and, for the most part, used with the greatest boasting and giving of thanks to the Creator for helping them do it."

"That's why it's called the Old Testament; it's ancient history," objected Levchenko.

"And the New Testament is such," replied Sokolovich, "that it would make the hair of a gorilla stand on end if he knew how to read . . . No," he said, knitting his brow and looking off to one side, "there's no comparison between Cain and our biped gorillas! They've left him far behind; they've long since lost their naivety—probably ever since they built Babylon at the site of their so-called paradise. Real gorillas haven't yet had any Assyrian rulers, Caesars, inquisitions, or any colonization of America, or kings who sign death sentences with cigars in their mouths, inventors of submarines that in one fell swoop send a thousand men to the bottom of the sea, or Robespierres or Jack the Rippers . . . What do you think, Levchenko?" he asked, once again fixing his stern gaze on the sailors. "Did those gentlemen suffer the agonies of Cain or Raskolnikov? Did all the murderers of tyrants and oppressors suffer torment, murderers who have their names inscribed in golden letters in the so-called annals of history? Do you get all agonized when you read that the Turks have slaughtered another hundred thousand Armenians, that the Germans are poisoning wells with pestilential bacilli, that the trenches are heaped up with putrefying corpses, that army aviators are dropping bombs on Nazareth? Do people feel tormented in some Paris or other, or in London, cities built on human bones and flourishing on the most ferocious and commonplace cruelty toward one's so-called fellow man? It turns out that only Raskolnikov was tormented and even then only because of his own anemic weakness, and because that was the way it was planned by his malicious creator, who had to shove Christ into all his trashy novels."

"Weigh them anchors! Cast off!" screamed Levchenko, hoping to make a joke of a conversation that had become oppressive.

Sokolovich was silent for a moment; then he spat between his knees and added dispassionately, "At present tens of millions of people are participating in warfare. Soon the whole of Europe will be crawling with murderers. But we all know perfectly well that the world won't let this bother it one iota. They used to say that a trip to Sakhalin Island was a dreadful undertaking, but I'd like to know who's going to be afraid to travel through Europe in a year or two, after this war has ended."

Pilnyak began telling about an uncle who had murdered his wife in a fit of jealousy. After listening for a moment, Sokolovich remarked with an air of gloomy reflection, "People are altogether much more prone to murder a woman than a man. Our sensory perceptions are never so acutely responsive to the body of a man as they are to the body of a woman, that base creature who gives birth to us all, and who revels in true voluptuousness only when she gives herself to the coarsest and strongest males of the species."

Then, placing his elbows on his knees, he fell silent once more and seemed to have completely forgotten his collocutors.

Sometime after ten he parted with the sailors in a casual, condescending manner; he left them in the restaurant and strolled off once again, toward Nevsky.

The resplendence of illuminations on Nevsky Prospect was smothered by the dense haze, which was so penetrating and cold that a policeman's mustache had acquired a whitish tint, seemed to have gone gray as he stood at the corner of Vladimirskaya, directing the maelstrom of carriages, sleighs, and goggle-eyed automobiles whirling toward one another. Near Palkin a sloe black stallion who had fallen on his side, onto the shaft, desperately thrashed about, flailing his hooves against the slippery roadway, struggling to right himself and get back up; hastily and frantically bustling about, looking outlandish in his monstrous overskirt, a foppish cabman was attempting to help him, while a red-faced giant of a constable, who had trouble moving his cold, benumbed lips, was screaming, waving a hand in its cotton glove, driving away the crowds. Sokolovich heard some muffled voice telling how an old white-bearded man in a long raccoon coat, said to be a famous writer, had been run down and crushed while crossing the street. Not even pausing to listen, he turned off onto Nevsky Prospect.

Pedestrians overtook him, peering up in astonishment at his face; he himself overtook others. His hands stuffed into his pockets, his shoulders slightly raised, hiding his scraggly fog-moist chin in his collar and looking askance at the feckless, dark mass of people flowing along in front of him, almost unnaturally conspicuous in that mass because of his stature, he sauntered along the sidewalk on his big feet, always stepping out first with the left leg and taking longer strides with the left than with the right. From the poles of streetlamps carbonic black shadows fell into the smoky haze. With a monotonous tramping of hooves compact droves of rime-frosted cab horses clattered along in that smoke; trotters were flying amidst them, their strength and impertinence conspicuous, their nostrils blowing vapor, which blended with the misty waves that rolled along on the wind. A man and woman flashed by and rushed away in a mad whirl—a budding young officer firmly clasping the waist of the lady, who was nestling against him and hiding her face in an astrakhan muff. Sokolovich slackened his pace and long gazed after that couple, which receded in the distance to the point where, amidst flarings of greenish heat lightning, the endless chain of wine red streetcar lights evanesced in the icy murk of that enormous torrent Nevsky seemed to be. His large face was ferocious with intense concentration.

He walked diagonally across Anichkov Bridge and set off along the other side of the street. The wind and fog bore down with still more vehemence; far away, high in the darkness and mist, loomed the reddish eye of the clock in the tower of the municipal duma. Sokolovich stopped and stood for quite a long time, lighting a cigarette and lowering at the prostitutes who had appeared on the sidewalk now and kept meandering by in a slow, endless stream. Behind him was the huge translucent window of a closed store with its mournful, nocturnal illumination; waxen, blond-haired dandies with large but sparse eyelashes peered out inertly from behind the window, dressed in expensive overcoats and fur mantles, wooden legs lifelessly protruding from their fashionable, splendidly pressed pantaloons. Then he plodded on, reached the Kazan Cathedral, now decapitated by the foggy darkness, and climbed the steps to the veranda of Dominick's.

Inside, amidst the cramped masses who ate and drank standing up and in their coats, as if they were still out on the street, he took a seat in a dark corner—the only lit spot was the snack counter, besieged by the mob—and ordered black coffee. With extraordinary abruptness a puny man in a derby, his small face frozen stiff, appeared at his table and hastily asked permission to take a sulfur fusee from the matchbox; striking it hastily, he asked in a quick patter of words, "Excuse me, please, but you look an awful lot like an acquaintance of mine from Vilnius, by the name of Yanovsky."

Sokolovich stared him straight in the eye and answered with a ponderous gravity, "You're mistaken, Mr. Plainclothes Man."

He stayed at Dominick's until one in the morning. The deserted restaurant resounded with banging chairs, which the flunkies, who had suddenly become boorish and coarse, were turning upside down and tossing onto tables. He glanced at his big silver watch and arose from his seat.

Nevsky Prospect in the dead of night and the fog is dreadful. Desolate, lifeless, it is covered by a murky brume that mists it in obscurity, that seems linked to the arctic murk that drifts in from the end of the world, from the land called the North Pole, where something beyond human comprehension lies concealed. The center of this misty torrent is still illumined from above by the off-white glow of electrical orbs. But on the sidewalks, beside black shopwindows and locked gates, it is darker. Humming, leisurely sauntering along these sidewalks, their cheap finery clashing with the surroundings, stroll the women, in the guise of insouciance but chilled to the marrow by that icy dampness, and some of their faces are so striking for the nullity they express that an uncanny fear arises, as if one had stumbled upon a creature of some other species, not a human being but some unknown breed.

After Sokolovich had left Dominick's and had walked roughly two hundred paces, he selected one of those prostitutes, later found to be a certain Korolkova, who called herself simply Kinglet, a small, meager woman whose tawdry and modish attire made her appear more ample, wearing a hat that was also of ample dimensions and very peculiar in style, of black velvet adorned with a cluster of glass cherries. Her small, broad-cheeked face with black, deeply sunken beady eyes had something about it reminiscent of a bat. Letting her head sway slightly with affected flippancy, even, so it seemed, with a certain awareness of the irresistible charm of her sex, one hand holding up her skirt, the other, in a large flat muff made of glittering black fur, covering her mouth, she had suddenly blocked the path of the round-shouldered, shuffling Sokolovich. He cast a sharp glance at her and immediately shouted in his hollow voice for a night-duty cabman, who was parked at the corner. Then, seating themselves in the tacky four-wheeler, this couple rolled away, first along Nevsky, then through the square, past the gleaming clock on the Nikolaev Station, which now was totally dark, having dispatched all its trains into the depths of snowy Russia, past the hideous, stout horse that eternally bows its large head, in sleet or in fog, begging its portly rider for free rein, then along Goncharnaya and still further—through foggy streets and alleyways, into that mysterious desolation of the capital's nocturnal outskirts.

As they rode Sokolovich smoked in silence. Apparently oppressed by this silence, Korolkova remarked that in her opinion the Golenishev-Kutuzov brand of cigarettes was better than the one called Lilac. This attempt to strike up a simple conversation, even what could be taken as a friendly move, as yet unrelated to the aim of their journey, was pathetic and touching; but Sokolovich remained silent. Then she started asking to be paid in advance and added with unnatural audacity that she would stay the whole night, but only for a very good price. Without replying he took out two silver rubles and handed them to her. She accepted them, checked one of them with her teeth, discovered it was counterfeit, and put it in her muff, stating that this one didn't count, that she would keep it for no special reason, as a souvenir, since it was wartime and silver was rare and illegal; after that she started asking for more. Sokolovich did not respond at first, then gave her one more ruble. Next she tried a different approach—being a woman; she suddenly shuddered and made a movement as if to nestle up to him. The shudder was affected but the feeling that had suddenly gripped her was, most likely, not; she felt a strong attraction toward him, so large, powerful, categorical in his ugliness and his merciless somber sobriety. But he made no response to her movement.

They rode far out of the city. Korolkova told the cabman to stop beside a two-storied brick building with the sign ROOMS FOR TRAVELERS—BELGRADE. By now it was a quarter to two; the area was deserted.

Having ascended the battered stair carpeting to the second floor of the Belgrade, the guests were met in a semidark corridor by the concierge Nyanchuk, who had been sleeping on a narrow, wooden settee beneath a sleazy winter coat with a threadbare lambskin collar. In his drowsy stupor he was dazed by the stature of Sokolovich, by the somberly intense countenance and the scanty, fog-moist American-style beard. He got up and asked in a hostile tone, "What is it you need?"

"As if you didn't know, blockhead," said Sokolovich through his teeth, walking presumptuously past him and putting a silver half ruble in his hand.

Nyanchuk was on the verge of taking offense and replying, "A blockhead is how a blockhead acts," but he felt the money in his hand and recognized Korolkova, who proclaimed as she walked by, "You didn't know me; that means I'll get rich!" So he only scowled. Grumbling something about how they already had problems with the police every day, he led the way for Sokolovich. After striking a match, he flung open the door to a very warm, stuffy room imbued with a peculiar cloying odor, half its window obstructed diagonally by the roof of some outbuilding. Beyond the window, beyond the dark glass pane, there was a dull sound of resonant voices, the rumble of some machine, and what seemed a vision of hell, the blazing crimson flame of a huge torch.

"What's that?" Sokolovich stopped and asked harshly, even anxiously.

"Night work, cleaning sewers," muttered Nyanchuk, still feeling offended; when he had lit two candles sitting on the windowsill in red rosettes, he lowered the puffy white blinds made of calico and inquired what the guests would like brought. Sokolovich ordered some kvass for himself and added with an odd smirk, "And let's have some fruit for the lady."

"We haven't got no fruit," Nyanchuk replied. "Except grapes. Ruble and a half a bunch."

"Lovely," said Sokolovich. "Bring on the grapes."

Korolkova was obviously flattered by such treatment. Trying her best to act the part of a noble-born lady treated to grapes in the middle of winter, glancing about the room, stamping her frozen feet and blowing into her muff, she said archly, "Oh my, they're probably cold!"

A moment later Nyanchuk brought in a big iron tray containing the grapes and two uncorked bottles frothing over with foam, and when he had gone Sokolovich immediately locked the door. As Nyanchuk left the room, Korolkova was standing beside the table, still breathing into her muff, nibbling on the firm green grapes mottled with sawdust, and her dreadful companion with that yellow necklace of beard below his freshly shaven face was removing his coat in the corner, unwinding a long scarf of coarse violet wool. After that the room, with the ominous flame still blazing and the cryptic night work still dully rumbling on outside its window, became shrouded in mystery.

At four o'clock a bell in the corridor began jangling. Nyanchuk awoke and jumped up from the settee, wearing long drawers with foot straps and felt slippers. When he reached the switchboard he found the third button clicked on. Behind the door of room 3 a woman's voice asked for a ten-pack of Zephyr cigarettes. Returning from the snack bar with the cigarettes, the drowsy Nyanchuk forgot which room had ordered them and rapped on number 8, the room he had given Sokolovich. Behind the door a coarse low bass asked in a slow drawl, "What is it?"

"Your little miss asked for some cigarettes," said Nyanchuk.

"My 'little miss' did not ask for cigarettes, and there's no way whatsoever that she could have," the bass voice answered peremptorily.

Recalling at once who had wanted the pack, Nyanchuk placed it in the plump female hand thrust through the crack in the door of room 3, lay down once more in the quiet, semidark hotel, and fell fast asleep to the measured ticking of the clock at the end of the corridor.

It was already past six when he awoke again; towering high above him in his coat and peaked cap, the lodger from room 8 was poking at his shoulder.

"Here's for the room and for your trouble," he said. "Let me out. It's time I was at the factory, and the lady said she'd like to be awakened at nine."

"But what about the grapes?" Nyanchuk asked quickly, in an anxious tone.

"I've accounted for everything," said Sokolovich. "According to my figures it comes to four rubles seventy. And I'm giving you five and a half. Understood?"

He started walking calmly toward the stairwell.

Eyes half closed with craving for sleep, squirming about to adjust the coat he had thrown over his shoulders, Nyanchuk once more led the way, tramping along down the steps of the staircase. Sokolovich waited patiently as he struggled with the key, which he had great difficulty turning in the keyhole. Finally the door swung open. He walked past Nyanchuk, raised the gate, and covering his throat with his hand, like an opera singer afraid of catching cold, he mumbled a hollow good-bye into his beard and stepped out on the street, into the damp and fresh air. It was still utterly dark and quiet, but in that darkness and hush the proximity of morning could be sensed. Above all the distant surrounding expanses, above the whole enormous nest of the still mute metropolis hung the muffled, faraway moan of the mills and factories, summoning the countless working masses from all their squalid shelters, from all their hovels and miserable dives. Standing with its black shadow opposite the hotel, a floodlight illumined part of the main road and the street. The fog had dissipated, a light snow had fallen in the night; soaring high in the air from behind the fence adjacent to the floodlight, a massive bulk of lumber exuded a funereal white glow against the blackness of night. Sokolovich turned to the right and vanished in the distance. Chilled to the bone, Nyanchuk slammed the door and ran back up the stairs.

There was no point in lying down again. He began searching for his boots under the settee when suddenly he noticed that the door of room 8 was ajar and light was spilling from within. He jumped up and rushed to the room. Inside there was a dreadful hush, the kind of hush that a room with someone in it never has, even a room occupied by only a sleeping person. The guttering candles crackled in their split rosettes, shadows were darting in the gloom, and on the bed, protruding from beneath a blanket, were the short bare legs of a woman lying flat on her back. The head was hidden beneath two pillows that were pressed down upon it.

1916

»»» «««

The Mad Artist

The sun glittered golden in the east beyond the hazy blue of remote forests, beyond the white, snowy flatland upon which an ancient Russian city gazed from a low bank of hills. It was Christmas Eve, a robust morning with temperature just below freezing and a mantle of rime frost.

The Petrograd train had just arrived. Up the hill from the railway station, along the smoothly packed snow, stretched a queue of cabmen, with passengers and without.

The large old hotel on that spacious square opposite the old merchant bazaar was quiet and empty, tidied up for the holiday. Guests were not expected. But a gentleman in a pince-nez rode up to the veranda, a man with dumbfounded eyes, in a black velvet beret with greenish curls falling from beneath it, in a long overcoat of sparkling chestnut fur.

The red-beard on the coach box let out an affected wheeze; this was his way of showing he was frozen through and deserved a bit extra. The passenger paid no attention, leaving it up to the hotel to settle accounts with him.

"Take me to your very brightest room," he said loudly as he walked with magisterial stride down the wide corridor, following a young bellboy who carried his expensive foreign valise. "I'm an artist," he said, "but this time I do not want a room facing north. By no means!"

The boy threw open the door to number 1, the luxury suite, which included a vestibule and two capacious rooms but had windows that were small and sunken deeply into the thick walls. It was warm, cozy and tranquil in those rooms, amber with the sunlight that was tempered by rime frost on the lower windowpanes. Gingerly setting down the valise on a carpet in the middle of the front room, the bellboy, a young lad with merry, intelligent eyes, stood waiting for the passport and for further instructions. Short of stature, youthfully nimble in spite of his age, wearing a beret and velvet jacket, the artist paced from corner to corner; letting the pince-nez fall with a movement of his brows, he rubbed his pale harrowed face with white, seemingly alabaster hands. Then he cast a strange glance at the servant, looking at him with the unseeing eyes of a very nearsighted and absentminded man.

"December 24, 1916!" he said. "You must remember that date!"

"Yes sir," answered the boy.

From the side pocket of his jacket the artist removed a gold watch, screwed up one eye, and took a quick look at it.

"Exactly half past nine," he continued, once more adjusting the lenses on his nose. "I've nearly reached the goal of my pilgrimage. Glory to God on high, and on earth peace, goodwill toward men! I'll give you the passport, don't worry; right now I can't concern myself with passports. I haven't one single moment to spare. I'm off to the city right now, and I have to be back here by eleven sharp. I must complete the crowning work of all my life. My young friend," he said, stretching out a hand toward the boy and showing him two wedding rings, of which one, on the little finger, was a woman's, "that ring represents a deathbed behest!"

"As you say, sir," answered the bellboy.

"And I will obey that behest!" said the artist in a menacing tone. "I will paint an immortal work! And I will make a gift of it—unto thee."

"We thank you most humbly," answered the boy.

"But, my dear fellow, the fact is I've brought with me neither canvas nor paints—because of the monstrous war it was impossible to get them through. I hope to acquire them here. At last I shall incarnate everything that drove me out of my mind for all of two years and that later was so marvelously transfigured in Stockholm!"

Continuing to speak, rapping out the words, the artist glared through his pince-nez straight at his collocutor.

"The whole world must know and understand that revelation, those joyous tidings!" he exclaimed with a theatrical wave of his hand. "Do you hear? The whole world! Everyone!"

"All right, sir," answered the boy. "I'll report it to the manager."

The artist put on his fur coat and made for the door. At breakneck speed the boy dashed to open it. The artist nodded to him pompously and strode off down the corridor. On the landing of the stairwell he paused and added, "In all the world, my friend, there's no holiday more lofty than Christmas. There's no sacrament that can equal the birth of a child. The final gasp of an old, bloody world! A new man is born!"

The dawn light outside had dissipated, the streets were full of sunshine. Already beginning to crumble and granulate, the rime frost on telegraph lines stood out against the pale blue sky with a delicate, dove gray hue. Clustered together on the square was a whole forest of thick, dark green Christmas firs. At butcher shops stood frozen white carcasses of naked pigs with deep slits on their stout napes; gray hazel grouse were hanging there, plucked geese, turkeys plump and stiffened. Conversing one with another, pedestrians hurried along, cabmen whipped up their shaggy nags, sleigh runners squealed.

"I know thee, Rus!" said the artist loudly, striding through the square and looking at the tightly girded and stoutly attired, robust hucksters and market women, who were shouting out beside stands that held homemade wooden toys and large white gingerbread cakes in the form of steeds, roosters, and fish.

He hailed an empty cab and asked to be driven to the main street.

"And make it fast; by eleven I must be back home working," he said, seating himself in the cold sleigh and placing the heavy, indurated rug across his knees.

The cabman's cap gave a nod, and the small, well-fed gelding set off at a rapid pace along that sparkling, smooth-pressed road.

"Faster, faster!" repeated the artist. "At twelve o'clock the sunlight will be at its brightest. Yes," he said, looking around, "familiar places, but thoroughly forgotten! What's that piazza called?"

"How's that, sir?" asked the cabman.

"I'm asking you what's the name of that square!" shouted the artist in a sudden frenzy. "Stop, you scoundrel! Why have you brought me to a chapel? I'm afraid of churches and chapels! Stop! You know, when a certain Finn once drove me to a cemetery, I immediately wrote letters to the king and the Pope and he was sentenced to death! Take me back!"

The cabman reined in the careering horse and cast a bewildered glance at his passenger.

"But where is it you want? You said Main Street . . ."

"I told you—I need a store that has art supplies!"

"You might better get you another cab, Your Honor; you got me all confounded."

"Well, go straight to hell then! Here, take your pieces of silver!"

The artist climbed awkwardly out of the sleigh, tossed three rubles at the cabman, and walked off in the opposite direction, down the middle of the street. His fur coat had come open and was trailing through the snow; his eyes, full of suffering and dismay, wandered from side to side. When he noticed some strips of gilded trimming in a shopwindow, he hastily entered the store. But he had scarcely begun asking about paints when the rubicund young lady, who sat at the cashier's booth in a short fur coat, interrupted him.

"No, no, we don't handle any paints. We have only window frames, decorative trimmings, and wallpaper. But then, you're not likely to find a canvas and oil paints anywhere in our city."

In genuine desperation the artist clutched at his temples.

"My God, is that true? Ah, horrendous! Now and precisely now the paints are a question of life and death! Back in Stockholm my idea had already ripened to the full, and when it becomes incarnate it will make an unparalleled impression. I must depict the hovel in Bethlehem, the Birth of Christ, and must imbue the whole painting—the manger, and the Child and the Madonna, and the lion and lamb reclining together—side by side!—with such exultation of angels, with such light, so that verily this shall be the birth of a New Man. Only I shall have it set in Spain, the land of our first trip, our wedding journey. In the distance blue mountains, blossoming trees on hills, against a background of broad, celestial expanses . . ."

"Excuse me, sir," said the young lady in a frightened tone. "There may be customers coming in. We have only frames, trimmings, and wallpapering."

The artist flinched, then raised his beret with exaggerated politeness.

"Ah, for the love of God forgive me! You're right, a thousand times right!"

And he walked out hastily.

A few buildings down the street, in a store called Educational Aids, he bought a huge sheet of rough pasteboard, colored pencils, and water colors on a palette made of paper. Then he leapt into another cab and urged the driver on, back to the hotel. In the hotel he immediately rang the call bell; the same boy appeared. The artist was holding his passport in both hands.

"Here!" he said, extending it toward the boy. "Render what is Caesar's unto Caesar. And after that, my dear fellow, you must bring me a glass of water for my aquarelles. Oil paints, alas, are nowhere to be found. The war! The Iron Age! The Age of the Troglodyte!"

After thinking for a moment, he suddenly beamed with rapture.

"But what a day! Lord, what a day! At exactly midnight the Saviour is born! The Saviour of the world! That's how I'll sign the picture: 'Birth of the New Man!' I'll base the Madonna on her whose name from this day forth shall be sanctified. I shall resurrect her, she who was murdered by the evil spirit together with the new life she bore beneath her heart!"

Expressing, once again, his earnest readiness to be of service, the bellboy departed, but a few minutes later, when he came back with a glass and a carafe of fresh water, the artist was sleeping soundly. His pale and thin face resembled an alabastrine mask. He lay supine on a bed in the second room high atop the pillows, his head cast back, his long, gray-green hair in disarray, and even his breathing was inaudible. The boy withdrew on tiptoe; outside the door he encountered the manager, a squat man with sharp eyes and short hair brushed up on the crown of his head.

"Well, what's going on then?" asked the manager in a hasty whisper.

"Asleep," answered the boy.

"Will wonders never cease!" said the manager. "And his passport checks out. There's just one notation, to the effect that his wife passed on. Ivan Matveich phoned from the police, told us to keep an eye on him. You be on your guard now, look sharp. It's wartime, brother."

"He said, 'I'll give it to you; just let me get the thing done,'" said the boy. "He didn't ask for a samovar . . ."

"There, there you see!" took up the manager and stuck his ear against the door.

But on the other side of that door all was quiet; there was only the aura of melancholy that always pervades the room of a sleeping person.

The sunlight slowly receded from the hotel suite. Then it was gone completely. The rime on the windows had turned gray, bleak. The artist suddenly awoke in twilight and rushed to the call bell.

"This is horrible!" he screamed as soon as the boy appeared. "You did not awaken me! And it was just on account of this very day that we undertook our terrible odyssey. Just imagine what it was like for her, in her eighth month of pregnancy! We passed through a thousand obstacles, everything imaginable, went without sleeping or eating for nearly six weeks. And the sea! The berserk pitching of the boat! And that incessant fear that at any moment you might be blown to pieces. 'Everyone up on deck! Ready the life preservers! First man to run for the lifeboat against orders gets his head smashed!'"

"As you say, sir," said the boy, nonplused by those strident cries.

"But what joyous light there was," continued the artist, calming down. "With the frame of mind I was in just now I'd have finished the job in two or three hours. But what's to be done! I'll work through the night. Just help me get a few things ready. That table, now, might do."

He walked up to the table in front of the settee, pulled the velvet covering away, and gave it a shake.

"It stands quite steady. But listen now—you have only two candles here. You must bring eight more; otherwise I cannot paint. I need light in great profusion!"

The boy left again and returned after a long absence with seven candles in a variety of candlesticks.

"We're one short; they're all being used in the rooms," he said.

The artist got upset all over again, started screaming.

"Ah, how vexing that is! I needed ten, ten of them! Obstructions at every step, base treachery! At least help me move this table into the very middle of the room. We'll augment the light with reflections from the mirror."

The bellboy dragged the table to the designated spot and set it firmly in place.

"Now it must be spread with something of a white color, which won't assimilate the light," muttered the artist, awkwardly helping out, dropping his pince-nez and putting it back on. "What could we use? I'm afraid of white tablecloths . . . That's it, my stack of newspapers; I had the foresight not to discard them!"

He opened the valise lying on the floor, removed several issues of a newspaper, covered the table, fastened the paper down with tacks, laid out his pencils and palette, set the nine candles in a row, and lit them all. With that plethora of flames the room took on a strange, festive, but also ominous aura. The windows had gone black. Candlelight was reflected in the mirror above the settee, casting a bright golden glow on the grave white face of the artist and the young, perplexed face of the boy. When everything was finally in order, the bellboy withdrew deferentially to the threshold and asked, "Will you be dining with us or elsewhere?"

The artist smiled bitterly and theatrically.

"The child! He fancies I could eat at such a moment! Go in peace, my friend. You will not be required again until morning."

The bellboy made a discreet departure.

Hours flowed by. The artist paced from corner to corner. He said to himself, "I must get prepared." Outside his windows lay the blackness of the frosty winter night. He lowered the blinds. All was silent in the hotel. Out in the corridor, on the other side of the door, cautious, furtive steps could be heard; they were spying on the artist through the keyhole, eavesdropping. Then even the sounds of those footsteps dwindled away. The candles blazed, their flames quavering, reflected in the mirror. The artist's face was becoming more and more haggard.

"No!" he suddenly shouted, coming to an abrupt stop. "First I must reconstitute her features in my memory. Away with this childish fear!"

He leaned over to the valise, long hair drooping down. Thrusting a hand beneath his linens, he pulled out a large white velvet album, then took a seat in an armchair by the table. Opening the album, he threw back his head resolutely and proudly, then froze in contemplation.

In the album there was a large photographic print: the interior of some empty chapel, with arches and sparkling walls of smooth stone. In the middle of the room, on a bier covered by the funereal pall stretched a long coffin containing a thin woman with eyelids closed and protuberant. Her narrow and beautiful head was encircled by a garland of flowers; her folded hands rested high upon her breast. At the head of the coffin stood three ecclesiastical candelabra; at the foot another, tiny coffin with an infant, who resembled a doll.

The artist peered intently at the sharp features of the dead woman. Suddenly his face was contorted with horror. He threw the album on the rug, jumped up, and rushed over to his valise. He dug everything out of it to the very bottom, scattered his shirts, stockings and ties on the floor . . . No, what he was seeking was not to be found! He looked all about in desperation, rubbed his forehead.

"Half my life for a brush!" he exclaimed hoarsely, stamping his foot. "I forgot, forgot, miserable wretch! Find one! Work a miracle!"

But there was no brush. He fumbled in his pockets, found a penknife, and went running to his coat. Would he be able to cut off a piece of the fur and tie it to a pen or to a sliver of wood? But where would he get the thread? Middle of the night, everyone's sleeping . . . they'd take him for a madman! And in a frenzy he snatched the pasteboard from the settee, hurled it on the table, ran into the bedroom for some pillows, placed them on the armchair to make a higher sitting position, and seizing first one colored pencil, then another, he threw himself into his work.

He worked without respite. Removing his pince-nez, he bent low over the table, set down forceful and confident strokes, flung himself back, fixing his eyes on the mirror, whose bright haze was full of quavering, parti-colored flames. The hair on the artist's temples was soaked from the heat of the candles, the veins in his neck were swollen with nervous tension. His eyes were watery and glittering, his facial features sharpened.

At last he saw that the sheet of pasteboard was hopelessly ruined—crammed with absurd and garish drawings that were completely contrary one to another in both inner substance and meaning. The feverish inspiration of the artist was completely out of control, doing exactly what he did not want done. He turned the pasteboard over, grabbed a blue pencil, and stood motionless for a short time. The open album lay beside his armchair. The long coffin and dead visage in that album kept flashing before his eyes. With vehement force he slammed the album shut. Sticking out from beneath the linen in his valise was a wickerwork flask of cologne. He jumped up, quickly unscrewed its top, and began drinking, burning himself with the liquid. Having emptied almost all of the flask, panting from the effects of that aromatic flame, his throat afire, he strode about the room once more.

Soon a youthful energy took possession of him—bold resoluteness, confidence in his every thought, every feeling, an awareness that he was capable of anything, dared to do anything, that there were no more doubts, no obstacles. He was suffused with hope and joy. It seemed to him that the somber, satanic delusions of life, which had flooded his imagination in black waves, were receding. Hosanna! Blessed is He who cometh in the name of the Lord!

Now with astounding, hitherto unprecedented clarity he could see in his mind's eye what his heart was craving, a heart belonging not to life's slave but to a creator of life, so he said to himself. He had an image of the heavens plethoric with eternal light, languishing in an Eden-like azure and wreathed with wondrous, though vaguely disquieting clouds; the coruscating visages and wings of innumerable exulting seraphim stood out amidst the eerie, liturgical beauty of the heavens; God the Father, menacing and joyous, beatific and triumphant as in the days of the Creation, towered among them like a mammoth iridescent vision; the Maid of Ineffable Grace, her sacred eyes filled with the bliss of the jubilant mother, standing in wreaths of clouds translucent with the blue of distant, earthly realms that extended beneath her, displayed to the world, raising high in her hallowed arms the Child, radiant as the sun, and the savage, mighty John the Baptist, girded with the pelt of a beast, knelt at her feet, kissing the hem of her raiment in a frenzy of love, tenderness, and gratitude . . .

The artist rushed back to his work. He kept breaking pencils and, in feverish haste, his hands trembling, sharpened them again with the knife. The dying candles, guttering, dripping wax down the scorching-hot candlesticks, flamed even more torridly beside his face, which was curtained along its cheeks by his wet hair.

At six o'clock he was frenetically jabbing the button to the call bell: he had finished, finished! Then he ran up to the table and stood there, his heart pounding, waiting for the boy. The pallor on his face was of such a hue that his lips seemed black. His jacket was covered all over with flecks of varicolored dust from the pencils. The dark eyes burned with inhuman suffering and, at the same time, with perfervid rapture.

No one came. A sepulchral quiet surrounded him. But he stood, he waited, transformed into sheer listening and anticipation. Just now, at any moment, the boy would come running in, and he, the creator, having consummated his labor, having poured out his soul at the bidding of the Lord God on High, would quickly say to him the words prepared in advance, awesome and victorious words: "Take. I give this *unto thee.*"

On the verge of blacking out from the furious throbbing of his heart, he held the pasteboard firmly in his hand. But that pasteboard, smeared all over in a variety of colors, contained monstrous heaps of images that had overwhelmed his imagination in absolute contrast to his passionate reveries. A savage black-blue sky was blazing to its very zenith with conflagrations, with the bloody flames of smoking, crumbling temples, palaces, and dwellings. Torture racks, scaffolds and gibbets with garrotted men hanging from them were black against that fiery background. Towering over all the painting, over all the sea of fire and smoke, majestic, demoniacal, stood a huge cross with a crucified man upon it, the ensanguined Martyr, his sacrosanct arms widespread, extended submissively along the crossbeam. Death, dressed in chain mail and serrated crown, its macabre bared teeth grinning, had taken a running start and thrust an iron trident deep in below the heart of the crucified Christ. The bottom of the painting depicted an amorphous pile of the dead—and the melee, the gnarring and biting clash of the living, a tangle of naked bodies, arms, and faces. And those faces, snarling, fanged, with eyes protruding from sockets, were so base and obscene, so distorted with hatred and spite, with the voluptuousness of fratricide, that one could readily have taken them for the faces of bovine creatures, wild beasts, devils, but in no way whatsoever for the faces of human beings.

Paris, 1921

»»» «««

Sempiternal Spring

. . . And what's more, my friend, a remarkable thing happened to me recently. In June I went out into the countryside, to the provinces (visiting an acquaintance of mine). Of course, I still recall the time when these trips were nothing out of the ordinary. I suppose that for you in Europe that's still the way it is. But many are the things we once had here and people still have in Europe! One-fifty or two hundred miles is no hop, skip, and a jump for us anymore. Russia has reverted to the times of ancient Muscovy, and the distance between points is, once again, enormous. So the Muscovite humanoid doesn't go in much for traveling these days. Of course, we have every variety of unbridled lawlessness here now; Lord, do we ever have that. But don't forget that all of this "freedom," which we couldn't imagine we would live to see, began only quite recently.

In a word, something unusual occurred, something I had not experienced for many years. One fine day I took a cab and set off for the railway station. In the letter that you somehow got through to me you wrote that you conceive of Moscow nowadays, even of its external appearance, as something "insufferable." Yes, it is indeed repulsive. I had an acute sense of that as I rode along to the station, exhilarated by the peculiarity of my situation, by my role as a traveler, in the sort of cab you used to see only in the most abysmal backwater regions, and one that charged not a billion rubles, but twenty kopecks for the ride. What Asiatic multitudes of people! How many hawkers there are, peddling from trays in all sorts of flea markets and roadside "nooks," to use that vile idiom that's becoming ever more fashionable here! How many buildings in ruins! How full of ruts the roadway is, and the foliage of the trees that are left has run rampant! On the squares in front of the railway stations there are nooks as well, constant selling and buying, mobs of the lowliest rabble, speculators, thieves, street women, vendors of assorted culinary slop. Inside the stations they have snack counters open again and waiting rooms for different classes, but all of these are nothing but barns, befouled to the point of hopelessness. And always so many people—it's such a struggle to push your way through. Trains are infrequent; the wholesale confusion and red tape make buying a ticket a difficult business, and you've really done something if you make it into a coach, which, of course, is also of backwoods provenance, with the wheels corroded to a rusty red. Many travelers show up at the station early, sometimes on the eve of their departure.

I arrived two hours before the train left and came near paying for my audacity, since I barely managed to get a ticket. But by some means or other (that is, by bribery, of course) the matter was arranged; I received a ticket, got into a coach, and even found a seat on a bench instead of on the floor. Then the train was off, Moscow was left behind, and I saw fields, forests and villages I had not seen for ages. A deeply rooted day-to-day existence had resumed here after that little holiday of dissipation by which Rus had amused herself at such an incredible price. Soon almost everyone packed into the coach began nodding, lolling back, and snoring, open mouthed. Opposite me sat a muzhik with light brown hair, big, self-assured. At first he smoked and kept spitting on the floor, making a rasping sound by rubbing across it with the toe of his boot. Then he took a milk bottle from the pocket of his *poddyovka* and started drinking in protracted gulps, breaking off only to avoid suffocation. Having drunk all his milk, he too flopped back, reclined against the wall, and started snoring like the others; and the rancidity that wafted from him began virtually driving me crazy. Unable to bear any more, I gave up my place and went out to stand in the corridor. And there in the corridor I came upon an acquaintance I had not seen for some four years, a former professor who once was rich; he stood there swaying along with each sway of the coach. I hardly recognized him; he had become a hoary old man who had the look of a pilgrim who wanders sacred places. His shoes, his sleazy coat and hat were ghastly, even worse than my own trappings. Unshaven for ages, gray hair down to his shoulders, he had a sackcloth bag in his hand, another on the floor by his feet. "I'm on my way home," he said, "to the country; they've given me a plot of land attached to my former estate, and, you know, I'm living just like that Muscovite turned rustic whom you're on your way to see. I feed myself by the sweat of my brow, but my free time is devoted to my former work: a broad historical monograph, which, in my opinion, could inaugurate a whole new scholarly era . . ." By now the silvery disk of the sun was floating low beyond the boles of trees, beyond the forest. A half hour later the founder of a new era disembarked at his cloistral substation—and began hobbling along with his sacks in the cold twilight, by the green path of a cutting through that birch forest.

When I arrived at my destination it was already after ten, and dusk had set in. Since the train was late, the muzhik who came to meet me had waited there for a while, then took off for home. What could I do? Sleep in the station? But they lock up the station at night, and even if they didn't lock it up there are no settees or benches left ("Ain't no more masters, my friend"), and even for "Soviet" subjects sleeping on the floor is not always a pleasant prospect. Could I hire some other peasant in the settlement by the station? But that's almost impossible these days. By the entrance to the depot sat a mournful and apathetic muzhik who had come for the night train to Moscow. When I asked he dismissed the whole idea with a wave of his hand.

"Who's going to drive you there now! Ain't hardly no horses, all the rigs is wore out . . . Wheel axle costs two billion, makes me sick even to talk about it."

"What about going on foot?" I asked.

"You got far to go?" I told him where.

"Well, that ain't over fourteen miles. You'll make it."

"But then, I'd have to go through the woods, and what's more, on foot."

"Why, that don't mean nothing, going through the woods! You'll make it."

But immediately after that he told me about how two "characters" of some sort had hired somehow "this here fellow" in their village last spring, and then both he and they had vanished: "Never seen no more, not them, not him, nor the horses, nor the rig. So that nobody ever did find out who done in who—them him or him them . . . No sir, it ain't like old times no more!"

Naturally, after hearing that story I lost all desire to travel by night. I decided to wait until morning and to ask for a night's lodging in one of the taverns by the station. "We got here altogether two of them," the peasant had said. But it turned out that spending the night in the taverns was also impossible—they wouldn't take me in. "Now if you want a little tea, we're at your service," the woman said in one place. "We got tea on the menu here . . ." I stayed for a long time in that dimly lit room drinking tea, that is, something nauseating made from well-stewed grass. Then I said, "At least let me sit out on the porch until morning."

"But you'd be uncomfortable on the porch . . ."

"Not more uncomfortable than on the road!"

"You unarmed?"

"Search me. Be my guest!" I turned out all my pockets and unbuttoned my coat.

"Well, maybe on the porch is all right—otherwise, nobody's going to let you in their huts either; they're already all of them sleeping by now anyway."

Soon after I went out and sat down on the porch the light in the tavern was extinguished (the adjacent tavern had long since been dark), and night, sleep, silence set in . . . What a long night that was! In the distant sky beyond the dark of the forest the scumbled sickle of the moon was rolling. Then it too disappeared, and in its place summer heat lightning began to glimmer . . . I sat, strode about in front of the porch along the dim white road, sat again, smoked cheap tobacco on an empty stomach. Sometime after one o'clock I heard the alternating modulation of wheel spokes, the thrust of naves on axles down the road—and a short time later someone drove up to the adjacent tavern, stopped, and began tapping on the window in a kind of stealthy, prearranged manner. First a head peered out from the passageway; then the proprietor cautiously emerged, a barefoot, disheveled old man (the very one who had refused my request for lodgings with such astounding spite and rudeness), and a mysterious operation commenced. Something resembling sheepskins was repeatedly dragged out of the passageway and loaded into the newcomer's cart, and all this took place in the glimmer of heat lightning, which illumined the forest, shacks, and road with increasing intensity. The wind had turned cooler now, and thunder rumbled threateningly in the distance. I sat there admiring the spectacle. Do you remember those thunderstorms in the dead of night at Vasilevskoe? Remember how everyone in the house was so afraid of them? Just imagine, I no longer have any sensation of fear, and that night on the porch of the tavern the storm that came to naught and brought no rain aroused only feelings of delight. But toward the end of my vigil I felt a horrible weariness. Besides that, my spirits were low. How was I going to walk fourteen miles after a sleepless night?

But at sunrise, as the storm clouds beyond the forest began to pale and thin out and my surroundings began taking on a humdrum, diurnal aspect, I ran into some unexpected luck. A carriage swept past the tavern and stopped at the station; a commissar had come for the Moscow train, the man who now managed Prince D——'s former estate, which was right in the locale where I was bound. The tavern keeper, who woke up and stuck her head out the window, informed me of this, and I rushed up to the coachman as he left the station for his return trip. It was strange how readily he agreed to let me go with him. He turned out to be a fascinating man, a childishly naive giant who kept repeating as we drove along, "Rather not even look; can't see nothing for the tears in my eyes!" Meanwhile the sun was rising, and the swayback, broad-rumped white stallion, crazed and deafened with age, pulled us briskly and lightly down the forest roads, in the carriage that was also quite old but was marvelous, as soothing as a cradle. Many a year had it been, my friend, since I last rode in a carriage!

The man I visited for a few days in this forestland is a curious type in some ways; self-taught, half educated, he had always lived in Moscow, but last year he abandoned the city and returned to his birthplace, the village and manor that had belonged to his ancestors. Since he hates the new city of Moscow vehemently, he kept sending me glowing descriptions of the beauties of his region, insisting that I come to see him and get away from it all. And it's true, the region is astonishing. Just imagine: a thriving settlement, peaceful, picturesque, looking as if nothing that has happened ever did, looking even as if the abolishment of serfdom and the French invasion never occurred. All around are pristine forest preserves, remoteness, and silence unparalleled. The forest, which is gloomy and resonant, consists primarily of pines. Walking through the depths of those woods in the evening I sensed an aura not of antiquity or olden times but of eternity itself. The evening glow presents itself in bits and pieces; here and there the red of the slowly expiring sun behind the treetops breaks through. The balsamic warmth of the pine needles, heated throughout the day, mingles with a pungent crispness that wafts from marshy depressions and the narrow but deep river, with its mysterious convolutions that blear with a cold haze in the evening. One hears no birdsong, just a death-laden muteness and a few nightjars flitting about. There's one and the same interminable sound, like the sound of a spinning wheel. When it goes completely dark and stars appear over the pine forest, the hoarse, blissfully grievous shrieks of eagle owls begin sounding all around, and in those shrieks there is something still inchoate, pretemporal, where a mating call, the baleful anticipation of coitus, blends the sounds of laughter and sobbing, rings out with the horror of some cataclysm, perdition. And so, in the evening I wandered the pine forest beneath the incantations of the nightjars, in the dead of night I sat on the portico listening to the owls, and I devoted my days to the captivating world of the former manor house—truly "former" since not a single one of its noblemen-lords remains alive. It's an unspeakably beautiful place.

The days were sunny and hot. On my way to the manor house I walked through alternating patches of sun and shade, down a sandy road amidst the stifling, sweet fragrance of pine needles, then along the river through the undergrowth by its bank, flushing kingfishers and looking at the open backwaters, smothered in white water lilies and dotted with dragonflies, at the shady rapids where the water was transparent as a tear, although it seemed black as well, where tiny fish gleamed with silver and some sort of blunt, green snouts gazed goggle-eyed. Then I crossed the ancient stone bridge and ascended to the manor grounds.

By some fortunate circumstance the manor has remained untouched, unplundered, and it has everything that is usually associated with such estates. There is a church built by a famous Italian architect; there are several marvelous ponds; there is a lake called Swan Lake with an island that has a pavilion, where fetes were held in honor of Catherine the Great, who often used to visit the manor. Farther on there are gloomy ravines full of firs and pines, so enormous that your hat nearly falls off when you gaze up at their crowns, which are burdened with the nests of kites and of some other large black birds with funereal fans on their heads. The house, or rather the palace, was built by the same Italian who built the church. I entered the grounds by way of huge, stone portals upon which two contemptuously somnolent lions reclined, surrounded by something growing dense and wild, truly the grass of oblivion. Most often I would make my way directly to the palace and enter its vestibule, where all day long a one-armed Chinaman with a short rifle across his lap was seated in an antique satin armchair; the palace is now a museum, you see, "the people's property," and must be guarded. Of course, only someone with a Chinese temperament could bear to sit there like an idiot in a completely empty building; there was something even a bit gruesome about that idle vigil. But the one-armed, short-legged dolt with the yellow wooden visage sat placidly, smoked cheap shag, occasionally whined something old-womanish and plaintive in an indifferent tone, and looked on with indifference as I walked past him.

"Don't be afraid of him, master," the coachman had told me in the voice one uses to speak about dogs. "I'll let him know; he won't bother you."

And so it was; the Chinaman didn't bother me. If he had been ordered to bayonet me, then of course he would have done so without blinking an eye. But since there was no need to bayonet me, he merely looked at me askance and I made myself at home, was free to pass hours on end in the *chambres* of the palace. Endlessly I wandered through them, endlessly looked around, lost in private thoughts . . . The ceilings sparkled with gilded ornamental festoonery, with gilded coats of arms, with Latin apothegms. (If only you knew how unaccustomed my eyes had grown not only to beautiful things but even to simple cleanliness!) Priceless furniture was reflected in the lacquered floors. In one *chambre,* under a red satin canopy, there was a towering bed made of some dark wood; there was also a Venetian chest, which opened to mysterious, mellifluent music. In another room the entire wall space between the windows was occupied by a clock with chimes; in a third stood a medieval organ. And everywhere busts and statues gazed down upon me, portraits and more portraits. Lord, the beauty of the women in those paintings! And what handsome men in full-dress uniforms or camisole-waistcoats, in wigs and faceted gems, with bright-shining azure eyes! But the brightest and most majestic of all was Catherine. With what beneficent good humor she stood resplendent, regnant in that sumptuous circle! And, strange to behold, on a small escritoire in one of the studies was a brown wooden plank containing a golden disk engraved with the information that this was a portion of the flagship *Saint Eustachius,* which had gone down in the Battle of Cheshme "with glory and honor to the Russian Empire . . ." Yes, with glory and honor to the Russian Empire. That sounds strange now, doesn't it?

I also spent a good deal of time in the assembly chambers downstairs. You know my passion for books; well, in those vaulted rooms below there was a book repository. It was cool down there, perpetually shadowed; the windows had thick iron bars, and through the bars you could see the joyous greenery of bushes, the joyous sunny day, still the same, exactly the same as a hundred or two hundred years ago. Bookshelves were built into niches in the walls and on those shelves glimmered the lusterless gold of ten thousand book spines, nearly all of the most important achievements in Russian and European thought over the last two centuries. One room had an enormous telescope, another a gigantic planetarium, and on the walls, once again, there were portraits and extremely rare engravings. I pried apart the pages of a magnificent little tome from the beginning of the last century and read these lines, printed on the rough paper:

> Be not consumed by mad desire;
> Rebellious spirits pacify.
> O shepherd lad, damp down the fire,
> Bestill thy reedpipe's doleful sigh.

For a long time I stood there enchanted. What rhythm and what charm, what grace and dancing modulation of feelings! Now, when only "roadside nooks" remain of the glory and honor of the Russian Empire, they write in a different style: "The sun, like a mare's piss puddle . . ." Another time I came upon a first edition of Baratynsky and, as if by design, opened the book at these verses:

> So be it; let all past times away like fleeting dreams,
> Still beautiful, wasteland Elysium, art thou;
> Thy puissant grace resplendent gleams,
> Becalms my soul as I gaze on thee now . . .

Just before my departure I visited the famous church. Pale yellow, circular in structure, it stands in the forest on the edge of a hollow, its golden crown sparkling in the blue sky. Inside there is a circle of yellowish marble columns supporting an airy cupola full of sunshine. In the circular gallery between the columns and walls there are paintings of saints with the stylized countenances of those who are buried in the familial crypt under the church. And through the narrow windows you can see how the wind sways the shaggy crests of the pines, which stretch their wild, majestic limbs up from the hollow to reach the same level as the windows, and you hear the soughing and roaring of that wind. I descended into the pitch-darkness of the crypt, using the red flame of a wax candle remnant to illumine the huge marble coffins, the huge iron lucernes, and the scabrous gold of mosaics along the arches. The chill of the netherworld wafted from those coffins. Could it be true that indeed they are here, those handsome men with azure eyes who stood so regnant in the palace *chambres*? No, I could not reconcile myself to that . . . Later I climbed back up to the church and gazed for a long time through the narrow windows at the feral and somnolent agitation of the pines. Somehow joyously and sorrowfully that temple, forgotten, forever deserted, reveled in the sun! Within it reigned the silence of the dead. But beyond its walls the summer wind roared and sang—the same, the identical wind that blew a hundred or two hundred years ago. And I was alone, absolutely alone, not only in that bright and dead temple but, so it seemed, in all the world. Who could have been with me, with a person who by some truly miraculous circumstance had been spared amidst the vast concourse of the dead, amidst the gross and swift collapse of the Russian Empire, a collapse without equal in the history of man!

And that was my last visit to the manor house. On the following day I departed.

»»» «««

Now, as you see, I am back in Moscow. More than a month has passed since my return, but I'm still living with the keen and, what's more, indescribably strange emotions that I brought back with me. I doubt they will ever leave me. You see, what I began to feel and understand so vividly, acutely during my trip had already long been ripening within me. And I cannot foresee, there just cannot be anything in the future that could alter my present state of mind. They, these people of the so-called New Life, are right—there is no return to former times, to the past, and the new way now reigns firmly, is setting in and becoming the everyday norm. In my present state of mind I constantly feel as if the very last link between me and the world around me were corroding or being ripped apart, as if I were withdrawing from it ever farther into that world to which I have been linked not only all my days, from childhood and infancy, from birth, but even before I was born. I am retiring to "Bygone Elysium," as if into some dream that glitters with a semblance of that realm, bright and strikingly vivid, where those dead people with azure eyes are now transfixed, in that empty palace in the woods near Moscow.

It goes without saying, you see, that a miracle has occurred. A certain someone, already moldering in the stench of a burial pit, turns out not to have perished altogether, like the thousands of others who were dumped with him into that pit. To his own great astonishment he begins gradually recovering his senses, finally makes a complete recovery, and even is able to climb up out of there and make his reentry into the wide world of the living. Now he is back, he acquires once more the familiar habit of being; like everyone—ostensibly like everyone—he sees the city again, the sky, the sun, concerns himself again with nourishment, clothing, shelter, and even with worldly circumstances and endeavors. But, my friend, can a person pass through death, even a temporary death, unscathed? And the most important thing is how much it changed, how incredibly that very wide world itself changed while we, who survived by some miracle, were immured in the grave! I repeat, such a rapid collapse, such a transformation of the whole face of the earth over a period of some five years is unprecedented. Imagine the almost instantaneous ruin of all the world of antiquity; and imagine a few people buried beneath the debris, beneath the avalanche of barbaric hordes, and then those people suddenly come to life after two or three centuries. What must they feel? God, above all else what loneliness, what ineffable loneliness! So, you see, a certain obsession has long been growing within me. The more I get used to the idea that my ascension from the dead is not a dream but is utter reality, the more I am struck by a sensation of the terrible upheaval that has taken place on earth. I speak, of course, not of external changes, although even in externals we must confront a baseness so unparalleled that the situation cannot be rectified for centuries. And I have begun looking around me more and more intently, recalling my life before the grave more and more vividly . . . The obsession has grown and grown. No, for me the world to which I once belonged is not the world of the dead; it is reviving more and more, becoming my soul's single, ever more joyous refuge, my private abode, inaccessible to anyone else!

Yes, on my way out of Moscow, riding through her streets, I felt with a special intensity something I had long experienced. I realized to what extent I am a man of another time and age, and how alien to me are all Moscow's "nooks" and all that new brand of offal that rolls along her streets in automobiles! And then, consider the station from which I departed, the coach where I found a seat, my traveling companion who was drinking milk right out of the bottle . . . Consider the professor with his sackcloth bags, his scholarly fancies, and that forest cutting through which he hobbled away—all alone, terribly alone . . . How touched I was as the train stood at the substation where he got off—those first impressions of silent fields, forest remoteness, the smell of birches, flowers, evening crispness! My God, my God, once again, after a thousand years of the most terrible travail on earth! Once again that pure sacred stillness, the setting sun beyond the forest, the distant expanses, the vista at the other end of the forest cutting, bitter and crisp aromas, the sweet chill of evening glow. And my sense of alienation from this "Soviet" coach on whose platform I stood and from the brown-haired muzhik who was sleeping in it suddenly struck me so deeply and intensely that tears of happiness welled up in my eyes. Yes, by some miracle I have survived, have not perished like the thousands of others who were butchered, tortured, who disappeared without a trace, who shot themselves or hanged themselves; once again I'm alive and even traveling. But what do I have in common with this new way of life, which has devastated my whole universe? I am living—and sometimes, as at this very moment, am even in a mood of rapturous bliss—but with whom and where am I living?

The night that I spent on the tavern porch was also just a part of my past. For could I perceive it as a night in June in the year 1923? No, that night was a night out of my previous life. The heat lightning and the thunder and the crisp wind that blew in with the approaching storm were also of the past. They carried me away completely into the world of the dead, blissfully ensconced for all time in their unearthly cloister. And now that sunny regnancy of the summer days hangs before me incessantly, that pine forest and fairyland-somnolent palace lost and forgotten in the pines, those portals with lions and the tall weeds growing above them, the somber ravines full of firs, shallow ponds with flocks of wagtails on their grassy banks, the lake overgrown with sedge, the forever-deserted church and empty, glistening assembly chambers full of the visages of the dead . . . I cannot describe to you the marvelous feeling that never seems to leave me; how terribly alive they are for me!

Do you remember that Baratynsky poem from which I quoted several lines and which harmonizes so well with what dominates all my present life, with what lies secreted in the inmost recesses of my soul? Do you remember how it ends, that elegy to a presentiment of the Elysium that Baratynsky apprehended, while burdened by his bereavement and sorrow? "Amidst the desolation of my native domain, amidst the ruins and the graves I feel," he says, "the hidden presence of some Spectre"; in reference to that "Lethean Shade," that "Spectre," he writes:

> And it prophesies with suasion an abode divine,
> Where a *sempiternal spring* shall lull me for all time,
> Where I shall not remark the lost destroyed design,
> Where e'er unwithering oaks cast down their blitheful umber,
> And streams flow on unceasing, without number.
> There that sacred Shade I'll meet, that world make mine.

The desolation that surrounds us is indescribable; countless, without end are the ruins and the graves. What do we have left except "Lethean Shades" and that "sempiternal spring" to which, "with suasion," they are calling us?

Maritime Alps, October 5, 1923

»»» «««

In a Never-Never Land

Paper ribbon spurts from the machine by the frozen window of the telegraph office—and Ivlev reads letter by letter the words full of wondrous meaning: "Ivan Sergeevich marries niece at Yuletide horses sent . . ."

The telegrapher, over whose shoulder he reads, shouts oddly that this is officially secret, this is Pushkin's Pskov exposé, but now Ivlev sees himself out on the road, in abysmal winter, in the depths of Russia.

He sees that evening is coming, that with evening comes the frost; he tells himself that no one can recall such a snowy winter since the time of Boris Godunov. And to this wintry Russian evening, to the snowy fields and forests Godunov lends something barbarous and gloomy, menacing. But among other items acquired for the wedding and the holidays, lying there in the sledge are a pair of magnificent Swedish skis, purchased by the niece in Moscow. Their presence brings a surge of joy, a promise of something that makes the heartbeat catch. Briskly, with an air of self-assurance, the troika pushes on.

The sledge is carpeted, plush. In imitation beaver cap and peasant greatcoat girded by a belt with silver studs, the coachman stands in the box. Immobile behind him sit two women who are corpulent with fur coats and shawls: a hale old lady and her black-eyed, rubicund niece. Like everything in the sledge they are powdered with snow spray. Both gaze intently ahead, at the coachman's back, at the bobbing croups of the outrunners, at the horseshoes glistening through clods of snow.

Now they have come out onto the highway; the outrunners jog along more easily, no longer stretching the traces. Their home is already visible in the distance, their village, the doleful, dense, frostbitten pine forests.

Suddenly the old lady speaks out, in a loud, steady voice.

"Well now, thank God we're home. I thought I'd never get out of that Moscow of yours. But here it's just like twenty years off my shoulders; can't get enough of looking around and feeling happy. Tomorrow I'm letting Ivan Sergeevich know—we won't put off your wedding any longer. Do you hear?"

"As you please, Auntie. Whatever you say is fine with me," answers the niece distinctly, with a naivety that sounds merry and sham.

The troika is already dashing smartly through the village, where above peasant huts and snowdrifts stand dark pines grown gray with frost. And beyond the village, in the midst of the forest itself the manor appears: a large, snowy yard; a large, low wooden house. Dusk, desolation, the lights are not yet lit. Reining in the horses, the coachman drives in a wide semicircle up to the porch.

White with snow spray they struggle from the sledge, mount the steps, and enter the warm spacious anteroom, covered cozily with horse cloths, almost pitch-dark. From the back chambers a bustling old granny in woolen stockings comes running; she bows, exults, helps them unbundle. They unwrap the shawls, liberate themselves from the snow-laden, fragrant fur coats. The more the niece unbundles, the more gay and vivacious she becomes, and she suddenly turns out to be slender, lissome; nimbly she takes a seat on the antiquated coffer beside the window and quickly removes her gray city overshoes, revealing one leg to the knee, to the lace of her pantalettes, her black eyes gazing expectantly at her aunt, who divests herself with vigorous but slow movements, breathing laboriously.

Then suddenly it happens, that terrible drawing near of something long since foreboding. Auntie drops her raised arms, gives a weak, sweet cry—and slowly, slowly sinks toward the floor. The granny seizes her under the arms but cannot cope with her weight and cries fiercely, "Miss!"

Through the window one sees the snowy yard, beyond it, amidst the forest, the glittering snowy fields; beyond the fields the low, bald moon looks on, glowing. And now the granny and the aunt are no more; there is only that landscape painting in the window, only the dark anteroom; there is only the joyous horror of that darkness and the absence now of any obstacle between Ivlev and the girl who was supposed to be the bride of some Ivan Sergeevich; there is that one marvelous gleam in the black eyes that suddenly have drawn so very near to him; there is the quick spark of dread that came when she removed her overshoe on the coffer and the very rapture that followed immediately in the weak, sweet cry of her aunt, sinking in death-deep languor onto the floor.

For the entire next day Ivlev is filled with an importunate sensation of passionate love. The secret of what occurred in some pristine country manor underlies all he does, thinks, says, and reads. This sense of being in love is a hundred times more intense than even the feelings he once experienced in his early, most callow youth. And in the depths of his soul he knows no logic will ever convince him that this black-eyed niece does not nor ever did exist in the world, or that, therefore, she does not know what agonizing and joyous memories—their *mutual* memories—have possessed him all day.

Maritime Alps, July 12, 1923

»»» «««

An Unknown Friend

OCTOBER 7

On this *carte illustrée* with such a mournful and sublime view of a moonlit night by the shores of the Atlantic Ocean, I hasten to send you my fervent gratitude for your latest book. These shores are my second home, Ireland—you can see from what a distance one of your unknown friends has sent regards. Be happy and may God keep you.

OCTOBER 8

Here is yet another view of that lonesome country, where fate has cast me forever.

Yesterday, in a dreadful rainstorm—the rain here never ends—I went to the city on some errands, happened to buy your book, and couldn't tear myself from it all the way back to the villa, where my husband and I live year-round because of my poor health. The rain and the storm clouds made the countryside almost dark, flowers and greenery in the gardens were uncommonly vivid, the empty streetcar sped along, discharging violet flashes, but I kept reading and reading, and without knowing why I felt almost tormented with happiness.

Farewell, once more I thank you. There is something else I want to say to you, but what? I don't know, I can't put it in words.

OCTOBER 10

I cannot refrain from writing you again. I suspect you receive too many of these letters. But they are all responses from the very human beings you create for. So why should I be silent? It was you who first established contact with me when you published your book; that is, it was published for me too . . .

The rain has been pouring down all day on our unnaturally green garden; my room is bleak, and the fire in the hearth has been lit since morning. I would like to tell you many things, but you know better than others how difficult it is, almost impossible—to express all of oneself. I am still under the effect of something elusive and equivocal, but beautiful, for which I am obliged to you. Explain it to me, just what is it, that feeling? And what is it people experience when they come under the influence of art? Fascination with human skills and powers? A sharpened desire for personal happiness, which desire ever and always lives within us but is aroused in particular by anything that functions sensuously—music, verses, some graphic recollection, some smell? Or is it a joyous sense of the divine splendor of the human soul, which only those few artists, such as you, can reveal to us, you who remind us that it does exist, nonetheless, that divine splendor? For example, I may read something—at times even something dreadful—and suddenly I say, "God, how beautiful this is!" What does that mean? Perhaps it means: how beautiful life is nonetheless!

Good-bye, soon I shall write you again. I don't think there is anything improper about that; I think it's acceptable—writing to writers. Besides, you do not even have to read my letters . . . although that, of course, would make me very sad.

Night

Forgive me, this may sound ugly, but I cannot help saying it: I am not young, I have a daughter fifteen years old, quite a young lady already, but at one time I was not so bad-looking and I've not changed too considerably since then . . . Nonetheless, I don't want you to imagine me as different from the way I really am.

OCTOBER 11

I have written you by virtue of my need to share with you the emotion stirred within me by your talent, which has the effect of mournful but lofty music. Why is it necessary—this sharing? I don't know, and you don't know either, but we both know full well that this need of the human heart is ineradicable, that without it life does not exist, and that herein lies some great mystery. For you too write only by virtue of that need; what's more—you devote utterly all of your being to it.

I had always read a lot—and kept many diaries, as do all people dissatisfied with life—I still read a lot even now. I had also read you, but only a few of your works, I knew you mostly by name alone. But then this new book of yours . . . How strange it is! A person's hand writes something somewhere, a person's soul conveys a minute fragment of his innermost life through the most minute of allusions—the word can convey so much, even in a style such as yours!—and suddenly space, time, differences in people's fates and circumstances disappear, and your thoughts and feelings become my own, ours in common. Indeed, there is only one soul in the world, a universal soul. Doesn't that explain my impulse to write you, to express something, to share something with you, to complain of something? Aren't your works really the same thing as my letters to you? For you also have something to express to somebody;

you project your lines out somewhere into space, toward a person who is a stranger to you. For you also complain, most often you simply complain, because complaining, in other words pleading for compassion, is utterly inseparable from the human spirit; how much of it there is in songs, prayers, verses, protestations of love!

Perhaps you will answer me, won't you, even if only a word or two? Do answer me!

OCTOBER 13

Once again I'm writing you at night, already in bed, tormented by an elusive desire to say something that very easily could be called naive, that in any case cannot be expressed the way one feels it. Actually, I want to say very little: only that I'm sad, that I feel very sorry for myself—and that, nonetheless, this sadness and this feeling sorry for myself make me happy. It's sad for me to think that I'm in some foreign country on the westernmost shores of Europe, in some villa outside the city, amidst the autumn darkness of the night and fog from the sea, which stretches all the way to America. It's sad that I'm alone, not only in this cozy and splendid room but in all the world. Yet the saddest thing of all is that you, whom I have invented and from whom I am now expecting something, are so infinitely far from me, such a stranger to me, and of course, despite everything I've said, you are alien to me and justifiably so . . .

Really, everything in the world has its charm, even this lamp shade and the golden glow of the lamp, and the glistening linen on my uncovered bed, and my robe, my foot in the slipper, my thin arm in the wide sleeve. And everything is infinitely pathetic—what's the use of it all? Everything passes, will pass, and everything is futile, just as my endless anticipation, which takes the place of life for me . . .

I beg of you—write. Of course only two or three words, just enough so that I know you hear me. Excuse my importunity.

OCTOBER 15

This is our city, our cathedral. The desolate, rocky shores—those on my first *carte postale* to you—are further up the coast, to the north. But even the city, the cathedral—everything here is doleful and somber. Granite, slate, asphalt, and rain, rain . . .

Do write me a brief note; I understand very well that you have no more than two or three words to say to me, but, believe me, I shall not be the least bit offended. Just write, write!

OCTOBER 21

Much to my distress, I've received no letter from you. And fifteen days have passed since I wrote you for the first time . . .

But perhaps your publisher has not yet sent my letters on to you. Perhaps you are distracted by urgent matters or society life. That's very sad; even so, it's better than thinking you have simply scorned my request. Such a thought is very offensive and painful. You may say that I have no right whatsoever to your attention and that, consequently, anything I say about offense or pain is beside the point. But is it true that I do not have that right? Perhaps that right becomes mine once I've experienced certain feelings for you? Wasn't there, for example, a certain Romeo, who demanded requital for his love with no grounds whatsoever for that demand, or Othello, who insisted he had the right to be jealous? Each of them said, "If I love, how can I not be loved, how can someone betray me?" Mine is not the simple desire to be loved; it's more than that, much more complex. Once I love someone or something, that person or thing is already mine, a part of me . . . But I cannot explain it to you properly; I only know that it seems and always has seemed that way to people . . .

But be that as it may, I have no answer from you, and I'm writing you once again. I suddenly conceived the fancy that you were somehow close to me—but then again, was it merely a fancy? I came to believe in the fiction I myself had concocted and began writing you persistently, and now I know that the more I write you, the more indispensable will it be for me to do so because some kind of bond between you and me will grow stronger and stronger. I cannot imagine what you are like; I have absolutely no conception of even your physical features. To whom, then, am I writing? To myself? But it makes no difference. After all, I am you.

OCTOBER 22

Today is a marvelous day, my soul is at ease, the windows are open, and the sun and warm air remind me of spring. How strange this land is! Rainy and cold in summer, rainy and warm in autumn and winter, but from time to time we have such beautiful days that it makes you wonder: is this winter or Italian spring? Oh, Italy, Italy, and my eighteen years, my hopes, my joyous credulity, my expectations on the threshold of life, all of which lay before me and all in a sunlit fog, like the mountains, the vales, and the blossoming gardens surrounding Vesuvius! Forgive me, I know there is nothing at all novel in any of this, but what do I care?

Night

Perhaps you have not written me because I am too abstract for you. Then here are a few more details about my life. I have been married now for sixteen years. My husband is a Frenchman; I met him one winter on the French Riviera, we were married in Rome, and after a wedding trip through Italy we settled here for good. I have three children, a boy and two girls. Do I love them? Yes, I do; even so, my love for them is not like that of most mothers, who cannot conceive of life apart from the family, the children. When my children were small, I looked after them incessantly, sharing in all their play and preoccupations, but now that they no longer need me I have a good deal of free time, which I spend reading. My relatives are far away, our lives have diverged, and our mutual interests are so few that we seldom even write one another. Due to my husband's position I am often obliged to go out in society, to receive guests and return their visits, to attend evening parties and dinners. But I have no friends, male or female. I have nothing in common with the local ladies, and I don't believe in friendship between men and women . . .

That's enough about me. If you reply, tell me at least something about yourself. What are you like? Where do you make your home? Do you prefer Shakespeare or Shelley, Goethe or Dante, Balzac or Flaubert? Do you like music and what kind? Are you married? Are you bound up in some dreary alliance, or perhaps you and your bride are in that tender and beautiful phase when everything is new and joyous, when there still are no memories, which are only wearisome, which give you the illusion of some former happiness, an inscrutable happiness once taken for granted.

NOVEMBER 1

No letter from you. What torment! Such torment that I sometimes curse the day and the hour when I made my decision to write you . . .

And worst of all, there's no way out of this. Despite the many times I have assured myself that no letter will come, that there's nothing to wait for, I keep waiting nonetheless: who can say for sure that a letter won't arrive? Oh, if only I could be certain that you wouldn't write! Just knowing would make me happy. But no, no, hoping is better nonetheless. I'm hoping, I'm waiting!

NOVEMBER 3

No letter, and my torments continue . . . But the only time it's really oppressive is in the morning hours, when after dressing myself with unnaturally calm, deliberate movements but with hands cold from suppressed emotion, I go down for coffee, then give a music lesson to my daughter, who works through the piece with such touching diligence and sits at the piano so straight, so charmingly straight, as only a girl of fifteen can sit. Finally, at midday, the post arrives; I rush to check it, find nothing—and I feel almost calm until the next morning . . .

But today is another splendid day. The low sun is limpid and meek. Autumn flowers bloom amidst the many bare black trees of the garden. Beyond the garden's branches, in the vales, there is something delicate, pale blue, uncommonly beautiful. And in my heart I feel grateful to someone and for something. For what? After all, one really has nothing and never will have anything . . . But is that so, does one indeed have nothing if it exists, that gratitude that moves the soul?

I am grateful also to you for giving me the opportunity to invent you. You will never know me, never meet me, but in this as well there is a good deal of mournful charm. And perhaps it's best that you don't write me, that you have not written me a single word and that I never see you at all as a living person. Could I possibly talk with you like this and perceive you as I do now if I knew you, even if I had but one letter from you? Certainly you would not be the same, certainly a bit worse, and I would be less open about writing you . . .

It's getting cooler, but I've yet to close the window; I keep looking at the pale blue haze of the lowlands and hills beyond the garden. And that blue is tormenting in its beauty, tormenting because one certainly must do something with it. But what should be done? I don't know. We know nothing!

NOVEMBER 5

This resembles a diary, but it's not a diary, nonetheless, because now I have a reader, even if he is only hypothetical . . .

What prompts you to write? The desire to tell about something or to express (even if only allegorically) the whole of yourself? The latter, of course. Nine of every ten writers, even the most renowned, are just storytellers; that is, they actually have nothing in common with what is worthy of being called art. But what is art? Music, a prayer, a song of the human soul . . . Oh, if only I could leave behind even a few lines about how I too once lived, loved, and took joy in my life, how I too had my youth, spring, Italy . . . about the existence of a faraway land on the shores of the Atlantic Ocean, where I live, love, and still keep on waiting for something even now . . . about some poor and savage islands on this ocean and some people who live a poor and savage life, a people alien to all the world, whose origin, obscure language, and reason for being no one knows nor ever will know . . .

Nonetheless, I keep waiting and waiting for a letter. Now this has become something like an obsession, a kind of mental disorder.

NOVEMBER 7

Yes, everything is marvelous. No letter has arrived, of course, not one single letter. And just imagine: because that letter has not arrived, because I have no answer from a person I have never seen nor ever will see, no response to my voice cast out somewhere into the distance, into my own dream, I feel a horrible loneliness, the horrible emptiness of the world! Emptiness, emptiness!

Rain, fog, humdrum existence once again. But there's even something good about this; that is, it's normal, just as it should be. That thought calms me.

Good-bye, may God forgive you for your cruelty. Yes, it is cruel nonetheless.

NOVEMBER 8

It's only three o'clock, but the fog and the rain make it seem just like twilight.

At five we're having guests for tea.

They'll drive up in the rain in their automobiles from the dismal city, which is even more black when rain is falling, with its black wet asphalt, black wet rooftops, and black granite cathedral, whose spire fades away in the rain and murk . . .

I'm dressed already and seem to be awaiting my entrance onto the stage. I'm awaiting that moment when I will say all the proper things, be gracious, animated, solicitous, and just a bit pale, but that can easily be attributed to the dreadful weather. Now that I'm dressed I seem to have grown younger, I feel like my daughter's elder sister, and I'm ready to burst into tears at any moment. I have experienced, nonetheless, something strange, something like love. For whom? On what account?

Farewell, I no longer expect anything—I say that with complete sincerity.

NOVEMBER 10

Farewell, my unknown friend. I break off this unrequited correspondence in the same way I began it—with gratitude. Thank you for not replying. It would have been worse had it been otherwise. What could you have said to me? At what point could we have stopped writing one another without a feeling of constraint? And what else could I have found to tell you besides what has already been said? I have nothing more to say—I've said everything. Actually, only two or three lines can be written about any human life. Oh yes. Only two or three lines.

Once again I'm alone in my house, with the foggy ocean nearby, with humdrum autumn and winter days, and with a strange feeling—as if I had lost someone. And I return once again to my diary, for which I have a strange need, though God only knows why this diary, and your writings, are so necessary.

A few days ago I dreamt of you. You were somehow strange, taciturn, sitting in the corner of a dark room, and you were invisible. But I could see you nonetheless. Even in my sleep I felt: how can someone you've never seen in your life appear visible in your dreams? For isn't it true that only God creates from a void? And I felt terrified and awoke full of fear, with a sense of oppression.

In fifteen or twenty years, possibly, neither you nor I will be on this earth. Till we meet again in the otherworld! Who can be sure that it does not exist? After all, we don't understand even our own dreams, the creative work of our own imaginations. Is it ours, the imagination, that is, to be more precise, what we call our imagination, our fancies, our reveries? Is it our own will we obey when we yearn for communion with this or that human soul, as I yearn for communion with yours?

Farewell. But no, I'll say au revoir nonetheless.

Maritime Alps, 1923

»»» «««

The Hare

The opaque murk of a snowstorm. Glass in the windowpanes is pasted over with fresh white snow, and the light in the manor house has a white, niveous hue; pounding incessantly, monotonously beyond the walls, monotonously knocking at regular intervals against the roof, a bough on the old tree in the front garden creaks and groans. As always during a snowstorm I take peculiar delight in the aura of olden times, in the coziness of the house.

Then the door slams in the vestibule and I hear Petya, who has returned from hunting, hear him stamp his felt boots, shake himself free of snow, then walk with soft steps through the parlor to his room. I get up and go into the vestibule. Did he have any luck?

He did.

Sprawled on a bench in the vestibule lies a hare, whitened with frost, front legs thrust forward and hind legs backward. I gaze at him and touch him with a feeling of wonder and rapture.

He has a broad forehead, with large and goggling, backward-staring glassy eyes that are golden at the pupil and still have all their luster—still the same aimless gleam they had in life.

But now his heavy carcass is utterly rock hard and cold.

Stretched taut and covered in coarse fur, his legs are also like rock. The gray-brown tuft of a tail has the screwed-tight appearance of a taut knot. There is congealed blood on the bristling, feline whiskers and the cleft upper lip.

Marvelous, simply a miracle!

An hour ago, no more than an hour ago, he was out in the fields twitching those whiskers, with those long ears flattened back, peering keenly, intently over his shoulder out of the glass of those eyes, golden at the pupil, crouched in a frozen depression beneath a snowdrift, filling that hole with his intense warmth, reveling in the raging haze of the blizzard, which blew from all sides and brought snow down upon him. Suddenly discovered and roused by the dog, he fled in a headlong dash, the mind-spinning beauty of which cannot be expressed in the words of man. And how hot and feral was the pounding of his terror-stricken heart when the shot stunned him, brought his flight to an abrupt end, and Petya caught him firmly by the ears, and with what a piercing, infantile scream did he respond to the last thing he felt—the quick sharp flame of the knife that pierced deep into his throat.

No words can convey the ineffable delight I take in this smooth fur and stone-rigid carcass, and in my very own being, and in the cold window of the vestibule, covered over, pasted with fresh white snow, and in all that blizzardly pale light spilling throughout the house.

August 19, 1924

»»» «««

The Cranes

A clear and cold day in late autumn. I ride on horseback at a steady jog-trot along the highroad. Gleaming low sun and empty fields; an autumnal mute anticipation in the air. Then, from behind me, in the distance, a clacking of wheels. I listen: a faint brisk clack, the clatter of a light *drozhky.* I turn around—someone is overtaking me. That someone comes nearer and nearer; now I can see his horse distinctly, racing at full speed, then the driver himself, glancing out occasionally from behind the horse and laying on first the whip, then the reins . . . What can the problem be? He keeps coming on and now he has almost reached me. I hear the furious panting of the horse over that clacking sound, then a desperate shout: "Master, give way!" Startled and confused, I swerve sharply off the road—and they flash past in a trice, first the marvelous bay mare, her eye, her nostrils, new reins the color of sealing wax, new gleaming harness, lather below her tail on the thighs, then the man himself: a muzhik, a black-bearded gallant utterly possessed by the swift ride and by a senseless, devil-may-care frenzy. He casts his rabid gaze upon me as he flies past, and I catch several striking details: his hearty red mouth and the pitch black of his handsome, youthful beard, his new peaked cap, his yellow silk shirt beneath a long black coat thrown open. I recognize him—the rich, provident miller from near Livny—and he rushes on like the wind. After barreling along for about one more verst, he suddenly leaps from the *drozhky.* I pick up my pace and ride hard to reach him, and this is what I see as I approach: the horse is standing on the road, sides heaving laboriously, the sealing-wax reins hang over the shafts, and the driver himself lies on the road nearby, facedown, the skirts of his long coat spread wide.

"Master!" he shouts fiercely into the earth. "Master!"

He flaps his arms about in despair.

"Ah, it's so sa-a-a-ad! Ah, master, the cranes is done flew away!"

And shaking his head from side to side, he chokes on drunken tears.

1930

»»» «««

The Calf's Head

A boy of about five, freckled, wearing a sailor suit, stands quietly in the butcher shop, as if enchanted; Papa has gone off to his job at the post office, Mama to the marketplace, taking him with her.

"Today we're having a calf's head with parsley," she had said, and he had conjured up something small, attractive, beautifully garnished with bright green leafage.

Now he stands there and gapes, surrounded on all sides by something huge and red, by short, truncated legs hanging to the floor from rusty iron hooks and headless necks hulking up to the ceiling. The front of each hulk has a long, empty, gaping belly covered in nacreous ingots of blubber, and the shoulders and rumps glitter with fine pellicles of dried fatty meat. But his torpid gaze is concentrated upon a head, which has turned up right in front of him, lying on the marble counter. Mama looks at it too as she haggles fervently with the shop's proprietor, who is also enormous and fat, wearing a coarse white apron horribly stained on the belly with what looks like rust, girded very low by a broad belt that hangs with thick, greasy scabbards. Precisely it, the head, is the object of Mama's haggling; the meat man is screaming something angrily and jabbing the head with a pulpy finger. All the controversy revolves around it, but it lies immobile, apathetic. Its bovine brow is flat and placid, the turbid blue eyes are half closed, the large lashes drowsy, and the nostrils and lips so dilated that they have an impudent, disgruntled look. And all of it is naked, flesh gray and resilient, like rubber.

Then with one terrible blow of his ax, the meat man cleaved it into two halves, and he flung one half, with one ear, one eye, and one thick nostril, in Mama's direction, onto a piece of cotton-thread paper.

1930

»»» «««

The Elephant

A thin, lively eyed little girl resembling a fox cub, uncommonly charming in her pale blue ribbon, which grips the platinum hair in a bow on the crown of her head, stands in a menagerie, gaping at the oblique, scabrous hulk of an elephant, obtusely and majestically facing her with his large, broad-browed head, ratty ears like burdock leaves, starkly protruding tusks, and thick, hummocky tube of low-hanging proboscis with a black rubbery funnel at its tip. In a very soft voice: "Mama, why are his legs swelled up?"

Mama laughs. But the elephant himself is laughing. Inclining the broad-browed head, he looks back at the girl, and there is clearly a glitter of something sly and merry in his porcine little eyes. He sways back and forth with pleasure, begins twitching the proboscis—and suddenly, out of pathetic helplessness, unable to express his feelings and thoughts any other way, he raises it up at a sharp angle, revealing the moist fleshy pulp of its underside, the horns of his bared tusks, and the absurdly small mouth between them; in anguished rapture he lets roll out of his terrible viscera a hollow, thunderous rumble, then emits a joyously doltish, mighty bellow that shakes the whole menagerie.

For dinner a special dish of cauliflower was served and there were guests—a plumpish but still youthful and attractive lady with a black-eyed boy, who was very quiet and attentive.

Mama told about the elephant, how the little girl had asked about his legs. The girl understood that she had said something funny, that she was the source of admiration, and she started twisting and turning, rolling her head round and round, then suddenly burst out with excessively loud guffaws.

"A lovely child!" said the lady in a pensive voice, gazing at her unabashedly.

And kicking out with her dangling feet, she repeated archly, "No, Mama, really: Why are his legs swelled up?"

But Mama's smile was no longer spontaneous; she was talking with the lady about something else now, something of absolutely no interest. Then, casting a sideways glance at the boy, the little girl fidgeted out of her chair, ran up to the buffet, and, in order to get their attention again, started guzzling water right from the mouth of a carafe, sputtering, burbling, and spilling it down her chin. When she had spilled it all over herself and had choked, she stopped and burst into tears.

1930

»»» «««

Indulgent Participation

In Moscow—let us say on Molchanovka—lives "a former artiste of the Imperial Theaters." Alone, very elderly, broad across the cheekbones, wiry and lean. She gives singing lessons. And this is what happens to her every year in December.

One Sunday—let us imagine a very frosty, sunlit morning—the bell in her vestibule rings.

"Annushka! It's the doorbell!" she cries anxiously to the cook from her bedroom.

The cook runs to get the door—and then steps back in astonishment: so dazzling, so smartly arrayed are the guests—two young ladies in furs and white gloves and their escort, a coxcomb of a student from the university, frozen through in his light uniform coat and thin boots.

The guests wait for quite some time in the cold sitting room, which admits an amber glow through the frosty mosaic of the windows; then they hear the brisk footsteps of their hostess and hurriedly arise to greet her. She is all in a flurry—knowing why they have come, she has heavily powdered her face and perfumed her large, bony hands.

"For goodness' sake, forgive me, ladies and gentlemen; it seems I've made you wait," she says with a captivating smile and the most worldly nonchalance. As she makes her swift entry, she has difficulty controlling the beating of her heart.

"But no, please forgive us for the imposition," the student interrupts with refined deference, bowing and kissing her hand. "We come to you with an assiduous and most humble request. The organization committee for the traditional literary-vocal-musical evening in aid of impecunious matriculants of the Fifth Moscow Gymnasium has bestowed upon us the honor of petitioning you in regard to your indulgent participation in that evening, which is to transpire on the third day of the Christmas holidays."

"Ladies and gentlemen, if possible, spare me!" she begins captivatingly. "The fact is—"

But the young ladies pounce upon her with such cordiality, with such ardor and flattery that she cannot manage even this feeble attempt to refuse or evade . . .

After that three whole weeks go by.

For three whole weeks Moscow works, does business, makes merry, but among all its most diverse occupations, interests, and distractions, it secretly harbors only one feeling—anticipation of the portentous evening performance on the twenty-seventh of December. Countless playbills of all colors and sizes mingle in motley assemblage on every street and intersection: *The Lower Depths, The Blue Bird, The Three Sisters,* Chaliapin in *Water Nymph,* Sobinov in *Snow Maiden,* Shor, Krein, and Erlich, Zimin's Opera, an evening with Igor Severianin . . . But now what catches all eyes? Only the small placard printed in large letters with the given name, patronymic, and surname of that indulgent participant in the literary-vocal-musical evening in aid of impecunious pupils of the Fifth Moscow Gymnasium. All this time the participant herself never goes out, sits at home working without respite so as not to disappoint the expectations of Moscow; endlessly she contemplates her repertoire, testing her voice from morning to evening, preparing first one selection, then another . . .

Now the days go by with extraordinary rapidity, and this rapidity horrifies her: before you have time to blink your eyes that terrible December 27 will be here!

She has stopped giving lessons, receives no one, never leaves the house for fear of catching bronchitis or a head cold. What, exactly, should she perform? The audience has no inkling of the difficulty this question presents to even the most experienced artiste! One must manifest the utmost in acumen, taste, tact, and savoir faire! After long, agonizing doubts and waverings, however, she settles the matter by retaining her old, unchanged repertoire. Once again she rehearses three pieces. The first is French, tender and sad, bewitching like a lullaby but concealing the enormous passion, strength, and pain of an enamored feminine soul, which madly thirsts for happiness but sacrificially abnegates this happiness; the second is full of scintillating coloratura and Russian impetuosity; and then—the pièce de résistance: "I would kiss you, but I fear the moon would see," in which, as always, she will display extraordinary resplendence, will perform "with fervor," wantonly, youthfully, and will break off on such a desperately high and exultant note that the entire concert hall will then shudder with applause. Besides these, she prepares twelve other pieces for encores . . . The days keep flashing by, and now a certain foreboding grows in her soul, as if the hour of her execution were approaching. She works, however, and works still more. And then, at last, that final, fateful day arrives!

On the morning of December 27 all her faculties are strained to the limits of intensity. In the morning still one more rehearsal, but this is the final, the dress rehearsal. Now she sings as if onstage, in full voice, with all the expressiveness of high art; she and her accompanist review her entire program—and she has that feeling: all the work was not in vain! But who knows, for all that, what awaits her in the evening? Triumph or perdition? Her face is aflame, her hands like ice . . . After the rehearsal she goes into her bedroom, undresses, and lies down. Annushka brings her something totally exceptional—impressed granular caviar, cold pullet, and port wine: on the day of a performance this is the lunch of all great artistes. Having eaten, she orders the cook to pull the shutters, to leave her, and to maintain absolute silence in the house. She closes her eyes and lies in the darkness completely quiescent, trying to think of nothing, to let nothing agitate her—for an hour, two, three, right up to six o'clock in the evening. At six she jumps up: a strident ring in the vestibule—the hairdresser!

Heart beating, ears and cheeks blazing, hands icy, she measures out forty whole drops of an etheric-valerian medicine, and in her robe, with hair let down, like a virgin they have come to adorn, to prepare for immolation, she takes her seat before the mirror. Having first warmed his hands over the stove in the kitchen, the hairdresser comes in and says encouragingly, "Marvelous weather! A little nippy, but marvelous!"

He works slowly, with refinement, feeling that he too is a participant in the forthcoming event, understanding completely and sharing her artiste's agitation since he himself is an artist at heart. With his casually light conversation, his jokes, and, in general, all his proficiency in these matters—together with his implicit faith in her forthcoming success—he calms her little by little, restores her vigor, fortitude, and hopes . . . But when he has completed his work, when he has examined it from all sides and is convinced that nothing better can possibly be made of these magnificent waves and coifs, he leaves, and the clock in the dining room slowly strikes seven. Once again her heart begins to founder: they are coming for her at half past eight!

Eight strikes and still she is not ready. She has taken drops again—this time Hoffmann's; she puts on her best linen, rouges and powders herself . . . Then at half past eight the bell rings once more, jolting her like thunder: they've come! Annushka runs clumsily into the vestibule; she too is beside herself, so agitated that she has trouble getting the door to open.

They—this time two university students—have arrived in a huge, antediluvian hired coach with two mammoth nags in harness. They too are men-about-town and they too wear no galoshes, and their feet too are rigid from the frost. The sitting room, as usual, is cold; lamps smelling of kerosene burn drearily. In only their dress coats they patiently sit, their mirror-smooth heads glistening, wafting the sweet scent of brilliantine and pomade, with large white satin bows on their chests like groomsmen at a wedding. They sit in silence, wait politely, steadfastly, look at the doors closed on all sides around them, at the frozen windowpanes flickering with fiery dots of blue and red, at the grand piano, at the portraits of great male and female singers on the walls; they listen to the numb knell and the din of trams beyond the windows, to the apprehensive steps of Annushka and the artiste herself behind the doors . . . Time passes, a quarter hour, a half hour, forty minutes . . . Then all at once one of the doors opens wide. As if on cue they jump from their seats, and with a captivating insouciant smile the artiste rushes to greet them.

"For goodness' sake, forgive me, gentlemen, it seems I've made you wait . . . What now, could it really be time? Well, all right then, we'll go if you wish. I'm ready."

Even through the rouge and powder on her cheeks crimson blotches burn; her breath is redolent of drops, lilies of the valley, her hands of cream, her airy, smoke-colored, gossamer dress of fragrances. She looks like Death setting off for a ball. She has thrown something lacy-black, Spanish over her intricate elevated coiffure, over the gray hair waved and fluffed on all sides, and has draped a coat of white curly goat's hair over the bare shoulders with the enormous clavicles . . . The students rush headlong after her into the anteroom. The slimmer and taller one seizes her overshoes, hastily drops to one knee and fits them adroitly over her black satin slippers with the diamond buckles; when she bends to help him and to make a modest attempt at straightening the hem on the white lace tips of her pantalettes, he smells how her armpits reek with the rankness of mice.

She sang of the storm cloud that met the thunder and of some kind of sanctuary—"the Lord has sent us to a sink-tuary here"—and with special resplendence, "I would kiss you . . ." A carping old gaffer sitting in the first row snickered sarcastically at this point, twisted his head back with unequivocal insinuation: my humble thanks, but please, no kisses . . . For all that he only made a fool of himself. The performance came off with colossal success; incessantly they called the artiste back and forced encores upon her—especially the sensitive young people, who stood in the aisles shouting even with menace and beating together their cupped palms with an awesome, booming resonance.

1929

»»» «««

The Idol

It was teeming and animated that winter too, as winters always were in the Moscow Zoological Gardens. Music was played at the skating rink from three o'clock on, and there were throngs of people arriving, swarming about, skating. But on the way to the rink they all paused for a moment to gaze curiously at something attracting their notice in one of the pens by the road. All the rest of the pens, together with the many artificial grottos, huts, and pavilions scattered about on the snowy meadows of the zoo, were deserted, and like everything deserted, they were doleful. All the strange beasts and birds who populated the zoo were wintering in warm lodgings, but this pen was inhabited; it contained something even more exotic than any pelican, gazelle, or duck-billed platypus: an Eskimo tent of skins and bark and a big, bearded dun reindeer with smooth rump and bobtailed, crowned by the high and heavy blades of gray antlers—a powerful beast who was somehow all firm and rigid, like everything northern, polar; he was meandering about, poking at the snow periodically with the hoof of his slender leg, searching for something beneath it. And beside the tent, sitting right on the snow, his short legs in skewbald fur stockings crossed and tucked under him, his bare head protruding from indurate sacking of reindeer hide, was what appeared to be some living idol, but it was simply an effeminate, beardless, savage muzhik, who had almost no neck, whose flat skull was striking for its brawn and for the thickness of the coarse and straight resinous black hair upon it, whose copper yellow face, with broad cheeks and narrow eyes, was marked by an inhuman obtuseness, which, however, appeared somehow blended with sorrow. From three o'clock until late evening this idol did nothing but sit there in the snow, paying no attention to the people swarming in front of him, but from time to time he put on a performance. Between his knees there were two wooden basins: one containing pieces of raw horse flesh and the other black blood. He would extend his short arm for a piece of the horse flesh, dip it into the blood, stuff it in his fish mouth, swallow, and lick clean the fingers, which were completely out of keeping with everything else: they were small, slender, and even beautiful . . .

That winter, among those who went to the skating rink at the Moscow Zoological Gardens and who, in passing, looked upon such an astounding specimen of humanity were a young man and his fiancée, both university students. And the image of those happy days remained in their memories forever: snow-laden grounds, frostiness, trees in the zoological gardens incrusted with curls of rime as if with gray coralline rock, the bars of a waltz drifting over from the rink, and him, sitting there, incessantly stuffing in his mouth the pieces of sopping meat black with blood, absolutely no expression in his dark narrow eyes, on his flat yellow iconic face.

1930

»»» «««

The Consecration of Love

I

Mitya's last happy day in Moscow was the ninth of March. So, at least, it seemed to him.

Near midday he was walking with Katya up Tverskoy Boulevard. All at once winter had yielded to spring; the patches of sun were almost hot. It appeared the skylarks had indeed returned, bringing with them warmth and joy. Everything was wet, everything was melting, dripping, dribbling from buildings; yardmen were clearing ice from the sidewalks, heaving down glutinous snow from the roofs; there was animation everywhere, masses of people all about. Lofty clouds drifted apart like faint white smoke, blending into the moist blue sky. In the distance Pushkin towered, assuasively pensive, and the Strastnoy Monastery gleamed. But best of all, Katya, who was prettier than ever that day, utterly guileless and intimate, would often take Mitya's arm with childlike trust and look up at his face, which was happy, even appeared a bit supercilious as he walked along with such lengthy strides that she barely could keep up with him.

When they had reached the Pushkin Monument she said abruptly, "How funny you are; when you laugh you stretch open that big mouth of yours with a kind of sweet, juvenile awkwardness. Don't get offended; it's for your very smile that I love you. And, of course, for your Byzantine eyes."

Trying not to smile, suppressing both a secret gratification and a vague resentment, Mitya answered congenially as he gazed at the monument that now rose high above them.

"As for juvenile behavior, it seems you and I have a lot in common there. And I'm about as similar to a Byzantine as you are to a Chinese empress. You're all so wild with ecstasy over these Byzantiums and Renaissances . . . I can't understand your mother!"

"Well, what would you do in her place—lock me up in some castle tower?" asked Katya.

"No, I'd simply bar the door to all those professed theatrical bohemians, those future celebrities from studios, conservatories, and drama schools," answered Mitya, still trying to be calm and amiably casual. "You told me yourself that Bukovetsky once asked you to have dinner at the Strelna and that Egorov suggested sculpting you naked, posing as some kind of moribund ocean wave, and of course you were terribly flattered by such an honor."

"All the same, I won't abandon my art, even for your sake," said Katya. "Maybe I'm repulsive, as you so often tell me," she said, although Mitya had never told her anything of the kind. "Maybe I'm depraved, but take me for what I am. And let's not quarrel; stop being jealous for at least today, on such a marvelous day! Why can't you understand that, even so, you're better for me than any of them, you're the only one?" she asked softly, emphatically, gazing into his eyes with affected seductiveness. Then pensively and languidly she declaimed, "Betwixt us there's a slumbrous secret. / A ring has passed from soul to soul."

This final touch, these verses pained Mitya to the quick. On the whole, much was unpleasant and painful even on that day. The jesting remark about his juvenile awkwardness was unpleasant; it was not the first time Katya had made such remarks, and made them in earnest. Now in one respect, now in another, Katya had often proved herself more grown up than he; often (and unwittingly, that is, quite naturally) she had demonstrated her superiority over him, and he was painfully aware of that, took it as a sign that she was versed in some secret profligacy. The "even so" was unpleasant ("even so, you're better for me than any of them") and the abrupt sotto voce that for some reason she put on when she said it; especially unpleasant were the verses, the mannered declamation. But Mitya could bear even the verses and the declamation, that is, what most reminded him of the set that was drawing Katya away from him, arousing his acute hatred and jealousy, he could bear all of this with comparative ease on that happy day, the ninth of March, his last happy day in Moscow, so it often later seemed to him.

As they were returning that day from Kuznetsky Avenue, where Katya had bought several Scriabin pieces at Zimmerman's, she spoke in passing about his, Mitya's, mother and said with a laugh, "You can't imagine how frightened I am at the very thought of meeting her!"

For some reason not once during the whole time they had been together had they touched upon the future, on what was to become of their love. Now suddenly Katya had brought up his mother and had spoken as if it were thoroughly understood that this was her future mother-in-law.

2

Then everything appeared to flow along as before. Mitya accompanied Katya to the studio of the Moscow Art Theater, to concerts, to literary evenings. He went to her house on Kislovka, overstaying himself, sitting until two in the morning and taking advantage of the strange freedom accorded Katya by her mother, a nice, kindly woman with vermilion-dyed hair, always smoking, always well rouged (long separated from her husband, who had another family now). Katya would also drop in at Mitya's student lodgings on Molchanovka, and just as before they spent nearly all their time in an oppressive daze, kissing incessantly. But Mitya was troubled by a persistent fear that something terrible had suddenly begun, that something had changed, or had begun to change, in Katya.

It had quickly flown by, that buoyant, unforgettable time when they had just met, when, barely acquainted, they suddenly felt that nothing was more interesting than talking (morning till night) only with one another—when so unexpectedly Mitya had found himself in that fairyland world of love that he had awaited secretly since childhood, boyhood. It was December—frigid, fine, day after day adorning Moscow with dense rime frost and the turbid red sphere of the low sun. Then January, February began whirling Mitya's love in a vortex of unremitting happiness, which already seemed finalized, or at least was just on the brink of realization. But already even then something had begun (more and more often) to aggrieve him, to poison the happiness. Already even then it often seemed, somehow, that there were two Katyas. One was she for whom Mitya had felt an urgent need, had begun desiring from the first moment of their acquaintance, and the other was the real, the commonplace Katya, grievously irreconcilable with the first. At that time, nevertheless, Mitya had experienced nothing comparable to his present feelings.

Everything could be explained. Spring's feminine concerns had commenced—shopping, placing orders, interminable alterations of one thing or another—and Katya did indeed have occasion to frequent the dressmakers with her mother; she also had examinations to face at the private school of dramatics where she studied. Her preoccupation, her distraction, therefore, could be entirely natural. Mitya kept seeking consolation in such thoughts, but consolations were to no avail. His morbidly suspicious heart produced counterarguments that were stronger, that were corroborated more and more manifestly. Katya's inner aloofness kept growing and with it grew his morbid suspiciousness and his jealousy. The director of the drama school made Katya's head whirl with praises, and, unable to restrain herself, she repeated his words to Mitya. The director had told her, "You, my dear, are the pride of our school" (he called all of his actress-pupils My Dear)—and during the Lenten season, in addition to her group lessons, he began working with her privately, so as to make a brilliant display of her at the examinations. It was well known that he debauched his young actresses; every summer he took one or another of them with him to the Caucasus, to Finland, or abroad. And Mitya began imagining that now the director had designs on Katya, who, although not at fault, probably sensed his intentions, understood them nonetheless, and therefore appeared to be in collusion with him, involved in a vile, illicit relationship. This thought was all the more tormenting since it was only too apparent that Katya's interest in Mitya had diminished.

By all indications something had begun drawing her away from him. Just thinking of the director was enough to upset him. But not only the director! It seemed some other preoccupations had begun taking precedence over Katya's love. Preoccupations with whom or what? Mitya did not know; he was jealous of everyone, of everything, but primarily of the way of life, as he imagined it, that she now appeared to have adopted behind his back. It seemed that she was gravitating irresistibly away from him and toward something, perhaps toward the sort of thing that was frightening even to contemplate.

Once, in her mother's presence, Katya had remarked, half in jest, "Mitya, where women are concerned, your reasoning is based altogether on the old *Rules of the Household.* You'll turn out to be an absolute Othello. I, for one, wouldn't ever think of falling in love with you, and I'd never marry you!"

Her mother objected.

"But I can't conceive of love without jealousy. Someone who is not jealous, in my opinion, is not in love."

"No, Mother," said Katya with her habitual penchant for repeating the views of others. "Jealousy shows a lack of respect for the person one loves. If I can't be trusted, I'm not loved," she said, pointedly looking away from Mitya.

"But in my opinion," objected her mother, "jealousy is what love is. I even read that somewhere. It was proved quite conclusively, and they even gave examples from the Bible, where the Lord God himself is called jealous and vengeful."

As for Mitya's love, it was now manifested almost exclusively by jealousy. This was not ordinary jealousy but, so it seemed to him, a special kind. Although they had allowed themselves too much, he and Katya had not yet taken the final step toward intimacy. When they were alone Katya was often even more passionate than before, but this had begun arousing his suspicions now, sometimes giving rise to a sense of horror. All of the feelings that contributed to his jealousy were horrible, but among them there was one that was most horrendous of all, one that Mitya could not formulate, was utterly incapable of comprehending. It consisted of the idea that these manifestations of passion, the very passion that was so beatific and sweet, that, when applied to them, to Mitya and Katya, was more lofty, more lovely than anything in the world, became unspeakably vile, seemed even somehow grotesquely unnatural when Mitya thought of Katya with another man. That was when he would feel an intense revulsion toward her. Everything that he himself did with her in private was full of paradisic captivation and chasteness. But as soon as he imagined someone else in his place it changed instantaneously, was transformed into something shameless, which provoked a craving to throttle Katya, not the fancied rival but Katya herself.

3

Katya's examinations, which were held at last (in the sixth week of Lent), seemed to confirm decisively that Mitya had good reason to feel tormented.

Katya did not even see him there, did not notice him at all, was utterly alien, promiscuous.

Her performance was a great success. She was dressed all in white, like a bride, and was captivating in her agitation. The audience applauded cordially and fervently, while the director, a smug thespian with impassive, dolorous eyes, sat in the front row, and simply to flaunt his exorbitant pride he gave her instructions from time to time, speaking softly but in such a way that the unbearable sound of his voice carried throughout the auditorium.

"Less preciosity," he said ponderously, calmly, with an imperious air that suggested Katya was every bit his own private possession. "Don't act, live the role," he said distinctly.

That too was unbearable. And even the reading was unbearable, although it prompted applause. Katya was burning with embarrassment, blushing furiously, her weak voice sometimes cracked, she had trouble catching her breath, and all that was touching and charming. But she read with a vulgar, singsong mellifluence, every sound full of pose and stupidity, considered the acme of declamatory art by those Mitya so detested, the actors' set that dominated her every move these days. She did not speak, but constantly vociferated, with a certain importunate, languorous ardor, with an excessive beseeching that had absolutely no basis for its urgency, and Mitya was so ashamed for her that he could not bear to look. But most horrendous of all was the blend of angelic purity and profligacy in everything about her, in her blazing face, her white dress, which seemed shorter onstage since those sitting in the auditorium viewed Katya from below, her small white slippers, her legs tightly encased by silk stockings. "In the church choir a young girl sang," read Katya with affected, excessive naivety about some girl who was, ostensibly, angelic in her innocence. And Mitya felt both poignantly close to Katya—as one always feels in a crowd toward the one he loves—and fiercely hostile toward her; he took pride in her, realized that, even so, she belonged to him and simultaneously felt a pain that rent his heart: no, she no longer belonged to him!

After the examinations the happy days returned, but Mitya could not believe in that happiness so easily as he once had. Recalling the examinations, Katya remarked, "How silly you are! Really, couldn't you sense that I was reading so well just for you and you alone!"

But he could not forget how he had felt at the examinations and could not admit that even now he was feeling the same way. During one of their arguments Katya, who could sense what he felt and was keeping from her, exclaimed, "I don't understand why you love me if, in your opinion, everything about me is so nasty! Just what is it, after all, that you want of me?"

But he himself could not understand why he loved her, although he felt that his love not only was not diminishing but was ever growing, together with the jealous struggle he was waging with someone, with something on account of it, this love, on account of its intensifying power, the increasing demands that it made of him.

"You love only my body, not my soul!" Katya once said bitterly.

Again these were someone else's words, histrionic words, but despite all their absurdity and banality they touched upon something grievously insoluble. He did not know why he loved her, could not say exactly what he wanted . . . What does it mean, after all—love? Answering this question was all the more impossible since in nothing that Mitya had heard about love, in nothing that he had read was there a single precise definition of the word. In books and in life everyone apparently had agreed once and for all to speak only about love that is almost discarnate or only about what is called passion, sensuality. But his love was neither the one nor the other. What did he feel for her? That which is called love or that which is called passion? Was it Katya's soul or her body that produced an almost giddy sensation, a kind of death-laden beatitude when he undid her blouse and kissed her breasts, paradisiacally captivating and vestal, bared with a kind of soul-stunning docility, with the shamelessness of purest innocence?

4

She was changing more and more.

Partly responsible was her success at the examinations. There were, however, other reasons for the change.

With the coming of spring Katya appeared somehow to have undergone an instantaneous transformation into a young society miss, elegantly dressed, always rushing somewhere. Now Mitya even felt ashamed of his dark corridor when she drove up—she never came on foot now, but always by cab—when she scurried along that corridor in her susurrous silk, veil lowered over her face. Now, invariably, she treated him with tenderness, but invariably she was late and cut short their meetings, saying she had to go to the dressmaker's again with her mother.

"You know, we're decking ourselves out with mad abandon!" she said gaily, widening her eyes with astonishment, perfectly aware that Mitya did not believe her but saying it all nonetheless, since they had utterly nothing to talk about anymore.

Now she almost never removed her hat, kept her umbrella in her hand, sat on Mitya's bed as she prepared to go, her calves, tightly encased in silk stockings, driving him mad. And after telling him that in the evening she would be out again—she had to visit someone again with Mother—just before leaving she invariably went through one and the same ritual, clearly aimed at duping him, at compensating for all his silly, as she called them, torments: with a sham-surreptitious glance over her shoulder at the door she slipped off the bed, brushing her hips against his legs, and said in a hasty whisper, "Well, kiss me then!"

5

Finally, at the end of April, Mitya decided to go to the country for a rest. He had thoroughly drained, thoroughly tormented both himself and Katya, and the torment was all the more unbearable since there appeared to be no reason for it whatsoever. Had anything really happened, was Katya really guilty of anything? One day, with the firmness of desperation, she told him, "Yes, do go, go away; I simply haven't the strength! We must part temporarily to clarify our relationship. You've got so thin that Mother has convinced herself you have consumption. I simply can't take any more!"

So Mitya's departure was fixed. But, although beside himself with grief, to his great amazement he was almost happy nonetheless. As soon as the departure was fixed, everything abruptly reverted to the way it had been before. He had always wanted desperately to deny the horrible suspicions that gave him no peace day or night. The slightest change in Katya, therefore, was enough to change his view of everything again. Once again she had become tender and passionate beyond all pretense—he sensed this with the unerring discernment of his jealous temperament—and once again he began sitting with her until two in the morning, again they found things to talk about, and the closer it came to the day of his departure, the more absurd their separation appeared, the need to "clarify the relationship." One day Katya even broke into tears—she had never wept before—and those tears suddenly made her frightfully dear to him, transfixed him with a feeling of acute pity and a vague sense of guilt.

At the beginning of June her mother was leaving to spend all summer in the Crimea and was taking Katya with her. They decided to meet in Miskhor, where Mitya would come later.

He prepared to leave, made ready for departure, wandered around Moscow in a strange stupefaction, peculiar to one who goes briskly about his business although inflicted with some grave disease. He was steeped in morbid sadness and at the same time morbidly happy, moved by Katya's renewed intimacy, her solicitude—she had even gone with him to buy straps for his luggage, as if she were his fiancée or wife—and by the rejuvenation of almost all the things that recalled the first days of their love. Everything around him gave rise to the same sensations as before—buildings, streets, people who were walking and riding along them, the weather, which was vernally dour each day, the smell of dust and rain, the ecclesiastical smell of poplars flowering in the side lanes beyond the fences. Everything bespoke the bitterness of separation and the blitheness of summer hopes, of hopes for their meeting in the Crimea, where all obstacles would disappear and everything would be realized (although he had no idea what, precisely, this everything was).

On the day of his departure Protasov dropped in to say goodbye. Among upper-form gymnasium pupils, among university students, you often meet youths who have adopted a cordially morose, derisive bearing, the air of being older and more experienced than anyone on earth. Such a person was Protasov, one of his closest friends, his only real friend, who, despite Mitya's reticence and taciturnity, knew all the secrets of his love. He watched as Mitya strapped up the suitcase, noticed how his hands trembled, then smiled with lugubrious sagacity and said, "You're nothing but children, Lord have mercy! And besides, *mein lieber* young Werther from Tambov, it's high time you realized that Katya is, above all, a most typical feminine individuum, and that the very chief of the gendarmes himself couldn't change that. You, a masculine individuum, are climbing the walls, presenting her your most lofty of instinctual demands for the perpetuation of the species, and, of course, all this is perfectly legitimate, even, in a certain sense, consecrated. Your body is the highest reason, as Herr Nietzsche so justly remarked. But equally legitimate is the fact that you can break your neck on that consecrated path. There are creatures in the animal world whose very prospectus of existence is based on the assumption that they pay the price of their own being for their first and last act of love. But inasmuch as that prospectus, presumably, has no absolute binding force on you, just you mind your p's and q's and look out for yourself. Generally speaking, don't be in any hurry. 'Junker Schmidt, my word of honor, summer will return!' Let's not assume this is the bitter end. After all, she ain't the only fish in the ocean. I see by your efforts to throttle the suitcase that you'll never buy that argument, that this is a cherished fish, indeed. Well then, forgive me for the unsolicited advice—and may God's servitor Saint Nicholas, with all his holy henchmen, preserve thee!"

Protasov squeezed Mitya's hand and left, and as Mitya strapped his pillow and blanket tightly to the suitcase, the sound of singing reached him through a window that was open onto the courtyard; testing his voice, the boy who lived across from him, a student of vocal music who practiced from morning to night, had burst out with "The Asra." Mitya hurried to finish with the straps, fastened them up perfunctorily, grabbed his peaked cap, and set off for Kislovka—to say good-bye to Katya's mother. The tune and words of the student's song were ringing in his head, repeating themselves so urgently that he wandered along more stupefied than ever, taking no notice of streets or pedestrians. It really did look like this was the bitter end, like "Junker Schmidt had drawn his pistol for to shoot himself!" "All right, so what, the bitter end is the bitter end," he thought, and once again his mind drifted back to the song, which told of a sultan's daughter who strolled in the garden, "her lustrous beauty gleaming," and how there in the garden she met a blackamoor thrall, who stood by the fountain "paler than death." One day she asked him who he was and whence he came and he answered, beginning ominously but humbly, with morose simplicity, "Mohamet is my name . . ." and ending with a rapturously tragic wail: "I'm of the unfortunate tribe of the Asra; once having loved, we die!"

Katya, who was dressing to go to the station and see him off, called out affectionately from her room—the room where he had spent so many unforgettable hours!—that she would be there before the first bell. The gentle and kindly woman with vermilion hair sat alone, smoked, and gazed at him sadly; most likely she had known the situation for some time, had guessed everything. Flushed scarlet, shuddering internally, he kissed her soft flaccid hand, bowing his head in a filial gesture, and with maternal endearment she kissed him several times on the temple and made the sign of the cross over him.

"Come now, dear boy," she quoted Griboedov with a listless smile, "life is meant for laughing! Well then, Christ be with you, go on now, go . . ."

6

After Mitya had disposed of the usual last-minute tasks before checking out of his lodgings, he and the hall servant stowed his bags in a listing horse-drawn cab, and finally he squeezed himself in beside the luggage, was jerked into motion. Immediately he experienced the peculiar sensations that grip a departing traveler (finished, forever, a certain portion of my life!)—and at the same time a sudden buoyancy, hopes for the beginning of something new. Feeling somewhat calmer, he brightened up, had a new perspective on things around him. The end, farewell to Moscow and to everything he had lived through there! It was drizzling, dour, the side streets were empty, the cobblestones dark and glimmering like iron, the buildings mirthless, dirty. His cabman drove at a tormenting, plodding pace, and from time to time the odor wafting from him forced Mitya to turn away and hold his breath. They drove past the Kremlin, crossed Pokrovka, once again turned off onto side streets, where crows in the gardens were screeching hoarse greetings to the rain and approaching evening, where in spite of everything it was spring, and spring smells were in the air. Then at last they arrived and Mitya rushed off at a run behind his porter, through the teeming station, out onto the platform, then to track 3, where the long, cumbersome train to Kursk already stood waiting. And instantaneously, amidst all the huge, hideous mob laying siege to the train, beyond all the porters who screamed forewarnings as they rolled their thundering baggage carts along, he caught sight of, singled out the one who stood all alone in the distance, "her lustrous beauty gleaming," who seemed an absolutely unique creature, not only in this mob, but in all the world. The first bell already had sounded—this time he, not Katya, had been late. It was touching that she had arrived before him; she was waiting for him and rushed to him once again with the solicitude of a wife or fiancée.

"Darling, quick, find a seat! It's time for the second bell!"

After the second bell she was even more touching, looking up at him from the platform as he stood in the door of the third-class coach, which was crammed full by now and reeking. Everything about her was captivating—her dear pretty face, her slender figure, her freshness, her youth (still an admixture of the womanly and the childish), her upraised, gleaming eyes, her plain pale blue hat with a certain refined panache in the way it was shaped, and even her dark gray suit, even its material and the silk of its lining, which Mitya gazed at adoringly. He stood there, thin, ungainly; for the trip he had put on coarse top boots and an old jacket with buttons copper red, rubbed bare of their surface lacquer. Katya looked at him, for all that, with sincere love and sadness on her face. The third bell tore through his heart so abruptly and stridently that Mitya threw himself from the coach like a madman, and just as frenetically Katya rushed horror-stricken to embrace him. He pressed his lips to her glove, and leaping back, onto the coach, started waving his cap in a frenzied rapture, his eyes full of tears, while she took up her skirts and floated backward with the platform, her upraised eyes still fixed upon him. She was floating more and more rapidly, the wind was blowing Mitya's hair more and more furiously as he leaned out the window, the locomotive was accelerating more and more swiftly, more and more mercilessly, its insolent, menacing bellow demanding the right of way—and suddenly both she and the end of the platform broke away as if sundered.

7

The lengthy spring twilight had long since set in, dark with rain-glutted storm clouds; the cumbersome train car went thundering through a bare, cool field—it was still early spring in the open country—conductors walked down the corridor of the coach, requesting tickets and setting candles in the lamps, but Mitya still stood by the audibly quavering window, the smell of Katya's glove on his lips, still glowing all over with that poignant flame left by the final instant of parting. And the long, happy and grievous Moscow winter, which had transfigured his whole life, rose up before him in its entirety, in a completely new light. Katya's image as well appeared now in a new light, once again changed . . . Yes, who is she, what is she? And love, passion, the soul, the body? What is that? None of that exists—something different exists, completely different! That smell of the glove—isn't that also Katya, love, the soul, the body? The muzhiks, the laborers in the coach, the woman leading her hideous child off to the toilet, the dim candles set in clattering lamps, the twilight on empty spring fields—everything is love, everything the soul, and everything is torment and unspeakable joy.

In the morning there was the town of Orel, a transfer to a provincial train that stood beside a distant platform. What a simple, calm, and kindred world this is, Mitya felt, in comparison to the Moscow world, which already has receded into some remote fairyland kingdom revolving around Katya, who now appears so solitary, pathetic, and so tenderly beloved! Even the sky, smeared here and there with the pallid blue of rain clouds, even the wind was simpler and calmer . . . The train from Orel ambled along leisurely and Mitya leisurely ate spice biscuits impressed with a Tula trademark as he sat in the almost empty coach. Then the train accelerated, began lulling him, muffling him in sleep.

He awakened only in Verkhovye. The train had stopped, there was quite a bustle, masses of people, but there was also a kind of backwoods aura. Pleasantly smelling vapors wafted from the station kitchen. Mitya consumed a delicious bowl of cabbage soup and drank a bottle of beer, then dozed off again—a profound fatigue had come over him. When he awoke the train was tearing through a vernal birch forest, a spot he recognized, located just before his final stop. Once again darkness was gathering with the dusky hues of spring; through the open window came the redolence of rain and of what seemed like mushrooms. The forest was still utterly bare, but the thundering train, nonetheless, reverberated more distinctly here than in the fields; vernally sorrowful station lights flashed briefly in the distance. Then came the high green light of the semaphore—especially captivating in the twilight of a bare birch forest—and with a thud the train switched over onto a different track . . . Lord, how rustically pathetic and dear was that farmhand who stood waiting on the platform to meet the young master!

The twilight and storm clouds grew denser as they left the station and rode out through a large village, also springlike, muddy. Everything was immersed in that extraordinarily soft twilight, the profoundest silence of the earth, of the warm evening, blending with the dark of amorphous, low-hanging rain clouds, and once again Mitya marveled and rejoiced. How calm, simple, and squalid is a country village, those stinking peasant huts with no chimneys, long since sleeping—after Annunciation Day the good country folk stop kindling their lights—and how fine it is in this dark and warm steppeland world! The tarantass plunged along over ruts, through mud; the towering oaks beyond the farmstead of a rich muzhik were still utterly denuded, inimical, mottled with the black nests of rooks. Near a hut, peering into the dusk, stood a strange muzhik who might have emerged from antiquity: bare feet; rough, torn peasant coat; sheepskin cap over long straight hair . . . A warm and blitheful, balmy rain began failing. Mitya thought of the girls, the young peasant wenches sleeping in those huts, of everything female, to which he had drawn so near that winter with Katya, and all was blended together—Katya, the girls, the night, spring, the smell of rain, the smell of earth upturned and prepared for fertilization, the smell of horse sweat, and the smell of a kidskin glove in his memory.

8

Life in the country began with lovely, placid days.

Katya's image appeared to have paled in the night, evaporated into the surroundings on the way from the station. But it only seemed that way, and it went on seeming that way for a few more days, until Mitya had slept off his trip, recovered his senses, become accustomed to the novelty of impressions familiar from childhood: the home where he grew up, the country village, spring in the country, the vernal nudity and emptiness of the world, once again pure and young, prepared for burgeoning anew.

The estate was small, the manor house old and modest, household management uncomplicated, requiring few menials. A quiet life began for Mitya. His sister Anya, a second-form gymnasium pupil, and his brother Kostya, a young military cadet, were still in Orel attending school, due to arrive no earlier than June. His mother Olga Petrovna was concerned, as usual, with managing the estate, aided only by her steward—the boss man, as he was called by the servants. After spending much of her day in the fields, she went to bed as soon as it was dark.

On the day after his arrival, when Mitya, who had slept twelve hours, emerged washed and dressed in clean clothing from his sunlit room—its windows faced east, toward the garden—and walked through all the other rooms, he experienced a vivid sense of their kindredness and their placid simplicity, which calmed both body and soul. All objects throughout the house were in their customary places, just where they had been for so many years, and there was the same familiar and pleasant redolence. Throughout the house they had tidied things up for his arrival, floors had been washed in every room. They were finishing off washing the parlor, which adjoined the vestibule and the footmen's chamber, as that room was still called even now. A freckled peasant girl, hired on as a day worker from the village, stood on the windowsill beside doors that led onto the terrace, stretching to reach the upper pane, making it whistle as she rubbed, her bluish, somehow remote image reflected in the lower panes. Taking a large rag from the pail full of hot water, the housemaid Parasha, sleeves turned up, feet bare, legs white, walked across the soaked floor on her small heels, and wiping the sweat from her flushed face with the bend of a wrist, she said in her amicable, free and easy patter, "Go on out get you some food; your mama and the boss man went off before sunrise to the depot. You likely never even heard them."

And immediately, forcefully, came the reminder of Katya. Mitya found himself physically drawn to that bare female arm and to the feminine curve of the girl who stretched upward from the windowsill, her skirt, beneath which the bare legs extended like firm columns, and he joyously sensed Katya's prepotency, his belonging to her, felt her secret presence in all the impressions of that morning.

That presence made itself felt more and more vividly with each new day and became more and more lovely as Mitya recovered his senses, calmed down, forgot that other, that commonplace Katya, who in Moscow had so often and so grievously failed to blend with the Katya his desires had created.

9

Now, for the first time, he was living at home as an adult, whom even Mother treated somehow differently than before. What's more, his first real love lived in his heart, and he was bringing to fulfillment what his whole being had secretly awaited since childhood, boyhood.

Even during his infancy something beyond expression in human speech had stirred wondrously and cryptically within him. Once somewhere on a certain day, probably also in spring, in the garden beside the lilac bushes—the piquant smell of Spanish blister flies stuck in his memory—still a very small child, he stood with some young woman (most likely his nanny), and all at once a celestial radiance appeared to flare up before his eyes—perhaps it was on her face, or perhaps on the sarafan over her full bosom—and something passed through him in a wave of heat, leapt up within him, veritably as a child moves in its mother's womb . . . But it all had a dreamlike air. Dreamlike too was everything that came later—in childhood, boyhood, and gymnasium years. There were certain peculiar, utterly unique transports over first one, then another of the little girls who came with their mothers to the children's fetes held for him, a secret, avid curiosity toward every movement of the enchanting, also utterly unique little creature in a frock, in tiny shoes, with the bow of a silk ribbon on her head. There were (and this was later, in the provincial capital) much more conscious transports, lasting nearly a whole autumn, over a schoolgirl who often appeared at evening in the tree beyond the fence of the neighboring garden. Her sportiveness, derisiveness, her brown frock, the round comb in her hair, dirty arms, laughter, ringing cries—it all so enchanted Mitya that he thought of her from morning to night, pined, sometimes even wept, ravenously desiring something of her. Then all this ceased somehow of its own volition, was forgotten, and there were new, some longer, some shorter (but all, once again, inscrutable) transports. There was the piquant joy and bitterness of sudden infatuations at gymnasium balls. There was a certain bodily languor and nebulous presentiments in the heart, anticipations of something . . .

He was born and grew up in the country, but while in gymnasium he had no choice but to spend spring in the city—with one exception, the year before last, when he came to the country for Shrovetide, fell ill, and stayed at home recovering for March and half of April. Those days were unforgettable. He lay in bed nearly two weeks, doing nothing each day but looking out the window, watching the skies change in harmony with the world's increasing warmth and light, watching the snow, the garden, its boles and branches. Morning, and the room so bright and warm from the sun that reinvigorated flies are crawling about the panes . . . After-dinner hour on the following day: sunlight from behind the house on its other side, the pallid, nearly sky blue vernal snow visible through the window, and large white clouds in the azure, nestling against the crowns of trees . . . Then, one day later, such bright interstices in the cloudy sky and such a wet glitter on the bark of trees, and it does so drip from the roof above the window that you never get enough of looking and rejoicing in it all . . . Later came the warm fogs and rain; the snow was devoured, disappeared in several days, the ice on the river broke into motion, and the earth in garden and yard began laying itself bare, became newly, joyfully black . . . Mitya long remembered one day at the end of March, when for the first time he rode out on horseback into the fields. Not brightly, but so vividly, so youthfully did the sky shine through the pallid colorless trees of the garden. The breeze in the field was still crisp, the crop stubble feral and rust red, and in the plowed section—they were plowing already for oats—greasily, with primordial vigor, the upturned black clods glistened. He rode across the entire field of stubble and clods to the forest, which he could see in the crystalline air from afar—bare, small, visible from end to end—then he descended into its lowland hollows and let the hooves of his horse rustle through the deep overlay of last year's leaves, which in some places were utterly dry, straw yellow, in others wet and brown; he crossed ravines strewn with those leaves, where floodwater still was flowing, and from out of the bushes swarthy gold woodcocks came ripping, crackling right beneath the horse's legs . . . What had it meant to him, all that spring and especially that day, when such a crisp breeze was blowing toward him over the field, when the horse, struggling to cope with the waterlogged stubble and the black, plowed earth, wheezed so loudly through his big nostrils, snorting and groaning internally with splendid, savage force? It had seemed at the time that his first real love was that spring itself, its days of sheer infatuation with someone or something, when he loved all the schoolgirls and all the peasant wenches in the world. But how remote those days appeared to him now! What an utter child he had been then, innocent, ingenuous, with his meager stock of modest sorrows, joys, and reveries! His aimless, discarnate love of that time had been a dream, or rather the recollection of some marvelous dream. But now Katya was in his world, a soul who incarnated that world in her person and who hovered triumphantly over all of it.

10

A reminder of Katya seemed ominous only one time during those early days in the country.

One late evening Mitya went out onto the back veranda. It was very dark, quiet, redolent of damp fields. Beyond the night clouds, above the nebulous contour of the garden, tiny tear-moist stars were glowing. Suddenly something far away in the distance gave a savage diabolic hoot, followed by a paroxysm of yelping and shrieking. Mitya winced, froze in his tracks, then carefully descended from the veranda, entered the dark tree-lined arborway, which appeared to be surveying him with enmity on all sides, stopped once more, and began waiting, listening. What could it be, where was it—that which had flooded the garden so abruptly and awesomely with its din? "A barn owl or a timber screech owl consummating his love, nothing more," he thought, but he stood dead still, as if he sensed the veiled presence of the Devil himself in that murk. And suddenly it resounded again, a low ululation that shook Mitya to the depths of his soul, booming and rumbling somewhere near, in the treetops of the avenue—and the devil bore himself noiselessly off to another part of the garden. There, first of all he began yelping, began puling and weeping beseechingly, plaintively, like a child, flapping his wings and caterwauling in grievous ecstasy, then went into a shrieking and loutish cackling, as if he were being tickled or tortured. Shuddering all over, Mitya strained his eyes and ears in the darkness. But that devil suddenly broke off, made a choking sound, and after rending the dark garden with a death-laden, anguished wail, he vanished as if the earth had swallowed him up. Having waited several more moments in vain for the resumption of this amatory horror, Mitya quietly returned to the manor house—and the whole night long he was tormented in his sleep by those aberrant and revolting thoughts and feelings into which his love had been transformed that March in Moscow.

In the morning sunlight, however, his nocturnal agonies quickly dissipated. He recalled how Katya had burst out weeping when they decided he must leave Moscow; he recalled with what delight she grasped at the idea that he too would come to the Crimea in early June, how touchingly she had helped him as he prepared to leave, how she had seen him off at the station . . . He took out her photograph and for a long time he just stared intently at her small head with the stylish coiffure, marveling at the purity and clarity in that direct, frank gaze of the slightly rounded eyes. Then he wrote her an exceptionally long and exceptionally earnest letter, full of faith in their love, and once again he was enveloped by the ceaseless sensation of her amorous, radiant omnipresence in everything by which he lived and rejoiced.

He recalled what he had experienced when his father died, nine years before. That too was in spring. On the day after his death Mitya walked timorously, bewildered and horror-stricken, through the parlor where his father lay on a table, elegantly arrayed in nobleman's uniform, chest raised high, large pallid hands crossed upon it, nose white, beard black and diaphanous. Stepping out onto the veranda, he glanced at the huge coffin lid standing by the door, covered on top in golden brocade—and suddenly the thought seized him: "Death is here on earth!" It pervaded everything: the sunlight, the vernal grass in the yard, the sky, the garden . . . He walked out into the garden, onto the linden-lined arborway splotched with light, then off onto branch pathways that were still more sunny, gazing at the trees and the first white butterflies, hearing the first birds warbling blithefully—and he recognized nothing: death, that horrible table in the parlor, and that long, brocaded coffin lid on the veranda pervaded everything! The sun was shining differently somehow, not as before, the grass was a different green; inert butterflies perched in a different way on the spring grass blades that were warm, as yet, only at their tops. Nothing was the same as it had been twenty-four hours ago, everything was transfigured as if the end of the world were near, and spring's captivation, its eternal youth, had gone pathetic and bleak! This lasted for a long time afterward, for the whole of that spring, just as he long smelled—or fancied—that awesome, vile, cloying smell in the well-scrubbed, frequently aired house.

And now Mitya was experiencing the same kind of dazed obsession—but one of an utterly different order. This spring, the spring of his first love, was also utterly different from all previous springs. The world once again had been transfigured, once again was full of what appeared to be some extraneous thing, but not at all something malign or horrible; on the contrary—something that wondrously blended with the joy and youth of spring. That extraneous something was Katya, or, rather, it was the summit of earthly captivation that Mitya wanted and demanded of her. Now, as each spring day passed in turn, he demanded more and more of her. And now that she was not here, now that there was only her image, a nonexistent, merely desired image, it seemed that in no way had she violated the immaculacy and magnificence that he demanded of her, and with each passing day she made her presence felt more and more vividly in all of Mitya's surroundings.

II

He became joyfully convinced of this during the very first week of his sojourn in the country. Spring seemed on the verge of arriving at any moment now. He sat with a book beside the open window of the drawing room, gazing through the fir and pine boles of the front garden at the dirty stream in the meadow, at the village on the slopes beyond the stream. In the bare, age-old birches of the neighboring squire's garden, tirelessly, from morning to night, steeped in the languor of their blissful ferment, the rooks were screeching as they screech only in early spring, and the view of the village on the slopes was still feral and drab; so far only the willows were overlaid with a yellowish greenery there . . . He went into the garden; it was still stunted and bare, transparent—only the grassy strips were green, dappled all over with tiny turquoise flowers. Acacia blooms along the avenue were like powdery rime, and in the hollow, in the southern, lower part of the garden a solitary wild cherry flowered pallidly with tiny white blossoms . . . He went out into the fields. It was still empty, still drab there in the openlands, the stubble still thistly like a brush, the desiccate field paths still violet and scabrous with hummocks . . . And all of this had the exiguity of youth, of the time of anticipation—and all of it was Katya. It only seemed that he was distracted by the peasant girls working as day laborers, who did now one chore, now another around the estate, by the farmhands in the workers' annex, by reading, strolls, visits to muzhiks he knew in the village, conversations with Mother, rides out into the fields in the light *drozhky* with the steward (a coarse, strapping retired soldier).

Then still another week went past. One night there was a torrential cloudburst, and then somehow the hot sun's power became ascendant, spring lost its meekness and pallidness, and right before his eyes everything around him began changing in leaps and bounds. They started plowing, transforming the stubble into black velvet; the boundary strips around the fields turned green, the verdure in the yard was more succulent, the blue of the sky more dense and bright. The garden was rapidly dressing itself in crisp greenery that was soft even to the eye; gray panicles on the lilac began turning mauve, became redolent, and a multitude of black and metallically blue, huge glittering flies appeared on its dark green glossy leafage and in the hot patches of light on the trails. Branches were still visible on the apple and pear trees, hardly touched by the tiny, grayish, uniquely soft leafage, but these apples and pears, which stretched out networks of skewed branches beneath other trees in all directions, had begun curling with lacteal snow, and with each passing day this bloom became more white, more dense, and more fragrant. Through all this wondrous time Mitya was intently and joyfully observing all the spring changes taking place around him. But Katya not only did not pale but also was not lost amidst them; on the contrary—she had a share in all of them and imparted to everything her presence, her beauty, which burgeoned in harmony with the burgeoning spring, with that ever more sumptuously white garden and the ever darker blue of the sky.

12

Then one day on his way to tea, as Mitya entered the parlor full of the early evening sun, the mail lying beside the samovar suddenly caught his eye, the mail he had awaited in vain all morning. He dashed up to the table—Katya was long overdue in answering the letters he had sent—and brightly, balefully it lay there glimmering, the small, highly elegant envelope with the superscription in that familiar, pathetic hand. Grabbing it up, he strode out of the house, then through the garden, along the central arborway. He walked to the most distant part of the garden, where the hollow passed through it; then he stopped, looked around, and quickly tore open the envelope. The letter was brief, only a few lines, but Mitya must have read it over five times before he could grasp the words, his heart was pounding so. "My beloved, my one and only!" he read again and again—and these exclamatory phrases made the earth float beneath his feet. He raised his eyes. The sky above the garden gleamed joyously and exultantly, the snowy whiteness of the garden was also gleaming all around; in the crisp greenery of distant bushes a nightingale, already sensing the early evening chill, sang distinctly, intensely, with all the sweetness of mindless nightingale rapture—and the blood drained from Mitya's face, tremors passed over his scalp.

He walked back slowly to the house; the chalice of his love was full to overflowing. And just as gingerly did he bear his love within him on the days that followed, in silent and happy anticipation of a new letter.

13

The garden was dressing itself in a variety of colors.

A huge old maple, towering over all the southern part of the garden, prominently visible from everywhere, became still larger and more prominent—arrayed in crisp, dense greenery.

Higher and more prominent too was the central arborway, upon which Mitya constantly gazed from his windows. The crowns of its old lindens, also covered, though still transparently, in a pattern of young leafage, rose and stretched over the garden like a light green row of hills.

And at a level lower than the maple, lower than the arborway, there was a sheer expanse of curly, aromatic, cream-colored blossoms.

All of this: the huge and splendrous maple crown, the light green hills of the arborway, the nuptial white of apple, pear, and bird cherry trees, the sun, the blue of the sky, and everything that was thriving and spreading in the bottomlands of the garden, in the hollow, along the branch pathways and trails, at the base of the manor's southern wall—lilac bushes, acacias and currants, burdock, nettles, wormwood—everything was strikingly lush, crisp, and new.

Since vegetation was encroaching from all sides, the fresh green yard appeared more cramped, the house somehow smaller and more beautiful. It seemed to be expecting guests. For days on end the doors and windows in all the rooms were open: in the white parlor, in the blue, old-fashioned drawing room, in the small divan room, also blue and hung with oval miniatures, in the sunny library, a large and empty corner room with old icons set in the front-corner shrine and low ash bookcases along the walls. Now the trees had moved right up against the house, gazing festively into the rooms with their variety of green colors, some light green, some dark, apertures of bright blue between their branches.

But there was no letter. Mitya knew how hard it was for Katya to write letters, realized how much trouble she had making herself sit down at a desk, find pen, paper, envelope, buy a stamp . . . But once again rational considerations were of little help. After several days the happy, even proud assurance he had felt as he awaited the next letter disappeared; he pined and worried even more. After such a letter as the first something still more lovely and blissful should follow immediately. But Katya was silent.

He stopped going out so often to the village, went riding in the fields less frequently. He sat in the library, leafed through journals that had been yellowing and withering on the bookshelves for decades. These journals were full of lovely verses by the old poets, marvelous lines almost always dealing with the same thing—that with which all verses and songs have been replete since the world began, the one thing that nourished his own soul now—and in one way or another he could invariably apply these verses to himself, to his love, to Katya. For hours on end he sat in the armchair beside the open bookcase and tormented himself, reading and rereading:

> The household sleeps, dear one; come out in the garden haze!
> The household sleeps, and only the stars upon us gaze.

All these enchanting words, these adjurations seemed his own, appeared to be addressed to only one person, to the one whom he, Mitya, saw persistently everywhere and in everything, and sometimes they had an almost menacing ring:

> Over smooth and tranquil river
> Fly the swans, their wings aquiver,
> And the waters undulate.
> Oh, come back! The star belts glimmer,
> Slowly trembling, green leaves shimmer,
> And the cloud banks congregate.

Closing his eyes, shivering, he repeated this adjuration several times in a row, this call of the heart overflowing with amorous force, a heart craving exultation, beatific deliverance. After that he sat for a long time staring straight ahead and listening to the profound, rustic silence surrounding the manor—and then bitterly shook his head. No, she did not respond, she was gleaming mutely somewhere out there, in that remote and alien Moscow world! And once again the tenderness streamed from his heart—once again something grew and spread, menacing, ominous, incantatory:

Oh, come back! The star belts glimmer,
Slowly trembling, green leaves shimmer,
And the cloud banks congregate.

14

One day after Mitya had eaten dinner—they dined at noon—and dozed a bit, he left the house and walked at a leisurely pace out into the garden. The peasant girls who often worked there, spading up the ground under the apple trees, were working that day too. Mitya was going out to sit with them and have a chat; this had become a habit of late.

The day was hot and quiet. Walking in the splotched shade of the arborway, he saw the curls of snow-white branches stretching far into the distance all around him. Especially lush and vigorous was the bloom on the pear trees, and the mixture of that white with the vivid blue of the sky produced a violet tint. The pear and apple trees were blooming and shedding; the tilled earth beneath them was strewn with faded petals. The warm air was permeated with their delicate, sweet-scented smell, together with the smell of hot and decomposing dung in the cattle yard. Cloudlets would congregate, and then the dark blue sky took on a paler hue, the warm air and those smells of putrefaction became still more delicate and cloying. All the balmy warmth of this vernal paradise hummed drowsily and blissfully with honeybees and bumblebees, who burrowed into its curly, mellifluent snow. And repeatedly, with beatific tedium, diurnally, now here, now there, first one, then another nightingale gave a metallic chirp.

The arborway ended far in the distance, at the gates of the barn. Far to the left, at the corner of the earthen wall that enclosed the garden, was a dark spruce grove. Two peasant girls were there beside that grove, splotches of color amidst the apple trees. As usual, Mitya turned at the midpoint of the pathway and walked toward them. Bending over, he made his way through ramifications of low branches, which caressed his face with feminine delicacy, redolent of honey and of something like lemon. As usual, one of the girls, the thin ginger-haired Sonka, had barely caught sight of him when she began wildly shrieking and laughing.

"Oy, the master's coming!" she screamed in sham alarm, and jumping down from the thick pear bough where she had been resting, she rushed to her spade.

The other girl, Glashka, responded in just the opposite way, pretended not to have noticed Mitya at all; leisurely, firmly implanting on the iron spade her soft black felt boot, white petals clustered within its top, she dug the spade into the ground with an energetic thrust, and turning over a slice of earth, she burst out singing loudly, in a strong pleasant voice, "Hey, my garden, garden of mine, who do you flower for!" She was a strapping wench, purposeful and always solemn.

Mitya walked up and sat in Sonka's place, on the bough of the old pear tree where the bole split into branchings. Casting her bright eyes upon him, Sonka asked loudly, with affected offhandedness and gaiety, "Oh-ho, now, just got up? Watch out you don't sleep through big things!"

She was fond of Mitya and she made every effort to hide it but could not; she behaved awkwardly around him, babbled whatever came into her head, always, however, hinting at something, vaguely surmising that there must be a reason why he wandered about incessantly in a daze. Suspicious that he was getting into Parasha's bed, or that he was at least making the effort, she was jealous, spoke to him tenderly and sharply by turns, sometimes gazed at him languidly, openly displaying her feelings, sometimes coldly and with enmity. Mitya was strangely pleased by all of this. There was no letter, still no letter, and he was not living now, but simply existing from day to day in ceaseless anticipation, languishing more and more in that anticipation, in the impossibility of sharing the secret of his love and torment with anyone, of speaking about Katya, about his hopes for the Crimea. Sonka's hints about some love in his life, therefore, were pleasant. These conversations, after all, somehow touched upon the secret anguish that oppressed his soul. It was also exciting to know that Sonka was infatuated with him, was, consequently, his intimate to some degree, which made her a secret participant in that love life he cherished in his heart, and sometimes he even felt a strange hope that in Sonka he might find either a confidante or a kind of surrogate for Katya.

Now, unaware of what she was saying, Sonka had touched upon his secret again. "Watch out you don't sleep through big things!" He looked around. The brightness of the day made that solid mass of the dark green spruce thicket seem almost black, and those bits of sky that filtered through the pointed crowns of the trees were a special, majestic blue. The vernal greenery of the lindens, maples, and elms, bright throughout with sunlight that pierced it from end to end, formed a buoyant, joyous canopy over all the garden, spread mottled shade and bright patches on the grass, the trails and clearings; the hot and balmy bloom, glowing white beneath that canopy, seemed porcelain, gleamed and shone in spots where it too was pierced by the sun. Smiling in spite of himself, he asked Sonka, "But what kind of things could I sleep through? There you've got my whole problem—I don't have nothing to do."

"Hush now, don't you go swearing that on the Bible; I believe you!" Sonka shouted gaily, coarsely, once again affording him pleasure by her refusal to believe he had no love affairs. Suddenly she gave another raucous screech and shooed away the ginger calf with the white kinky tuft on his forehead; he had ambled out of the spruce grove, walked up behind her, and began munching on the flounce of her cotton print dress.

"Ow, confound you and blast your eyes! One more of his sons hath the good Lord sent us!"

"Is it true they're trying to marry you off?" said Mitya, at a loss for words but wishing to continue the conversation. "They say it's a rich farmstead and a handsome fellow, but you turned him down, won't listen to your papa . . ."

"Rich, all right, but dull as sin; ain't got molasses for brains," answered Sonka spryly, somewhat flattered. "Just might be I got me somebody else in mind."

Without interrupting her work the solemn and taciturn Glashka shook her head.

"You do shovel it thick, girl, from the Don River to the ocean and back!" she said softly. "Just stand there gabbling all sorts of trash and you'll soon have a name for yourself in the village."

"Shut up your cluck-clucking!" shouted Sonka. "I ain't no crow, I can hoe my own row!"

"And just who might be this somebody else you got in mind?" asked Mitya.

"Well, I'll own up!" said Sonka. "I done fell for that old grandpa herdboy of yours. Just look at him and I go hot right down to my heels! I ain't no worse than you folks; I like riding old horses too," she said provocatively, hinting, apparently, at the twenty-year-old Parasha, who was already considered an old spinster in the village. Then all at once, with the audacity she somehow was entitled to because of her secret infatuation with the young master, she threw down her spade and sat on the ground, stretching out and slightly spreading her legs in their old, coarse half boots and skewbald wool stockings, letting her arms drop feebly.

"Whew, I ain't done a thing and I'm dead give out!" she shouted, laughing. "They're worse for wear," her shrill voice rang out. "They're worse for wear, these boots of mine, / But on the toes they spark and shine." Then she laughed again and screamed, "Come off with me for a rest in the shed. I'm hot to trot!"

Her laughter was infectious. Smiling broadly and awkwardly, Mitya jumped off the bough, walked up to Sonka, and lay down with his head across her knees. Sonka pushed it away, but he lay back again, his mind flowing with poetry, which he had been reading so much of for the last few days:

Petals' scroll now brightly open,
Blooming rose, of joy a token,
Sprinkles, moistens all with dew.
The abounding and unbounded,
Aromatic, involuted
World of love is mine anew.

"Don't you touch me!" shrieked Sonka, now really alarmed, trying to lift his head and push it away. "I'll yell so loud all the wolves in the woods'll start howling. I ain't got nothing for you; it burned for a spell and then died out!"

Mitya closed his eyes and said nothing. The sun, shattering into fragments as it passed through leaves, branches, and pear blossoms, formed hot patches that dappled and tickled his face. Tenderly and spitefully Sonka tugged at his wiry black hair—"Just like horsehair!" she cried—and pulled down his cap to shield his eyes. He could feel her legs beneath his head—the most awesome thing on earth, female legs!—her stomach was touching him, he smelled her cotton print skirt and blouse, and all of this was mingled with the burgeoning garden and with Katya. The languorous chirping of nightingales both near and far, the perpetual, voluptuous, somnolent buzz of innumerable bees, the warm mellifluent air, and even the simple sensation of the earth beneath his back tormented him, produced an oppressive thirst for some superhuman happiness.

And suddenly something began rustling in the spruce grove, began laughing gaily and maliciously, then gave a low resonant hoot—"Coo-coo, coo-coo"—so balefully, so clearly, so near and so distinct that the rasp and the tremor of a sharp tongue were audible, and his desire for Katya, the desire and imperative that right now, at any cost, she must give him precisely it, that superhuman happiness, gripped him with such a fervency that, to the astonishment of Sonka, he leapt up impulsively, and stepping out with enormous strides he rushed away.

Together with that fervent desire, that demand for happiness, in accord with the low, resonant voice that abruptly sounded with such awesome clarity right over his head in the spruce grove, that appeared to rive the bosom of this spring world to its core, the thought had suddenly entered his mind that there would not be and could not be a letter, that something had happened in Moscow, or was on the verge of happening, and that he was finished, lost!

15

Back in the house, he stopped for a moment before the mirror in the parlor. "She's right," he thought. "My eyes may not be Byzantine, but they certainly are the eyes of a lunatic. And that thinness, the coarse and bony ungainliness, the somber swarthiness of the brows, the hair's wiry blackness; is it really almost like horsehair, as Sonka said?" Then he heard the quick tramp of bare feet behind him. Embarrassed, he turned around.

"Must be the young master's in love; he keeps on admiring hisself in the looking glass," said Parasha with affectionate drollery, running by on her way to the terrace with a boiling samovar.

"Your mama was looking for you," she added as she swept the samovar up on the table, set for tea, and turning around she cast a quick keen glance at Mitya.

"Everyone knows, they've all guessed!" thought Mitya and forced himself to ask, "Where is she?"

"In her room."

Having skirted the house, crossing already to the western sky, the sun peered translucently through pines and firs, which screened the terrace with their coniferous branches. The spindle shrubs beneath them also had an utterly summerish, glazy sheen. Covered with fine shade and spotted with hot patches of light, the tablecloth gleamed. Wasps were hovering above the basket that held white bread, above the cut-glass jam bowl and the cups. This whole scene bespoke a lovely summer in the country and a life both happy and carefree. In order to forestall the appearance of his mother, who, of course, understood his situation no less than the others, and to demonstrate that he had no secret burdens whatsoever weighing upon him, Mitya left the parlor and entered the corridor, which extended past the doors of his room, Mother's, and two more rooms, occupied by Anya and Kostya in the summer. The light was dusky in the corridor, bluish in Olga Petrovna's room. This whole room was crammed snugly and cozily with the most antiquated furniture in the house: chiffoniers, commodes, a large bed, an icon case with the usual lamp burning in front of it, although his mother had never shown any particular religious inclinations. Beyond the open windows, on the neglected flower bed by the entry to the central arborway, there was a broad shady spot, and beyond that shade, directly facing it, the luminous garden glowed a festive green and white. Ignoring all this long-familiar view, eyes in spectacles lowered over her knitting, Olga Petrovna, a large but spare, solemn dark-haired woman of forty, sat in an armchair by the window and rapidly plied her needles.

"Were you asking for me, Mother?" said Mitya, stopping at the door of the room.

"No, no, I just wanted to have a look at you. I almost never get to see you now, except at dinner," answered Olga Petrovna without interrupting her work, speaking in a special, immoderately calm tone.

Mitya recalled how, on the ninth of March, Katya had said that for some reason she was frightened of his mother, recalled the charming implication clearly there in her words . . . He muttered awkwardly, "But did you, perhaps, have something to tell me?"

"Nothing, except that it seems to me you've got a bit bored these last few days," said Olga Petrovna. "Maybe you could take a little ride somewhere . . . over to the Meshersky manor, for example . . . They've got a house full of nubile young ladies," she added, smiling. "And, on the whole, I think they're quite a nice, sociable family."

"In a few days I really might like to ride over there," answered Mitya with an effort. "But let's go have our tea now; it's so pleasant out on the terrace . . . And we can talk there," he said, knowing full well that Mother, with her penetrating mind and her reticence, would not resume that fruitless conversation.

They sat on the terrace until almost sunset. After tea Mother continued knitting and speaking about the neighbors, household matters, about Anya and Kostya—just imagine, Anya has to retake an examination again this August! Mitya listened, answered now and again, but all this time he was feeling something like what he had felt just before his departure from Moscow: the stupefaction again, as if he were in the throes of some grave disease.

For nearly two hours that evening he strode incessantly back and forth through the house, through parlor, drawing room, divan and library, up to the library's southern window, open onto the garden. On the windows of the parlor and drawing room the soft red of sunset glowed amidst branches of pines and firs; the voices and laughter of farmhands could be heard as they gathered for supper beside the kitchen annex. Into the passages between rooms, through the library window gazed the steady and achromatic blue of the evening sky, with one motionless, rosy star hanging there; picturesquely sketched upon this blue was the green crown of the maple and the whiteness, somehow wintry whiteness, of everything blooming in the garden. And he kept striding, pacing, utterly unconcerned about how this would be interpreted in the house. His teeth were clenched so tightly that his head ached.

16

From that day on he stopped observing the many changes that approaching summer was consummating around him. He saw and even felt them, those changes, but they had lost their discrete value and his delight in them was only a grievous delight; the better everything was, the more grievous it was for him. Katya had become an utter obsession; now Katya was in everything and behind everything to the point of absurdity, and since each new day was an ever more terrible confirmation that she no longer even existed for him, for Mitya, that now she was in the power of someone alien, was giving some other man herself and her love, which must by all rights be exclusively his, Mitya's, everything in the world began to seem unnecessary, grievous, and the more lovely it was, the more unnecessary and grievous it became.

He hardly slept at night. The captivation of those moonlit nights was incomparable. Quiet, ever so quiet, lay the milky white garden. Nocturnal nightingales sang assiduously, languished in indolent transports, contending with each other in the sweetness and refinement of their songs, in purity, painstaking care, sonority. The silent, delicate, utterly pallid moon hung low above the garden, was accompanied invariably by a tiny, unspeakably captivating swell of pale bluish clouds. Mitya slept with curtains undrawn, and the garden and moon peered in his windows all night. Every time he opened his eyes and looked up at the moon, immediately, like one possessed, he pronounced the word in his mind: "Katya!" And he said it with such rapture, such pain, that he himself realized how bizarre this was. How could it be that the moon reminded him of Katya, but it did remind him all the same, reminded him of something, and, what was most amazing of all, there was even some visual resemblance! But ofttimes he simply saw nothing; his desire for Katya, the recollection of what had been between them in Moscow, enveloped him so forcefully that he shuddered all over in a feverish tremor and prayed to God—but, alas, always in vain—to have her right here, with him in this bed, at least in a dream. Once that winter he had gone with her to the Bolshoy Theater to hear Sobinov and Chaliapin in *Faust.* For some reason everything had seemed especially delightful that evening: the radiant chasm gaping beneath them, torrid and balmy with masses of people, the red velvet, golden-fringed tiers of loges overflowing with glittering raiment, the iridescent gleam of a gigantic chandelier above that chasm, the overture streaming out far below in accord with the conductor's gesticulations, its sounds now blaring, demoniacal, now infinitely tender and sad: "Once in far Thule there lived a good king . . ." After the performance, having accompanied Katya through the hard frost of that moonlit night to Kislovka, Mitya stayed with her later than ever, lost himself more than ever in the torpor of their kisses, and took with him the silk ribbon that Katya had used to tie up her braid for the night. Now, on these grievous May nights, he had come to the point that he trembled just to think of that ribbon, which he kept in his desk.

In the daytime he slept, then rode on horseback to the large village where the railway station and post office were located. Fine weather continued. Sporadic rain would fall, thunderstorms, downpours would quickly come and go, and once more the hot sun would gleam, ceaselessly performing its rapid labor in the gardens, fields, and forests. The garden had stopped flowering, lost its blooms, but continued to grow rampantly more lush and dark. The forests were now immersed in countless flowers, high grass; their sonorous depths, steeped in the songs of nightingales and cuckoos, ceaselessly beckoned him into the marrow of their greenery. Now the bareness of the fields had disappeared—an opulence of grain shoots covered them throughout in variegated patterns. And for days on end Mitya lost himself in those forests and fields.

He was too ashamed to hang about every morning on the terrace or in the yard, waiting in sterile anticipation for the steward or a farmworker to arrive from the post office. Besides that, the steward or the worker would not always have time to ride eight versts for trifles. So he himself began riding to the post office. But he too would return, invariably, with only an issue of the Orel newspaper or a letter from Anya or Kostya. His torments were becoming almost unbearable. The fields and forests through which he rode so crushed him with their beauty and their happiness that he even had a pain in his chest.

Once, just before evening, he was riding from the post office through a deserted neighboring estate, which stood in the midst of an old park that blended into the birch forest surrounding it. He rode along the festal prospect, as the muzhiks called the central arborway of this estate. Two rows of huge, dark spruces lined the avenue. Majestically somber, broad, covered with a thick layer of slippery rust red needles, it led to an ancient manor house standing at the end of its corridor. The red, dry and calm light of the sun, which was sinking to his left beyond the garden and forest, obliquely illumined the lower part of this corridor between the boles, glittered amidst the golden panoply of needles. And such spellbound silence reigned all around—only the nightingales were blaring their song from one end of the park to the other—there was such a sweet redolence of spruces, of jasmine bushes, which were clustered about the manor on every side, in all of this Mitya sensed such prodigious joy (someone else's, some pristine joy), and with such awesome distinctness did she suddenly appear to him on the huge decrepit terrace amidst the jasmine bushes, Katya, in the image of his young wife, that he felt his face convulsed by a deathly pallor, and he said aloud, firmly, his voice resounding over all the arborway, "If I don't get a letter in a week I'll shoot myself!"

17

The next day he arose very late. After dinner he sat on the terrace, held a book on his knees, gazed at the pages covered with print, and thought vacantly, "Should I go for the mail or not?"

It was hot. One behind the other, white butterflies hovered in pairs above the heated grass, above the glazy sheen on the spindle shrubs. Watching the butterflies, he asked himself again, "Should I go, or should I break off these shameful trips once and for all?"

From behind a rise the steward appeared in the gates, riding a stallion. He glanced up at the terrace and turned straight toward it. Drawing near, he pulled up the horse and said, "A good morning to you! Still reading?"

He looked around with a grin on his face.

"Is your mama sleeping?" he asked softly.

"I think she's asleep," answered Mitya. "Why?"

The steward was silent for a moment, then said abruptly, in a solemn tone, "Look here, young master, I ain't got nothing against no books, but a man ought to know the right time for things. Why is it you're living like some kind of monk? Ain't there enough women or young wenches around?"

Lowering his eyes to the book, Mitya did not respond.

"Where have you been?" he asked, without looking up.

"Been to the post office," said the steward. "And, sure enough, there weren't no letters there at all, just this paper here."

"And why do you say 'sure enough'?"

"Because, what I mean is, somebody's still writing; they ain't finished yet," answered the steward rudely and derisively, offended by Mitya's refusal to continue the conversation he had begun.

"If you please," he said, stretching out the newspaper to Mitya, and spurring his horse, he rode away.

"I'll shoot myself!" thought Mitya resolutely, gazing at the book and seeing nothing.

18

Certainly Mitya understood that there was nothing more savage and bizarre imaginable: to shoot yourself, to shatter your skull, to cut off in a single instant the beat of a sound young heart, to break off your thoughts and feelings, go deaf, go blind, to vanish from this unspeakably magnificent world, which for the first time only now had shown itself to him in all its scope, to be deprived instantaneously and for all time of any share in the life that included Katya and approaching summer, where there were sky, clouds, sun, warm wind, grain in the fields, villages, country hamlets, peasant girls, Mother, manor, Anya, Kostya, verses in old journals, and somewhere out there—Sevastopol, the Baidar Gates, torrid, lilac-hued mountains with pine and beechen forests, the dazzlingly white, stifling highway, the gardens of Livadia and Alupka, scorching sands by the gleaming sea, suntanned children, suntanned women bathing—and once again Katya, wearing a white dress, sitting beneath a white parasol on the shingle right beside the waves, which emit a blinding glare and provoke an unwitting smile of gratuitous joy.

He understood, but what could he do? Where could he go, how could he break out of that vicious circle, where the better everything was the more grievous, the more unbearable it became? This, precisely this, was insufferable—the very happiness in the world that was crushing him, happiness that lacked something indispensable.

In the morning he would awaken, and the first thing to strike his eye was the joyous sun, the first thing he heard was the joyous pealing, familiar from childhood, of the village church bells—out there beyond the dewy garden, full of shade, glitter, birds and flowers. Even the yellow wallpaper was joyous and dear, the same paper that had cast its yellowish gleam on his childhood. But immediately one thought would transfix his soul with rapture and horror: "Katya!" The morning sun sparkled with her youth, the crispness of the garden was lambent too with the beauty and grace of her image; the wallpaper of his ancestors demanded that she share with Mitya the whole of this precious, rustic antiquity, the life his fathers and grandfathers had lived here till they died, on this estate, in this house. And Mitya would throw aside the blanket, leap out of bed in just his open-necked nightshirt, long legged, thin, but sound for all that, young, warm with sleep; quickly he would pull out the desk drawer, snatch up the cherished photograph, and lapse into a stupor, gazing at it avidly, perplexedly. All the captivation, all the grace, the ineffable gleaming and beckoning something that comprises the maidenly, the female, all of this was in her slightly serpentine head, in her coiffure, in her faintly provocative yet innocent gaze! But that gaze gleamed enigmatically, with inexorable joyous muteness. Where could he find the strength to bear it, so near and so remote, and now, perhaps, alien forever, the gaze that had revealed such unspeakable happiness in life and had so shamelessly, terribly deceived him?

On the evening when he had ridden from the post office through Shakhovskoe, that ancient, deserted estate with its black spruce arborway, his outcry, which came as a surprise to Mitya himself, was the perfect expression of that extreme state of enervation he had come to. Watching from the saddle at the postal window, waiting as the clerk rummaged in vain through a pile of newspapers and letters, he heard behind him the din of a train approaching the station, and that sound, together with the smell of locomotive smoke, overwhelmed him with a happy recollection of the Kursk station and, on the whole, of Moscow. As he rode from the post office through the village, in each peasant girl of small stature who walked ahead of him, in the movements of her hips, he sensed some alarming aura of Katya. Out in the fields he met someone's troika; in the tarantass, flying along at a brisk pace, he saw two hats flash by, one of them a girl's, and he nearly shouted it out: "Katya!" The white flowers on the boundary strip were linked in a trice with the thought of her white gloves, the blue bear's ears with the color of her veil . . . When he had ridden, by the light of the setting sun, into Shakhovskoe, the dry and sweet odor of spruces and the sumptuous fragrance of jasmine gave him such a keen feeling of summer and of someone's ancient summer life in this lovely and opulent estate that when he glanced at the red-gold twilight on the arborway, at the house standing in the evening shade, in the depths of the avenue's corridor, he suddenly saw Katya in the full bloom of female captivation, descending from the terrace into the garden, almost as distinctly as he saw the manor house itself and the jasmine. He had long since lost any concrete, true-to-life conception of her; with each passing day she appeared to him more singular, more transfigured. But on that evening her transfiguration had been so intense, so victoriously exultant, that Mitya was even more horrified than he had been that noonday, when the cuckoo abruptly started hooting above his head.

19

He stopped going for the mail; by a desperate, extreme exertion of his will he forced himself to break off those trips. He also stopped writing. He had already tried everything, written everything: the frenetic protestations of his love, a love such as the world had never seen, the groveling entreaties that she love him or at least be his "friend," the unconscionable tales about how ill he was, how he was writing from his sickbed—aimed at provoking at least her pity, at least attracting some attention—and even the menacing hints that there was, it seemed, only one recourse: to relieve Katya and his "more fortunate rivals" of his presence on this earth. Having stopped his writing and his dogged pleadings for an answer, forcing himself with all his strength to expect nothing (secretly hoping, nonetheless, that the letter would come precisely when he had deceived fate by shamming perfect indifference or when he really had become indifferent), trying in every way possible to avoid thinking of Katya, searching in every way possible for some salvation from her, once again he began reading whatever he came across, riding out with the steward into neighboring villages on matters concerning the estate, silently repeating over and over, "It's all the same; what will be will be!"

Then one day he and the steward were returning from a small farmstead in the light *drozhky,* riding at a brisk pace as usual. Both sat astride the bench, the steward in front—he was driving—and Mitya in back, and both were jounced about by the bumpy road, especially Mitya, who kept a firm grip on the cushion as he gazed by turns at the red neck of the steward and the bouncing fields before him. As they approached the manor house, the steward released the reins, let the horse go at a jog, and began rolling a smoke; smiling complacently, he looked into the open tobacco pouch and said, "There wasn't no use for you to take umbrage at me back then like you did, young master. Wasn't it the truth I was telling you? I ain't got nothing against no books, why not do some reading when you got a minute or two, but books ain't going to run away nowhere; a man ought to know the right time for things."

Mitya flushed and answered in a tone that came as a surprise to him, with a forced casualness and an awkward grin, "But I don't see that there's anybody available . . ."

"How do you mean?" said the steward. "There's slews of women and wenches!"

"The young ones just tease," answered Mitya, trying to adopt the steward's manner. "You don't have no chance with wenches."

"They don't tease; you just ain't learned how to handle them," said the steward, switching to a preceptorial tone. "Then again, you're tightfisted. A empty sack don't stand upright."

"I wouldn't be tightfisted if things was set up to work out smooth, without any hitches," Mitya suddenly answered shamelessly.

"Don't you bother yourself none about that; everything'll be worked out just fine," said the steward, and lighting his smoke, he switched over to a slightly aggrieved voice. "It ain't your cash nor none of your presents I got in mind; I'd just like to give you a little cheer. Every time I look, there sets the young master bored to tears! I think to myself, 'No, I just can't let it go on like that.' Ain't I always looked out for the masters? Nearly two years I been with you here, and, thank God, I ain't heard a bad word from you nor the madam. Take some, now, they don't give a damn for the master's livestock. Is them cows fed?—fine; they ain't?—well, the hell with 'em. But I'm not like that. For me them cows means more than anything. That's what I tell the boys: you do what you like with me, but I want them cows fed right!"

Mitya had begun thinking the steward was drunk when suddenly he dropped the air of aggrieved sincerity and said with a sidelong, questioning glance, "Well then, could we do any better than Alyonka? A fine little piece, full of piss and vinegar, plenty young, and her husband's off at the mines . . . Course, you got to slip her a little gewgaw of some kind. It'll cost you, let's say, when all's said and done, a five. One ruble, let's say, on her treat, then hand her two more. And for me just a bit of something for tobacco . . ."

"That won't be any problem," answered Mitya, once again instinctively. "Only, what Alyonka is it you're talking about?"

"Why, the forester's, naturally," said the steward. "Can't be you don't know her. Married the new forester's boy. I believe you may've seen her in church last Sunday . . . That's when it come to me outright: that there is just the thing for our young master. Married less than two years, keeps herself clean."

"Well, sure, all right," answered Mitya with a grin. "Go on and get it set up."

"In that case, then, I'll give it a try," said the steward, taking up the reins. "I'll sound her out, then, in a day or so. And meantime you keep your eyes open too. Tomorrow she'll be out with the wenches fixing up the garden bank, so you just mosey on out in the garden . . . And them books ain't going to run away nowhere; could be you can still get a bellyful of reading in Moscow."

He whipped up the horse, and once again the *drozhky* began to shake and bounce. Holding firmly to the cushion and trying not to look at the stout red neck of the steward, Mitya gazed into the distance, through the trees of their garden at the willows in the village, which sat on a slope leading down to the river, to the meadows beside its bank. It was already half done, something bizarre and unexpected, absurd, something that, nonetheless, sent a chilling languor passing through his body. And now in some new way, not as before, the bell tower that was so familiar since childhood, its cross glittering in the early evening sun, jutted up in front of him, beyond the crowns of the garden's trees.

20

The peasant girls called Mitya Wolfhound because of his thinness; he was the type whose black eyes appear to be constantly dilated, whose mustache and beard hardly grow even in adulthood—just a few sparse and wiry curls stick out. All the same, on the morning after his conversation with the steward he shaved, then put on a yellow silk shirt that gave his emaciated, somehow inspired face a strange and beautiful glow.

Sometime after ten he walked slowly out into the garden, trying to adopt a kind of bored air, as if he were strolling about for lack of anything else to do.

He left the house from the main veranda, which faced north. To the north a slate blue murk hung above the roofs of the coach house and cattle yard, above that part of the garden directly in front of the bell tower. There was a dimness about everything; steam and redolence flowed into the air from the chimney pipe of the kitchen annex. Gazing at the sky and at crowns of trees in the garden, Mitya turned the corner of the house and set off for the linden arborway. From beneath the amorphous clouds gathering beyond the garden in the southeast, a hot feeble wind was blowing. No birds were singing, not even the nightingales. There were only masses of bees, rushing soundlessly through the garden with their nectar.

The peasant girls were working by the spruce grove again, repairing the earthen wall, evening out the crannies left by cattle hooves, filling them in with earth and with fresh and steamy, pleasant-reeking dung, which from time to time the farmhands carted in across the arborway from the cattle yard—the ground was strewn with moist, glittering dollops. There were about six of the girls. Sonka no longer was with them; they really had arranged a match for her now, and she was staying home to make preparations for her wedding. There were several quite scrawny little girls, there was the stout, comely Anyutka, there was Glashka, who seemed to have become even more austere and purposeful—and Alyonka. Mitya noticed her at once amidst the trees, he knew at once it was she although he had never seen her before, and he was taken unawares; the resemblance shocked him like a flash of lightning, the something in common that he saw—or that he fancied he saw—between Alyonka and Katya. He was so amazed that he even paused, momentarily dumbfounded. Then he walked toward her resolutely, keeping his eyes trained on her.

She too was small and agile. In spite of the dirty work she had come to do, she was wearing a pretty cotton print blouse (white with red polka dots), a black patent leather belt, a skirt of the same pattern, a pink silk kerchief, red wool stockings, and soft black galoshes, which suggested again (rather, her whole small, lithe foot suggested) something of Katya, that is, something of the womanly mixed with the childish. Her head was also small, and her dark eyes were prominent and gleaming in much the same way as Katya's. When he walked up she alone was not working, as if sensing that in some way she was special, different from the others; she stood on the earthen wall talking to the steward, resting her right foot on a pitchfork. Propped up on his elbows, the steward lay beneath an apple tree smoking, his jacket with its torn lining spread beneath him. When Mitya walked up he politely moved over onto the grass, giving him his place on the jacket.

"Set down, Mitry Palich; have a smoke," he said in a friendly, offhand manner.

Mitya cast a quick, stealthy glance at Alyonka—the pink kerchief gave her face a lovely glow—then he sat down, keeping his eyes lowered, and lit a cigarette (many times that winter and spring he had given up smoking, but now he had started again). Alyonka did not even bow to him, appeared not to have noticed him. The steward continued telling her something that made no sense to Mitya because he had not heard the beginning of the conversation. She laughed, but in a way that indicated her mind and heart were not in the laughter. Contemptuously and derisively the steward kept throwing smutty allusions into every sentence. She answered him nimbly and also derisively, giving him to understand that in chasing after someone he had conducted himself stupidly, had been too brazen and at the same time chickenhearted, afraid of his wife.

"Well, I see nobody's going to outgabble you," the steward finally said, cutting short the argument on the pretense that it was all too wearisome and useless. "Better you come set with us a spell. The master's got something to say to you."

Alyonka looked off to one side, tucked in the dark ringlets of hair on her temples, but remained standing in the same spot.

"I said get over here, you idiot!" said the steward.

Alyonka hesitated for a moment, then suddenly made a nimble leap from the wall, ran up to within two paces of where Mitya lay on the jacket, and squatted on her haunches, staring at his face with a genial curiosity in her dark, dilated eyes. Then she broke out laughing and asked, "Is it true you don't have no truck with women, young master? Like some kind of deacon in the church?"

"And how do you know he don't?" asked the steward.

"I just know," said Alyonka. "I heard. No, he ain't allowed. He's got a little somebody in Moscow," she said with a mischievous gleam in her eyes.

"There ain't nobody here fit for the master, so he don't mess with nobody," answered the steward. "A lot you know about his business!"

"How do you mean, 'nobody'?" said Alyonka, laughing. "There's slews of women and wenches! Anyutka over there, now; you couldn't do no better. Anyut, come on over here, we got some business for you!" she shouted in a ringing voice.

Anyutka, who had a broad, fleshy back and short arms, turned around—her face was attractive, her smile kind and pleasant—she shouted something in her singsong voice and went back to working even harder.

"I said come on over here!" repeated Alyonka, her voice ringing out still more loudly.

"No use me coming over; I got no experience in that sort of business," sang out Anyutka merrily.

"We don't need Anyutka; we want something a little bit cleaner, more dignified," said the steward in a preceptorial tone. "We know exactly who we want."

He gave Alyonka a very pointed glance. She was embarrassed and blushed faintly.

"Oh no, oh no," she answered, hiding her embarrassment with a smile. "Anyutka, now, you won't find nothing better. And if it ain't her you want, well, there's Nastka; keeps herself clean too, once lived in town . . ."

"That's enough, hush up," said the steward with abrupt rudeness. "Get back to what you're doing; you had your gabble and that's it. The madam's been on to me anyhow, says, 'With you all they do is get into mischief.'"

Alyonka jumped up—once again uncommonly nimble in her movements—and grabbed her pitchfork. But just then a farm-hand, who had finished dumping out the last cartload of manure, cried "Lunchtime!" Then, tugging at the reins he drove off smartly down the avenue, his empty cart bed clattering.

"Lunchtime, lunchtime!" screamed the girls in a variety of voices, throwing down their spades and pitchforks, leaping over the earthen wall, jumping down from it with their bare legs and multicolored stockings flashing, and running into the spruce grove to get their bundles of food.

The steward cast a sideways glance at Mitya, winked at him as if to say that things were moving right along, and raising himself a bit, he assented to the break with the pompous air of one in authority.

"Well, if it's lunchtime, I guess lunchtime it is."

Splotches of color beneath the dark wall of spruces, the girls sprawled out gaily, haphazardly on the grass, began untying their bundles, removing their flat cakes and spreading them on the hems of their skirts between outstretched legs, began munching, drinking milk or kvass from their bottles, still talking loudly and rambunctiously, laughing at every other word, and glancing over at Mitya with curious and provocative eyes. Alyonka bent toward Anyutka and whispered something in her ear. Unable to hold back a charming smile, Anyutka pushed her away roughly (choking with laughter, Alyonka collapsed, head on knees), and with sham indignation she cried out in her melodic voice, which carried throughout the spruce grove, "Idiot! Cackling away over nothing. What's so funny?"

"Let's get away from sin, Mitry Palich," said the steward. "Whew, just look there, they got the demons in their blood!"

21

The next day no one worked in the garden; it was a holiday, a Sunday.

Rain had poured in the night, pounded its wet patter on the roof; now and then the garden was illumined by a pallid but far-reaching, phantasmal glow. By morning, however, the skies had cleared; once again all was simple, full of equanimity, and Mitya was awakened by the sunlit, joyous peal of bells.

Leisurely he washed, dressed, drank a glass of tea, and set off for mass. "Your mama's done left," scolded Parasha affectionately. "But you behave like you're a Tatar or something."

He could reach the church either by way of the pasture, by going through the gates of the manor and turning right, or through the garden, along the central arborway and then to the left, by the road between garden and barn. Mitya went through the garden.

Everything was quite summerlike now. He walked down the arborway straight toward the sun, which cast a dry glitter on the barn and fields. That glitter, and the pealing bells blending somehow perfectly and placidly with it and with all this country morning, the fact that he had just washed, had just combed his wet, glossy black hair and put on his peaked university cap, all of this suddenly seemed so fine that Mitya, who had not slept all night again and who once again had been plagued with the most discrepant thoughts and feelings, felt a sudden spasm of hope for some happy deliverance from his agonies, for salvation, liberation from them. The bells gamboled and beckoned, the barn ahead of him was glittering with heat; a woodpecker paused, perked up his crest, scurried up the rugged linden bole to its sunny, bright green crown; velvet, black-red, purposeful bumblebees were burrowing into flowers in the blazing sun of the clearings, birds were flooding all the garden with their sweet and carefree song . . . Everything was just as it had been many, many times in his childhood and boyhood. This memory of all the captivation, the carefree former times, was so vivid that suddenly he was sure God was merciful; perhaps it would be possible to live on earth even without Katya.

"I really will go visit the Meshersky family," Mitya suddenly thought.

But then he raised his eyes—and not twenty steps from him he saw Alyonka, who at that very moment was walking past the gate. She was wearing the pink silk kerchief again, a smart, pale blue dress with flounces, and new shoes with taps on the heels. Swinging her buttocks, she walked along rapidly, not seeing him, and he leapt aside impulsively, behind the trees.

When she was out of sight he returned hastily to the house, his heart pounding. He suddenly realized that he had set off for church with the secret aim of seeing her there, and he knew that he could not, must not see her in church.

22

While they were eating dinner a special messenger from the station brought a telegram—Anya and Kostya had wired that they would arrive tomorrow evening. Mitya received this news with absolute indifference.

After dinner he lay on the terrace, supine on the wickerwork settee, eyes closed, feeling the hot sun approach the terrace, listening to the summery buzzing of flies. His heart was shuddering, the insoluble question was on his mind: what next in this Alyonka business? When would it definitely be settled? Why hadn't the steward asked her outright yesterday: would she, and if yes, then where and when? There was another torment as well: should he or should he not break his resolution to make no more trips to the post office? He could go once more today, for the last time. Wasn't this pathetic hope just another senseless self-torment? But what could one trip (really, just a simple ramble) add to his agony now? Wasn't it perfectly obvious that for him everything out there, in Moscow, was finished forever? What, after all, could he do about anything now?

"Young master!" a soft voice suddenly rang out beside the terrace. "Young master, you sleeping?"

Quickly he opened his eyes. The steward was standing there in a new cotton print shirt and a new peaked cap. His face was festive, sated, and slightly drowsy, drunken.

"Young master, quick, let's ride on out to the woods," he whispered. "I told the madam I had to see Trifon about them bees. Quick now, while she's still snoozing; she might wake up and change her mind . . . We'll pick us up a little snort for the old man; after he's potted you get him to talking, and I'll sneak around and have a whisper in Alyonka's ear. Come on out quick, I got the horse harnessed up."

Mitya jumped up, ran through the footmen's room, grabbed his cap, and rushed out to the coach house, where a spirited young stallion stood harnessed to the light *drozhky*.

23

The stallion tore away like a whirlwind and flew past the gates. They stopped off at the shop opposite the church, bought a pound of lard and a bottle of vodka, and sped away.

Near a peasant hut that flashed by at the edge of the village they saw Anyutka, smartly dressed but having nothing better to do than stand there. The steward cried out something to her in a jocular but coarse tone; with drunken, senseless and malicious bravura he jerked aside the reins and used them to lash the stallion's croup. The horse dashed on at even greater speed.

Sitting there jouncing about in the *drozhky*, Mitya held on with all his strength. The back of his neck baked pleasantly in the sun, a warm breeze blew in his face, bearing the heat from the field, now redolent of rye breaking into bloom, of road dust and axle grease. The rye was swaying, flecked with silvery gray ripples—like some kind of marvelous fur; skylarks were soaring up continuously above it, crying out, skimming obliquely, then falling, and far ahead lay the soft blue of the forest . . .

In fifteen minutes they had reached the forest, and keeping up the same brisk pace, knocking against stumps and roots, they sped along its shaded road, which was joyous with patches of sun and countless flowers in the dense, high grass on each side. Wearing her pale blue dress, her legs in half boots stretched out evenly, straight in front of her, Alyonka sat embroidering amidst the oak saplings that were breaking into leaf beside the sentry hut. The steward barreled past her, making a threatening gesture with his whip, and immediately reined in near the threshold. Mitya marveled at the bitter and crisp scent of the forest and the vernal oak leafage; he was deafened by the ringing yelps of puppies, who surrounded the *drozhky* and filled all the forest with echoes. They stood there pouring out ferocious howls in all sorts of pitches and timbres, but their shaggy muzzles were kindly and their tails were wagging.

After they had climbed down and hitched the stallion beneath the window, to a desiccate little tree that had been singed by lightning, they went into the hut through the dark entrance hall.

Inside it was very clean, cozy and snug, hot because the sun shone in both its tiny windows from beyond the forest and because the stove was lit—they had been baking bread loaves made from sifted flour that morning. Alyonka's mother-in-law, Fedosya, a neat, respectable-looking old woman, sat at the table, her back to the sunny window, which was specked with small flies. When she saw the young master, she stood up and made a deep bow. They greeted her, sat down, and began smoking.

"Whereabouts is Trifon?" asked the steward.

"Having a rest in the storeroom," said Fedosya. "I'll go fetch him for you."

"Things is moving!" whispered the steward as soon as she had left, winking with both eyes.

But so far Mitya could see nothing moving at all. Everything so far was unbearably awkward; it seemed that Fedosya knew perfectly well why they had come. Once again the thought that had horrified him for three days flashed through his head: "What am I doing? I'm losing my mind!" He felt as if he were walking in his sleep, under the power of some alien force, moving faster and faster toward a lethal but relentlessly beckoning abyss. Yet he sat smoking, looking around the hut, trying to appear casual and calm. Especially shameful was the thought that any minute Trifon would come in, a man who was said to be testy and clever, who would size up the situation even quicker than Fedosya. But at the same time he was thinking of something else. "Where does she sleep? Right here on this plank bed or in the storeroom? In the storeroom, of course," he thought. A summer's night in the forest, the tiny windows of the storeroom, with no frames, no glass, the somnolent whisper of the forest all night long, and she sleeps . . .

24

When Trifon came in he too bowed low to Mitya but said nothing and kept his eyes averted. Then he sat down on a bench by the table and began speaking with the steward in a dry hostile tone: "What is it, what you here for?" The steward hastened to reply that the madam had sent him, that she would like Trifon to come have a look at the apiary. Their beekeeper was a deaf old imbecile, and he, Trifon, with all his cleverness and know-how, why he just might be the top beekeeper in the whole province. Thereupon he pulled out the bottle of vodka from one of his trouser pockets and the lard in its rough gray paper, now soaked with grease, from the other. Trifon gave him a cold, derisive glance but rose from his seat and took a teacup from the shelf. The steward served Mitya first, then Trifon, then Fedosya—with great relish she swilled hers down—and finally himself. Tossing off his drink, he immediately set about pouring another round while munching on a piece of bread and puffing out his nostrils.

Trifon got drunk quite rapidly, but he maintained his dry manner, the hostile derisiveness. After only two glasses the steward grew extremely muddled. Outwardly the conversation took on an amiable guise, but the eyes of both men were mistrustful and rancorous. Fedosya sat in silence, looked on politely but discontentedly. Alyonka did not appear. Having lost all hope that she would come, clearly realizing that only a fool would dream of counting on the steward—

on his "having a whisper" in her ear even if she did come—Mitya stood up and announced sternly that it was time to go.

"Directly, directly, there ain't no hurry!" responded the steward in a dour and insolent tone. "I got something to tell you in private."

"Well, you can tell me on the way back," said Mitya, controlling his temper but speaking even more sternly. "Let's go."

But the steward slapped his palm on the table and repeated with an air of drunken mysteriousness.

"Listen here, now; this is something that can't wait to be said going back! Come on out with me for a minute."

Rising sluggishly from his place, he flung open the door to the entrance hall.

Mitya followed him out.

"Well, what is it?"

"Hush up," whispered the steward cryptically, staggering as he tried to close the door behind Mitya.

"Hush up about what?"

"Hush up!"

"I don't understand you."

"Just keep quiet! Our lady'll be here! Take my word for it!"

Mitya pushed him away, went out of the entrance hall, and stopped on the threshold of the hut, not knowing what to do next. Should he wait a bit longer or drive home alone, or should he simply leave on foot?

Ten paces from him lay the lush green forest, now covered in evening shade, which made it even more fresh, pure, and lovely. The kind of sun that goes with clear, perfect weather was setting behind its crowns, radiantly spreading through them its carmine gold. And suddenly a melodic female voice rang out, low and resonant, reverberated through the forest depths, seemed to be somewhere far on the other side, beyond the ravines, its modulation so charming, so invocatory, as a voice sounds only in the forest amidst the evening glow of summer.

"A-ooo!" resounded the protracted cry of that girl, apparently amusing herself with forest echoes. "A-ooo!"

Mitya leapt down from the threshold and ran through flowers and grass to the forest, which descended into a rocky ravine. There in the ravine, chewing on cowslip stems, stood Alyonka. Mitya ran to the edge and stopped. She gazed up at him in astonishment.

"What are you doing here?" asked Mitya softly.

"I'm hunting for our Maruska and the cow. Why?" she answered, also softly.

"Well then, will you come?"

"Well, what am I supposed to do, come for nothing?" she said.

"Who said for nothing?" asked Mitya, now almost in a whisper. "Don't worry about that."

"When?" asked Alyonka.

"Well, tomorrow . . . When can you?"

Alyonka thought for a moment.

"Tomorrow I'll be going to shear sheep at my mama's," she said, after pausing and carefully surveying the forest on the knoll behind Mitya. "In the evening, soon as it's dark, I'll come. But where? Can't use the barn, somebody'd walk in . . . What about the shed, in the hollow of your garden? Only look out you don't pull no tricks—I won't do it for free . . . This ain't Moscow," she said, gazing up at him with laughing eyes. "They say them women there pay for it theirselves."

25

The journey back was chaotic.

So as not to feel indebted, Trifon had produced his own bottle, and the steward got so drunk that at first he could not mount the *drozhky;* he fell against it, causing the frightened stallion to lunge forward and nearly gallop off alone. But Mitya kept silent, looked at the steward insensibly, waited, patiently, while he took his seat. Once again the steward drove the horse on with absurd ferocity. Mitya kept silent, held on firmly, looked at the evening sky, at the fields rapidly shuddering and bouncing before him. Above those fields, toward the sunset, the skylarks sang their last meek songs; in the east, now blue with the coming night, there were flares of the distant, placid heat lightning that promises nothing but fine weather. Mitya took in all this twilight captivation, but now it was utterly alien to him. There was only one thing on his mind and in his heart: tomorrow evening!

At home he was greeted with the news that a letter had come from Anya and Kostya, confirming their arrival tomorrow on the evening train. He was horrified; they would drive up in the evening, run out in the garden, possibly into the hollow, approach the shed . . . But immediately he recalled that they could not be driven here from the station until after nine, and then they would be fed, given tea . . .

"Are you driving in with me to meet them?" asked Olga Petrovna.

He felt himself go pale.

"No, I don't think so . . . I don't feel much like it. And there won't be any room . . ."

"Well, maybe you could ride in on horseback."

"No, I don't know . . . What's the point, anyway? At least right now I don't feel like it."

Olga Petrovna looked at him intently.

"Are you well?"

"Perfectly well," said Mitya in an almost rude tone. "I'm just awfully sleepy."

Right after that he went to his room, lay down on the sofa in the dark, and fell asleep, still dressed.

In the night he heard torpid faraway music and saw himself hanging above a huge, vaguely illumined abyss. It kept getting brighter and brighter, became ever more bottomless, ever more golden, more luminous, ever more swarming with masses of people, and then with utter clarity, with unspeakable sorrow and tenderness, the words began sounding and resounding within it: "Once in far Thule there lived a good king." He trembled with emotion, turned over on his other side, and went back to sleep.

26

The day seemed interminable.

Mitya came out in a daze for tea and for dinner, then went back to his room again, lay down once again, took up a volume of Pisemsky that had been lying on his desk for ages, read without understanding a word, spent hours gazing at the ceiling, listened to the steady summerlike and satin hum of the garden in the sun beyond his window . . . Once he got up and went into the library to find a different book. But that room, captivating for its antiquity and its calm, for the view of the beloved maple outside one window and the bright western sky out the others, aroused such an acute reminder of those (now infinitely remote) spring days when he had sat in this room reading verses in old journals, and it all seemed so full of Katya that he turned and rushed back out. "To hell with it!" he thought in exasperation. "To hell with all that poetic tragedy of love!"

He recalled with indignation how he had thought of shooting himself if Katya did not write, and then he lay down again, once again took up Pisemsky. But just as before he understood nothing of what he was reading, and from time to time, as he gazed at the book and thought of Alyonka, he would begin shuddering all over from a tremor in his stomach that grew more and more intense.

And the closer it was to evening, the more often the tremor gripped him, churned within him. Voices and footsteps throughout the house, voices in the yard—now they were harnessing the tarantass for the trip to the station. Everything had the kind of resonance it has when you are ill, when you lie alone and normal, humdrum life flows on all around, indifferent to you and therefore alien, even malign. Finally Parasha cried out from somewhere, "Madam, the horses are ready!" Then the dry, hollow jangle of harness bells became audible, the tramp of hooves, the rustle of the tarantass rolling up to the veranda . . . "Ah, when will all this end!" muttered Mitya, beside himself with impatience, not moving, listening avidly to the voice of Olga Petrovna as she gave final instructions in the footmen's room. Suddenly the harness bells came alive, their hollow jangle grew ever more steady and categorical in accord with the din of the carriage rolling downhill, then began dying away . . .

Mitya quickly got up and went into the parlor. That room was empty and bright with the clear, yellowish sunset. All the house was empty, somehow strangely, terribly empty! With a strange, somehow valedictory feeling, Mitya glanced into the mute open rooms—into the drawing room, the divan room, the library, where through the window he could see the vespertine blue glow of southern sky above the horizon, the picturesque green crown of the maple, and, above it, the pink dot of Antares . . . Then he looked into the footmen's room to see if Parasha was there. Having assured himself that it too was empty, he grabbed his cap from the hook, ran back into his room, and leapt out the window, throwing his long legs far out toward the flower bed. He froze dead still in that flower bed for an instant; then, stooping, he ran across to the garden and veered immediately onto a secluded branch pathway, which was densely overgrown with acacia and lilac bushes.

27

Since there was no dew, the smells of the evening garden could not have been especially pungent. But for all the spontaneity of his every movement that evening, it seemed to Mitya that never in his life—with the exception, perhaps, of early childhood—had he encountered such strong and such diversified smells. Everything was redolent—acacia bushes, lilac leafage, currant foliage, burdock, wormwood, blossoms, grass, earth . . .

After Mitya had taken a few quick steps, he was struck by a frightening thought: "What if she tricks me and doesn't come?" It seemed now that all of life depended on whether Alyonka appeared or not. Catching amidst the smells of vegetation another smell, that of evening smoke, which drifted over from somewhere in the village, he stopped once more and looked around. A crepuscular beetle was slowly floating and droning by not far from him, as if sowing quiet, tranquillity, and dusk, but everything was still bright from the evening glow, which enveloped half the sky with the steady, long-undying light of early summer gloaming, and above the manor roof, visible in blotches through the trees, the skewed and sharp sickle of the newborn moon glittered high in transparent, celestial emptiness. Mitya glanced at it, crossed himself with a brief, perfunctory gesture below his chest, and strode out into the acacia bushes. The pathway led to the hollow but not to the shed—to reach it he had to go catercornered, bearing left. After making his way through the bushes, Mitya began running headlong, amidst the low and extensive network of outstretched branches, sometimes bending, sometimes pushing them out of his way. A moment later he arrived at the designated spot.

Fearfully he plunged into the shed, into its darkness, which smelled of dry fusty straw, looked around attentively, and almost felt a surge of joy when he realized no one was there. But the fateful moment was drawing near; he stood beside the shed all keen sensitivity and strained concentration. The whole day long, nearly every minute, he had experienced an extraordinary physical agitation. Now it had reached a peak of intensity. But even now, strangely enough, as throughout the day, it was somehow discrete, did not imbue the whole of him, possessed only his body and had not captured his spirit. But his heart was pounding terribly. And all around there was such staggering quiet that this was the only thing he could hear—the pounding heartbeat. Soundlessly, tirelessly they hovered and whirled, the soft colorless moths in the branches, in the gray apple-tree leafage, etched in all sorts of lacework patterns against the evening sky, and these moths made the quiet seem even more quiet, as if the moths were spinning incantations and casting their spells upon it. Suddenly behind him there was a snapping sound and it jolted him like a thunderclap. He flinched and turned around, looked back through the trees in the direction of the earthen wall—and beneath the apple boughs he saw something black rolling toward him. But before he had time even to think what it could be, this dark thing came swooping right up upon him, made some kind of sweeping movement—and proved to be Alyonka.

She pushed down the hem of her short skirt made of black homespun wool, flung it away from her head, and he saw her frightened face, beaming with a smile. She was barefoot, wearing only a skirt with a plain, austere blouse tucked into it. Her pointed, girlish breasts were prominent beneath the blouse. Its collar was cut wide, so that he could see her neck and part of her shoulders; the sleeves were turned up above the elbows to reveal her rounded arms. Everything about her, from the small head, covered by a yellow kerchief, to the tiny bare feet, womanly and childish at the same time, was so fine, so lissome and charming, that Mitya, who previously had always seen her smartly dressed, who for the first time saw her in all the captivation of that plainness, gasped inwardly.

"Well, hurry up, then," she whispered gaily and surreptitiously, and taking a quick look around she darted into the shed, into the rank-smelling murkiness.

There she paused, and clenching his teeth to stop their chattering, Mitya hastily reached in his pocket—his legs were tensed, as firm as iron—and slipped a crumpled five-ruble note into her palm. Quickly she hid it in her shirt front and sat down on the ground. Mitya sat beside her and put his arms around her neck, at a loss what to do next—wondering whether he had to kiss her or not. The smell of her kerchief, her hair, the oniony smell of her whole body mixed with the smell of a peasant hut, of its smoke—this was all so lovely that his head spun, and Mitya could comprehend that with his mind and his senses. Nonetheless, it was just the same as before. The awesome power of physical desire did not pass over into spiritual desire, into beatitude and rapture, the sweet languorous something that all his being craved. She pulled away and lay down on her back. He lay beside her, pressed against her, stretched out his hand. Laughing quietly and nervously, she took it and pulled it down lower.

"Absolutely not permitted," she said, half joking, half serious. Then she moved his hand away and held it tenaciously in her own small hand. Her eyes looked through the shed's triangular window frame at the apple branches, at the now darkened blue sky beyond those branches and the motionless red dot of Antares, still hanging there in solitude. What did those eyes express? What was he supposed to do? Kiss her neck, her lips? Suddenly she pulled up on the short black skirt and said hastily, "Well, hurry up then . . ."

When they arose—and Mitya got up overwhelmed with disillusionment—putting her kerchief back on and straightening her hair, she asked in an animated whisper, now in the tone of an intimate, a lover, "They say you was just over in Subbotino. Priest there sells sucking pigs cheap. Is that true or not? Ain't you heard?"

28

On Saturday of that same week the rain, which had begun as early as Wednesday and poured from morning to night, was still falling in torrents.

Time and again that day it intensified, showered down with a special vehemence and somberness.

All day Mitya wandered incessantly through the garden, weeping so hard and so long that at times he himself was amazed at the force and abundance of his tears.

Parasha searched for him, cried out for him in the yard and on the linden arborway, called him for dinner, then for tea. He did not respond.

It was cold, piercingly damp, dark with storm clouds; against their blackness the thick greenery of the wet garden was prominent, especially lush, crisp, and bright. The wind that gusted from time to time cast still another downpour from the trees—a deluge of spattering raindrops. But Mitya paid no attention to anything, saw nothing. His white peaked cap was drooping and had turned dark gray, his university jacket had gone black, his boots were muddied to the knees. He was a terrible sight, soaked through and through, dripping water, his face completely drained of blood, his eyes tear-blanched and insane.

He smoked one cigarette after another, walked with lengthy strides through the mud of the pathways, sometimes simply dashed off at random, headlong, into the tall wet grass amidst the apple and pear trees, stumbling against their skewed, rugged boughs splotched with sodden gray-green lichens. He would sit on the swollen, blackened benches, go out to the hollow, lie on the damp straw of the shed, in the very spot where he had lain with Alyonka. The cold, the icy dampness of the air, turned his large hands blue, his lips had gone mauve, his deathly pallid face with its gaunt cheeks had taken on a violet hue. He would lie on his back, legs crossed, hands behind his head, glaring savagely at the black straw roof, from which large rusty raindrops were falling. Then his cheeks went tense, his brows began to twitch. Impulsively he leapt up, pulled from his trousers pocket the stained and rumpled letter, which he had read over and over since receiving it late yesterday evening—the surveyor who came to the manor for several days on business had picked it up at the post office—and once again, for the hundredth time, he avidly devoured the words:

> Dear Mitya,
>
> Try not to think badly of me, forget, forget all that has been! I'm nasty, I'm repulsive, spoiled, I'm not worthy of you, but I'm madly in love with art! I've made my decision. The die is cast, I'm going away—you know with whom . . . You're sensitive, intelligent, you'll understand; I beg of you, my dear, don't torment yourself and me! Don't write me at all, it's no use!

When he reached that point in the letter Mitya wadded it up, and burying his face in the wet straw, clenching his teeth rabidly, he choked on his sobs. The incidental "my dear," which was such a terrible reminder of their intimacy and appeared even to restore that intimacy, which flooded his heart with unbearable tenderness—that was beyond human endurance! And right after this "my dear" came the firm declaration that even writing her now was no use! Yes, he knew it: no use! It was all over, finished forever!

Just before evening the rain assailed the garden with tenfold greater force, and sudden blasts of thunder finally drove him back to the house. Wet from head to foot, his teeth chattering from the icy tremor that had spread through all his body, he looked out from beneath the trees to make sure no one could see him, then ran up below his window, raised it from the outside—with its antiquated frame it could be opened by lifting the bottom half—

and leaping into his room, he locked the door and hurled himself on the bed.

Darkness was quickly approaching. The din of the rain was everywhere—on the roof, all around the house, in the garden. It had a dualistic quality, that din, two disparate sounds—one sound in the garden, but by the house, in accord with the unremitting gurgle and plash of the drainpipes pouring water into puddles, a different sound. That dichotomy of sound produced an impalpable apprehension in Mitya, who had lapsed immediately into a lethargic torpor, and together with the fever that burned his nostrils, his breath, his head, it steeped him in something like narcosis, created what appeared another world, some other early evening in what seemed some other, some alien house, where there was a horrible presentiment of something.

He knew, he sensed that he was in his own room, now nearly dark with the rain and approaching evening, that out there, at the tea table in the parlor were the voices of Mother, Anya, Kostya, and the surveyor, but simultaneously he was walking through someone else's manor house, following, lagging behind a young nanny, and he was seized by impalpable, ever-growing horror, mixed, however, with concupiscence, with a presentiment of someone's intimacy with someone, an act that contained something unnaturally, grotesquely abhorrent, but in which he himself somehow was taking part. He experienced all of this through the intermediary figure of a child with a large white face, whom the young nanny carried in her arms, leaning backward and rocking him to sleep. Mitya hurried to overtake her, overtook her, and tried to look at her face—to see if this was Alyonka—but suddenly he found himself in a dusky gymnasium classroom, its panes smudged with whitewash. She who stood there at a mirror, in front of a chest of drawers, could not see him—he had abruptly turned invisible. She was wearing a yellow silk petticoat that tightly encompassed her rounded hips, high-heeled slippers, and sheer black openwork stockings through which her flesh was gleaming; sweetly timorous and shamefaced, she knew what was about to occur. Already she had managed to hide the child in one of the drawers. Throwing her hair over her shoulder, she quickly began braiding it, and casting sideways glances at the door she gazed in the mirror, at the reflection of her powdered face, her bare shoulders and small, milky bluish breasts with their pink nipples. The door was flung open; looking around briskly and ominously, a gentleman in a dinner jacket came in, his face anemic, clean shaven, his hair black, short, and curly. He took out a flat, golden *porte-cigare* and lit up a cigarette with an air of free and easy nonchalance. Her braiding now almost done, she looked at him timorously, knowing his intentions, then tossed the braid back over her shoulder and raised her bare arms . . . He put his arms around her waist in a condescending gesture—and she embraced his neck, showing her dark armpits, nestled against him, and buried her face in his chest.

29

Mitya came to his senses covered in sweat, with the astoundingly vivid realization that he was lost, that this world was monstrously somber and hopeless, more than any netherworld beyond the grave could ever be. The room was full of murk, the dinning and spattering continued beyond the windows, and his body, which shuddered all over with chills, could not stand this din and this patter (unbearable for the sound alone). But most unbearable and hideous of all was the monstrous, grotesque unnaturalness of human coitus, which he himself and the clean-shaven gentleman seemed just now to have shared out between them. There were voices and laughter in the parlor. They too were hideous and grotesquely unnatural in their estrangement from him, in the coarseness of life, its indifference, its mercilessness toward him.

"Katya!" he said, sitting up on the bed and throwing his feet to the floor. "Katya, what is this, anyway!" he said aloud, absolutely convinced she could hear him, that she was there, that she was silent and unresponsive only because she herself was crushed, because she herself understood the irremediable horror of all that she had done. "Ah, it doesn't matter, Katya," he whispered bitterly and tenderly, meaning that he would forgive her everything if only she would rush to him as she once had done, so that together they could be saved—could save their beautiful love in this most beautiful of all spring worlds that only so recently had been like a paradise. But having whispered it—"Ah, it doesn't matter, Katya!"—he knew immediately that he was wrong, that it did matter, that salvation, a return to that wondrous apparition he had been given to see at Shakhovskoe, on the terrace overgrown with jasmine, did not exist, could not be, and he began quietly weeping with the pain that was rending his chest.

It, the pain, was so intense, so unbearable, that without thinking what he was doing, without realizing what all this would lead to, passionately desiring only one thing, to escape from it at least for a moment and to avoid being engulfed again in that horrendous world where he had spent the whole day and where he had just been enveloped in the most hideous and abominable of all earthly dreams, he fumbled around for the drawer of his night table, pulled it out, found the cold and heavy lump of the revolver, and heaving a deep and joyous sigh, he opened wide his mouth; then, with a sense of delight, he firmly squeezed the trigger.

Maritime Alps, September 14, 1924

»»» «««

Somber Pathways (Linden Lined)

A tarantass sped along through the cold nastiness of autumn, down one of the main highways near Tula, flooded with rains and cut up into a multitude of black ruts. Spattered with mud, its hood half raised, it was pulled by the usual sort of troika, with the horses' tails tied up out of the slush. The tarantass rolled up to a long, wooden structure, one wing of which accommodated a government post station, the other a private roadhouse, where you could rest or spend the night, dine or drink tea. On the coach box sat a robust muzhik in tightly belted, crude peasant coat; dark of visage and grave, with his sparse tar black beard, he looked like some ancient brigand. His passenger was a trim, old military man in large peaked cap and gray army coat with beaver collar raised. His brows were still black, but his mustaches were white and blended with sideburns of the same color; his chin was clean shaven, and his whole face had that resemblance to Alexander II that was so widespread among military men in the years of his reign. He had the same inquisitive look about him as well, something severe and at the same time weary.

When the horses stopped he flung one leg, in a military boot cut level at the top, out of the tarantass; then, holding up the flaps of his greatcoat with hands in suede gloves, he ran up onto the porch of the building.

"To the left, Your Excellency," called out the coachman from the box in a rough voice. Stooping at the threshold to compensate for his height, he went into the vestibule, then entered the inn on the left.

It was warm inside, dry and tidy: in the left corner a new, golden-gleaming icon, beneath it a table covered with a clean austere tablecloth, cleanly washed benches on the other side of the table. A cooking stove that occupied the far right corner was newly whitewashed; closer to him there was an ottoman of sorts, covered with skewbald horse cloths and supported by a board propped against the side of the stove. The sweet smell of cabbage soup wafted from behind the stove door—along with aromas of cabbage long boiled, beef, and bay leaves.

The traveler threw his greatcoat on a bench, appearing still slimmer in just his uniform and boots. He took off his gloves and cap and with a weary gesture rubbed a thin pale hand over his head. His gray hair had slightly curling fringes around the temples, near the corners of his eyes; there were traces of smallpox scars on the handsome, oblong face with dark eyes. The roadhouse was empty, and he opened the door to the vestibule and called out angrily, "Hey! Anybody here?"

Immediately a dark-haired woman came in; she too had black eyebrows and was still good-looking despite her age, resembling an elderly gypsy woman, with dark fluff on her upper lip and along her cheeks. Her step was brisk, although she was plump, with large breasts beneath a red blouse, with a triangular stomach like a goose's beneath her black woolen skirt.

"Welcome, Your Excellency," she said. "Would you care to eat or shall I just bring a samovar?"

Glancing briefly at her rounded shoulders and graceful legs, at the red, worn Tatar slippers, he answered distractedly and abruptly, "Just the samovar. Are you the owner here, or just serving?"

"I'm the owner, Your Excellency."

"So you keep the inn yourself?"

"That's right, sir. By myself."

"How's that, then; are you a widow? Is that why you're running a business by yourself?"

"I'm not a widow, Your Excellency, but one must live somehow. And I like being in charge."

"I see. Well, that's good. And you keep things so nice and clean here."

The woman kept looking at him curiously, slightly narrowing her eyes.

"I like cleanliness too," she answered. "After all, I grew up with the gentry, so how could I not know what decent manners are, Nikolai Alekseevich?"

He stood up straight, opened his eyes wide, and his face reddened.

"Nadezhda, is it you?" he said hastily.

"It's me, Nikolai Alekseevich," she answered.

"My God, my God!" he said, sitting down on a bench and staring at her. "Who would have thought! How long has it been since we saw each other? About thirty-five years?"

"Thirty, Nikolai Alekseevich. I'm forty-eight now, and I would guess you're almost sixty."

"Close to it . . . My God, how strange!"

"What do you find strange, sir?"

"Well, everything, all of this . . . Don't you understand!"

His weariness and absentminded manner had disappeared; he got up and began pacing resolutely about the room, looking at the floor. Then he stopped, and flushing through the grayness of his hair, he spoke.

"I don't know anything about you since back then. How did you end up here? Why didn't you stay with the masters?"

"Soon after you left the masters gave me my freedom."

"And where did you live after that?"

"That's a long time in telling, sir."

"You say you were never married?"

"No, never."

"Why not? Beautiful as you were?"

"I couldn't do that."

"Why couldn't you? What do you mean?"

"What's there to explain? I dare say you recall how I loved you."

He reddened to the point of tears, frowned, and began striding around the room again.

"Everything passes, my friend," he muttered. "Love, youth—everything. It's a banal story, the ordinary thing. With the years everything goes. How is that in the book of Job? 'Thou shalt recall it as the waters that pass away.'"

"God grants different things to different people, Nikolai Alekseevich. Everybody's youth will pass, but love—that's another matter."

He raised his head, stopped, and smiled a sickly smile.

"But you could not have loved me for all time!"

"It seems I could. No matter how much time went by, I lived for only one thing. I knew that the former you was long since gone, that for you it was as if nothing had ever happened, but then . . . It's too late for reproaches now, but, you know, it really was heartless the way you threw me over. How often I felt like laying hands on myself, just because I was so hurt, not to speak of everything else. After all, Nikolai Alekseevich, there was a time when I called you Nikolenka, and remember what you called me? And you used to read me all those poems about 'somber pathways,'" she added with a bitter smile.

"God, how beautiful you were!" he said, shaking his head. "How full of fire, how lovely! What a figure, what eyes! Do you remember how everyone looked at you?"

"I remember, sir. And you yourself were ever so handsome. You were the one I gave my beauty to, my passion. How could anyone forget a thing like that?"

"Ah! Everything passes. All is forgotten."

"Everything passes, but not all is forgotten."

"Leave me," he said, turning away from her and walking over to the window. "Go, please."

Taking a handkerchief out and pressing it to his eyes, he added in a rapid patter of words, "If only God would forgive me. You, apparently, have forgiven."

She got as far as the door and stopped.

"No, Nikolai Alekseevich, I haven't forgiven you. If we're to touch upon our feelings in this conversation, I'll tell you straight out: I never could forgive you. Just as there was nothing dearer than you on earth way back then, so it remained later on. That's why I can't forgive you. But then, what's the point of recalling all this; dead bodies are not brought back from the graveyard."

"Yes, yes, there's no point to it. Send for the horses," he answered, stepping away from the window with his face set firm. "Let me say one thing. I never have been happy in my life; please don't think that. Excuse me if this should wound your pride, but I'll tell you frankly—I was crazy with love for my wife, and she betrayed me, threw me over in a more insulting way than I did you. I adored my son—the hopes I placed on him while he was growing up! And he turned out to be a good-for-nothing, a wastrel, insolent, heartless, and without honor or conscience . . . But then, all of this is also quite the ordinary, banal story. I wish you health, dear friend. It seems that in you I, as well, lost the most precious thing that I had in life."

She walked up to him and kissed his hand, and he kissed hers.

"Tell them to bring the horses."

After they had driven off, he thought gloomily, "Yes, how charming she was! Enchanting, lovely!" He recalled his final words with shame, and the way he had kissed her hand, but immediately he felt ashamed of his shame: "Isn't it true that she gave me the best moments of my life?"

Toward sunset pale rays of light broke through. The coachman drove his team at a trot, continually switching black ruts, selecting those less muddy and thinking some thoughts of his own. Finally he said, with a graveness in his crude voice, "She was all the time looking out the window as we drove off, Your Excellency. Could be you've knowed her for quite a while?"

"A long time, Klim."

"Some skirt, that one, sharp as a tack. They all say she's getting rich. Lends out money on interest."

"That doesn't mean anything."

"Well, I don't know! Who is there don't want to live a better life! If you lend it out listening to your conscience, ain't no great harm in that. And they say she's fair-minded. But she's tough! You don't pay it back on time, well, it's only yourself to blame."

"Yes, you've only yourself to blame . . . Whip it up a bit, please, so we're not late for the train."

The low sun gleamed yellow on the empty fields, the horses sloshed with measured tread through mud puddles. Knitting his black brows, he gazed at the scintillating horseshoes and thought, "Yes, blame only yourself. Of course those were my best moments. If not the best, then the truly enchanting moments! 'The wild rosebush red, in bloom, the pathways somber, linden lined.' But my Lord, what would have come next? What if I had not left her? How stupid! This very Nadezhda, not the keeper of a roadhouse inn but my wife, the mistress of my home in Petersburg and the mother of my children?"

Closing his eyes, he kept shaking his head.

October 20, 1938

»»» «««

Sunstroke

After dinner they left the hot, brightly lit dining room, went out on deck, and stood by the railing. She closed her eyes, placed her hand, palm out, to her cheek, and burst out laughing in that easy, charming way; everything about this small woman was charming.

"I must be drunk," she said. "Where did you come from? Three hours ago I had no idea you existed. I don't even know where you boarded the ship. In Samara? But it makes no difference. Is that my head spinning, or is the boat swinging around?"

Up ahead there was darkness and there were lights. A brisk soft wind blew out of the darkness into their faces and the lights rushed off to one side. As it completed its rapid approach to a small landing, the steamship executed a sharp turn and made a wide arc, flaunting the cockiness of a Volga cruise boat.

The lieutenant took her hand and placed it to his lips. Small and strong, the hand smelled of suntan. And when he thought of how firm and dusky the whole of her must be underneath that light linen dress, after a month of lying on hot beaches in the southern sun (she said she was coming from Anapa), he felt a sinking in his heart, a mix of awe and bliss.

"Let's get off," he muttered.

"Where?" she asked, surprised.

"At this landing."

"What for?"

He didn't answer. Once again she put the back of her hand against her burning cheek.

"It's like going crazy."

"Let's go, let's get off," he repeated obtusely. "Please."

"Oh, whatever you like," she said, turning away.

As if at full tilt the cruise ship struck the dimly illumined landing with a soft clunking sound, and they nearly fell over each other. The end of the mooring cable flew past above their heads, then the boat rushed backward, the water was churning noisily, and the gangplank clattered into place. The lieutenant dashed off to get their bags.

A moment later they walked through a drowsy waiting room, emerged where the sand was hub-deep on the carriages, and silently got into a light cab covered in dust. The gradual ascent, up the hill, along a road that was soft with dust, passing an occasional crooked lamppost, seemed endless. But then they were finally on top, they came out onto a cobblestone byway and went crepitating along it. There was a kind of town square, administrative buildings, a fire tower, the warmth and smells of a district capital city, summertime, late at night. The cabman stopped by an illumined entryway, and beyond its wide-open gates an old wooden staircase made a steep ascent upward. An unshaven old porter in rose-colored peasant shirt and frock coat took their things peevishly and ambled off on his dilapidated legs, leading the way. They entered a large but sweltering room, searing with the heat built up by the sun all day; it had white curtains lowered over the windows and two unlit candles on the vanity table. As soon as the porter closed the door behind them the lieutenant made a headlong rush to embrace her, and they kissed with such a frenzied breathlessness that for years afterward they would recall that moment; never had he or she, throughout the whole of their lives, experienced anything like this.

At ten in the morning, a hot and sunny, happy morning with church bells pealing, with a bazaar on the square out front of the hotel, with the redolence of hay, tar, and once again all those complex and aromatic smells that a Russian provincial city wafts, she left, that small nameless woman, she who never had revealed her name, jokingly calling herself the beautiful stranger. They had not slept much, but after she came out from behind the folding screen beside the bed, having washed and dressed in five minutes, she looked so fresh that she might have been seventeen. Was she embarrassed? No, hardly at all. Just as before she was straightforward and merry—but back in a rational frame of mind.

"No, dear, no," she said when he asked her to travel on with him. "No, you must stay here and wait for the next boat. If we travel on together, everything will be spoiled. That would be very unpleasant for me. I give you my word of honor that I'm not at all what you may take me to be. Never has anything even faintly like this happened to me, and it won't happen again. With me it was like an eclipse. Or rather, we both had something like sunstroke."

For some reason the lieutenant readily agreed with her. In a light and buoyant mood he drove with her back to the landing—just in time for the departure of the rose-colored *Aeroplane.* On the deck, in front of everyone, he kissed her and then had to jump to make it back onto the gangplank, which they were pulling away.

In the same light spirit, carefree, he returned to the hotel. But now something had changed. Without her the room seemed utterly different than it was while she was there. It was still full of her—and empty. That was strange! The scent of her fine English eau de cologne was still in the air, the cup she had left, with a bit of coffee, was on the tray, but she was not in the room. Suddenly the lieutenant's heart was squeezed with such tenderness that he quickly lit a cigarette and paced several times, back and forth, across the room.

"A strange adventure!" he said aloud, laughing and feeling the tears welling up in his eyes. "I give you my word of honor that I'm not at all what you may take me for." And now she's gone.

The folding screen was pushed back, the bed still not made. He felt as if he simply could not bear to look at that bed. He put the screen in front of it, shut the windows to block out the din of the bazaar and the squealing of wheels, lowered the white curtains puffing out in the breeze, and sat down on the sofa. So that's the end of this "one-night stand"! She's gone, and now she's already far away from here, sitting, probably, in a glassed-in white salon, or she's out on deck looking at that enormous river as it sparkles in the sun, at the barges they meet, at yellow spits of sand, at the distant gleam of water and sky, at all that boundless amplitude of the Volga. So farewell, and now forever, for all time. Because where would they ever meet again?

"I just can't," he thought. "I can't just suddenly show up in that city out of the blue, where her husband lives, her three-year-old daughter, her whole family, and all of her everyday life!" Now that city seemed to him somehow special, inviolable, and the thought that she would go on living her solitary life there, often, perhaps, recalling him, recalling their casual, so transient encounter, that never again would he see her, this thought astonished and appalled him. No, that can't be! That would be just too wild, unnatural, unbelievable! Then he felt such pain, imagined the uselessness of the whole rest of his life without her, and he was seized with horror and despair.

"What the hell!" he thought, standing up, pacing around the room again, and trying not to look at the bed behind the screen. "What is going on with me? What's so special about her anyway, and what, in fact, happened? It really is like some kind of sunstroke! But now the main thing is how do I kill a whole day in this backwoods town without her?"

He still remembered everything, every special little feature; he remembered the smell of her suntan and linen dress, her firm body, the vivacious, simple and merry sound of her voice. Especially vivid in his mind were all the pleasures of her feminine charms, which he had just enjoyed, but now the main thing, nonetheless, was something completely new: a strange, puzzling sensation that was not at all there when they were together. Could he have imagined he would feel this way when yesterday he initiated what he thought of as simply a pleasant diversion? And now it was impossible to tell her that! "There's the main thing," he thought, "that I'll never be able to tell her! And what's to be done, how can I live through this endless day, with these recollections and this incessant torment, in this godforsaken hole of a town, built up here above the glistening Volga, the same river she and that rose-colored boat just sailed off on!"

He had to save himself, somehow occupy or distract his thoughts, go somewhere. With an air of determination he put on his visored cap, picked up his swagger stick, walked briskly, spurs jingling, along the empty corridor, and skipped down the steep staircase to the entryway. Yes, but go where? A cabman was parked by the entry, young, in a stylish long-skirted coat, calmly smoking a cigarillo. The lieutenant looked at him bewildered and amazed: how could somebody sit there calmly on a coach box, smoking and acting so thoroughly ordinary, carefree and indifferent? "I must be the only one in all of this city who is so miserably unhappy," he thought, setting off for the bazaar.

The marketplace bazaar was already breaking up. For some reason he started wandering around it, stepping on the fresh dung, walking past wagons, carts with cucumbers, new washbasins, and chamber pots, and the peasant women who squatted there on the ground vied with one another in calling out to him. They picked up the chamber pots and drummed their fingers against them, making them sing to show their durability, while the men deafened him with shouts: "Right over here, Your Honor, we got first-class cukes!" This was all so stupid, absurd, that he fled the bazaar. He went into the cathedral, where they were singing in loud, happy, and resolute voices, with a sense of duty fulfilled. Then he shambled about for a long time, circling a small, hot and overgrown garden on the precipice of the cliff, above the boundless, steely bright expanse of the river. The shoulder straps and buttons of his tunic were so hot that he could not touch them. The headband on the inside of his cap was damp with sweat, his face flaming.

Returning to the hotel, he felt relieved when he entered the cool, large and empty dining room on the lower floor; it was a relief as well to take off his cap and sit down at a table beside an open window, through which hot air wafted, but all the same it was air. He ordered iced fish and vegetable soup. All was well, in everything there was immeasurable happiness and great joy; even in the torrid heat and the myriad smells of the bazaar, in all of that unfamiliar backwoods city and that old provincial hotel, joy prevailed, and in the midst of the joy his heart was simply ripped to pieces. He drank several glasses of vodka, taking bites of lightly salted cucumbers covered in dill, feeling that without a second thought he would gladly die tomorrow if only by some miracle he could bring her back, could spend one more day with her, today—and for one solitary reason: to tell her and somehow prove to her, convince her, how tormented he was and how ecstatically he loved her. Why prove it? Why convince her? He did not know why, but it was something he needed more than life.

"My nerves have gone totally haywire!" he said, pouring out a fifth glass of vodka.

He pushed away the soup, asked for black coffee, started smoking, concentrating all his thoughts. What was he to do now, how could he rid himself of this sudden, unexpected love? But getting rid of it—and he sensed this with utter clarity—was impossible. He suddenly jumped to his feet again, picked up his cap and swagger stick; asking directions to the post office, he rushed off with the phrasing of the telegram already formulated in his head: "From this day on all my life forever, to the grave, is yours, in your power." But when he arrived at the old building with its thick walls, containing the post office and telegraph service, he stopped in his tracks, horrified. He knew what city she lived in, he knew she had a husband and a three-year-old daughter, but he did not know either her surname or her given name! He had asked her several times yesterday at dinner and in the hotel, but she had always laughed and said, "But why do you need to know what my name is?"

On the corner next to the post office there was a display of photographs in a showcase window. He stood looking for a long time at an oversized portrait of some military man in thick epaulettes, with bugged-out eyes and a low forehead, strikingly magnificent sideburns, and the broadest of chests adorned with medals. How bizarre, how hideous are all these everyday, mundane things when your heart has been smitten—yes, that was the word, now he understood—by this horrible "sunstroke," by too large a love, too large a happiness! He glanced at the picture of a newlywed couple—a young man in long frock coat and white tie with his hair in a crew cut, standing stiffly at attention, arm in arm with a girl in nuptial gossamer. Then he turned to a portrait of a pert, comely young lady wearing a university cap cocked sideways on her head. After that, tormented with envy toward all these people he did not know, people who were not suffering, he began looking intently up and down the street.

"Where should I go? What should I do?"

The street was deserted. The buildings were identical, white, two-storied, merchant-class buildings with expansive gardens, and it seemed to him there was not a soul inside them; a thick white dust had settled atop the cobblestone. All of this dazzled him, all of it was infused with sunlight, hot, flaming, and joyous, but the sun appeared to have no reason for being here. In the distance the street ascended, humped over, and leant up against a cloudless, grayish sheen of horizon. There was something southern in that, recalling the cities of Sevastopol, Kerch . . . Anapa. This, in particular, was unbearable. Head down, squinting against the light, concentrating his gaze on the ground in front of his feet, staggering, stumbling along and entangling his spurs, he shambled back to the hotel.

He arrived in such a state of enervation that he might have been returning from a lengthy campaign somewhere in Turkestan or the Sahara Desert. Summoning up what strength he had left, he walked into his large and empty room. It was made up now, deprived of the last traces of her—but a single hairpin she had forgotten lay on the night table! He took off his tunic and looked at himself in the mirror. His face—an ordinary officer's face tanned a gray color, with an off-white mustache that was hot from the sun and a light blue whiteness to his eyes, which seemed even whiter in contrast to the tan—that face had an agitated, insane expression on it now, and there was something youthful and profoundly unhappy about the lightweight shirt with its standing starched collar. He lay down on his back in the bed, put his dusty boots up on the frame. The windows were open, the curtains lowered, and from time to time a light breeze puffed them out, blowing in the torrid heat from the searing iron roofs, redolent of all that luminous and now desolate, mute Volga world. He lay with his hands behind his head and gazed intently straight in front of him. Then he clenched his teeth, closed his eyes, and felt the tears running out from beneath his eyelids onto his cheeks; finally he went to sleep. When he opened his eyes again the evening sun was already gleaming a reddish yellow beyond the curtains. The wind had died down, the room was stuffy and dry, like the air in a cooking stove. And he recalled all of yesterday and this morning as if it were ten years ago.

In no hurry he got up, slowly washed his hands and face, raised the curtains, rang and requested a samovar and the bill, spent a long time drinking tea with lemon. Then he sent for a cab, had his bags taken out, and settling himself in the light carriage, on its rust red, burning hot seat, he gave the porter a large tip of five rubles.

"You know, Your Honor, it seems like I was the one brought you up here last night!" said the cabman gaily, seizing the reins.

By the time they descended to the landing a blue summer night was hanging out its cerulean glow over the Volga, a multitude of varicolored lights lay spread upon the river, and still more lights were hanging in the masts of the cruise ship as it made its rapid approach to the shore.

"Got you here just in time!" said the cabman fawningly.

The lieutenant gave him five rubles too, bought his ticket, and went out to the landing. Just as yesterday there was a soft knocking sound as the ship was moored and a slight dizziness from the vibrations underfoot; then came the flying end of the moorage cable and the noise of the water, which was roiling up and running forward beneath the wheels of the slightly backward-moving ship. That ship seemed particularly fine and hospitable, with the throngs of people aboard and the kitchen, already brightly illumined all over and smelling so good.

A moment later they rushed away upriver, in the same direction that she had been borne so recently, that morning.

A dark summer sunset was dying out far up ahead, duskily, sleepily, in a variety of colors reflected in the river, which far beneath it, beneath that sunset, was glittering in shudders of ripples, and the lights were floating and floating ever backward, dissipating in the darkness all around.

The lieutenant sat beneath an awning on the deck, feeling as if he had aged ten years.

Maritime Alps, 1925

»»» «««

Shere Monday

Dark was descending upon Moscow that gray winter day, the streetlight flares of cold gas pierced the gloaming, while warmly illumined were the showcase windows of the stores—and the Moscow life of eventide, freeing itself from diurnal routine, burst into flame. Taxi sleighs raced along in thicker, brisker clusters now, trams packed full of passengers emitted a more ponderous clatter as they dove into the murk, where hissing green stars burst sparking from the trolley wires and turbid shadows of bedimmed passersby hustled along in a livelier, a vespertine way. Every evening at that hour my coachman drove me, behind a brisk trotter straining his traces, from Krasnye Vorota to the Cathedral of Christ the Saviour—she lived opposite it—and every evening I took her to dine at the Prague Restaurant, the Hermitage, or the Metropole, then, after dinner, to various theaters, concerts, and later to the Yara or the Strelna.

How all this was to end I had no idea and I did my best to keep my mind off that, tried not to think it all the way through. It was useless, equally as useless as bringing it up with her; from the very beginning she had refused to discuss our future. She was such a puzzle to me, so enigmatic, and our relations were strange. We were not yet sexually intimate, and that kept me in a state of perpetual unresolved tension, agonizing anticipation. Notwithstanding this, every hour I spent beside her made me unspeakably happy.

For some reason she was taking courses, attending her lectures infrequently, but attending them nonetheless. Once I asked her why. She shrugged. "Why is anything done on earth? Do we really understand why we act the way we do? I'm just interested in history." She lived alone. Her widowed father, an enlightened man from a distinguished merchant family, was retired, living in Tver, and like all such merchants he busied himself with collecting something or other. In the building opposite the Cathedral of the Saviour she was renting, for its view of Moscow, a corner apartment on the fifth floor; it had only two rooms, but they were spacious and well furnished. In the front room a wide Turkish ottoman took up a lot of space, and there was an expensive piano on which she was constantly practicing the slow, somnambulic, and lovely first movement of the *Moonlight* Sonata (she never got past that beginning part). On the piano and on her vanity table there were always elegant arrangements of flowers in faceted vases—I ordered fresh ones delivered to her every Saturday. When I arrived on Saturday evenings she would be lying on the ottoman, above which, for some reason, a painting of the barefoot Tolstoy was hung, and she would slowly extend her hand for me to kiss and say with an air of detachment, "Thanks for the flowers."

When I brought her boxes of chocolates or new books—Hofmannsthal, Schnitzler, Tetmajer, Przybyszewski—I would get that same "Thanks" with the warm hand extended, and sometimes she would tell me to sit beside the ottoman, still wearing my coat. "I don't know why," she said, lost in thought and stroking my beaver collar, "but that smell of winter air you bring into the room with you from the courtyard, somehow that's the loveliest thing imaginable." It appeared as if she needed nothing: not the flowers, the books, not the dining out, the theater, the suppers at suburban restaurants, although she did, nonetheless, have certain flowers that she liked and others that she didn't. She always read all the books I brought her, and she finished off a whole box of chocolates in one day. When dining out afternoons or late evenings she ate no less than I, and she loved open-topped pastries with fish soup of eelpout, pink hazel grouse well roasted in strong sour cream. Sometimes she said, "I can't understand why people don't get sick of the tedium of their lives: every day having dinner, then supper." She herself, for all that, would eat dinner and supper with the savoir faire of a Moscow gourmand. Other than that her only obvious weakness was for fine clothing: velvets, silks, and expensive furs.

We both were well to do, healthy, young, and so good-looking that in restaurants or at concerts people's eyes were always drawn to us. Having grown up in the Penza area, I was handsome back then in a sort of ardent southern way, even "indecently handsome" as a certain renowned actor once told me, a monstrously stout man who was a tremendous glutton and sage. "The devil only knows what you are, some kind of Sicilian or something," he said in his drowsy voice. My personality was southern as well, lively, ever ready to smile cordially or make a kind joke. Her beauty, on the other hand, had overtones of the Hindu or Persian: an amberlike duskiness about her face, something a bit ominous in the thickness of her marvelous black hair, brows that gleamed softly, like black sable fur, black eyes like velvet coals. She had a dark downy fluff above velvetish crimson lips and that lent a special touch to her captivating mouth. Most of the time when she went out she would wear a velvet garnet red dress and shoes of the same color with golden buckles. But she attended her lectures dressed like a lowly student and bought meals for thirty kopecks at a vegetarian place on the Arbat. Just as I was prone to loquacity, to a simple-hearted gaiety, so she was equally prone to keep her silence. She was always pondering over something, always delving deeply into thought. Lying on the ottoman with a book in her hands, she would often lower the book and gaze into the distance with a quizzical look. I would see this when I dropped in sometimes in the afternoon, on the three or four days each month when she did not go out at all, refused to leave the house. She would just lie and read, forcing me as well to sit in an armchair beside the ottoman and read in silence.

"You're so awfully talkative and restless," she would say. "Let me finish this chapter."

"If I weren't so talkative and restless I might never have met you," I answered, reminding her of how we first got acquainted. Once in December I happened to be at the Art Club attending a lecture by Andrej Bely. He was singing his lecture, prancing and cavorting onstage, and I was fidgeting about and laughing so much that she, who by chance had the seat next to mine and who at first looked at me somewhat bewildered, finally laughed out loud, and then I turned to her and said something funny.

"That's how it was," she said. "But all the same, keep quiet for a little while, read something or have a smoke."

"How can I be quiet! You can't imagine how much I love you! But you don't love me!"

"Yes, I can imagine. As for my love, you know full well that besides Father and you I have no one on earth. In any case, you are my first and my last. Isn't that enough for you? But let's not talk any more about that. When you're around it's impossible to read; let's have some tea."

So I would get up, boil water in an electric teakettle on the table behind the ottoman, take out cups and saucers from a walnut cabinet in the corner behind the table, saying whatever came into my head.

"Did you finish reading *The Flaming Angel*?"

"I finished looking through it. It's so puffed up I feel embarrassed to read it."

"And why did you suddenly walk out of Chaliapin's concert yesterday?"

"He was just too reeking in panache. And then again, I don't like that spirit of 'golden-haired Russianness' in the first place."

"You don't like much of anything!"

"That's true, not much."

"What a strange love!" I thought as the water boiled and I stood looking out the window. The room smelled of flowers and my love was blended in my mind with their aroma. Out one window I could see, like a low-hung, huge and far-distant painting, the opposite side of the river, Zamoskvoreche: snowy, dove blue Moscow. Out the other one, to the left, part of the Kremlin was visible, and opposite it, somehow excessively close to me, was the whiteness of the massive, too new Christ the Saviour, with one golden cupola reflecting bluish splotches of the jackdaws that hovered perpetually around it. "A strange city!" I said to myself, thinking of Okhotny Ryad, of the Iverskaia icon of the Mother of God, of Saint Basil's—Basil the Blessed, Holy Fool—of the Church of the Saviour in the Pinewood, the Italian cathedrals, of something Kirghizian about the spires on the towers of the Kremlin walls.

Arriving at twilight I sometimes found her lying on the ottoman, wearing only a silk quilted robe edged in sable—"Inherited from my grandmother in Astrakhan," she had said. I sat beside her in the semidarkness, not putting on the lights, and I kissed her hands, legs, her so incredibly soft body. She made no move to resist but kept silent all the time. I was seeking her hot lips, and she gave them to me, breathing hard now, but still silent. When she felt I no longer had the strength to control myself she pushed me away, sat up, and in a low voice asked me to turn on a lamp; then she went off to her bedroom. I put the light on, sat down on the revolving stool beside the piano, and gradually recovered, coming out of that fervid stupor. A quarter hour later she emerged from her bedroom dressed and ready to go out, calm and down to earth, as if nothing had happened.

"Where should we go tonight? To the Metropole, maybe?"

Then once again, all evening, we would speak of other things. Soon after we had become close I mentioned marriage to her, and she said to me, "No, I'm not the kind to be a wife. Not suited for it, no."

That answer did not discourage me. "We'll see about that!" I said to myself, hoping to change her mind with time, and I didn't bring up the subject of marriage again. Our unconsummated intimacy sometimes seemed unbearable, but with this, too, what did I have except hope for the future? One day, sitting beside her in that evening darkness and silence, I took my head in my hands and cried out, "No, I can't stand this anymore! And what's the idea, why do you have to torment me and yourself so cruelly?"

She said nothing.

"Well, whatever this is, it's not love, not love."

Out of the darkness came her steady voice in response: "Maybe not. Yet who knows what love is?"

"I do, I know!" I exclaimed. "And I'll keep waiting until you figure out what love is too, what happiness is!"

"Happiness . . . 'Our happiness, my friend, is like water in a seine: you pull and it swells out, but you drag it in and there's nothing there.'"

"What's that?"

"That's what Platon Karataev said to Pierre."

I waved my hand in a gesture of dismissal.

"Ah, forget it, all this wisdom of the Orient!"

Then once more, for the whole evening, we spoke only of incidental things—the new play at the Moscow Art Theater, the new story by Andreev. Once again it was enough for me, first of all, that I could sit close to her in a sleigh that went dashing along pell-mell, holding her through the smooth fur of her winter coat, that, second, we could walk together into a restaurant full of people, to the march from *Aida*, that I could eat and drink beside her, listen to her languid voice, look at the lips I had been kissing an hour ago. "Yes, I kissed them," I said to myself, gazing at those lips in enraptured gratitude, at the dark fluff above them, at the garnet red velvet of her dress, her sloping shoulders, and the oval of her breasts, breathing in the somehow spicy smell of her hair, thinking, "Moscow, Astrakhan, Persia, India!" In the suburban restaurants, toward the end of the evening meals, when everything was swathed in tobacco smoke and growing ever more boisterous, when she was smoking, getting tipsy, she would sometimes lead me off to a private room and ask me to call in the gypsies. They would enter with that deliberate show of clamor and unbridled dash. At the head of the choir, a guitar on a light blue strap over his shoulder, strode an old gypsy man in a knee-length, side-pleated coat with galloons; he had the dove blue mug of a drowning victim, a bare head like a cast-iron sphere. Following behind him came the lead singer, with a low forehead beneath her fringe of hair the color of tar.

She listened to the songs with a strange languid smile. At three or four in the morning, I would take her home. By the entryway, eyes closed tight with happiness, I would kiss the wet fur of her collar, and in a state of enraptured despair I would dash back to Krasnye Vorota. "Tomorrow and the day after will be exactly the same," I thought, "that very same torment and that same happiness. But so what? It's happiness all the same—enormous happiness!"

So January passed, February; Maslenitsa came and went. On Forgiveness Sunday she told me to come to her place between four and five in the evening. When I arrived she met me already dressed, in a short astrakhan fur coat and an astrakhan hat, in black felt overshoes.

"All in black!" I said, entering as usual in a joyful mood.

Her eyes were tender and still.

"Tomorrow, after all, is Shere Monday," she answered, taking her hand, in its black kid glove, out of an astrakhan muff and holding it out to me. "'Lord, Sovereign of all my life . . .' Would you like to go to Novodevichy Convent?"

I was amazed, but without hesitation I answered, "Let's go!"

"What do we need with one tavern after another?" she added. "Yesterday morning I was at the Rogozhskoe Cemetery."

I was even more amazed.

"Cemetery? Why? Is that the famous Old Believer cemetery?"

"Yes, the sectarian one. Pre-Petrine Rus! They were having a funeral for their archbishop. And just imagine, there was a coffin made from an oak log, like in ancient times, the golden brocade looked like forged iron, the face of the dead man was covered by a white Eucharist cerecloth with a large ornamental pattern sewn on it in black—the beauty of it and the horror. And deacons were standing by the coffin, holding rhipidions and trikeria."

"How do you know all that? Rhipidions, trikeria!"

"It's you who don't know me."

"Well, I didn't know you were so religious."

"It's not a matter of religion. I don't know what it is . . . But, for example, I often go to the Kremlin cathedrals in the mornings, or on evenings when you don't drag me off to restaurants, and you had no inkling of that. Well, so that's how it was: deacons, and what deacons they were! Peresvet and Osliablia! They had two choirs up in the stalls for the singers, and they were all Peresvet types too: tall, powerfully built, in long black caftans, singing and playing off one another—first one choir sang, then the other—and all in harmony, using the old church musical notes instead of a modern score. They had sparkling evergreen branches laid out in the burial crypt, and out in the courtyard there was frost, sunshine, a dazzling sun . . . But no, you don't understand that! Let's go."

The evening was placid, sunlit, with rime frost on the trees. Perched in silence on the brick red blood of the monastery walls there were jackdaws that looked like nuns; now and again the clock chimes on the bell tower would toll out in delicate, mournful tones. We walked, squeaking our way through the snow in silence, entered the gates, then set off along the snowy paths of the cemetery. The sun had just set now, it was still quite light, the gray coralline of branches in rime frost struck a marvelous pose against the golden enamel of sunset, and all around us, glimmering mysteriously in flames both serene and mournful were the lamps that burned perpetually over graves. I walked behind her, gazed tenderly at the tiny footprints, at the little stars her new black overshoes left in the snow; sensing my gaze, she suddenly turned around.

"It's true, you really do love me!" she said in quiet bewilderment, shaking her head.

We stopped beside the graves of Ertel and Chekhov. Hands folded inside the muff, she gazed for a long time at Chekhov's gravestone monument, then shrugged. "What a disgusting blend of the saccharine Russian style and the Moscow Art Theater!"

It started getting dark, frosty; we slowly made our way back out the gates, beside which my Fyodor sat forbearing on his coach box.

"Let's drive around awhile longer," she said, "and then we'll go to Egorov's place and eat up the last of the Shrovetide pancakes before Lent. Only not too fast, Fyodor—all right?"

"Yes, ma'am."

"Somewhere in Ordynka there's the building where Griboedov lived. Let's go find it."

So for some reason we went to Ordynka, meandered for a long time around back alleyways with their gardens, found the Griboedov byway. But who was there to tell us what building he had lived in? Not a soul was out on the streets, and who among them would have needed Griboedov anyway? Now it had long grown dark, and beyond the rime-frosted trees bright windows were casting a rosy glow.

"The Marfo-Mariinsky Cloister is around this area too," she said.

I laughed. "Are we off to another nunnery?"

"No, I just happened to mention it."

The bottom floor of Egorov's tavern in Okhotny Ryad, steamy like a bathhouse, was full of shaggy cabmen in thick layers of clothing, cutting up heaps of pancakes slathered in a plethora of butter and sour cream. In the rooms upstairs with their low ceilings, also very warm, merchants of the old style were using icy champagne to wash down flaming-hot pancakes and granular caviar. Passing through to the second room, where an icon lamp was burning in the corner, in front of the Three-Handed Mother of God painted on a black slab of wood, we sat down on a black leather ottoman at a long table. The fluff on her upper lip was rime-frosted, the amber of her cheeks had a slightly rosy sheen, the blackness of her irises was blended right into the pupils of her eyes—I gazed at her face enraptured. Pulling a handkerchief out of the fragrant muff, she said, "This is wonderful! Downstairs we've got savage muzhiks, and here we have blini with champagne and the Three-Handed Mother of God. Three hands! That's like India, you know! You're gentry class, you can't understand Moscow the way I do, in all its variety."

"Oh yes, I can! And let's order a dinner today stalwartlike!"

"How do you mean, 'stalwart'?"

"It means 'sumptuous.' Haven't you heard that? 'Thus spake Giurgy.'"

"That's wonderful! Giurgy!"

"Yes, Yury Dolgoruky, Prince George the Long-Armed. 'Thus spake Giurgy unto Sviatoslav, prince of the North: "Come hither, to me, my brother, into Muscovy," and he made ready, for to hail and wassail him, a stalwartlike feast.' "

"How lovely. And now all we have left are vestiges of that old Rus, in a few northern monasteries. And in the songs they sing in church. Recently I was at the Zachatev Monastery—you can't imagine how marvelously they perform the ancient lauds there! It's even better at the Chudov Monastery. Last year I kept going there during Holy Week. Oh, how fine it was! Puddles all around, the air already soft, a kind of tenderness, a sadness in your soul, and that perpetual feeling of the homeland, its ancient days . . . All the doors of the cathedral were wide open, all day long the common people were going in and coming out, services went on continuously . . . Ah, I think I'll just go off and join a convent somewhere, in one of the most backwoods places, Vologda, Viatka!"

I started to say that if she ever did that then I would go away too, or I'd kill someone, so they'd send me off to hard labor on Sakhalin Island. My emotions got away from me and I lit up a cigarette, but a waiter came up, wearing a white shirt and white trousers with a raspberry-colored fascicled belt, and reminded me deferentially, "Excuse me, sir, but smoking is not allowed."

And without pausing, in a special fawning tone, he went into his rapid spiel.

"What will you take with your pancakes? The house herbal tea? Caviar, bit of salmon? Today we have a sherry of quite rare quality to go with the fine fish soup, and, complementary to the *navaga* dish, we have . . ."

"And with the *navaga* you've got a rare sherry too," she added, lifting my spirits with that gentle air of loquacity, the mood she had been in all evening. I felt so invigorated that I listened with only half an ear to what she said next. She said it with a soft gleam in her eyes.

"I love the Russian chronicles and the age-old legends so much that I keep on rereading my special favorites until I have them down by heart. 'There was once in the Russian Realm a city called Murom, and reigning over it was a true-believer Orthodox prince who went by the name of Pavel. And it so came to be that into the quarters of his wife the Evil One insinuated a flying serpent, that he might engage her in lechery. That serpent manifested itself unto her in the guise of a human being, a man of exquisite beauty . . .' "

Jokingly I opened my eyes wide in fright.

"Ugh, how terrible!"

Ignoring me, she went on. "That was how God tempted her. 'When the time came for her hallowed demise, they made their plea unto the Lord, this prince and his consort, that they in one day together might part this earth. And they arranged to be interred in a single coffin, and they mandated a proviso that two sepulchres be squared off from one piece of granite. And they arrayed themselves, likewise, at one and the same time, in monastic vestments.' "

Once more my air of detachment gave way to amazement, even alarm: what was going on with her today?

Then later that evening, when I took her home much earlier than usual, before eleven, she suddenly stopped me at the entryway when I was already back in my sleigh.

"Wait. Drop by tomorrow night, but not before ten o'clock. They're giving one of those actors' 'charivaris' at the Moscow Art Theater."

"Come again?" I said. "You mean you want to go to this charivari?"

"Yes."

"But you once said you couldn't imagine anything more vulgar than that stuff!"

"I still can't. But I want to go anyway."

In my thoughts I was shaking my head—all these whims, these Moscow caprices! But I responded cheerfully, in English, "All right!"

The next day at ten in the evening I rode the elevator up to her floor, opened the door with my key, and paused for a moment in the dark anteroom. It was unusually bright inside, all the lights were lit: chandeliers, candelabra on both sides of the mirror, and a floor lamp with a delicate shade at one end of the ottoman. The piano was playing the beginning of the *Moonlight* Sonata. The sounds were intensifying, ever more languorous as they proceeded, ever more invocatory, with that blissfully somnambulistic sadness. I slammed the door of the anteroom and the music broke off; I heard the rustle of a dress. When I went in she was standing up straight beside the piano in a somewhat theatrical pose, wearing a black velvet evening dress that made her look thinner, basking in its elegance, in the festive coiffure of her tar black hair, the dusky amber of her bare arms and shoulders, the delicate ample cleft of her breasts, the glitter of diamond earrings that hung by her lightly powdered cheeks, the coal black, velvet eyes and velvety purple of her lips. Black glossy locks of hair, in semicircles of ringlets, were folded in toward her eyes, giving her the look of an Oriental beauty on a primitive folk painting.

"Now if I were a singer and were singing onstage," she said, looking at the bewilderment on my face, "I would respond to applause with an affable smile and the slightest of bows, to the right and left, then toward the upper tiers and the parterre, all the time imperceptibly but carefully pushing aside the train of my dress with one foot, so as not to step on it."

At the charivari she smoked a lot and kept sipping champagne, intently watching the actors, who, with boisterous shouts and refrains, were depicting something supposed to be Parisian: thick-set Stanislavsky with his white hair and black eyebrows and stout Moskvin, a pince-nez perched upon his oblong washtub of a face. With a studied earnestness and assiduity the two of them were falling backward, improvising, to the horselaughs of the crowd, a desperate cancan dance. Kachalov walked up to us with a wineglass in his hand, pale with tipsiness, large drops of sweat on his forehead, a tuft of blond Belorussian hair hanging down; he raised the glass, and gazing at her with a mannered somber avidity, he intoned in his low actor's voice, "Maiden queen, mistress of all Shamakha, to your health!"

She gave him a slow smile and clinked glasses with him. He took her hand, tottered in her direction, and almost lost his footing. Regaining his balance, he glared at me with clenched teeth.

"And who might be this handsome cavalier? I hate him."

Next came the wheeze, whistle, and rumble of a barrel organ, and then it went stomping into the gamboling strains of a polka. At this point, with his ever-present snigger and his air of scampering haste, little Sulerzhitsky came dashing, slithering up to us; he bent down, portraying the gallantry of old merchant-class Rus, and hastily muttered, "May I have the pleasure of this Tranblan polka?"

Smiling, she arose, and with agile, short tapping steps, all agleam in her earrings, her dark complexion, her bare shoulders and arms, she walked off with him between the tables, accompanied by glances of delight and hand clapping, while he, throwing back his head, bleated out like a goat: "Look alive, let us go, hurry up, / I must dance this polka with you!"

It was after two in the morning when she stood up, shielding her eyes. As we were getting our coats, she looked at my beaver hat, ran her hand across the beaver collar, and set off for the exit, saying in a half-joking, half-serious tone, "It's true, you are handsome. Kachalov was right . . . 'A serpent in the guise of a human, a man of exquisite beauty.'"

On the way home she kept silent, inclining her head away from the bright moonlit blizzard that was blowing in our direction. A full moon dove about in the clouds above the Kremlin. "Like a shining skull," she said. The clock on the Tower of the Saviour chimed three times. Then she added, "What an ancient sound, somehow tinny and cast-iron. It was just the same, the hour of three chimed out just like that back in the fifteenth century. And in Florence the bells ring that way too; it reminded me of Moscow."

When Fyodor reined in the horse by the entryway, she issued, in a lifeless voice, one brief command: "Let him go."

Astounded—never before had she allowed me up to her apartment at night—I said to him in bewilderment, "Fyodor, I'll come home later on foot."

We were silently drawn upward in the elevator, entered the night warmth and quiet of the apartment with its hammers knocking in the radiators. I helped her out of her coat, which was slippery with snow; she removed the wet, downy shawl from her hair and tossed it into my hands, then quickly went into the bedroom, her silk underskirt rustling. I took off my coat, entered the front room, and with sinking heart, as if on the brink of a precipice, I sat down on the Turkish ottoman. Her steps resounded beyond the open doors of the illumined bedroom, I could hear her catch her dress in the hairpins as she pulled it off over her head . . . I arose and walked up to the doors. Wearing only a pair of swan's down slippers, she was standing, her back to me, in front of the vanity mirror, combing out with a tortoiseshell comb the black strands of long hair that were hanging down beside her face.

"Well, you always claimed I didn't give much thought to that business," she said, tossing the comb on the vanity. Throwing her hair back over her shoulders, she turned to me. "But no, I did think about it."

At dawn I felt her moving around. I opened my eyes—she was staring point-blank at me. I raised up a bit, out of the warmth of the bed and of her body; she bent toward me and said in a quiet, steady voice, "Tonight I'm leaving for Tver. Only God knows for how long . . ."

She pressed her cheek against mine—I felt the blink of a wet eyelash.

"I'll write and tell you everything as soon as I get there. Everything about the future. Forgive me, can you leave now? I'm very tired."

And she lay back down on the pillow.

Gingerly I dressed, timidly kissed her hair, and on tiptoe I went out onto the stairwell, which was already brightening with a pale light. I set off on foot through the wet, sticky snow. The blizzard was done, all was calm; you could see far distant things down the street, it smelled of snow and of bakeries. I reached the Iverskaia Chapel, which was burning and glittering inside with bonfires of candles; amidst the mob of old crones and beggars I got down on my knees in the tramped-solid snow, took off my hat. Someone touched my shoulder. I glanced up and saw a most pitiable old woman looking at me, her face twisted into a grimace of compassionate tears.

"No, don't do it, don't go killing yourself that way! It's a sin, a sin!"

The letter, which I received some two weeks later, was short—an affectionate but firm request not to expect her back, not to try to find her. "I won't be returning to Moscow. I'll start by doing penance; then, perhaps, I'll take vows as a nun . . . May God give you the strength not to answer me—it's useless to drag out and exacerbate our sufferings."

I fulfilled her request. For a long time I lost myself in the most filthy of taverns, drinking heavily, sinking lower and lower in every possible way. Then, little by little, I began recovering—indifferently, hopelessly. Almost two years had passed since that Shere Monday.

New Year's Eve of 1914 was the same quiet, sunlit evening as that one, the unforgettable one. I left my home, caught a cab, and drove to the Kremlin. Once there, I went inside the empty Archangel Cathedral, stood for a long time without praying in the half-light, gazing at the faint glimmer of the old golden iconostasis and the plaques on the sepulchres of the Moscow tsars. I stood as if in expectation of something, in that peculiar silence of an empty church, when you dare not even draw breath. When I came out of the cathedral I told the cabman to take me to Ordynka. We drove at a slow pace, as we had then, through the dark back alleyways with their gardens and bright windows, passed through the Griboedov byway—and all the while I was crying, crying.

In Ordynka I told the cabman to stop by the gates of the Marfo-Mariinsky Cloister. Inside the courtyard I could see the dark silhouettes of carriages and the wide-open doors of a small, illumined church, from which the mournful and tender strains of a girls' choir poured out. For some reason I felt I must, without fail, go in there. The yard porter by the gates blocked my path, saying gently, in entreating tones, "No sir, no, it's not allowed!"

"Not allowed? You mean I can't go into a church?"

"Wellsir, yes, of course you can, but I'm only asking you, for Lord's sake, don't go in now; the Grand Duchess Elizaveta Fyodorovna is in there, and the Grand Duke Dmitry Pavlovich."

When I slipped him a ruble he heaved a sigh of distress but let me pass. No sooner had I entered the courtyard when icons appeared, gonfalons were borne out of the church, and behind them, dressed all in white, long-limbed and delicate of visage, in a white ceremonial kerchief with a golden cross embroidered on the forehead, tall, stepping devoutly along with eyes lowered and a large candle in her hand, came the Grand Duchess. Behind her stretched a lengthy chain of that same whiteness, singers with flamelets of candles in their hands, nuns or lay sisters—I'm not sure who they were or where they were bound. For some reason I looked very intently at them. And one of those walking in the middle of the group suddenly raised her head, covered by a white kerchief; a candle was cupped in her hand, and her dark eyes threw a sharp glance out into the darkness, apparently right at me . . . What could she have seen in the dark, how could she have sensed my presence? I turned and quietly walked back out the gateway.

May 12, 1944

»»» «««

The Cold Fall

In June of that year he was a guest at our estate. He always had been like one of the family; his late father was a friend and neighbor of my father. On June 15 Francis Ferdinand was killed in Sarajevo. They delivered the newspapers from the post office on the morning of the sixteenth. Holding the Moscow evening paper, Father came out of his study into the dining room, where he, Mother, and I were still drinking tea, and said, "Well, my friends, it's war! They've killed the Austrian archduke at Sarajevo. That means war!"

On Saint Peter's Day we had a number of guests—for Father's name day—and at the dinner table our engagement was announced. But on July 19 Germany declared war on Russia.

He came in September but stayed only a day and night—to say good-bye before his departure for the front (at that time everyone thought the war would end soon; our marriage was postponed until spring). And so we were spending our last evening together. After supper, as was customary, they brought in the samovar, and looking at the windows, all misted over with its steam, Father said, "An incredibly early and cold fall!"

We sat quietly that evening, merely exchanging meaningless words from time to time, exaggeratedly calm, concealing our secret thoughts and feelings. Even Father's remark about the autumn was full of feigned nonchalance. I walked up to the door of the terrace and wiped the glass with a handkerchief; out in the garden clear, icy stars were glittering brightly and distinctly in the black sky.

Leaning back in his easy chair, Father smoked, gazing vacantly at the hot lamp hanging over the table; Mother sat under its light in her spectacles, carefully stitching together a small silk pouch. We understood its purpose—and felt both touched and frightened. Father said, "So you want to go early in the morning all the same, and not after lunch?"

"Yes, with your permission, in the morning," he answered. "Sad to say, I still have things to get arranged at home."

Father let out a brief sigh.

"All right, my dear boy, whatever you think. But in that case it's time for Mama and me to get some sleep; we don't want to miss seeing you off tomorrow."

Mother stood up and made the sign of the cross over her future son; he bent to kiss her hand, then Father's. Left alone, we stayed for a time in the dining room—for some reason I decided to lay out a game of solitaire. He paced silently from corner to corner, then asked, "Want to take a little walk?"

Feeling more downhearted than ever, I responded impassively, "All right."

Still in a pensive mood as he found his coat in the anteroom, he recalled Fet's verses with a sweet, wry smile: "The autumn's so frosty this year! / Put on your capote and your shawl . . ."

"I don't have a capote. How does it go after that?"

"Can't remember. Like this, I think: 'Look there, in the pine wood, my dear; / It's a fire, so it seems, rising tall.' "

"What kind of fire?"

"The rising moon, of course. There's a sort of rural autumn charm in those lines: 'Put on your capote and your shawl.' The days of our grandfathers and grandmothers . . . Oh God, my God!"

"What's wrong?"

"Nothing, dear. It's sad, all the same. Sad and good. I love you so very much."

When we had put on our coats we went through the dining room, onto the terrace, then down into the garden. At first it was so dark that I had to hold on to his sleeve. Then the ever brighter sky began revealing black branches strewn with the mineral glitter of stars. Pausing for a moment, he turned toward the manor house.

"Look how the windows of the house are shining in some absolutely special way, in an autumn way. I'll remember this evening as long as I live, forever."

I turned to look, and he embraced me in my Swiss wrap. I pushed aside the downy kerchief from my face and let my head fall back so he could kiss me. After we had kissed he looked in my face.

"How your eyes are gleaming," he said. "Aren't you cold? The air is just like winter. All the same, if I'm killed, you won't forget me right away?"

I thought, "And what if he is killed? Could I really forget him in a short time—for isn't everything forgotten in the end?" Frightened by my thoughts, I answered hurriedly, "Don't say that! I could never go on living without you!"

After a brief silence he said slowly, "Well then, if I'm killed, I'll wait for you there. You just live, enjoy your life on earth, then come to me."

I burst into bitter tears.

In the morning he left. Mama hung around his neck the ominous little pouch that she had sewn the previous evening—it contained a golden icon worn by her father and grandfather in time of war—and in a paroxysm of desperation we made the sign of the cross over him. Watching as he rode away, we stood on the porch in that state of torpor that one always experiences when seeing off someone for a long separation, feeling only the amazing incongruity between us and the joyous sunny morning all around, with its glistening rime frost on the grass. We stood there awhile, then went back into the emptiness of the house. I walked through the rooms, hands behind my back, not knowing what to do with myself, whether to start sobbing or to sing out as loud as I could.

He was killed—what a strange word!—a month later, in Galicia. Thirty whole years have passed since then. And I have lived through so very much during those years, which seem to have lasted for ages when you think about them attentively, when you turn over in memory all that magical, inscrutable something, a mystery to both mind and heart, that is called the past. In the spring of 1918, after Father and Mother had both died, I was living in Moscow, in the cellar of a trader-woman from the Smolensk market who always used to mock me: "Well, now, Your Excellency, how's your life expectancy?" I too was engaged in huckstering. As so many others were doing at that time, I was selling what few things I still possessed to soldiers in Caucasian fur hats and unbuttoned greatcoats—some sort of ring, or a small cross, or a moth-eaten fur collar. And there, selling things on the corner of Arbat and the market, I met a rare, beautiful person, an elderly retired military man, whom I soon married and with whom I went away in April to Yekaterinodar. It took us nearly two weeks to get there. We traveled with his nephew, a boy of about seventeen, who was working his way south to join the volunteer forces. I went as a peasant woman in bast sandals; my husband wore a tattered Cossack smock and let his black and gray-streaked beard grow out. We remained in the Don and Kuban regions for more than two years. In a winter storm we sailed with a huge mob of other refugees from Novorossisk to Turkey, and during the voyage, at sea, my husband died of typhus. After that I had only three relations left on all the earth: my husband's nephew, his young wife, and their daughter, a baby of seven months. But soon the nephew and wife sailed away to the Crimea to join Wrangel's forces, leaving the baby in my hands. There they disappeared without a trace. After that I stayed on for a long time in Constantinople, earning a living for myself and the child by the most burdensome manual labor. Then, as did so many others, she and I began wandering here, there, and everywhere: Bulgaria, Serbia, Czechoslovakia, Belgium, Paris, Nice . . . Long since grown, the girl remained in Paris, became altogether French, quite comely, and absolutely indifferent to me. She worked in a chocolate shop near the Madeleine; her sleek hands with the silver nails wrapped boxes in satiny paper and tied them up with thin, golden twine. And I lived and still live in Nice on whatever the Lord happens to send me . . . I had first been to Nice in 1912—and in those happy times I never could have imagined what it would become for me someday!

So I went on living after his death, having once rashly sworn that if he died I could never go on. But in recalling everything that I have lived through since then, I always ask myself, "What, after all, does my life consist of?" And I answer, "Only of that cold fall evening." Was there ever really such an evening? Yes, all the same, there was. And that's all there ever was in my life—the rest is a useless dream. And I believe, I fervently believe that somewhere out there he's waiting for me—with the very same love and youthfulness as on that evening. "You just live, enjoy your life on earth, then come to me . . ." Well, I've lived, I've had my joy; now I'll be coming soon.

May 3, 1944

»»» «««

Night

The dacha is dark, the hour late; a ceaseless murmur streams all around me. After a long walk by the precipice over the sea I lie in a chaise longue on the balcony. I am thinking—and listening, listening: a crystalline murmur, mesmerization!

The abysmal night sky is replete with multicolored stars suspended within it, and there is the fragile, gray Milky Way, transparent and also full of stars, inclining in two uneven wisps of haze toward the southern horizon, which is starless, consequently almost black. The balcony faces the garden, which is strewn with shingle and has only the occasional stunted tree. From the balcony the night sea unfolds. Pale and silent, smooth milk white, it lies lethargically quiescent. The stars as well seem disposed to keep their silence. And, as in some jangling dream, a monotone, crystalline din, never ceasing even for a second, pervades all this mute night world.

What am I thinking?

"And I decided to seek and search out by wisdom concerning all things that are done under the sun; but this sore travail hath God given to the sons of man that they may torment themselves . . . God hath made men reasonable, but alas, they have lost themselves in the wildest of fancies." And the Preacher counsels paternally, "Be not righteous over much, and burden not thy mind with philosophy." But I am forever "philosophizing." I am "righteous over much."

What am I thinking? When I asked myself this, I wanted to recall precisely what I was thinking, but immediately I began thinking about my thought, about how thought seems the most marvelous, the most incomprehensible—and the most fateful—thing in my life. What was I thinking, what was within me? Reflections (or a semblance of reflections) about my surroundings, and for some reason a desire to remember, preserve, retain those surroundings within me . . . What else was there? Boundless happiness because of the great serenity and the boundless harmony of the night, but also a nebulous anguish and some sort of cupidity. Why the anguish? Because of the dim sensation that in me alone there is no serenity—my perpetual secret torment!—and there is no mindlessness. Why the cupidity? Because of the craving to make use somehow of this happiness and even of the anguish and craving, to create something from them . . . But this too, O Preacher, is anguish: "In days to come all will be forgotten. There is no remembrance of former lives. Also their love and their hatred and their envy is now long perished; neither have they any more a portion in any thing that is done under the sun."

What was I thinking? But the precise subject of my thought is not important—what is important is my thinking, a process that is an absolute mystery to me, and still more important and more of a mystery is my thinking about this thinking, about how "I understand nothing, neither of myself nor of the world," and at the same time *I understand my nonunderstanding,* I understand that I am lost amidst this night and amidst this incantatory murmur, which seems now living, now dead, now senseless, now revealing the most vital and most imperative truths.

This reflection about my own reflections, this understanding of my own nonunderstanding, is incontrovertible proof of my involvement in something a hundredfold larger than I am; it is, therefore, proof of my immortality. Apart from all that is my private self, there is obviously within me a certain something that is fundamental, incorruptible—truly a particle of God.

Yes, but a particle of that which has neither form nor time nor space, of that which means my ruin. Eat thereof and ye shall be as God. But "God is in heaven, and we upon earth." In eating thereof we die, we pass from the earth, from earthly forms and laws. God is infinite, unbounded, ubiquitous, innominate. But for me these very divine properties are horrendous, and if they grow continually within me, then my earthly "being" and "doing," my life as a man expires.

The small trees stand immobile and dark in the garden.

Gray shingle gleams between them, flowers glow white in the flower bed, and beyond that is the precipice—and the sea ascends into the sky like a milk white Shroud of Christ.

This milkiness has a mirror smoothness; but the horizon is gloomy and baleful—because of Jupiter and because there are almost no stars in the southern sky above the skyline.

Golden, enormous Jupiter burns so regally at the end of the Milky Way that barely visible shadows from the table and chairs are cast onto the balcony. It seems like a minute satellite of some other world; in a misty golden column its radiance falls from the immense heights of the heavens into the mirror-smooth milkiness of the sea, while on the horizon, clashing with the light, what seems like a dark knoll stands in dismal silhouette.

The incessant din never ceases for an instant, suffusing the silence of sky, earth, and sea with some diaphanous murmur, like millions of streaming, merging rivulets or like wondrous flowers that seem ever growing in crystalline spirals.

Only man marvels at his own existence and meditates upon it. This is what most distinguishes him from other creatures, who are still in paradise, mindless of themselves. But men also differ one from another—by the degree, the extent of this marveling. Why is it God has so deeply marked me with the fatal brand of the marveler, the reflector, the "philosophizer," why does all this keep growing and growing in me? Do they philosophize, these myriads of nocturnal steppeland cicadas, who appear to suffuse me and the whole universe with their song of love? They are in paradise, in the beatific sleep of life, but I have awoken and sit keeping my vigil. The world is within them and they within it, but I seem to be outside looking in. "The fool sitteth idly and devoureth his own heart. He that observeth the wind shall not sow."

I listen and think. As a result I am profoundly alone in this midnight hush, jangling bewitchingly with myriads of crystalline wells, which flow inexhaustibly, with utmost acquiescence and mindlessness, into some abysmal Womb. The sublime light of Jupiter eerily illumines the vast expanse between heaven and sea, the great temple of night above whose royal portals it hangs as a sign of the Holy Spirit. But I am alone in that temple; I sit within it keeping my vigil.

Day is the hour of deeds, the hour of bondage. Day exists in time and space. Day is fulfillment of earthly duty, service to earthly being. And the law of day decrees: be thou active in toil; interrupt it not for consciousness of thine own self, of thy place and thy goal, for thou art a slave of earthly being, and a certain task has been allotted unto thee, a calling, a name. But what is night? Does it behoove man to sit before it keeping vigil, in that inscrutable state of mind that we call "philosophizing"? We were enjoined to eat not of the forbidden fruit; listen, just listen to them, those selflessly ecstatic singers: they have not eaten, they do not eat! And what but exaltation of them did the Preachers derive from all their wisdom? It was they who said, "All is vanity of vanities, and man reapeth no profit from all his endeavors!" But it was they too who added—with bitter envy—"The sleep of a labouring man is sweet! And there is nothing better for a man than that he take delight in his labour, and merrily eat his bread, and drink his wine in the joy of his heart!" What is night? That which makes free for a certain interval the slave of time and space, takes from him his earthly task, his earthly name and calling—and makes ready for him, if he sits keeping vigil, a great temptation: sterile "philosophizing," sterile striving for understanding, that is, redoubled nonunderstanding: an incomprehension of the world, of one's very self within it, of one's beginning and one's end.

Neither of them exists for me, neither beginning nor end.

I know how many years old I am, but I was told this, that I was born in such a year, on such a day, and at such an hour. Otherwise I would be unaware of the day of my birth and, consequently, of the sum of my years; I would not even know that I exist by reason of birth.

Birth! Just what is birth anyway? By no means is my birth my beginning. My beginning lies in the (absolutely inscrutable) murk where I was conceived before birth, and in my father, mother, in grandfathers and great-grandfathers, for they too are I, only in somewhat different form, of which a great deal has been reproduced almost identically in me. "I remember that once, myriads of years ago, I was a goat yeanling." I myself had a similar experience (in the very land of the one who made this statement, in the tropics of India); I experienced the awesome sensation that I had been there before, in that paradisiacal warmth.

Self-delusion? Autosuggestion?

But it is quite probable that my forebears dwelt precisely in the tropics of India. How could they, in passing on so many times to their descendants and, finally, in passing on to me almost the exact form of ear, chin, brow, how could they not pass on as well the more delicate and imponderable, their very carnality, which was bound up with India? There are those who fear snakes or spiders "irrationally," that is, in a way contrary to the reason; this is a sensation from some previous existence, the dark recollection, for example, that once an ancient forebear was threatened constantly with death from cobra, scorpion, or tarantula. My forebear dwelt in India. So why, when I see coconut palms bent back from the ocean strand, when I see naked dark brown people in the warm tropical water, why should I not recall what I once felt when I was my own naked dark brown ancestor?

But neither do I have an end.

Not understanding my birth, insensible to it, neither do I understand nor apprehend my death, of which, again, I would not have had the remotest conception, awareness, or perhaps even sensation had I been born and lived on some island altogether uninhabited, without a single living creature. All my life I have been living under the augury of death—and all my life, nonetheless, I have felt that I will never die. Death! But every seven years a man is regenerated; that is, imperceptibly he dies as imperceptibly he is reborn. Therefore, many times I too have been regenerated (that is, have died while being reborn). I was dying yet was living, have died even repeatedly—yet in principle I am just the same, and, furthermore, I am replete with the whole of my past.

Beginning, end. But my conception of time and space is terribly shaky. Not only do I sense this more and more as years go by, but also I become more conscious of it.

I have been singled out from others of my kind. Even though I have a lifelong awareness of how agonizingly weak and inadequate my talents are, in comparison to some I am quite an extraordinary man. But precisely because of this (that is, by virtue of a certain singularity, by virtue of my belonging to a special category of men) my conception, my sense of time, of space, and of my very self is especially shaky.

What category, what men are these? Men who are called poets, artists. What must they possess? The ability to grasp with special intensity not only their own time, but also that of others, the past, not only their own country, their own lineage, but also different, other countries, tribes, not only themselves, but also everyone else—that is, what is usually called the ability to reincarnate, and, besides that, an especially vital and especially graphic (sensuous) Memory. One numbered among such men must have traversed the long path of incarnations in the chain of his ancestors, until suddenly he becomes the peculiarly consummate image of his savage forebear, with all the crispness of his sensations, all the graphicness of his thoughts, with his enormous subconsciousness. But he also must have been immeasurably enriched on the long path, must have acquired enormous consciousness.

Does such a man suffer tremendous torment or is he blessed with tremendous good fortune? Both. The curse and the joy of such a man is a keenly intense ego, a craving for the uttermost confirmation of that ego and also (by virtue of vast experience during his abode in the enormous chain of incarnations) uttermost awareness of the vanity of that craving, an acute sensation of the All. And so: the Buddha, Solomon, Tolstoy.

In youth and maturity gorillas have awesome physical strength, are immeasurably sensual in disposition, merciless in pursuing satiation of their lust, characterized by extreme spontaneity; but by old age they have become indecisive, pensive, doleful and compassionate . . . The resemblance to the Buddhas, Solomons, and Tolstoys is striking! And then again, in the regal breed of these saints and geniuses how many there are whose very looks suggest a comparison to gorillas! Everyone is familiar with the eyebrow arches of Tolstoy, the gigantic stature of the Buddha and the lump on his skull (and the fits of Muhammad, when the angels revealed amidst lightning "the mysteries and abysses not of this earth," and "in the trice of an eyewink," that is, beyond all laws of time and space, they bore him from Medina to Jerusalem—to the Rock

Moriah, which was "incessantly oscillating between heaven and earth," as if blending earth with heaven, temporal with eternal).

At first all the Solomons and Buddhas embrace the world most greedily, then most passionately they curse its temptations. At first they are all great sinners, then great foes of sin, at first great amassers, then great dissipaters. They are all insatiable slaves of Maya—there, that's her you hear, the jangling conjuring Maya; listen, just listen to her!—and each is distinguished by something that intensifies with the years, a sensation of the All and of one's inevitable dissolution within It.

Suddenly, with a faint stir of air, the smells of ocean crispness and of blooms from the flower bed drift up to my balcony. And presently a rustle is heard, the soft sigh of a wave half asleep, slowly rolling in somewhere down below to the shore. Happy, somnolent, mindless, submissive, dying unaware of its death! It has rolled in, splashed, illumined the sands with a pale blue radiance—the radiance of innumerable lives—and just as slowly has receded, returned to its cradle and grave. The innumerable lives seem to sing all around still more frenziedly, and Jupiter, its golden torrent pouring into the great mirror of waters, seems to glitter in the heavens still more awesomely and regally.

Am I really not beginningless, endless, ubiquitous?

Decades now separate me from my infancy and childhood. Long, infinitely long ago! But I need only think for a moment and time begins to melt. Frequently I have experienced something miraculous. How frequently this has happened: I return to those fields where I was once a child and a youth, and as I look around I suddenly feel that the many long years I have lived since then seem never to have been. This is absolutely not, by no means a recollection; no, I simply have become my former self. Once again I have the same relationship to these fields, to this air of the openlands, to this Russian sky, the very same apprehension of all the world that I had right here on this country path, in the days of my childhood and adolescence!

Frequently at such moments I have thought, "Every instant of all by which I once lived here has mysteriously imprinted its vestige as if upon some innumerable, infinitely minute recording disks within what is most fundamentally me; and now some of the imprints have suddenly burst into life and manifested themselves." Another second and they will fade once more in the murk of my being. But let them; I know they exist. "Nothing perishes—all things are but altered." But could there be something that is subject not even to alteration, that undergoes no modification, not only during my lifetime but even over the course of millennia? A great multitude of such imprints have been passed on to me by my ancestors, my forebears. A wealth of capabilities, genius, talent—what is all this but a wealth of those imprints (both inherited and acquired), but various kinds of sensitivity to them and the totality of their manifestations in rays of the Sun that fall intermittently from somewhere upon them?

Having chanced to awaken recently at dawn, I suddenly was staggered at the thought of my age. Once it seemed that this was some unique, almost awesome creature—a man who had lived forty or fifty years. And now, at last, I too had become such a creature. "What, then, am I?" I said to myself. "What exactly have I become?" And by slightly exerting my will, by looking at myself as one looks at a stranger (how marvelous that we can do this!), I felt, of course, totally convinced that even now I was exactly the same person I had been at age ten or twenty.

I lit a lamp and looked in the mirror: yes, there was gauntness now, a rigidity of the features, silvery patches on the temples; the color of the eyes was somewhat faded. But so what?

And with a particular nimbleness I arose and walked through the other rooms. They were still just barely brightening, still nocturnally serene, but already embracing the new, slowly dawning day, which feebly, mysteriously divided their semidarkness at the level of my chest.

A special predawn serenity still reigned as well in all that enormous nest of humanity called a city. The houses stood mutely, posing in a special, nondiurnal way, with a great many windows and a profusion of inhabitants, who all apparently were so diverse and so identically devoted to sleep, nonconsciousness, and helplessness. The streets lay mute (and still empty, still pure) beneath me, but by now the gaslights burned green in pellucid twilight. And suddenly once again came that inexpressible something I have felt all my life when I chance to awaken at daybreak; I felt great happiness, a childlike credulity, the soul-touching sweetness of life, the beginning of something altogether new, good, lovely—and my intimacy, brotherhood, and unity with all others living on earth. How well I can understand at such moments the tears of the apostle Peter, who precisely at dawn sensed so keenly, so youthfully and tenderly, all the force of his love for Jesus and all the evil that he, Peter, had perpetrated the night before in his fear of the Roman soldiers! Once more I felt as if I myself had lived through all the events of that remote, evangelic morning in the Grove of Olives, the denial by Peter. Time disappeared. With all my being I felt, What an insignificant period that is—two thousand years! I have already lived half a century; I need only multiply my life by forty to reach the time of Christ, of the apostles, "ancient" Judea, "ancient" humanity. *The very same sun* that the pale, teary-eyed Peter once gazed upon after his sleepless night will rise again at any moment over me. And almost the same feelings that overwhelmed Peter at Gethsemane now overwhelm me, evoking in my eyes as well the same sweet, grievous tears that Peter shed by the fire. So where is my time and where is his? Where am I and where is Peter? If we are so fused, though only for an instant, just where is that ego of mine, which all my life I have desired so passionately to affirm and set apart? No, it means absolutely nothing—my living on earth not in the days of Peter, Jesus, Tiberius, but in the so-called twentieth century! Besides which, I have lived so much through my imagination in others' lives, remote lives, feeling that I have existed always and everywhere! Where is the line between my reality and my imagination, my feelings, which, after all, are reality too, something indubitably existing?

All my life, consciously and unconsciously, I have been striving to surmount, to destroy space, time, and form. Unappeasable, immeasurable is my craving for life. I live not only in my present but also in all my past, not only in my own life but also in thousands of others' lives, in everything contemporaneous with me and in something back there in the haze of distant ages. But for what? In order to destroy myself by so doing, or, on the contrary, to affirm myself, to enrich and strengthen myself?

People fall into two categories. One enormous category includes those of their own fixed time, mundane builders, doers, men who seem almost without past, without ancestors, faithful links in the Chain of which the wisdom of India speaks; what do they care that both beginning and end of that Chain slip away so awesomely into boundlessness? The other category, very small in comparison, includes those who not only are not doers, not builders, but are outright annihilators, who long have known the vanity of doing and building, men of dreams and contemplation, who marvel at themselves and at the world, men who "philosophize," who have responded in secret to the ancient call: "Withdraw from the Chain!" Who now crave disappearance, dissolution in the One, and who, simultaneously, suffer fierce excruciations, grieve for all the visages, the incarnations within which they have abided, and, especially, for every second of their present existence. These men are endowed with a great wealth of apprehension received from their innumerable predecessors; they sense the infinitely remote links of the Chain, of Being. Marvelously (and perhaps for the last time?) they have resurrected in their person the strength and vigor of their forefather in paradise, his corporeality. These men are paradisiacally sensual in disposition but already deprived of Paradise. This accounts for the great fissure within them: the torment of leaving the Chain, of separation from it, the consciousness of its vanity—and of its redoubled, awesome charm. And each of these men is fully justified in intoning the ancient plaint: "O Eternal and All-Embracing All! Once thou didst not know Desire, Craving. Thou didst abide in peace but thyself destroyed it. Thou didst conceive and lead forth the immeasurable Chain of incarnations, of which it is incumbent upon each to be ever more incorporeal, ever nearer the beatific Beginning. Now ever more stridently sounds unto me thy call: 'Withdraw from the Chain! Withdraw and leave no trace, no legacy, no heir!' Yes, Lord, I hearken unto thee now. But still bitter to me is my severance from the fraudulent, bitter sweetness of Being. Still am I in awe of thy Without-Beginning and thy Without-End."

Yes, if only one could engrave this fraudulent yet unspeakably sweet "Being" at least in word, if not in flesh!

In the most ancient of my days, thousands of years ago, I spoke in measured tones of the measured sounding of the sea, sang of my joy and sorrow, of how the blue of the skies and the white of the clouds were remote and magnificent, of how the form of the female body was agonizing in its inscrutable charm. And now I am just the same. By whom and for what am I impelled to bear this burden without respite—to express incessantly my feelings, thoughts, ideas, and to express them not simply, but with exactitude, beauty, and power, which must enchant, enrapture, arouse sadness or happiness in men? Who instilled in me and why the unappeasable need to infect them with what I myself am living, to pass on myself to them, and to seek in them for sympathy, for unity, fusion with them? Since infancy never do I feel anything, never do I think, see, hear, or smell without that "cupidity," without the craving for enrichment, which I need to express the utmost richness of myself. I am obsessed by the eternal desire not only to amass and then dissipate but also to stand out among millions of men like me, to become known to them and worthy of their envy, rapture, wonder, of eternal life. The crown of every human life is the memory of it; the best promise made to man over his coffin is memory eternal. There is no soul that would not pine in secret dream of that crown. And my soul? How weary it is with that dream—for what, why?—the dream of leaving myself in the world for eternity, my feelings, visions, desires, of prevailing over what is called my death, which will come for me indisputably in due time and in which, nonetheless, I do not believe, don't want to and can't believe! Relentlessly, with all my being, I scream without words, "Sun, stand thou still!!" And all the more passionately do I scream because in truth I am destroying rather than preserving myself. I cannot do otherwise since I have been given the skill to surmount them—time, space, form—to sense my nonbeginning and my without-end, that is, the All, which draws me back into Itself as a spider draws its web.

But on and on sing the cicadas. They too have been given to know it, this All, but their song is sweet; for me alone it is sad—a song full of paradisiacal mindlessness, of beatific selfless ecstasy!

Jupiter has attained to its apogee. And the night has attained ultimate silence, ultimate quiescence before Jupiter, the ultimate hour of its beauty and grandeur. "Night unto night passeth knowledge." What kind? And when? Perhaps during this, its cryptic, most lofty hour?

The unbounded, abysmal temple of the star-glutted sky has become still more regal and menacing; a myriad of large early-morning stars have ascended into it. And now the misty golden column of radiance falls precipitously into the milky mirror smoothness of the sea swathed in lethargy. In that barren southern garden strewn with pale shingle the small, dark trees appear still more immobile, seem to have become even smaller. And the incessant din, never ceasing even for an instant, suffusing the silence of sky, earth, and sea with what seems a diaphanous murmur, now resembles still more some wondrous flowers that appear to be growing in crystalline coils . . . What then, at last, will it attain to, this jangling silence?

But there it is again, that sigh, the sigh of life, the rustle of a wave rolling onto the shore and spilling over, and afterward another slight stir of the air, ocean crispness and the smell of flowers. I seem to awaken. I look around and stand up. I run down from the balcony, walk through crunching shingle in the garden, then go running down from the precipice. I walk through the sand and sit down at the very edge of the water; ecstatically I plunge in my hands, which ignite instantaneously, blaze with myriads of glistening drops, innumerable lives . . . No, my time has still not come! Still there is something that outweighs all my philosophizing. Like my passion for woman it still is there, my lust for this aqueous night womb.

God, let me be!

Maritime Alps, September 17, 1925

»»» «««

The Case of Cornet Elagin

I

It's a horrendous business, this—a strange case, enigmatic, insoluble. On the one hand it's elementary, yet on the other very complex. It's like cheap pulp fiction—that's what everyone in our city called it—and at the same time it could motivate the plotline for a profound work of literature. In his courtroom remarks the lawyer for the defense could not have put it more precisely.

"In this case," he said at the beginning of his presentation, "there would seem to be no room for argument between myself and the representative of the prosecution. After all, the defendant himself admits to his guilt. After all, his crime and his personality—just as the personality of his victim, whose will he is said to have brutally violated—are, ostensibly, so vacuous and pedestrian that virtually anyone present in this courtroom would find them unworthy of philosophical speculation. But all of that is just not so, it simply appears to be that way. We have grounds for dispute here; we have a great many topics worthy of polemic and deep reflection."

Then he went on to say, "Let's hypothesize that I had only one aim: to get leniency for the defendant. If so, then I would have very little to say. In cases such as ours the law code does not stipulate what, exactly, should govern the decisions of judges. It has left an enormous amount of discretion to their apprehension of the case, to their conscience and perspicacity, by means of which they must, in the final analysis, select this or that legal framework through which to punish the done deed. Therefore, I would attempt to influence their apprehension, their conscience, I would try to bring to the forefront all of the best qualities to be found in the defendant and all that mitigates his guilt; I would arouse benevolent sentiments in the judges and would do so the more persistently since, after all, he denies but one fact about his actions: premeditated evil intent. Even if I took such an approach, however, could I avoid clashing with the prosecuting attorney, who has defined the criminal as no more, no less than 'a beastly fiend'? In any court case, facts can be perceived in various ways, lit from one angle or another, presented in unique perspectives, in this or that musical key. What, then, do we have here, in our case? It appears there is not a single aspect of it, not a single detail which the prosecutor and I would view identically, present in the same fashion, light from the same angle. 'It's all cut-and-dried, but it's not at all cut-and-dried!' That is the point I must repeat to him incessantly. That is the most important fact, what lies at the heart of the matter: things are just not what they seem to be."

The beginning of this business was horrendous as well.

Last year, the nineteenth of June. It was early in the morning, sometime between five and six, but the dining room of Captain Likharev (Household Troops, hussars regiment) was already bright, stuffy, dry, and hot from the summer sun that bathed the city. It was, however, still quiet, understandably so, since the captain's apartment was in a complement of hussar barracks situated on the outskirts of town. Basking in that silence, the captain lay in a deep sleep commensurate with his young years. On his table there were liqueurs, cups of coffee half full. In the next room, the living room, another officer, Count Koshis, staff captain, was sleeping, and in the study still another, Cornet Sevsky. The morning was, in a word, just like any other, the scene unpretentious, but, as usual when something extraordinary happens in the midst of the ordinary, what happened next in Captain Likharev's apartment, early in the morning of June 19, was all the more horrible, astounding, and somehow unbelievable. Suddenly, amidst the total silence of that morning, the bell in the anteroom jangled; next came the sounds of the orderly, running cautiously and lightly on bare feet to open the door, and then a deliberately loud voice rang out, "Is he in?"

The newly arrived guest entered with that same deliberate clamorousness, flinging open the door to the dining room with a pointed lack of restraint, stomping his boots and jingling his spurs with a particular brashness. The captain raised up, a look of amazement on his sleepy face. Standing before him was his fellow regimental officer, Cornet Elagin, a small puny man, ginger haired and freckled, with bowed and uncommonly thin legs, wearing fancy boots, such dandiness being, as he loved to say, his "primary" weakness. Hastily he removed his light greatcoat, threw it on a chair, and said in a loud voice, "There you are, take my epaulettes!" Then he walked over to the divan by the opposite wall, sprawled out on his back, and placed his hands behind his head.

"Wait a minute, wait," muttered the captain, following his movements with widened eyes. "Where have you been, what's wrong?"

"I killed Manya," said Elagin.

"Are you drunk? What Manya?" asked the captain.

"The actress, Maria Iosifovna Sosnovskaya."

The captain put his legs down on the floor. "What is this, are you joking?"

"Alas, unfortunately, or maybe fortunately, I'm quite serious."

"Who is that out there? What happened?" shouted the count from the living room.

Elagin stretched his body and pushed open the door with a gentle kick.

"Stop the bellowing," he said. "It's me, Elagin. I've shot Manya."

"What?" said the count, and after a brief pause he burst out laughing. "So that's how it is!" he shouted merrily. "Well, the hell with you, we'll forgive you this time. It's good you woke us up, anyway. We'd have slept in for sure, what with partying again till three last night."

"I give you my word, I killed her," repeated Elagin insistently.

"You lie, brother, you lie!" yelled Likharev, reaching for his socks. "You almost had me scared there, thinking something really happened . . . Efrem, bring some tea!"

Elagin reached into the pocket of his trousers, pulled out a small key, and tossing it quite skillfully over his shoulder, right onto the table, he said, "Go take a look for yourselves."

In the courtroom the prosecutor frequently made reference to the cynicism and horror of certain episodes that figured in the Elagin drama; in so doing he often focused on this very scene. He forgot that only at the beginning that morning did Captain Likharev fail to notice what he later called the "supernatural" pallor of Elagin's face, along with something "inhuman" about his eyes, and then, when he did notice, he was "simply astonished by both of these things."

2

And so, here's what happened last year, on the morning of June 19.

A half hour after the scene described above Count Koshis and Cornet Sevsky already were standing at the entryway to the building where Sosnovskaya lived. They were no longer in a joking mood.

Goading on the cabman till the horse was half dead, they leapt out of the carriage in a mad rush, stuck the key into the keyhole, and started desperately ringing the bell. But the key did not fit, and on the other side of the door there was only silence. Losing patience, they ran out into the courtyard to look for the house porter. He rushed into the kitchen from the service entrance, then returned to tell them that Sosnovskaya, so the maid reported, had not spent the night at home. She had gone out early in the evening, carrying something wrapped up in a bundle. The officers were at a loss; now what should they do? They thought things over, shrugged their shoulders, and drove to the police station, taking the porter with them. From there they phoned Captain Likharev, who yelled like a madman into the receiver.

"That idiot, he's got me in such a state I could bay at the moon. He forgot to tell us not to go to her apartment at all but to their love nest, at 14 Starogradskaya Street. Did you get that? Starogradskaya, number fourteen. It's something like a *garçonnière* in Paris; the entry is right off the street."

They headed off at a gallop for Starogradskaya.

The porter sat up on the coach box. With an air of restrained self-importance a policeman from the local ward took his seat in the cab opposite the military men. It was hot, the streets were noisy, teeming with people; it was hard to believe that on such an animated sunny morning a person could be lying dead somewhere, and the thought that twenty-two-year-old Sashka Elagin could have done it was bewildering. How could he bring himself to do something like that? What did he kill her for, why, and how did he kill her? There was no sense in any of this, and all the questions remained unanswered.

When, finally, they arrived at the dreary, old two-storied building on Starogradskaya, the count and the cornet, in their words, "completely lost heart." Could it be that *this thing* was here, that they would have to look at *this thing* now, although they wanted to see it, did feel drawn to it, even irresistibly so? In contrast the police officer, immediately savoring his authority, became livelier and more self-assured.

"If you please, the key," he said to them in a dry and firm tone of voice. The military men hastened to hand it over with the same meekness that the porter might have shown.

The gateway was at the middle of the building, and beyond the gates there was a small courtyard and a sapling, with green foliage somehow unnaturally bright, or it seemed that way in contrast to the dark gray of the stone walls. To the right of the gates was that mysterious door that gave directly onto the street, the door that must be opened. And so, frowning, the policeman stuck the key in the door, it swung open, and the military men saw something like a totally dark corridor. As if he had some instinct for finding the right spot, the police officer stretched out his hand and scraped it along the wall to the switch. The light revealed a cramped and gloomy room with a table standing at its far end between two armchairs. There were plates on it, with the remains of chicken and fruits. But still gloomier was the sight they saw when they went a bit farther. On the right side of the corridor they came upon a small entry into the next room, also quite dark, but illumined in a mortuary way by an opaline lamp that hung from the ceiling, beneath an enormous umbrella drapery made of black silk. All the walls of that room, completely blank walls with no windows, were also draped from top to bottom in some black material. Here, once again far back into the room, there was an ample Turkish divan built low to the ground, and lying on it, wearing only a negligee, with half-open eyes and lips, with head sunken onto her breast, upper and lower extremities extended and legs slightly apart, was the white figure of a young woman of rare beauty.

The men who entered that room paused and stood for a moment, frozen in fear and astonishment.

3

The beauty of the dead woman was rare because it fulfilled, to a rare degree, the standards that, for example, modish artists set for themselves when depicting ideally beautiful women. All the attributes were there: an exquisite physique, skin of an exquisite hue, a petite foot void of any blemish, a childlike, ingenuous charm about the lips, delicate and exact facial features, marvelous hair . . . And now all of that was dead, had begun fading away, turning to stone, and her beauty made the dead woman even more awesome. Her hair was in perfect order, her coiffure looked ready for a ball. Her head, slightly elevated, was lying on the pillow of the divan and the chin was just barely touching the breast, which gave her fixed, half-open eyes and all of her face what appeared to be a somewhat perplexed expression. All of this was eerily illumined by the opaline lamp hanging from the ceiling, in the depths of a huge black umbrella that resembled some rapacious bird, spreading its membranous wings over the dead woman.

In a word, even the policeman was taken aback by that scene. Afterward they all proceeded, in a hesitant way, to examine the woman more closely.

The lovely bare arms of the deceased lay stretched straight alongside the body. On her breast, on the lace of the nightdress, there were two of Elagin's visiting cards and alongside her legs a hussar's saber, which seemed a crude thing to be lying there next to that feminine nakedness. Struck by the absurd idea that it might contain traces of blood, the count made a move to grab it and draw it out of its scabbard, but the policeman stopped him from making that unlawful move.

"Oh, yes, of course, of course," muttered the count in a whisper. "For now, nothing, of course, must be touched. But I'm amazed that I don't see blood anywhere, or any signs of a crime whatsoever. Is it an obvious poisoning?"

"Remain patient," said the policeman in a preceptorial tone. "We'll wait for the inspector and the doctor. But it certainly does look like a poisoning."

And it really did. There was no blood anywhere—not on the floor, not on the divan, not on the body or the nightdress of the dead woman. Lying on the armchair were a pair of women's underpants and a peignoir, and beneath them a blouse that was light blue with a pearly tinge, a skirt made of excellent dark gray material, and a gray silk manteau. All of these things were tossed there haphazardly, but none of them had a single drop of blood. On the ledge jutting out from the wall above the divan there was still another confirmation that this was a poisoning. Amidst champagne bottles and corks on that ledge, amidst burned-down candles and women's hairpins, torn pieces of paper with writing all over them, there was a glass with stout left half drunk and a small vial. The white label of the vial contained these ominous, black-lettered words: *OP. PULV.*

At the very moment when the policeman and the two officers were taking turns reading those Latin words, they heard the clatter of the carriage bringing the inspector and the physician, and a few minutes later came confirmation that Elagin had told the truth. Sosnovskaya really had been killed with a revolver. There were no bloody spots on the nightdress, but beneath the dress they discovered a scarlet stain around the heart, and in the middle of it a round-shaped wound with traces of burns at its edges. From that wound a thin stream of dark blood had flowed out but had not soiled anything because the wound was stuffed with a wadded-up handkerchief.

What other conclusions did medical expertise reach? Quite a few. It was established that the right lung of the dead woman had traces of tuberculosis. That she was shot at close range and that death was instantaneous, although the woman could, nonetheless, have uttered a short phrase after the shot. That there was no struggle between the killer and his victim. That she had drunk champagne and had taken a small dose of opium with the stout (not enough to kill her). And, finally, that on that fateful night she had had sexual intercourse.

But why, for what reason had she been murdered? In answer to this question Elagin stubbornly insisted: because they—he himself and Sosnovskaya—had been in a "tragic position," that they saw no way out except death, and that, in killing Sosnovskaya, he had only done what she had ordered him to do. This testimony, however, seemed totally at variance with notes written by the woman right before she died. On her breast they found two of his visiting cards, with scribblings in her hand in Polish (quite illiterate, by the way). One of them read as follows: "To General Konovnitsyn, chairman of the directorate of the theater. My friend! I thank you for your noble friendship of many years standing . . . I send my final greeting and ask you to give my mother all of the proceeds from my final appearances."

The second one read, "This person was justified in killing me . . . Mother, poor unhappy Mother! I ask no forgiveness because I am dying not of my own volition . . . Mother! We'll see each other . . . we'll meet up there, on high . . . I feel that this is my final moment . . ."

On the same sort of visiting cards Sosnovskaya had written other last-minute notes. They were strewn about the ledge on the wall and were thoroughly torn into bits. When put together and pasted they read as follows:

"This person demands my own and his death . . . I won't get out of this alive."

"And so, my final hour has come . . . Lord, abandon me not . . . My final thoughts are with my mother and with my sacred art . . ."

"The abyss, the abyss! This person is my fate . . . Lord, save me, help me . . ."

And, finally, the most enigmatic of all: "*Quand même pour toujours . . .*"

All of these notes, the ones on the visiting cards that lay on her breast untorn and the ones on the ledge in bits and pieces, seemed to contradict Elagin's protestations. But that's just it: they only seemed to. Why were they not ripped up, the two cards on Sosnovskaya's breast, one of which contained the words so disastrous for Elagin: "I am dying not of my own volition"? Not only did Elagin not rip them up and not take them with him, but it was he himself (who else could have done it?) who placed them in the most conspicuous spot. Was it the haste of the moment that kept him from ripping them up? If he were in a hurry, he could, of course, have forgotten to do that. But how could he, in the haste of the moment, have placed on the dead woman's breast notes that so incriminated him? And was he really in such a hurry? No, he put the body of the dead woman in order, he covered her with the negligee, after having stanched her wound with a handkerchief. Then he tidied himself up, got dressed. No, in regard to that the prosecutor was right: there was nothing hasty about the way this was done.

4

The words of the prosecuting attorney: "There are two types of criminals. Firstly, accidental criminals, whose malfeasance is the fruit of provocation plus an unfortunate concatenation of circumstances, termed, in juridical parlance, temporary insanity. Secondly, criminals who commit the actions they commit pursuant upon evil and malice aforethought. These are the born enemies of society and the social order, these are the criminal fiends. So to which category does he belong, the man sitting before us at the dock, the accused? To the second, of course. He is, without question, a fiend, who committed this crime because his idle and profligate life had turned him into an animal."

This tirade was exceptionally strange (although it expressed virtually the consensus in our city about Elagin), and it was all the more strange because during the trial Elagin sat grief-stricken, perpetually propped up on one arm, shielding himself with his hand from the spectators and answering every question quietly, in jerky phrases, with a heartrending meekness. But then again, the prosecutor was right in a way, for at the dock sat a criminal who was in no way ordinary and who by no means had been in a state of "temporary insanity."

The prosecutor posed two questions. The first, naturally, was this: was the murder committed in a fit of passion, that is, was it provoked? The second was this: was there some secondary consideration that served as a stimulus to the murder? He answered each of these questions with absolute certainty: no, and again no.

"No," he said, in answer to the first question. "A fit of passion must be totally excluded, first of all because fits do not last for several hours. And then again, what could have thrown Elagin into such a state?"

In dealing with the second question the prosecutor proposed a whole series of ancillary possibilities, then proceeded to refute, or even ridicule, each of them.

"On that fateful day had Elagin drunk more than usual? No, he always drank a lot, and on that day no more than usual.

"Was and is the defendant in sound health? I concur with the opinion of the doctors who examined him: he is in perfect health, but he is certainly not in the habit of controlling his behavior.

"Could he have become unhinged by the impossibility of marriage between him and the woman he loved, assuming he did indeed love her? No, because we know with certainty that the defendant was not concerned about that, had made no effort whatsoever to arrange a marriage."

He continued. "Did the purported plans of Sosnovskaya to travel abroad bring about his derangement? No, because he had long known that such a trip was planned.

"But then, perhaps, it was the thought of breaking with Sosnovskaya, a split that would come consequent upon that trip? No again, because before that night they had spoken of separating a thousand times. And if all of this is so, then what, finally, led to his fit of passion? Was it the conversations about death? Was it the strange ambience of the room, its, so to speak, eerie mystery, its oppressiveness, along with the oppressiveness of that whole morbid and gruesome night? As for the conversations about death, by no means could they have been anything new for Elagin; he and his beloved had conversed incessantly on that topic, and he was, of course, long since fed up with it. And it is simply ludicrous to speak of the eeriness of the room. That quality was tempered in the extreme by elements of the utterly prosaic: the supper, the remains of that supper on the table, the bottles, and even, forgive me, the chamber pot. Elagin ate, drank, relieved himself as nature requires, went off a time or two to the other room to get some wine or a knife for sharpening pencils."

The prosecutor concluded as follows: "As to the contention that the murder committed by Elagin fulfilled the wishes of the dead woman, well, one need not discourse at length on that. In dealing with that issue we have Elagin's unsubstantiated assertions that Sosnovskaya herself asked him to kill her. And we have her note, which destroys his credibility absolutely: 'I am dying not of my own volition.'"

5

One could take issue with many particulars of the prosecutor's speech. "The defendant is a man in perfect health." But where is the line to be drawn between sound health and unsound, between normality and the abnormal? "He made no effort whatsoever to arrange a marriage." But, in the first place, he made no effort only because he was firmly convinced that it would be useless. And, in the second place, are love and marriage really so closely bound one unto the other? Would Elagin have calmed down and finally resolved definitively the drama of his love had he been joined in holy matrimony with Sosnovskaya? Isn't it common knowledge that any strong and far from ordinary love is characterized by a strange avoidance of marriage?

But all these objections, I repeat, relate to the particulars of his speech. In regard to basics the prosecutor was right: there was no fit of passion.

As he put it, "Medical expertise has reached the conclusion that Elagin was 'rather' in a calm than in an aberrant state of mind. And I submit to you that he was not only calm but amazingly calm. This is substantiated if we examine the tidiness of the scene of the crime, the room where Elagin remained long after that crime was committed. Then again, we have the testimony of a witness, Yaroshenko, who observed how calmly Elagin exited that apartment on Starogradskaya, and how scrupulously, in no hurry at all, he locked it with his key. And, finally, we have Elagin's conduct at Captain Likharev's place. What, for example, did Elagin say to Cornet Sevsky, who pleaded with him to 'come to his senses' and try to recall if Sosnovskaya had not really shot herself? He said, 'No, brother, I remember everything *perfectly well*!' And he proceeded to describe exactly how he had fired the pistol. The witness

Budberg was 'put off and shocked by Elagin's cold-blooded behavior: after his confession he sat nonchalantly drinking tea.' And the witness Fokht was shocked even more. 'Staff Captain, sir,' said Elagin to him ironically, 'Request permission to be excused today from training exercises.' 'That was so horrible,' said Fokht, 'that Sevsky just lost it and burst out crying.' True, there came a time when Elagin himself burst into tears. That was when the captain returned from the regimental commander's, where he had gone to get orders about what to do, when Elagin understood by the looks on the faces of Likharev and Fokht that he, in essence, was no longer an officer. That was the moment when he broke down and sobbed," concluded the prosecutor. "Then and only then!"

Of course, that last part is, once again, quite strange. Who is not aware of how often it happens, this sudden awakening from the stupor of grief or misfortune? It may be triggered by an absolutely trivial detail, something that catches the eye and abruptly reminds a person of all his previous happy life and all the hopelessness, the horror of his present situation. And, after all, the thing that reminded Elagin was not something trivial or incidental. After all, he had, in effect, been born an officer; ten generations of his forebears had served in the military. Now he was no longer an officer, but that was not the worst of it—he was no longer an officer because one whom he had truly loved more than himself was gone from this world, and he, he himself was responsible for that monstrous deed!

Yet then again, these, as well, are only discrete details. The main thing is that there really had been no "temporary insanity." But if not, then what happened? The prosecutor acknowledged that "in this dark business we must, first of all, concentrate on examining the personalities of Elagin and Sosnovskaya; we must clarify their relations." And he firmly proclaimed, "Two persons who had nothing in common between them came together."

But is that so? There's where the essence of the matter lies: is that really true?

6

About Elagin I should mention, first of all, that he is twenty-two—a fateful age, a terrible time, which defines a man for all of his future. Usually at that age one experiences what in medical terms is called sexual maturation and in life is called first love, which people view almost always in a totally poetic light and, in general, with extreme frivolity. That "first love" is often accompanied by dramas and tragedies, but absolutely nobody takes into account that this involves something much more profound, more complex than the agitation and sufferings usually termed adoration of the dear beloved. In the throes of first love one experiences, unawares, a fearful blossoming, a tortured discovery, a celebration of the first mass of sex. And so, were I Elagin's defense attorney, I would have asked the judges to take note of his age precisely from that point of view; I would also have asked them to note that before them sat one quite extraordinary in that regard. "A young hussar, a madcap type living at fever pitch," said the prosecutor, repeating the generally accepted opinion, and in support of his words he cited the account of a witness, the actor Lisovsky. About how once Elagin had come to the theater in the afternoon, when the actors were gathering together for rehearsal, and how, when she noticed him, Sosnovskaya skipped off to one side, hid behind Lisovsky, and said quickly, "Uncle, don't let him see me!"

"I shielded her," said Lisovsky, "and that little hussar, who was reeking of wine, suddenly stopped and went off the wall—he's standing there with his legs spread and he's looking around bewildered: where in the world did she get to?"

There you have it, exactly: off the wall, a madcap. But what drove him off the wall? Was it really his "idle and profligate life"?

Elagin came from a rich, aristocratic family. Very early he lost his mother (who was, please note, inclined to states of extreme exaltation). What separated him from his father, an austere and stern man, was, primarily, the fear he always lived with, growing up and even after he was grown. With cruel effrontery the prosecutor denigrated not only Elagin's moral fiber but also his physical appearance.

"That's how he was, gentlemen, our hero arrayed in his picturesque hussar's uniform. But look at him now. Now he has nothing to disguise him. Before us sits a short-of-stature, stooped young man with pale yellow mustache and an utterly featureless, niggling expression on his face; in his little black frock coat he's as far as one could imagine from Othello. This is a person, in my opinion, with acutely developed degenerative characteristics, at times meek to extremes—for example, in his relationship with his father—and at other times bold to extremes, unfazed by any and all obstacles; that is, when he felt free from his father's supervision and could hope to escape punishment."

Well, yes, in that rough characterization there is a lot of truth. But, first of all, in listening to it I wondered how you could take so lightly those horribly complex and tragic things often associated with people who have a sharply defined hereditary lineage. In the second place, even in what I accept as true there is only a small dose of genuine truth. Yes, Elagin had grown up in trepidation, fearing his father. But trepidation is not cowardliness, especially where parents are concerned, and furthermore, where the person in question has a redoubled sense of the legacy that binds him to his fathers, grandfathers, and great-grandfathers. Yes, Elagin's features are not the classical features of the hussar, but to me that proves the uniqueness of his nature. Take a closer look, I would tell the prosecutor, at that ginger-haired, stoop-shouldered man with the skinny legs, and you may be almost awestruck to see how far from "niggling" is the freckled face with small greenish eyes (which avoid meeting your gaze). Then again, take note of his degenerative stamina. On the day of the murder he was in training exercises—from early morning, of course—and at breakfast he drank six shots of vodka, a bottle of champagne, and two shots of cognac, and after all that he remained almost completely sober!

7

The generally accepted low opinion of Elagin is greatly at variance with the testimony of his many comrades in the regiment. All of them spoke of him in the highest of terms. Here, for example, is the opinion of the squadron commander: "When he joined our regiment Elagin established himself with remarkable ease among the officers; he was also always extraordinarily kind, solicitous, and just to the lower ranks. In my view the one thing that stood out was his instability, which manifested itself, however, not in some unpleasant way, but only in frequent and rapid transitions from merriness to melancholy, from the glib to the taciturn, from self-confidence to hopelessness about his merits and overall destiny."

Next comes the opinion of Captain Likharev: "Elagin was always a good and kindhearted comrade, only he had some strange things about him. First he would be modest and secretive in a shy way, then he would go off into some kind of recklessness and bravado. When he came to me and confessed to murdering Sosnovskaya, after Sevsky and Koshis had rushed off to Starogradskaya Street, he alternated between passionate weeping and sarcastic, raucous laughter. And when they arrested him and were taking him off to the lockup, he put on this bizarre smile and asked our advice about which tailor he should order his civilian clothing from."

Then Count Koshis: "In general, Elagin had a jolly and tenderhearted disposition, nervous, impressionable, even inclined to get ecstatic over things. The theater made a strong impression on him, as did music, which often left him in tears. And he himself had an unusual talent for music; he could play just about any instrument."

All of the other witnesses said approximately the same things.

"A person easily carried away, yet one who seemed always awaiting something genuine, something out of the ordinary."

"Most of the time at parties with comrades he was convivial and was something of a pest, in a nice sort of way. He would be the one most often to call for champagne and would then treat any and all to it. When he got involved with Sosnovskaya he desperately tried to hide his feelings for her from everyone, but he was much changed. Frequently pensive, sad, he would say that he was ever more convinced that suicide was the answer."

Such was the information about Elagin that came from people who lived with him in closest proximity. "So where," I was thinking as I sat in the courtroom, "where did the prosecutor get the dark colors he used to paint his portrait? Or did he have access to some other information?" No, he did not. So we must assume that the dark tones were inspired by his stereotype of how the "golden youth" behaved, or by what he had learned from the one letter at the disposal of the court, written to a friend in Kishinev. Here Elagin was totally straightforward in speaking of his life.

"I've reached the point, old friend, of being somehow indifferent; nothing matters whatsoever! Today may be fine, and I say thank God for that, but what happens tomorrow I don't give a damn; mornings are wiser than evenings, as they say. I've achieved a glorious reputation: number one drunk and fool in virtually the whole city."

This sort of self-evaluation seems to gibe with the eloquent opinions of the prosecutor, who said that "in the name of an animal-like pursuit of voluptuous pleasure, Elagin placed the woman who had given him everything before the judgment of society, and he deprived her not only of life but even of her final honor—a Christian burial." But does it really gibe? No, the prosecutor took from that letter only a few lines. Here's how the text reads in toto: "Dear Sergey, I received your letter and though I may be late in answering, what's to be done? When you read my letter you'll probably be thinking, 'What a scribble, as if a fly had fallen into an inkwell and then had himself a good crawl!' Well, handwriting, so they say, if not the mirror of one's character, is, to a certain degree, the expression of it. I'm still the same worthless layabout that I was before, or, if you like, even worse, since two years of independent life plus *a few other things* have left their mark. There have been, my friend, some developments that the wise King Solomon himself could not express! Therefore, don't be surprised if you hear one fine day that I put the big hurt on myself. I've reached the point, old friend, of being somehow indifferent; nothing matters whatsoever! Today may be fine, and I say thank God for that, but what happens tomorrow I don't give a damn; mornings are wiser than evenings, as they say. I've achieved a glorious reputation: number one drunk and fool in virtually the whole city. But, besides that, would you believe it? I sometimes feel within my soul such power and such torment, plus an attraction to all that is elevated and fine, in a word to the devil only knows what, that my chest aches with it. You'll tell me it's all a matter of youth. If so, then why do people the same age as me feel nothing of the sort? I've become horribly nervous. Sometimes in the winter, when it's cold and there's a snowstorm at night, I'll jump out of bed and go galloping on horseback through the streets, astonishing even the beat patrolmen, who are so jaded that nothing surprises them; and this, please note, is when I'm completely sober, not off on a spree. I want to capture some elusive motif, which I seem to have heard somewhere, but I can't get it back, just can't! All right, then, I'll confess to you. I've fallen in love, and not at all, not at all with the kind of woman the whole city is full of. But enough about that. Write me, please, you know the address. Remember how you said it should be? 'To Russia, Cornet Elagin.' "

It's amazing. How, after reading just this one letter, could anyone say that "two persons who had nothing in common between them came together!"

8

Sosnovskaya was, by nationality, pure Polish. She was older than Elagin, twenty-eight years old. Her father had been a minor government clerk who committed suicide when she was only three. After remaining a widow for a long time, her mother remarried, once again to a petty clerk, and she soon was widowed again. As you see, Sosnovskaya's family was quite pedestrian, so where did the strange spiritual qualities that distinguished her come from? And what about her passion for the stage, which, as we know, was manifested quite early? I would think, certainly, that these things had no basis in her family upbringing or in her education at the private boarding school where she studied. She was, by the way, quite a good student who read a lot in her spare time. While reading she would sometimes copy from the book ideas and sententiae that she liked—of course, as usual in such cases, she would link them somehow or other to herself. She would also jot down remarks, keeping something like a diary, if that's the right word for bits and pieces of paper, which she might not touch for whole months at a time and by which she vented her disjointed dreams and her views on life. Sometimes she just scribbled on the laundry bills or those from her seamstress, things of that sort. What, exactly, did she write?

" 'The best happiness is not to be born; second best is to return in short order to nonbeing.' A marvelous thought!"

"Worldly life is boring, deadly boring; my soul aspires to something extraordinary . . ."

"'People understand only those sufferings by which they die.' Musset."

"No, I'll never be married. That's what they all say, but I swear it by God and by Death."

"It's either love or death. But where in the universe is one to be found whom I can love? There is no such one, there cannot be! But how can I die when I adore life like a woman possessed?"

"There's nothing in heaven, nothing on earth, more awesome, more enticing and puzzling than love."

"Mother says, for example, that I should marry for money. Me, me, for money! What a celestial word it is, 'love,' how much hell and charm there is in it, although I myself have never loved!"

"All the world is looking at me with its millions of carnivorous eyes, the way it was when I was small, at the menagerie."

"'Being a human is not worth it. Or being an angel. Because even the angels murmured against God and rose up against Him. What's worth being is a God or a nonentity.' Krasinski."

"'Who can boast that he has delved into her soul, when she directs all her life's force toward barring the depths of her soul?' Musset."

When she completed her course at the boarding school, Sosnovskaya immediately announced to her mother that she intended to devote herself to art. At the beginning Mother, a devout Catholic, was of course dead set against this plan to become an actress. Her daughter, however, was certainly not one to defer to anyone else's wishes. Besides that, even earlier she had managed to convince her mother that by no means was her life, the life of Maria Sosnovskaya, to be a mundane and inglorious affair.

At about age eighteen she went off to Lvov and quickly realized her dreams: she had no difficulty whatsoever getting onstage and soon became a standout. Shortly after that she acquired such renown, both with the audience and in the theatrical world, that in her third year of work she was invited to perform in our city. But then, even in Lvov, she was scribbling in her notebook much the same things as before.

"'Everyone talks about her, they cry and laugh over her, but who really knows her?' Musset."

"If not for Mother I would kill myself. That is my constant desire."

"Whenever I drive somewhere out of the city, when I see the sky, so lovely and boundless, I don't know what's going on with me. I want to scream, sing, declaim, weep . . . to love and die . . ."

"I'll arrange a lovely death for myself. I'll rent a little room, have it draped in funereal fabrics. Music must be playing on the other side of the wall, and I'll lie down in a modest white dress, envelop myself in a myriad of flowers, and die of their aroma. Oh, how marvelous that will be!"

And still more.

"They all, all of them demand my body and not my soul."

"If I were rich I would circumnavigate the globe and would make love all over the world."

"'Does a person know what he wants? Is he sure of what he is thinking?' Krasinski."

And, finally: "That scoundrel!"

And who was the scoundrel, the man who did to her what, of course, we can easily guess? All we know is that he existed and had to exist. "Even back in Lvov," said the witness Zauze, a colleague of Sosnovskaya's there, "she didn't dress for her performances but rather undressed. At home she received all of her acquaintances and suitors in a transparent peignoir, with legs bare. The beauty of those legs had everyone, especially the newcomers, rapt with ecstasy. And she would say, 'Don't be surprised, they're my very own,' and would lift her hem to show her legs above the knee. In those days she repeated to me endlessly—often in tears—that no one deserved her love and that her only hope lay in death."

This was when the "scoundrel" appeared, the man she traveled with to Constantinople, Venice, Paris, the one she visited in Kraków and Berlin. He was some Galician landowner, a man of immense wealth. The witness Volsky, who had known Sosnovskaya since childhood, spoke of him.

"I always considered her a woman of very low morals. She didn't know how to conduct herself as behooves an actress and a resident of our region. She loved only money, money and men. It was cynical, when she was still barely more than a little girl, the way she sold herself to that Galician warthog!"

Sosnovskaya told Elagin about that very "warthog" in the conversation they had prior to her death. That was when she complained to him, speaking in a slow and haphazard way, "I grew up alone, nobody watched out for me. In my family, and in all the world too, I was alien to everyone. A certain woman—and may all of her offspring be damned!—introduced me to debauchery, me, a pure trusting girl. And in Lvov I truly loved one person like a father, and he turned out to be such a scoundrel, so despicable that I'm horrified even to think of him now! He got me taking hashish, drinking wine, he took me to Constantinople, where he maintained an entire harem. He lay there in his harem looking at his naked slave girls, and he forced me to undress too, vile, base creature that he was."

9

After she arrived in our city Sosnovskaya soon became the talk of the town.

"Even back in Lvov," testified the witness Meshkov, "she would often suggest to men that they die in exchange for one night with her, and she kept repeating that she was looking for a heart capable of loving. She went about persistently searching for that loving heart, and she would say repeatedly, 'My main goal is to live and take advantage of life. The taster must try all varieties of wines and not become intoxicated with one. That should be a woman's attitude toward men.'"

"And it's just what she did," said Meshkov. "I'm not sure she tried every wine, but I do know that she surrounded herself with a huge assortment of brands. But then again, maybe she did it primarily to create a furor around herself and get a group of claqueurs at the theater. 'Money,' she would say, 'money means nothing. I'm greedy, sometimes as miserly as the world's last Philistine, but for some reason I don't think about money. The main thing is fame, with that everything else will come.' The only reason she kept harping constantly about death was, in my opinion, the same: to get people talking about her."

In our city she continued behaving the same way she had in Lvov, and she wrote down almost exactly the same thoughts.

"Lord, what languishment, what tedium! If only we could have an earthquake or an eclipse!"

"One evening I was in the cemetery. It was so lovely there! It seemed to me . . . but no, I cannot describe that feeling. I wanted to stay there all night, to declaim my lines over the graves, and to die of enervation. On the following day I performed so wonderfully, like never before."

And again: "Yesterday I went to the cemetery at ten in the evening. What an onerous spectacle! The moon bathed gravestones and crosses in its rays. It seemed I was surrounded by thousands of corpses. Yet I felt so happy, joyous! It was so fine for me there."

After she met Elagin he once told her that a sergeant major in the regiment had died, and she demanded that he take her to the chapel where the dead body lay. Later on she wrote that the look of the chapel and the body in the moonlight made a "strikingly ecstatic impression" on her.

By that time her thirst for fame and attention had become simply frenetic. Yes, she was extremely good-looking. Her beauty was not especially original; nonetheless she had some special, rare charm that was out of the ordinary, a blend of the simple-hearted and ingenuous with an animal cunning, and, in addition, a constant mix of playfulness with sincerity. Take a look at her portraits, note the pose so characteristic of her—the way she scowls up at you from slightly beneath her brows, with those lips that are always barely parted, the somber look, a look that in most pictures is endearing, that beckons and makes a promise, as if agreeing to some secret and unseemly thing. And she knew how to take advantage of her beauty. Onstage she had a variety of ways of making herself appealing, a knack for letting all her charms flourish. It was not only the sound of her voice and vivaciousness of her movements, the laughter or the tears; it was also because most of the time she played roles that let her display her body. Meanwhile, at home she would don seductive Oriental and Greek garments to receive her multitude of guests. She set aside one of her rooms, as she expressed it, for the special purpose of suicide—there she had revolvers, daggers and sabres in the form of scythes or spiraling scimitars, and vials with all kinds of poisons—and she made death the constant, the favorite subject of all conversations. But that wasn't all—frequently, while expatiating upon various methods of depriving herself of life, she would suddenly seize a loaded pistol from where it hung on the wall, cock it, and pressing the barrel to her temple, she would say, "Kiss me, quickly, or I'll fire!" Either that or she would put a strychnine tablet in her mouth, then declare that if her guest did not get down on his knees and kiss her bare foot, she would swallow it. And she did all that and said all that in such a way that the guest would go pale with fear, and later he would depart twice as enraptured with her as before. He would spread throughout the city the very gossip that so titillated everyone and that she herself so wanted spread.

"She just almost never was her real self," testified at the trial the witness Zalessky, who had known her well for a long time. "Playing around, teasing, these were the things she constantly did. Driving a person mad with her tender, enigmatic looks, smiles so full of meaning, or the sad sigh of a defenseless child—she was an expert at all of that. She behaved the same way with Elagin. She would get him all fired up and then dash his hopes with cold water. Did she want to die? Well, she had a carnivorous love for life, and an extraordinary fear of death. There was in her nature, above all, a great deal of gaiety and the buoyancy of life. I recall how once Elagin sent her a gift—the pelt of a polar bear. At that moment she was entertaining a crowd of guests, and she forgot them all, she was so ecstatic over that bearskin. She threw it down on the floor, and paying no attention to anyone, she started doing somersaults on it, tossing off moves that any acrobat would have envied. What a charming woman she was!"

But then, that same Zalessky told about how she suffered from fits of depression and despair. The doctor Seroshevsky, who had known her for ten years and treated her even before she left for Lvov—back when her consumption was in its early stages—also testified that recently she had been so tormented by an acute nervous disorder, by memory loss and hallucinations, that he feared for her ability to think rationally. She was treated for that same disorder by Dr. Schumacher, to whom she kept insisting that she would not die a natural death (and from whom she once borrowed two volumes of Schopenhauer, "which she read quite attentively, and most surprising of all, which she comprehended extremely well, as it turned out later"). And another doctor, Nedzelsky, testified as follows: "She was a strange woman! Most of the time when she was entertaining guests she was high-spirited and coquettish. But sometimes, for no particular reason, she would suddenly fall silent, roll back her eyes, and drop her head down on the desk. Or else she might start throwing things, smashing tumblers and glasses on the floor. When that happened you had to say to her quickly, 'All right, all right then, break some more,' and immediately she would stop."

It was this "strange and charming woman" that, finally, Cornet Aleksandr Mikhailovich Elagin was to meet.

10

How did that meeting come about? How did the intimacy between them originate, and what were their feelings for each other, their relations? Elagin himself spoke of this on two occasions: first briefly and in a fragmentary way, to the police investigator, a few hours after the murder; the second time during questioning three weeks after the initial interrogation.

"Yes," he said, "I am guilty of depriving Sosnovskaya of her life, *but it was what she herself wanted.*

"I met her a year and a half ago, at the box office of the theater, through Lieutenant Budberg. I fell deeply in love with her, and I thought she shared my feelings. But I wasn't always sure of that. Sometimes it seemed she loved me even more than I loved her, but sometimes it was just the opposite. Besides that, she was constantly surrounded by admirers, she would flirt around, and I was tormented by ferocious jealousy. Nonetheless, that in the end was not the basis for our tragic situation; it was something else, something I can't express . . . At any rate, I swear that I didn't kill her because of jealousy.

"As I said, I met her last February at the theater, by the box office. I made a call on her then, but until October I never visited her more than twice a month, and always in the daytime. In October I confessed my love for her, and she allowed me to kiss her. A week after that she and I went with my comrade Voloshin to dine at a suburban restaurant. We, just the two of us, were returning from there, and although she was merry, affectionate, and slightly tipsy, I felt so timid with her that I was afraid to kiss her hand. Then one time she asked to borrow Pushkin's *Egyptian Nights,* and after she read it she said, 'Well, could you bring yourself to give your life for one night with the woman you loved?' When I quickly answered yes, she smiled mysteriously. I already loved her very much, and I saw clearly and felt that this would be a fateful love for me. As we became closer I got bolder, I started speaking to her of my love more and more often, telling her I felt that this was killing me . . . if only because Father would never allow me to marry her; and living with me out of marriage would be impossible for her, an actress whom the Polish public would not forgive an open, illicit liaison with a Russian officer. And she complained of her fate as well, of her strange soul. She avoided responding to my protestations of love, to my unvoiced question: did she love me too? But she seemed to leave me a certain hope by those complaints, their intimate tone.

"Then, from January of this year, I began visiting her every day. I sent bouquets to the theater, flowers to her apartment, gave her gifts. Two mandolins, the pelt of a polar bear, a signet ring, and a diamond bracelet. I decided to give her a brooch in the shape of a skull. She adored things emblematic of death, and she had often said she wanted me to give her just such a brooch, with an inscription in French: *QUAND MÊME POUR TOUJOURS!*

"On March 26 of this year I received an invitation to dine with her. After the meal she gave herself to me for the first time . . . in the room that she called the Japanese room. We had our subsequent meetings in that same room; she would send her maidservant off to sleep after dinner. Afterwards she gave me a key to her bedroom, which had an outside door giving directly onto the stairwell . . . In memory of March 26 we ordered wedding rings, which had, as she stipulated, etchings on the inside of them—our initials and the date of our first intimacy.

"On one of our excursions to a village outside of town we went up to a cross beside a Catholic church, and I swore my eternal love before that cross, said that in the eyes of God she was my wife, and I would be faithful to her until death. She stood there sad and pensive, saying nothing. Then, in a simple, firm voice she said, 'I love you too. *Quand même pour toujours!*'

"Once in early May, when I was dining with her, she took some opium in powder form and said, 'How easy it is to die! All you have to do is sprinkle a little bit in, and it's ready!' Then she sprinkled the powder into a champagne glass and put it to her lips. I grabbed it out of her hands, threw the wine into the fireplace, and broke the glass on my spur. The next day she said to me, 'Instead of a tragedy yesterday it turned out to be a comedy!' Then she added, 'What am I going to do? I can't bring myself to it, and you can't either, you don't dare . . . How shameful!'

"After that we started seeing one another less frequently. She said she could no longer receive me at home in the evenings. Why? I was going out of my mind, suffering terribly. And, besides that, she changed the way she treated me, became cold and sarcastic, sometimes received me as if we were barely acquainted, and she would mock me for my lack of character. But then suddenly everything changed again. She started driving around to pick me up for promenades, acting playful with me—maybe because I had begun mastering a cold reserve in my behavior toward her. Finally, she told me to rent a separate apartment for our liaisons, but she wanted one on a secluded street, in some sort of gloomy old building. She wanted it to be extremely dark, and she would tell me how to furnish it. Well, you know exactly how that apartment was decorated.

"And so, on the sixteenth of June I went to her place at four o'clock, told her the apartment was ready, and gave her one of the keys. She flashed me a smile and returned the key, saying, 'We'll talk about that later.' Just then the doorbell rang and a certain Shkliarevich came in. I quickly put the key in my pocket and started talking about trifling things. But as he and I were leaving together she said loudly to him in the anteroom, 'Come on Monday.' Then she whispered to me, 'Come tomorrow, at four,' and whispered it in such a tone that it made my head spin.

"The next day I arrived at four sharp, but to my astonishment the cook, who opened the door, informed me that Sosnovskaya could not receive me, and handed a letter to me! In it she wrote that she felt unwell, that she was going to see her mother at the dacha, that 'it's too late now.' Beside myself, I walked into the first confectionary shop I came to and wrote her an awful letter, asking her to explain what she meant by that word 'late,' and then I sent a messenger to deliver the letter. But he brought it back—as it turned out she was not at home. After that I decided she must want to break things off with me for good, and when I got home I wrote her another letter, in which I rebuked her sharply for all the games she had played with me. I asked her to return the wedding ring, which was probably just a joke to her, while to me it was the most precious thing on earth, something that would go with me to my grave. By that I meant that all was finished between us and I wanted her to know that nothing was left for me but death. Along with the letter I returned her portrait and all of her letters and personal items that I had: gloves, hairpins, hat. The orderly came back and said that she was not at home but that he had left the letter and the parcel with the porter.

"In the evening I went to the circus, ran into Shkliarevich there, a man I didn't know well, but dreading being alone, I drank champagne with him. Suddenly he said, 'Listen, I can see what you're going through and I know the reason why. Believe me, she's not worth it. All of us have been through this, she's led us all by the nose.' I felt like grabbing my sword and cutting his head off, but I was in such a state that I did nothing of the sort. I didn't even break off the conversation, I was secretly glad to have him with me, happy there was at least someone to get some sympathy from. I don't know what happened to me. Of course, I didn't say a word in response to that, didn't mention a thing about Sosnovskaya, but I drove him to Starogradskaya Street and showed him the apartment that I had so lovingly selected for our liaisons. I was really bitter, so ashamed that I was made such a fool over that apartment business.

"From there I told the cabman to take us to the Nevyarovsky Restaurant and make it fast. A light rain was falling, the cab was racing along, and even the rain and the lights up ahead were painful and scary for me. At one in the morning I returned home with Shkliarevich from the restaurant, and I had already begun undressing when suddenly the orderly brought me a note. She was waiting for me out on the street, asking me to come down immediately. She had arrived in a carriage with her maid; she told me she was so worried about me that she couldn't stand to come alone, so she brought the maid. I told my orderly to take the maid home, I got in the carriage with her, and we drove over to Starogradskaya. On the way I kept rebuking her, told her she had been playing around with me. She said nothing, just kept looking straight ahead, occasionally wiping away tears. But then she did seem calm, and since her emotional state almost always influenced mine, I started calming down too. When we arrived she brightened up altogether—because she liked the apartment so much. I took her hand, begged forgiveness for all my accusations, asked her to return the portrait, that is, the one that I had sent back to her when I was irritated. We often had arguments, and in the end I always felt guilty and always asked forgiveness. At three in the morning I drove her home. On the way our conversation became strained again. She sat looking straight ahead, I couldn't see her face, I could only smell her perfume and hear the icy, spiteful tone of voice. 'You're no man,' she said. 'You have no character whatsoever. I can enrage you or calm you down whenever I please. If I were a man I would grab a woman like me and cut her up into little pieces!' Then I shouted, 'In that case take your ring back!' and I forced it onto her finger. She turned to me with a bewildered smile and said, 'Come tomorrow.' I answered that on no account would I come. She started pleading with me in an awkward, timid way, saying, 'No, you'll come, you'll be there . . . at Starogradskaya.' Then she added resolutely, 'No, I beg you to come, I'll soon be going abroad, I want to see you for the last time; the main thing is I need to say one very important thing to you.' Then she started crying again and added, 'It just amazes me, you say you love me, that you can't live without me, you'll shoot yourself, and then you don't want to see me for the last time.' Trying to control myself, I said if that was how it was, I would let her know tomorrow what time I would be free. As we said good-bye at the entry to her courtyard, in the rain, my heart was breaking with pity and love for her. When I returned home I was surprised and disgusted to find Shkliarevich sleeping at my place.

"On Monday morning, the eighteenth of June, I sent her a note saying I would be free from twelve o'clock on. She answered, 'At six, come to Starogradskaya.'"

II

Antonina Kovanko, Sosnovskaya's maid, along with her cook, Wanda Linevich, testified that on Saturday the sixteenth Sosnovskaya had been lighting a spirit lamp so she could curl the hair of her bangs. She absentmindedly dropped the match on the hem of her flimsy peignoir, it caught fire, and she started screaming wildly, tearing it off and getting it away from her body. She was so thoroughly terrified that she got in bed, sent for the doctor, and kept repeating, "There, now you'll see; that forebodes some great misfortune."

The dear unhappy woman! It's extraordinary how touched and distressed I am by that story of the peignoir and her childlike horror. In some amazing way this trifling detail ties together and illumines all of the fragmentary and contradictory things that we always heard about her, things that, since her death, we've heard everywhere, out in public and in the courtroom. Primarily, it gives me an amazingly vivid sense of the true Sosnovskaya, whom almost no one really understood or intuited—just as no one knew Elagin—in spite of all the interest she aroused, all their wanting to understand her, to solve her riddle, all the gossip circulating perpetually for the past year.

So I'll say it one more time: how incredibly mediocre are the judgments of man! It's the same old story whenever people have to deal with an event of even the most minor significance: they look but don't see, they listen but don't hear. At odds with everything obvious, as if on purpose, they must needs distort to the utmost both Elagin and Sosnovskaya and everything that went on between them! As if everybody had agreed to speak nothing except banal vulgarities: "What's so hard to figure out? He's a hussar officer, jealous and drunken, living in the fast lane. She's an actress, all tangled up in her haphazard, immoral style of life.

"Private quarters, wine, kept women, debauchery," they said about him. "All the loftier sentiments deafened by the rattle of his saber."

Loftier sentiments, wine? But what does wine mean to a man like Elagin? "I sometimes feel such torment, plus an attraction to all that is elevated and fine, in a word to the devil only knows what, that my chest aches with it . . . I want to capture some elusive motif, which I seem to have heard somewhere, but I can't get it back, just can't!" But then, with alcohol one breathes easier, expands one's horizons, with alcohol that elusive melody sounds clearer and closer. And let's face facts: alcohol, and music, and love are all deceptive in the end; they only exacerbate that inexpressible something, that sense of the world and of life already too acute and pronounced.

"She didn't love him," they said about her. "She was just scared of him—because he was constantly threatening to kill himself; that is, he would not only bring her the heartbreak of his death, but he would also make her the heroine of a tremendous scandal. There is testimony that she experienced 'even a certain loathing' for him. Did she belong to him all the same? But does 'belonging' really change anything? Many were those she belonged to! But Elagin wanted to transform into a drama one of those innumerable romantic comedies she loved to act in."

And still more: "She was horrified by the awful extremes of jealousy ever more characteristic of his behavior. Once, when he was at her place, the actor Strakun dropped in for a visit. At first Elagin just sat there calmly, but he was turning pale with jealousy. Suddenly he got up and walked out quickly, into the next room. She rushed after him, and when she saw the revolver in his hands she fell down on her knees in front of him, begging him to have mercy on himself and her. Apparently the playing out of such scenes was far from rare. So isn't it understandable, her decision, finally, to rid herself of him, to depart on a trip abroad, for which she had made all preparations on the eve of her death? He brought her the key to the apartment on Starogradskaya, the apartment which she had, obviously, thought up only as a pretext not to receive him at home before her departure. She did not take that key. He began insisting she take it. She announced to him, 'It's too late now,' meaning there's no point in my taking it now, I'm leaving. But he dashed off such a letter to her that, upon receiving it, she scampered over to his place in the middle of the night, beside herself, afraid she would find him already dead."

Let's assume this is all true (although every one of these suppositions is totally contradicted by Elagin's confession). Then why, all the same, was Elagin so "terribly" and "excessively" jealous and why did he want to transform the comedy into a drama? What did he need that for? Why didn't he simply shoot her in one of his fits of jealousy? Why was there "no evidence of a struggle between the murderer and his victim"? And then: "She sometimes felt even a certain loathing for him. In the presence of outsiders she would make fun of him, give him insulting nicknames. She called him, for example, Bowlegged Pup." But, my Lord, that captures the very essence of Sosnovskaya! In the notes she made while still back in Lvov there is one about loathing somebody: "So he still loves me! And I? What do I feel for him? Both love and loathing!" Did she used to insult Elagin? Yes. Once when they were having an argument—which they had with extreme regularity—she called for the maid and threw her wedding ring down on the floor, shouting, "Take it, you can have this disgusting thing!"

But what had she done prior to that? She had run into the kitchen and said to the maid, "I'm going to call for you in just a minute, and I'll throw this ring down on the floor and say you can have it. But don't forget—this is just a comedy. You must give it back to me this very day, because with this ring I am betrothed to him, to that fool, and it's dearer to me than anything on earth."

There was good reason why she was called a woman "of easy virtue," and good reason why the Catholic Church refused her a Christian burial, "as befitting a person of bad and dissolute character." She belonged in toto to that feminine type that includes both professional prostitutes and votaries of free love. But what type of woman is that? One with an extremely pronounced and insatiable, unslaked sexuality. It just cannot be satisfied. For what reason? But how would I know for what reason? And look what always happens. Men of that terribly complex and profoundly interesting type, which is (to one degree or another) atavistic, those who in their very essence are acutely sensual, not only with regard to women but also in everything about their view of the world, these men, with all the force of body and spirit, are attracted to just that type of woman. Consequently they play the hero role in huge numbers of romantic dramas and tragedies. Why? Due to their lack of taste, their dissolute nature, or simply because such women are accessible? Of course not, no, a thousand times no. If for no other reason than this: because such men can see and sense perfectly well how agonizing a liaison, an intimacy with such women always is, how truly horrendous, even fatal it can be. They sense that, they see it, they know, and all the same they are drawn most frequently to just that sort of woman—relentlessly drawn to their torment and even death. Why?

Of course she was only acting out a comedy when she wrote her little notes in advance of dying, as if hypnotizing herself into believing her final hour was indeed at hand. And absolutely nothing to the contrary is suggested by her diaries—which, by the way, are banal and naive in the extreme—or by her visits to cemeteries.

No one denies the naivety of her diaries or the theatricality of her graveyard visits, just as no one denies that she loved to hint at her resemblance to Maria Bashkirtseva or Marie Vetsera. But why, nonetheless, did she select that sort of diary and not some other, and why did she feel an affinity for precisely those women? She had everything: beauty, youth, fame, money, hundreds of admirers, and she used all of those things passionately, rapturously. But she lived her life in perpetual languishing, thirsting incessantly to get away from this repellent earthly world, where everything is always not quite it, just not quite right. How did it come to this? Because she playacted her way into behaving like that. But why did she choose to play out precisely this role and not some other? Because all of this is typical of women who dedicate themselves, as they put it, to art? But why is it typical? Why?

12

On Sunday morning the little bell on her bedside table rang out sometime after seven; she had awoken and was calling for her maid much earlier than usual. The maid brought in a tray with a cup of hot chocolate and pulled back the blinds. Sitting on the bed, she followed her movements, scowling up, as was her habit, from beneath her brows, pensively and absentmindedly with lips half parted. Then she said, "You know, Tonya, I went to sleep yesterday right after the doctor left. My oh my, Mother of God, how scared I was! But just as soon as he got here I felt so nice and calm. In the night I woke up, got on my knees in the bed, and prayed for a solid hour. Just think how I would have looked if I was burned all over! With my eyes burst and my lips puffed out. I would have been a frightful sight. They'd have bits of cotton sticking all over my face."

She didn't reach for the chocolate for a long time, kept sitting there thinking of something. Then she drank the chocolate, took a bath, and sat in her bathrobe at the small desk, hair let down, writing letters on stationery with a funereal border around the edges; she had ordered that stationery long ago. After dressing and having breakfast, she drove away. She went to her mother's dacha and returned from there only sometime after eleven that evening, along with the actor Strakun, who "was always like one of the family to her."

"They were both of them in a happy mood when they arrived," said the maid. "After I let them into the anteroom, right away I called her off to one side and gave her the letter, with the things

Elagin had sent while she was away. She whispered to me, 'Hide these things quick; don't let Strakun see them!' She was in a rush to open the letter, and when she read it she went suddenly pale, lost her composure, and cried out, paying no attention now to Strakun, who was sitting in the drawing room: 'For God's sake, run for all you're worth and find a cab!' I ran for a carriage and found one right by the entryway. We galloped off at full speed, and on the way she kept crossing herself and saying, 'Oh my, Mother of God, if only we find him alive!' "

On Monday she went out early in the morning to the bathhouses on the river. That day Strakun had dinner at her place, along with an Englishwoman (who came almost every day to give English lessons but almost never gave any). After they ate the Englishwoman left, and Strakun stayed for about another hour and a half. He lay smoking on the divan, with his head on the lap of the hostess, who "was wearing just a dressing gown and Japanese slippers on her bare feet." Finally Strakun left, and in saying good-bye to him she asked him to come back "this very evening at ten o'clock."

"Won't that be a bit too often?" said Strakun, laughing as he searched about for his walking stick in the anteroom.

"Oh, no, please!" she said. "But if I'm not here, don't get angry with me, Lucian."

After that she spent a long time burning some sort of letters and papers in the fireplace. She was humming, joking around with her maid.

"I'll burn everything now, since I didn't burn up myself! But it would have been a good thing, had I burned! Only all of me, though, right down to the ashes."

Then she said, "Tell Wanda to have supper ready for ten o'clock in the evening. I'm going out now."

She left between five and six, taking with her "something wrapped in paper, resembling a gun."

She set off for Starogradskaya Street, but on the way she dropped in on the seamstress Leshinskaya, who was altering the peignoir that had caught fire on Saturday, shortening it. In Leshinskaya's words, "she was in a nice, happy frame of mind." After examining the peignoir and wrapping it up in paper, along with the package she had brought from home, she sat for a long time in the workshop amidst all the girls who sewed things there, and she kept saying, "Oh my, Mother of God, I'm so late, it's time for me to go, my little angels!" But she kept on sitting there. Finally she arose with an air of resolution and a sigh, but she said gaily, "Farewell, Pani Leshinskaya. Farewell, my little sisters, my angels, thank you for blathering on with me. It's so pleasant to sit with this dear little group of women; otherwise I'm all the time with men, only with men!"

And nodding from the threshold, smiling once more, she left.

Why did she take a revolver with her? The gun belonged to Elagin, but she kept it at her place, afraid he would shoot himself. "She intended to return it to its owner now, because in a few days she was leaving for a long stay abroad," said the prosecutor, and he added, "Thus she set off for the assignation that was to prove her undoing, but as yet she had no inkling that this would be a fatal assignation. At seven o'clock she arrived at building number fourteen Starogradskaya, apartment one. And so the door to that apartment closed and was opened once more only on the morning of June 19. What occurred there in the night? There is no one to tell us about that except Elagin. Let us listen to his words once again."

13

So one more time all of us, the whole packed courtroom, sat in absolute silence and heard those pages from the official indictment, which the prosecutor deemed necessary to read in order to refresh our memory of the case, and with which Elagin's account concluded.

"On Monday, June 18, I sent her a note, saying I was free from twelve o'clock on. She answered, 'At six, Starogradskaya.'

"At a quarter to six I was there, bringing with me some snacks, two bottles of champagne, two bottles of stout, two glasses, and a vial of eau de cologne. But I had to wait for a long time—she didn't get there until seven.

"After she arrived she kissed me in a distracted way, went into the next room, and threw the package she had brought with her on the divan. 'Leave me,' she said in French; 'I want to get undressed.' I went out and once again I sat alone for a long time. I was completely sober and terribly depressed, feeling vaguely that all had ended or was ending. By the way, even the atmosphere inside that place was weird. I sat with the light on as if it were night, and meanwhile I knew and felt that outside, beyond the walls of those desolate and dark rooms it was still daylight, a lovely summer's evening . . . She didn't call out to me for ages, I don't know what she was doing. On the other side of that door it was totally quiet. At last she shouted, 'Come in, it's okay now.'

"She was lying on the divan, wearing only a peignoir, with bare legs, no stockings or slippers, and she said nothing, just scowled up at the ceiling, at the lamp there. The package she had brought was opened, and I could see my revolver. 'But why did you bring that with you?' I asked. She didn't answer at once. 'Just because . . . I'm leaving, you know . . . Better for you to keep it here and not at home.' A terrible thought flashed through my mind: 'No, it's not that simple!' But I didn't say anything.

"After that we began quite a lengthy, strained and cold conversation. I was terribly agitated, but hiding it—I kept wanting to get a grip on something, expecting that at any moment I would gather my thoughts and tell her, finally, something important and decisive.

After all, I understood that this was, perhaps, our last meeting, or, at any rate, that the separation would be long. But I couldn't come up with anything, I felt totally powerless. She said, 'Smoke if you want to.' 'But you don't like that,' I answered. 'No, it's all the same *now*,' she said. 'And give me some champagne.' I rejoiced at that as if it were my salvation. In a few minutes we finished off the whole bottle. I sat down beside her and began kissing her hands, saying that I would not survive her departure. She ruffled my hair and said vacantly, 'Yes, yes . . . What a misfortune that I cannot be your wife . . . Everything and everyone is against us, maybe only God is on our side. I love your soul, I love your *fantasies*.' What she meant to express by that last word I do not know. I glanced up, at the umbrella drapery, and I said, 'Look, you and I are here together as if in a crypt. And how quiet it is!' In response she just smiled sadly.

"At about ten she said she wanted to eat. We went into the front room. But she ate very little, and so did I—most of all we drank. Suddenly she glanced at the snacks I had brought and exclaimed, 'Silly, *błazen,* you bought so much again! Next time don't you dare do that.' 'But now when will it be, that next time?' I asked. She gave me a strange look, then dropped her head and rolled her eyes up. 'Jesus, Mary,' she whispered. 'What can we do? Oh my, I want you madly! Come on, quick.'

"Sometime later I looked at the clock, and it was already after one. 'My, how late,' she said. 'I have to go home this very minute.' But she made no move to get up and then she added, 'You know, I have this feeling that I must leave as soon as possible, but I can't budge from the spot. I feel that I'll never get out of here. You are my fate, my destiny, the will of God.' I couldn't understand that either. Apparently she was trying to say something like what she wrote later on: 'I die not of my own volition.' You may think that in using that sentence she expressed her defenselessness before me, but in my opinion she meant something else: that our unfortunate meeting was fate, God's will, that she was dying not of her own will, but God's. But then, I didn't place any particular importance on her words at the time; I was long accustomed to her eccentricities. Then she said abruptly, 'Do you have a pencil?' I was amazed again; why would she need a pencil? But I hastened to hand her one; I had it in my notebook. She also asked me to give her a visiting card. When she started writing something on it, I said, 'But listen, isn't it awkward, writing notes on my visiting card?' She answered, 'No, it's nothing, just some things I'm jotting down for myself. Let me think for a bit and doze.' Then she put that card, with scribblings all over it, on her breast, and she closed her eyes. It became so quiet that I fell into a kind of stupor.

"That must have gone on for at least a half hour. Suddenly she opened her eyes and said coldly, 'I forgot—I came to return your ring. You yourself wanted to finish it all yesterday.' And raising up a bit, she tossed the ring on the ledge by the wall. 'You mean you really love me?' she almost screamed. 'I don't understand how you could calmly suggest that I go on living! I'm a woman, I can't make decisions. I'm not afraid of death—I'm afraid of suffering, but with one shot you could finish me off, and then yourself.' That's when even more, with a terrible clarity, I understood all the horror of our situation, the dead end we were in, and I knew that it must, at last, be somehow resolved. But to kill her, no, I felt that was something I couldn't do. I was feeling something else—the decisive moment had come for me. I took the revolver and cocked it. 'What? Only yourself?' she exclaimed, jumping up. 'No, I swear by Jesus, that will never be!' And she snatched the gun away from me.

"Then once again the agonizing silence set in. I sat, she lay there, neither of us moved. Suddenly she said something to herself, something unclear, in Polish, and then to me, 'Give me my ring.' I passed it to her. 'Yours too!' she said. I quickly gave her mine as well. She put her ring on her finger, told me to put mine on and started talking. 'I have always loved you and I love you now. I drove you out of your mind and tormented you, but that's just the way I am and such is our destiny. Give me my skirt and bring some stout.' I passed her the skirt and went for the stout, and when I returned I saw there was a vial of opium beside her. 'Listen,' she said firmly, 'Now comes the end to all the comedies. Can you live without me?' I answered that I could not. 'Yes,' she said, 'I've taken all of your soul, all of your thoughts. You won't hesitate to kill yourself? If that's so, then take me with you. I can't live without you either. And if you kill me you'll die with the knowledge that finally I belong to you totally—and for all time. But now listen to the story of my life.' And she lay down again, kept silent for a moment, calming down, and then began slowly recounting to me all of her life, from childhood on . . . I recall almost nothing of that account."

14

"And then again, I don't recall which of us started writing first. I broke the pencil in half . . . We started writing and wrote all the time without speaking. I wrote, I think, first of all to my father. You may ask why I rebuked him for 'not wanting me to be happy,' when I had never tried a single time to get his permission to marry her. I don't know. All the same, he never would have consented . . . Then I wrote to my comrades in the regiment, bidding farewell to them. And then who else? I wrote to the regimental commander, asking him to arrange a decent burial for me. You say, 'Does that mean I was certain I would commit suicide?' Of course. But then, how was it that I didn't do it after all? I don't know.

"She, I recall, was writing slowly, stopping to ponder over things; she would write a word and then scowl up at the wall. It was she who tore the notes into bits, not I. She would write something, tear it up, and throw the pieces about haphazardly . . . It seems to me that even in my grave it won't be as horrible as it was sitting there with her in silence beneath the lamp, so late at night, writing all those useless notes . . . It was what she wanted, that we write them. I just unquestioningly obeyed her that night, I did everything she commanded, right down to the final moment.

"Suddenly she said, 'Enough. If it's to be done, then quickly. Give me some stout, bless me, Mother of God!' I poured out a glass of the stout, and she, raising up slightly, took a pinch of powder and with no hesitation she put it in the glass. After drinking down more than half, she ordered me to drink the rest. I drank it. She began tossing about on the divan, taking my hands, then asking me to do it: 'And now kill me, kill me! Kill for the sake of our love!'

"How, exactly, did I do that? It seems I embraced her with my left arm—yes, of course it was the left—and I put my lips to hers. She said, 'Farewell, farewell . . . But no: hello to you, and now that hello is forever. If it didn't work out here, then it will up there, on high.' I pressed up against her, holding my finger on the trigger of the gun. I recall feeling how my whole body was twitching . . . And then, somehow, the finger twitched all by itself. She managed to say in Polish, 'Alexander, my beloved!'

"At what time did it happen? I think it was three o'clock. After that what did I do for another two hours? It took me something like an hour to walk to Likharev's place. The rest of the time I sat there beside her; then, for some reason, I put everything in order.

"Why didn't I shoot myself? But I just somehow forgot about that. When I saw her dead I forgot everything on earth. I sat there and just looked at her. Then, in some kind of wild, unconscious state of mind, I started tidying her up, and the room . . . I couldn't break the promise I had given her, that after her death I would kill myself, but I was overcome by total indifference . . . I feel the same indifference now to the fact that I'm alive. But I can't reconcile myself to one thing: that people think I'm an executioner. No, no! Maybe I'm guilty before the law of man, guilty in the eyes of God, but in her eyes no—not guilty!"

Maritime Alps, September 11, 1925

»»» «««

Light Breathing

In the graveyard, above a fresh clay mound, stands a new cross made of oak, sturdy, ponderous, smooth.

April, gray days. The tombstones here, in this spacious provincial graveyard, can be seen from afar through the bare trees, and a cold wind keeps jangling and rattling the porcelain wreath at the foot of the cross.

There is a large convex porcelain medallion set into the cross, and the medallion contains a photographic portrait of a schoolgirl with joyous, strikingly living eyes.

This is Olya Mesherskaya.

As a small girl she was indistinguishable from all the others in that mass of brown school frocks; what could be said about her except that she was one of those comely, rich and happy little girls, that she was a capable student but was mischievous and reacted with utter nonchalance to the exhortations of her form mistress? Then she began blossoming out, developing in leaps and bounds. At the age of fourteen her waist was slender, her legs well formed, and already clearly defined was the shape of her breasts and all those other curves whose charm has never been expressed in the human word; at fifteen she was already renowned for her beauty. How attentive were some of her girlfriends to their coiffure, how well groomed they were, how devoted to the demureness of their every bodily movement! But she was afraid of nothing, neither ink stains on her fingers nor a blush somewhat too florid, neither hair in disarray nor a knee that was bared as she fell on the run. Without any effort whatsoever on her part, somehow imperceptibly, it all came to her, everything that so distinguished her from all others at the school during those last two years: elegance, stylishness, grace, the bright gleam of her eyes . . . No one could dance at the school balls as Olya Mesherskaya could, no one could skim along on ice skates in quite the same way, no one at the dances was ever so ardently pursued as she, and, for some reason, no one was more adored by the lower-form schoolgirls. Imperceptibly had she become a young lady and imperceptibly had her fame grown ever more splendrous at the school, and already there were rumors in the air, that she was capricious, that she could not live without admirers, that the schoolboy Shenshin was madly in love with her, that she was said to love him too but was so inconstant in her treatment of him that he had attempted suicide . . .

In that last winter of her life Olya Mesherskaya, so they said at the school, was out of her mind with gaiety. The winter was snowy, sunlit, frosty; the sun set early behind the tall fir trees in the snowy school yard and the weather was invariably fine, radiant, holding the promise of more frost and more sunshine tomorrow, of strolls along Sobornaya Street, skating at the municipal gardens, of a rosy tinge in the evening sky, music, and masses of people glissading about that rink in all possible directions, amidst whom the one who appeared most carefree and happy of all was Olya Mesherskaya. But then one day, during the long noon recess, as she dashed like a whirlwind across the school assembly hall chased by a mob of blithefully shrieking first-form girls, she was suddenly called to the office of the headmistress. She stopped on the dead run, breathed just one deep sigh, straightened her hair with a brisk, womanly gesture that was now quite natural for her, hitched up the straps of her apron on her shoulders, and ran upstairs, eyes glistening. The headmistress, a woman still young but gray haired, sat calmly plying her knitting needles at a desk beneath a portrait of the tsar.

"Good day, Mademoiselle Mesherskaya," she said in French, not raising her eyes from the knitting. "Unfortunately, this is not the first time I've been obliged to summon you here to have a word with you concerning your behavior."

"Yes, madame," answered Olya as she approached the desk, looking at her with those clear and lively eyes but without any expression on her face; then, with the delicacy and grace peculiar to her alone, she dropped a curtsey.

"You'll pay scant attention to my words; unfortunately I'm convinced of that," said the headmistress. She raised her eyes and tugged up on the knitting, making the ball of wool spin on the lacquered floor so that Olya looked down with an inquisitive glance. "I have no intention of repeating myself; I shall not speak at length," she said.

Olya was very fond of this uncommonly clean and large office, which, on such frosty days, wafted the lovely warmth of the sparkling Dutch stove and the crisp fragrance of lilies of the valley on the desk. She sat silently and expectantly, glancing at the full-length portrait of the young tsar, who was standing in the middle of some lustrous drawing room, at the even parting in the milk white, neatly permed hair of the headmistress.

"You are no longer a little girl," said the headmistress in a momentous tone, holding back her irritation.

"Yes, madame," answered Olya simply, almost gaily.

"But not yet a woman," said the headmistress with still greater moment in her tone, and her sallow face reddened slightly. "First of all, what sort of hairstyle is that? It's a grown woman's hairstyle!"

"It's not my fault, madame, that I have nice hair," answered Olya, lightly touching both hands to her beautifully done coiffure.

"Ah, so that's it, not your fault!" said the headmistress. "The hairdo is not your fault, those expensive barrettes are not your fault; it's not your fault that you're ruining your parents with spending twenty rubles on shoes! But, I repeat, you simply fail to take into account that you're still a mere schoolgirl—"

At that point Olya interrupted, maintaining her simple, calm and polite manner.

"Excuse me, madame, you're mistaken; I'm a woman. And do you know whose fault it was? Papa's friend and neighbor and your brother, Aleksei Mikhailovich Malyutin. It happened last summer in the country . . ."

And within a month after that conversation a Cossack officer, ugly and plebeian in appearance, having utterly nothing in common with the set to which Olya Mesherskaya belonged, shot her on the platform of the railway station, amidst a whole throng of people who had just arrived on the train. And the incredible confession of Olya Mesherskaya, which had so astounded the headmistress, proved to be absolutely true. The officer declared at the coroner's inquest that Mesherskaya had led him on, had been intimate with him, and had sworn to be his wife, but at the railway station on the day of the murder, as she was seeing him off for Novocherkassk, she suddenly told him that the idea of loving him had never even entered her head, that all the talk of marriage was just her way of mocking him; and she showed him the page in her diary describing the episode with Malyutin.

"I quickly scanned the lines while she promenaded around, waiting for me to finish reading, and then, right there on the platform, I shot her," said the officer. "You have that diary here; look at what she wrote on the tenth of July last year."

The entry in the diary read as follows: "It's past one in the morning. I fell into a deep sleep but awakened immediately . . . I've just become a woman! Papa, Mama, and Tolya, all of them went off to the city; I was left on my own. I was so happy to be alone! In the morning I strolled about in the garden and openlands, went out into the forest; it seemed to me that I was the only one in the whole wide world, and never in my life had my thoughts been so clear. I also dined alone, then played the piano for a whole hour; the sounds of that music made me feel as if I would live forever and would be happier than anyone on earth. After that I fell asleep in Papa's study, and at four o'clock Katya woke me up and said that Aleksei Mikhailovich was there. I was very pleased he had come, it was so nice to receive him and entertain him. He was driving a pair of Vyatka-breed horses, very beautiful, and they stood out by the porch the whole time. He stayed on because it started to rain, and he was hoping the roads would be dry by evening. He was sorry he hadn't caught Papa in, was quite animated, and behaved with me like a gallant young admirer, kept joking about how he had long been in love with me. When we went for a stroll in the garden before tea the weather was lovely again, the sun was glistening throughout the wet garden, though it had turned quite cold, and he took me by the arm and said that he was Faust with his Margarete. He's fifty-six years old but still very handsome and always well dressed—the one thing I didn't like was that he was wearing one of those cloaks with a cape. He smells of English cologne and has quite young black eyes and an absolutely silvery beard, elegantly parted into two long halves. For tea we sat out on the glassed-in terrace, I felt as if I were not so well and lay down on the ottoman, and he smoked, then came over and sat down beside me, began paying me compliments again, then taking my hand and kissing it. I covered my face with a silk handkerchief, and he kissed me several times on the lips through the silk . . . I don't understand how that could have happened, I was out of my mind, I never thought I could be that sort! Now there's only one way out . . . I feel such revulsion for him, I just can't live through this!"

Over the course of these April days the city has turned clean and dry, its cobblestones have taken on a white hue, and one walks along its streets with a pleasant sense of buoyancy. Every Sunday after mass a small woman in mourning attire, in black kid gloves, carrying an umbrella with an ebony handle, makes her way along Sobornaya Street, which leads her out of the town. On the way she crosses a muddy square full of smoke-blackened smithies, where the crisp air from the openland blows. Further on, between the monastery and the dungeon, appears the white cloud-strewn slope of the sky, the gray spring fields, and then, after getting past the puddles beneath the monastery wall and turning left, one sees what appears to be a large, low-lying garden enclosed by a white fence, above whose gates are written these words: THE DORMITION OF THE HOLY MOTHER OF GOD. The small woman crosses herself perfunctorily and walks, as if accustomed to the path, down the central avenue. When she has reached the bench opposite that oak cross, she sits there in the wind and the spring cold for an hour, for two hours, until her feet in the light boots and her hands in the narrow kid gloves are frozen through and through. As she listens to the birds of spring, blithefully singing on despite the cold, as she listens to the jangling of the porcelain wreath in the wind, she sometimes thinks she would give half her life if only that dead wreath were not hanging there before her eyes. That wreath, the mound, the cross of oak! Is it possible that she lies there beneath it, the one whose eyes shine so immortally from the convex porcelain medallion on the cross, and how can one reconcile the pure gaze of those eyes with the ghastly business now associated with the name of Olya Mesherskaya? But in the depths of her soul the small woman is happy, as are all people who dedicate their lives to some passionate dream.

This woman is the form mistress of Olya Mesherskaya, a spinster no longer young, who has lived for years in some fantasy world that takes the place of her real life. The first of her fanciful creations was her brother, a poor and utterly undistinguished junior officer;

all of her most cherished thoughts were of him, his future, which, for some reason, she imagined to be full of sparkling promise. After he was killed in the Battle of Mukden, she tried to convince herself that her work was her sacred mission. Now the death of Olya Mesherskaya has inspired yet another captivating dream. Olya Mesherskaya is the object of her every thought and feeling. On every day off work she visits her grave, spends hours staring at the oaken cross, conjuring up the pallid face of Olya Mesherskaya in her coffin amidst flowers, and she recalls a conversation she once overheard. One day, while strolling about the school yard during the midday recess, Olya Mesherskaya had been speaking in a quick rapid patter to her favorite classmate, the tall plump Subbotina girl.

"Once I was reading one of Papa's books—he has scads of curious old books—and I read what a woman must have to be truly beautiful . . . Well, you know, there was so much there that I can't remember it all, but, of course, it said black eyes, smouldering like pitch. Really and truly, that's what it said: smouldering like pitch! Then, eyelashes black as the night, a gentle blush about the cheeks, a slender form, hands somewhat longer than the usual—you understand? A bit longer than ordinary! A small foot, a moderately large bosom, a calf that is rounded just so, a knee the color of seashells, sloping shoulders. I learned a lot of it almost by heart, it's all so perfectly right! But the main thing, you know what the main thing is? Light breathing! And I've got it, you know. Just you listen how I can sigh . . . It's true, I've got it, don't I?"

Now that light breathing has dissolved anew in the vapors of the world, in the cloud-strewn sky, the cold spring wind.

1916

»»» «««

Aglaia

In the secular world, in the forested village where she was born and grew up, Aglaia was known as Anna.

She lost her mother and father early. Smallpox dropped in on the village one winter, and a host of dead bodies were carted off to the graveyard at the large settlement beyond Holy Lake. Suddenly two coffins made their appearance in the Skuratov hut as well. The little girl felt neither fear nor pity; but she never forgot the odor that wafted from the coffins, unlike any other smell, alien and oppressive to the living, and she recalled the winter briskness of the Lenten thaw and the cold that blew into the hut with the peasants, who came to carry out the coffins to the sledge beneath the windows.

In that forested region the villages are rare and small, their rough-hewn farm shacks are scattered about—built close to streams and lakes if the loamy hillocks don't get in the way. Poor but not poverty-stricken, the people there look after what little they have, keep to the old ways, although for as long as anyone recalls the men have left their womenfolk, gone off to do hire work. The women remain, they plow the infecund earth in spots free from woodlands, they scythe the grass in the forest and spend winters clattering away at their spinning wheels. In childhood Anna's heart was enveloped in those old ways; dear to her were the dark hut with no chimney and the wooden splint light burning in its holder.

Her sister Katerina had long been married. It was she who ran things, at first with her husband, whom she had taken into her household, and later alone, after he had begun going off to work elsewhere almost year-round. Under her watchful eye the girl grew steadily and swiftly, never feeling ill, complaining of nothing, but always lost in thought. If Katerina called to her, asked what was the matter, she responded artlessly, saying that her neck was making creaking sounds and she was listening. "There!" she said, revolving her head and her pallid face. "Can you hear it?"

"But what are you thinking about?"

"Nothing, I guess. I don't know."

As a child she did not associate with girls her age and had no desire to go anywhere. Only once did she make a trip with her sister, to the old settlement beyond Holy Lake, where pinewood crosses are sticking up in the graveyard beneath its pine trees and a rough-timbered chapel stands, roofed with the black scales of wood shingles. That was the first time she was arrayed in bark sandals and a *sarafan* made of homespun cloth, with a newly bought necklace and yellow kerchief.

Katerina grieved and cried over her man; she bemoaned her childless state as well. But after she was done with shedding her tears she made a vow not to know her husband. When he arrived she greeted him joyfully, calmly spoke of household matters, examined his shirts carefully, and mended what needed mending. She busied herself about the stove and felt happy when something pleased him, but they slept apart, as if unrelated. When he left she lapsed back into dreariness, fell silent. She spent more and more time away from home, at a women's cloister not far off, or visiting the elder Rodion, who was saving his soul in a forest hovel just beyond that cloister. She doggedly taught herself to read, brought holy books back from the cloister and read them aloud in a peculiar voice, eyes lowered, holding the book in both hands. The girl stood beside her, listening, gazing around the hut, which was always tidy. Drunk with the sound of her own voice, Katerina read of saints and martyrs who despised our dark earthly things and embraced the ethereal, who wished to mortify their flesh with its passions and lusts. Anna listened to the reading, as if to a song in a foreign language, attentively. But when Katerina closed the book she never asked to be read more; she was always an enigma.

Approaching age thirteen she became wondrously thin, tall, and strong. She was delicate, fair in complexion, blue eyed, and she loved the simplest and crudest of jobs. When summer came and Katerina's husband arrived, when the village went out to reap, Anna went along with them and worked like a grown-up. But the northern latitude provides a meager summer season. Soon the sisters were alone once more, back in their monotone life, and once again Anna cleared away manure in the cattle yard, cleaned the stove, and sat with her sewing or weaving while Katerina read—of the seas and deserts, of the city of Rome, of Byzantium, of the first Christians with their wondrous and miraculous deeds. Words full of rapture resounded those evenings through the crude hut amidst the forest: "In the realm of Cappadocia, during the reign of the pious Byzantium emperor Leo the Great . . . In the days of the patriarchate of the most-like-unto-Christ Joachim of Alexandria, in the faraway land of Abyssinia."

And so Anna learned of maidens and youths torn apart by wild beasts in the amphitheaters, of the celestial beauty of Barbara, who was beheaded by her fierce progenitor, of relics preserved by angels on Mount Sinai; of the warrior Eustachius, summoned unto the true God by the voice of the crucified Redeemer himself, who beamed in the form of a sunray between the horns of a deer that he, Eustachius, had driven into a snare he had set; of the travails of Sabbas the Enlightened, who dwelt in the Vale of Fire; and of many, many more, passing their bitter days and nights by wasteland springs, in crypts or mountain cenobies . . . During her adolescence she once saw herself in a dream, wearing a long, flaxen shift, with an iron crown on her head. And Katerina said to her, "That foretells death for you, my sister, an early demise."

In her fifteenth year she became quite the young woman, and people marveled at her comeliness: the pale gold of her oblong face was lambent with a faint blush, her brows were thick and light brown, her eyes blue; she was graceful, shapely, albeit still a bit ungainly: tall in stature, slender, with arms elongated. She had a fine, quiet way of raising her long lashes. Winter that year was uncommonly harsh. The forests and lakes were enveloped in snow, holes cut in the ice were soon fettered in thick frost, a frozen wind seared the air, and two suns, their iridescent rings mirroring one another, played games with the dawns of each morn. As the Yule season approached Katerina ate oatmeal and a soup made of bread and water, while Anna took only bread.

"I want to fast my way through to another prophetic dream," she told her sister.

And on the eve of the new year she dreamt again. She saw an early frosty morning, a dazzling, glacial sun had just rolled out from beyond the snowbanks, a sharp wind took away her breath. Into that wind, that sun, she flew along on skis through a white field, chasing after some marvelous ermine, then suddenly plunging into an abyss—and was blinded, suffocating in a cloud of snow dust that swirled up from beneath her skis toward the precipice above.

Nothing comprehensible could be made of that dream, but not once, on the whole first day of the new year, did Anna look up to meet her sister's eyes. The local priests made their rounds of the village, dropped in on the Skuratovs as well, but she hid behind a curtain beneath the sleeping shelves. That winter, still not fully resolved to go through with her plan, she was often out of sorts, and Katerina said to her, "Why don't you do as I say and go see Father Rodion? He can relieve you of all your burdens!"

In the winter she read to her tales of Alexis, Man of God and of Ioann the Anchorite, both of whom died in penury at the gates of their aristocratic parents; she read of Simeon Stylites, who rotted alive while standing on a stone pillar. Anna asked her, "And how is it that Father Rodion doesn't stand on a pillar?" She answered that the feats of the saintly ones are of many kinds, that zealots of old were more likely to have saved themselves in the Kiev caves, and later in the primeval forests, or they attained to the Heavenly Kingdom in the guise of naked and scabrous freaks.

Also that winter Anna learned of the Russian servitors of the Lord, her spiritual forebears: Matthew the Perspicacious, unto whom it was given to view only the dark and base things of this world, to see through to the most abject depths of vileness within human hearts, to spy out the visages of subterranean devils and hear their impious insinuations; Mark the Digger of Graves, who devoted himself to the burial of the dead, and in his perpetual proximity to Death achieved such power over it that Death came to shudder at the sound of his voice; Isaaky the Hermit, who covered his body in the fresh, raw hide of a goat, whereupon that hide attached itself and grew to his skin, Isaaky, who gave himself over to madcap whirling with demons in the midnight hours, when they enticed him into their prancing and reeling dances to the raucous sounds of shrieks and the music of fifes, timbrels, and gusli.

"From him, Isaaky," said Katerina, "devolved all of the Fools in Christ. And so many there were to come later, countless numbers of fools! Father Rodion hath so avowed it: that no other country had them, that only unto us did the Lord appear manifest through them, for the amplitude of our sins and in the amplitude of his grace." Then she added what she had heard in the cloister: the grievous story of how the people of Rus had left Kiev for the forests and impassable bogs, for its towns built of bast under the cruel suzerainty of the Muscovy princes, how Rus had endured the travails—times of troubles, internecine wars, the truculent Tatar hordes, and other God-given retributions—pestilence and famine, conflagrations and heavenly portents.

"So many," she said, "whole masses upon masses of those Folk of God, suffering for Christ's sake and playing the holy fool, so many there were back then that the very divine liturgy in churches was drowned out by their squeals and shrieks. And no small number of them," she said, "were conjoined with the canonized saints. There was Simon from the Volga forests, who wore only a tattered shift, who roved about and shrunk from the gaze of man in wild thickets, who later, when living in the city, was beaten daily by the locals on account of his scabrous conduct, and who died of the wounds he received in those beatings. There was Prokopius, who embraced perpetual torments in the city of Vyatka, forasmuch as he would scamper up onto the bell towers in the night and ring the bells again and again in the call to alarm, as in the time of a fiery inferno. There was another Prokopius, who was born in the Ziryan region amidst savage trappers of beasts, who went about his whole life long carrying three iron pokers and who doted on empty spaces, the gloomy forested banks above the Sukhona River, where he perched upon a rock, shedding tears and praying for those who traversed the waters below him. There was Jacob the Blessed, who sailed in a coffin made from a hollow log, down the River Msta to the uncouth inhabitants of that poor region. There was Ioann the Hirsute, from near Great Rostov, whose head of hair was in such derangement that all who beheld him were dumbfounded with fear. There was Ioann of Vologda, called Big Cap, small of stature, face furrowed with wrinkles, body bedizened with crosses, who never once in his life removed the cap, which was like unto cast iron. There was Vasily the Naked Walker, who in winter frost or the sweat of summer wore iron chains in lieu of clothing while holding a handkerchief in his hand.

"And now, my sister," said Katerina, "they all stand before the Lord rejoicing in the assemblage of his saints, while their incorruptible relics repose in cypress and silver shrines, within cathedrals sculpted in sanctity, side by side with the tsars and archbishops!"

"But why did Father Rodion never play the Fool in Christ?" asked Anna again. Katerina answered that he was among those who walked in the steps not of Isaaky, but of Sergius of Radonezh, those who languished in the forest monasteries. "Father Rodion," she said, "first began seeking salvation in an age-old and glorious wilderness, based on the forest primeval where once a certain great saint had lived, in the hollow trunk of an oak that was three centuries old. In that wasteland he, Rodion, perdured through a period of strict obedience and took vows as a monk; there, for his penitent tears and intractable gainsaying of flesh he was vouchsafed the honor of laying eyes upon the Queen of Heaven herself; there he kept his vow to live seven years in seclusion and seven years in silence, but even this did not quench his zeal. He left the monastery and came—many, many years ago—into our forests, put linden-bark sandals on his feet, donned a loose overall of sackcloth, a black epitrachelion with an octangular cross and a depiction of the skull and crossbones of Adam. He consumes only water and uncooked weeds, covers over the window of his hovel with an icon, sleeps in a coffin beneath a lamp that burns perpetually. And in the midnight hours howling beasts besiege him without surcease, throngs of frenzied revenants and devils."

At the onset of her sixteenth year, when it is meet and proper for a girl to be betrothed, Anna abandoned the secular world.

Spring of that year came early and was hot. Berries ripened in the forests by untold numbers, the grasses were waist high, and by the time of the Peter-Paul fast haymaking had begun. Anna worked with a will, became tanned in the sun amidst grasses and flowers; a dark flush was aflame on her face, and the kerchief pulled low on her forehead hid the warm gaze of her eyes. But one day while they were mowing a large, glittering snake with an emerald head wound itself around her bare leg. Reaching down with her long and thin arm, Anna seized its frigid slimy thew of a body and flung it afar. She never even looked up from the ground, but she was terribly frightened and turned whiter than a shroud. And Katerina said to her, "That, my sister, is the third premonition. Beware of the Tempter Serpent; a dangerous time is in store for you!"

Due to the fright or because of those words, for a week after that the pallor of death never left Anna's face. And on the eve of Peter-Paul Day, out of the blue she asked to attend all-night vesper services at the cloister. She went there, spent the night, and on the morn she was vouchsafed to stand in the crowd of country folk at the threshold of the hermit. That was when he bestowed upon her a great honor: of all those in the crowd he spied her out and beckoned for her to come inside. And she left him that day with head bowed low and kerchief covering half her face, pulled down over the fire of her effulgent cheeks, and so confused were her feelings that she was barely aware of the ground beneath her feet. He had called her a chosen vessel, an immolation for the Lord; he had lit two waxen tapers, took one for himself, gave her the other, stood for a long time praying in front of the holy icon, and commanded her to press her lips to that image.

Then he gave her his blessing to join, in the near future, the women's cloister and to receive instruction.

"My happiness, guileless sacrifice!" he said to her. "Be not the bride of earth, but heaven's bride! I know, I know that thy sister hath prepared thee. Sinner that I am, I too shall do my best in thy behalf!"

Dwelling as a nun in the cloister, detached from the world and from her own will for the sake of her spiritual godfather, Anna, rechristened Aglaia upon taking the veil, lived for thirty-three months. And as the thirty-third expired she passed on.

How she lived there, saving herself, of that no one can know to the full—it was a time that was so long before ours. One or two things, nonetheless, remain in the folk memory. One day a group of old women from a number of faraway regions were trudging along, making a pilgrimage to that forested spot where Anna was born. On the bank of a small river, as they were about to cross it, they encountered the usual sort of man who wanders holy places. He was ragged, ill favored, even, to put it simply, weird, wearing an old-fashioned gentleman's derby beneath which his eyes were blindfolded with a kerchief. They began inquiring about directions, how to get to the cloister, about Father Rodion and Anna. By way of reply he spoke first of himself: "I don't know God knows what about nothing, my sisters," he said, "but I can, however, converse with you to a degree, for I am presently on my way back from those very parts.

"As for me, now," he said, "I might, perchance, just give you the creeps and that's no big surprise, for many find me a rough row to hoe: be they on foot or be they on horse folks come upon me and what do they see? A little drifter-pilgrim toddling through the forest, ambling along all on his lonesome and humming Psalm-songs to boot, got him a white kerchief tied over his eyes. Stands to reason they're flabbergasted. These eyes of mine, by virtue of my sinful soul, are just too greedy and quick; my vision is so uncommon and keen that even at night I can see like a cat, being, as I am, sighted beyond measure, on account of me having no truck with folks but keeping apart from them. Wellsir, so that's how come I decided to foreshorten, just a teeny bit, my corporeal vision."

Then he began telling the pilgrims how far, by his reckoning, they had yet to go, which region they should make for, where they could spend the night and find rest, and how the cloister looked.

"First off," he said, "you'll come to the settlement on Holy Lake, and then to the very village where Anna was born, and there you'll see still another lake, the convent one, which is shallow and is yet substantial, and you'll have to get you a boat across that lake. And as soon as you land on shore, well, right there you'll see the convent, a stone's throw away. Of course, on that bank there's no end of woods, but, as a rule, you can see the walls of the convent through the trees, the church domes, the cells, and the hostels for folks on pilgrimages."

Then he spent a long time narrating the hagiography of Rodion, the childhood and adolescence of Anna, and he concluded by speaking of her sojourn at the cloister: "Her time there was, mercy, oh so short!" he said. "It's a pity, you might declare, the loss of such beauty and youth? Well, we, of course, in our ignorance, find it pitiful. But Father Rodion knew well what he was doing. After all, he treated everybody the same—he was affectionate, humble, he was full of joy and persistent to the point of mercilessness, especially with Aglaia. I was there, Grandmothers, at the spot where she reposes. A long grave, lovely it is, all grown over with grasses, green . . . And I won't try to hide it, nosiree: it was there by the grave that I got the idea of binding up my eyes, Aglaia's example prompted me. For she, you have need of knowing, never, for the whole of her stay in the cloister, never a single time did she raise her eyes. She pulled a shroud cloth down over them and there it remained, and she was so sparing of words and meek in spirit that even Father Rodion marveled at her.

"And you know, perchance, it was no easy thing for her, such a feat of zealotry—to bid farewell to the earth, to the face of man for all time! And in the cloister she took upon herself the most toilsome work, then spent nights standing in prayer. That's how come, they say, that Father Rodion came to so love her! He singled her out from all others, admitted her daily into his hut, had long conversations with her about the future glory of the cloister, even revealed his visions—of course with strict admonishings to keep silent about them. Well then, so she burned out, and in such short order, like a candle. Are you sighing again, despondering? Me, well I got to agree with you—it's sad! But I'll tell you something even more fascinating. For her great humility, her averting of eyes from the earthly world, for her silence and backbreaking travails Rodion did something unheard of. As the third year of her great feat was waning, he had her made a nun, and then, after prayer and holy contemplation, he summoned her at a certain terrible hour—and told her to accept her demise. Yes, he said it outright and straightforth: 'My happiness, thy time has come! Remain in my memory just as beautiful as thou standeth here now before me. Depart unto the Lord!' And what do you think? A day later she passed on. She laid down, flared up like a flame, and expired. True, he consoled her. He disclosed to her right before her death that inasmuch as she, in the early days of her instruction, had failed to keep secret a minuscule portion of the things he told her, that her lips, but only her lips, would decay. He gave a bounty of silver for her funeral, coins for distribution at her burial, a fascicle of tapers to be lit at her fortieth-day memorial service, a large yellow candle that cost a whole ruble for her coffin, and that coffin itself—round, hollowed from an oak trunk. And with his blessing they laid her out, thin and so wondrously long she was in that coffin, with hair let down, wearing two shroud shifts, in a white cassock girded by a black, woman's cincture. Over that she was clad in a black mantle with white crosses, and on her head they placed a green velvet cap with gilded embroidery, and atop that cap a kamelaukion, the cylindrical headdress that honors Orthodox clergy. At the last they wrapped a blue shawl with tassels about her and put a leather rosary strap in her hands. They decked her out, in a word, like nobody's business!

"Yet all the same, Grandmothers, there persists a nasty, demonic rumor that she did not wish to die, oh mercy, how she wanted to live! Departing at such a young age, in such comeliness, they say she bid farewell to all in tears, in a loud voice proclaiming unto them all: 'Forgive me!' The last thing she did was she closed her eyes and said quite distinctly: 'And thou, Earth Mother, against whom I have sinned most grievously in body and spirit—wilt thou forgive me?' And those same terrible words were the ones folks cried out, falling down and pounding their heads on the ground, in the penitential prayer for Holy Rus of yore at vesper services on the eve of Whitsun, right before the pagan Day of the Water Sprites."

1916

»»» «««

Temir-Aksak-Khan

"A-a-a, Temir-Aksak-Khan!" savagely wails the lilting, passionate, hopelessly grievous voice in the Crimean village coffeehouse.

The spring night is dark and humid, the black wall of the mountain precipice barely visible. Beside the coffeehouse, which coheres to the cliff, an automobile with an open top stands on the main road in the dun white mud, and two long columns of bright smoke stretch forth into the darkness from its terrible, dazzling eyes. Out of the distance far below the roar of the unseen ocean drifts up, and a moist, restive wind wafts from the darkness on all sides.

The air in the coffeehouse is thick with tobacco smoke; the interior is dimly illumined by a lamp made of tin hung from the ceiling and heated by a pile of red-hot embers glowing on a hearth in the corner. The wretched mendicant, who began his tale of Temir-Aksak-Khan with that agonizing cry, is seated on the clay floor. He is a one-hundred-year-old monkey in a sheepskin jacket and a shaggy astrakhan cowl that has gone rust red from the rain, the sun, and time. On his lap he holds something resembling a crude wooden lyre. He is bent over and his listeners cannot see his face; they see only the brown ears protruding from beneath the cowl. Periodically ripping out harsh sounds from the strings of his instrument, he wails with insufferable, despairing grief.

Seated on a stool near the hearth is the proprietor of the coffeehouse, an effeminately plump, handsome Tatar. At first he wore a smile that expressed in turn affection and a bit of melancholy, then condescension and mockery. But later he froze motionless with brows raised, and that smile was tinged with perplexity and suffering.

On a bench beneath the small window sits a hadji, smoking; he is tall, with thin shoulder blades and gray beard, wearing a black robe and a white turban that is in perfect contrast with the dark swarthiness of his face. Neglecting his chibouk, he has thrown his head back against the wall and closed his eyes. One leg, in a striped woolen stocking, is bent at the knee and propped up on the bench, the other hangs down, its slippered foot dangling.

Seated at the table beside the hadji are the travelers who, on a sudden whim, had stopped their car to have a cup of miserable coffee in this village coffeehouse: a heavyset gentleman in bowler and English macintosh and a beautiful young lady, pale with strained attentiveness and agitation. She is from the southern regions; she knows the Tatar language, understands the words of the song . . . "A-a-a, Temir-Aksak-Khan!"

Nowhere in the universe was there a khan more resplendent than Temir-Aksak-Khan. All of the sublunar world was trembling at his feet, and the most lovely of women and maidens on earth were ready to die for the pleasure of being, if only for one brief moment, his slaves. But just before his demise Temir-Aksak-Khan sat in the dust on the flagstones of the marketplace, kissing the tatters of passing cripples and beggars.

"Tear out my soul, ye afflicted and poor, for my soul is bereft of the wish to desire!"

And soon thereafter, when the Lord God had at last taken pity on him and released him from the vain magnificence of this earth and the vain delights of earthly existence, all of his kingdoms disintegrated, his cities and palaces crumbled into desolation, and the powder of sands covered their ruins beneath the eternally blue sky (blue like the glaze on fine china) and the eternally blazing sun (blazing like the flames of the inferno) . . . *A-a-a, Temir-Aksak-Khan! Where are thy days and thy deeds? Where thy battles and victories? Where are those young, tender, petulant ones who loved thee, where are the eyes that came into thy bedchamber shining like black suns?*

All are silent, all are captivated by the song. But the effect is strange: the despairing grief, the bitter reproach that lacerates the whole tale is sweeter than the most lofty and passionate joy.

The traveling gentleman stares intently at the table and fervently draws on his cigar. The eyes of his lady are open wide; tears are flowing down her cheeks.

After sitting there enraptured for a short time they leave, step out across the threshold of the coffeehouse. The beggar has finished his song and begun gnawing and tearing at the spongy flatcake given him by the proprietor, but it seems as if the song has not ended, as if it has no end and never will have.

Before leaving the lady gave the beggar a large tip, a gold piece, then had the disquieting notion that this was not enough; she would like to go back and give him still another, no, two or three, or would like even to take his rough hand and kiss it right in front of everyone. Her eyes are still burning with tears, but she feels she has never been happier than at that very moment, after hearing the tale about how everything under the sun is vanity and sorrow, on that dark and damp night with the faraway roar of the unseen ocean, with the smell of spring rain, with the restless wind that penetrates to the depths of the soul.

Half reclining in the motorcar, the driver hastily leaps out and bends over into the light of the headlamps; he sets about doing something, looking like a wild animal in his fur coat, which seems turned inside out. The automobile suddenly comes to life, drones, shudders with impatience. The gentleman helps his lady get in, then sits down beside her; she thanks him in a distracted way when he covers her knees with the lap rug . . . The car rushes along, following the beveled highroad downhill, ascends an incline, resting its bright columns of light on shrubbery and then whisking them off, dropping them into the darkness of another declivity . . . Stars are glistening through fragments of clouds high on the summit, above the outline of barely visible peaks that seem gigantic; far up ahead there is a glimpse of the almost imperceptible whiteness of surf at the bend of the gulf; the wind blows softly and forcefully into their faces.

O Temir-Aksak-Khan, went the song, never in the sublunary realm had there been one more bold, more happy and resplendent than thee, swarthy of visage, fiery of eye, as bright and beneficent as Gabriel, as wise and magnificent as King Suleiman! More radiant and green than the foliage of Paradise was the silk of thy turban, and its diamond-studded glittering plume was lambent with the starry fire of those precious stones, and the most lovely of slave girls and queens in the world were ready to die for the joy of touching their lips to thy dark and narrow hand, refulgent with the rings of the Orient. But having drunk to the dregs that chalice of earthly delights, in the dust of the marketplace didst thou sit, Temir-Aksak-Khan, and thou didst clutch at and kiss the ragged vestments of the cripples passing by.

"Tear out my anguishing soul, ye afflicted!"

And the centuries have rushed past above thy forgotten grave, and the sands have covered the ruins of thy palaces and mosques beneath the eternally blue sky and the ruthlessly joyous sun, and wild dog-rose bushes grow through the remnants of the azure faiences of thy sepulchre, so that ever and ever again, with each new spring, the hearts of nightingales might languish upon that sepulchre, bursting asunder with their grievously blitheful songs, with the misery of ineffable joy . . . *A-a-a, Temir-Aksak-Khan, where is it, thy bitter wisdom? Where are the torments of thy soul, which spewed out in bile and tears all the nectar of earthly delusions?*

The mountain peaks have passed, faded away; now the sea is dashing along beside the highroad, running up with its roar and its cankerous, shellfish smell onto the white shingle of the beach. Far up ahead, in the dark lowlands, red and white lights are sprinkled about, a rosy glow hangs over the city, and above it all, city and gulf, the night is black and soft, like soot.

Paris, 1921

»»» «««

Night of Denial

A somber stormy night near the end of the rainy season; darkness, raging winds and cloudbursts.

The shores of the sacred Isle of the Lion, black forests that extend to the very edge of the ocean, which seems about to engulf them.

A tremendous roar of waves, advancing relentlessly upon the island in frothing, inwardly glittering masses to cover not only the littoral sandbars, where glutinous rings of starfish lie emitting a cryptic glow and susurrous crabs by the thousands writhe about, not only the shoreline cliffs but even the feet of the palms, which bow down, their thin trunks curving sinuously back from those shoreline bluffs.

From time to time the damp and warm tempest blows through with redoubled vehemence, with incredible force, so majestic and puissant that the fierce rumble rolling out of the forest toward the sea is no less awesome and harsh than the rumble of the sea itself. Then the palms, swaying from side to side like living creatures tormented by a vexing somnolence, suddenly bend low in the face of those storm winds that come tearing up to the shore, fall in unison toward the vale, while myriads of dead fronds tumble noisily down from their tops and heady fragrances pervade the air, wafted from the interior of the island, from its cryptic wooded heartland.

Glutted and bleak as they were on the nights of the Flood, the storm clouds hang ever lower above the ocean. But in the boundless expanse between them and that watery abyss there is a certain semblance of light; to the mute blear of its depths the ocean is replete with the secret flame of innumerable lives.

Sea billows with fiery-roiling manes roll roaring toward the shore, then flare up with such brilliance just before collapsing that a man who is standing in the forest above the beach is illumined by the green light they reflect.

The man is barefoot, dressed in the tatters of an anchorite, his hair shorn and his right shoulder bared.

Amidst the majesty surrounding him he is small of stature, like a child, and was that a look of horror that gleamed for a fleeting second upon his emaciated face, in the luster and din of the collapsing wave?

Outshouting the din and the blended rumble of forests and tempest, he proclaims in firm and sonorous tones, "Glory to Thee on High, the Hallowèd One, the All-Seeing-Most-Lucidly, the Subduer of Desire!"

Whirling in with the raging winds, what appear to be myriads of fiery eyes spark in the black murk of the forest, and the voice of that man who stands on the shore resounds ecstatically: "All in vain, Mara! In vain, Thousand-Eyed One, dost thou tempt me, soaring above the earth in life-giving storms and cloudbursts, fecund and fragrant anew with the putrescence of graves, which give birth to new life out of dust and rot! Get thee hence, Mara! As a drop of rain runneth down and away from the taut leaf of a lotus, even so doth Desire glissade from my soul!"

But the vortex of countless fiery eyes whirls triumphantly amidst the downpour of tumbling palm fronds, eyes that illumine what seems a gigantic graven image sitting on the ground beneath the black canopy of the forest, its head towering up to the very tops of the palms.

Its legs are crossed.

Wound about it from neck to loins are the gray coils of a snake, which puffs out its rose-colored throat, stretching its flat, narrow-eyed head above the head of the image.

Despite the prodigious weight of those serpentine coils, he who sits is unconstrained and stately, erect and majestic.

On the crown of his head is the divine excrescence, the pointed lump. The blue-black, curly but short hair is like the blue in the tail of a peacock. The rubicund visage is regally serene. The eyes gleam like semiprecious stones.

And his awesome voice, a voice that rings with untrammeled freedom that is like the thunder in its force, rolls majestically out of the depths of the forest toward the man who is standing on the shore.

"Verily, verily I say unto thee, my disciple: again and yet again wilt thou deny me for the sake of Mara, for the sake of that sweet deceit that is mortal life, on this night of earthly spring."

Paris, 1921

»»» NOTES «««

Russia (soon to be the Soviet Union) adopted the Gregorian calendar in 1918; dates cited in the notes are frequently given in Old Style (Julian calendar, lagging behind the Gregorian by twelve days in the nineteenth century and thirteen days in the twentieth century), followed by Gregorian (for example, June 6/19). The King James Version is the source for all biblical citations, unless otherwise specified.

Abbreviations

Sob. soch.	Ivan Bunin. *Sobranie sochinenij* [*Collected Works*]. 9 vols. Edited by A. S. Mjasnikov, B. S. Rjurikov, and A. T. Tvardovskij. Moscow, 1965–67.
Lit. nasled.	*Ivan Bunin: Literaturnoe nasledstvo.* No. 84. 2 vols. Edited by V. R. Shcherbina et al. Moscow, 1973.
Bab.	A. Baboreko. *I. A. Bunin: Materialy dlja biografii (s 1870 po 1917).* Moscow, 1967.
Bab. 2	Aleksandr Baboreko. *Bunin: zhizneopisanie* (in series *Zhizn' zamechatel'nykh ljudej*). Moscow, 2004.
Bab. notes	A. Baboreko. Annotations to Ivan Bunin, *Sobranie sochinenij* [*Collected Works*]. 8 vols. Jubilee ed. Moscow, 1994.
Bakh.	Aleksandr Bakhrakh. *Bunin v khalate.* N.J.: Tovarishchestvo zarubezhnykh pisatelej, 1979.
Barsk.	N. A. Barskaja. *Sjuzhety i obrazy drevnerusskoj zhivopisi.* Moscow, 1993.
Dal'	Vladimir Dal'. *Tolkovyj slovar' zhivogo velikorusskogo jazyka* [*Interpretive Dictionary of the Great Russian Language*]. 4 vols. Moscow, 1955–56. Reprinted from publication of 1880–82.

Engle. — Omer Englebert. *The Lives of the Saints.* Trans. Christopher and Anne Freemantle. New York: David McKay, 1951.

G.d. — Galina Kuznetsova. *Grasskij dnevnik.* Washington, D.C.: Victor Kamkin, 1967.

Gold leg. — F. S. Ellis, ed. *The Golden Legend or Lives of the Saints as Englished by William Caxton.* London: J. M. Dent, 1800.

Guerney — Ivan Bunin. *The Elaghin Affair and Other Stories.* Trans. B. G. Guerney. New York: Alfred A. Knopf, 1935.

Henry — Peter Henry, ed. *I. A. Bunin: Selected Stories.* 2nd ed. London, 1993.

I. B.: pro contra — D. K. Burlaka, B. V. Averin, et al., eds. *Ivan Bunin: Pro et Contra.* St. Petersburg, 2001.

Ivanits — Linda Ivanits. *Russian Folk Belief.* New York: M. E. Sharpe, 1989.

Mar. — Thomas Gaiton Marullo, ed. *Ivan Bunin: Russian Requiem, 1885–1920: A Portrait from Letters, Diaries, and Fiction.* Vol 1. Chicago: Ivan R. Dee, 1993. *Ivan Bunin: From the Other Shore, 1920–33.* Vol. 2. Chicago: Ivan R. Dee, 1995. *Ivan Bunin: The Twilight of Emigré Russia, 1934–53.* Vol. 3. Chicago: Ivan R. Dee, 2002.

Mikh. — Oleg Mikhajlov. *Zhizn' Bunina: lish' slovu zhizn' dana . . .* Moscow, 2002.

Murom.-Bun. — V. N. Muromtseva-Bunina. *Zhizn' Bunina.* Paris, 1958.

Orekh-mest. — Dmitrij Orekhov. *Svjatye mesta Rossii.* St. Petersburg, 2000.

Orekh-svjat. — Dmitrij Orekhov. *Svjatye ikony Rossii.* St. Petersburg, 1999.

Shang. — I. I. Shangina. *Russkie traditsionnye prazdniki.* St. Petersburg, 1997.

STDF — Maria Leach, ed. *Standard Dictionary of Folklore, Mythology and Legend.* New York: Harper and Row, 1972 (paperback ed., 1984).

Unbe. B. O. Unbegaun. *Russian Surnames.* Oxford: Clarendon Press, 1972.

Ust. Bun. Militsa Grin, ed. *Ustami Buninykh: dnevniki.* 3 vols. Frankfurt, Germany: Possev-Verlag, 1977, 1981, 1982.

Vrem. goda Vl. Sokolovskij, compiler. *Vremena goda, Pravoslavnyj narodnyj kalendar' (Kniga dlja chtenija na kazhdyj den').* Perm: Ural-Press, 1996.

Wood. James B. Woodward. *Ivan Bunin: A Study of His Fiction.* Chapel Hill: University of North Carolina Press, 1980.

The Grammar of Love

Bunin noted precisely the time he completed this story: 12:52 A.M., February 18, 1915.

3 *a certain Ivlev* In describing the origins of the story, Bunin mentions that his nephew Nikolai Pusheshnikov bought him a present, a rare book called *The Grammar of Love.* "After I read it I had a hazy recollection of something my father had told me in the early years of my adolescence, about some neighbor of ours, a poor landowner who went crazy with love for one of his serf girls." Bunin also notes that he used the beginning letters of his own name (Ivan Alekseevich Bunin, or, as he signed his works, Iv. Bunin) to form the surname Ivlev (see *Sob. soch.*, 9:369). The impressionable Ivlev also appears in other stories, such as "A Winter Dream" (1918) and "In a Never-Never Land" (1923). Bunin may have been unaware of further implications of the surname. *Unbe.* (48, 54) finds its derivation in the baptismal name Iov (Job), and *Henry* (61) says it is the kind of truncated family name given to illegitimate children and may originate with Putivlev.

3 *tarantass* A low, four-wheeled carriage with two long poles connecting front and rear axles. The carriage body rested on the poles, which served as springs. In snowy weather the body was mounted on a sledge.

6 *Khvoshinskoe* The name of Khvoshinsky's estate. At one point the peasant lad calls the estate, or the village located near it, Khvoshino.

11 *There is a state . . . upon the truth* First four lines of E. A. Baratynsky's long poem "The Last Death" (1827).

13 *"An Explication of the Language of Flowers"* The so-called language of flowers used by lovers ostensibly came to Europe in the eighteenth century, but exactly from where is not clear. In some interpretations one flower could stand for a whole sentence, including a question, an answer, or a wish. The Russian poet and translator D. P. Oznobishin supposedly translated from the Persian and published in the 1730s a book titled *Sélam, or The Language of Flowers,* including more than four hundred flowers, each having a meaning in words. If, for example, you sent your chosen one a lily of the valley, it meant, "Long and secretly have I loved you." A geranium: "I need to speak with you in private." A poppy: "You make me dream." As the last two examples suggest, floral language was none too precise (in the passages from Khvoshinsky's book the geranium and poppy have other meanings and do not express complete sentences). Some believe that lovers actually used this symbolic language, but more likely floral language consisted of little more than vocabulary lists, with meanings provided for various flowers. The *sélam,* supposedly a Turkish language of objects used by harem girls to communicate with their lovers outside the harem, has dubious validity. As Beverly Seaton writes (37–38), the *sélam* was "neither floral nor symbolic. But the editors and commentators of the nineteenth century joined the *sélam,* the flower symbolism of China (about which they knew very little), and the religious flower emblems of the Christian Middle Ages into a type of Indo-European floral language which was never specifically set forth but was widely accepted. It gave the language of flowers a worthy ancestry—which, in reality, it has; but not in the way in which they presented it." Seaton's book, *The Language of Flowers: A History* (University Press of Virginia, 1995) has a wealth of information. She finds no antecedents for books on floral language prior to the French publications of the early nineteenth century, but she may

have missed Eastern (Chinese, Persian, Turkish) sources. The idea that flowers have symbolic meanings originates far in the past, as illustrated by the scene in *Hamlet* in which the mad Ophelia strews flowers about. Seaton includes (167–202) "A Combined Vocabulary," listing the meanings assigned to certain flowers from five different sources (French, English, and American). Here is a comparison of meanings for the flowers listed in Khvoshinsky's *Grammar:* (1) poppy ("sorrow" in the *Grammar*) is most widely interpreted in the other vocabularies as "consolation"; (2) spindle tree has two sources that provide the same interpretation as in the *Grammar*—"your charms are engraven on my heart"; (3) periwinkle has four sources for a similar interpretation ("sweet memories, tender recollections, pleasures of memory"); (4) somber (sad) geranium twice has "melancholy spirit," which is also the same ("spleen"); (5) wormwood is not listed (although it has the widespread connotation in a European context of "harsh or embittering feelings, sadness"), but absinthe (same plant) is listed in Seaton's "Combined Vocabulary" with the consistent interpretation of "absence." Judging by the correspondences above and the French provenance of the *Grammar* in Bunin's story, the most likely source for its section on floral language is Charlotte de Latour (possible pseudonym of Louise Cortambert), *Le langage de fleurs* (Paris: 1819).

Just before arriving at the Khvoshinsky estate, Ivlev comes upon a flowering shrub called God's tree. This, according to *Dal'* (1:107), is *Artemisia abrotanum* (*procera*?) [Dal's question mark]. According to a botanical source, it is *Artemisia campestris* (N. N. Brezgin, *Lekarstvennye rastenija verkhnevolzh'ja* [Yaroslavl', 1984], 195–96, illustration 100). It is not listed in Seaton's vocabularies, but it is of the same genus as wormwood (*Artemisia absinthium*). So in some skewed way the presence of this beautiful plant signifies the "absence" of Lushka from Khvoshinsky's (and Ivlev's) world and the "bitterness eternal" of wormwood (and love). And yet, if we look under "artemisia" in Latour's listing, we find (alongside the other sources, who, once again, cite "absence") the meaning "happiness." But then, this is the message of Bunin's whole literary career: love is happiness and eternal bitterness!

Published in Russian translation in Moscow in 1831, *The Gram-*

mar of Love, or The Art of Loving and of Being Loved in Return was entitled in French *Code de l'amour* (Paris, 1829). The author was Hippolit (Hippolyte?) Jules Demoliere (Demolièr?) (*Bab. notes,* 5:492). See also A. V. Bljum, "Iz buninskikh razyskanij: I. Literaturnyj istochnik 'Grammatiki ljubvi,'" in *I. B.: pro contra,* 678–81.

First Love

This story was written in 1930, "Light Breathing" in 1916. The schoolboy-cadet here is a kind of adumbration after the fact of the lovelorn schoolboy Shenshin of "Light Breathing," who attempts suicide after Olya Mesherskaya toys with him. The long-legged girl of this story foreshadows (again in reverse chronological sequence) Olya herself.

Typical of many Bunin narratives, "First Love" is dominated by nature descriptions. We don't get to the human characters until the last paragraph, although the drama they are playing out is in harmony with the natural beauty and the labyrinthine entanglements of nature preceding that paragraph.

The stork here is a male, and the clacking sound he makes with his bill is a mating call: "In calling the female to the nest, the male assumes a characteristic pose: he stands in the nest, throws his head far backward, so that the back of the head touches the spine, and emits a loud clack by knocking the upper half of his bill against the lower half" (S. Ismailova and A. Majsurjan, eds., *Entsiklopedija dlja detej,* vol. 2, *Biologija* [Moscow: Avanta Plus, 1994], 450–51). The parallel between the stork and the young cadet in the throes of first love is obvious. In European folklore the stork is the bird who brings happiness and babies (a prominent piece of stork folklore that carried over to the United States).

In Paris

Bunin's discussion of the origins of the story, attributed to information from A. Bakhrakh, appears in Valentin Lavrov's documentary novel about Bunin's life, *Katastrofa* (Moscow, 1997), 2:345–48. Sometime in the twenties, Bunin was sitting in a café in Paris, where he overheard one phrase, "Patience is the medicine of the poor," from the conversation of a couple much like the one described in the story. He ran into this same couple, very much in love, at another café later. A year or two later he came across the woman again. She was alone, wearing mourning dress, her face frozen in "a deathly despair." On the basis of those three encounters he made up the story.

17 *Rien n'est plus difficile . . . une femme de bien* "There's nothing more difficult than picking out a good watermelon or a decent woman."

17 *zubrovka* A vodka made from woodland and meadow grasses.

19 *L'eau gâte le vin . . . et la femme—l'âme* "Water ruins wine just like a carriage ruins the roadway and a woman the soul."

20 *chachlyks* Also *shashlik;* shish kebabs.

20 *rassolnik* Meat or fish soup with pickled cucumbers.

22 *Le bon Dieu envoie toujours . . . de derrière* "The Good Lord always gives pants to those who have no backside."

24 *Qui se marie par amour . . . mauvais jours* "He who marries for love has lovely nights and miserable days."

24 *Patience—médecine des pauvres* "Patience is the medicine of the poor."

28 *L'amour fait danser les ânes* "Love makes even donkeys dance."

On the Night Sea

29 *Evpatoria* Seaport on the western Crimean Peninsula.

30 *Alupka* Crimean resort seventeen kilometers southwest of Yalta.

30 *Gagry* Also Gagra; resort on the Black Sea about eighty kilometers northwest of Sukhumi.

32 *Some Gaius once was mortal* Gaius is Gaius Julius Caesar. This is a paraphrase from a syllogism in a textbook of logic by J. G. Kiesewetter (1766–1819), a book widely used in nineteenth-century Russian schools. Bunin most likely recalled Tolstoy's prominent citation of the same passage in "The Death of Ivan Ilich" (chapter 6).

32 *Novodevichy Cemetery* Located at the Novodevichy Convent in Moscow, this is the most celebrated cemetery in the country, a burial place of famous Russians of the nineteenth and twentieth centuries. Also mentioned in "Shere Monday."

34 *Prince Gautama beheld Yasodhara* Gautama Buddha; Yasodhara was his legendary wife.

36 *I heard the fatal tidings . . . was my response* Slightly misquoted lines from Alexander Pushkin's famous elegy on the death of Amalia Riznich, "Beneath the Blue Skies of her Native Land," a poem that expresses much the same emotions experienced by the writer in Bunin's story: indifference upon hearing of a former mistress's death. These same lines are also quoted in Ivan Turgenev's *First Love.* Of course, here we also have an echo of the doctor's diagnosis in "On the Night Sea." His colleagues dispassionately inform him that he has a terminal illness, and his response to the tidings is dispassionate.

Bunin's wife, Vera Nikolaevna Muromtseva-Bunina, suggests that this story has its origins in a meeting between Bunin and A. N. Bibikov, the man who married the first love of Bunin's life, Varvara Pashchenko. Bibikov came to see Bunin on the day of Pashchenko's death, May 1, 1918. Bunin did not attend the funeral. See *Murom.-Bun.*, 90.

Antonov Apples

For details on the autobiographical backgrounds of this story, see *Bab. notes,* 2:538–40. The young Bunin expressed sentiments very similar to those of his narrator in letters to Varvara Pashchenko. He mentioned, for example, his love for the smell of Antonov apples and the gentry way of life. Passages from these letters are cited in English in A. F. Zweers, *The Narratology of the Autobography: An Analysis of the Literary Devices Employed in Ivan Bunin's "The Life of Arsen'ev"* (New York: Peter Lang, 1997), 83–84. On Pashchenko, see also *Mikh.*, 70–76.

39 *holiday of Saint Lavrenty* Also Saint Lawrence's Day; August 10/23. Archdeacon Lawrence was martyred in A.D. 258 under the reign of the emperor Valerian. Pope Sixtus, who was being led off to prison, commanded Lawrence to sell all the Church treasures in aid of beggarly Christians. Later arrested and taken before the emperor, he was asked where the treasures were. "Give me three days and I'll show you those treasures," said Lawrence. After gathering together all the mendicants who were feeding themselves on the alms he had distributed, he declared, "Here are those vessels into which the treasures have been deposited. And all those who vouchsafe their treasures into such vessels will have them returned many times over in the heavenly kingdom." After this, subjected to horrendous tortures, Lawrence gave up the ghost with the words, "Thank you, Lord Jesus Christ, for having found me worthy to enter thy gates" (*Vrem. goda*, 191–92).

Apples and apple eating are also associated in Russian folk belief with the holiday of the Transfiguration. For more about this major Eastern Orthodox holiday, which falls on August 6/19, see notes to "Transfiguration." One of the folk names for Transfiguration Day is "Apple Saviour Day" (*Jablochnyj Spas*). According to folk sayings, ripe apples are harvested and "even a beggar can have an apple to eat" on this day. Another belief is that in the heavenly kingdom dead children whose parents have not eaten apples before Apple Saviour Day are given apples to eat, but those whose parents have eaten apples before that day get none. Therefore parents, especially those who have lost children, may consider it a sin to eat apples before August 19. See *Vrem. goda*, 189–90.

39 *When cobwebs abound . . . be fruitful* *Dal'* (4:398) has other expressions: "Many cobwebs presage a long (dry) autumn" and "Autumn cobwebs presage clear weather."

42 *dooly-pears* *Dulia* is a dialect word for small pears grown in Bunin's native region.

44 *holiday of Saints Peter and Paul* June 29/July 12, holiday of Saints Peter and Paul. This holy day makes frequent appearances in Bunin's works.

48 *red kvass* An earlier translator of this story, Olga Shartse, suggests that the kvass is red because it is made from fermented beets. Kvass is more typically made from fermented black bread. See Ivan Bunin, *Stories and Poems,* stories trans. Olga Shartse, poems trans. Olga Shartse and Irina Zheleznova (Moscow: Progress Publishers, 1979), 41.

53 *The Nobleman-Philosopher* Reference to the book by the writer Fyodor Ivanovich Dmitriev-Mamonov (1727–1805), first published in 1769 and republished in Smolensk in 1796.

53 *Erasmus* Erasmus Desiderius (1466?–1536), Dutch philosopher and theologian. His satirical work *In Praise of Folly* appeared in 1509.

54 *The Secrets of Alexis . . . Victor, or A Child in the Forest* Novels of the French writer D. Dumesnil (1761–1819).

Drydale

The title of this novella has previously been translated as *Dry Valley.* The Russian title is one word, *Sukhodol.* "Dale" means a "valley" or "vale," and it is commonly used in English as a combining form: "Rochdale," "Glendale," and so forth. Hence "Drydale."

There is at least one similar place-name, Sukhodol'e, near the area where this work is set (Bunin's native region). It is located north-northeast of the city of Verkhov'e. See I. Eroshkin, ed., "Orlovskaja oblast': topograficheskaja karta" ["Topographical Map of Orlov District"] (Moscow: Voenno-topograficheskoe upravlenie General'nogo shtaba, 1997), maps 15 and 16.

59 *Natalya* Bunin alternates between using Natalya and Natashka in reference to his main character. Natashka, which first shows up in chapter 5, right after she takes the folding mirror, is a peasant pejorative-affectionate diminutive of Natalya. It is as if the character must be renamed at this climactic moment—when her dreams of love are about to be smashed and her life irreparably ruined.

63 *Book Six* The book of genealogy, which recorded the names of hereditary nobles, those at the highest level of the Russian nobility. The surname Bunin appears in this listing.

68 *Saint Mercurius of Smolensk* Bunin's wife Vera Nikolaevna wrote that the Bunin family had a copy of this icon in its possession from his grandfather's times. On the hagiographical legend of Saint Mercurius of Smolensk, see Ad. Stender-Petersen, ed., *Anthology of Old Russian Literature* (Columbia University, 1966), 189–92 (in original Old Russian), and Serge Zenkovsky, ed., *Medieval Russia's Epics, Chronicles and Tales* (New York, 1974), 208–11 (English translation). Neither of these sources has the story of the voice speaking out of the icon or the role of the Hodegetria. This variant of the tale, the one Bunin paraphrases, is discussed in N. K. Gudzij, *Istorija drevnej russkoj literatury* (Moscow, 1966), 311–12. There are apparently at least four different variants. Gudzij mentions that the motif of a hero who carries his own severed head also appears in Catholic and Islamic legends and in Russian folk legends. Even in its written hagiographical form, of course, it is heavily infused with folklore. On the leitmotif of decapitation in *Drydale,* see Tamara Nikonova, "Obshchaja sud'ba i chastnaja zhizn' v povesti I. A. Bunina *Sukhodol,*" in *Bounine revisité: Cahiers de l'émigration russe* (Paris: Institut d'Études Slaves, 1997), 4:17. See also my notes to "The Snow Bull" and N. L. Eliseev, "Bunin i Dostoevskij," in *I. B.: pro contra,* 695–96 (where a passage from Dostoevsky's *The Brothers Karamazov* [part 1, chapter 2] is discussed, describing the monastery scandal scene in which old man Karamazov mocks two Russian Orthodox clergymen by asking them questions about a saint who walks along with his own decapitated head, kissing it all the while).

68 *he whose iron sandals . . . cathedral at Smolensk* In the Eastern Orthodox Church the solea is a raised part of the floor in front of the inner sanctuary, where the parishioners receive communion. The cathedral mentioned here is the most renowned in Smolensk, the Cathedral of the Dormition, built in the seventeenth and eighteenth centuries (architects were Korolkov and later Sedel). The gigantic iron sandals were still there as of January 2000; the helmet was stolen in Soviet times, and there was also once a pike or staff (appropriated by the Poles during their occupation of the city in the seventeenth century). The cathedral has several iconic representations of Saint Mercurius of Smolensk, but the icon described by Bunin is not there (nor had anyone I talked to in Smolensk ever even seen a copy of this particular icon, the headless Mercurius with the severed head in one hand and the Hodegetria in the other).

68 *Hodegetria the Guide* A copy of this famous icon is the main object of reverent worship in the Smolensk Cathedral of the Dormition. The name (in Russian, Odigitrija) comes from a Greek word meaning "guide" or "one who shows the way." According to legends it was painted by the apostle Luke. See Brokgauz-Efron encyclopedia (1916), 29:280. On the iconic tradition of the Hodegetria Mother of God, see also *Barsk.,* 38–39. The original, situated in Constantinople, was one of the most sacred of icons in the Byzantine Empire. Copies were made especially frequently by Russian artists of the fifteenth and sixteenth centuries. One of the most famous is that done by the icon painter Dionysius (1482), now held by the Tretyakov Gallery in Moscow. The icon depicts the Virgin, cradling in her left arm a very grown-up-looking, very grave Christ Child and holding up her right hand in a gesture of presentation: "Here He is; this is the Way." According to the ancient Russian Annals (*letopisi*), the oldest copy of the Hodegetria brought to Russia came to Smolensk. For details on the Smolensk Cathedral of the Dormition, its Hodegetria icon, and the legend of Saint Mercurius, see *Orekh-svjat.,* 28–33.

In Roman mythology Mercury is the psychopomp (analogous to the Greek Hermes) who guides souls through the world of the dead; if we take this parallel into account, we have a strange concatenation of two different guides (the Virgin and Mercurius) in one icon. See T. A. Nikonova, "Dusha russkogo cheloveka v glubokom smysle (povest' *Sukhodol*)," in *Tsarstvennaja svoboda: o tvorchestve I. A. Bunina* (Voronezh: Kvadrat, 1995), 63.

71 *Tatar thistle* Also called eriophorum. The word *tatarka* is a leitmotif of *Drydale.* It can mean (1) "Tatar woman," (2) "hunter's crop" (*chabouk*), (3) "winter wheat" (southern dialect), or (4) the plant *Cirs. eriophorum* (*Dal'*, 4:392).

76 *Kalmyk* The Kalmyk peoples live in the Lower Volga and around the Caspian Sea. Their ancestors, the Oirats, migrated from Central Asia in the late sixteenth and first third of the seventeenth centuries.

79 *the imp, the house spirit* In Russian, *domovoj,* a poltergeist sort of beast thought to be resident in every home. The home's grandfather figure and protector, his behavior can be erratic and destructive, so he must be appeased. The *domovoj* lives behind the stove, is associated with the hearth and fire, and "one of his punishments when the family displeases him is to burn down the house" (*STDF,* 321). There is at least a hint of the raging *domovoj* in the fireball that races through the manor house of Drydale late in the narrative.

82 *drozhky* A low, open four-wheeled carriage with a long narrow bench, which the riders straddle.

85 *Fora!* An Italian expression of approval: "Encore!"

86 *folktale of the scarlet flower* A folktale written by S. T. Aksakov and first published in his *Childhood Years of the Bagrov Grandson* (1858). The tale has a beauty-and-the-beast plot; unlike Natalya's love story, this one ends happily, with the beast transformed into a handsome prince and the girl married to him.

88 *upon awakening she found herself in the city* The city described here is surely Yelets, where Bunin was a gymnasium pupil and where he frequently sets scenes from his stories (see, for more

detail, notes to "Light Breathing"). The smell of the iron roofs, the cobblestone streets, and other details also appear in *The Village.* The town square described here is most likely on Torgovaja (Market) Street, called Peace Street (Ulitsa Mira) in Soviet times.

89 *the cathedral, which at that time had just been built* The massive Voznesensky Sobor (Ascension Cathedral) was a long time in the making (1845–89). Natalya would be looking at it early on, in the 1850s. Its architect was the renowned Konstantin Ton (1794–1881), who built the original Cathedral of Christ the Saviour (desecrated and destroyed by Stalin—more on this cathedral in "Shere Monday") and the Great Kremlin Palace in Moscow. The Yelets Ascension Cathedral is second in size among Orthodox cathedrals in Russia, after Saint Isaac's in St. Petersburg (third if we take into account the recently reconstructed Cathedral of Christ the Saviour).

90 *yellow jailhouse . . . opposite that monastery* A repetitive descriptive detail from the city of Yelets, used in many of Bunin's stories.

90 *Nogai tribesmen* The Nogai are Muslim Turkish peoples living in the northern Caucasus region.

91 *polonaise by Oginski* M. K. Oginski (1765–1833), Polish composer.

93 *Intercession Day* *Pokrov;* literal translation: "Day of the Protective Veil of the Theotokos." Celebrated on October 1/14. In the tenth century, Constantinople, the capital of the Orthodox Byzantine Empire, was under attack by the forces of Islam (the Saracens). The people in the Vlakhern Cathedral, which contained holy relics of the Virgin (including her head covering and part of a belt brought from Palestine in the fifth century), prayed fervently for deliverance. Among those praying was the holy fool Andrej, who had a vision of the Virgin Mary shining with a heavenly radiance and accompanied by angels, John the Baptist, and John the Theologian. She removed the veil (called the *pokrov* or *omophorion*) from her head and spread it over those who were praying in the temple in

token of her protection (or the protection of God through her intercession) against all seen and unseen enemies. The *pokrov* shone with a resplendence brighter than the rays of the sun (as described in Orthodox sacred documents, the miracle of the *pokrov* is analogous to the episode of Christ's transfiguration). Consequently, the Muslims besieging the city retreated and no blood was shed. In memory of the miracle the holiday of the Protection (Intercession) of the Theotokos was instituted in the twelfth century (see *Vrem. goda,* 236–38). Many churches take their name from the Intercession of the Virgin, including the most famous church in all of Russia (popularly called Saint Basil's) on Red Square in Moscow. This is Pokrovskij Sobor—named after what Ivan the Terrible saw as a different intercession on the part of the Mother of God—the aid she provided in defeating the Tatar Khanates in the mid-sixteenth century. The folkloric implications of Pokrov and its syncretistic aspects are treated in discussion of the story "Aglaia" (in the afterword).

93 *the marshal of the nobility* Elected representative of the landed nobility of a province or district, he saw to the interests of the nobility in local government organs and, in general, helped manage the affairs of the squires.

94 *velvet cap with the relic* A previous translator of Bunin's novella, B. G. Guerney, writes that "scull-caps sanctified by contact with the bones of saints or martyrs were worn to ward off . . . headaches, and were also considered a sovereign remedy against all sorts of maladies" (296). But here we seem to have Grandfather wearing a cap with a relic actually attached to it. This most likely is an amulet worn as protection against evil forces.

95 *One half of the double doors . . . never opened* Russia is full of double doors and one half is always locked, making it difficult to go in and out of rooms or buildings. I used to think this was something dating to Soviet times, a means of better controlling people as they came and went. Now I think that it dates, originally, back to some ancient superstition related to the folklore of thresholds and doors.

I have asked Russians repeatedly why one door of every room or at the entry to every building has to be kept locked, and no one has a good answer. One Russian folklorist told me that this has nothing to do with folklore; it's just to keep the cold out (a specious argument, since even inside heated buildings, or on scorching summer days, one door of the double doors at any threshold is always locked). On the folklore of doors and thresholds, see *STDF,* 321. By opening both doors Grandfather apparently is observing a private ritual that marks the special nature of the occasion. But in the world of superstition that dominates *Drydale,* there is an implication that he breaks a threshold taboo and soon pays for this violation with his life.

95 *"Lyudmila"* A ballad by V. A. Zhukovsky (1783–1852), published in 1808. Bunin was proud of the fact that Zhukovsky was really a Bunin, since he was the illegitimate son of a landowner, Afanasy Bunin, and a captive Turkish woman. He was one of the founders of Russian Romanticism, and "Lyudmila" became a work emblematic of that school of literature. See *Mar.*, 3:252–53, 354.

95 *to a dead man betrothed* Inexact quotation from the Mikhail Lermontov poem "The Dead Man's Love" (1841). Voitkevich's behavior places him in the pose of the Romantic military officer popularized by Lermontov in Russia, and Bunin borrowed this character almost shamelessly from the poseur-officer and Lermontov lover Solyony in Chekhov's play *The Three Sisters.* Here is an unrhymed, unmetered translation of the Lermontov poem "The Dead Man's Love":

> So let it cover me over,
> The cold earth,
> O friend! Forever, evermore with thee
> Will be my soul.
> In the land of calm and oblivion
> I, denizen of the tombs,
> Still have not forgotten
> The mad languor of love.

In hour of final torment without fear
Departed this world did I,
And with that separation consolement I awaited,
But there was no separation!
I viewed the charms of things discarnate
And grieved,
For thy image in the features of the heavens
I could not discern.
What to me the gleam of Godhead's power
and sacred Paradise?
I've brought the earthbound passions
Here with me.
Ever one dear reverie
I caress everywhere.
I desire, weep, am jealous,
Just as in olden times.

Should the breath of a stranger
Touch thy lovely cheeks,
My soul in mute torment
Will tremble through and through.
Should thou whisper perchance,
Drifting into sleep, another's name,
Then, flaring into flame, thy words
Will waft through me as fire.

Thou must not love another,
No, thou must not!
To a dead man by the sanctity of word
Thou art betrothed!
Thy fears, alas, and thy entreaties,
What use are they?
Thou knowest: peace, oblivion,
I need them not!

97 *A mouth that runs from ear to ear* In D. Sadovnikov's *Riddles of the Russian People* this is cited as a riddle for "cheekbones." But the

compiler also mentions that it is just a humorous expression for a person with a big mouth. See the English edition of Sadovnikov, trans. and ed. Ann Bigelow (Ann Arbor, Mich., 1986), 288, 428.

97 *Parsee from Drydale* A parsee is an adherent of the Zoroastrian or ancient Persian religion; he is also a fire worshiper, and the use of the term here is connected with the fire motif that is such an integral part of *Drydale.* See Tamara Nikonova, "Obshchaja sud'ba i chastnaja zhizn' v povesti I. A. Bunina *Sukhodol,*" in *Bounine revisité: Cahiers de l'émigration russe* (Paris: Institut D'Études Slaves, 1997), 4:18–19.

100 *Martin Zadeka* Or Zadek; publisher or author of a well-known book on interpretation of dreams, mentioned in Pushkin's *Eugene Onegin,* 5:22. See Vladimir Nabokov's notes in his translation of Pushkin's *Eugene Onegin* (New York, 1964), 2:514–16. See also the text of *Eugene Onegin,* ed. D. Chizhevsky (Harvard University, 1967), 260.

100 *May the sun not set upon our wrath!* "Let not the sun go down upon your wrath" (Ephesians 4:26).

100 *Psalm 50* The primary mood of Psalm 50 (Psalm 51 in the King James Version) is penitential: "Have mercy upon me, O God, according to thy loving-kindness: according unto the multitude of thy tender mercies blot out my transgressions." One verse alludes, apparently, to illegitimacy: "Behold, I was shapen in iniquity; and in sin did my mother conceive me." The Khrushchov family has a history of illegitimate births and intermingling of peasant and gentry bloodlines. At least one of Grandfather's sons may not really be his, and family folklore has it that the man who murders him, Gervaska, is his illegitimate son. Note also allusions to this psalm in "The Gentleman from San Francisco."

101 *Old man's here . . . you'd buy him back!* An expression common in Bunin's native region, it is sometimes shortened: "*Ubit' by ego,*

kupit' by ego" ("Could just kill him; like to buy him"). Most frequently used in a situation of remorse (when a person who has been a nuisance dies), it means, "We didn't appreciate him when he was alive, but now we'd be willing to pay to bring him back." Thanks for this information to Professor S. A. Sionova of Yelets Pedagogical Institute.

The beautifully lyric nature scene in which Bunin allows his character Pyotr Kirillovich one last look at the earth he is about to depart recalls the death of the poet Afanasy Fet, one of Bunin's favorites. Fet, who died on November 21, 1892, had been ill for some time. He got up from his sickbed, walked out onto the porch of the country house, breathed in the fresh air, and took one last look at life; then he walked back inside, sat down in an armchair, and died. The serenity of this final scene is belied by the fact that he died of severe asthma and had just made an unsuccessful attempt to commit suicide. On Fet (Shenshin), see also notes to "Light Breathing" and "The Cold Fall."

109 *besieged Pochaev* The Pochaevsko-Uspenskaia Lavra is a monastery in western Ukraine (Kremenets subdistrict of Ternopol' district). Historically it has been constantly embroiled in political struggles between Poland and Russia linked to religious rivalries. From the 1770s the monastery was in the hands of the Uniates (supported by the Polish government). After the monks participated in the Polish Uprising of 1830 to 1831, it was transferred to the Orthodox Church (*Great Soviet Encyclopedia,* 20:247). Following the First World War Pochaev reverted to Polish control and remained a part of Poland until 1939. The monastery, supposedly founded a hundred years before Rus embraced Orthodox Christianity, is known for its wonder-working icon of the Mother of God (in the Dormition Cathedral). It also has the relics of the reverend Job of Pochaev (celebrated for their power to heal) and a famous spring also noted for healing the sick. See *Orekh-svjat.*, 49–57.

116 *age-old ditties . . . in the nursery* The bogeyman with his bag coming for the screaming child is in the tradition of the threat lullaby.

Examples may be found in the lullaby section of V. P. Anikin, ed., *Mudrost' narodnaja: zhizn' cheloveka v russkom folk'lore: Vypusk pervyj, Mladenchestvo, detstvo* (Moscow, 1991), 70–72. Here is one:

Hushaby, hushaby,
Hushaby, my child!
A little old man will come,
Will whip you with a switch;
Will whip you, you know why?
'Cause you don't sleep at night,
All you do is yell!

Lullabies steeped in violence, threats, death are commonplace worldwide. On the universality of this phenomenon, see part 2, "Lulling," in Marina Warner, *No Go the Bogeyman* (New York, 1998).

116 *traditional funeral dish of frumenty* In Russian, *kut'ja,* this dish is associated with a variety of folk rituals. It is prepared (in its purest, traditional peasant variant) from whole grains of wheat and bird-cherry berries. The more recent, urban variant is made from rice mixed with raisins and honey.

118 *On ocean's expanse, on sea's watery waste* Bunin often collected and transcribed oral folklore. See, for example, *Lit. nasled.,* 1:402. This type of charm, called *otsushka,* is aimed at removing the travails and grief of love. Its rhythmic first line is a formulaic beginning for a multitude of Russian charms. The pattern of invoking a faraway, mystical realm at the beginning is typical. It is as if one must leave one's present existence and go out to some mysterious world where the power of the charm will be more effective. On the mythical Isle of Buyan, see E. Grushko and Ju. Medvedev, eds., *Slovar' slavjanskoj mifologii* (Nizhnij Novgorod: 1995), 222–23. The mysterious Sea-Ocean (Ocean-Sea) is discussed in the same work two pages earlier. Joseph Conrad (citing V. Vilinbakhov, "Tajna ostrova Bujana," in the journal *Nauka i religija* [1967, 9:52–55]) writes that Buyan was thought to be the home of Elijah the Prophet; he identifies Buyan (endemic in Russian charms and other Russian folk genres) precisely:

"It is the present-day Baltic island of Rügen, and was once a mecca-like goal for Slavic pilgrims" (*Slavic and East European Journal,* no. 3 [1989], 438). For more on Buyan (Ruyan/Rugen) see A. N. Afanas'ev, *Poeticheskie vozzrenija slavjan na prirodu* (3 vols., 1865–69), Moscow 1994 reprint, 2:131–33. See also Maria Kravchenko, *The World of the Russian Fairy Tale* (New York: Peter Lang, 1987), 142–46. Of course, the Buyan of Russian folklore is not a real Baltic island; it's a never-never land.

121 *Mary of Egypt* Sixth-century saint (died in 522), commemorated in the Orthodox Church on April 1/14. According to the traditional tale, she abandoned her parents and went off to Alexandria, where she lived a licentious life. From her own words, as told to Father Zosima, "I thought that the whole meaning of life consisted of satisfying the lustings of the flesh." From Alexandria she decided to go to Jerusalem, committing acts of fornication all the way there. She was repulsed by a heavenly force when trying to enter the holy temple in Jerusalem. She prayed to the Virgin, and a voice from an icon of the Mother of God spoke to her, saying, "If you go out beyond the Jordan, there you will find a blessed tranquillity." She departed into the desert and lived forty-seven years in total isolation, doing penance for her sins. She is said to have walked on water, and when she prayed she levitated up from the earth, leaning on one elbow. Since Mary of Egypt herself had lived a life of profligacy, she is thought to be merciful to harlots and fornicators. Parents of sons or daughters who have lapsed into lechery address their prayers to her. See A. V. Kozlov, ed., *Prazdniki i znamenitye daty pravoslavnogo i narodnogo kalendarja* (St. Petersburg, 1993), 73–74. See also *Vrem. goda,* 96–97. For the English-language version of her life, see *Gold leg.,* 3:106–10.

122 *Kiev Cave Monastery* Founded in 1051, this is the oldest and most venerated monastery in the Russian world and the cultural center of ancient Rus.

124 *the gray goat* "In Christian Europe goats are thought to have been familiars of witches or of the Devil . . . The lechery of the goat is part

of European proverbial lore . . . Ritual intercourse between women and goats is indicated in Semitic and Latin areas" (*STDF,* 456).

125 *Saint Elijah the Ministrant, the ancient caster of flame* Saint Elijah's Day in the Russian Orthodox calendar is July 20/August 2. As usual in his treatment of Russian religion, Bunin emphasizes here the inevitable mixing of pagan folkloric belief and Christianity (dual belief, or syncretism). Elijah the Prophet, while a biblical figure (see 1 Corinthians 14:26–40 and Matthew 21:12–14, 17–20), is also closely associated with the pagan sky god Perun. Russian peasants imagined him riding a fiery chariot across the sky and throwing down thunderbolts. If not pacified he could destroy a peasant's crops with fire or hail. Peasants did not work on Saint Elijah's Day for fear of angering the prophet. They also prayed to him for rain. In the folk imagination he was simultaneously one who provided succor (ministrant) and a fearsome force for destruction (caster of flame). The peasants sometimes imagined Elijah as pursuing the devil and throwing down lightning bolts wherever he might take refuge. "Since the devil was prone to hide anywhere, measures were taken to keep him away during storms: the candles from Holy Thursday were lit, houses were censed, black cats and dogs, possible transformations of the devil, were thrown outside, and everything was sealed with the sign of the cross, for, according to general belief, the prophet might strike a house, animal, or person in which the unclean force sought refuge" (*Ivanits,* 29–30, citing S. V. Maksimov).

In *Drydale* the devil himself is resident in the manor (chapter 9), in the person of the despicable Yushka. Less than two months after Yushka leaves, a fireball races through the house (in September) and nearly burns it down. Ironically (or perhaps logically in the uncanny world of *Drydale*), Yushka may have a direct connection not only to the forces of the devil, but also to the folkloric-Christian Elijah. From the Russian name Il'ya or Iliya (Elijah) comes Il'yusha (affectionate diminutive), which leads to Il'yushka (pejorative-affectionate diminutive), which leads to Yushka (truncated version of Il'yushka). If this formulation holds, Yushka is a perverted representative of Saint Elijah in the flesh. He also appears to be in league with the *domovoj* (see above). In Bunin's diary entry for May 20, 1911, he describes the prototype for Yushka. See *Bab. 2*, 160.

In Bunin's story from 1913 "The Sacrifice," the syncretistic figure of Elijah plays a prominent role.

126 *her house serf Tkach* The name, which Unbegaun associates with Ukrainian, means "weaver." It, like names taken from professions (such as Baker or Cooper in English), became a surname in Russian, but surnames arrived late historically. In *Drydale* the name seems more like a nickname (see *Unbe.*, 277). The novella is full of incidental, nebulous characters, but Tkach is mentioned only this once. Like a lightning flash he flares briefly into the narrative, and the revelation that he was Grandmother's lover is one of the most astonishing facts in the whole saga of Drydale.

127 *God's Servitor of Voronezh* The prelate Mitrofan (more on him in notes to "Ioann the Weeper").

128 *the comet that steeped the whole country in terror* The only comet that appeared between the end of the Crimean War and the emancipation of the serfs in 1861 was one of the brightest ever, Donati's Comet, discovered on June 2, 1858, by Giovanni Donati (*Great Soviet Encyclopedia*, 8:364).

131 *citizens of the first rank* Designation under the reign of Catherine II (1762–96) for those who had scholarly degrees, for artists, capitalists, bankers, and shipping tycoons (*Dal'*, 2:43).

Way Back When

135 *the Arbat* At one time a prosperous district of Moscow; by the time of this story (early twentieth century) it had long since fallen into decline. The main street (in the 1990s it was made into a pedestrian street and tourist center) is also called Arbat. For detailed notes on the Moscow streets and landmarks mentioned in "Way Back When," see *Henry*, 70–74.

136 *the title of prince* Prince (*knjaz'*) is a title indicating high standing within the Russian landed nobility and implies no connection with royalty.

140 *Muir-Merrielees* Muir-Merrielees (or, in English, Muir and Merrielees) is a Moscow department store on Petrovka Street. Bunin's friend, the famous Anton Chekhov, once named two of his puppies Muir and Merrielees in honor of the store. See Donald Rayfield, *Anton Chekhov: A Life* (New York, 1997), 265, 613. In Soviet times the store remained at the same location but was called TSUM (acronym for "Central Department Store").

140 *a new Strastnoy and a new Petrovka* Strastnoy (Strastnoy Bul'var), Petrovka, and Kuznetsky (Kuznetsky most) are famous Moscow streets.

140 *pneumatics* Inflated rubber tires, recently introduced at the time the story is set.

141 *vats of bay leaves stood at the entrance of the Prague* The Prague Restaurant still is there in the Old Arbat district. The bay leaves are used for flavoring soups.

142 *the Trinity Monastery or the New Jerusalem* Famous Russian Orthodox monasteries near Moscow, much visited by Russian believers on pilgrimages. The Trinity–Saint Sergius Monastery, founded by Sergius of Radonezh, is located in Sergiev Posad, while the New Jerusalem, associated with the Patriarch Nikon, is in the town of Istra. See *Orekh-mest.*, 109–31.

A Passing

In one of his early stories, "The Golden Pen" (1920), the Soviet writer Valentin Kataev ironically portrays Bunin in Odessa, in the process of writing what was to become "A Passing" as the Russian Civil War raged around him. Other writers have also made Bunin a character in their works of fiction. For example, Yury Nagibin's story "The Literature Teacher" portrays a precocious and arrogant young Vanechka Bunin during his years as a student in Yelets. See Nagibin's *Tsarskoselskoe utro* (Moscow: Sovetskij pisatel', 1983), 389–404.

145 *the prince* See note to "Way Back When."

146 *Bestuzhev* The history of Russian surnames can be traced only for the nobility, since no documents exist for any other class prior to the eighteenth century. A Russian family of the nobility often attempted to shore up its claims to an ancient provenance by pointing to an ancestor from a foreign land (the Bunins, for example, did this themselves). Purely Russian origin was considered somehow not quite respectable. The name Bestuzhev probably comes from the nickname Besstuzhij (Shameless), but family legend concocted an English forebear, a certain Gabriel Best, who supposedly entered the service of the Grand Duke of Moscow early in the sixteenth century. See *Unbe.*, 22–24. Incidentally, *Unbe.* (161) lists Bunin in the category of "Surnames derived from personal nicknames" and says the nickname meant "haughty person" (quite an appropriate etymology for Ivan Bunin's name!). One of Bunin's nicknames within his family was Sudorozhnyj (the Convulsive), indicative of his irascible and quick-tempered personality (*Mikh.*, 20).

147 *several bins of newly reaped grain* These are *chetveriki*, each equivalent to 26.239 liters (Old Russian dry measure).

149 *Praise ye the Lord from the heavens* Psalm 148.

151 *tarantass* See note to "The Grammar of Love."

The Snow Bull

This is a story full of colors (aquarelle paintings of a wintry night in the countryside: whites, blacks, blues, greens), along with all sorts of light effects: gleams, shimmers, and glimmers. It has an ominous tone; something foreboding is suggested by the sinister figure of the snow ogre. On the other hand, it describes an artist, a contemplator (like Bunin) who takes sheer pleasure in looking at the world and marveling at its wonders. After he destroys the snow creature, Khrushchov seems, in his own mind, to have eliminated the uneasiness in himself and his sleeping son. But something about the ending suggests otherwise—in particular the green color of the horses that intrudes upon the azures and whites. Here is one possible interpretation of "The Snow Bull": it depicts an artist reveling in the joys of life just before a horrible tragedy is about to befall him. Everything in the house is asleep in the night: the white-haired doll with the wide-open eyes rolled back, the wooden horses, and the boxes of the little boy, who awakens frightened. He too, Kolya, is soon to be sleeping the eternal sleep. We have no way of confirming this interpretation in the context of the story itself, but the subtext suggests that "The Snow Bull" is about the death of Bunin's own son, Nikolai (Kolya). In an earlier variant of the story the contemplative Khrushchov is, apparently, a writer. Having obliterated the snow ogre, he thinks, "Now if I could go back to my study and simply, in very simple terms, write down everything that I've just seen and felt" (*Sob. soch.*, 3:479–80). In the purist view of literary hermeneutics, autobiographical details are supposed to be kept apart from the artifice of the story, but if you know that Bunin's only son was named Kolya and that he died in the winter, you can't help reading this story beyond the boundaries of the text. In my view, Bunin would never have used the name of his own dead son without good reason. He wrote the story in midsummer but chose a background of winter. Only six years before that Kolya Bunin had died at age four, on January 16, 1905. You wonder if he really had once built a snow monster, or if something like what is described in the story actually occurred.

154 *Khrushchov* The name derives from that of an insect, the may beetle, *khrushch* (*Unbe.*, 191). Of course, Bunin would not have used this surname for a sensitive protagonist of the landed nobility had he known that a man of peasant origins named Khrushchov would become Soviet premier fifty years later. It is, however, also the surname Bunin uses for his family of squires in *Drydale*, a work completed in 1911. This suggests that Bunin saw an affinity between the narrator of that novella and the artist-protagonist of "The Snow Bull." Both of these characters, to some extent, are

alter egos of Bunin himself. Another connection is the decapitation leitmotif (Khrushchov knocks the head off the snow monster). In *Drydale* a central image is the decapitated Mercurius. In addition, Natalya's head is sheared, and Grandfather and Pyotr Petrovich die from blows to the head; both Natalya and Aunt Tonia "lose their heads" over love.

The Saviour in Desecration

This is one of many Bunin stories using the same narrative frame: a man of the gentry (sometimes, like Bunin himself, a creative artist) is driven in a cab or carriage by a peasant, who either tells him a story or contributes to the narrative in his colloquy with the gentleman. See, for example, in this collection, "The Grammar of Love," "Transfiguration," and "Somber Pathways."

The remark about icons used as covers for chamber pots is a paraphrase of a peasant saying that Belinsky quotes in his famous "Letter to Gogol" of 1847. See V. G. Belinskij, *Estetika i literaturnaja kritika* (Moscow, 1959), 2:636: "According to you the Russian people are the most religious in the world. It's a lie! At the basis of religion is pietism, reverence, the fear of God. But a Russian pronounces the name of God while scratching his backside. In speaking of an icon he says, 'if it's worth its salt you pray to it, and if it's good for nothing you use it as a cover for chamber pots.' Take a closer look, and you'll see that by their very nature the common people are deeply atheistic. They still have a great deal of superstition, but not even a trace of religiosity."

Bunin may have not been this straightforward about his views of the "folk," but I think that he would have agreed with the opinion Belinsky expresses. Notwithstanding this, and despite the ironic tone of the narrative, "The Saviour in Desecration" is, in its own odd way, one of Bunin's most religious stories.

159 *the Empress Vasilisa* The maiden Vasilisa appears most prominently in a popular Russian folktale that has a Cinderella-type plot: "Vasilisa the Lovely." The Eastern Orthodox tradition also has a martyress Vasilisa (died in A.D. 309), who is commemorated on September 3/16.

The Sacrifice

According to a diary note by Vera Nikolaevna Bunina (June 9, 1923), Bunin spoke about the original inspiration for the story as follows: "I was on my way to Yelets and I saw a hut being built beside the highroad, and the shavings were gleaming in the moonlight" (*Ust. Bun.*, 2:112). In his own diary (June 17, 1912; *Ust. Bun.*, 1:126) Bunin writes about being in a tiny peasant hut near Glotovo, where he saw a boy of about fifteen who had been killed by lightning and a little girl whose head had been singed (*Bab. notes*, 3:544).

"The Sacrifice" is one of Bunin's most important stories on the theme of syncretism (dual belief) in Russian life. It is striking that in the Russian folk conception of Elijah the Prophet so much pagan residue remains, since in his biblical persona he is the staunch defender of the One True God and the castigator of pagan ways. Elijah fought to preserve Israel's worship of the true God against corruption by Queen Jezebel and the Phoenician priests of Baal (1 Kings:17–19, 21). The Bible story of Elijah goes roughly as follows: Elijah lived the life of an ascetic, letting his hair grow long and dressing in animal skins. He prophesied a horrible drought, to be visited upon those who did not accept the one God. Later he engaged in a kind of competition with the high priests of the pagan god Baal to see whose God would accept a sacrifice and send down fire. The priests of Baal could not get any reaction out of their god; then it was Elijah's turn. He placed a fatted calf upon his sacrificial altar and sprinkled the calf and the wood with water three times. After God sent down fire to consume the wood, water, and calf, the people began glorifying the One True God; then a cloud rose up and rain fell. Elijah ordered the priests of Baal to be seized and executed. After this he went back out into the desert, spent forty days and forty nights wandering there. A voice ordered him to stand before God and hear his commands, which would be audible not in the winds, not in an earthquake, not in fire, but in a quiet breeze. At the end of his life Elijah was taken up alive to heaven in a fiery chariot sent down by God.

The biblical story of Elijah is reflected in Russian iconography. There is a thirteenth-century icon from the village of Vybuty, near Pskov, showing a majestic but very tranquil Elijah listening to the voice of God in the air (Tretjakov Gallery, Moscow). A fifteenth-century icon painted in Novgorod (now also in Tretjakov) portrays a mean-eyed, very imposing old prophet staring out at the viewer with a penetrating gaze. Here we have the kind of wrathful, threatening image that is reflected in "The Sacrifice." For depictions of these two icons see *Barsk.*, 150–53. A third icon is "The Fiery Ascension of Elijah the Prophet," which portrays Elijah in the center, episodes from his life around the borders, and the fiery chariot at the top (a copy is displayed at the Ethnographic Museum in St. Petersburg).

In the Russian folk tradition Elijah is an irrational, avenging heavenly figure who sends down thunder and lightning bolts (see notes to *Drydale*). Peasants prayed to him in times of drought and brought sacrifices to him (a shoulder of lamb or a calf). He also was closely associated with fertility and with control over the harvest. See *Vrem.goda*, 173–78. Bunin's "The Sacrifice" is based loosely on a Russian folktale, "Elijah the Prophet and Saint Nicholas." See A. N. Afanas'ev, *Narodnye russkie skazki i legendi* (Berlin, 1922), 2:500–3. For an English translation, see *Ivanits*, 138–40. In this story a certain peasant always observes Saint Nicholas Day but not Saint Elijah's; he even works on July 20. Elijah decides to punish him, but Saint Nicholas warns the peasant that his grain is about to be scorched, and he sells it off cheaply to the priest of Saint Elijah's Church. This sort of thing is repeated twice more, until, finally, the peasant appeases Saint Elijah by buying a big ruble candle to place before his icon while buying a little kopeck candle for Saint Nicholas. The tale ends happily for the peasant (and there is nothing about his relatives dying of lightning strikes at any point in the story). On the history of sacrifices in the Slavic world, see also Afanas'ev, *Poeticheskie vozzrenija slavjan na prirodu*, 2:249–64.

161 *Peter-Paul Fast* June 29/July 12.

161 *Brod* Ovsjanyj Brod is a place-name on the map even today, located a few kilometers south of the estate of Bunin's grandmother, Ozerki.

161 *Saint Elijah's Day* July 20/August 2.

165 *splint light* A long dry stick used to provide illumination in a peasant hut. For an illustration of how such sticks (wood splints) were mounted, see Genevra Gerhart, *The Russian's World: Life and Language*, 2nd ed. (New York: Harcourt Brace Jovanovich, 1995), 104.

Transfiguration

On the Transfiguration (*Preobrazhenie*) of Jesus Christ, which is celebrated on August 6/19 in the Russian Orthodox Church, see Matthew 17:11–13, Mark 9:2–9, Luke 9:28–36. The Russian verb from the same root (*preobrazit'sja*) is also a high-style word for "to die"; therefore, the Russian title has the additional connotation "death." Christ's transfiguration is at least obliquely applicable to the meaning of Bunin's story. See, for example, Joseph Campbell, *The Hero with a Thousand Faces,* 2nd ed. (Princeton University, 1968), 229–30, 236–37. Campbell (as Bunin) sees the transfiguration in terms of Eastern religious concepts. There are two more transfigurations suggested by the title of the story: that of the old lady who dies and that of her son Gavril, whose life is transfigured on the night he reads the Psalms over his dead mother, watching her as she is transfigured. Another transfiguration of sorts is implied by the narrative method of the story. It is Gavril's tale, but not a word in the story is directly his. We learn in the tack-on at the end that he has told this story, while working as a coachman, to "a worthy man." This is another of Bunin's favorite "Ivlev" types, the educated man riding in the carriage and talking to the peasant (see "The Saviour in Desecration" and "The Grammar of Love"). Gavril's story of his transfiguration is obviously filtered through "Ivlev's" literary imagination, and it is he who retells it in literary terms.

Note that in the biblical account the Prophet Elijah, along with Moses, appears to Christ during the Transfiguration. Elijah is also to return with Jesus at the time of the Last Judgment. On Elijah in Russian Orthodoxy and in the Russian folk tradition, see notes to "The Sacrifice" and *Drydale.* For parallels in this story with iconic representations of the transfiguration of Christ, see the afterword.

On the history and design of the Russian peasant hut, see *Bol'shaja sovetskaja entsiklopedija,* 2nd ed., 17:352–53. See also Gerhart, *The Russian's World,* 96–105.

The Gentleman from San Francisco

The model for the hotel on Capri is the Grand Hotel Quisisana, where Bunin and his wife stayed three winters in a row. In the Bunin Museum at

Orel there is a postcard of the hotel that Bunin sent to his brother, with the windows of Bunin's room circled. See this postcard reproduced in Asja Olejnikova, ed., *Vernis' na rodinu, dusha (fotoal'bom)* (Orel: Izd. Orlovskoj gosudarstvennoj teleradioveshchatel'noj kompanii, 1995), 88. His memoir of Chaliapin (*Sob. soch.*, 9:392) mentions that the great singer visited him at the hotel and once sang for a group of people there. See the photograph of Chaliapin, Bunin, Gorky, and others (dated 1913) in Olejnikova, 86. Hazzard notes that many of Capri's hotels were originally built for ambulatory tubercular patients and that the Quisisana took its name from an Italian phrase meaning "Here one is healed." This has a particular irony in light of what happened to the gentleman at this hotel. See Shirley Hazzard, *Greene on Capri* (New York: Farrar, Straus, and Giroux, 2000), 122.

In notes entitled "The Origins of My Stories," Bunin describes the impetus for "The Gentleman from San Francisco." He recalls having seen Mann's *Death in Venice* in the window of a bookstore in Moscow, after which he thought of the sudden death of an American on Capri and immediately decided to write "Death on Capri," which he finished in four days. "I made up San Francisco and everything else (except for the fact that some American really did die after having dinner in the Quisisana)." See *Sob. soch.*, 4:483. On why Bunin domiciled his American businessman in San Francisco, see the afterword. If you read newspaper accounts of the devastating earthquake and raging fires in San Francisco (April 18, 1906), you can't help wondering how the "hero" of the story managed to restore his business (whatever his business was) and make a substantial profit (enough to allow for his long trip around the world) just a few short years after much of the city and its business district were destroyed.

On the Naples area and the Isle of Capri, see the guidebook *Naples: The City and Its Famous Bay, Capri, Sorrento, Ischia, and the Amalfi Coast down to Sorrento* (Touring Club of Italy, 1999), especially 145–50. Many things described by Bunin in 1915 are still there: the funicular still operates, and the Grand Hotel Quisisana, most probable death site of the gentleman from San Francisco, remains the most luxurious hotel on the island. The Blue Grotto (Grotto Azzurra) is still the most famous tourist attraction. The Phoenician Path mentioned in Bunin's story is the Scala Fenicia, "a steep and ancient path with more than 500 steps carved out during the time of the Greek colonists and resurrected by the Romans"

(145; see also Hazzard, 120). The little donkeys (called *ciucci*) that used to carry tourists up the steep paths have now been replaced by electric carts. (Hazzard, 100).

173 *tarantella* A lively, passionate Neapolitan folk dance, usually performed by couples accompanied by the tambourine, popularly supposed to be a remedy against the bite of the tarantula (*Webster's Second International Dictionary*). According to the reminiscences of Vera Bunina, the writer himself once performed a brisk imitation of a tarantella on board an Italian ship sailing for Odessa (see *Bab.*, 131). The same passage describes an argument Bunin had about social injustice with a student of right-wing views; Bunin emphasized how the ship was made up of different levels (with the stokers slaving away on the lower level and the passengers sitting up above drinking wine). Vera Nikolaevna assumes that this conversation was the genesis of "The Gentleman from San Francisco."

173 *Miserere* (Latin, "have mercy") (1) Psalm 50 in the Vulgate, one of the most popular of the penitential Psalms, so called from its first words: "Have mercy upon me, O God, according to thy lovingkindness; according unto the multitude of thy tender mercies blot out my transgressions" (Psalm 51 in the King James Version). (2) A musical setting of Psalm 50 as the *Miserere* of Allegri, written (about 1635) for nine voices in two choirs (*Webster's Second International Dictionary*). Note that in *Drydale* Pyotr Kirillovich (Grandfather) potters about muttering Psalm 50 on the eve of his murder.

181 *Tiberius* Second emperor of Rome, reigned A.D. 14 to A.D. 37. His initially benevolent rule degenerated into a reign of terror, and in A.D. 27 he retired to Capri, where he led a life of brutish sensuality (*Henry*, 68). Most historians assume that the stories of the brutality of Tiberius on Capri have been embellished by folk legend.

184 *his soul had lacked even a mustard seed of so-called mystical feelings* The original metaphor is biblical (Matthew 17:20): "For verily I say unto you, If ye have faith as a grain of mustard seed, ye shall say

unto this mountain, Remove hence to yonder place; and it shall remove: and nothing shall be impossible unto you."

184 *Reuss XVII* The German principalities of Reuss (Reuss-Greiz, the older line, and Reuss-Schleiz-Gera, the younger line) were incorporated into Thuringia in 1918 (*Henry*, 69).

188 *a man resembling Ibsen* Henrik Ibsen (1828–1906), Norwegian playwright. Why the mention of Ibsen here? Because Bunin appears likely to have been familiar with an Ibsen poem, "A Letter in Verse" ("Et rimbrev," 1875). See E. A. Jablokov, "Pozhar na kovchege (Rasskazy I. Bunina i proza M. Bulgakova nachala 1920–kh godov)," in *Tsarstvennaja svoboda: o tvorchestve I. A. Bunina* (Voronezh, 1995), 105n4. "Et rimbrev" has been translated by John Northam as "A Rhyme-Letter" in *Ibsen's Poems* (Olso: Norwegian University Press, 1986), 125–29. It has many details in common with "The Gentleman from San Francisco": (1) the ship in the poem is called *Europa*, and it seems to be on a voyage that marks the end of European civilization (this apocalyptic theme was on Bunin's mind when he wrote his story); (2) there is a description of the ship's bowels ("the boilers bubble; the pistons shrug their shoulders at the double") and of the captain, who "deserves the confidence of all on board"; (3) a general malaise infects the ship because, for some unknown reason, everyone, both crew and passengers, suspects that "we're sailing with a corpse for cargo." This imagery of the corpse in the hold of *Europa* is repeated twice, and with its second mention the poem ends.

194 *two Abruzzian mountaineers* Bunin probably encountered such men on Capri, but he may have borrowed the scene of the mountaineers from a painting by Karl Bryullov, *Pifferari before the Image of the Madonna* (1825), now in the collection of the Tretjakov Gallery in Moscow. This painting depicts two Italian wandering musicians, one with bagpipes and the other with a fife, standing in front of a half-ruined chapel. At the top of the facade is a painting (not an alabaster statue) of the Virgin.

The Saints

Bunin considered this story one of his best (see *Novyj zhurnal,* no. 107 [1972], 161–70). The original title in manuscript was "The Harlot Alina."

In speaking of the main character, Bunin wrote Boris Zaitsev that Arsenich was totally fictitious and that he had never met anyone like him in real life (*Bab. notes,* 3:557, citing *Novyj zhurnal,* no. 136 [1979]).

198 *poddyovkas* A *poddyovka* is a man's light coat, collarless, gathered at the waist, its skirts reaching below the knees. This word appears repeatedly in the stories translated in this volume, but to avoid constant use of a foreign word in English, I have normally translated it as "waisted coat" or "long, tight-waisted coat."

200 *the old rag, so long and carefully preserved* Arsenich's handkerchief hints that he is akin to the Christian saints. See the mention of Thecla's small white handkerchief, which she gave to a beggarly old man (whereupon that gift outweighed all her sins). Note also that the most famous of all holy fools in Russia, Vasily (Basil) the Blessed (sixteenth century), went around naked but always carried a handkerchief in his hand.

203 *Niobe* In Greek mythology, the daughter of Tantalus. She offended the gods by denigrating the newly born twins Apollo and Artemida and bragging about her many children (she had seven boys and seven girls). After all of her children fell dead, pierced by Apollo's golden arrows, her inordinate pride was blamed for their deaths. Then, out of grief, she turned to stone, her mouth open as if still voicing her sorrow, and eternal tears were frozen in stone on her eyes. See I. S. Javorskaja, *Mify drevnej Gretsii* (Lenizdat, 1990), 31–35.

206 *There where the flesh consumeth away* Zechariah 14:12: "And this shall be the plague wherewith the Lord will smite all the people that have fought against Jerusalem; Their flesh shall consume away while they stand upon their feet, and their eyes shall consume away in their holes, and their tongue shall consume away in their mouth."

209 *the kind of pine tree they call a cedar* The word in Russian is *pevg* (see *Dal'*, 3:27, where it is described as a tree mentioned in the Bible). The reference is to 1 Kings 6:14–19, depicting Solomon's building of the house of the Lord. The wood most frequently mentioned for the structure is cedar.

210 *the elders of Valaam Monastery* The Valaam Monastery of the Transfiguration is located on the island of Valaam (Lake Ladoga); founded by Novgorodians not later than the beginning of the fourteenth century (*Sovetskij enstiklopedicheskij slovar'*, 190).

210 *the gift of tears* In the world of Eastern Orthodox asceticism the shedding of penitent tears is considered a gift. Mary of Egypt, for example, shed such copious tears that she could no longer see the secular world for the aqueous veil over her eyes. True believers who desire the gift of penitent tears are advised to pray to the venerable Saint Ephrem the Syrian (fourth-century theologian of Eastern Christendom). Heavy weeping is also an integral part of the institution of Russian holy foolery. See Panchenko, "Jurodstvo kak zrelishche," in D. S. Likhachev and A. M. Panchenko, "*Smekhovoj mir*" *drevnej Rusi* (Leningrad: Nauka, 1984), especially 104–12. Here the contradictory aspects of holy foolery are discussed. The *jurodivyj* (holy fool) "acts out" unseemly behavior in the marketplace square during the daylight hours but spends his nights alone, standing in prayer and weeping voluminous tears.

211 *the great martyr Boniface* Boniface of Tarsus (died A.D. 306). A man "much given to wine and debauchery," he was converted to Christianity, and in order to please Aglae (in Arsenich's variant of the legend she is called Aglaida), the wealthy Roman lady who was his patron, he made a trip to the East in search of relics. "Having reached Tarsus, he saw some confessors of the faith being led to torture, took their part, kissed their chains, and for this was condemned to death. It was his relics that Aglae received, and she placed them in an oratory fifty stadia from Rome" (*Engle.*, 188). One wonders if Bunin (or the original hagiographers) grasped the

irony of this odd tale, in which a dissolute man goes in search of relics, dies owing to a rash act of bravura, and returns home sanctified, in the person of his own holy relics!

212 *Shamakha* Also mentioned in "Shere Monday."

Zakhar Vorobyov

For a description of Bunin reading this story to a group including Maxim Gorky on Capri in 1912, see *Mar.*, 1:157–58. See also *Bab. notes*, 3:542. Gorky is described as weeping, enraptured with the story. The theme of common Russian man as epic hero is in tune with much of what he himself wrote. The very word "man" "sounds proud" in the famous Gorky phrase, and the proud hero has parallels with heroes of the Russian epic tales (*bylina*) and the tall tales of the American West (the Paul Bunyan sort of thing). Zakhar can outstare the sun and win a race with it (but he can't outdrink Death). The story also has something in common with the parable by Tolstoy, "How Much Land Does a Man Need?" in which the protagonist drops dead from extreme physical exertion (but in Tolstoy's tale the theme is greed and the character is negative).

On the "duel" with the sun, see the proverb cited in *The Life of Arseniev* (*Sob. soch.*, 6:113): "Death is like the sun; you can't look at it." See also the Bunin poem "Stop, Sun" ("Sun, Stand Thou Still" [1:403]) and the use of this biblical citation in the story "Night."

"Zakhar Vorobyov" has an unexpected subtheme: the theme of the artist and his audience. Zakhar the storyteller is the folk artist enveloped in his own creative imagination, but his listeners are dull and unimaginative, totally unreceptive to the creative art that he presents them. Consciously or subconsciously, Bunin may have had his own readers, or literary critics, in mind. He often treated the theme of writer and reader (teller and listener) in oblique ways. In, for example, "The Saints," the children (audience) ask the storyteller Arsenich, "Did you make all that stuff up yourself?" Bunin's answer to that question was almost always a resounding yes, even when his materials were clearly based on personal experiences. For a broad discussion of the theme of art and the creative artist in Bunin's works (treated most prominently in this volume in "An Unknown Friend" and the "Ivlev" stories), see Ol'ga Berdnikova, "Buninskaja kontseptsija khudozhnika," in *Bounine revisité: Cahiers de l'émigration russe* (Paris: Institut d'Études Slaves, 1997), 4:53–60.

215 *Zakhar Vorobyov* The title and name of the main character are equivalent in English to Zacharias Sparrowson.

215 *Aspen Grange* (Osinovye Dvory) The home village of Zakhar Vorobyov actually existed. It was not far from Glotovo, where Bunin himself lived for a number of years (*Bab. notes*, 3:542). Livelong (Zhiloe), death site of Zakhar, is also still to be found on a map of the region.

216 *First Saviour Day* (Pervyj Spas) August 1/14. Also called Honey Saviour Day or Wet Saviour Day, this is the first of three holy days dedicated to Jesus Christ. It was established to honor the signs that issued forth from the icons of the Saviour, the Holy Virgin, and the Venerable Cross during the battle of the saintly prince Andrej Bogoljubskij (1157–74) against the Volga Bulgars in 1164. It is the first day of the Dormition Fast (which Zakhar, obviously, does not observe). Second Saviour Day (Apple Saviour Day) is August 6/19, Transfiguration. Third Saviour Day (Nut Saviour Day) is August 16/29; it is associated with the legend of the Icon Created Not by Human Hands. See *Vrem. goda*, 184–86, 189–90, 196–97.

221 *hand scale* In Russian, *bezmen;* a simple weighing scales with a hook, held in one hand. The word has overtones of violence in certain expressions, and the implication here is that the peasant is threatening to strike the local magistrate with the instrument. See, for example, *Dal'*, 1:66, the expression "I'll weigh you on a (knuckle) bone *bezmen*" is like the modern threat in English "I'll give you a knuckle sandwich."

229 *Tatar thistle* See notes to *Drydale.*

234 *meekly placed copper coins at the head of that heap* The ritual of placing copper coins at the head of a corpse has various explanations, but it most likely is a way of "laying the ghost," that is, gift

giving to the deceased as a gesture of pacification, so that his spirit will not return to haunt the living. The common people sometimes explain that the money is used by the deceased for paying off sentinels who guard the gates into the otherworld. See Anne Ingram, "Marking Death: Representations of Beliefs about the Dead in Ukrainian Cemeteries," *SEEFA Journal* (*Journal of the Slavic and East European Folklore Association*) 3, no. 2 (fall 1998): 21.

Glory

The title might also be translated as "Fame."

This story barely makes it into the category of fiction. Bunin invents a somewhat eccentric narrator to express his own ideas, and there is not any plot or development of the action. Quite frequently Bunin's works do not fit exact categories of fiction. For example, "Night" is a lyrical-philosophical meditation, not really a short story.

Bunin was interested in holy fools, God's People, pilgrims, false messiahs, and village eccentrics for his whole writing career. See, for example, among works not translated for this volume, the story "The Chalice of Life" (1913; *Sob. soch.*, 4:201–21) and the poem "Nearing the End" ("Na iskhode," 1916; *Sob. soch.*, 1:436). As "Glory" illustrates, the author marveled at how such misfits came to be so revered among the Russian people. Writers like Tolstoy and Dostoevsky took the phenomenon of holy foolery in Russia more seriously; in debunking the God's People as, basically, charlatans, Bunin is more in line with Chekhov, who maintained, largely, a rationalist position in regard to Russian culture and peasant life. As Bunin and Chekhov, however, understood, it is difficult to grasp the irrationalist side of Russian culture (still vital today) without an understanding of the phenomenon of holy foolery. See, for example, D. S. Likhachev and A. M. Panchenko, *"Smekhovoj mir" drevnej Rusi*—especially the part written by Panchenko, titled "Smekh kak zrelishche" ("Laughter as Spectacle"), 91–194. See also Ewa Thompson, *Understanding Russia: The Holy Fool in Russian Culture* (New York: Lanham, 1987).

Biblical sources most widely cited as justification for the asceticism and self-abnegation of holy foolery are "Whosoever will come after me, let him deny himself" (Mark 8:34); "We are fools for Christ's sake" (1 Corinthians 4:10); and "If any man among you seemeth to be wise in this world, let him become a fool, that he may be wise" (1 Corinthians 3:18).

When asked about his plans for the future (in an interview very late in his life, in the indigent years), Bunin replied that his main concern was heating his apartment. The interviewer then asked him, "What about fame [glory]?" Bunin replied that fame meant little to him under the present circumstances and that coal and wood were the main thing. See *Mar.*, 3:283.

235 *Klyuchevsky* V. O. Klyuchevsky (1841–1911), renowned Russian historian.

239 *a ram's horn of Jericho* For the story of Joshua and how the walls of Jericho fell after the blasts of the seven trumpets of rams' horns, see Joshua 6.

242 *Danilushka of Kolomna . . . Semyon Mitrich* Bunin may have garnered some of the facts for this story from the book on charlatan holy fools by I. G. Pryzhkov, *26 moskovskikh lzhe-prorokov, lzhe-jurodivykh, dur' i durakov* (Moscow, 1865). Semyon Mitrich enjoyed enormous popularity despite his near inability to speak; he died in 1861 and five priests presided over his funeral (see Ewa Thompson, *Understanding Russia*, 40–41, citing Pryzhkov, who also mentions Danilushka's presence at the funeral).

243 *knucklebones* This game is described briefly in Gerhart, *The Russian's World*, 367. See also *Shang.*, 56. Knucklebones was a popular game played by males throughout much of Russian history. It consisted of throwing thin metallic "kickers" or "dingers" (*bitki*—small enough to be held in the hand, of various shapes, oblong or round, sometimes made by fusing knucklebones with lead) at mounted knucklebones (*babki*—the actual joints on the hooves of cattle) and trying to knock them down. The game was like boys' marbles today, in that whoever made the right hits got to keep the knucklebones he knocked down. There were many varieties of the game. Most commonly players would stand at a distance of some

ten to fifteen meters to make their tosses. The Russian Ethnographic Museum in St. Petersburg has on display some knucklebones and dingers.

Ioann the Weeper

On crying and weeping (the gift of tears) as an integral part of Orthodox asceticism and holy foolery, see notes to "The Saints."

246 *prince* See note to "Way Back When."

247 *a penitential psalm of David* Which psalm has the prince chosen for his epitaph? Various psalms of David express repentance, often blended with lamentation. The personal appeal or lament, "the cry of an individual to God for succor," is the most common type of psalm (*Interpreter's Bible,* 4:7).

247 *the bitter and terrible words of the prophet Micah* Bunin cites the passage (from Micah, 1:8) not exactly as the Russian Bible has it: "For this will I cry and weep, will I walk about like one plundered [robbed] and stripped naked, howl like the jackals and cry like the ostriches." *The Interpreter's Bible* (6:906) translates the passage as "For this I will lament and wail; I will go stripped and naked; I will make lamentation like the jackals, and mourning like the ostriches." The prophet Micah is bemoaning the fate of Samaria and Jerusalem, which must be punished for worshiping false gods. He hopes his people will change their ways and avoid imminent doom. "His was a desperate attempt to bring a nation to her senses" (*Interpreter's Bible,* 6:907).

248 *God's Holy Servitor of Voronezh* The prelate Mitrofan (1623–1703), a contemporary of Peter the Great. His relics, returned to the Orthodox Church in 1989, are now venerated at the Intercession Cathedral of Voronezh. When Mitrofan died in 1703 he was buried in the Annunciation Cathedral. In 1717 his body was disinterred and found to be whole (not decomposed), and after that the relics were considered to have healing powers. Especially begin-

ning in the 1820s, large numbers of pilgrims flocked to Voronezh; many miraculous healings were reported. See *Orekh-mest.*, 151–59. Among those who prayed at the relics of Mitrofan were Aunt Tonia and Natalya in Bunin's *Drydale* (after which Tonia's nervous illness abated).

248 *But in the village of Sinful itself, here is the story they tell of him* What follows is a skewed version of an official hagiography, with the "hagiographer" attempting to stick to the requisite devices and *topoi* (for example, the saint is described as coming from a devout family, loving the Gospels from his earliest years), while deviating radically at times from the formulas. For example, the storyteller gets carried away by the beauty of the priest's grain-fed horse and often lapses out of high-style language into ungrammatical colloquialisms. Some of the details (such as the way the hero is forcibly married off by his parents but has no sexual congress with his new wife) are borrowed from the popular hagiography of Alexis, Man of God.

248 *the Athos monastery* According to *Bab. notes*, 3:547, this is New Athos, on the Black Sea coast of the Caucasus.

I'm Saying Nothing

A lot of the folk material used in this story was collected by Bunin himself. On the description of beggars and cripples and the folk songs from Bunin's diaries (in English translation), see *Mar.*, 1:150, 176–77. See also *Ust. Bun.*, 1:110 (entry for July 15, 1911, on the beggars at Kiriki festival day), 118–19 (entry for May 19, 1912, the passage Shasha wails out to end the story)—this is the spiritual song, *dukhovnaja pesnja*, beginning, "Three sisters once lived, three Marys of Egypt." At one point in *Drydale* (chapter 8), the crazed Aunt Tonia calls herself Mary of Egypt, after the sixth-century saint. See notes to *Drydale*.

253 *Shasha* The normal Russian nickname for Alexander (Aleksandr) is Sasha, and this variant makes for a peculiar baby-talk effect.

According to Vera Nikolaevna Bunina there was an actual prototype for the Shasha of this story, a peasant from Glotovo named Alexander Ivanov. Some of the details, including a few of Shasha's favorite expressions and the description of his wedding, are based on reality. When the story first appeared in the newspaper *Russian Word,* somebody showed it to Shasha. After reading it he remarked indignantly, "Well, if you're going to write you ought to at least tell the truth and not make everything up!" Cited in *Bab. notes,* 3:555, from *Murom.-Bun.*, 46.

257 *lezginka* A brisk dance native to the Caucasus region and originating with the Lezgis of Daghestan. This is a wooing dance performed by a man whirling and leaping around an impassive woman, who turns slowly in place. It may also be performed as a wild saber dance by a man alone (*STDF,* 616).

257 *summoning up the memory of his dead mother* A typical example of how un-Freudian Bunin can be. This is the only mention in the story of Shasha's dead mother, and Bunin makes no attempt to explain the psychological underpinnings of his hero, why he behaves in the self-destructive way he does.

259 *Kiriki* (Or Kirika) Religious festival, the saint's day of Kirik and Ulita (Quirine and Juliet—Christian martyrs), celebrated on July 15/28. For the hagiographical account, see *Vrem. goda,* 170. The English translation can be found in *Gold leg.*, 3:225–26. There is a strange congruence between Bunin's tale of a man wallowing in voluptuous masochism and this brutal story. About A.D. 330 a noble lady, Juliet, flees from Iconium because she is persecuted for her Christian beliefs, taking with her a three-year-old son, Quirine. In Tarsus (Cilicia) the provost Alexander has her scourged with raw sinews. Later he throws down the child against a staircase, and "the tender brain fell abroad out of his head upon the steps." Juliet rejoices that her child has gone to heaven before her. "Then it was commanded that Juliet should be flayed, and burning pitch cast on her, and at the last her head to be smitten off." In a variant of the story the son declares himself Christian, "howbeit that he was over-

young to speak, but the Holy Ghost spake in him." Then mother and child are hewn into pieces and "disperpled abroad," but a heavenly angel appears to put the pieces back together, and Christian people give them a decent burial.

263 *ancient patriarchs . . . cave tombs where they were immured* Allusion to the Kiev Cave Monastery. See notes to *Drydale.*

264 *Alexis, Man of God* Son of Roman patricians, he wandered for seventeen years, returned home, and lived another seventeen years incognito, enduring the cruelties of the servants in the household. He was recognized only after his death, and a series of miraculous healings occurred at his funeral. His day of commemoration in the Orthodox calendar is March 17/30. His hagiography is one of the most popular in Russia, and Bunin borrowed details from it for the pseudo-hagiography in the story "Ioann the Weeper" (see *Vrem. goda,* 87–88). For an English translation of the hagiography, see *Gold leg.*, 6:205–12.

Noosiform Ears

On the decapitation leitmotif (the headless pool players, the decapitated Kazan Cathedral, and the head of the murdered Korolkova, invisible beneath the pillows), see notes to "The Snow Bull" and *Drydale.*

268 *Nevsky Prospect* Main thoroughfare of St. Petersburg. For descriptions of many of the Petersburg place-names, bridges, cathedrals, and other landmarks mentioned in "Noosiform Ears," see the guidebook *S.-Peterburg: Putevoditel' po stolitse* (St. Petersburg: Izd. S.-Peterburgskogo gorodskogo obshchestvennogo upravlenija, 1903).

268 *the statue of Alexander III* Unveiled May 23, 1909, on Znamensky Square, next to what is now the Moscow Railway Station, the monument honored Tsar Alexander for his role in constructing the Great Trans-Siberian Railway. The sculptor was P. P. (Paolo) Tru-

betskoj (the son of a Russian diplomat in Florence and an American woman, he was born and raised in Italy). This odd-looking equestrian statue (stout rider on exhausted horse) has had an equally odd history. It was, from the beginning, widely perceived as a caricature. The sculptor Trubetskoj is supposed to have said (this is probably apocryphal), "I don't know what all the fuss is about; I just depicted one animal sitting on another." At least publicly he defended the sculpture as a serious depiction of Russian might embodied in the figure of the tsar, and he remarked that perhaps his work was not appreciated because it deviated from the stereotypical portrayal of a royal figure. The statue was so widely ridiculed that within three years after it was unveiled the city duma was considering dismantling it or shipping it off to Vladivostok (the other end of the Trans-Siberian Railway). This occasioned even more jokes: "Now they're sending not only revolutionaries to Siberia; they've got around to exiling tsars there too!" After the victory of the Socialists in the October Revolution the statue was left standing but was publicly shamed. The "poet laureate" of socialism, Demian Bednyj, composed a four-line ditty, "The Scarecrow," which in 1919 was engraved on the pedestal:

> My son and my father were both executed in their time,
> And my destiny was to find posthumous ignominy.
> A cast-iron scarecrow, I stand here now in honor of the country
> That has cast off for all time the yoke of autocracy.

On October 15, 1937, declared to be of no historic value, the monument was removed. It became the property of the Russian Museum in 1939 and stood for a number of years in an isolated courtyard, where it survived the German bombs of World War II. It was finally rehabilitated only after the fall of the Soviet Union and was placed in the early nineties in front of the Marble Palace, where for years Lenin's famous armored car had stood. The sign there (as of spring 2000) reads that this is only a temporary location. Efforts are being made to transfer the statue back to its original site next to the Moscow Station. Therefore, that gasping, portly horse with its overweight rider (possibly influenced by Vrubel's strange painting *The Epic Hero*) may be destined to plod off again sometime soon, looking for a new home in the chaotic annals of Russian history. See the guidebook *Uznaj i poljubi Sankt-Peterburg,* compiled by V. F Pomarnatskij (St. Petersburg: Lenizdat, 1997), 161–63. For a full accounting of the history of the statue, with photographs, see L. P. Shaposhnikova, *Pamjatnik Aleksandru III: Skul'ptor Paolo Trubetskoj* (St. Petersburg: State Russian Museum, 1996). Note that Bunin based "Noosiform Ears" loosely on a crime committed in St. Petersburg in 1909, the same year the statue was unveiled. See V. N. Afanas'ev, *I. A. Bunin: ocherk tvorchestva* (Moscow, 1966), 252–53.

270 *pink peppermint sweets* Peppermint was thought to disguise the smell of alcohol on one's breath.

271 *I'm what they call a degenerate* The English word "degenerate" has its origins in *de* + *genus* ("that departs from its race or kind"). The Russian word *vyrodok* has the same etymological basis and the same meaning but has an additional (archaic) meaning surely known to Bunin: "the very worst or the *very best* of a given category of persons, having no similarity to any of them; unique, original" (italics mine). See *Slovar' sovremennogo russkogo literaturnogo jazyka* [Seventeen-volume dictionary of the Russian literary language] (Moscow: Izdatel'stvo Akademii nauk S.S.S.R., 1950–65). On Bunin's treatment of degeneracy in a variety of works, see *Wood.*, 108.

271 *By the ears, for example* In his ironic lecture on "noosiform" ears, Sokolovich seems to be mocking the theories of Cesare Lombroso (1835–1909), the famous Italian psychiatrist and criminal anthropologist, who visited Russia in 1896 and met with Tolstoy. Lombroso considered criminal behavior atavistic and listed physical features associated with different criminal types. Murderers were supposed to have cold glassy eyes, long ears, dark hair, and prominent canine teeth. Although Lombroso's theories have been discredited, they had some influence on Bunin, who was inclined to judge a person's character according to physical features. See, for example, *Wood.*, 109, citing a statement by Bunin that seems to

come directly from Lombroso or his disciples: "Modern criminal anthropology has established that the vast majority of natural criminals have pale faces, large cheekbones, a crude lower jaw, and deeply set eyes. Taking this into account, how can one not recall Lenin and thousands of others?"

272 *I read Dostoevsky's Crime and Punishment* Much of "Noosiform Ears" is a polemic with Dostoevsky and a parody of *Crime and Punishment,* Sokolovich being a travesty of Raskolnikov and Korolkova a travesty of Sonya Marmeladova. The critic Baboreko (*Bab. notes,* 4:503) points out similarities between Sokolovich and the "long-eared Shigalev" from Dostoevsky's novel *The Devils:* "his unnaturally large ears, long, wide and thick, with each sticking out, standing apart in its own special way" (citing Dostoevsky's *Polnoe sobranie sochinenij,* 10:110, 302). Bunin's vehement rejection of Dostoevsky's writings appears repeatedly in memoirs, letters, and the like. See, for example, *Mar.,* 3:29, 40, 184–85.

273 *murderers who have their names inscribed . . . annals of history* This very thing happened in the city where "Noosiform Ears" is set. Many Petersburg/Leningrad place-names were changed to honor revolutionaries who were, in fact, murderers. The most prominent example is Lenin himself. Another, less spectacular example: a footbridge right down the Griboedov Canal from the Church of the Saviour on the Blood (the church built on the spot where Alexander II was assassinated in 1881) was renamed in honor of the man who murdered him. Only recently, since the fall of the Soviet Union, have many of the assassins' names been removed and the original names of streets and bridges (and the city) restored.

274 *a trip to Sakhalin Island* Allusion to the trip made by Anton Chekhov in 1890. Sakhalin Island was the location of a notorious penal settlement.

276 *by the name of Yanovsky* The real name of Nikolai Gogol was Yanovsky; in "Noosiform Ears" Bunin's polemical tone is directed

not only at Dostoevsky but also at the whole "Petersburg Spirit" in Russian literature (for example, there is one dig at Aleksandr Blok's image of the feminine essence, the "beautiful lady"). Prominent among Gogol's works are those set in Petersburg, and the passage a few paragraphs later (beginning "Nevsky Prospect in the dead of night") is a takeoff on a famous description in the Gogol story "Nevsky Prospect." Bunin's attitude toward Gogol was predominantly negative, although at times he acknowledged Gogol's greatness and even influence on his own fiction. See *Mar.*, 3:39, 199, 249.

277 *Korolkova, who called herself simply Kinglet* Her surname resembles the Russian word for a type of bird, the kinglet (*korolyok*).

278 *the hideous, stout horse* Another allusion to the equestrian statue of Alexander III.

279 *You didn't know me; that means I'll get rich* A Russian superstition. If someone fails to recognize you, it is a sign that money is coming to you.

The Mad Artist

Deeply disturbed by the horrors of World War I and the Russian Revolution, Bunin was preoccupied with apocalyptic matters at the time he wrote this story. His works in the years directly preceding the revolution anticipate the end of the world as he knew it (see, for example, "The Gentleman from San Francisco," which had an epigraph, later deleted, from the book of Revelation). Replete with allusions to the New Testament, "The Mad Artist" treats apocalyptic themes best manifested in that final book of the Bible.

Sempiternal Spring

The theme of this story is the collapse of the Russian Tsarist Empire, but many of the descriptions of Moscow bear an uncanny resemblance to the city as it looked right after the collapse of the Soviet Empire seventy years later (the "New Russians" in their automobiles, the frenzied buying and selling, and so forth).

This story originated with Bunin's visit to the estate of Count Vladimir Grigorievich Orlov called Otrada, located about sixty miles from Moscow. Orlov came from a celebrated family of five brothers, one of whom (Aleksei, 1737–1808) was a hero of the Battle of Cheshme, for which he was granted the honorific "Orlov-Cheshmensky." The most famous Orlov brother was Grigory (1734–83), a favorite and lover of Catherine the Great, instrumental in helping her overthrow and murder her husband, Emperor Peter III, when she seized power in 1762. Vladimir Orlov (1743–1831), a cultured and highly educated man, had the Otrada palace built during the years 1775 to 1779 on the banks of the river Lopasni near the village of Semyonovsky. Many of the episodes in the story are taken from Bunin's direct personal experience, including the night spent on the porch of the inn. For all the details, see *Bab. notes,* 4:515–18. Baboreko provides even the name of the horse that pulled the carriage mentioned in the story: Harlequin.

An article by S. Kondakov from the magazine *Stolitsa i usad'ba* (nos. 83–88, 1917) describes the Otrada estate much as Bunin does in "Sempiternal Spring": the library of thousands of books, the somnolent lions at the entry, the piece of wood from the ship at Cheshme, the lake called Swan Lake, and so forth. See the reprint of that article, including photographs and paintings of the palace and mausoleum, in the journal *Pamjatniki otechestva* (*Mir russkoj usad'by*), 1992, no. 25:7–11.

296 *poddyovka* See note to "The Saints."

302 *the grass of oblivion* This phrase, taken from Alexander Pushkin's *Ruslan and Ljudmila,* was later used by Valentin Kataev as the title for his book on Bunin and Mayakovsky.

303 *the Battle of Cheshme* Naval battle on the Aegean Sea during the Russo-Ottoman War of 1768 to 1774. Fought in early July 1770, it resulted in a decisive victory over the Turks. Bunin has a poem whose title is the name of the flagship mentioned here, "Saint Eustachius." See *Sob. soch.*, 1:369–70.

304 *The sun, like a mare's piss puddle* Parody of two lines from a poem by the Soviet poet Sergei Esenin, "Mare Ships" ("Kobyl'i korabli," 1919): "Even the sun freezes, like a puddle / Pissed full by a gelding."

304 *So be it; let all past times away like fleeting dreams* Inexact citation from the poem by E. A. Baratynsky, "Desolation" (1834), which provided Bunin with the title for his story (the concluding lines of this poem are cited at the end of "Sempiternal Spring"). Evgeny Baratynsky was born on the family estate of Mara, near Tambov, in 1800. He was struck by the deterioration of the manor when he returned there from Moscow in the summer of 1833. The "spectre" who "prophesies with suasion an abode divine" is apparently the shade of Baratynsky's father. See Benjamin Dees, *E. A. Baratynsky* (New York: Twayne, 1972), 96–97. The name of the estate, Mara, with its Buddhistic connotations, would have had a special appeal for Bunin.

In a Never-Never Land

The title comes from the formulaic beginning of a Russian folk tale: *V nekotorom tsarstve, v nebyvalom gosudarstve* (Once upon a time in a far distant realm, in a never-never land).

There is a manuscript entitled "The Niece" held at the Bunin Emigré Archive (Leeds University, England). The title "In a Never-Never Land" ("*V nekotorom tsarstve*") has been added to this manuscript by V. N. Bunina. See Anthony J. Heywood, *Catalogue of the Bunin, Bunina, Zurov and Lopatina Collections,* Leeds Russian Archive, ed. Richard D. Davies with the assistance of Daniel Riniker (Leeds: Leeds University Press, 2000), 9. This archive contains manuscripts and drafts of many other stories translated for the present volume.

310 *Pushkin's Pskov exposé* (*Pskovskaja povest' Pushkina*—literally "Pushkin's Pskov novella") Most likely a nonsense phrase that reflects the dreamlike atmosphere of the story. Its alliterative sounds are more important than any meaning the words may

express. Alexander Pushkin, who was exiled to Pskov Province (the estate of Mikhailovskoe) for two years (1824–26), is the author of the play *Boris Godunov.* The mention of Godunov (Russian tsar, 1598–1605) later in the story, together with the mention of Pushkin, suggests that the protagonist may have derived inspiration for the imagery of his dream by reading Pushkin before going to bed. Ivlev, the imaginative artist type (who is an alter ego of Bunin himself), appears in other stories, most prominently in "The Grammar of Love."

An Unknown Friend

This story was inspired by Bunin's correspondence with a certain Natalya Esposito over a two-year period (1901–3). Mrs. Esposito, a Russian who married an Italian composer and lived near Dublin, first wrote him from Ireland in 1901, but, unlike the author in the story, Bunin answered her. Ten of her letters have survived (now held in the archive of the Turgenev Museum in Orel), but Bunin's replies to her have not. In one of her letters she uses the expression *l'ami inconnu,* which, in Russian, became the title of the story; many other passages from her letters are cited almost verbatim in "An Unknown Friend." See the article by L. N. Afonin, "O proiskhozhdenii rasskaza 'Neizvestnyj drug,'" in *Lit. nasled.*, 2:412–23. Bunin seems to have found a kindred spirit in Mrs. Esposito; at any rate, he and she share the Romantic conception of the high spiritual mission of art. He even seems to have been influenced to some extent by the ideas and style of Mrs. Esposito's letters. Although Bunin sometimes commented on the origins of his stories, he never publicly acknowledged the Esposito letters as the source of "An Unknown Friend." Bunin may have begun the story before his emigration or at least made extensive notes for it, since the Esposito letters were left behind when he emigrated and it is unlikely he could have remembered so many detailed passages from them in the year the story was written (1923). For a look at the postcard mentioned at the beginning of the story, with its "mournful and sublime view of a moonlit night," see the Afonin article, 415. The card, with the caption "Portrush by Moonlight," is in the archive at the Turgenev Museum.

The Hare

The title in Russian, "Rusak," refers to the gray hare (also called *serjak*), which is slightly larger than the European hare; unlike the white hare, also native to Russia, the *rusak* maintains its gray color year-round. The word *rusak* may also refer to a person with light brown hair.

The Cranes

In the Russian folk calendar the cranes fly away (*Zhuravlinyj lyot*) on September 18/October 1, which is the day of the Holy Martyress Arina (Ariadna). Traditionally you are supposed to shout "*Kolesom doroga!*" (which is a way of wishing them a good flight and literally translates as "May your road have wheels"); this will inspire them to return in spring. A rival date for the beginning of the flyaway comes much earlier, on Transfiguration Day, August 6/19 (see *Vrem. goda,* 225, 190). The peasant in this story, who wants to fly away with the cranes but ends up floundering on the ground like a bird shot down, resembles, at least in his impetuous drunken greediness for life, the protagonist of the story "Zakhar Vorobyov," written in 1912.

Avian imagery runs throughout Bunin's works (see, for example, in this collection the stork in "First Love"; the owl in *Drydale;* the owls, skylarks, and nightingales in *The Consecration of Love;* a variety of birds in "Sempiternal Spring"). Migratory birds, in particular the crane, are especially dear to the Russian folk psyche. One of Bunin's earliest prose works (1891) is a folk parable called "The Holiday," describing how a flock of wise albatrosses revel in a storm and survive it, while a flock of migrating birds perish (see *Lit. nasled.*, 1:160–61). Bunin once wrote in his diary: "The migration of birds is caused by an internal secretion: in autumn by a deficiency of a hormone, in spring by an excess of it . . . This agitation in birds may be compared to the time of sexual maturity and to periods of 'seasonal stimulation of the blood' in human beings . . . I've been just like a bird all my life!" Cited in *Bab.*, 61. In one of his interviews, Bunin remarks that "our fate has long been connected with birds," then goes on to enumerate the many literary works with avian names (*The Blue Bird,* "The Ugly Duckling," *The Seagull,* and so forth). See *Bakh.*, 167.

326 *drozhky* See note to *Drydale.* Mitya and the steward ride on a *drozhky* in *The Consecration of Love;* in "Zakhar Vorobyov" I have translated the word as "sulky."

The Calf's Head

Children and child psychology are not widely featured in Bunin's works. Two of the miniatures of 1930, "The Calf's Head" and "The Elephant," are exceptions to that tendency.

Indulgent Participation

The singer/artiste may be modeled partially on the famous actress Maria Nikolaevna Yermolova (1853–1928). In an interview that Bunin concocted to promote his own literary readings in the years of emigration he mentions how he frequently appeared with her at philanthropic literary evenings: "If only you knew what went on with her before she appeared onstage! Her hands were shaking, she kept taking valerian drops or Hoffmann's drops and was continually crossing herself" (*Bakh.*, 165). Yermolova, whom Stanislavsky was said to consider the greatest actress he had ever seen, was the first performer in the Soviet Union proclaimed "People's Artist."

332 *Molchanovka* There are two Molchanovka streets (*Bol'shaja* and *Malaja*), both located near the large bookstore Dom knigi.

332 *Imperial Theaters* The connection of the "former artiste" with the Imperial Theaters emphasizes her ostensible ludicrousness and obsoleteness, since at the time this story is set (second decade of the twentieth century) those state-run theaters were considered bastions of conservatism. The new mode was exemplified by the Moscow Art Theater, established by Stanislavsky and Nemirovich-Danchenko in 1898.

333 *the Fifth Moscow Gymnasium* Located on Povarskaya Street (in Soviet times, 1923–92, called Vorovsky Street), this school was known for the philanthropic concerts that it regularly organized.

333 *The Lower Depths* Maxim Gorky's famous play (also translated as *Down and Out*). Staged by Stanislavsky at the Moscow Art Theater in December 1902.

333 *The Blue Bird* Written by the Belgian symbolist Maeterlinck, this play was very popular in Russia in the early twentieth century and still sometimes appears at the Moscow Art Theater, where Stanislavsky staged it in 1908.

333 *The Three Sisters* Anton Chekhov's famous play, first performed at the Moscow Art Theater on January 31, 1901.

333 *Chaliapin* F. I. Shaljapin (1873–1938), world-famous bass, sang the role of the miller in *Water Nymph* (*Rusalka*) by A. S. Dargomyzhsky, an opera based on Pushkin's poem of the same title. On Chaliapin, see also notes to "The Gentleman from San Francisco" and "Shere Monday."

333 *Sobinov* L. V. Sobinov (1872–1934), renowned Russian tenor.

333 *Snow Maiden* (*Snegurochka*) A folklore fantasy by the playwright Aleksandr Ostrovsky. Rimsky-Korsakov's opera based on it was first staged by the Mamontov Opera in 1882.

333 *Shor, Krein, and Erlich* Moscow chamber musicians. Still a popular trio in postrevolutionary years. While traveling in the Near East in 1907 Bunin met D. S. Shor and accompanied him to Jerusalem (*Ust. Bun.*, 1:56; see also *Mikh.*, 215–16).

333 *Zimin's Opera* A Moscow opera house that functioned 1904–17. Founded by S. I. Zimin (1875–1942).

333 *Igor Severianin* Pseudonym of I. V. Lotarev, 1887–1941. Futurist poet who was extremely popular when this story is set. Bunin despised him. In fact, Bunin disliked almost everything mentioned on the long listing of playbills in "Indulgent Participation." The passage has an ironic subtext that culminates with the reference to a

writer whom Bunin considered the quintessence of early-twentieth-century modernist vulgarity.

335 *etheric-valerian medicine* Valerian was (and is) a common remedy for nerves. It supposedly has a calming effect on the heart and central nervous system.

335 *She has taken drops again—this time Hoffmann's* A remedy for nerves or upset stomach; after the German doctor Friedrich Hoffmann (1660–1742).

336 *lilies of the valley* Drops made from the lily of the valley are taken for a heart condition.

337 *the Lord has sent us to a sink-tuary here* This pronunciation of the word "sanctuary" reflects the artiste's old-fashioned, pseudoaristocratic style. In a diary note Bunin mentions that his first wife, Anna Tsakni, once played this song for him in the days before their marriage (see *Ust. Bun.*, 1:33). On Tsakni, see *Mikh.*, 138–53. See also *Mikh.*, 137–38, where the song (*Lied*) is attributed to Benjamin Louis Paul Godard.

The Idol

In Russian the title of this story is especially appropriate since the Russian word *idol* has two meanings: (1) "idol, image of a divinity," and (2) "callous or obtuse person, blockhead."

The Consecration of Love

On backgrounds of the story and possible prototypes for Mitya, see *Bab. notes*, 5:576. See also *Mikh.*, 374. A partial prototype was D. A. Shakhovskoj (later Archbishop John of San Francisco), and the scene of the assignation with Alyonka (including the participation of the steward as pimp) is taken from an episode in the life of Nikolai Pusheshnikov, Bunin's nephew. See *Bab. 2*, 270.

The critic Baboreko has also pointed out a possible prototype for the director of Katya's school. Just before the beginning of World War I a certain A. I. Adashev, an actor at the Moscow Art Theater and founder of his own private drama school, departed hastily for the provinces after the press devoted a number of articles to his scandalous behavior with his female students. See V. Afanas'ev, *I. A. Bunin* (Moscow, 1966), 297. See also *Bab. notes,* 5:576.

In May 1938, Bunin wrote, "In French the title I used for 'Mitya's Love' is much better: 'Le sacrement de l'amour.'" The French translation was published in 1925 (*Bab. notes,* 5:576–77). Based on this statement I have chosen my English title (rather than the literal but more pedestrian *Mitya's Love*).

340 *Tverskoy Boulevard* Probably the most famous and surely one of the most beautiful boulevards in Moscow; it now runs into Tverskaja (Gorky) Street at the Pushkin Monument (from 1932 to 1990 Tverskaja Street was part of Gorky Street).

340 *the skylarks had indeed returned* The mention of skylarks returning, bringing warmth and joy, alludes to a ritual observed by peasant girls as an invocation to spring. The skylarks supposedly return on March 9/22, Day of the Forty Martyrs. The peasants baked pastries in the shape of small birds, attached string to them, or mounted them on sticks. They flapped their arms as if they were the wings of larks, milled about like a flock of birds, and cried out, "Fly back, little larks, carry off the frosty winter, bring to us the warmth of spring; we're sick and tired of winter, it's eaten all our bread." By the nineteenth century this was mostly a game, but in ancient times it was thought that by imitating the flight of larks you magically summoned spring. See *Shang.*, 36. See also *Vrem. goda,* 84–85.

340 *the Strastnoy Monastery* Once located on what is now Pushkin Square; demolished in Soviet times.

340 *the Pushkin Monument* Famous statue of Pushkin, erected in 1880 on Pushkin Square, across from the termination of Tverskoy Boulevard. Sculpted by A. M. Opekushin.

341 *the Strelna* A fashionable restaurant in prerevolutionary times.

342 *Kuznetsky Avenue* "Kuznetsky" is short for "Kuznetsky most." Then and now a main thoroughfare and important commercial street in Moscow.

342 *the Moscow Art Theater* See notes to "Indulgent Participation." Bunin, who disliked this theater for its modernism, often criticizes it subtly (or not so subtly) in his works.

342 *Kislovka* Two streets near the center of Moscow were called Kislovsky Lane: Upper Kislovsky Lane (Bol'shoj pereulok), in Soviet times Semashno Street, and Lower Kislovsky Lane (Malyj pereulok), in Soviet times Sobinov Street.

342 *Molchanovka* See notes to "Indulgent Participation."

344 *Rules of the Household* (*Domostroj*) A document of the sixteenth century containing a detailed list of rules for social, religious, and especially home and family conduct. According to *Domostroj*, the exemplary family was patriarchal, ruled firmly by the male lord and master.

346 *In the church choir a young girl sang* First line of a famous untitled poem (1905) by the symbolist poet Aleksandr Blok. In making another of his frequent critical allusions to modernist art, Bunin chooses a poem that was extremely popular all over Russia. It remains one of Blok's most well-known and most beautiful poems.

349 *Miskhor* Seaside resort on the Crimean Peninsula near Yalta.

350 *young Werther from Tambov* The allusion is to Goethe's *Sorrows of Young Werther* (1774), a popular sentimental novel about a young man who brooded over a lost love and finally committed suicide. Tambov is a Russian city often taken as emblematic of backwoods provincialism.

351 *Your body is the highest reason* The following quotation expresses the Nietzschean idea: "Body am I entirely, and nothing else; and soul is only a word for something about the body" ("On the Despisers of the Body," *Thus Spoke Zarathustra*, trans. W. Kaufmann).

351 *Junker Schmidt* Here is a literal, nonpoetic translation of the poem entitled "Junker Schmidt":

> The leaf fades. The summer passes.
> Rime frost sparkles silver.
> Junker Schmidt with a pistol
> Wants to shoot himself.
> Wait, you madman, once again
> The verdure will come alive!
> Junker Schmidt! Word of honor,
> Summer will return!

The author, Koz'ma Prutkov, is a parodic invention of A. K. Tolstoy and the Zhemchuzhnikov brothers, poets of the nineteenth century. The poem is one of Prutkov's most famous parodies of the romantic pose, and Junker Schmidt himself "has become the archetypal Prutkovian romantic hero" (Monter). Although "Junker Schmidt" was once printed with the subtitle "From Heine," it is not clear precisely which Heine poem is parodied. See B. H. Monter, *Koz'ma Prutkov: The Art of Parody* (The Hague: Mouton, 1972), 80–81. Monter includes a poetic translation.

351 *"The Asra"* A romance (*Lied*) by the Russian pianist and composer Anton Rubenstein (1829–94), based on the words of a Heine poem ("Der Asra," 1846). Bunin, who was much impressed by this song as a young man, mentions it in at least one other work, "Without Kith or Kin" ("Bez rodu-plemeni"). See *Sob. soch.*, 5:525 and 2:504. The passages cited in *The Consecration of Love* differ somewhat from those in the original Heine poem. See *Bab. 2*, 215.

352 *she quoted Griboedov . . . life is meant for laughing* In Russian, *zhivite-ka smejas'*. This is from Griboedov's famous play *Woe from Wit* (act 1, scene 5). Appropriately, in terms of Bunin's novella, the

laughter here is mixed with tears. In speaking of Chatsky's departure, Liza tells how he wept. Liza: "'Why, dear sir, are you crying? Life is meant for laughing.' And he replied, 'With good reason do I weep, Liza, for who can tell what I will find upon my return? And how much there is, perchance, that I will lose!'"

353 *Kursk* Mitya takes the train bound for southern and southwestern points; it departs from the Kursk Station, located east of the Kremlin near what is now the main or outer ring road (Sadovoe kol'tso). Mitya changes trains in Orel, takes a train through the town of Verkhovye, and debarks, presumably at a small station between Verkhovye and Yelets.

356 *Annunciation Day* March 25/April 7. This is one of the major Eastern Orthodox holidays, marking the angel Gabriel's revelation to the Virgin Mary that she is to conceive the Son of God. In folk thought it is considered the day spring overcomes winter. See *Vrem. goda,* 92–93.

358 *Spanish blister flies* A pharmaceutical preparation called cantharides, commonly known as Spanish fly, is made from Spanish blister beetles. It is used as a blister-inducing agent or aphrodisiac.

358 *sarafan* Sleeveless dress, buttoning in front, worn by Russian peasant women; tunic dress.

368 *The household sleeps . . . upon us gaze* First two lines of untitled poem by A. A. Fet (1820–92).

368 *Over smooth and tranquil river . . . cloud banks congregate* From a poem by Ivan Turgenev, "Prizvanie" ("An Invocation," 1844); quoted by Bunin inexactly. The first line is not in the Turgenev poem.

371 *I don't have nothing to do* In speaking with the peasants or the steward, Mitya sometimes uses substandard locutions in an attempt to approximate their speech patterns.

372 *They're worse for wear, these boots of mine* In an earlier published version Bunin used all four lines of this *chastushka* (folk ditty). Here is a loose translation that is more directly vulgar than the original but that makes the meaning clear:

> They're worse for wear, these boots of mine,
> But on the toes they spark and shine;
> Married, single, fat, two-faced:
> All girls are the same below the waist!

373 *Petals' scroll now brightly open* From the Fet poem entitled "The Rose" (1864). The quotation is not exact.

375 *spindle shrubs* On the language of flowers, see notes to "The Grammar of Love." Spindle shrub translates "Thy charms are engraven on my heart." Many other plants mentioned in *Consecration* have meanings in various vocabularies of flowers. See note for page 402.

376 *Maybe you could take a little ride . . . over to the Meshersky manor* You wonder if the nubile young ladies mentioned here include the seductive Olya Mesherskaya (from "Light Breathing"). But Olya died (aged fifteen), presumably at some time between 1905 and 1916, so at the time Mitya is in the country (May–June 1900; see chronology below), she would not be very old.

378 *Sobinov and Chaliapin* See note to "Indulgent Participation." In Gounod's opera *Faust* (staged at the Moscow Bolshoy Theater, beginning September 24, 1899), Chaliapin played Mephistopheles and Sobinov played Faust. This detail establishes the exact chronology of the novel's action (all dates old style): December 1899, Mitya and Katya first meet; March 9, 1900, Mitya's "last happy day in Moscow"; one week before Easter 1900, Katya's examination; late April 1900, Mitya leaves for the country; early June 1900, Mitya's suicide.

378 *Once in far Thule there lived a good king* This same line from Gounod's *Faust* is sung by the rakish officer Petritsky, a friend of Vronsky, in Tolstoy's *Anna Karenina* (part 2, chapter 20).

379 *eight versts* One verst equals 1.067 kilometers. This indicates only one way; the round-trip to the station is sixteen versts.

381 *Sevastopol* Crimean city made famous by the siege of English, French, and Turkish forces during the Crimean War.

381 *Baidar Gates* A pass between the principal range of the Crimean Mountains, extending from the Baidar Valley to the Black Sea coast. For Bunin's mention of this in his letters home as he traveled in the region (April 1889), see *Mikh.*, 65.

381 *Livadia* Crimean town located on the Black Sea three kilometers from Yalta.

381 *Alupka* See notes for "On the Night Sea."

382 *Shakhovskoe* According to Bunin's wife, V. N. Muromtseva-Bunina, Shakhovskoe was modeled on the estate Kolontaevka, located in Bunin's native district, and it was named after a partial prototype for Mitya, D. Shakhovskoj.

388 *Mitry Palich* Mitya's name and patronymic (Dmitry Pavlovich) in the steward's pronunciation.

394 *sentry hut* The forester's family lives in a sentry hut or guard hut (*karaulka*) since it is his job to protect the trees in the forest from timber thieves.

395 *storeroom* In Russian, *klet';* a room in a peasant hut used as storage room and summer sleeping room. The visit to the forester amounts to a travesty of the peasant matchmaking ritual, with the drunken steward ineptly playing the role of the matchmaker and Mitya awkwardly parodying the prospective bridegroom. The whole scene is strange, since the steward could have arranged the assignation in private with Alyonka. There is at least a hint that Mitya's mother has asked the steward to make such an arrangement; it was quite common for women of the gentry to arrange for their sons to be "broken

in" with peasant girls. There is also a suggestion that the steward delays setting things up in hopes of getting more out of the deal. When Mitya finally takes the initiative, Alyonka readily agrees but says she is not willing to do this for nothing, as if to suggest that the steward had been pressuring her while hoping to keep all the money he received (from Mitya and from his mother) for himself. You wonder why Parasha, the house servant, is not the girl chosen. She is single, readily available, fond of Mitya, but Mitya's mother probably would not want this business going on right in her own household.

400 *Pisemsky* A. F. Pisemsky (1820–81), Russian novelist and dramatist.

401 *Antares* Antares is Mars, brightest star in the constellation Scorpio.

402 *acacia bushes, lilac leafage, currant foliage, burdock, wormwood* Assuming that Bunin had access to Latour's interpretations of the language of flowers (see notes to "The Grammar of Love"), here are the given meanings: (1) acacia: platonic love, (2) lilac: first emotion of love, (3) currant: not listed, (4) burdock: importunity, (5) wormwood (absinthe): absence. Since Mitya so often wanders down the linden arborway of his manor, it is also worth mentioning the meaning given for linden: conjugal love.

Somber Pathways (Linden Lined)

No title in English properly captures the old gentry spirit of the Russian title. The problem is the word for a tree-lined walkway in the park of a country estate: in French *allée* is fine, but there is no good word in English ("avenue" does not quite work). "Dark Alleys" conjures up images of pulp fiction or Mickey Spillane. In other stories translated in this collection I have most often used "arborway." In this story I have tried to express the old manorial spirit by planting (in parentheses) the lindens lining the pathways from the Ogarev poem.

413 *the book of Job* The complete citation (Job 11:16) goes as follows: "Because thou shalt forget thy misery, and remember it as waters that pass away."

415 *The wild rosebush* For complete citation of the poem from which this is borrowed ("An Ordinary Tale," by N. P. Ogarev), see *Sob. soch.*, 7:382. Bunin has slightly changed the quoted lines.

Sunstroke

Bunin was in awe of the act of carnal love, and "Sunstroke" is his most well-known story manifesting that awe. His wife, Vera Nikolaevna, was often uncomfortable when he spoke frankly in the company of others about sexual matters. Once, late in his life, she said, "Jan, it's like you've got some kind of devil standing beside you. Don't be sinful." Bunin answered as follows: "Well, just where is there anything sinful about what I'm saying? After all, I'm speaking of the most lovely thing on earth. Only for the sake of that is it worthwhile to be born. I can't always be cogitating over theological issues or writing stories about young priests, the way you'd like me doing nowadays. In love, in the act of love there's something divine, mysterious and awesome, but we don't value that enough. You have to live to be as old as I am to sense to the full all of the ineffable mystical charm of love. Describing it in words is impossible. It can't be communicated. Because the main thing always slips out of your grasp. No matter how I try it doesn't quite work out, or it comes out approximate, somewhere close to it, but the essence cannot be captured in words, you can't get your hook into it. And it's not only me who can't do it—nobody ever has expressed that and nobody ever will" (*Bakh.*, 101).

Here is a note from Galina Kuznetsova's diary of August 8, 1927: "Yesterday we spoke about writing and about the genesis of stories. With Ivan Alekseevich it almost always begins with nature, with some pictorial image that flashes in his brain, often just a fragment. 'Sunstroke,' for example, came from his imagining a walk out on deck after dinner, from a light in the darkness on a summer's night on the Volga. Then the ending came later" (*G.d.*, 24).

416 *Anapa* Resort town on the Black Sea, near Novorossisk.

Shere Monday

The title of this story is the term for the first day of Lent in the Eastern Orthodox tradition. It translates literally as "Pure Monday." There is no exact appellation for this holiday in English; I use the obsolete word "shere" on analogy with an old term for Maundy Thursday: "Shere" or "Sheer (Pure) Thursday." Shere Monday is a day of ritual purification; people wash themselves, put on fresh linen, clean their teeth, and bid farewell to the rambunctious (and often licentious) practices of the week preceding Lent (Maslenitsa Week).

One critic finds a strange incongruence in the fact that although the story is called "Shere Monday," on the Monday in question there is a huge gap (nothing happens). The unnamed heroine parts with the narrator on Forgiveness Sunday, the day before the beginning of Lent (Shere Monday), and tells him to come back no earlier than 10:00 P.M. on the following evening (when the "charivari" takes place). One presumes that she spends much of her time on this holy day contemplating her future life and praying. Of course, she then commits an act of deliberate sacrilege (fornication in the early morning hours on the second day of Lent). But there is a peculiarly Russian logic to this act. Before you can begin doing penance on the path to saving your soul, you first commit an act for which you then begin doing penance. On the time gap in the story, see E. A. Jablokov, "'Posle bala' i 'Chistyj ponedel'nik' (k probleme 'Bunin i Tolstoj')," in the book *I. A. Bunin: dialog s mirom* (Voronezh, 1999), 131. On the business of having to sin first, see the Prashcheruk article in the same book (51–52; full citation below).

For an account of Bunin's experiences in Moscow, where he stayed when visiting there, literary acquaintances he made there, and place-names he incorporated into his fiction, see the article by O. Tochenyj in L. P. Bykovtseva, ed., *Russkie pisateli v Moskve* (Moscow, 1973), 734–48. On some of the place-names mentioned in "Shere Monday," see my notes to "Indulgent Participation" and "Way Back When."

The ending of the story (the procession of women with candles and gonfalons) is reminiscent of a painting by Mikhail Nesterov (1862–1942), *Taking the Veil,* now in the collection of the Russian Museum, St. Petersburg.

425 *Cathedral of Christ the Saviour* Constructed 1839–83, consecrated in 1889, razed by Stalin in a deliberate act of desecration in 1931. In Soviet times a huge swimming pool occupied the site. This monumental cathedral has now been rebuilt from scratch at its former location.

426 *Moonlight Sonata* Beethoven's famous sonata has been played in a lot of fictional works, but Bunin probably recalled Tolstoy's *Family Happiness,* in which the heroine plays the piece at a number of points in the novel. In book 5 of *The Life of Arseniev* the heroine Lika is reading *Family Happiness,* and since the heroine of "Shere Monday" appreciates Tolstoy, she too has probably read the work and is, subconsciously or consciously, mimicking the behavior of the young woman in Tolstoy's novel. In "Shere Monday" she plays only the first, serene movement, but if you listen to the fury of the ending (the pounding emotion in the third movement, marked *presto agitato*), there is a suggestion of the ruin of the hero's life, and perhaps of the heroine's too (since she is about to take the veil right before the coming of the Bolshevik Revolution and the subsequent rape and murder of Orthodox nuns).

426 *a painting of the barefoot Tolstoy* This famous painting (1901) by Ilya Repin is in the collection of the Russian Museum, St. Petersburg.

426 *Hofmannsthal, Schnitzler, Tetmajer, Przybyszewski* Hugo von Hofmannsthal (1874–1929), Austrian writer in the spirit of the neo-Romantic; Arthur Schnitzler (1862–1931), Austrian dramatist and prose writer; Kazimierz Tetmajer (1865–1940), Polish writer of poetry and short stories; Stanislaw Przybyszewski (1868–1927), Polish writer with decadent leanings who wrote in Polish and German.

428 *Andrej Bely* Real name: Boris Bugaev (1880–1934). Symbolist writer whom Bunin consistently mocked and excoriated. In payback, Bely described Bunin as a scrawny man with a beaklike profile that gave him the appearance of a carrion crow and lips "that

looked like they were perpetually wrapped around a lemon" (*Mar.*, 2:85, citing Bely's book *The Beginning of the Century*).

428 *The Flaming Angel* First novel of the modernist poet Valery Briusov (1873–1924), published in 1908. Bunin was personally acquainted with Briusov, as he was with most of the Russian literary figures and actors mentioned in "Shere Monday."

428 *Chaliapin's concert* On the famous Chaliapin, see notes to "Indulgent Participation" and "The Gentleman from San Francisco." In "Shere Monday" Bunin's attitude toward his contemporaries, most of the writers and theatrical figures mentioned, is negative. In reality, his relationships with them were not always antagonistic. For more on Chaliapin, see Bunin's memoirs, *Sob. soch.*, 9:383–92.

429 *Iverskaia icon of the Mother of God* The chapel of the Iverskaia (Iveron) Mother of God is located at the entrance to Red Square, next to the Historical Museum. Destroyed by Stalin in the thirties, it has now been rebuilt in its former location. A copy of the wonder-working Iverskaia icon was brought from Mount Athos and reinstalled in the chapel. See *Moscow Times Russian Review*, January 15, 1996, 22–24. Bunin wrote "Shere Monday" in 1944, after many of the famous Moscow monuments he describes had been desecrated and demolished. He, in effect, rebuilt them in his artistic imagination. Now, by a strange irony of history, those very monuments have been rebuilt in fact. This makes a reading of the story today different from a reading in 1944. Back then the reader would have had to visualize the monuments as recalled by Bunin's artistic imagination, but today one can see them rebuilt in stone. This re-creation in tangible fact of what had been re-created imaginatively is one of the most interesting things about the story "Shere Monday."

Here is how a nineteenth-century German traveler to Moscow, Johann Georg Kohl, described the popular adoration of the Iverskaia icon in 1842: "There is really something touching in seeing the most sumptuously-clad ladies, glittering with jewels, leave their splendid equipages and gallant attendants, and prostrate themselves in the dust with the beggars." As for his description of the icon itself: "Her hand and the foot of the child are covered with dirt from the abundant kissing; it sits like a crust in little raised points, so that long since it has not been hand and foot that have been kissed, but the concrete breath of pious lips." See Laurence Kelly, ed., *Moscow: A Traveller's Companion* (New York, 1984), 162–63.

429 *Basil the Blessed, Holy Fool* Vasily (Basil) is the most renowned *jurodivyj* (holy fool) in Russian history. The famous sixteenth-century Intercession Church on Red Square (built 1555–60) took on the appellation Saint Basil's Cathedral after his remains were interred there. See notes to "Glory."

429 *Church of the Saviour in the Pinewood* Fourteenth-century Kremlin cathedral, no longer extant.

429 *the Italian cathedrals* Kremlin cathedrals built by Italian architects. They include (1) the Archangel Cathedral (1505–9), which contains the sarcophagi of the Moscow tsars and whose architect was Aleviz the New, now thought to be the Venetian Alvise Lamberti da Montagnana, and (2) the Cathedral of the Dormition, built by the Bolognese architect Aristotele Fioravanti in 1475–79.

430 *Platon Karataev said to Pierre* Prominent characters in Tolstoy's *War and Peace.*

430 *Moscow Art Theater* See note to "Indulgent Participation." Bunin's friend Anton Chekhov was closely associated with this theater. At a ceremony organized by its actors in honor of what would have been Chekhov's fiftieth birthday (January 17, 1910), Bunin's appearance made quite a sensation. After reading from his memoirs of Chekhov, he played out several conversations he had had with him, perfectly mimicking Chekhov's voice and intonations. Chekhov's mother and sister, who were in the audience, were brought to tears. After the performance, Stanislavsky offered Bunin the role of Hamlet in an upcoming production at the Moscow Art Theater. Years later, while living in France, Bunin and his wife attended a performance of the Moscow Art Theater in Paris

(December 1922) and social gatherings in the presence of, among others, Stanislavsky, Kachalov, Moskvin, and Olga Knipper (Chekhov's wife). See Vera Bunina's description of those events in *Ust. Bun.*, 2:102–5. See also *Bab. 2*, 265.

430 *Andreev* Leonid Andreev (1871–1919) wrote plays and stories, often on topics dealing with abnormalities and sex. He was extremely popular at the time "Shere Monday" is set (1912).

431 *Maslenitsa* Pagan pre-Lenten carnival week, coincides with the Christian Shrovetide.

431 *Forgiveness Sunday* Last day before Lent begins. On Forgiveness Sunday, after the vesper services, the priests and parishioners go through a special ritual of asking forgiveness of one another for wrongs and slights committed throughout the year. Then they can enter the Lenten season with a clear conscience, newly purified.

432 *Novodevichy Convent* See notes to "On the Night Sea." The Novodevichy Convent, along with its cemetery, is one of the most famous historical sites of Moscow.

432 *rhipidions and trikeria* A rhipidion is a fan used to keep flies from the wine in the chalice during the celebration of the liturgy (*Webster's Second International Dictionary*). In the Russian Orthodox Church it is a round image of a cherub on the top of a long staff (*Dal'*). A trikerion (Eastern Orthodox Church) is a three-branched candlestick symbolizing the Trinity, used ceremonially, especially by bishops, as in pronouncing a benediction (*Merriam-Webster's Unabridged Dictionary*, 3rd ed.).

432 *Peresvet and Osliablia* Fourteenth-century monks at the Troitse-Sergieva (Holy Trinity–Saint Sergius) Monastery north of Moscow, heroes of the Kulikovo battle (1380). In that battle, which marked the first military success against the Tatars since their invasion of Russia, the Russian troops were led by the Grand Prince of Moscow and Vladimir, Dmitry Donskoj.

433 *Ertel* Aleksandr Ivanovich Ertel (1855–1908), Russian realist writer. His primary subject matter was the life of the poor peasantry, merchants, and landowners. Bunin, who rated his work highly, wrote about him in his memoirs (see *Sob. soch.*, 9:414–22).

433 *Chekhov* Anton Pavlovich Chekhov (1860–1904), world-famous Russian writer. This imaginary visit that Bunin makes together with his characters to the graves of Ertel and Chekhov is touching, considering that he had known both men personally and had been one of Chekhov's best friends. By 1944, when "Shere Monday" was written, Nikolai Gogol's grave was located immediately across from Chekhov's. He had been disinterred and moved to Novodevichy Cemetery in 1931. Bunin, who has his heroine express his own disgust with the monument over Chekhov's grave, probably would disapprove even more vociferously of burying a writer so uncongenial to him right across from his beloved Chekhov.

433 *Egorov's* This famous tavern in Okhotny Ryad is also described in Bunin's *Life of Arseniev* (book 5, chapter 17), *Sob. soch.*, 6:253.

433 *Griboedov* Aleksandr Sergeevich Griboedov (1798–1829), author famous for his play *Woe from Wit* (1823). As a Russian diplomat in Persia, he was murdered during anti-Russian riots there. Bunin's diary entry for January 1, 1915, reads as follows: "Day before yesterday I went with Kolya [nephew of Bunin—Nikolai Pusheshnikov] to the Marfo-Mariinsky Cloister in Ordynka . . . In the Griboedov Byway no one was able to point out to us Griboedov's building." On Griboedov, see also notes to *The Consecration of Love.*

434 *Marfo-Mariinsky Cloister* Formerly located at 34 Bolshaja Ordynka Street, it was a commune where orphans and the wounded from World War I were cared for. The Church of the Intercession of the Mother of God was built there, from 1908 to 1910 ("Shere Monday" is set in 1912). In the diary note from January 1, 1915, Bunin mentions that he and his nephew were not admitted right away into the church because the Grand Duke Dmitry Pavlovich was there. When he wrote his story Bunin mentioned this detail but

added another character from real life, the Grand Duchess Elizaveta Fyodorovna. This was a woman who had dedicated herself to a life of religious zealotry after her husband, the Grand Duke Sergei Aleksandrovich, was assassinated in 1905. Along with her sisters, she met the same fate in July 1918. In 1920 the relics of the martyrs were taken to Jerusalem, where they remain to this day at the Church of Saint Mary Magdalene in Gethsemane. The Russian Orthodox Church declared Elizaveta Fyodorovna a saint in 1922. See N. V. Prashcheruk, "Transformatsija temy religioznogo prizvanija ('Aglaia' i 'Chistyj ponedel'nik')," in I. A. Bunin, *Dialog s mirom* (Voronezh, 1999), 54–55. Knowledge of these facts sheds new light on the ending of "Shere Monday." Writing in France in 1944, Bunin chose to conclude his story with a description of a religious procession of nuns and novices led by a woman soon to be martyred. Of course, the young women marching in that procession are also soon to face (from the Soviet regime) brutal mistreatment and even death. The characters in the story, who are living in 1912, have no foreknowledge of what is soon to occur in Russian history, but the author and his readers do, and this lends a special poignancy to the ending. On reading beyond the bounds of the text of a story, see notes to "Light Breathing."

434 *Three-Handed Mother of God* The Byzantium philosopher, theologian, and poet John of Damascus (Saint John Damascene—born about A.D. 675, died before 753) was a defender of the image in the iconoclast controversy that consumed the Byzantine world. According to his hagiography, the Emperor Leo III sent a forged letter to the caliph, in which John supposedly advocated invading and conquering Syria. In response to this slander, the caliph ordered that John's right hand be cut off, but after John prayed to the Mother of God, the hand miraculously reattached itself. In token of his gratitude, John crafted a votive hand out of silver and pasted it on an icon of the Mother of God. This icon, given the name the Three-Handed, was taken to Mount Athos in Greece and a copy was sent to the New Jerusalem Monastery near Moscow. "The third hand gradually acquired an allegorical interpretation: the help-giving hand of the Mother of God, who is perpetually

ready to extend aid to any believer" (Mahmoud Zibani, *The Icon: Its Meaning and History* [Collegeville, Minn.: Liturgical Press, 1993], 25–26). See also *Shang.*, 87–88.

434 *Yury Dolgoruky* Yury Dolgoruky (1090–1157), son of Vladimir Monomakh of Kiev. Dolgoruky is the legendary founder of Moscow.

435 *Zachatev Monastery* Founded in 1584 by Tsar Fyodor in hopes that his religious gesture would cure his wife of infertility. No longer extant.

435 *Chudov Monastery* Built on the grounds of the Moscow Kremlin, 1365.

435 *navaga dish* *Navaga* is a small fish of the cod family.

436 *Murom* A city on the Oka River in the principality of Riazan. The story of the temptation by the evil serpent comes from the first section of the Muscovite hagiographical tale "The Life of Peter, Prince of Murom, and His Wife Fevronia," probably composed in 1547. See Ad. Stender-Petersen, ed., *Anthology of Old Russian Literature* (Columbia University Press, 1954), 192–202. See also Serge Zenkovsky, ed., *Medieval Russia's Epics, Chronicles, and Tales* (New York, 1974), 290–300. Neither of these sources has the detail about the beauty of the serpent in the guise of a young man, but the description of the demise of the saintly couple is there: "When death was nearing, Peter and Fevronia prayed to God that they both might die in the same hour. And they requested that they be buried in the same tomb and in a common coffin in which their bodies would be separated only by a partition. And together they took monastic vows" (Zenkovsky, 299).

In the Russian Orthodox Church, the Day of Peter and Fevronia is commemorated on June 26/July 8, the day on which they supposedly died in 1228. This is considered an especially fortunate day for lovers. See *Vrem. goda,* 157.

436 *charivaris* The word in Russian, *kapustnik,* means an amateur comic spectacle. It comes from the word for "cabbage."

437 *Stanislavsky* Konstantin Sergeevich Stanislavsky (originally Konstantin Sergeevich Alekseev; 1863–1938), famous director and founder (with Nemirovich-Danchenko) of the Moscow Art Theater in 1898.

437 *Moskvin* Ivan Mikhailovich Moskvin (1874–1946) began acting in 1896 and appeared at the Moscow Art Theater beginning in 1898.

438 *Kachalov* Vasily Ivanovich Kachalov (real name: Shverubovich [1875–1948]) began his acting career in 1896; with Moscow Art Theater beginning in 1900. Known for his roles in Chekhov plays (*The Three Sisters, The Cherry Orchard*). Also in Gorky's *Down and Out* (*Na dne*).

438 *Shamakha* (Also spelled Shemakha) The capital of the eighteenth-century Shirvan Khanate in the Caucasus Mountains. In the Russian literary imagination it embodies the notion of some fairyland Oriental realm. See *Slovar' jazyka Pushkina* (Moscow, 1961), 4:964. In "Shere Monday" Kachalov is quoting from Pushkin's folktale in verse "Zolotoj petushok" ("The Golden Cockerel"), where the beautiful maiden queen of Shamakha fascinates Tsar Dadon. The tsar perishes at the end of the tale, and at that point the queen of Shamakha vanishes into thin air. The final lines (given below in unrhymed, unmetered translation) echo the disappearance of the heroine of "Shere Monday" and that of Galya Kuznetsova from Bunin's life:

> And then the Queen suddenly vanished,
> As if she had never been there at all.
> A folktale's a lie, but it contains a hint!
> A lesson for young gallant lads to learn.

The Queen of Shamakha, Rimsky-Korsakov's opera based on the Pushkin tale, was staged frequently in the first decade of the twentieth century. The artist Ivan Bilibin (1876–1942) did a costume design for the opera in 1908 as well as stage-set designs and illustrations for the tale itself ("Tsar Dadon Stands before the Queen of Shamakha," 1906).

438 *Sulerzhitsky* Leopold Antonovich Sulerzhitsky (1872–1916), director and organizer of theatrical activities. He helped Stanislavsky teach and popularize his acting system; together they staged a number of productions at the Moscow Art Theater.

The Cold Fall

The Austrian archduke was assassinated in Sarajevo on June 28, 1914 (Gregorian calendar). All dates in this story are based on the prerevolutionary Julian calendar.

443 *Saint Peter's Day* June 29/July 12.

444 *The autumn's so frosty this year* Literal translation: "What a cold fall!" Bunin uses the first stanza of a two-stanza poem by A. A. Fet; the quotation is slightly incorrect.

446 *Yekaterinodar* Renamed Krasnodar in 1920.

Night

This story was originally published under the title "Cicadas." Bunin may have been aware of the origin myth about cicadas and song. When song came into the world, so it went, some men were so ravished by its sublimity that they forgot to eat and drink and died of inanition. From those men the cicadas were created. The Muses granted them the privilege of not eating, so they could just sing and sing from birth to death. See Marina Warner (citing Socrates writing in Plato, *Phaedrus*), *No Go the Bogeyman* (New York, 1998), 284. Note the line in the Bunin story: "Listen to them, those selflessly ecstatic singers; they have not eaten, they do not eat!"

Bunin quotes extensively (but seldom with exactitude) from the Bible. In my translation I have attempted to retain the inexactness of quotations. Notes below refer to passages in the King James Version.

For a treatment of Bunin's major works, interpreted within the context of Buddhism, see Thomas Gaiton Marullo, *If You See the Buddha* (Evanston, Ill.: Northwestern University Press, 1998). For more on the story "Night," see M. S. Shtern, "Rasskaz I. A. Bunina 'Noch,'" in *I. B.: pro contra,* 613–24. Shtern finds a source for the part about Christ's disciple Peter in the Chekhov story "The Student," and, in reference to the Islamic passages in "Night," he draws a parallel with Bunin's article called "The Stone," which appeared in the book *Shadow of the Bird* (1907–11).

448 *And I decided to seek and search out* Ecclesiastes 1:13.

448 *God hath made men reasonable* Ecclesiastes 7:29.

448 *Be not righteous over much* Ecclesiastes 7:16.

449 *In days to come all will be forgotten* Ecclesiastes 1:11.

449 *Also their love, and their hatred* Ecclesiastes 9:6.

450 *Eat thereof and ye shall be as God* Genesis 3:5.

450 *God is in heaven, and we upon earth* Ecclesiastes 5:2.

450 *Shroud of Christ* A large rectangular piece of cloth on which the body of Christ in his coffin is depicted. Used in Orthodox Church rituals.

451 *The fool sitteth idly* Ecclesiastes 4:5.

451 *He that observeth the wind* Ecclesiastes 11:4.

451 *royal portals* Or royal gates; central doors in iconostasis of Russian Orthodox churches.

451 *All is vanity of vanities* Ecclesiastes 1:2–3.

451 *The sleep of a labouring man is sweet* Ecclesiastes 5:12.

451 *And there is nothing better for a man* Ecclesiastes 2:24, 5:18, 9:7.

452 *once, myriads of years ago, I was a goat yeanling* Metempsychosis (transmigration of souls) is important in both Hinduism and Buddhism; in the 550 births of the Buddha he supposedly appeared not only as human, but also as animal, vegetable, and divine.

452 *the one who made this statement* Gautama Buddha.

454 *the fits of Muhammad* This experience has been called the analogue of the Christian Transfiguration or the colloquy of Moses on Sinai. See James Hastings, ed., *Encyclopedia of Religion and Ethics* (New York: Charles Scribner's Sons, 1917–27), 8:878.

455 *Maya* (Māyā) Illusion, appearance. A Hindu philosophic term "applied to the illusion of the multiplicity of the empirical universe, produced by ignorance . . . when in reality there is only One" (*Encyclopedia of Religion and Ethics,* 8:503.) "Māyā causes a state of *moha* . . . 'delusion,' in which consciousness of the ultimate reality is lost, and bewildered men believe in the reality of the manifest world presented to their senses. It is a cosmic delusion which draws a veil across men's perception, leading them to error and infatuation with the world and the flesh, obscuring from the mind the vision of their true destiny" (Benjamin Walker, *The Hindu World* [New York: Praeger, 1968], 2:53–54).

456 *Nothing perishes—all things are but altered* From Ovid's *Metamorphoses: Omnia mutantur, nihil interit.*

458 *Withdraw from the Chain* Allusion to the Buddhist concept of continuous reincarnation and the idea of withdrawal from the chain of incarnations to attain Nirvana, which is referred to in an earlier published version of the story (under the title "Cicadas"): "Nirvana with its eternal bliss, which is sad, nonetheless, for the mortal, who never on earth can completely renounce Maya, the sweetness of 'being.'"

460 *Sun, stand thou still* Joshua 10:12–13. Bunin has a poem with this title, written in 1916. See *Sob. soch.*, 1:403. The full text (Joshua 10:12–14) describes how Joshua, the successor to Moses, chosen by the Lord to lead the Israelites into the Promised Land, is engaged in battle with the Amorites: "Sun, stand thou still upon Gibeon; and thou, Moon, in the valley of Ajalon. And the sun stood still, and the moon stayed, until the people had avenged themselves upon their enemies . . . So the sun stood still in the midst of heaven, and hastened not to go down about a whole day. And there was no day like that before it or after it, that the Lord hearkened unto the voice of a man: for the Lord fought for Israel."

460 *Night unto night passeth knowledge* Psalm 19:2.

The Case of Cornet Elagin

The story is based on an actual court case in which Cornet Aleksandr Mikhailovich Bartenev was tried for murdering the actress Maria Wisnowska in Warsaw (1890). Widely covered in the Russian press, the trial took place in February 1891. The defense attorney was the renowned Plevako (*Bab. notes,* 5:583). For Bunin's account of how he came across a cheap, true-detective brochure on the case and used it as a source, see *Bakh.*, 117–18.

Upon preparing the novella for its final publication (very late in his life), Bunin cut the final, fifteenth chapter:

> Elagin must expiate his guilt before the law of man by serving ten years at hard labor.
>
> But what about his guilt in the eyes of God and in her eyes?
>
> God's judgment is unknown. But if we had the power to bring her back from the dead, what would she say? And who would then dare stand between them?

462 *cornet* In the tsarist army, a junior-grade officer rank of the cavalry troops.

466 *garçonnière* French for "bachelor apartment."

469 *OP. PULV.* Apparently an abbreviation of the Latin term for "pulverous (powdery) opium" (Latin: *pulvis, pulveris* is dust, powder).

471 *Quand même pour toujours* (From Musset?) "Nonetheless, it's forever." This was one of Bunin's early titles for the story.

482 *Musset* Alfred de Musset (1810–57), French dramatist, poet, and short-story writer.

482 *Krasinski* Zygmunt Krasinski (1812–59), Polish poet, novelist, playwright, and epistolographer. His letters form an extensive literary work, called by one critic the greatest novel in Polish Romantic literature.

489 *Pushkin's Egyptian Nights* The main theme of this 1835 Pushkin work is artistic inspiration. An Italian improvisor puts on a performance in St. Petersburg, enacting in verse the story of Cleopatra and her lovers. Cleopatra announces at a festive banquet that she will allow any man access to her charms, one night of love, but in return his head will be lopped off on the morning after. She has three takers: Flavius, a bold military man; Criton, a young sage and poet; and an anonymous, fuzzy-cheeked youth who is "like a spring flower, barely developed" (and who is a kind of prototype of Elagin). The improvisation ends right in the middle (Pushkin did not finish the story), so we never get to the nights of love and the executions.

497 *Maria Bashkirtseva* Maria Konstantinovna Bashkirtseva (1860–84), Russian artist whose diary, published in French, was popular in Russia. She died of tuberculosis.

497 *Marie Vetsera* Czech woman who died in a suicide pact with her lover, the Austrian Archduke Rudolph of Hapsburg, in 1899.

502 *błazen* Polish for "clown," "fool," "buffoon." Note the similarity to the Russian word *blazhennyj* (holy fool). See note to "Aglaia," pp. 620–21.

504 *Now comes the end to all the comedies* Echoes a phrase mouthed by Pechorin after he kills Grushnitsky in a duel (in Lermontov's *Hero of Our Time*): "*Finita la commedia!*" That phrase is also used by the doctor in Bunin's "On the Night Sea." Note that V. Khodasevich suggested a parallel between Bunin's young, dashing (but unprepossessing and bowlegged) officer Elagin and Lermontov himself.

505 *If it's to be done, then quickly* Paraphrase of a line from Shakespeare's *Macbeth* (act 1, scene 7): "If it were done . . . then 'twere well it were done quickly!" See note in *Guerney*, 289.

Light Breathing

"Light Breathing" is foreshadowed by a Bunin poem of 1903, "The Portrait," which describes a graveyard, a chapel with a crypt, and a portrait of a girl with "large bright eyes" and a "coquettishly simple hairstyle." Here is the final stanza (unrhymed, unmetered translation):

> Wreaths, icon lamps, the smell of rot . . .
> And nothing else but the lovely gaze
> Of eyes that look with joyous amazement
> Upon all this sepulchral absurdity. (*Sob. soch.*, 1:178–79)

In choosing his title, which furnishes the musical tonality for the entire story, Bunin may also have been influenced by the sounds in the first line of a famous poem by Afanasy Fet (Shenshin), "Whispers, Timid Breathing" ("Shjopot. Robkoe dykhan'e," published in 1850). His use of the name Shenshin for the schoolboy may be a tip of the hat to Fet, for providing him with the sounds for the breathing leitmotif. For Bunin's note on the origins of this story, see *Sob. soch.*, 9:369. There he describes how one winter, while strolling about a small cemetery on the Isle of Capri, he came upon a cross containing a photograph of a young girl with uncommonly vivacious, joyful eyes. He immediately made this girl into Olya in his imagination, and he wrote the story with that "exquisite rapidity" that characterized the happiest moments of his writing life. When setting up the action, Bunin transported his newly invented girl back to Russia, precisely to Yelets, a town he knew well. The building housing the women's gymnasium later became the Yelets Pedagogical Institute (granted the status of a university in October 2000 and renamed the I. A. Bunin State University at Yelets). You can still run up the same black cast-iron stairs that Olya ran up on her way to inform the headmistress that she had become a woman (as of September 2000, there was a portrait of Bunin in the stairwell). The prototype for the office of the headmistress is in that building as well, and you can visit the cemetery (Staroe kladbishche) where Olya Mesherskaya is (fictitiously) buried (on Tolstoy Street, formerly Kladbishchenskaja). Closed to new burials in the 1970s, the cemetery is now deteriorating. A commemorative chapel containing the remains of Yeletsians who died fighting Tamerlane (see notes to "Temir-Aksak-Khan") was rebuilt in 1995, in commemoration of the six hundredth anniversary of the defense of the city. Also on Tolstoy Street is what remains of the men's monastery (Trinity Monastery, completed in 1835), which was located across the street from the jail. Only part of the bell tower and some dilapidated walls are left, and the interior of the monastery grounds is now occupied by an automobile and taxi base. On her way to the cemetery the form mistress walks "between the monastery and the dungeon." Bunin was in the habit of bringing his characters back almost obsessively to that spot. For example, Natalya in *Drydale* passes the same place (chapter 5, *Sob. soch.*, 3:155). See also *The Life of Arseniev* (6:12–13, 67, 90) and "Belated Hour" (7:42), a story that describes how a ghostly narrator makes a midnight visit to Yelets, to the grave of his long-dead beloved. The jail, incidentally, was still there, across from the ruins of the monastery bell tower, and it was still functioning as a jail (as of the year 2000). For a photograph of the Trinity Monastery as it looked in the first half of the nineteenth century, see V. Gorlov and A. Novosel'tsev, *Elets vekami stroilsja* (Lipetsk, 1993), 250. The same book contains information on the monastery and graveyard (243–55) and a sketch of the cemetery gates and the Kazan Church within the cemetery grounds (253); this church is still holding services and, according to Yeletsians, never stopped holding services even during Soviet times. Sobornaja Street, mentioned in "Light Breathing," was renamed October Street in Soviet times. On that street is the Intercession Church, from the bell tower of which Bunin discovered a panoramic view of Yelets as described in the early story "Above the City" (*Sob. soch.*, 2:201): "Like a multicolored schema the city lay far below us, small and congested, and in our hearts we were feeling what swallows must feel on the fly." On such details, see the guidebook *Buninskie mesta v gorode El'tse* (*Places Associated with Bunin in the City of Yelets* [Yelets, 1994]).

The city unveiled a statue of its most famous native son in 1995, placing it prominently in the central square. The sculptor, Yury Grishko, depicts Bunin seated, relaxed, in something of a tranquil mood. Grishko eschews the pose of fastidious haughtiness that Bunin so characteristically put on for artists and for the lenses of cameras; in so doing he has created, in my view, one of the best artistic portrayals of the writer.

Writing in his emigration years, Bunin once visualized such a monument in his honor, "in some city square, where, early on a summer evening, slender-legged working-class children will chase each other around that statue with idiotic shrieks, while it stands there eternally mute and unmoving" (cited in *Mikh.*, 13–14). The Grishko statue, in fact, has suffered even worse indignities. The last time I was in Yelets, vandals had written graffiti on its head, and one leg looked to have been broken off, then reattached.

There is another Bunin statue in Yelets (by Nikolai Kravchenko, of Bunin in his gymnasium years) in the city gardens, where Olya Meshcherskaya skated in the winters and danced in the summers. Finally, there is also a bust (the older Bunin of the Nobel years) just across the street from the Ascension Cathedral. At least two other Russian cities now feature Bunin monuments: Orel (the writer in his favorite supercilious stance) and Voronezh. The statue in Voronezh, by the Moscow sculptor A. Burganov, depicts a seated Bunin of about forty, with a dog at his knees, recalling the story "Dreams of Chang" or Bunin's best-known poem, "Loneliness," which ends with the following declaration by the artist whose love has just left him: "I'll light a fire in the hearth, I'll be drinking / Might just buy me a dog, I'm thinking."

Two churches named after the Presentation of the Blessed Virgin in the Temple are also associated with Bunin; each of them has been restored since the fall of the Soviet Union and completely redone in the interior. Bunin attended services as a gymnasium student in the Yelets Presentation Church and was baptized in the Voronezh Presentation Church.

In *G.d.* (103–4) Kuznetsova relates a conversation between her and Bunin about "Light Breathing." Bunin told her that he was surprised this story was more popular than "The Grammar of Love," which he rated higher. On more details from that conversation, see my afterword in this volume.

For a detailed critical treatment of "Light Breathing," including discussion of its musical motifs, see L. S. Vygotskij, "Legkoe dykhanie," reprinted in *I. B.: pro contra,* 435–55.

507 *Mesherskaya* This name (in an exact transliteration from the Cyrillic, Meshcherskaja [feminine] or Meshcherskij [masculine]), a genuine Russian surname with the *-skij* suffix (many such names are of Ukrainian, Polish, or Jewish origin), is associated with the aristocracy and gentry; it is among the oldest of Russian family names, deriving from *Meshchera,* "originally the name of a Turkicized Finnic tribe and of the region inhabited by it" (*Unbe.,* 126–27).

508 *the schoolboy Shenshin* Possible allusion to one of Bunin's favorite poets, Afanasy Fet, who was born at the estate of his stepfather, Afanasy Shenshin, in 1820 and illegally registered as his son. Later the documents were annulled by ecclesiastical authorities and he was forced to use the name of his German father, Fet (until 1873, when Tsar Aleksandr II granted him permission, finally, to use the name Shenshin). Allusions to Fet and citations from his poetry run throughout Bunin's works. See, for example, *The Consecration of Love* and "The Cold Fall."

509 *the full-length portrait of the young tsar* Recalls the portrait of Nicholas II by Ilya Repin (1895), which is in the collection of the Russian Museum in St. Petersburg. This detail brings up the idea of what you might call retroactive reading, or reading beyond the boundaries of the text. "Light Breathing" was written in 1916. Those who first read the story after July 1918 have a totally different perspective on the painting of the handsome young tsar because they invariably will recall that only a few years after the murder of Olya Mesherskaya, this man, together with the whole of his family, was brutally murdered in Ekaterinburg. On the way that facts beyond the text of a story change one's perspective on that story, see also notes to "The Snow Bull" and "Shere Monday."

513 *the Battle of Mukden* Final and greatest battle of the Russo-Japanese War, fought from February 19 to March 10, 1905, near the Chinese city of Mukden (Sheniang). The Russian troops suffered horrible losses.

513 *what a woman must have to be truly beautiful* This passage may come from Bunin's copy of *The Grammar of Love* (see notes to the story of the same title).

Aglaia

Bunin once read this story aloud to Galina Kuznetsova in 1931 and commented on it as follows: "'You know, they view me only as the author of *The Village*!' he complained. 'But this is me too! I've got this in me as well! After all, I'm Russian myself, and I have both of these things in me! And the way it's written! Such a variety of rare words, and the way nature is described, that landscape of Northern (and iconographic) Rus: those pines, the sand, her yellow kerchief, her elongation—I mention that several times—the way Aglaia is built, the long arms . . . Her sister is an ordinary person, but she already has that something, blue eyed, fair complexioned, quiet, long armed—it's already a degeneration. And the catalogue of Russian saints! And that character the pilgrim women come across, how well he's conceived! In his derby hat with his eyes blindfolded! A real devil! Seen too much of life! "He consoled her by saying that only her lips would rot!" What a cruel consolation that is, a terrible consolation! But nobody understood that! Everybody started howling about *The Village,* just because it was a novel! But they didn't even notice the charm of "Aglaia"! How offensive that is, having to die and everything you've carried in your soul, everything you've accomplished is still not understood by anyone, not valued the way it should be! And there's so much diversity here, such a variety of rhythms, such diverse mentalities! I've been all over the place, sniffing things out—and I sensed right away the spirit of the country, of the people'" (*G.d.,* 212–13).

The two names of the heroine: Aglaia is from the Greek, meaning "brightness, radiance," and Anna is a variant of Hannah, Hebrew for "grace." Bunin apparently took the name Aglaia from *The Lives of the Saints,* where it appears several times. For example, Saint Boniface of Tarsus (see notes to "The Saints") was "master of the revels of Aglae," a dissolute Roman woman who was later converted, became a true believer, and subsequently a saint (see *Engle.*, 188). The mother of the famous Alexis, Man of God was also Aglaia (see reference to *The Golden Legend*). In Greek mythology Aglaia is one of the Three Graces, sister goddesses and beautiful maidens represented as intimate with the Muses and serving as attendants upon Eros, Aphrodite, and Dionysus. Probably the most prominent Aglaia in Russian literature is Dostoevsky's Aglaia Epanchina in *The Idiot.*

On the ending of the story: Linda Ivanits writes that "in remote areas of Vladimir Province, old people observed a ritual of asking the earth's forgiveness prior to death into the twentieth century" (citing Fedotov, *The Russian Religious Mind,* 2:135–37 and a G. K. Zavoiko article in *Etnograficheskoe obozrenie;* see *Ivanits,* 15, 209, 244). On the Christian premises of this story, see N. V. Prashcheruk, "Transformatsija temy religioznogo prizvanija ('Aglaia' i 'Chistyj ponedel'nik')", in the book *I. A. Bunin: dialog s mirom* (Voronezh, 1999), 45–50. Prashcheruk appears to assume, as do I, that the ending of "Aglaia" calls into question some of the most essential principles of Russian Orthodox asceticism.

514 *splint light* See notes to "The Sacrifice."

516 *Cappadocia* Ancient, mountainous, eastern province of Asia Minor (now Eastern Turkey).

516 *Byzantium emperor Leo the Great* Leo I, fifth-century ruler (457–74).

516 *Joachim of Alexandria* Christianity spread to Ethiopia (Abyssinia) from neighboring Alexandria, Egypt, in the fourth century.

516 *Barbara* Legend has it that Saint Barbara was born in Egypt, daughter of a rich pagan grandee. After she converted to Christianity her father imprisoned her in a tower, and she desecrated the pagan idols placed there. Later she escaped but was captured, subjected to horrendous tortures, and executed by beheading in A.D.

306 (her father himself cut off her head). Her day of commemoration in the Orthodox calendar is December 4/17. In the twelfth century the holy relics of Saint Barbara were supposedly brought to Kiev from Constantinople, where they remain to this day in the Vladimir Cathedral (*Vrem. goda,* 21–22). For a complete version in English of the life of Saint Barbara, see *Gold leg.*, 6:198–205.

By a strange concatenation of circumstances Saint Barbara has now become the patron saint of the Strategic Rocket Forces of Russia. This came about after the fall of the Soviet Union with the recrudescence of Russian Orthodoxy. Patron saints were selected for various branches of the armed services. Soviet premier Nikita Khrushchev had formally inaugurated the Rocket Forces in 1960, and by sheer coincidence he signed the order on the saint's day of Barbara (see Michael R. Gordon, "Atheism Discarded," *International Herald Tribune,* June 15–16, 2000).

516 *the warrior Eustachius* Aristocratic Roman general Eustachius (Placidus), who accepted Christianity, lost all his riches and died under torture (in the reign of Emperor Hadrian, A.D. 117–38). Placidus adopted the name Eustachius upon being baptized. He "was converted while deer hunting; a young stag with a cross between its antlers suddenly turned to him and made a long speech which transformed his soul" (*Engle.*, 358). After refusing to make sacrifices to pagan idols, Eustachius, his wife, and sons "were shut up in a bronze bull, roasted over a fire for three days, and perished together without their bodies being consumed" (*Engle.*, 359). See the Bunin poem "Saint Eustachius" in *Sob. soch.*, 1:369–70. In its last stanza this poem describes, obliquely, the vision Eustachius sees between the horns of the trapped animal. In the earlier stanzas he bids farewell to the sensual ardor of his younger days, to the "innocent [virginal] havens of my native [dear] pagan haunts":

> You have shattered [dealt a crippling blow to] my knees,
> O humble Gaze, o Cross of Golgotha.

The image of Christ's "gaze of humility" ("meek gaze") appears three times in this poem, but the third time, when

Eustachius sees the vision through the horns, it is a "Gaze both meek and threatening." The eye imagery in the poem is especially relevant to the leitmotif of the eye in "Aglaia."

The flagship of the Russian navy, *Saint Eustachius*, is mentioned in "Sempiternal Spring."

516 *Sabbas the Enlightened* Probably Saint Sabbas, the hermit who was born in Cappadocia in 439 and died in the monastery he founded southeast of Jerusalem in 532. The Basilica of Saint Sabbas in Rome is named after him.

518 *Alexis, Man of God* See notes to "I'm Saying Nothing."

518 *Ioann the Anchorite* Apparently from Constantinople. He also returned home after living as a monk, set up his dwelling in a hut next to his parents' house, and revealed himself to his mother only shortly before he died (*Sob. soch.*, 4:491).

518 *Simeon Stylites* Saint Simeon was the earliest of the Christian ascetics who lived on top of pillars practicing mortification of the flesh. He supposedly stayed atop a pillar near Antioch, Syria, from 423 until his death in 459. See Charles Kingsley, *The Hermits* (New York, 1891), 167–96.

518 *naked and scabrous freaks* Allusion to the *jurodivye*, holy fools.

518 *Matthew the Perspicacious* Bunin has a poem with this title dated January 24, 1916 (see *Sob. soch.*, 1:388–89). While dwelling in a dark cave, Matthew is accosted by the devil, who calls him the seer (perspicacious one) and points out that even in his dark abode Matthew is still as "keen-sighted as a snake." He says that Matthew is "no less an enemy of man than we are" and proposes that he join the devil and his minions in dogging the steps of humanity:

> You are a master at spying out their contemplations,
> You, holy father, are by no means a stranger
> To taking root in the mystery of their hearts,

And my eyesight, too, is not all that bad.
Why then be inimical to demons?
Aren't you a demon no less than we?

The devil further accuses Matthew, who is "hundred-eyed and hundred-eared," of seeking out so avidly the darkness of asceticism because he hates earthly life, because he can't stand the stench of carnality and finds silt in all of life's springs. He says Matthew's "merciless soul" is full of unquenchable pride. The devil has quite a point here, and although Matthew continues to defend the "darkness and famine" of his cave, he feels compelled to call out to God in the final two lines:

O Lord! Give sustenance to my faith
And send strength unto me for the struggle!

518 *Mark the Digger of Graves* Not identified.

518 *Isaaky the Hermit* Isaaky Pechersky (eleventh century), who was associated with the Kiev Cave Monastery. He is generally considered the first known Russian *jurodivyj* (holy fool), and he was the first to be canonized (1547). See Ewa M. Thompson, *Understanding Russia: The Holy Fool in Russian Culture* (New York: University Press of America, 1987), 83.

519 *Simon from the Volga forests* Not identified.

519 *Prokopius, who embraced perpetual torments in the city of Vyatka* Died in 1627. His hagiography, written about fifty years later, describes how he went into a trance during a storm and awoke a changed person. He walked around naked, tore up any clothes he was given, and rolled in the dirt like a dog. He was beaten for his habit of sneaking up into church belfries and ringing the bells at night, but later this was interpreted as his way of warning the denizens of Vyatka that they must change their sinful lives. See Thompson, *Understanding Russia,* 92.

519 *Prokopius, who was born in the Ziryan region* Prokopius of Ustiug, died 1285 or 1303, canonized in 1547. Some consider him the first genuine Russian *jurodivyj*. His hagiography epitomizes the problems of actually learning much about the life of a holy fool. It was put together long after his death (sixteenth century) and blends events from the twelfth century and the fifteenth. In this account Prokopius supposedly came to Ustiug from Novgorod and (this is hard to believe) was originally "from foreign lands, of the Latin tongue." See S. S. Bychkov, ed., *Zhizneopisanija dostopamjatnykh ljudej zemli russkoj (X–XX vv.)* (Moscow, 1992), 117–26; 320. See also Thompson, *Understanding Russia*, 83–85.

519 *Jacob the Blessed* Jacob (Iakov) of Borovichi (died 1540). His body floated in a hollow log down the River Msta to Borovichi. Three times the peasants of the village tried to push it back out into the river, but each time it returned to shore. They buried the body in the village cemetery, after which miracles began occurring there and Borovichi became renowned for its "saint." See Thompson, *Understanding Russia*, 88–89.

519 *Ioann the Hirsute* (Or Hairy) From Rostov the Great. Died in 1580 or 1622, apparently never canonized. See Thompson, *Understanding Russia*, 91.

519 *Ioann of Vologda, called Big Cap* Like the famous Vasily Blazhenny (Saint Basil), this Moscow *jurodivyj* (died 1589) was buried in the Intercession Cathedral (Saint Basil's) on Red Square. In 1876 he was canonized by decree of the Holy Synod. See Thompson, *Understanding Russia*, 82.

519 *Vasily the Naked Walker* Vasily Blazhenny, Saint Basil the Blessed Fool, most renowned holy fool ever to live in Russia. He died about 1552. After Ivan the Terrible built the Cathedral of the Intercession (sixteenth century) to commemorate his victories over the Tatar Khanates, Vasily was reburied in that church (on Red Square in Moscow). Pilgrims began thronging to his shrine, and people called the church Saint Basil's. It is still known by that name today. Vasily

was canonized at some point near the end of the sixteenth century. See Thompson, *Understanding Russia,* 78–82. For more information on Saint Basil and his connection with the Intercession Cathedral (including depictions of him on icons and a photograph of his reliquary-sepulchre in the church), see A. L. Batalov and L. S. Uspenskaja, *Sobor pokrova na rvu (Khram Vasilija Blazhennogo)* (Moscow: Severnyj palomnik, 2002).

520 *Sergius of Radonezh* Sergius of Radonezh (1314–92), the founder of the Saint Sergius Monastery of the Holy Trinity near Moscow (1337), probably the most well-known saint in Russia. For an account of his life, see *Vrem. goda,* 230–32.

520 *his penitent tears and intractable gainsaying of flesh* On the gift of penitent tears, see notes to "The Saints."

520 *epitrachelion* A long, narrow stole worn by bishops and priests of the Eastern Orthodox Church.

524 *kamelaukion* A tall, brimless hat worn by priests and monks; in the Orthodox Church it is a sign that the wearer has done something to deserve special honor.

525 *Whitsun* Weeklong Christian festival that begins with Whitsunday, the seventh Sunday after Easter, observed as a festival in commemoration of the descent of the Holy Spirit on the day of Pentecost (2 Acts: 1–4). In the Orthodox Church, Whitsunday always comes ten days after the holiday of the Ascension, which is observed on a Thursday, the fortieth day after Easter.

525 *the pagan Day of the Water Sprites* (*Rusal'nyj den'*, the Thursday after Whitsunday) The water sprites (*rusalki*) were supposedly spirits in the form of naked girls who lived in underwater homes. Thought to attack men and drag them into the water to drown them or to tickle men to death, they represented the afterlife of souls of unbaptized babies or of girls who drowned themselves over unrequited love. Like almost all pagan images they were closely

associated with the forces of the devil but also embodied fertility. Water Sprites' Week, which predated the Christian festival of Trinity Week, was one of the pagan Russian fertility festivals, during which a number of games and semirituals celebrated the vegetative forces (especially the birch tree). Normally a birch was cut and brought into the village, and peasant girls decorated the tree and wove garlands out of its twigs. On Whitsunday they played fortune-telling games connected with throwing the garlands into the river. The water sprites were unclean (of the devil) and dangerous but also had a positive force (promoting fertility and pacification of the dead). When the Christian festival of Trinity Week was superimposed upon the older pagan festival, the two became inextricably blended in the folk imagination. On Water Sprite Week, see *Ivanits,* 75–81. See also Maria Kravchenko, *The World of the Russian Fairy Tale* (Berne: Peter Lang, 1987), 45–46.

Temir-Aksak-Khan

The story revolves around an Eastern legend about Temir-Aksak, also known as Timur the Lame or Tamerlane (1336–1405), the renowned medieval military commander in Central Asia. The words *temir-aksak* in Turkish mean "the iron limper" or the "iron man lame man" (*Bab. notes,* 4:508). Tamerlane's grave, unlike that of the Temir of this story, is not forgotten and his blue-green sepulchre is not overgrown with wild dog-rose bushes. The Tamerlane mausoleum, called the Gur Emir, is still a central tourist attraction and Muslim shrine in the ancient Uzbekian city of Samarkand.

Bunin would have special reason to commemorate Tamerlane's life, since the city where he studied, Yelets, was invaded and sacked by Temir-Aksak in 1395. So a different legend goes, Tamerlane, "who held mastery over half the globe, from the Caspian and Mediterranean Seas to the Nile River and the Ganges," was encamped on the old Moscow road outside of Yelets when he was treated to a mantic dream. The Queen of Heaven appeared unto him, surrounded by a host of warriors, and ordered him to abandon forthwith the realm of Rus. Immediately he retreated, leaving Russia and Europe in peace. On the spot of the dream the Russians built a church named after the icon of the Blessed Yelets Mother of God. Copies of this icon abound in Yelets to this day. The legend of the Yelets icon derives from a more famous legend, the one describing how the most venerated icon in all of Russia, the Vladimir Mother of God, was brought to Moscow from Vladimir, in order to forestall Tamerlane. After the Muscovites prayed to the icon, the Theotokos appeared in Tamerlane's dream, holding both arms high toward the heavens. The Yelets icon depicts her the way Temir-Aksak supposedly saw her, arms raised.

There are two different shrines in Yelets containing the remains of those who died unsuccessfully defending the city in 1395. One of these is behind the mammoth Ascension Cathedral (see notes to *Drydale*); the other is in the old cemetery next to the Church of the Kazan Mother of God, near where Olya Mesherskaya is buried (see notes to "Light Breathing"). On Tamerlane and Yelets, see also V. Gorlov and A. Novosel'tsev, *Elets vekami stroilsja* (Lipetsk, 1993), 226–27.

Night of Denial

The story is set on Ceylon (Sri Lanka).

532 *Mara* In the Buddhist scriptures Mara is the sovereign of the world, god of death and god of the living. "Māra is Kāma, 'Desire,' since desire is the *raison d'être* of birth and death; and, because Buddha is the deliverer from death and birth, Mara is the personal enemy of Buddha . . . Māra embodies desire, the universal fetterer, the sensual life both here and in the other world" (*Encyclopedia of Religion and Ethics,* 8:406–7). From Bunin's story "Brothers" (1914): "Everything in the forests was singing, glorifying Mara, the god of Life-Death, the god of 'craving for existence'" (*Sob. soch.,* 4:258). Another quote from that story (278): "In India and Ceylon, where in the febrile darkness of black, searing-hot nights one has the sensation of man's melting, dissolving in this black murk, in the sounds and aromas, in the awesome All-One—only there do we faintly comprehend what this Personality of ours really means."

533 *the divine excrescence* This protuberance on the skull of the Buddha is also mentioned in "Night."

For more on the topic of Buddhism, see the Thomas Marullo book mentioned in notes to "Night." Bunin wrote poetry with Buddhist themes (for example, two poems entitled "Ceylon"; see *Sob. soch.*, 1:372, 406). See also *G.d.*, 274–75. Here (in conversations that took place in the fall of 1932) Bunin tells Galina Kuznetsova about his visit to a Buddhist library on Ceylon and speaks of Buddhism. He remarks that he could have become one of the immortals ("one of those whose name is remembered") had he laid his life upon "the bonfire of labor," and had he not "delivered it over to the devil-tempter of quotidian life. But . . . as the Buddha told Ananda, 'Verily, verily I say unto thee, many more times wilt thou deny me again in this night of thy earthly incarnations.'"

The Buddha's beloved disciple Ananda (also mentioned in the story "Brothers"), is obviously the prototype for the anchorite in "Night of Denial." In discussing in terms of Buddhism his failure to devote his life relentlessly to the labors of art, Bunin is getting himself wrapped up in a contradiction. Buddhist principles are not compatible with the desire of the modern artist to immortalize himself through art. This is just one more vainglorious and earthbound delusion (but it is an idea that Bunin was obsessed with all his life). He, of course, understood the fruitlessness of such an obsession: "I wanted glory, praise, even to be remembered after death (which is the most senseless thing of all)" (cited in *Mikh.*, 13).

»»» AFTERWORD «««

Ivan Bunin (1870–1953), the first Russian writer to be awarded the Nobel Prize for Literature (1933), had one of the longest careers in Russian literary history. Having published his first poem in 1887, he continued to write poetry and prose works for another sixty years. His reputation as an exacting stylist was well established in Russia before the revolution and civil war, which forced him into emigration in 1920. He spent the remainder of his life in France, writing works set primarily in prerevolutionary Russia.

Bunin is often taken to be a scion of the great Russian realist movement of the nineteenth century, but packaging him neatly as a realist is a vast oversimplification. Certainly he has affinities with the realists (he is obsessed with realistic detail and with describing things precisely), and he has also been considered something of a classicist—for the perfection of his form. His preoccupation with romantic love (the central theme of his whole literary life) suggests, of course, Romanticism, and Bunin is indeed a Romantic in other ways as well: in his desire to transcend the bounds of the mundane in both life and art, in his ornate style and his use of Romantic catchphrases. Since his fear of death is inordinate, his emphasis on the Romantic theme of escape is not surprising: escape through love, Eastern religions, idealization of a bucolic past, or art. In a number of stories included in the present collection, Bunin blends the love theme with the theme of art. Most surprising, perhaps (at least for literary critics who have put Bunin in the box labeled "realist"), he is, to some extent, a modernist writer. This would come as a surprise, as well, to the neo-Romantic symbolists, his contemporaries, whom Bunin engaged in internecine conflict for so many years and who laughed off his works as outmoded, but his best prose is also his most modernist.

ART AND LOVE

Important points are easy to miss. If you think that the great classic of country music, David Allan Coe's "Take This Job and Shove It," is a song about quitting your job, you have missed the main point. This is a song about trying to get up the nerve to quit your job and fantasizing about storming out in a burst of rancorous glory. Most obvious in "The Grammar of Love" is the landowner Khvoshinsky's obsessed love for the peasant girl Lushka. It's a story in the vein of Romanticism, but it is also neo-Romantic (modernist) or even postmodernist in the unique way a casual observer is converted into a central character. The main point may be the way this story treats a strange ménage à trois, since the creative dreamer and narrator Ivlev, modeled after Bunin himself, is shown in the process of becoming Khvoshinsky's alter ego. In a deliberate act of artistic creativity, Ivlev assumes the identity of another dreamer like himself, falls in love with a figment of his own imagination, the "legendary Lushka," and achieves a creative, semi-insane escape into the other being described in the Baratynsky poem. This story, consequently, is not only about Khvoshinsky and Lushka but also about that fantasist who wants, imaginatively, to get in bed with them. Furthermore, it may be the closest thing Bunin has written to a ghost story, since the presence of the dead Lushka is manifested in any number of details. In reading this fine work about art and the semi-insane imagination, we are reminded how much the great Vladimir Nabokov owed to his older émigré colleague.

Ivlev is also the protagonist of a later story, "In a Never-Never Land," in which he dreams the plot (another in the Ivlev series is

"A Winter's Dream" [1918], not translated in the present collection). As dreamer-narrator he views the action and creates it simultaneously, like a director making a film. This is the ideal situation for the artist who would like to build the events of his own life in the same way he constructs his fiction. In a distant dreamland (the title is the formulaic first line of a Russian folktale), Ivlev creates an ideal love for himself and calmly destroys all obstacles to that love (for example, by "murdering" the old aunt). The story ends with the creative artist in the role of Pygmalion, worshiping his creation and asserting that this love is more real for him than any woman made of flesh and blood.

The art theme, overlapping with the love theme and featuring a Pygmalion twist, shows up in a number of other works. In one of his best stories in this vein, "An Unknown Friend," Bunin puts his own ideas about art into the mouth of the heroine. He treats the complicated relationship between writer and reader, artistic communication and the creativity inspired by the right kind of communication. The woman reads a writer's stories, concocts a fictional image of that writer in her mind, falls in love with the concoction, and begins writing love letters to her own creation. While pleading for an answer, she dimly comprehends that if the real writer ever answered, her fictional reality would be destroyed. It is not surprising to find this theme in an artist as self-centered as Bunin. While writing his semiautobiographical *Life of Arseniev* in the thirties, he described how he had fallen in love with his own character, Lika, about whom he began having dreams: "I once awoke and thought, Lord, this could be the greatest love in all my life. And it turns out that she did not exist."[1] As suggested above, the Ivlev cycle of stories presents another Pygmalion, the artist in love with his own imaginative fancies, but despite the attraction of the Pygmalion myth, "An Unknown Friend" demonstrates the ultimate failure of solipsism in art, which cannot be disentangled from life, where there are no goddesses around to incarnate the statues you sculpt. Communication is essential; if the only reader this solitary woman has is herself, the process is incomplete. That is why she so pleads for an answer to her letters. She needs a reader, but, paradoxically, that reader cannot be the artist who inspired her since he is the character whom she has invented. What complicates the issue inordinately is her attempt to substitute an invented love for an incarnate love. Notwithstanding the inclinations of the creative dreamer Ivlev, Bunin, a writer obsessed with carnality, is not one to believe that the statue of Galatea, left in marble rather than flesh, is enough. But apart from the issue of art, this story is very much about love (and about why romantic love has always worked so poorly): in the process of "falling in love" and picking our "partners for life," we reinvent them to fit our own ideal picture rather than taking them for the way they are. First we sculpt our statues or paint our paintings, using our partners for models; then we complain that they, in their fleshy reality, can't live up to the Galateas we have created.

Bunin writes about love primarily in terms of sensuality; in Russian literature he is the great cataloger of flesh. Throughout his life he was both fascinated and perplexed by the enigma of human sexuality, especially by the all-enveloping power of the female body. In discussing one of his favorite Western writers, Maupassant, he once remarked that "he was the only one who dared to repeat incessantly that human life is ruled utterly by the craving for woman."[2] Toward the end of a career dominated by the theme of sensual love, however, Bunin remained dissatisfied with literary treatments of love, both in his own works and in other works of world literature:

> I am often amazed and saddened, even horrified . . . when I think about the stupidity, the inattentiveness toward women that was

> characteristic of me during the early years of my life in France (and even before that). *No one ever has* managed to write about that wondrous, ineffably beautiful something, utterly unique of all earthly things, the body of woman. And not only the body. One must, must make the attempt. I have tried—the result is filth and banality. I must find different words.[3]

THE EVOLUTION OF A PROSE WRITER

The progress of Bunin's career as a prose writer is marked by a series of starts and stops. Although he was much recognized and honored in Russia by the time he was in his early thirties, that recognition came mainly as a response to his poetry and his translations from Western literature. Anton Chekhov, who died in 1904, regarded his good friend and colleague Bunin as his logical successor, the one best suited to carry on the grand traditions of Russian literature, but had Bunin died before 1910, he would have quite a meager reputation in Russian letters today. After the new vogue of symbolism took center stage, his poetry was, largely, unappreciated, and even later few readers (with important exceptions, such as Nabokov) ever placed the poetic works on the same high level as the prose. But the prose was itself poetic from the start, and it remained so for the whole of Bunin's career. Early on, however, Bunin was not interested in telling a story with plot and character development. His short stories were much criticized for their *etjudnost'*, their lack of a structural focal point and their dependence on lyrical mood. This criticism was, for the most part, justified. In the Ivlev cycle mentioned above, two of the stories lack artistic focus: only "The Grammar of Love" has the successful integration of lyricism and plot intrigue that makes it a wonderful work of art. The tendency to write plotless stories with characters vaguely developed was something Bunin never got totally away from. Even after emigrating, for example, at age fifty-four, he could write a piece like "Glory" (1924), which barely makes it into the category of fiction.

Beginning about the turn of the century, however, Bunin began working his way out of the *etjudnost'* into something big, culminating in the best series of prose works he ever wrote (in the six years preceding the revolution, 1910 to 1916). With the still rather formless "Antonov Apples" (1900), the beginnings of the changeover are apparent, and in many ways this work foreshadows the novella *Drydale* (*Sukhodol*), which represents Bunin at his very best. "Antonov Apples" is a series of descriptive passages stuck together, vignettes from the life of the petty landowner-squires. The characters have prototypes easily identified in Bunin's own life, and the narrator, to a large degree, is based on Bunin too. The story is about memory conjured up through sensuous impressions, in particular the sense of smell. In earlier passages (later cut) Bunin wrote that he had heard Schiller liked to have apples lying about in his room, since their fragrance inspired his creative moods. Bunin described the smell of Antonov apples as a blend of honey and autumnal crispness (*Sob. soch.*, 2:505–6).

The narration of "Antonov Apples" involves an intricate mix of verbal tenses and time sequences that was to become a hallmark of Bunin's best prose later on. No critic has treated this device in all its complexity. We get paragraphs beginning in the present tense, then capturing the immediacy of certain former experiences by telling them in the past tense, then throwing in a code word (*byvalo,* meaning repetitive action in the past—"as it used to happen"), then sometimes coming back to the present tense again. One effect, probably deliberate, is to mangle time sequences so as to suggest that time is a fiction and that life repeats itself endlessly in the same patterns. Related to this is the way the nebulous narrator of this sketch grows, imperceptibly, as he narrates. At the beginning he seems quite a young boy (eight to ten years old?). His aging process is left deliberately vague. In the scenes when he participates in the hunt he appears to be in early adolescence, and at the end of the story he may be a grown man, out on another hunt. This reduplication of the narrator, his appearance in various guises, suggests what might be termed Bunin's doppelgänger device. Characters often double each other, or themselves, within a story. Toward the conclusion of "Antonov Apples," we are informed that the madcap squire-hunter Arseny Semyonich has shot himself. But then comes a description of the life of the middling landowners, told in the same exalted, nostalgic terms as before, with the implicit message that things haven't changed much with the passing of the old order. At the bottom of the same page where Arseny's suicide is revealed an alter ego of Arseny appears. He may have no borzoi dogs, but he is essentially the same person, the rough-hewn passionate lover of the hunt. Utilizing, therefore, an uncanny artistic device, Bunin kills off his character and resurrects him on the same page. Life goes on, and the story ends with men like Arseny out on the hunt again, drinking in the outbuilding of some isolated estate and singing sad songs to the accompaniment of a guitar. Of course, the implication is that this is the same and yet not the same. Soon these men will have died off too, and perhaps nothing of the old spirit will remain. An added complication, at the end, is the position of the narrator, the only character who pulls together the fiction as a whole. Is he one of those squires out there singing the valedictory songs? Maybe so, but more important he is a writer writing the valedictions, the alter ego of his creator Bunin; his main function is to keep the squires and their way of life alive in the only way he can: by describing them and it in creative art.

Although "Antonov Apples" has the structural diffuseness of Bunin's early prose works, Bunin is already doing some of the things that he later does best. "Apples" presents his extensive knowledge of life on the country manors, his eye for significant detail and dedication to descriptive accuracy, his amazing grasp of the flora and fauna of his native region, his acute apprehension of all things sensuous. It also serves as an example of how Bunin's art was steeped in nostalgia years before his forced emigration. Born into a family of the declining gentry class, Bunin idealized the past of the landowning squires and liked repeating that he had come along one hundred years too late. He was, indeed, at age thirty, something of an anachronism, "the last of the classics" of nineteenth-century Russian literature. Emigration, of course, intensified his nostalgia, but the traditional life of the gentry was already long gone by 1917, and even had the Russian Revolution never occurred, Bunin would have produced a good many works bemoaning the passing of the old ways. Two of the stories in the present volume, "Way Back When" and "Indulgent Participation," are, in part, nostalgic evocations of prerevolutionary life in Moscow. In my view, "Way Back When" ("Dalekoe") is the best thing he wrote in that vein. "A Passing" is an elegy to Bunin's dying gentry class (already dead by the time the story was published in France). It also presents a different take on the love theme from "The Grammar of Love," with the gruesome Anyuta loving the master unrequitedly ("I was the onliest one that truly loved you"), and the master, who had wasted away with love for some Lyudmilochka (she may be the counterpart of the illustrious Lushka), passing on unaware that Anyuta's love ever existed. "Sempiternal Spring" combines yearning for return to an idealized bucolic world of the eighteenth century with revulsion for the twentieth century as embodied in the new Soviet state.

A CRUEL TALENT

In publishing *The Village* (written 1909 to 1910), Bunin forced the reading public to develop a new perception of him as a writer. This long work (novella length) is remarkable in the way it depicts the squalor and degradation of Russian country life. It also is the first major work to embody what might be described as Bunin's "cruel talent." He leaves nostalgic and lyrical evocations of rural scenes behind him to reveal the baseness of peasant life. Bunin's onetime friend Maxim Gorky was always split between his admiration of Bunin's aesthetics and his dislike for his "gentry" politics. In a letter of November 1901, for example, he wrote that "Antonov Apples" smelled good, but it was hardly democratic. With *The Village,* the elegiac tone was absent, and Gorky found passages with a social message that he could really get his teeth into. Bunin's harsh depictions of peasant life were (like some of Chekhov's stories) an attempt to counter what he saw as overidealization of the peasants in countless works of Russian literature (most prominently in the works of Tolstoy). In *The Village* there are descriptions of rape, callous brutality, persistent violence. That was only the beginning; descriptions of cruelty and beastliness became a hallmark of Bunin's prose after 1910, although fictional works centered on those themes are fewer in the emigration years. Bunin seems to be making a broad statement about humanity in general, belaboring a truth embodied laconically in the Russian proverb "*Chelovek cheloveku zver'*" (literally, "Man is an animal to man"). In the present collection the cruel vein is represented, primarily, by "The Mad Artist," "I'm Saying Nothing," and "Noosiform Ears."

The expression "cruel talent," of course, was a label that one critic tacked on Fyodor Dostoevsky, a writer Bunin considered the precursor of repulsive modernist literary tendencies (godfather of the schools of decadence, symbolism, futurism, and so forth), a writer he never tired of excoriating, but one who, nonetheless, influenced him. In "I'm Saying Nothing" (1913), where he depicts a character who for no known reason revels in masochism, Bunin is getting over onto Dostoevsky's turf. Characteristically, the author makes no attempt to explain the psychology behind his character. Shasha just is the way he is. Even after he acquires a wife and children he remains utterly alone (so choosing to remain); he is the Underground Man of country life, but, of course, unlike Dostoevsky's urban Underground Man, he has no education and no ability to reason. Dostoevsky has been accused (by Bunin, among others) of enjoying the way he grabs the reader by the hair and shoves his nose down into the vomit of life, deriving, so they say, a perverse, almost voluptuous delight in describing the basest side of humanity. At times Dostoevsky may be justifiably accused of that, although he redeems himself by the truth and depth of his art. It is, however, an accusation that can sometimes be directed at Bunin as well. Shasha revels in the squalor of his life, enjoys being degraded; it is as if he will not be satisfied until he is crippled and blinded. Simultaneously, the narrative force behind the story seems also to be reveling in the nastiness. This is especially apparent in the long and detailed descriptions of hideous, malformed cripples and beggars toward the end of the story. It's as if the keen-eyed narrator just can't get enough of looking at the hideousness and depicting it in extensive detail. He is something like the jolly "impresario" boy who acts as barker for one of the freaks: "Step right up and have a look, folks. Here we have the leprosy of human life in all its splendor!" The author (after all, the lengthy descriptions come right out of Bunin's own diary entries) might justifiably be accused of rolling in the grotesquery like a dog in excrement. You sometimes get a similar feeling when reading detailed descriptions of beastliness in works like *The Village.*

The influence of Dostoevsky on Bunin's works is sometimes unmistakably there,[4] but Dostoevsky is largely absent in the best of Bunin, and even works written in protest against Dostoevskian tendencies are not wholly successful. A case in point is "Noosiform Ears" (1916), a story in which Bunin takes on the whole of the so-called Petersburg Spirit in Russian letters, including, most prominently, Dostoevsky and Gogol. But the implicit argument (quite true) that the average murderer is not a half-repentant schizophrenic like Raskolnikov in *Crime and Punishment* doesn't really need to be made. After all, Dostoevsky had already presented something of a Sokolovich type (Svidrigailov) in the same novel. Then again, "Noosiform Ears" is an attempt at parody and irony, and the simple truth is that Bunin is not one to handle this sort of thing very skillfully. His lack of appreciation for the more subtle effects of irony, along with the paucity of humor in his fiction, are traits that most firmly place him in the tradition of nineteenth-century Russian realist literature. Dostoevsky *does* appreciate irony and *does* manifest a sense of humor (true, it's very dark humor), and those traits are part of what make *him* essentially a twentieth-century writer.

The weakness of "Noosiform Ears" as a work of art may, additionally, be attributable to things that were going on in Bunin's life and the world around him at the time that work was written. The same thing may be said for "The Mad Artist" (1921), another story that is not among Bunin's best. After a period during which his art flourished, political events intruded into Bunin's world and made writing a difficult business. The bloody mess of World War I was followed by the successive revolutions of 1917, and then came the civil war, which eventually forced Bunin's immigration to France. In view of those tumultuous historical events, it is no surprise that his production tailed off for a few years, and much of the fiction he did write was colored by things he found profoundly disturbing.

"The Mad Artist" deals with the limitations of art in a world gone berserk. The Russian artist, Bunin himself as well as the hero of the story, cannot live in a cork-lined room, insulated from the world around him. The disturbed painter of the story wishes to "give birth" to a creative work that will resurrect in the creative act his dead child and wife, defeat the insane trends of the time, and save the world. But the artistic imagination refuses to lie, and the final creation embodies all the earthly horrors that the artist himself has lived through. Written before Bunin had recovered his equilibrium after leaving his native country, "The Mad Artist" may be a reflection of his own confused state of mind. You wonder to what extent he would have continued his wonderful streak of artistic success had the revolution and civil war not intruded into his life. No other period in his writing career can compare with the second decade of the twentieth century, when he wrote "The Grammar of Love," "Light Breathing," "Aglaia," "Zakhar Vorobyov," "The Gentleman from San Francisco," and what is, without doubt, his best longer work, *Drydale.* Even things that are not quite first rate (but date to this period of efflorescence) show him utterly confident, writing with verve and willing to take chances. One such story is "The Dreams of Chang," in which he filters Eastern philosophy through the imagination of a drunken anthropomorphic dog.

DRYDALE

In speaking of "The Gentleman from San Francisco" (1915), Bunin once told the young Valentin Kataev that with this story he had succeeded in writing the sort of "symphonic prose" that he had been striving toward for some time. But *Drydale,* composed four years earlier, is already a supreme achievement of musical construction. It would take a long scholarly treatise to explain Bunin's pointillist technique, how skillfully he uses his artistic leitmotifs, how he weaves together the strands of the plot, starting with adumbrations of important events, leaving them for several pages (or chapters), then returning to amplify them, sketching in a few more things, switching to a new musical movement, sprinkling in leitmotifs from a previous movement. Here is one example among countless others: Pyotr Petrovich is described as dead only four pages into the story; then come repetitive allusions to that death, details that amplify what we know of it and how we view it, but the actual description of the accident appears only seventy pages later, near the very end (and even then we are left wondering if it really was an accident). Of course, the musical analogies involve not only the artistic structuring of *Drydale* but also the writing itself. Descriptive passages have a music of their own; the prose rings with beautiful music, even when the events being described are far from uplifting.

We recall that previous to his publication of *The Village* in 1910 Bunin had been writing lyrically evocative short compositions centered around a narrative presence resembling himself. The characters in his stories had no flesh and blood; they were nebulous presences. This feature, characteristic to some extent of Bunin's whole career, seems paradoxical. Here is a writer preoccupied inordinately with flesh, but his characters often don't come across as firmly fleshed out on the page. It's something Bunin never learned, or may not have been interested in learning, from the writer he most revered, Lev Tolstoy. After reading *Anna Karenina* you find it hard to believe that Stiva Oblonsky never really existed. Here is a character so tangibly portrayed in flesh and blood that he cannot *not* have existed! In fact, Stiva is much more a real person than, say, Count Beust, the diplomat whose memoirs he is reading in the early chapters of the novel. Count Beust really did live, and he left a multivolume set of memoirs as testament to his time on this earth, but for us readers Stiva is still a more tangible human being. No character in Bunin's works ever steps forward on the page with such insistence on being perceived as a creature of flesh and blood, and Stiva is only one of countless Tolstoyan characters who get up in the reader's face, meat on their bones, demanding to be taken as *real.*

The comparison, nonetheless, is not fair, since who else in world literature is as good, in that respect, as Tolstoy? Much criticized early in his career for lyrically diffuse characters, Bunin, with *Drydale,* performed an amazing feat of acrobatics. He took the nebulousness of the characters and made that into a literary virtue. What do we know about the denizens of *Drydale*? We know something about the major characters, especially Natalya, who is at the center of everything and helps narrate the story. We know that Aunt Tonia went mad over love. But what motivates the behavior of Pyotr Petrovich? What do we know about Klavdia Markovna, except that she married Pyotr Petrovich (why? how?) and that she has a lively disposition? The other brother, Arkady Petrovich, father of the main narrator, is carefree, shiftless, and good hearted, but he never quite achieves tangibility either. With the exception of Natalya, most of the peasant characters are equally hazy. Evsei has a bit of substantiality, as do the villains of the story, Gervaska and Yushka. Others, such as the peasant lad Fomka and the centenarian Nazarushka, stick their noses into the narrative for one brief interlude. It is as if most of the characters are out of focus, and that is the way Bunin wanted it to be. He apparently intended for one major character to dominate everything: the personified Drydale estate itself. His human characters are little more than ants crawling the grounds of that estate. *Drydale* is the story of the slow death of a manor, and the insubstantial existence of human Drydalers is part of the artistic pattern. The fluid sense of time and fluidity of verbal tense add to the effect of impalpability. Right from the beginning we already know nearly everything that happens to the characters, and we have only to wait while the narration fills in missing details. All is foreordained; mired in superstition and fatalism, the Drydalers also know what will happen to them and can only wait for it to happen. Time is irrelevant. At one point (chapter 5) the narrative grades subtly over from Natalya's dread-laden anticipation of her future life on the Soshki farmstead into a detailed description of exactly what she will be doing out on that farmstead. It, in all its intricate detail, is surely not her future anticipation of such a scene; it is the exact scene from a future day in her life—an abrupt skip forward in time that, once again, illustrates the irrelevance of time in the world of *Drydale.* This sort of unique artistic device in Bunin's art has been insufficiently appreciated.

When an author decides that most of his characters have the tangibility and free will of ants, he risks alienating the affections of his readers, who want more than the vicissitudes of a manor house to relate to. Bunin gets around the problem by vividly portraying a number of striking events: the romance of Aunt Tonia and her subsequent madness, the love of Natalya for Pyotr Petrovich, her theft of the mirror and banishment, her rape by the despicable Yushka, and the uncanny presence of satanic forces in the manor house at the climax of the story. There are scenes of striking originality and artistic power. Voitkevich is little more than a stock Romantic figure, but the one scene in which he appears is wonderful. Tonia sits playing at the piano, pausing continuously to adjust her sleeves, while the somber Voitkevich stands behind her in the pose he considers proper for the Romantic military man steeped in Lermontov, aping Napoleon in the way he holds one hand in his tunic, "propping up his waistline," while into the room float a multitude of brightly arrayed butterflies, emblematic of the couple's budding love. Each butterfly is portrayed with exactitude, its raiment precisely delineated, and one can be sure that they are not fabricated out of sheer imagination; the sharp-eyed realist in Bunin had observed exactly such butterflies and noted the exact contours and colors of each. Then the gruff Voitkevich, frustrated in his every attempt to express his love for Tonia, takes aim at one of those delicate, palpitating presences, perched for a moment on the piano lid, and gives it a furious whack (we can almost hear the jarring clang of the piano resounding through the manor house). All that is left of Tonia's love afterward is a delicate bit of fluff on the piano lid, and when the maids wipe off that silvery dust her madness and hysteria commence.

Equally powerful, although of a totally different order, is the scene of Natalya's rape. Yushka the rapist represents many things simultaneously. He is the embodiment of raw carnality, the emissary of the devil, and yet, at the same time, he is the representative of the Prophet Elijah in his weird syncretistic aspect: a Russian Orthodox Christian saint but also a pagan caster of flame. How is it that the manor house is destroyed by fire? We are given to understand that, in the view of the characters (and in the view of the narrative presence), it is no accident. It is fated, just as all of the trials of the main characters seem inevitably fated to occur. If the reader has not reached this conclusion earlier, here is where one fact becomes patently obvious: *Drydale* is far from being a realistic novel. In fact, after an encounter with this work, only an extremely imperceptive reader could ever again describe Bunin as a realist writer. Despite the precise detail (like the butterflies), *Drydale* represents Bunin at his neo-Romantic best: symbolic events, musical prose and the musical structure of a symphonic composition, ghostly characters, strange narrative presences.

Who is telling us the history of *Drydale*? Past critics have often assumed that Bunin divides the narration between the house servant Natalya and the scion of the Khrushchov family, son of Arkady Petrovich (some assume that his daughter is involved in the narration as well). But while Natalya does provide the narrator, that son, with much of the necessary detail, it is only he who delivers the story to us. His role in the work is probably the best illustration of what a unique and modernist thing *Drydale* is, for here we have the narrator as spectral presence. What do we know of the two characters who stand apart from Drydale and view the estate as outsiders, "my sister and I"? The sister barely exists at all—she steps into the narrative for only a scene or two—and the brother is little more than a figment himself. Who did Arkady Petrovich marry? We are never told, and that is one of many amazing lapses of the man narrating the story. After all, this is his mother and the mother of his sister, but never do we hear a single word about her. The narrator is so circumspect or inattentive—or, more likely, made so deliberately spectral—that he leaves out myriads of things the reader might be expecting to learn. A real person would at least mention the name of his cousin (son of Pyotr Petrovich, who ends up being the last male to live at Drydale). This novella is an uncanny tale of fated characters told by a ghost, whom the most powerful personage in the fiction, the manor itself, has hired as ghostwriter.

In numerous respects, *Drydale* is not a gentry novel at all, but a takeoff on the kind of novels written in the grand tradition of gentry literature (Tolstoy, Turgenev). In statements he made at the time it was published, Bunin made clear that the type of petty landed gentry he describes is everywhere but has not been depicted in fiction. Tolstoy's squires, for example, speak French, but in *Drydale* the learning of and speaking of French is a farce. Tolstoy's landowners stand clearly apart from the peasants on their estates. The *Drydale* landowners, on the contrary, are often dominated by their own peasant servants, and bloodlines are vaguely defined. In the grand tradition of service to the state, Russian noblemen serve as officers in time of war, but the participation of the Khrushchov brothers in the Crimean War is, once again, more farcical than anything else. In many ways *Drydale* is the most subtle work Bunin ever wrote, a novella in which he leaves a multitude of facts unexplained or double-edged. The characters are motivated, primarily, by superstition and vague premonitions; peasant folklore (dating back to the Neolithic Age) runs their lives. We have little idea why they behave as they do, and neither, apparently, do they. We don't even know (nor do they) what their origins are. There are hints that the brothers Pyotr Petrovich and Arkady Petrovich have different fathers, that Grandfather himself may be illegitimate. Peasant blood freely intermingles with the blue blood of the Khrushchov landed nobility. In a sudden revelation far into the novella, we learn that Grandfather's beloved wife, Anna Grigorievna, an "imperious beauty," has allowed herself to be carnally used by the Gervaska-like servant Tkach (whose name shows up just this one time in the whole long story). So we are left with the supposition that either Arkady or Pyotr (or both?) may be the scions not of Grandfather Pyotr Kirillovich, but of a man who resembles Gervaska (who himself may be the illegitimate son of Pyotr Kirillovich). And Bunin was accused of writing works devoid of intrigue!

What is the "slight wound" that kept Pyotr Petrovich from returning immediately from the Crimean War? It is mentioned only once, but knowing what we do of his character, there is at least a hint of venereal disease. Did Yushka rape Aunt Tonia as well as Natalya? Here is a man who says he has "more rut" in him than a monastery goat, but is he copulating with both women? We can never be totally sure, but there are hints that "the devil" who got into Tonia and made her moan voluptuously in the dark was really the devil's minion Yushka. How did the narrator's father, Arkady Petrovich, die? We don't know that either, since the odd, disembodied narrator never bothers to tell us. In his summation of the fates that befell the denizens of the Russian landed nobility (final chapter), he mentions that some of them laid hands on themselves, but no suicide appears in the action of the novella. Could the carefree and irresponsible Arkady Petrovich, like the squire he resembles from "Antonov Apples," the lover of the hunt Arseny Semyonich (they both are loosely based on Bunin's father), have shot himself? We don't know, just as we don't know how the main character of the book, Natalya, met her end. She simply dissipates into thin air, and in the final chapter, describing the narrator's visit in search of his relatives' graves, she (probably the most sympathetic female character in all of Bunin's works) is not even mentioned.

This ending of the novella, with its graveyard pastoral scene, is reminiscent of Turgenev (for example, *Fathers and Sons*), but *Drydale* is eons away from Turgenev's works. It is very much a neo-Romantic, impressionistic novel of the twentieth century, much more modern, for example, than Bunin's last collection of stories, *Somber Pathways,* which, while written in the 1940s, is deliberately anachronistic. Here, in a work from 1911, Bunin is at his modernist best. Who is the ghostwriter and psychopomp leading us and the narrator through the land of the dead that is Drydale? As suggested above, this may be a voice conjured up by the legendary power of the estate itself. One of the joys of interpreting artistic literature is crawling way out on limbs and waiting for later critics to climb the chinaberry tree with their chain saws. To push my interpretation to its outer limits, one might use as a point of departure what we are told near the end of the story. Whenever the narrator sees Natalya and hears her relate the tale of her ruined life (chapter 10), he recalls the image of the beheaded Mercurius of Smolensk, relating his own tale from the mouth of the severed head beneath his arm. So that, in sum, the weird and spectral narrative presence of *Drydale* is something like a decapitated talking head, held under the author's left arm and dictating the story to him as he writes.

THE SLAVIC SOUL

Of course the main theme of *Drydale* is one of Bunin's favorite: the self-destructive nature of the Slavic soul, and like so many Russian intellectuals, while bemoaning the purposeful abnegation, he can't help finding some glory in it. Bunin often exalted the institutions of Ancient Rus (see, for example, a very late story, "Shere Monday"). In the icon featured in *Drydale,* Mercurius is holding his bloody head in one hand, while in the other he holds the Guide to the True Way, the Hodegetria Mother of God. In stories throughout his career, Bunin stressed both the horror and the somehow redemptive obverse of the horror, and then, again, the reverse of that, the horror again—but, after all, isn't this sort of alternation the most characteristic feature of the whole Russian literary tradition? As for Russian Orthodoxy, Bunin could never have been a true believer; his eye and mind were too keen to accept the oversimplifications. In conversation with Galina Kuznetsova, he once remarked, "Everything about us is somber. They speak of our bright joyous religion . . . it's a lie, there's nothing so dark, terrible, cruel as our religion. Just think of those black icons, the terrible hands and feet . . . And all the standing for eight hours, the night-time services . . . No, don't talk to me about our 'bright' and merciful religion."[5]

The thing that comes through most clearly, in work after work about the Russian soul, is Bunin's apprehension of how thoroughly primitive superstition and pagan folklore were blended with the spirit of Russian Orthodoxy. Wherever there is Russian religion in Bunin there is *dvoeverie* (dual belief, or syncretism), and this is obvious on nearly every page of *Drydale.* Where else but in Russia could *jurodstvo* (holy foolery) have had such an impact, that institution reeking in Dionysian ecstasy and asceticism, reveling in contradiction? In the many works where he treats *jurodstvo,* Bunin lumps it together with similar phenomena, describing mendicants, low-life wandering minstrels, pilgrims, former monks, beggars, and cripples, in a word, "God's People," anyone who has rejected settled day-to-day existence and the quotidian decencies of bourgeois life: "Holy Rus, thirsting for self-abnegation, despising all restraint and labor, all things mundane, with a passion for any and all masks" ("I'm Saying Nothing"). In exploring this tendency in the Russian mentality, Bunin, of course, is interested in broader issues. The extremes of the "Russian Way" are frequently manifestations of human nature pushed to its limits—and Bunin wants to know what there is about human beings that makes them so eager to destroy themselves.

Bunin, nevertheless, is not one to overglorify the ways of the "God's People," as so many intellectuals have done throughout Russian history. Great masters of Russian literature, such as Tolstoy and Dostoevsky, great philosophers, such as Berdiaev, are prone to propagate certain "Russian ideas": that the Russian peasant has intuitive access to an irrational Great Truth, that the Russian people have a God-given mission to save the world, and so forth. Nonsense such as this is displaced periodically, stuck down into some deep nook in the national consciousness, but it always gets dredged back up. Bunin represents (along with Pushkin, Chekhov, and Nabokov, among others) the more rationalist line on this phenomenon. As his short piece "Glory" demonstrates, his primary response to holy foolery is to marvel at how the God's People, basically charlatans or madmen, came to be so respected, even revered among the general populace in the nineteenth and twentieth centuries. But this is not to say that he underestimates the importance of the phenomenon in Russian history and culture. People venerate what they choose to venerate. Whether the object is worthy of veneration becomes, eventually, beside the point. This is a central issue in "Ioann the Weeper." Ivan Riabinin, who is nothing more than an unbalanced peasant, is made into a creature of mythical proportions. In the end the villagers of Sinful (and even visitors such as the aristocratic lady) believe the myth they have fabricated and are living their lives by that myth, so what Ivan Riabinin was in his lifetime does not matter anymore. Of course, this is how human history operates universally: people make historical events into myths, distorting the reality of history in the process, but never mind—myths to live by are much more important than historical facts.

"Ioann the Weeper" is a story about the great gulf separating educated upper-class Russia from peasant Russia and, simultaneously, about how readily that gulf is narrowed or eliminated. It begins with the image of the primordial peasant who comes to look at the express train, which represents a world that has nothing, apparently, in common with that of his village. It ends with an aristocratic woman getting off that very train and communing with the religious legend by which that village lives. Another way of reading the story is to see it as the tale of two eccentrics, prince and fool, who are not so different as they appear and who end up in exactly the same place. We are not told what psalm is quoted on the prince's grave, but an appropriate verse would be the first line of Psalm 132 (133 in the King James): "Behold, how good and how pleasant it is for brethren to dwell together in unity!"

The story has an interesting structure in that it implies a narrator who rides up to Sinful on the express train at the beginning and then goes about learning and retelling the tale of the legendary fool. The Englishman with a pipe, a cosmopolitan traveler intent on observing things with the keen eye of the artist, is close to Bunin himself in his sojourning persona. But when the Englishman rides off with the express train, the artist-narrator separates himself from him and temporarily joins the muzhik on his walk over to the graveyard. After the peasant ambles on, the narrator spends the rest of the story observing things on his own and talking, presumably, with residents of Sinful, who fill in the details about the life of Ivan Riabinin. After a description of the gravestones with their epitaphs, we are provided a few episodes from the life of the eccentric prince, followed by the skewed hagiography of Ioann the Weeper, as related by some peasant voice. This narrator within the narration attempts to retain traditional hagiographic conventions in style, but he or she gets carried away by the beauty of a grain-fed horse and frequently lapses from high-style phrasings into illiterate locutions. Next come a few more realistic details from the life of Ivan, possibly gleaned by the principal narrator from the same old folks who provide the hagiography. Here we see Ivan in his genuine persona, as a frenetic and unseemly madman, continually whipped for his hectoring of the grandee-prince. Toward the conclusion of the story we learn that the prince himself, on his deathbed, saw something transcendent about the madman and asked to be buried beside him. After that we get a detail taken apparently from the narrator's observations inside the church at the graveyard. There, on the walls, are depictions of a half-naked savage and saintly figure—the prophet that Ioann has become in the eyes of the people after his death.

So ends "Ioann the Weeper," or so we might expect it to end, but Bunin uses one of his favorite devices, a tack-on scene (the critic Woodward calls this a rider or postscript), in which new characters are introduced, personages whose images and actions provide us with a final look at the major themes.[6] An unidentified aristocratic woman, separating herself from the world of rational enlightenment (represented by the express train), walks out once a year to weep and pray at the grave of the holy fool. With her is a young officer (a cornet, like Elagin in the longer story), who has little interest in the ritual but who is still Russian enough (that is, superstitious enough) to go through the ritual motions in a perfunctory way. The story ends with the Prophet Micah, ancient model for Ioann, wailing and lamenting through the words on the gravestone, while the aristocratic lady weeps in homage to the bedlamite and, implicitly, to the threadbare and irrational soul of Russia.

CARNAL LOVE AND THE DISSOLUTION OF FLESH

Just as he returns repetitively to the theme of the Slavic soul, so too does Bunin belabor the issue of sensual love. In his inordinate fear of death and his preoccupation with flesh, he resembles his idol, Lev Tolstoy, but he has little of Tolstoy's social conscience or even his concern for ethical issues. Bunin prefers to emphasize the metaphysical, above all the transience of life and the way people adjust to the inevitable fact of their mortality. Sensual love is so appealing because it allows you to forget, at least for a few seconds, about death. But Bunin's adolescent experiences with love reinforced what he had learned from reading Romantic literature, especially the idea that Eros is inevitably linked to Thanatos. Already present in Bunin's early fiction, this conjunction of Eros-libido-Thanatos is later embodied in important works written over a twenty-year period: "The Grammar of Love," "Light Breathing," "Sunstroke," *The Case of Cornet Elagin, The Consecration of Love (Mitya's Love), The Life of Arseniev.* Furthermore, romantic love walks hand in hand with death in nearly every story he wrote in his last decade as an active writer (the *Somber Pathways* compilation).

In the present collection the love-death theme is extensively aired out in one of the longest works of his émigré production, *The Consecration of Love.* Clearly stated is the central question of much of Bunin's art, a question he realized had no definitive answer, but one that, nonetheless, had to be asked: What is love between man and woman? Bunin simply does not believe in platonic love. In his view carnality is the foundation of relationships between the sexes, since human beings are ruled by animal instincts. Whatever rational impulses we may have developed, over the millennia since we crawled out of the sea in the person of our reptilian ancestors, remain subordinate to instincts. Prometheus hardly exists in the world of Bunin's art; Mother Nature is in control, constantly peering through the windows of the decrepit manor houses where his protagonists live, stretching out her arms to take these, her children, back into her embrace.

Furthermore, Mother Nature, or, more appropriately in regard to Bunin, the Mother Earth Goddess of ancient Russian folk belief—*Matushka-syra-zemlja*—is not at all the nurturing type when it comes to love. She is interested only in doing her job, promoting propagation of the species and death, since, in the endless cycle of life, the old must be cleared away as the new are conceived. In *The Consecration of Love* Mitya is one of those creatures of the animal world mentioned by his friend and Bunin's spokesman Protasov, those who "pay the price of their own being for their first and last act of love." After the Earth Goddess has forced him to do what she has put him on earth for—to copulate—she is ready to absorb him, to take his flesh back into the serenity of the moist earth. Most astounding of all is that Mitya, like many of Bunin's protagonists, is secretly in love with Mother Earth. Subconsciously rejecting the precepts of the Enlightenment, Mitya is driven by his instincts to the sacrament of coitus-quietus, to a symbolic copulation (through copulation with woman) with the spirit of the earth, womb and tomb of all transient creatures. Bunin, as Freud, believes that Thanatos exists in the energy of Eros, that all living things are in secret mourning for the inorganic state, subconsciously yearning for the nullity out of which they were propelled into Being. A Freudian death wish (derived, however, from his knowledge of Russian agricultural folk mythology and his reading in Eastern religions, rather than from Freud) is firmly ensconced in Bunin and his characters, whose fear and hatred of death are tempered by a secret wish to embrace it. The ruttish sensuality of some stories in the *Somber Pathways* collection, written when Bunin was approaching eighty years of age, more likely reflects his subconscious wish to come to terms with death than (as some have unkindly suggested) the striving of a lascivious old man to relive youthful sexual ecstasies in his creative imagination.

One of the strengths of Bunin's art is his willingness to face the darkest of contradictions in the human psyche. Love as animal instinct, carnal love often is transmogrified into cruelty in the Bunin protagonist, even into the perverse sort of sensuality characteristic of Sokolovich in "Noosiform Ears." Although he is repelled by Sokolovich's behavior, Bunin is not one to deny the imperative of human sensuality. After all, who, according to this Jack the Ripper philosopher, has noosiform ears? Not only the degenerates, but also the artists and geniuses. In certain stories from his miniature series (written, largely, in 1930), "The Idol," "The Calf's Head," "The Elephant," Bunin dwells upon the animal nature of humanity. But even such a beast as the man putting on a display in the zoo ("The Idol") has slender, beautiful hands that are "completely out of keeping with everything else," and the last word in the story, describing his "flat yellow face," is *lik,* a lofty Old Church Slavonic word suggesting a description of a saint in an icon. Perhaps this is irony, but perhaps something more.

Bunin admires, as does Nietzsche, "all those happy, soundly constituted mortals who are far from regarding their precarious balance between beast and angel as an argument against existence."[7] But he himself, like characters such as Mitya, is often unable to accept this precarious balance with equanimity. At the moment he shoots himself, Mitya is too distraught to be consciously aware of his motivations. He may be rebelling against the human condition of limbo, refusing to accept it, or, to view this from a different angle, he may be subconsciously accepting the role Mother Earth has assigned him and resigning himself to return his fleshy existence to her. In "On the Night Sea," Bunin slips into a despairing attitude toward the way life is organized, annihilating all justifications for going on living. With its leitmotifs of "nothing" and "absolutely nothing," the story recalls the lost generation of American writers who were in Paris at the same time Bunin lived there. One is reminded of the Lord's Prayer full of "*nada*" in Hemingway's "A Clean Well-Lighted Place." Like the collocutors we are all drifting on a sea of night, surrounded by senseless emptiness and bound for an absurd nothingness. Here you find none of the marveling joy and ecstatic horror that are the hallmarks of a Bunin story. Fortunately, "On the Night Sea" is an exception to the general tenor of Bunin's work, but the kind of pessimism it manifests explains his need to find transcendence of life's contradictions through art.

The impetus for "On the Night Sea" apparently came from an autobiographical incident. Upon the death in 1918 of Bunin's first, and perhaps greatest, love, Varvara Pashchenko, the man who had married her came to see him, and the former rivals had a long conversation. An oblique theme of the story involves the way in which men who have slept with the same woman, notwithstanding the intensity of their rivalry, end up somehow becoming the same person. This is one more manifestation of the doubling theme that shows up in Bunin's works, particularly in regard to sensual love. His early affair with Pashchenko had a profound influence on his fiction throughout his entire career. When Bunin writes about immature young men in love with actresses (*The Consecration of Love, The Case of Cornet Elagin, The Life of Arseniev*), he always seems to begin with a backward look at himself and Varvara Pashchenko (or, sometimes, at Anna Tsakni, his first wife, who aspired to a career as a performer of music). There is also a doubling involved in Bunin's depictions of women his heroes love, and that doubling began with Pashchenko. Once again we recall the Pygmalion theme of "An Unknown Friend." There was the real

Varvara Pashchenko, and then there was the idealized Pashchenko whom the young creative artist Bunin invented and fell in love with. In reading accounts of this early love, including letters he wrote at the time, one realizes that even as a young man Bunin was well aware he was falling in love with a figment of his imagination.[8] Mitya too is aware, at least vaguely, that he has invented the Katya he loves. The doubling of her image is obvious when he sees something in common between her and the peasant girl Alyonka. Of course, the ultimate lesson Mother Earth teaches him is that sexual love with one woman is, from her point of view, the same thing as sexual love with any other woman (see the *chastushka* cited in my annotations to *The Consecration of Love:* "all girls are the same below the waist").

The doppelgängery in Bunin's works is inherent in his worldview. Just before his suicide Mitya has a confused nightmare in which he sees himself and his rival somehow simultaneously making love to Katya (which is to say that all men, as well, are the same below the waist). By the end of "The Grammar of Love" Ivlev has become a double of the insane Khvoshinsky. We all, ultimately, ride the same bicycle and come in the same box. As "The Gentleman from San Francisco" illustrates, we all go out in the same box too. Perhaps the overriding message of the doubling is that of Bunin's story "Brothers" (1914) or that of the psalm cited above in reference to "Ioann the Weeper": in the end we're all brethren dwelling together in unity, although, due to our insistence on pumping up the individual ego, we refuse to accept that truth and embrace the fraternity.

Had Bunin himself been able to accept the immersion of his own ego in the great All-One, things may have gone easier for him in life, but he, like Mitya, was pulled in two different directions. One side of him wanted to revel in the sensuous joys of the world, while the other side wanted to give up the ego and resign itself to the universal rhythms. In stories that reflect his reading of Ecclesiates and Eastern religions, along with his intuitive comprehension of the agricultural mentalities (deeply fatalistic) that form the underpinnings of the collective Russian psyche, Bunin meditates on life's ephemerality and the ultimate dissolution of the flesh. In "Transfiguration" there is none of the love-death blend so typical of his works; this story, all about death, seems to be saying that if you can comprehend the ultimate grandeur of life's grand climacteric, then you've grasped something essential about life and can live easy from then on. In Russian iconic representations of Christ's transfiguration the dazzling white light from the figure of Jesus spills out over all the icon, ultimately stabbing in streaks of white at the figures of the three prostrate disciples (Peter and the brothers James and John), who lie terrified at the bottom of the painting. See, for example, the icon of the transfiguration done about 1403, from the Cathedral of the Transfiguration in Pereslavl-Zalesskij (now held in the Moscow Tretyakov Gallery); see also the fifteenth-century Andrej Rublyov *Transfiguration* from the iconostasis of the Kremlin Annunciation Cathedral, now in the State Museum of the Moscow Kremlin.[9] In his story Bunin suggests interesting parallels with the biblical episode. It is the old woman herself (as corpse) who is transfigured, yet she has something vaguely in common with the image of the transfigured Christ in his dazzling raiment. The color white dominates descriptions of the corpse, and the whiteness of death spreads over the hut (Bunin sets the scene during a snow squall, and bits of gleaming snow are sticking to the windowpanes). Most important, the whiteness infuses the peasant Gavril, son of the dead woman. Like Christ's terrified disciples up on the mountain he is penetrated by a dazzling essence that alters his life irreparably, transfigures him. The tack-on ending of the story reveals that after his transfiguration Gavril has no desire to participate in the aspirations of the bourgeois workaday world. Furthermore, his contemplation of the grandeur of death has left him happy and calm. The story describes (at least) two transfigurations and two deaths. For Gavril has, in a metaphorical sense, died in his previous life and been reborn into a new, transfigured life.

In many iconic representations of the transfiguration the two disciples on either side of the painting are depicted in poses of terror, throwing up their hands to protect themselves from the penetrating rays of light, but the center figure, young John, while depicted as prostrate with body contorted, is looking in the opposite direction from the transfigured Christ. His face is strangely contemplative, devoid of fear. See, for example, the Pereslavl-Zalesskij icon from 1403, mentioned above, or the transfiguration fresco (restored) from the fourteenth-century Church of the Transfiguration at Kovalyov (outskirts of Novgorod). In the Novgorod icon the central figure of John has already undergone his own transfiguration. His sandals appear to have been singed off his feet (he is the only character in the paining not sandaled), and the feet, grotesquely swollen, might have been painted by Picasso six hundred years later. But judging by the look on his face (certainly not scared but profoundly disturbed) he already has his mind not on the events at hand but on what this might all mean to him in his future life. This is a fascinating and bold stroke on the part of the iconographer: showing a human character already transfigured because of, and at the very moment of, Christ's own radiant transfiguration. We have no way of knowing whether Bunin deliberately modeled his Gavril on the central figure at the bottom plane of such icons, but there is certainly a parallel.

Confronted by the stark presence of death and the transience of all things material, Gavril follows the path suggested by the Preacher in Ecclesiates. He resembles some of Tolstoy's serene peasant characters, rejecting earthly striving and taking joy in the simple pleasures of nature. Bunin can allow his character to find such serenity in rejection of ego, but the autobiographical "Night," a philosophical mood piece steeped in Ecclesiastes, reveals that he himself is always divided between rejection of striving and a joyous reveling in the individual ego. Probably better than any other work, "Night" reveals what Zinaida Gippius once called Bunin's simultaneous acceptance and rejection of life. In the final lines the narrator, who is almost certainly Bunin himself, cries out to God to be left with flesh and earth. But here too there is a contradiction, since, as discussed above, Bunin's obsession with sensuality and nature reveals his desire to embrace simultaneously the joys of life and the serene consolations of death. The same dichotomy is there in "Night of Denial," in which the message of eternal striving for both sensual ecstasy and dissolution of ego is told within a Buddhist context. Once again the lessons of Ecclesiastes and the East pervade the story titled "Temir-Aksak-Khan," but that story embodies another lesson, applicable to Ecclesiastes and to much of Bunin's art. As Anthony Burgess has written in a different context, "Here is the old paradox of art. The denial of human joy is made through language which is itself a joy."[10] The story is a song like that of the beggar, and the effect on the reader (at least this reader) is the same as the effect of that song on the young woman: "the despairing grief . . . that lacerates the whole tale is sweeter than the most lofty and passionate joy."

While Bunin may sometimes despair in the face of art's inadequacies or even disparage the artistic consciousness (in a work such as "On the Night Sea"), he often succeeds in demonstrating the redeeming qualities of artistic form. Art, in fact, is all he has, the only weapon at his disposal in his struggle with life's contradictions. His study of Oriental religions and his pretensions to acceptance of the great truths of Buddhism do not run very deep. Nirvana cannot, ultimately, have much to offer to a man who takes ultimate joy in looking intently at the beauty and smelling, savoring the multitude of smells and tastes of the earth.

STRENGTHS, WEAKNESSES, AND INFLUENCES

Bunin's art (and life) are replete with contradictions. The contradictions are neither surprising nor, necessarily, detrimental to his reputation, since all great artists contradict themselves. More difficult to take are the philosophically unconvincing ideas that he keeps sticking into his stories. These ideas are at least loosely connected with Oriental religions. One is his insistence on some sort of mystical connection between all human souls down through the ages (the universal soul). This theme appears in "Night," "Scarabs" (1924), and in many other works, of both fiction and nonfiction (such as *The Liberation of Tolstoy,* 1937). Similarly lacking in conviction is the idea that through a succession of reincarnations one, having received and developed certain traits from one's forebears, pushes on toward Nirvana. In reference to the central character in *The Case of Cornet Elagin* the concept is irreconcilable with another of Bunin's pet theories: that there is a kind of degeneracy working its ways upon the human race (an idea frequently associated with the faulty theories of the criminal anthropologist Lombroso—see my annotations to "Noosiform Ears"). Bunin brings up his hypothesis about degeneracy repeatedly throughout his career (often using the word in both a positive and a negative sense; see, for example, his comments on "Aglaia," cited in my notes), but he does not define exactly what he means by degeneracy, and I doubt that he ever worked it out definitively in his own mind. As Yury Ivask once remarked, however, the art of Bunin is wiser than Bunin the man. One could expand this further to assert that Bunin is a better creative artist than deep thinker. In fact, the philosophical side of his work is not what makes him worth reading. The best of his art, nonetheless (aesthetically), is good enough to transcend his lack of philosophical depth, even to make us look with indulgence upon another of his delusions, the grand delusion of the nineteenth- and twentieth-century Western artist: immortalization of self through art. In a book full of interesting insights James Woodward remarks that with every work Bunin wrote "he was inflicting on time and death yet another defeat. He looked forward to a victory over time."[11] I doubt it. Maybe he sometimes felt that way, but deep down he realized that this sort of thinking scintillates on the same level as the ruminations of the drunken dog in "The Dreams of Chang." Or then again, maybe he did not want to admit it to himself, but he knew that the "universal soul" stuff as well as "art as immortality" would never work for him. He would end up as we all do, the same way Temir-Aksak-Khan ends up, and ultimately the great edifice of art (at least that produced by an individual artist) will be one more grand mausoleum that crumbles away into dust.

Above all, as man and writer, Bunin is ruled by passion. Being passionate means, inevitably, having strong feelings about any number of things. Bunin was known for his revulsions, directed in particular at (1) the Soviets, who deprived him of his homeland and destroyed the Russia of his past (see "Sempiternal Spring") and (2) the modernists in art and literature, who were in vogue in Russia from the 1890s on and who viewed the "anachronistic" Bunin with contemptuous disdain. His polemics with political movements and modernist art (along with its godfather Dostoevsky), his public excoriations often spill over into his fiction (see, for example, *The Consecration of Love*, "Shere Monday," "Indulgent Participation," "Noosiform Ears"). The downside to this passionate expression of strong opinions is that Bunin is often less successful aesthetically in works where he vents personal animosities and tries to settle scores. "Sempiternal Spring" could do with less venom. "Shere Monday" might be better off without so many guest appearances by actors from the Moscow Art Theater, to all of whom Bunin assigns the role of buffoon. One sometimes feels that the pokes he takes at his contemporaries in literature and theater are better left for works of nonfiction, or maybe still better left altogether undelivered (indeed, in his memoirs he takes pokes with a vehemence unrestrained, and in so doing sometimes makes himself look bad).

This is not to say, nevertheless, that Bunin is unable to create fresh art by taking off on the themes of literary artists past and present. *The Consecration of Love,* in part a polemic with Tolstoy's later works on concupiscence, has strong links to Goethe's *Faust* and *Werther.* "The Grammar of Love" is like one of Turgenev's *Hunter's Sketches* (in a number of details it recalls "Living Relics," in which a different Lushka [Lukerya], appears) pushed in a new direction, and another of the Turgenev sketches, "The Singers," provides the basis for the plot background of "Temir-Aksak-Khan." "Transfiguration" takes off from Gogol's "Vij," "I'm Saying Nothing" owes much to Dostoevsky, as does *The Case of Cornet Elagin.* "The Gentleman from San Francisco," a masterpiece of stylistic creativity, is told in a voice borrowed from Tolstoy. The story "Somber Pathways" is something like a retelling of Pushkin's "The Stationmaster," while "Sunstroke" and "Light Breathing" are fresh variations on things Chekhov had done in his best-known works. Even one of Bunin's most original creations, *Drydale,* reads at times like an encyclopedia of influences: (1) the crude dwarf peasant in Natalya's mantic dream resembles the peasant whom Anna Karenina dreams of (and Anna, of course, hearkens back in her dream to that of Tatyana in Pushkin's *Eugene Onegin*); (2) Voitkevich comes right out of Chekhov's play *The Three Sisters* (the Lermontov-loving, wood-headed charlatan Solyony); (3) to a remarkable degree the parricide Gervaska resembles Dostoevsky's Smerdyakov from *The Brothers Karamazov;* (4) the scene where the narrator and his sister encounter the androgynous figure of Aunt Tonia beating a cow in the fields is a rehash of the scene where Plewshkin first appears in Gogol's *Dead Souls.*

As a rule Bunin can handle satire, heavy sarcasm, but can't do (or is not interested in doing) irony in its most intricate incarnations. In this respect his mentor and friend Chekhov is much more a writer of the twentieth century. As mentioned above, Bunin's sarcasm can become excessive, but in his best works he manages to restrain his own strong feelings or temper them with lyricism. "Indulgent Participation" is an example of a story full of sarcasm combined with a subtle lyricism; the combination makes for a trenchant artistic blend. The old actress, while presented sarcastically, ends up being sympathetic all the same. Though decrying the phoniness inherent in her theatricality, Bunin seems to admire the way she struggles on in life, creating year after year, in the face of declining health, her art. It is as if the author insinuates himself into the story twice, playing two different roles: that of the carping old critic sitting in the first row at the performance and that of the old artiste herself. As Professor Ivask once remarked in discussing "Indulgent Participation," Bunin too was devoted to what was attacked as anachronistic art, and he too struggled on, year after year, to write what he considered genuine artistic literature. In the end it is the sarcastic old critic who makes a fool of himself, while the artiste soars out of the story in a burst of lyricism (half-ironic lyricism, true, but lyricism nonetheless).[12]

Here we have Bunin at his strongest. In his best works he has an acute feel for the structure of literary art, a way of finding the right tones, or combination of tones, putting things together successfully. This musical structuring allows him to overcome certain deficiencies of style. For example, Bunin is sometimes awkward or old-fashioned in the way he moves his characters around and pushes the action forward. It appears that he can't be bothered with the small stuff, since he has bigger things in mind (those bigger things being the musical structuring of the composition as a whole). For example, *The Case of Cornet Elagin* is masterfully structured (the moving backward and forward in time, the presentation of facts from various points of view), but literary devices for advancing the plot come out of the early nineteenth century. Written in 1925, *Elagin* has military officers racing around in horse-drawn cabs, practically goading on the drivers with pokes in the neck (as do so many passengers in the cabs of nineteenth-century Russian literature). Considering that the story is set about 1890, this sort of thing is passable, but the way the action is advanced is harder to take. The author employs a series of factotum characters, anonymous couriers, to deliver messages between the main characters. These retainers move obscurely about through the novella but never become anything more than cardboard mannequins playing messengers. I find myself wondering what the orderly sent to return Sosnovskaya's effects is thinking about the whole melodramatic mess. In a word, Bunin is often content to let things flow along by using the plotting conventionalities of Turgenev or Lermontov.

Examples abound of Bunin's cavalier attitude toward certain basics. In the late story "In Paris," he first leads his characters into a movie theater and only later, in the middle of a long descriptive passage, bothers to inform us that they are seated in the balcony. This is along the lines of casual storytelling, when the guy relating the anecdote says, "And then they heard some shots from down below, and, oh yeah, I forgot to tell you that they were up in a tower and that's why the sounds came from down below." This flawed or awkward stance in basic plotting shows up even in some of the best of Bunin's stories. For example, when the author needs to inform us of an important event in the life of Olya Mesherskaya ("Light Breathing"), he ushers us into the inquest proceedings of her murderer and has that man tell us to take a look at her diary. Then somebody, presumably a Russian variant of a coroner, opens that diary and we get to read what happened in the words of the main character. Giving that narration to the main character (the dead Olyenka) at the end of the story (through the introduction of the diary) is a stroke of genius, but the diary is introduced awkwardly.

Critics contemporaneous with Bunin, among them fellow writers, didn't have a lot to say about the careless things, but they did respond, early on, to what they saw as an excess of detail in Bunin's style. Too much is crammed onto one page, into one paragraph or one sentence. Chekhov, apparently, was the first to mention the "too thick soup" and was echoed by Gorky in his well-known comment on *The Village:* "Every page is a museum." Even some of the best stories were subjected to this criticism (see Olesha's comments on "The Gentleman from San Francisco"). Bunin never really got away from the problem of density of style or from a certain overlavishness, what his younger émigré colleague Nabokov later described as *parchovaja proza* (brocaded prose). The use of long nature descriptions overloaded with adjectives plus ornate rhythmic riffs is not much in vogue today, and the problem is compounded by Bunin's fondness for literary devices characteristic of Romanticism. Especially strong in the émigré period is the profusion of oxymorons, something like "in bliss and horror his heart sank," or combinations like "blissfully horrible," and "grievously joyous." The Romantic style becomes, at times, excessive; it is a particular problem in *The Consecration of Love.* Twice in this novella, for example, Mitya's face takes on a "deathly pallor" (*smertel'naja blednost'*). Despite the Romantic clichés, however, this novella may be the best thing Bunin wrote on the insanity of romantic love, and its ending is one of the most powerful passages of prose in his whole career.

Of course here, as in stories such as "Sempiternal Spring," Bunin is deliberately using an old-fashioned style. His Mitya, who idealizes the life of his dying class and prefers Romantic poets of the early nineteenth century, is himself an anachronism, and the style is in concord with the character. But in the age of irony such archaic stylistic effects cause problems, since an expression like "deathly pallor" may now appear to have been deliberately employed with ironic intent. Although Bunin uses his own brand of irony subtly and effectively in some works (such as "Indulgent Participation" and "Light Breathing"), it was never his strong suit, and the reader sometimes has the disturbing feeling that the irony perceived in characters or situations was not intended by the author—rather, it has sneaked into the work at hand through a window left open by dated Romantic style. Here is an example. In a beautiful passage near the end of "Light Breathing," we are informed of "what a woman must have to be truly beautiful." The informant is the dead heroine Olya (as channeled through the mind of her weirdly romantic form mistress), and, coming from this young girl, the descriptions of "black eyes smouldering like pitch" and "eyelashes black as the night" are clearly ironic. Given the circumstances (we already know that the same lovely girl has lived a short life and gone out in a blaze of romantic glory), the description is simultaneously moving. There is nothing to jar the sensibilities of the reader, no false note. But look at the description of the heroine of "Shere Monday," given to us straight by the narrator, unfiltered through the mind of a young girl or anyone else: "Her beauty . . . had overtones of the Hindu or Persian: an amberlike duskiness about her face, something a bit ominous in the thickness of her marvelous black hair, brows that gleamed softly, like black sable fur, black eyes like velvet coals." In the first place, a work of the twentieth century can't get away with (as straight narrative) details like the black sable and the black eyes like velvet coals. They make the reader smirk. In the second place, for anyone who has read "Light Breathing" (and anybody who has read Bunin has read "Light

Breathing," his best story), what is perceived in the black sable fur and eyes like velvet coals is something like self-parody, but it is not deliberate self-parody. Unbeknownst to the author, his lovely Olya has suddenly taken control of the narration. Returning to the world of 1944 from that cemetery in Yelets where Bunin buried her in 1916, she has begun, once again, describing her ideal image of womanhood. The effect is ironic, but the author wants it straight. A false note is struck, and that is one (of several) reasons why "Shere Monday" can't live up to its author's high opinion of it (he once declared it the best story he had ever written).

I'm not sure if Bunin was aware of these problematic kinks in his stylistics; he probably would assert rather vehemently, and in unseemly terms, that there was no such problem. At several points in his career he did try, for reasons not totally clear, to find quite different directions for his art. The miniature stories, written mostly in 1930 but including works from other years (such as "The Saviour in Desecration," 1926), constitute an interesting artistic experiment—the pursuit of ultimate brevity. Many of them come off remarkably well, and most of them reflect, in abbreviated form, Bunin's major themes: love and the entanglements of nature ("First Love"), the mystery of the Slavic soul ("The Cranes"), the simultaneous loftiness and beastliness of mankind ("The Idol"). In the forties, after writing his semiautobiographical masterpiece *The Life of Arseniev,* he resumed his search for an economical prose with the *Somber Pathways* collection, but the brevity here is not so pronounced. The style of "The Cold Fall," however (from this final compilation), is probably as simple as that of any story he wrote. It is modeled on the starkness of the Fet poem from which the story's title is taken, almost as if in his last years Bunin were attempting to utilize the laconic simplicity of much of his own poetry (strongly influenced by Fet) in his prose style.

DARK ALLEYS

Bunin spoke in the highest terms of his *Somber Pathways* stories (represented in the present collection by the title story, by "The Cold Fall," "In Paris," and "Shere Monday"), stating that they represented the best work of his career, that in them he had found a musical structure and tonality in harmony with the chaos of twentieth-century life. Try as I might, I can find no way to agree with him. Take the title story. In some small degree it is a retelling of Pushkin's "Stationmaster" with the outcome reversed: the upper-class character did not end up marrying the peasant girl. But Pushkin's story is more complex, since it is steeped in light ironic humor, something Bunin never had much use for. "Somber Pathways" has nothing in common with twentieth-century literary art. It owes something to Tolstoy, especially for the way Bunin accumulates a mass of detail, as in the long descriptions of the dress and mannerisms of the main characters at the beginning. K. Leontiev had criticized Tolstoy for this overdetailing of descriptions long, long ago, and in the short parable stories of his late period Tolstoy had abandoned the method. Bunin seemed to have found a similar economy in his miniatures of 1930, but to get back to that he would have to cut his first paragraph in "Somber Pathways" by half.

This story is deliberately and aggressively old-fashioned. To take an architectural parallel, it is something like the Church on the Blood in St. Petersburg, designed by Alfred Parland with something like the sixteenth-century Saint Basil's on Red Square in mind but built in 1883 (completed in 1907). The building grates on the aesthetic sensibilities of architectural purists. Why construct a sixteenth-century church in St. Petersburg at the end of the nineteenth century? Likewise, why write a story from the nineteenth century in 1938? It is incredible to think that at the same time Nabokov was on the verge of publishing something as creatively new and fresh as *The Real Life of Sebastian Knight* (his first English-language work), Bunin, who at one time had himself had certain modernist tendencies, was reverting wholeheartedly to the Russian realism of the previous century (sweetening it with his usual dollop of the Romantic).

The story "Somber Pathways" is set in the nineteenth century, its language is archaic, its literary devices and structure are creaking with age: the detailed descriptions of the characters and their dress, the rusty mechanisms used to crank things along (the officer reddening in reaction to his old lover's words, the pacing back and forth, the conversation with the coachman at the end, whom the author has provided with inside knowledge about the woman so that he can impart this information to the officer character and the reader). Compare this heap of literary stale black bread to the yeasty originality, the stylistic and structural creativity of "The Grammar of Love," "Aglaia," "The Gentleman from San Francisco," *Drydale,* "Light Breathing," works written twenty years earlier.

Not only the story "Somber Pathways" but the whole collection of stories under that title provided, essentially and foremost, a reason for Bunin to go on living. He was written out and worn out, both physically and emotionally. One more disastrous event in world politics (World War II) had encroached upon his life, as if the First Great War, the Russian Revolution, and the Russian Civil War had not been enough for one writer's lifetime. Even worse on a personal level, he had lost the last great love of his life, Galina Kuznetsova, and when Galya left him he suddenly found himself in a humiliatingly familiar position: he had become one of his own characters, Mitya, or, say, the lieutenant in "Sunstroke." Then again, the fact that his best work was already done is not so surprising. I don't know if a survey has ever been taken, but I doubt that many writers blossom out into new creativity after the age of sixty. At that age Vladimir Nabokov resigned from his job as a professor in the United States and moved to Switzerland, finally relieved of the burden of teaching and hoping to push his creative modernism in new directions. But then a propensity for playing games (always there, even in his best works) came to the fore and overwhelmed him. Nothing written in Switzerland can compete with the brilliant things he had done earlier, in Berlin, Paris, and the United States.

Bunin sometimes complained about a kind of mass hypnosis affecting everyone who read Dostoevsky. How could readers be impressed with this haphazard and hysterical writer? "Not only do they dare not say that the king is naked, but they don't even dare admit it to themselves."[13] In reading the stories of the *Somber Pathways* collection, I get a similar feeling. Bunin emphatically declared it his best collection because he desperately needed to believe that it was, but why do so many readers and critics take him at his word? Bunin's best prose was written between 1910 and 1916, with another clump of works (almost as good, but not quite) between 1921 and 1930. Then, before *Somber Pathways,* came *The Life of Arseniev* in the thirties, almost equally brilliant but something of an anomaly for its length and semiautobiographical nature. None of the stories in the final collection can be compared to the best of the earlier works. Of course, I can anticipate the reaction of the lovers of the dark allées: "Yeah, well we happen to appreciate St. Petersburg's 'Church on the Blood,' magnificently glittering with its cupolas over Griboedov Canal, and Bunin was wrong about Dostoevsky too!"

MAKING A CASE FOR *ELAGIN*

Just before he left Russia, to go abroad to a German resort, where he died, Anton Chekhov said to the writer Teleshov, "And you tell

Bunin to keep on writing and writing. He's going to be really big someday. Be sure to tell him that from me. Don't forget." This, coming when it did, was a prescient remark, for within a few years after Chekhov's death, Bunin's artistic potential burgeoned. He wrote a series of prose works that still shine today with creative energy; he was on the verge of that something big, and then somehow he could not maintain himself at quite that high level. Why not? One wonders whether Bunin would have pushed his art in totally new directions had not the Great War and the turmoil in Russia and the forced emigration knocked him off kilter. In the brilliant creativity of their aesthetics, *Drydale* and "The Gentleman from San Francisco" stand out from almost everything else he had done. Why did he back up somewhat during the years in France, return to the kind of writing he had long since perfected?

Why, for example, did he not produce a few more things like *The Case of Cornet Elagin,* which was written in 1925 as a kind of literary experiment? The novella seems to me insufficiently appreciated. I think it is one of Bunin's best longer works, although it is written in a style unusual for him. There is something fresh about the way it eschews nature description and the excessive embellishments of style. In this story the overwrought modes of Romanticism (or of the neo-Romantic) belong to the characters, not to the style of narration itself (as in *The Consecration of Love*). Bunin incessantly repolished the stories he loved, and the fact that he never came back to *Elagin* is attested by some critics as proof that he did not appreciate the work. Only two months before he died he scribbled on the margins of *Elagin,* "All of this story is an *extremely* repulsive story!" (see *Sob. soch.*, 5:527). But this is not necessarily a judgment of the literary merits of *Elagin;* it may be an expression of Bunin's irritation with the characters, or with their original prototypes, with the melodrama they insist on playing out to the end. If Bunin did indeed consider the story a failure, he was simply wrong.

The author made one excision (of the last chapter) very late in his life; in its final form the novella was published in a New York collection posthumously. Of course, an interesting question with regard to his revisions of stories already published is this: Are the final and definitive versions always better than the earlier ones? It is problematic for an aging and ill author to make major changes (in Bunin's case they usually amounted to cuts) in works that had come out decades earlier. It recalls, somehow, the way an old man, late in life, decides to change his will and cut out his scapegrace nephew. Maybe the nephew is more worthy than he is given credit for being. For example, I prefer the original title "Cicadas" for the story retitled "Night."

In considering *Elagin,* the literary critic is reminded, once again, that no one reads Dostoevsky in depth and walks away unscathed. Although Bunin never tired of raging about Dostoevsky's demerits as a writer, the influence keeps showing up in his works. Perhaps one of the reasons *Elagin* irritated him was precisely this: he could not help admitting to himself that the main point of the novella is a point incessantly made in Dostoevsky's fiction—that everything cuts both ways, or to use the proverb favored by the police inspector in *Crime and Punishment,* everything about human psychology is a "stick with two ends." We incessantly strive to find simple answers to complex questions about why people behave the way they do. That's what the narrator of *Elagin* keeps telling us over and over. For every logical explanation about the behavior of Sosnovskaya or Elagin, you can make an equally logical case for the opposite explanation. This is a typically Dostoevskian thing.

Elagin is a masterpiece of structure, interweaving characterizations of the two major personages from a multiplicity of viewpoints. The narrator himself is an interesting character; resembling somewhat Dostoevsky's narrator in *The Brothers Karamazov,* he is a local resident who takes an interest in a local scandal. The novella is built around the recapitulation of a case that has already been tried (we get the verdict in the final chapter, but then Bunin excised that chapter). The narrator has attended the trial, and now he, in effect, restages it, rehears the arguments for the prosecution and defense, then makes his own commentaries on any number of issues, sometimes assuming the role of defense attorney after the fact.

Bunin is particularly good at showing the two major characters as simultaneously ludicrous and sympathetic. Elagin is misguided and confused but not a bad sort, and in no way does he fit the stereotype provided by local gossip (and reinforced by the prosecuting attorney). Sosnovskaya is an idiot, a poseur, and yet she reads Schopenhauer and comprehends his ideas. Just when you might think the narrator views her totally in a negative light, he suddenly reveals that he too, like so many of the men who have crossed her path, is captivated: "The dear unfortunate woman! It's extraordinary how touched and distressed I am by that story of the peignoir." Everything cuts both ways, and Bunin's major theme, the Dostoevskian lesson about the impossibility of stereotyping human beings (or ever really pinning down anything about life), is extremely well expressed.

You wonder for whom the narrator is writing the story. Does he hope to reeducate his fellow townspeople, whom he views as simpleminded gossips stubbornly unwilling to consider life's complexities? Has he taken it upon himself to plead for a new trial by exposing the errors of the first? After all, letting Elagin have the last word, his assertion that he will never be guilty in the eyes of his beloved, reinforces the narrator's basic sympathy for the hapless cornet. Or is our narrator simply half in love with the late Sosnovskaya, or with the image of her he has invented through listening to witnesses describe her? There is at least a dollop of the impressionable Ivlev-type artist in this man. We don't know much about the narrator, but the haziness of his image is one more way of reinforcing the main point: on a deeper level we don't know much about why any individual behaves the way he does, nor does that individual himself.

In a word, this may be a Dostoevskian story filtered through the prisms of modernism and the writings of Freud, but it is nonetheless a Dostoevskian story. While echoing Dostoevsky in all his profundity, Bunin also belabors the artistic ambiance that most irritated him about Dostoevsky's fiction: the hyperhysterical atmosphere, the sentimentality, the melodrama. Sosnovskaya's behavior often reminds the reader of characters like Nastasya Fillipovna in *The Idiot.* Her description of how "a certain woman" led her, "a pure trusting girl," onto a wayward path (end of chapter 8) could have come out of Dostoevsky's sentimental first novel, *Poor People,* which features several older women who make a living by procuring young girls. Fyodor Dostoevsky, of course, was in many respects thoroughly steeped in the Sentimental Age, while being, in other ways, far advanced into the twentieth century as a writer. *The Case of Cornet Elagin* has a similar mix. Despite the antiquated plot devices, in its complex structure, its enigmatic narrator, its theme of the complexities and contradictions of the human psyche, it holds up well as a work of twentieth-century literature. It is regrettable that Bunin did not try writing more works free of rural Russian settings and not dominated by nature descriptions. Somehow he felt out of his element in *Elagin,* but you wonder what he might have achieved had he written other works in this vein.

THE NOWHERE (GENTLE)MAN

And to what exotic realms of inspiration would his literary career have led him had he been able to write more stories resembling "The Gentleman from San Francisco"? His most anthologized piece, the best in his cosmopolitan vein, still his best-known story outside of Russia, it is an anomaly in his creative works as a whole. True, he did write a number of other things set in foreign countries with non-Russian characters (such as "Brothers," "The Dreams of Chang," "The Son"), but none of them can compete in artistic merit with "The Gentleman." When this long story was published in 1915 critics hailed Bunin as the successor to Tolstoy and Chekhov. It is, in fact, a great story, one that manifests his incredible range of vocabulary. Due to the profusion of Russian dialectical words, the translator can't get through a paragraph of a work like *Drydale* without the help of the great Vladimir Dal' and his dictionary, but you don't need Dal' at all for "The Gentleman." You do, however, require a dictionary of foreign words and expressions, which demonstrate Bunin's familiarity with the Western European culture and milieu.

In terms of style, the story exemplifies, once again, the overloaded nature of Bunin's prose, the sort of ornateness and density that Chekhov and Gorky had criticized. Although repelled by Bunin personally, the writer Yury Olesha was fascinated with his precision in descriptive passages, but he too criticized the overload:

> Is it necessary to write with such lavishness of colors, as Bunin does? "The Gentleman from San Francisco" simply smothers you in colors; they make a reading of the story hard going. Each vivid image in itself, of course, is marvelous, but while reading the story you get the impression of being in attendance at some performance, where a certain exclusive skill is being demonstrated—in this case the ability to define objects. In addition to the development of themes and expression of thoughts, something else is going on in the story, something with no direct connection to the tale itself, and that something is precisely this performance at giving names to vivid images. It lowers the value of the story.[14]

I agree with Olesha only in part. It seems strange that he, with his own fondness for vivid metaphors, would pick one of Bunin's strongest stories to criticize in that regard, but he does have a point about the tough going for a reader. The sentences (and paragraphs) are lengthy, adjectives, participles, and gerunds are piled up, and we see the ultimate development of a lifelong tendency in Bunin: his refusal to let go of a sentence or paragraph, to stop one line of thought and make a clear transition to a new thought. Sometimes the reader gets lost in the middle of a sentence, waiting for the subject to show up, and that subject makes its appearance only near the end of a long breathless riff (the highly inflected Russian language allows for more flexibility in word order than English does). To use a water metaphor, you, as reader, are on that luxury liner, *Atlantis*, traversing the ocean amidst the howling storm. Ominously looming over the narration of "The Gentleman from San Francisco" is the memory of the *Titanic* (the story was written only three years after that spectacular tragedy). At times you feel as if a catastrophe had already occurred; you've been swept overboard and are desperately swimming through the heavy waves of Bunin's style, the *prichastija* and *deeprichastija* (participles and gerunds) that maintain the perpetual flow of the sentences. On a particularly weary night of reading you might feel as if you can't make it through another wave. In the descriptive passages of "The Gentleman from San Francisco" Bunin's style seems deliberately contrived to place the reader/swimmer in that situation—in midocean clinging to driftwood, water streaming off arms, legs, and head, like the shipwrecked sailors in a famous painting by Ivan Aivazovsky, *The Ninth Wave* (Russian Museum, St. Petersburg). At the center of that painting lies a small naked figure on a barely perceptible board, beneath an enormous, multicolored wave that is about to break over it. From the flotsam in the foreground one man waves a red rag toward that figure, in what may be a gesture of desperation (or valediction?). In terms of "The Gentleman," you might say that the waver of the rag is someone like Bunin himself, saying, "Swim on through it all, reader, swim through my style to the end, just as you must swim through the impossibly gigantic billows of life!"

Or, to look at this in slightly different terms, like the gentleman on his way across the Bay of Naples to Capri, the reader may get seasick. Maybe that dull disorientation is just what the author wants the consumer of his story to feel when reading about the amoral forces of nature and the stark facts of human mortality. Bunin emphasizes that in both directions of its voyage the *Atlantis* is putting up a fake show of aplomb, but that at any moment Mother Nature could pounce upon the ship, just as she has waylaid the gentleman from San Francisco at the Grand Hotel Quisisana. In his final appearance the captain of the vessel, a kind of fat Buddha idol upon whom the passengers place their implicit reliance, is shown to be none too reliable, or even confident.

Great stories are made great by their use of significant detail, and Bunin is wonderful in "The Gentleman from San Francisco" at selecting his details. Here are just a few of many examples:

1. The repetitive imagery of the dance of life. The meretricious lovers (hired by the cruise company) dance both coming and going, and they are clearly fed up with the phony dance of pretend romance; the tarantella that does not come off, since the gentleman pulls his little act and deprives the guests of Carmella and Giuseppe (two more meretricious whirlers); the gentleman's performance itself, his donning of ballroom slippers in preparation for dancing his final dance, the fandango of death in the reading room (with a special dance step featuring his heels pushing up the carpet as he twitches about in his death throes).

2. The image of death as a marriage ceremony. Up in his room before descending to die the gentleman carefully dresses and

grooms himself: "he went through something like preparing for a wedding." Bunin must have been aware of the close parallel in folklore worldwide between wedding rites and funerals. In some Russian rural peasant settings, upon being betrothed the future bride went into a state of seclusion that resembled mourning; she received no one and dressed in black. She was preparing to die in her status as a single girl in order to be reborn into a new life as a married woman. In the intricate peasant marriage ritual itself the girl had to memorize a long series of lamentations, partially as a way of expressing her sorrow at parting from her own family and entering into a different world. In any rite of passage the idea of dying comes into play. Unbeknownst to himself, the gentleman is about to go downstairs and be married to Death. Note that in preparing her performance "every year in December," the old artiste in "Indulgent Participation" also prepares metaphorically for death. Awaiting the arrival of the hairdresser, she is described as if about to be sacrificed, "a virgin they have come to adorn, to prepare for immolation." But the university students who arrive to accompany her to the performance are wearing white satin bows on their chests, "like groomsmen at a wedding." One of the striking aspects of this story is the way the old lady, despite all the foreshadowing, leaves Death, her bridegroom, bewildered and stranded at the altar. She triumphs and lives on to perform once more, presumably the following December.

3. The words of the gentleman standing before his mirror, having completed his struggle with the collar stud and all preparations for his marriage to Death: "Oh, this is awful." He apparently does not know what is awful, but his subconscious knows, and so he repeats the same words, this time "with conviction": "It's awful." Then, at the door of his wife, comes his final spoken word, as if all his subconscious energies have resigned themselves to what is about to occur, are now even eager to embrace nullity: "Wonderful."

4. The struggle with the collar stud, which is such an integral part of the scene where he dresses for dinner, and for the "wedding." Oleg Mikhailov[15] has drawn an interesting parallel between the rebellious collar stud and another inanimate object, the perfidious pouf in a different story about death (and a story that Bunin knew well), Tolstoy's "The Death of Ivan Ilich." Coming to pay his respects at the funeral of his friend Ivan, Pyotr Ivanovich sits down on a pouf that supports his weight unevenly and, with its springs, gives him an occasional fillip on the buttocks. In Tolstoy's morally edifying tale, the inanimate pouf is there to remind Pyotr and us not to waste our lives on the inessential and the material (as the dead Ivan Ilich has), to wise up and embrace the spiritual life before it's too late. Pyotr Ivanovich, of course, pays no heed to the message of the pouf. Bunin's story is not nearly so big on moral edification, but the collar stud does indeed seem to be trying to say something, and, like Tolstoy's character, the gentleman is not listening. Maybe the stud is saying, "You need me now, but in a few more minutes you won't need anything." In the final seconds of his life the gentleman struggles with things (the stud, the collar, the rug) that will outlive him and never miss him. "They will endure beyond our vanishing; / And they will never know that we have gone."[16] You find yourself wondering what happens to the independent-minded collar stud when the hotel lackeys tear away the tie and waistcoat from the gentleman in his death dance. Maybe the little lady, who is waddling down to the dining room chicken-style, hears the commotion at the reading room, comes running up at a waddle, and sees a bright shining object on the carpet. Or the German tourist "with the dumbfounded eyes of a lunatic" picks it up off the floor and takes it back, as a memento of Capri, to his home in Dusseldorf. At any rate, the collar stud will continue its material existence in a much more tangible way than will its erstwhile owner.[17]

What is "The Gentleman from San Francisco" about? Well, it's no big secret that the major theme is death. The story is about how insubstantial and friable any life is in the face of heartless and uncaring Mother Nature, who is prepared to kill us off at any moment. But many who read the story at the time it was published, and many who have read it over the years, see a different major theme. They interpret the story as morally and socially edifying, like "The Death of Ivan Ilich." They see it as a criticism of the idle rich philistines of the world and a defense of the insulted and humiliated lower classes. This is another (rather facile) reason for the story's popularity. Readers like the reassuring feeling that they have got the meaning of a modern story. "Here's what it's about: you have your good guys, and they're the stevedores and the Chinese coolies and the Abruzzian mountaineers, and you have your bad guys, and they're these rich bourgeois types like the main guy, the ones who take advantage of the good guys." I plead guilty to having just done something similar (producing a pat summary of the story) in the third sentence of this paragraph. Not only everyday readers, but specialists on artistic literature like that feeling of having understood a work of art to the point of being able to state the major theme in simple words. Question: What is the message of *Anna Karenina*? Answer: Adultery doesn't pay. Ah, now I feel better. Why is a first-rate story like "Aglaia" less widely read and less appreciated (at least in the Western world) than "The Gentleman from San Francisco"? One big reason is that it is much harder to stick a label on that story. "Aglaia" is about some very complicated and very Russian things.

"The Gentleman from San Francisco" is also about some very complicated (and universal) things, but it appears, on the surface and most obviously, to be about social and class inequities and about the democratic propensities of death. Not one to preach ethics much or plug for rectifying social ills in his fiction, Bunin may have been bothered by the easy social interpretation, but he set himself up for it by throwing in constant details about oppressed lower-class types (the Chinese laborers in San Francisco, the servants and stokers on the *Atlantis,* lackeys of various sorts in Naples, at the hotel on Capri, and the like). He also chose to tell the story in a voice that leaves no doubt about the narrator's disapproval of his main character. In fact, Bunin's critical approach to the idle rich probably has its origins in his reading of his favorite author, Lev Tolstoy, whose preachy intonations seem to be ventriloquizing through Bunin's narrative voice in "The Gentleman from San Francisco." Consider, to take only one example, the passage from *Anna Karenina* (Bunin's favorite novel) in which that disapproving voice describes a different foreign traveler, a frivolous prince from Western Europe, who comes to Russia to hunt animals, drink wine, and chase women. The man telling us about this could be the slightly more sarcastic twin brother of Bunin's narrator:

> Vronsky, who was, as it were, chief master of ceremonies, was at great pains to arrange all the Russian amusements suggested by various persons to the prince: races, and Russian pancakes, and bear hunts, and troikas, and gypsies, and drinking feasts with the Russian accompaniment of broken crockery. And the prince, with surprising ease, fell in with the Russian spirit, smashed trays full of crockery, sat with a gypsy girl on his knee and seemed to be asking—what else is there? Does the whole Russian spirit consist of no more than this?
>
> But in truth, of all Russian entertainments, the prince was most fond of French actresses and ballet dancers and white-seal champagne. (*Anna Karenina,* part 4, chapter 2)

Of course, Bunin knew that sentences dripping with such implicit narrative disgruntlement can be overdone. He also must have known that few readers ever heed the message writers preach, at least in personal terms. Most of us are too busy dancing and eating in the dining rooms of the luxury liners of the cruise ships of the world (or in bars or hash houses at a lower social level) to bother about social inequities (the coolies in San Francisco) or the metaphysical message (threatening billows outside the portholes). Well, we know the coolies and the billows are there, but we prefer not to look. In "The Death of Ivan Ilich" Tolstoy is saying, "Repent, before it's too late!" But, of course, if that is the only message you derive from reading that powerful story, there's not much point in your reading artistic literature at all. In fact, Bunin himself complained about the overemphasis on the moral edification of "Ivan Ilich" (in a conversation with Bakhrakh, when he was old and ill):

> In "Ivan Ilich" Tolstoy's approach is somehow not right. There's Ivan Ilich lying there and thinking, I didn't manage to get this done, I forgot about that, what a nasty life I've lived. But that's not the main thing (he was shuddering when he said this and not trying to hide it)—the main thing is the hideousness (*uzhas*) of death itself, the hideousness of nonbeing, of departing from life . . . The fuller the life you've lived, the more terrible is the approach of its end.[18]

So if the major themes of "The Gentleman from San Francisco"—(1) life is unfair and the upper classes are reprehensible in their treatment of the lower classes, and (2) do something soon about the way you're living, for death is waiting around the bend—are too obvious to be worth talking about, then what is? Well, lots of things: significant details such as those discussed above; the complicated style of the story and its symphonic structure; the role of incidental characters (including the devil); the voice of the narrator as borrowed from Tolstoy; the way Bunin uses that voice to indict, convict, and execute the main character, who is, after all is said and done, the brother of that narrator.

Bunin's stories took on a new excellence in the decade before the revolution primarily because he refined his ability to structure sentences, paragraphs, and entire works symphonically. As for "The Gentleman from San Francisco," Bunin once referred directly to its music in a conversation with the writer Valentin Kataev. Speaking of himself as an international writer, one who can delve into the universal soul and encompass the whole human race, he linked this philosophical concept to the structure of his prose:

> But the main thing is *what* I have developed here, in "The Gentleman from San Francisco"—the symphonic quality that is, to the highest degree, characteristic of every soul on earth; what I mean is not so much a logical as a musical structuring of artistic prose, with changes in rhythm, variations, switches from one musical key to another—in a word, the counterpoint that, for example, Lev Tolstoy made a certain effort to apply in *War and Peace:* the death of Bolkonsky and so forth.[19]

It's no easy undertaking, analyzing the music of "The Gentleman from San Francisco," but in reading the story you can sense the music in the paragraphs. This is true not only of that story but of all Bunin's best prose works. (I make an attempt at a musical analysis in my treatment of "Light Breathing." See also the mention of similar attempts by two Russian critics, Mikhajlov and Vygotskij, in my notes.) Suffice it to say here that the rhythms of "The Gentleman" have a relentless, ominous quality. You're on that ship or in those waves, you're listening to that dogged funeral procession (as in Gustav Holst's *The Planets,* part 5, "Saturn"), and you're getting seasick, or you're overboard, swimming as best you can through the bass notes in the billows (see above). Or you're wishing you were back in San Francisco, listening to Tony Bennett sing a simpler song with a nicer message and watching the sunshine on the Golden Gate Bridge.

Why, by the way, did Bunin decide that his character would come from San Francisco and not, say, from Chicago or New York? In my opinion his choice of the city is connected with the horrendous earthquake that occurred there only a few years before he wrote the story. The theme of the Apocalypse was much on his mind in the years of World War I; he even had an epigraph (later cut) from the book of Revelation: "Woe unto thee, Babylon, mighty city!" The *Titanic* had just gone down in April 1912, and there were implications that the *Atlantis* (named after the famous sunken island kingdom) may have been in for the same fate. Life was precarious and so was human civilization; the end of the world was near, and Bunin wanted to emphasize the shakiness of human prospects in California and everywhere else. (Another major earthquake fault runs across the same Mediterranean area where the gentleman is bound.) Another reason for the choice of San Francisco lies in the origin of its name. Saint Francis of Assisi (1182?—1226) may represent for Bunin the closest we can come to the ideal human being. He rejected the temptations of the world and went off to live with animals. Saint Francis has something in common with the musician-mountaineers on Capri, whom Bunin presents as foils to the gentleman and his ilk. In the Catholic tradition Saint Francis is also the closest we can come to the image of the ideal holy fool in Russian culture (not the kind of charlatan Bunin often presented in his works about holy foolery, but a genuine saintly figure).

Bunin, who dares to break the rules in much of his best fiction, is especially intrepid in the ways he uses incidental characters, players of bit parts. Not many writers have enough confidence in the structural durability of their narrative to bring in totally new personages right at the end: the strange form mistress through whose consciousness the story line is channeled at the end of "Light Breathing"; the aristocratic lady who prays at the grave of Ioann the Weeper; the bizarre pilgrim who takes over the narrative and finishes off the telling of "Aglaia." The boldest stroke in "The Gentleman" involves introducing the devil himself as a character, perched squinting on the Rock of Gilbraltar and trying hard to make out the lights of the *Atlantis* through the snow squall. I leave it to the individual reader to decide if this scene works in an aesthetically acceptable manner. Other interesting bit players are (1) the Oriental prince, who sticks his nose briefly into the tale and appeals to the daughter of the gentleman, but who, most important, seems to be one of the foreboding messengers of death, sent to presage the approaching event; the main character doesn't understand the implicit message of his presence, just as he shrugs off the appearance of the Quisisana hotel manager (before they ever meet) in a mantic dream; (2) the tyrant Tiberius, whose home on Capri the gentleman anticipates visiting, but he never gets to go (although Bunin himself has obviously been there); (3) the carefree idler Lorenzo, famed all over Italy and posing in the story for Bunin's pen the same way he poses perpetually, in his favorite insouciant macho stance, for famous painters; (4) the Abruzzian mountaineers, whose bagpipes and praises to the Virgin Mary the reader gets to hear about (the main character, once again, dies too soon and misses out on this).

It is not always easy (nor is there any reason why it should be) to figure out what an incidental character is doing in a Bunin story. The easiest thing to say about the lower-class characters living in close communion with nature (Lorenzo, the mountaineers) is that they serve as foils to the rich philistines who have no appreciation for the important things in life. Once again, however, that interpretation is overly facile. Is there a genuinely positive character in the story? Not really, or, at least, not obviously. The Abruzzian mountaineers singing their praises to Mary, Mother of God, seem overidealized, resembling some of Tolstoy's unbelievably spiritualized peasants. Making icons out of low-class types is, once again, not the usual thing for Bunin, and again we wonder to what extent the ventriloquizing Tolstoyan voice may be in charge. At any rate, the reader does not know enough about the mountaineers to be sure that they don't beat their wives at night or kick their dogs. As for Lorenzo, he may be content with the life he lives and the role he has chosen to play, but he is a poseur, not only in the literal sense of that word but also in the pejorative sense.

In "The Gentleman from San Francisco" there are (in my view) two main characters: an insensitive American capitalist and a narrator of unknown provenance and nationality (but he's probably Russian, since he writes his story in the Russian language). At first glance it may seem strange to be discussing a Bunin story in terms of its narrative presence. After all, Bunin did not much go in for the kind of twentieth-century fiction in which the teller of a story, often an unreliable teller, plays a major role. In many respects he is a nineteenth-century writer, and his angriest reaction to Vladimir Nabokov, who did very much go in for that sort of thing, was to call him a circus clown.[20] But whether he was totally conscious of it or not, Bunin often did rather modernist things with his narrators and intermediaries.[21] One of the most intriguing aspects of "The Gentleman from San Francisco" is the role played by the narrator himself and his relationship to his main character.

Bunin's commentary on the origins of "The Gentleman from San Francisco"(*Sob. soch.*, 9:368) is revealing. He begins by establishing how Thomas Mann's *Death in Venice* did *not* influence him. He was inspired only by its title, when he glanced at the cover of the book in the show window of a Moscow bookstore. To make sure we get this point he returns to it later—telling us how he subsequently read *Death in Venice* and did not like it. While staying at his cousin's estate of Vasilevskoe in September 1915, Bunin recalled that title in the shopwindow and the sudden death of an American tourist at the Grand Hotel Quisisana, where he and his wife frequently stayed when visiting Capri. That's when he decided to write "Death on Capri," changing the title as soon as he had the first line of the story down on paper. He wrote the draft in four days, "leisurely, calmly, in harmony with the autumnal placidity of the gray, and now quite short and brisk days and the quietude of the estate and the manor house." Here is a telling detail: he would sometimes take a break from his writing, go out into the garden with a double-barreled shotgun, and *shoot pigeons.* This activity gets refracted into the story itself, where the shooters are idle aristocrats killing pigeons for their own jaded recreation. One thing this conjunction of circumstances (writer killing pigeons, characters killing pigeons) suggests is that the teller of this story may have more than a casual connection with the upper-class characters, including the protagonist.

We need not get into the labyrinthine issue of the differences between a writer and the teller of his story. The narrator, for all that, is certainly the alter ego of the author and world traveler Bunin, a man who can describe, in intricate detail, life on a luxury liner or in a luxury hotel because he has been there. And he was there certainly not in the capacity of those underclass characters who populate the story in such profusion and whose prominence has led many to interpret it as social criticism. Bunin was in everyday contact with Maxim Gorky in the years he visited Capri, and you sometimes wonder if he may have been attempting, subconsciously, to show his friend Gorky that he too, while never having bummed and tramped with the dregs of society, was capable of inventing believable representatives of the underclass. (Note also his depiction of a Gorky type, the epic hero Zakhar Vorobyov.) At any rate, the narrator, Bunin's alter ego, rubs elbows in "The Gentleman" primarily with the idle rich, with people like the crass businessman from San Francisco, the Oriental prince, the cosmopolitan beauty with the mangy little dog, and the famous Spanish writer (whom the author could have made a famous Russian writer, but that would have been too obvious). Our narrator/writer is the one with the sharp eyes, noting how the tramontana cleaves the waves while the sunlight glitters on the foam. Later on he accompanies the gentleman into his hotel suite in Naples, after which he provides the splendrous imagery of Vesuvius viewed from the balcony, with the miniature donkeys and toy soldiers trekking along down below (things that the gentleman, sitting stolidly on that same balcony, may not bother to notice and certainly could never describe with the same panache).

The main point I am making here is that the narrator/author can describe so well how the idle rich luxuriated because he has luxuriated along with them. Astonishing as it may seem (given the totally negative portrayal of the main character), Bunin's narrator, in many respects, *is* the gentleman from San Francisco, or at least his fellow pigeon shooter. Of course, in the description of pigeon shooters in the story there is a big dollop of Tolstoyan disapproval (as in Tolstoy's passage about the foreign prince shooting animals for sport in *Anna Karenina*). But while implying the disapproval, agreeing with it, Bunin does something in his description that Tolstoy would not normally do—he makes the passage aesthetically lovely: "the shooting of pigeons, which soar up from their columbaries so beautifully above the emerald lawn, against a backdrop of seascape the color of forget-me-nots, and then come crashing right back down to the earth in small white clumps." No blood here, no gore, but lots of beauty. Lots of horror, too.[22]

It's as if Bunin's subconscious were telling him (and, implicitly, telling his readers): "I am an artist, a describer of the beautiful and sublime. I can make even dead pigeons beautiful, and, well, yes, I shot pigeons in the Russian countryside, but I shot them as a way of relaxing from my labors while engaged in the act of creation. So my pigeon shooting while writing the story has nothing in common with the pigeon shooting described in the story. Furthermore, I sailed on the liners and stayed at the Quisisana *in the service of high art,* in order to absorb the necessary details from the life of the capitalist rich, so as to write about them in a satirical way." But the argument is not totally convincing. At the summit where the funicular stops on Capri the narrator throws in a ragtag group of Russians, the only Russian characters who appear in the cosmopolitan story. This may be an inside joke, a description of Gorky and his friends, fellow intellectuals among whom Bunin himself may well have been standing. If so, it may be another implicit assertion that this is where Bunin stands as an artist, apart from the dim-witted and uneducated rich men like the gentleman from San Francisco. But, in fact, when he and his wife Vera Nikolaevna rode up on that funicular and waited for hotel transportation at the top (as they surely must have), the blue-blooded, well-dressed academician Bunin would have been standing over with the gentleman and his family, bound for the Quisisana, not with ragtag Russians and roundheaded Germans in lederhosen, who wouldn't even think of crossing the threshold of that luxury hotel.

Just as he sits with the dour and unimpressionable gentleman on the balcony in Naples, so too does the narrator ride up that slope with him in the funicular. We know this because somebody is sitting there noticing things that the so recently seasick family from San Francisco would never notice, even at the best of their observational powers: the vineyards and the glossy leafage of the orange trees are described with the keen eye of the artist. At the summit we get a confirmation of the narrator's presence in the funicular; the artist steps out of that coach and directly into the story to comment on his love for Italy (recalling the way the narrator of Gogol's *Dead Souls* periodically takes time out from his story to voice an exclamatory personal opinion): "Sweet is the smell of the earth in Italy after a rain, and each of the islands has its own special aroma!" Right after this comes the separation into the two groups: (1) ragged Russians and roundheaded Germans versus (2) luxury-liner types who stay at the Quisisana. The most interesting dichotomy in the narrative structure of the story is the way the narrative presence has something in common with each of those groups.

Of course, the paean to the smells of Italy is one way the narrator can distance himself totally from his hero, just as are the descriptive details from the balcony and the funicular. Unlike the dunderheaded capitalist, the narrator appreciates the natural beauty of the sensuous world, and, of course, an easy way of separating the characters into good guys and bad guys is to place the good guys among those who can appreciate the beautiful and spiritual. This is where the Abruzzian mountaineers come in. In "The Origin of My Stories" Bunin says that after returning with five or six dead pigeons he sat down to write again: "I became agitated and wrote through tears, even ecstatic tears, the part about how the *zapon'jary* (later the Abruzzians) come up and glorify the Madonna." As Chekhov frequently remarked (and as he must have told Bunin personally), beware the tears of ecstasy while you're writing your fiction. If you want to produce emotion, keep your own emotions off the page. Is this why the ecstatic passage about the encomiums to the Virgin moves me so little? Or is it because implicit in the story is the fact that the author/narrator has had no direct contact with the common people whom he exalts, that he has observed them only as the gentleman would, from the back of a tourist donkey with a little red saddle?

If the traveler from San Francisco could come back from the dead and face his creator, he might have a good case for defamation of character in a court of law. If we provided him with a voice, gave him a chance to testify, what would he say? He might say, "At least give me a name; don't just make me the nameless representative of all things crass and mercantile on earth. I am Frank Pirelli and my forebears immigrated to the United States from Italy and that's why I wanted to make a trip back there, and you left all that out. And I had to work my ass off from very humble origins to get to where I got, and I think that's a thing to be commended, not condemned. Furthermore, you don't give me credit for having an ounce of creativity or sensitivity. I'm not as dumb as you make me out to be. I once read *Moby Dick,* you know, and any human being (this is what they said about Captain Ahab in that book), any human being 'has his humanities.' You didn't allow me one iota of humanity. After all, as they say, schmucks are people too. Why not at least give me a modicum of religious inspiration or a good solid sniff of God's green earth before killing me off? Like, say, you did with Grandpa in your story *Drydale,* letting him have one last look at the beautiful world he is about to leave, before coming back into the room to get murdered. Or, say, let me listen to that performance of the Miserere and come away from it feeling inspired, sort of like your character in 'Way Back When' feels when he gets home from the circus.

"What you did, you know, is you convicted and executed me without a trial. I never got to say a single word in my own defense and there I was dead. And you complain about how people interpret your story in too easy social terms. Well, you're setting yourself up for that very thing when you make a cardboard figure out of me, or a dummy in a tailor's shop (that thing about how he's sitting there in the ballroom, 'with a cut to him not quite right but solidly sewn'). You know what your problem is? Your problem is that you don't want to face the very disturbing fact that you, my creator, are *me.* The way you treat me without mercy can be explained by your desperate attempt not to admit that we have a lot in common. And, of course, you're just like your idol Tolstoy in his 'Death of Ivan Ilich.' You don't want to face death on a personal level any more than anybody else does—so you distance yourself from it by describing it in terms of a person who is light-years (supposedly) away from you. But I'll tell you one thing, buster, you're in that coffin with me, or at least part of you is, and when you kill me off and ship me away, you are, in some degree, killing off and shipping off yourself. And I can prove it by a close reading of what you write. You see, your own style gives you away.

"Remember how you allow me only a couple of words upstairs, before I have to go down to the reading room and do my dance with death? I get to say something pedestrian, like 'Awful.' But then you provide me with a final thought. You have me conjuring up an image of the sexy dancer Carmella, but you don't present that thought in a way I would (supposedly) think it. 'Cause I ain't one (so you keep implying) to observe fine details or think in images. Let's take a look at your sentence. What I've done here is I've italicized the part of the sentence that is in your way of talking and left unitalicized the part that is me: 'This Carmella,' he thought, '*with her dark skin and the fakey look in her eyes, resembling a mulatto, in her florid outfit with the color orange prevailing,* I bet she can put on quite a dance.' There we have it, brother, you and me mixed up inextricably in the same sentence. You, the 'Author,' whose descriptive style in the story sure does wear an outfit of a bright orange color, are putting your own self right into my mind and helping me think my thought (or, rather, thinking your own thoughts and getting them mixed up with mine). If you'd just make me a teensy bit articulate in that last upstairs scene, you know what I'd say to you? I'd say, 'Before you send me down that staircase to die, try rereading your own story "Brothers," or take a look at the doubling of characters that runs through so many of your works, the way you keep proving that we're all in the same boat and we all go out in the same box. Take a good long look at the guy they named my city after. You could learn a few things from him too.'"

Notwithstanding the cri de coeur of Frank Pirelli, which I have invented as a way of presenting a different angle on "The Gentleman from San Francisco," and with which I agree in part, I still think that this story is one of the best Bunin ever wrote. If Chekhov could have read it, eleven years after he died, he would have been confirmed in his assumption that here was the writer who would replace him as the best prose writer Russia had to offer. He might say, "Well, sometimes the soup is still a bit too thick, and maybe you've let a variant of Lev Nikolaevich's voice do too much of the talking, but yes, Bukichon, it's good—even exceptionally good."

TWIN SISTERS

The best short story Bunin ever wrote is "Light Breathing." This is not only my opinion but also is the consensus among any number of readers and critics. What makes it great, essentially, is the pathos communicated by its music. "Light Breathing" treats Bunin's favorite love-death theme in a form that breathes art. Considering its length (only five pages) the story is extremely complex, in themes, tone, and structure. As usual in Bunin, Romantic overtones are strong. The story, at times, seems like a melodrama, and much of the plot is, indeed, melodramatic. There is the jealous Cossack officer, a stock figure in Russian Romantic literature. There is the young man Shenshin, "madly in love" with the heroine Olya and driven to attempted suicide. But, especially, there is the fifteen-year-old Olya herself in her role of femme fatale. She mocks the officer and invites him to kill her, just as she has, instinctively, invited the seduction by Malyutin. But Bunin, at his best, like Chekhov, is able to take absurdity or melodrama and mix it with his own subtle lyricism to produce pathos.

One can never make exact parallels between works of fiction and musical compositions, but approximations may be instructive.

"Light Breathing" consists of five movements and a coda. Within the movements certain leitmotifs are repeated: leitmotifs of the characters, of melodrama, and of Romantic conjuring. Breathing sounds constitute still another leitmotif; the blowing of the wind, sighs, exhalations waft through the composition. The first movement (in our hypothetical scoring) is marked adagio (to be played slowly; in an easy graceful manner). The first sentence, beginning with the words "In the cemetery," establishes a slow and mournful tempo; it ends with the same lugubrious chord sounded three times: "sturdy, ponderous, smooth." That mournful music is maintained for the first four paragraphs, and the last of these introduces the character's name (which is repeated incessantly throughout the story), with its hushing sounds in the surname (the breathing leitmotif). Then comes the second movement, andante (moderately slow, but flowing), a sudden switch into longer sentences and fluent rhythms, hinting at the liveliness that is the Olya leitmotif.

The new movement also begins with a temporal switch. As James Woodward has written,[23] there are "six abrupt changes of temporal perspective" in this brief story, and each of them is associated with a change in rhythm and pace. This manipulation of temporal perspective is a hallmark of Bunin's best work. The abrupt switching between present and past does a number of things in "Light Breathing." For example, it kills off and resurrects the main character repeatedly. It produces the effect of annulling time as time passes in the lives we live, making time appear irrelevant in the grand scheme of things. By beginning the story after Olya is already dead, Bunin writes what in reference to *Crime and Punishment* has been called a whydunit rather than a whodunit. We know who commits the crime near the beginning of Dostoevsky's novel, and we read on through hundreds of pages trying to find out why (while the criminal himself, Raskolnikov, is also agonizing over his motivations, wondering why he did it!). In "Light Breathing" (as well as in *The Case of Cornet Elagin, Drydale,* "Zakhar Vorobyov," and the like), we know who is dead right from the start, and the story keeps circling back around (or in Zakhar's case progressing onward toward the death in a straight line) to get us told, eventually, how it happened.

With the return to Olya's early years and description of her blossoming into young womanhood, the tempo quickens (andante con moto). We watch Olya skating, dancing at balls, and being admired by the smaller girls, and then, at the end of this movement, a few notes of the melodramatic are sounded—she's fickle, she loves to play games, and poor young Shenshin is an early victim. After the three dots of an ellipsis, beginning with the words, "In that last winter of her life," we get another slow and stately effusion of sounds, the description of the beautiful winter, "strolls along Sobornaya Street" and skating ("masses of people glissading about that rink in all possible directions"), the kind of elongated graceful euphonious passage (un poco maestoso) so typical of Bunin's nostalgic evocations of bygone days (this sort of thing is especially well done in, for example, "Way Back When"). The leitmotif of utter vitality, which is always associated with Olya, is particularly vivid in the description of her dashing across the assembly hall, pursued by those "blithefully shrieking first-form girls," only to come to a sudden halt. In music the pauses are sometimes as important as the musical notes, and "Light Breathing" has several significant full stops.

She stops on the dead run and heaves a deep sigh (the shushing, breathing leitmotif), puts herself in order, ready to face up to the conventional blandness awaiting her upstairs, but her eyes are gleaming (radiant eyes—another leitmotif of Olen'ka), and she is so full of life that she can't resist running up that staircase. So we get one last touch of the vitality before beginning something new with the third movement (andante moderato). That something new is the leitmotif of bourgeois conventionality embodied in the figure of the headmistress, with her portrait of the tsar hung on the wall, with every hair in place, doing the thing any good woman should do: knitting. She intones the usual admonishments to her wild young charge, who, of course, is not really listening. Olya is too busy taking delight in the sensuous details that life sneaks into the scene (a few isolated notes of the recurrent vitality leitmotif): even the image of ultimate domestic muliebrity, the knitting ball, betrays the cause of the headmistress when it spins wonderfully on the lacquered floor, putting on a scintillating show for the ever-observant Olen'ka.

Next, most prominently, comes the repetition, five times, of one insistent note: not guilty, not guilty, not guilty, not guilty, not guilty, and then a few lines later: guilty (in the English translation this is "not my fault, not your fault," and so forth). She is too young to be held responsible, she is not guilty. That fifty-six-year-old man who seduced her, brother of the headmistress, he's the one who's guilty, and the word without the "not" is applied by Olya to him. Of course, the headmistress is addressing all those "not guilties" to Olya sarcastically, and Bunin makes it clear (as have Dostoevsky and Nabokov) that in the matter of pedophilia things are not so simple as simpleminded people like to imagine. Olya may not be totally guilty, but she does invite the seduction, at least subconsciously; she is, as the Russian expression goes, not guilty, but it's still her fault. The revelation that ends the scene with the headmistress reverberates as a jarring prolonged chord sounded by the entire orchestra: "It was your brother who did it." At this point, were we filming the story, we would have a sudden zoom-in on the flabbergasted face of the headmistress, then a fade-out. The revelation is jarring in more ways than one. In reality would a girl blurt out such a statement, throw it in the face of her headmistress? Bunin's lover and protégé, Galina Kuznetsova, once told him that she found it hard to believe. She could not imagine herself as a schoolgirl or any other schoolgirl acting as boldly and recklessly as that. Bunin answered that he was always attracted to the idea of portraying a woman at the extreme limits of her *utrobnoj sushchnosti* (her essence as a carnal, childbearing creature). "Only we call this the carnal pregnant feminine essence (*utrobnost'*), and I called it light breathing. That naivety and lightness in all respects, both in daring behavior and in the act of dying, that's what 'light breathing' is, acting without thinking."[24]

After the revelation the music stops again for a moment; there is another interval of silence before the leitmotif of melodrama takes over: first the calm description of how she was murdered at the train station (with a quick glance back at Bunin's favorite novel, *Anna Karenina*), then the testimony of the plebeian Cossack officer, who describes how she tormented him, in the way we presume she had learned was proper form from the Romantic novels she had read. This reckless behavior, in the spirit of what Bunin defined for Galina as light breathing, is, obviously, suicidal. Olya is "asking for" what she soon is to receive: death at the hands of the Cossack. To paraphrase her words at the station: "Here, read my diary. I had a few men in my life before stupid you ever came along." The introduction of the diary into the narrative is awkwardly done (the whole paragraph describing the testimony of the officer at the inquest would be best omitted), but Bunin gets away with it because, with the diary, the vitality leitmotif returns, and when a writer presents liveliness and passion, and presents it passionately, the reader is eager to forgive. The long diary passage takes up almost a whole page of the story in Olya's own words; it is the longest passage we hear told in her voice. It constitutes the fourth movement, which is allegretto (molto vivace).

This is where the lightness of the story reaches its apogee. When Olya is speaking, a number of things are blended in the music of her voice: naivety, gracefulness, vitality, melodrama. The most touching thing about the passages in which she speaks is that naive and lively feel of the way a little girl would speak. Here is someone who only yesterday was, presumably, parading around in her mother's dresses and high heels, playing at being a grown-up lady. Above all, here is someone who is living life to the full, determined to find joy in her every second on earth. This is the only passage where we get a description of music within the music of the story. She plays the piano, and the "music made me feel as if I would live forever and be happier than anyone on earth." Bunin does not tell us what composition she plays, but, again, were we filming the story, this would be the perfect scene to begin with: long shot of a beautiful manor house amidst birches and lindens, slanting sunlight through the foliage, soft music (Beethoven's "Für Elise") getting progressively louder as we approach the house and enter the drawing room, where she sits at the piano in a white dress. Or we could have her doing the first part of *Moonlight* Sonata in the opening scenes and then return later to show her engrossed in the violent and jarring emotions of the third part.

The lightness and vitality of the fourth movement overwhelms the melodrama, although there is still plenty of that too. Olya is the little girl playing at being a big girl, subconsciously seductive ("I felt as if I were not so well and lay down on the ottoman . . . I covered my face with a silk handkerchief, and he kissed me several times on the lips through the silk."). Then the game ends and real life takes over. She's not in a Romantic novel anymore, and she's just had carnal relations with a man her father's age. The passage concludes with a series of clichés from Romantic novels: "I never thought I could be that sort! Now there's only one way out."

That one way out is the self-destructive path of the Romantic heroine, determined to avenge herself on men and, simultaneously, to destroy herself. We need not consider whether this is necessarily the way it has to end for Olya, any more than we need argue, as many critics have, that Anna Karenina was not compelled to destroy herself after the affair with Vronsky began. Bunin's favorite conjunction is love-death; he appreciates parallels with the insect world. The male human being is akin to the male praying mantis, who is eaten by the female while engaged in the act of love. Once you've done what Mother Nature put you on this earth to do, or even while you're doing it (the mantis), you're on your way out. This is the sad lesson that Mitya learns in *The Consecration of Love.* But you can't help thinking that, logically, Olya's reaction to her first act of love would have been entirely different had the male involved been, say, young Shenshin, not her father's friend. Similarly, young Mitya might have survived had the gentle Parasha, the house servant, taken him into her bed. But stories about people who fall in love, who then copulate and go merrily on living out their lives, these were not the stories Bunin wanted to write.

To return to the musical transitions, the next movement (the fifth, which is first adagio, then molto vivace), beginning with the words "Over the course of these April days," reverts to the description of the graveyard in spring. With that switch back to present time we encounter, once again, the music of stately gloom. We're back where we started, Olya is dead again, and we've suddenly got a new character in the story, Olya's more than strange form mistress, through whose consciousness the remainder of the story is filtered. She wanders, accompanied by mournful music, out to the cemetery, down what is, in Bunin's imagination, Kladbishenskaja (Cemetery) Street in Yelets, passing by the spot where the monastery is on one side of the road and the jail on the other (the spot that Bunin repeatedly has his characters pass and that he himself must have walked by countless times). The form mistress is engaged in some kind of obsessive ritual that she has decided she must go through. She brings to the story one more musical leitmotif of character to blend with what we have already encountered at the beginning. That is the leitmotif of the weirdly uncanny. She has devoted her life to a series of strange romantic dreams, but her romantic pose has nothing in common with the femme fatale business that Olya had adopted at age fifteen. The form mistress is a Romantic dreamer and not a Romantic doer.

Why bring in a new character at this late point in the story? One reason is that the form mistress, like the headmistress, is clearly intended as a foil to Olya. Each of the three women who appear in the story represents one possibility of what a woman can make of her life. In accord with the idea of the irrelevancy of time, Bunin may be suggesting that despite her short life Olya Mesherskaya has spent more time actually living than either of the other two, one of whom is steeped in safe conventionality, the other of whom dwells in the solipsism of a dream world. A more practical reason why the form mistress is brought into the narrative is because Bunin needs a character to overhear and report to the reader Olen'ka's conversation with her friend on the school grounds.

The penultimate temporal switch in the story is the flashback to the living Olya in that conversation. This is prepared by the conjuration leitmotif (in Russian, *naklikanie*). Throughout the story the name of the main character is perpetually repeated like a mantra, its sound effects accentuating the breathing leitmotif and adding to the effectiveness of the music: the lovely palatalized shushing sounds in the surname and the soft *l* in Olya (pronounced roughly "Oil-yuh"). It is as if the author or his characters (the form mistress?) were using the magic of incessant repetition of the name to conjure the girl back into life. In one brief passage (describing the form mistress) the name Olya Mesherskaya is repeated six times. And the conjuration works, because right after that she comes to life one last time, and Bunin gives her the story to finish off in her own vivacious voice. For the final time Olya Mesherskaya is alive and for the final time the vitality leitmotif (molto vivace) returns in full force. This last long paragraph, which moves me every time I reread the story, is Olen'ka's description, culled from a Romantic book, of "what a woman must have to be truly beautiful." It is the most ludicrously Romantic passage in the whole story, but in reading the enthusiastic account of sloping shoulders and calves that are "rounded just so," one comes to the poignant realization that the form mistress is right: it simply is impossible that someone whose eyes in the photograph shine with such immortal vitality and whose voice has rung out with the sheer joy of being alive is no more. Besides that, Olya didn't ever really "become a woman," as she wrote in her diary in the dead of night after the seduction. She was, essentially, still a little girl when she went out in a blaze of melodramatic glory. Here's how the music of the vitality (Olen'ka) motif, the music of Olya's voice, comes to an end: "But the main thing, you know what the main thing is? Light breathing! And I've got it, you know. Just you listen how I can sigh . . ." Once again the pause in the music for effect (the ellipsis). Then the sigh itself. Then her final words: "It's true, I've got it, don't I?"

After Olya's last words there's another pause while we start a new paragraph. Then comes the coda, the end of the vivacity and of Olya's life, a final temporal switch into a world beyond all temporality and a final change in the rhythms and sounds: one brief sentence that returns to the death theme and the stately gloom of the beginning: "Now that light breathing has dissolved anew in the vapors of the world, in the cloud-strewn sky, the cold spring wind."

One cannot, of course, be scientifically precise when treating a story in terms of musical movements, transitions, tempi, leitmotifs, and the like. But there is no doubt that "Light Breathing," which cries out to be read aloud in the original Russian, is structured musically. It derives much of its power from the music of the paragraphs, sentences, even individual words. The breath of lovely Olen'ka wafts through the story and is still there breathing in the wind at the end. The very title in Russian has a soft respiration in the *kh* sound of each word—"Lyokhoe dykhanie"—and this *kh* sound is used effectively at several other points in the story. A certain Soviet critic once made use of a special apparatus for measuring the respiration of those engaged in reading "Light Breathing." The pneumatographic tape of the machine revealed that while reading about murder, torment, death, and "the ghastly business now associated with the name of Olya Mesherskaya," the reader was breathing *lightly,* as if respiring in harmony with the respiration of the story. "Light Breathing," like so much of Bunin's art, is sad, but the music makes it somehow *beautifully* sad and recalls the paradox mentioned by Anthony Burgess (see above): "The denial of human joy is made through language which is itself a joy." To recall, once again, part 5 ("Saturn") of Holst's *The Planets,* the funeral procession in the music of "Light Breathing" (as in "Saturn") takes us in the end (through the consoling joys of musical aesthetics) to a warm and comforting afterlife.

The broad range of Bunin's themes and methods is sometimes astounding. In the same year that he wrote "Light Breathing," a story that has universal appeal, he wrote what amounts to a companion piece, "Aglaia," which is thoroughly steeped in Russian culture and history. The main character of "Aglaia" is much less accessible to Western readers comfortable with the literary type presented in "Light Breathing." Yet each story treats the death of a girl in the bloom of adolescence; they are the obverse of each other, and they end up saying similar things. If "Light Breathing" presents, through three female characters, three possible ways a woman can choose to live her life, "Aglaia" presents a fourth: the ascetic path. Olya Mesherskaya bids farewell to life in a blaze of sensuality, burning herself out in an act of self-destruction. The circle closes as her wild desire to live blends with an equally frenzied desire to die. "Light Breathing" is a story about self-immolation. But so is "Aglaia." The girl in that story sacrifices herself to the opposite dream, the ascetic ideal, shielding her eyes from all things sensuous, but she too goes out in a blaze ("she flared up and died"), and in some strange way her life is also voluptuous—because she takes a voluptuous joy in the denial of the flesh. One of Bunin's repetitive implications is that human beings will find a way to experience sensual joy in every aspect of life (even in the act of denying the senses). In a word, the two stories are complementary because the romantic dream and the ascetic dream are akin to each other.

Another congruence, central to an understanding of Russian culture, is a major theme of "Aglaia." As mentioned above, Bunin practically never wrote about Russian Eastern Orthodoxy without suggesting syncretism, that blending of Christianity with pagan religion as manifested in the traditions of Russian folk belief. "Aglaia" is one of his most profound stories on that theme. It is written somewhat in the pattern of a hagiography, but it calls into question certain dark sides of Russian Orthodoxy. Bunin implies that in its most excessive and fanatical ways, the Russian Orthodox religion is not that different from shamanism and other highly ecstatic pagan or semipagan practices. For Orthodoxy sanctions voluptuous mortification of the flesh, standing rotting on pillars. It places great emphasis on the healing powers of relics (dead pieces of saints' bodies) and looks with approval on the deliberately obscene, frenetically irrational behavior of the *jurodivye* (holy fools). While never coming right out and saying it, Bunin implicitly makes the same statement over and over in his works with peasant settings: Mother Earth and the Mother of God (the Virgin Mary) are congruent in the Russian folk imagination. Bunin, of course, was not the first Russian writer to make that point, nor will he be the last, since the congruence is as vital today as it was in 1916. The topic is prominent in Dostoevsky's works; he, for example, has his eccentric Maria Lebyadkin, resident in a convent, remark that "God and nature are the same thing" and speak approvingly of a lay sister who tells her, "The Mother of God is Great Mother Earth, and therein lies a great joy for men."[25]

Just as in "Light Breathing," Bunin takes a daring stylistic-structural tack toward the end of "Aglaia." In "Light Breathing" he introduces a strange new character and filters the end of the story through her; in "Aglaia" he brings in an eccentric, even bizarre narrator, the pilgrim wanderer, to finish off the telling of the story. That narrator provides confirmation of what we may already expect, if we are aware of the congruences mentioned above. According to his tale, for example, Aglaia blindfolded herself with a cloth, or *pokrov,* a word that can mean any kind of cloth used as a covering but also has strong religious overtones. In the Russian Orthodox Church it can be a pall, chrismal cloth (used for covering sacred relics), or brocaded hearse cloth (shroud placed over a coffin). It is also, and most important, the name of one of the most sacred iconic types in the Church tradition, an icon depicting the origin of a Church holiday (October 1/14, Protection Day or Intercession Day), the most significant holy day consecrated to the Mother of God.[26] In covering her eyes with *pokrov* and refusing to look at the carnal side of life, Aglaia is symbolically pleading for the patronage and intercession of the Virgin Mary. But in the Russian countryside Intercession Day was clearly associated with pagan fertility rituals, and Mother Mary was blended with Mother Earth. Traditional appeals to the spirit of the holiday make it clear that the Virgin Mary is not the only intercessor; the appeal is to some pagan force: (1) "Old Man Pokrov, cover (protect) Moist Mother Earth and me too, young lass!" (2) "Old Man Pokrov, cover the earth with snow, and me, young lass, with a bridegroom!" (3) "Pokrov will come, and will cover the head of a maiden" (*Dal'*, 3:247). Willy-nilly, Aglaia, in covering her eyes with the pall of the Virgin, is also placing upon them the pall of paganism, appealing for personal fertility. But that's what the whole story is about.[27]

This parallel sets us up for the shocking revelation that the (unreliable?) narrator provides at the end of the story. Following Aglaia's example, he blindfolds himself, incidentally, so as not to look at life, but in so doing he forces himself to look down at the ground, at Mother Earth, instead of regarding the monotheistic sky god of Judaism and Christianity. Aglaia, so the pilgrim tells us, did not really want to die in the end. Even though she had lived a life of total denial of material, earthly things, she was ever so reluctant to part with the earth (unlike her wild twin sister, Olya Mesherskaya, who embraced all earthly things with a fervid joy that somehow encompassed the joy of self-destruction). Most shocking of all, she, Aglaia, addressed her final words to a pagan goddess, the Earth Mother: "And thou, Earth Mother, against whom I have sinned most grievously in body and spirit, wilt thou forgive me?" In *Russian Folk Belief* Linda Ivanits writes that "in remote areas of Vladimir Province old people observed a ritual of asking the earth's forgiveness prior to death into the twentieth century" (see my notes to "Aglaia"). The supreme irony of the ending comes as a shock only if one is unaware of Russian syncretism. Aglaia addresses her final words to Mother Earth, who would (if She could express herself in rational words) strongly advocate the path of Olya Mesherskaya, who burned herself out in the service of ecstatic sexuality (Mother Earth's favorite thing). She (Earth) could only frown upon the negation of flesh preached by Father Rodion, the principles by which Aglaia has lived her life. But, in the end, the servant of asceticism and denial of flesh, the maiden Aglaia, it seems, is also the unconscious handmaiden of flesh and earth.

ALL EYES AND EARS AND FLESH

The vitality of Olya's life shines through her radiant eyes, and in "Aglaia" the imagery of the eye plays a central role as well. As an act of Christian asceticism Aglaia covers her eyes so as not to look and not to be looked at. Beautiful eyes are very much of the flesh, and her blue eyes may attract unclean glances. She might have to rip them out, as Santa Lucia did, send them to her admirer on a platter. In the spirit by which she lives Aglaia would be capable of doing that. Better not to be looked at or to look either, since through the eyes one views all worldly temptations. Aglaia does not wish to look through to the depths of earthly carnality, but (if we are to believe the pilgrim's tale) she has to some extent been "fascinated," "overlooked" (the original meaning of both words is "eyed," "hexed") by the forces of Mother Earth. Aglaia's ascetic example has inspired the weird pilgrim to blindfold himself. The original inspiration for this may have been Matthew the Seer (Perspicacious), about whom Bunin also wrote a poem (dated January 24, 1916). Matthew (see my notes to "Aglaia") goes off to live a life of Christian asceticism in a dark cave, where he can avoid looking at earthly life. But the devil visits him in that cave, tempts him, calls him "hundred-eyed and hundred-eared," and seeks to lure him back out to feast his eyes, once again, on the flesh-laden world. As the final lines of the poem suggest, Matthew is sorely tempted. The pilgrim (in "Aglaia"), as well, has cat eyes and greedy eyesight that can penetrate through to the deeper levels of life, and he feels that his Christian faith compels him to bind up his eyes.

The story "Aglaia" and the confluence of the heroine with her twin sister Olya Mesherskaya perfectly expresses the ever-present dichotomy in Bunin's worldview. Woodward (71) mentions "the conflicting emotional impulses that underlie the entire development of his art—the conflicting tendencies toward self-detachment from life in all its futilities and horror and self-abandonment to its sensual delights." Like the weird pilgrim in "Aglaia" and like Matthew the Seer, Bunin himself was characterized by the greediness of his eyesight. He looked upon every sensual thing with the utmost concentration, avid to embody in his art the details he apprehended. If, like Matthew, he went off into a dark cave (such as the cave of Buddhist asceticism that sometimes attracted him), he would always let the devil tempt him back out to look at the world. If, like Aglaia and the pilgrim, he tried to put a blindfold over his greedy eyes, he would still find a way to peep out from beneath it at Mother Earth. His conflicting emotional impulses, therefore, are always tilted, ultimately, in favor of earth and flesh. "Again and yet again wilt thou deny me for the sake of Mara, for the sake of that sweet deceit that is mortal life, on this night of earthly spring." That's what the Buddha says, and what is Ivan Bunin's answer? "Lord, let me *be*!"

Notes

1. *Bab.*, 49.

2. *Lit. nasled.*, 1:41.

3. *Novyj zhurnal*, no. 113 (1973), 135. From a Bunin diary note dated February 3, 1941.

4. See the article by Ju. Lotman, "Dva ustnykh rasskaza Bunina (k probleme 'Bunin i Dostoevskij')," in the book *O russkoj literature* (St. Petersburg, 1997), 730–42. See also my article, "Dostoevskij i 'dostoevshchina' v proizvedenijakh i zhizni Bunina," in *I. B.: pro contra*, 700–13.

5. *G.d.*, 102.

6. *Wood.*, 100–3. For additional examples of the postscript device see the endings of "Light Breathing," "Aglaia," and "Transfiguration."

7. F. Nietzsche, *The Birth of Tragedy*, trans. Francis Golffing (New York: Doubleday Anchor, 1956), 232–33.

8. On this issue see Alexander F. Zweers, *The Narratology of the Autobiography: An Analysis of the Literary Devices Employed in Bunin's "The Life of Arsen'ev"* (New York: Peter Lang, 1997).

9. *Barsk.*, 80–81.

10. *Harper's,* August 1976, 80.

11. *Wood.*, 169.

12. For a detailed treatment of this story, see my article, "Bunin's Sardonic Lyricism," in *Russian Language Journal* 33, no. 116 (fall 1979), 112–22.

13. Bunin cited in *G.d.*, 195.

14. Juryj Olesha, *Izbrannoe* (Moscow, 1974), 512–13. For an English translation of the whole of Olesha's comments, see *No Day without a Line,* trans. Judson Rosengrant (Ann Arbor: Ardis, 1979), 250–52.

15. Mikhajlov, *I. A. Bunin: ocherk tvorchestva* (Moscow, 1967), 131.

16. From the poem "Things," by Jorge Luis Borges, trans. Stephen Kessler.

17. For pictures of things that outlived Bunin and, apparently, never missed him, see the photo album *Vernis' na rodinu, dusha,* ed. Asja Olejnikova (Orel, 1995), 172–73: cigarette holder, passport papers, travel guidebooks, pipe, safari hat, and more. Those items are in the collection of the Bunin Museum in Orel. At the counterpart of that museum in Yelets you can see, for example, the forlorn-looking suitcases that accompanied Bunin to Stockholm when he traveled there to be awarded the Nobel Prize for Literature in 1933. Among other fascinating artifacts in the Bunin Archive at Leeds University is Bunin's wedding ring from his first marriage (engraved, in Russian, "Anna. 23 September 1898").

18. Aleksandr Bakhrakh cited in *Bab.*, 45.

19. Valentin Kataev, *Svjatoj kolodets. Trava zabven'ja* (Moscow, 1969), 193. For an English translation of the entire passage see Valentin Kataev, *The Grass of Oblivion,* trans. Robert Daglish (New York: McGraw-Hill, 1970), 73.

20. The comment is tempered by a grudging admiration: "There you have probably the most adroit writer in all of the boundless realm of Russian literature, and he's a red-headed circus clown. But, sinner that I am, I love talent, even in clowns" (*Bakh.*, 110).

21. See my discussion of "The Grammar of Love," in which Ivlev is much more than just the medium through which the story of Lushka and

Khvoshinsky is told. See also the strange narrative presence in *Drydale* and the role of the narrator in *The Case of Cornet Elagin.*

22. Julian Connolly writes that shooting pigeons in "The Gentleman" is "presented as an aesthetically pleasing experience" (*Ivan Bunin* [Boston: Twayne Publishers, 1982], 85).

23. *Wood.*, 154.

24. *G.d.*, 104.

25. *The Devils,* part 1, chapter 4, subsection 5.

26. Note that early climactic scenes of *Drydale* (the party and subsequent murder of Grandfather) are set on the Pokrov holiday. On the legend of the *pokrov* as holy protective veil of the Theotokos, see notes to *Drydale.*

27. On blendings of the Virgin Mary and Mother Earth and on the Pokrov holiday, see Joanna Hubbs, *Mother Russia* (Bloomington: Indiana University Press, 1988), 114–16.

»»» ON TRANSLATING BUNIN «««

In his famous book on the art of literary translation, *Vysokoe iskusstvo* (*A High Art*), Kornej Chukovsky insists that the best way to capture the spirit of a literary work in another language is to get far away from the original in order to come back to it. My method of literary translation is based on Chukovsky's ideas. He wants a translated work to read like an original work of art in the target language, and his greatest foes are the literalists, who slavishly stick to exact meanings of words in the language from which they are translating. My aim is to make Bunin read well in English without distorting the sense and the stylistic feel of the original Russian. This, of course, is a formidable task. The "getting away and coming back" amounts to a journey in two directions on a tightrope, with intervals of dancing on thin air. Paradoxically, the literary translator does some of his best work when he is totally off that tightrope, out on his own in the stratosphere. Of course, the abyss called *Otsebyatina* (Ownself Chasm) yawns below. You have to be close enough to grab ahold of the wire if you're on the way into free fall, but Providence gives you split seconds of hang time in space (somewhat like Wile E. Coyote in the old Road Runner cartoons). The best literary translators make use of those seconds while hoping that, like Wile E., they can survive the worst falls. In rereading my previously published translations (from Ivan Bunin's *In a Far Distant Land*) I was satisfied (more or less) with most of the stories. I feel fortunate, however, to have been given an opportunity the translator seldom gets: to take another look at those same stories. The changes I have made in them for this volume (which contains those twenty-three prose works revised plus seventeen more) are, largely, attempts at making the English sound more natural, which process involves more dancing in thin air. Of course, it never is going to sound totally natural, because you've always got the original archaic language text tugging at your ballet slippers as you teeter on the tightrope.

—Hold it, hold it. So what you seem to be implying, if I understand you correctly, is that the whole business of literary translation is, in its essence, *impossible.*

—Well, strange miracles do sometimes happen on this earth, and, when all is said and done, to look at the matter from a multitude of vantage points, they seldom happen, but they do, so that, when you come right down to the nitty-gritty . . . Well, yes . . .

—Then why try?

—Well, it's sort of like the thing called Life. When you're slithering along the greased tightwire of Life, you're not really getting anywhere either, are you? But you keep on going.

—No, no. That's not a valid comparison. Your reasoning is specious. Furthermore . . .

At any rate, I would like the success or failure of my efforts judged not on mistakes in interpretation of individual words or phrases (we all make those) but on the overall effect of the old-fashioned dance on and off the tightrope.

Some of the problems in translating Bunin amount to common problems for a translator of Russian writers, especially those who set their works on the landed estates of the nineteenth or early twentieth century. It is, for example, difficult to be consistent with names for the rooms in a manor house. The room called the parlor is where the family dines in *Drydale,* and the name survives, apparently, from sometime in the past when the room had another function. In *The Consecration of Love* the narrator himself mentions the persistence of an old term for the room where the serf-servant footmen once lived (*lakejskaja*—the lackey room). I have tried to be consistent by using the same names for manor house rooms in all the stories I have translated, but the problem is compounded when one room (*ljudskaja*) can have three different meanings: (1) servants' quarters in a manor house, (2) servants' annex, and (3) kitchen. Then again, nature descriptions present special difficulties. Names of the flora and fauna of the Russian countryside may not even have equivalents in English, especially if they appear in colloquial or dialectical form. Even if there is a word in English it often means little to the reader, especially the non-European reader, who may have never seen the most common of European trees, the linden (let alone numerous Russian flowering shrubs or birds that show up in Bunin's stories). Similarly, the non-Russian reader probably has no idea what a *kaftan, poddyovka,* or *ponyova* looks like, and there are no exact English words for these articles of clothing once worn by Russians living in the countryside. Bunin's word stock, furthermore, is replete with highly unusual dialectical and archaic words. Equivalents for such words in English are difficult to find.

Ideally, every translation would include a CD-ROM containing (1) illustrations of clothing worn by the characters, the wagons and carts they ride in, and the flora and fauna of their milieu and (2) audio of the sounds described in the works. For Bunin this would include, for example, the creak of a tarantass, the labored breathing of a horse and the sound its spleen emits, the cries of cuckoo birds, nightingales, and eagle owls (*Bubo bubo*), and the roar of a tramontana. It also wouldn't hurt to have a scratch-sniff-and-lick section of the book, where the reader could smell and savor the stories. Again for Bunin, this would include the taste of *kut'ja* (frumenty), *shchee* (cabbage soup), and Antonov apples, the smell of red-hot iron roofs in the summer, the stench of dung in the cattle yards, the pungent reek of disinfectant in the corridors of a cheap Russian hotel, the fragrances of all the flora he so carefully sniffs out in so many works. Maybe the best we have now (in lieu of that ideal CD-ROM and the scratch-taste-sniff) is the second edition of Genevra Gerhart's *The Russian's World: Life and Language.* But that book contains only words and pictures, not smells, tastes, sounds.

Another problem for the translator (the most maddening of all) is what to do about substandard speech. Translators intrepid enough to attempt works with dialogue featuring the underclass usually make their peasants, merchants, or workers speak something relatively close to standard literary English. Why do they do this? Because they know that if you make them speak substandard English, you have to choose what kind of substandard English (the way noneducated speakers speak English in the American South or in Yorkshire or in New Zealand?). As soon as you make this choice you run into the weirdly incongruous situation of having a Russian peasant woman speaking, for example, as if she grew up in the hills of West Virginia. Well, there really is no solution, but in my opinion you have to at least make the effort. If you don't, you are left with what Chukovsky calls *gladkopis'* (Lauren Leighton translates this as "blandscript"), a leveling out of earthy speech that ends up smoothing all the earthiness out of it, like building a Wal-Mart Supercenter on what was once pristine forestland. As far as I know, two of Bunin's best stories with peasant heroes, "The Saints" and "Zakhar Vorobyov," have never before been rendered into English. In these translations, as in all other incidences of Russian substandard speech in my book, I have made do with an approximation of the countrified English spoken widely all over the South and southern-midwestern regions of the United States. Readers jarred by the apparently American setting may further assert, disgruntledly, that I have translated Bunin not into English but into American English. I wouldn't argue with that, but when the issue is not substandard speech I sometimes try using European words for the European context. That's why the "headmistress" and "form mistress" are working in a Russian girls' gymnasium ("Light Breathing"). That, by the way, is not a place where they play basketball, but a private school in Europe.

—Now, that's what I call *inconsistent.* Having said that, let me say further . . .

—Okay, okay, I already told you it was impossible.

Some stories call for special effects, and "The Saints" is one of them. Its narrator speaks in a mixture of ungrammatical peasant speech from the nineteenth century, gallicisms he apparently picked up from his French-speaking masters in the days of serfdom, and highly literary locutions he has learned by reading hagiographies. In an attempt to approximate the third component I have sprinkled the text with outdated words from F. S. Ellis, *The Golden Legend, or Lives of the Saints as Englished by William Caxton.*

Some Russians I meet say, "What? You translate *Bunin*? But he's *hard* to read." True, he is, in the original Russian as well as in translation. There is, for example, his massive vocabulary and his use of words that sometimes appear in no dictionary. The easy way out (some translators have taken it) is to use ten-cent words in English for the thousand-ruble words in Russian. This makes for easier reading, but it's just one more variant of "blandscript." I once was naive enough to think that I did not know the recondite words because I am not a native speaker of Russian, but the fact is that plenty of Russians don't know them either. The greatest of aides is Vladimir Dal', whose four-volume dictionary of Russian is invaluable. Another is the seventeen-volume *Dictionary of the Academy of Sciences of the U.S.S.R.* After you find the word, however, you are faced with another daunting problem: how to find a word in English with the same stylistic feel. Roget (the third edition of his *International Thesaurus*) is a great help, as is Webster (second edition of the unabridged *New International Dictionary*). Of course, after you've discovered the word you need (the English word that nobody knows, which translates a Russian word that nobody knows), you have to deal with the exasperated gasps of a copy editor: "If it's a match you're talking about, why not call it a match instead of a sulfur fusee! After all, finding readers these days is hard enough without making things even harder for them!" My answer to that is this: the typical dumbed-down reader of modern America, he who consumes *The Idiot's Book for Idiots,* won't make it past the first page of any story by Bunin anyway, so let's not worry about him.

In addition to lexical problems there are, primarily, two big stylistic issues that complicate the translation of Bunin. The first of these relates to the overloaded nature of his style. Early in his career Bunin's colleagues Chekhov and Gorky both complained of the excessively compact, too detailed, overly descriptive writing. Chekhov said it was like a bouillon that was cooked too thick, and Gorky (in speaking of *The Village*) said, "Every sentence squeezes together three or four objects; every page is a museum!" Bunin writes long, long sentences and paragraphs, full of adjectives, participles, and gerunds. Instead of beginning a new paragraph, he will frequently just knock off the three dots of an ellipsis and continue on. The reader must hack through dense thickets of prose without a chance to stop and take a breath. The translator has to decide if such a breathless pace can be maintained in English; almost all translators of Bunin (including me) decide that it cannot. Russian is a highly inflected language with resources not available to English; it allows for longer and more complicated sentences and greater variety in syntax. If you try to stick to the same length of sentences and paragraphs in English, you risk ending up with an awkward mess. So, with one exception, my translations often break up Bunin's long sentences and start new paragraphs where they would logically begin. The exception is a story much translated previously, one of the most well known in this volume, "The Gentleman from San Francisco." Here, as a kind of experiment, I have tried to keep, where humanly possible, the original sentence and paragraph structure. In this work the long, uninterrupted riffs quite clearly have a stylistic function in harmony with the story's themes (see my afterword), and of everything that Bunin wrote the overloaded style may work best here. I have also tried to maintain, as closely as possible, the original punctuation of "The Gentleman." I have used, occasionally, a semicolon instead of a comma, when the English sentence just could not bear pushing on without a longer pause.

The second major stylistic problem relates to the Romantic movement. Born in 1870, Ivan Bunin was, in his formative years, heavily influenced by Romantic literary stylistics. This is what most dates him as a writer. There are, for example, too many exclamation points in his works, too many ellipses, and a profusion of oxymorons. There is an overuse of Romantic catchwords such as *uzhasno* and *strashno* ("horrible" and "terrible"). The problem here is exacerbated in modern English by overuse in colloquial contexts of those words. "Terrible" and "horrible" just don't sound as horrible and terrible as they did a hundred years ago. At times the context calls for "horrendous," "hideous," or "awesome" (another word, unfortunately, already tainted now by its casual use in a colloquial setting). The ellipsis device—that is, using three closely spaced dots to indicate a kind of pause for reflection or a brief sigh on the reader's or writer's part (not an omission in the text)—is pretty much gone in modern literature. I have chosen to eliminate a good many of these dots from Bunin's prose, especially where I cannot see any particular function for them. On the other hand, I have left the exclamation points mostly as they are in the original. The oxymorons ("blissfully tormented," "grievously joyful") are in tune with the overall Romantic ornateness of Bunin's prose, but they are sometimes overdone to the point where they verge upon the fustian. I as a translator, nonetheless, resist toning them down. Similarly, I force myself (for the most part) not to tamper with passages that are so over-Romanticized and lush that the modern reader may take them as ironic (see my discussion of "Shere Monday" in the afterword). The result, obviously, is an English deliberately stylized and archaic, just as Bunin's Russian is stylized and archaic.

Despite the luxuriant and floriferous, sometimes old-fashioned feel of Bunin's works, the best of them still stand proudly in the pantheon of nineteenth- and twentieth-century Russian literature. I can only hope that my translations convey the strengths of Bunin as a prose writer to the modern English-language reader, who may have grown unaccustomed to adjectives and long brocaded sentences. To such a reader I would say, "Give Melville and Faulkner a go; after them you'll be ready for Bunin." The translator, inevitably, must stand between the reader and the original writer. Whether he wants to be there or not, his job is that of intermediary. In order, however, to efface myself as fully as possible, I have chosen to place this note on the translations and my critical article on Bunin *after* the stories. This gives the reader the best chance at head-to-head contact with the writer, impeded (true) by the intermediary as translator, but unimpeded, at least at the start, by the strong opinions of the go-between.

Those opinions, of course, are also necessarily reflected in the stories and novellas selected for this volume. They constitute what I view as a representative sample of Bunin's prose fiction over his writing career, minus the weaker works that came early in that career. I think that his strongest stories were written between 1910 and 1916, and between 1921 and 1930, and my preference for those periods is reflected in the stories I have chosen. Four of his most significant longer works (novella length) are included in the present volume. Excluded are *The Life of Arseniev,* his only novel-length work of prose and a wonderful piece of art, which has been published in translation by Northwestern University Press, and *The Village,* an important early novella—I had to choose between it and *Drydale,* which, aesthetically, is a much better work. There are at least ten other short stories I would like to have included, but given the present length of the manuscript, I was already verging upon a multivolume collection. Twenty-three of the stories presented here were published by Hermitage in 1983. All have been revised for this volume. The additional seventeen stories, in total pages, represent a much larger proportion of the volume than the twenty-three. The order in which I have chosen to place the prose fiction reflects an interweaving of themes that show up throughout Bunin's literary career. The love theme is so important that we begin with it, leave it for a time, and then return to it periodically. Quite often the love theme is intertwined with the theme of death. Also represented are (1) the elegiac and nostalgic vein (stories on the decline of the landed gentry and the disappearance of traditional life in the countryside), (2) the "cruel" Bunin (peasant and lower-class brutalities and sordidness), (3) the interdependence of gentry and peasants and their basic communality, (4) the mentality of the Russian folk (the ways of holy foolery, the syncretism of Russian Orthodoxy), (5) the theme of art (including connections between writer and reader, storyteller and listener, plus the semi-insanity of the creative artist or imaginative dreamer), and, finally, (6) the Buddhist theme. I choose to end the volume with one of the Buddhistic stories, and I take the title of the whole book from that story, because I believe that "Night of Denial" is the perfect expression of Bunin's lifelong struggle (both in his art and in his personal existence) to choose between mutually contradictory paths.

The Russian source for all translated works is Ivan Bunin, *Sobranie sochinenij v devjati tomakh* (Moscow, 1965–67). In case of inconsistencies or misprints in this source, I have checked earlier texts and incorporated the necessary changes in the translations. From time to time I have also checked difficult passages in previous translations of Bunin's prose fiction, but, for the most part, harried translators from the past provide little help. As a rule, when the literary translator runs into big trouble (that is, he or she doesn't really understand a word or passage or he simply can't drag it across successfully into his native language), he just distorts the passage as best he can (or even omits it entirely). At least three of Bunin's translators into English, however, deserve a lot of credit for their conscientious efforts: B. G. Guerney, Olga Shartse, and the team of David Richards and Sophie Lund.

»»» ACKNOWLEDGMENTS «««

Much of the material in the critical afterword and the notes originated from talks I presented on Bunin at Russian universities in 1999 to 2000 (in Smolensk, St. Petersburg, Yelets, Voronezh, and Novgorod) while teaching as a Fulbright Scholar. I would like to thank Susan Harris, who originally accepted the proposal for this translation project at Northwestern University Press, as well as Susan Betz, editor in chief at Northwestern, for her willingness to further promote the cause of Bunin and for her persistent and relentless efforts to secure copyright permission. In regard to such efforts, my special thanks go out to Richard Davies, curator of the Bunin archive at Leeds University in England.

In addition, I am grateful to Igor Yefimov, who first published my Bunin translations at Hermitage Press in 1983, to the many Russians who answered detailed questions on Bunin's texts, and to the Russian students with whom I interacted when teaching a Bunin seminar at Novgorod University (plus one brilliant scholar there: Vladimir Shadursky). I also would like to thank the American scholars who encouraged my efforts and made suggestions about which works to translate at the outset. These include Mary Petrusewicz, Professor Maxim Shrayer of Boston College, and the dean of all American Bunin fanatics, Professor Thomas Marullo of Notre Dame University. Running into the usual computer glitches near the end of the project, I was gratified to have my son around. He (James Ian Bowie, Ph.D.) helped me prepare the computerized version of the manuscript in the eleventh hour (with the additional aid of Brian Nelson, who graciously provided the printer).

Finally, I would like to acknowledge the contribution of Natalya Isatchenko, who gave me private lessons on syncretism, and of two dead scholars: the poet Juryj Pavlovich Ivask, who introduced me to Bunin's works in a seminar at Vanderbilt University way back when (1969), and the kindest of men, Sergej Aleksandrovich Zen'kovskij, who steered me through the doctoral program there.